KENZIE KIRSCH MEDICAL THRILLERS 8-10

KENZIE KIRSCH MEDICAL THRILLERS 8-10

P.D. WORKMAN

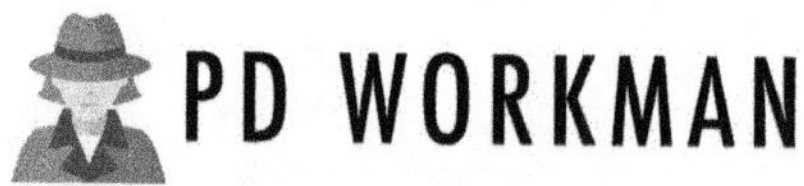

ISBN: 9781774688991 (KDP Paperback)
ISBN: 9781774688984 (ePub)

ALSO BY P.D. WORKMAN

FIND MORE BOOKS AT PDWORKMAN.COM

MYSTERY/SUSPENSE:

Kenzie Kirsch Medical Thrillers

Unlawful Harvest

Doctored Death

Dosed to Death

Gentle Angel

Rushin' Death

Posed for Death

Death of a Corpse

Endowed with Death

Shattered to Death

Captured in Death

Currying Death (Coming Soon)

Healed to Death (Coming Soon)

Death's Charm (Coming Soon)

Zachary Goldman Mysteries

Private Investigator

She Wore Mourning

His Hands Were Quiet

She Was Dying Anyway

He Was Walking Alone

They Thought He was Safe

He Was Not There

Her Work Was Everything

She Told a Lie

He Never Forgot

She Was At Risk

He Drowned in Memory

Their Walls Were Empty

They Came for Him

They Sought Vengeance

She Was Their Target

His Fear Was Real

She Was Out of Reach

He Was Deceived

She Once Vanished

A Bleeding Hearts Valley Thriller

An Abrupt Departure (Coming Soon)

High-Tech Crime Solvers Series

Virtually Harmless

Cowritten with D. D. VanDyke

California Corwin P. I. Mystery Series

The Girl in the Morgue

Stand Alone Suspense Novels

Looking Over Your Shoulder

Lion Within

Pursued by the Past

In the Tick of Time

Loose the Dogs

AND MORE AT PDWORKMAN.COM

ENDOWED WITH DEATH

Kenzie's ringer sounded. That wouldn't have been unusual except that she had it turned to silent mode during their visit with Lorne Peterson and his partner Patrick Parker. The ring wasn't just her generic ringtone, but the "urgent" trill that meant it was a work call, and it was programmed to bypass silent mode so that she couldn't miss it.

Zachary's head went up and he looked at her, dark eyes surprised. "What's that?"

He knew very well that it was her ringtone for the Medical Examiner's Office.

"Sorry," Kenzie apologized, standing up from the breakfast table. "I need to take this."

"You're not supposed to be on call today," Zachary objected as she hurried away from the table.

"I know that," Kenzie snapped. Which meant that something serious was going on. A mass casualty event? What would justify Dr. Wiltshire's calling her when she was supposed to be off all weekend for their visit to the Petersons?

She retreated to the guest room she and Zachary were sleeping in, pulling out her phone and swiping the answer slider so that it wouldn't go to voicemail before she had a chance to pick it up in private. She closed the door and raised the phone to her ear.

"Kenzie here."

"Kenzie, I'm sorry to call you on your weekend off," Dr. Wiltshire apologized, his voice sounding stressed. "Believe me, I didn't forget you were supposed to have the day off today."

"What's happened?"

"The perfect storm. We have an autopsy that needs to be done right away. Urgent political pressure. Which is fine; normally, that would not be a problem and I would just take care of it."

"Right."

He was a well-trained, experienced medical examiner, the man who was teaching Kenzie everything she needed to know. There was no one better qualified to do the autopsy.

Especially one that apparently had political repercussions.

"The thing is… I broke my hand."

"What?" Kenzie heard her own voice go up several notes higher than usual. "How did you do that?"

"A stupid accident. That is not important right now. What is important is that this autopsy cannot be put off, and I'm sidelined. I haven't had a chance to line up someone who can do overflow work for us while my hand is healing, and they want it done now."

"Yes. I understand. I'm sorry about your hand. I guess… I'll say my goodbyes here and get packed and come back. I'll be a couple of hours." Kenzie ran one hand through her long, spiraling curls.

"I apologize. It shouldn't have happened. You need your downtime. But…"

"It is what it is," Kenzie agreed, shrugging. He couldn't control the fact that he was getting pressure from above to do the important autopsy immediately. And he certainly had not planned to break his hand.

How bad was the break? He could be out of commission for anything from a few weeks to months of healing and physio. Or if he were unable to regain full use of his hand… Her stomach plummeted at the thought of his having to leave the medical examiner's office.

"I appreciate it, Kenzie. I'll be here to provide any assistance or advice. I just can't do the manual work."

"Okay. I'll see you in a few hours, then."

Kenzie terminated the call and looked around the room. They hadn't brought much with them. They had only stayed over one night so Zachary would have time to visit his sister Joss as well as the Petersons. Lorne was an old foster father of Zachary's, the only parent he had stayed in touch with over the years, bonded by a love of photography and Lorne's dedication to a lost and broken boy he thought he could do something for.

Rather than immediately telling Zachary about having to return to Roxboro and pulling him away from the discussion with his chosen family, Kenzie started packing. Pajamas, Zachary's meds, and charging cables went into the suitcase. The door opened and Zachary peeked in.

"You're off the phone?"

"Yeah."

Zachary looked at her for a moment, then down at the suitcase. The smile disappeared from his face, replaced with an expression of concern.

"What happened?"

"They need me to come back to do an autopsy. Something urgent. Dr. Wiltshire broke his hand."

"Oh, no!" He sounded immediately concerned for Dr. Wiltshire, which made Kenzie feel guilty because she had expected him to be upset about cutting their visit short and had been prepared to defend herself, pointing out that she had no control over the circumstances. "Is he going to be okay?"

"It sounded like it. He said he'll be waiting for me at the office, so he must not be at the hospital." The morgue was in the basement of the police department building, not at the hospital. "I'll find out when I get there. I didn't ask for details."

Zachary looked around the room. "Do you need help with anything else?"

"I've got this. Check the bathroom to make sure neither of us left anything in there. And… I'll make apologies to Lorne and Pat."

"It's fine. They understand that sometimes things come up. You can't exactly control when people die."

Kenzie appreciated the support. He was being understanding and supportive, but she was angry. It was the first time in a year that she had specifically booked off a full weekend for some downtime with Zachary and his family. She couldn't blame Dr. Wiltshire for the circumstances, but she was ticked off and wanted someone to take it out on. She closed the suitcase, which was soft-sided and did not respond with a satisfying bang.

"Let's just get ready."

Zachary left the bedroom ahead of her and walked down the hall to check the bathroom while she walked the suitcase to the door.

"I'm so sorry," she apologized to the two men. "I'm not supposed to be on call. Nothing was supposed to happen to interrupt me this weekend. But…"

"Things happen," Lorne said understandingly.

Pat nodded his agreement. "I'll put the coffee in travel cups for you. And I could make some breakfast sandwiches while you guys get ready…"

Kenzie looked toward the table, where they had just started to eat the delicious breakfast spread Pat had prepared. She hated having to leave so abruptly. Having Pat make it into sandwiches for them would take a few minutes and be extra work on his part. Still, the alternative was leaving all of the food and not being able to appreciate his efforts. Her mother's voice in her head told her it was rude not to eat it after he had gone to so much work.

"Uh… sure. That would be lovely."

Pat brightened at her words, obviously having anticipated that she would say no. "Great! It will take no time at all. Just give me a couple of minutes while you put your bags in the car and say goodbye."

Kenzie smiled and nodded. Pat picked up the eggs, ham, and other ingredients to make into breakfast sandwiches and retreated to the kitchen.

"Thank you," Lorne said with a smile, laugh lines fanning out around his eyes and mouth. "You made his day."

"Happy to help. And it saves us having to stop somewhere on the way for gas station snacks or fast food. My body and my taste buds will thank me for it."

Kenzie gave the older man a quick hug as Zachary returned from the bathroom, holding up his empty hands to show that there wasn't anything else to go in the suitcase. Kenzie took the luggage out to the car, leaving him to say his goodbyes.

2

"Did he say who died?" Zachary asked, as he smoothly maneuvered the car through multiple lanes of traffic, the speedometer climbing.

"He knows it will take a couple of hours," Kenzie told him. "Slow down."

Zachary looked at the speedometer and touched the brakes to slow the car down just slightly.

"He didn't say who it was," Kenzie said. "And I didn't stay on the phone to ask. The sooner I get there, the sooner I'll know everything and be able to get started on it. He said it was political, so I assume…" Kenzie shrugged as she thought about it. "Probably some old guy. Dropped dead in his club or mistress's bedroom and they want to stay ahead of the gossip and headlines."

Zachary grinned. "But you're not cynical or anything."

"I know too much about how politics works from Dad's work. Dr. Wiltshire didn't give me any details, but just the fact that he said it is political makes me assume it's not someone who just died in their sleep last night."

"No, you're probably right about that," Zachary admitted. He made a quick lane switch that made Kenzie's heart race. But no one honked and, so far, she had never seen him pulled over by the cops for speeding. If he were, they would probably let him off with a warning if Kenzie apologized and pled that she was trying to get back to Roxboro quickly to get to a law enforcement matter. And maybe it would teach Zachary to take things a little more slowly.

But probably not.

They got into a clear lane, and he leaned back, relaxing, getting into the groove of a highway drive, which always seemed to calm his ADHD brain.

It didn't take the full two hours to get to the medical examiner's office, and Dr. Wiltshire didn't mention anything about the time when he met with Kenzie.

"Again, I'm sorry for doing this to you," he apologized, "Thank you for making the time. I know this is not how you expected to spend your Sunday. Can I get you something? You probably need lunch."

"No, I ate on the way. I'm good for a while. So, what have we got?"

The first shock was that it was not an old man. Dr. Wiltshire led Kenzie to her usual autopsy table and pulled back the sheet from a very small figure. A boy, a toddler of two-and-a-half or three, by Kenzie's guess. Slight build. Blond hair and a round face.

Kenzie shook her head. "I thought you said this was political."

Dr. Wiltshire sighed. "Michael Wade, son of Crispin 'Cash' Wade. Friend of the governor, currently a congressman, moves in all the right social circles."

Kenzie took this in. She shook her head, thinking about it. "So he and the governor are putting pressure on the medical examiner's office to have the autopsy done instantly, so there are no questions raised in the newspapers or social media."

Wiltshire nodded. "People like this don't want there to be any lingering questions about a death in the family. They want a statement as to the cause of death. A tragic accident, unavoidable, all that kind of thing. We'll oblige them the best we can. It looks like a simple open-and-shut case, but you can never predict complicating factors."

"No," Kenzie agreed. She looked at the body on the table.

It was, at first glance, unremarkable. The child looked as if he had been healthy in life. The cavitation in the front of his skull indicated he had met with a pretty strong force. A car accident or fall from a significant height, most likely. She shuddered, glad that she did not have any children of her own. She couldn't imagine trying to deal with the sudden and tragic death of a child she had thought healthy and happy. It had been hard enough when they had lost Amanda, Kenzie's sister, as a young adult, after a long and protracted battle with kidney disease. At least they had known what was coming and knew that she was no longer suffering.

"What's the story?" Kenzie asked. She picked up the file on the counter, which should have the basic scene details, but she wanted to hear everything Dr. Wiltshire thought might be important from the start.

"Fall from a third-floor window. Apparently, the boy's caregiver was not with him, didn't realize he had gotten into a room he wasn't supposed to be in. There was a balcony. He went climbing like kids do and went over the rail." Wiltshire's voice was flat and clinical, removing himself from the situation. There was no point in their getting wrapped up in the emotions of a tragic case. They carried a lot of burdens and couldn't spend a lot of time and energy grieving over the loss of a person they hadn't even known. Enough of the tragedy of a case would seep in through the cracks in the walls they built around themselves without their opening the door.

Kenzie nodded and followed his lead, not letting herself think about the family's loss and the tragedy of a young life cut short. She was lucky to live in modern times when the death of a child was a rare event rather than something that every family went through multiple times. In days gone by, it had not been unusual to lose several children in infancy or early childhood. They were privileged. There were places in the world where that was still true.

She dressed, scrubbed, and tapped the button on the floor to make her initial recording. She introduced the case with the patient name, date, and details of the death they had been given. It was clear that George had already examined the body for any forensic evidence and washed it in preparation for Kenzie's arrival. Kenzie hadn't seen him in the outer suite when she had come in. He had probably been called in especially for this case, as she had, and had gone home when he was finished preparing the body for her.

Kenzie proceeded with a gross examination of the body, carefully noting any defects, bruises, cuts, or anything else that might be important later. No birthmarks. A variety of bruises, as was the case for most toddlers. Kenzie studied them closely, and moved the body from front to back and then front again

"Something of note?" Dr. Wiltshire asked.

"No. I don't know. There are bruises on his arms, upper and lower, and on both his back and front."

"Recent? From today?"

He could see the coloring as well as Kenzie could, and had drilled her in the past about the colors the bruises went through from the time they were inflicted until a week or two later. Everyone healed at different rates, of course, but the order of the colors was always the same, and the timeline could be estimated.

"No, nothing that is obviously today. But they wouldn't be, would they? How long before the accident did he get out of bed?"

"Not long. It wasn't clear from the report from the police at the scene whether he had been up interacting with a caregiver before the incident, or went straight from bed to the balcony before they knew he was up."

There would be a number of people to interview, Kenzie suspected, and anyone who was closely connected to the boy might be too distressed to give a clear statement in the first few hours of the investigation.

"The bruises are a variety of ages," Kenzie observed. "I know that kids get into trouble, some of them more than others. And some kids bruise quite easily. But… it seems like a lot."

"Make sure they are all documented. You may want to try an alternative light source as well. You may be able to see other bruising under ALS."

Kenzie nodded. It was tedious to measure, take pictures of, and describe each bruise. And the ones on the shins, knees, and elbows seemed to be the typical accidental injuries of a child just learning to get around in the world. But the documentation needed to be done before moving on to other things.

"What position was the body in when the police got there?" Kenzie asked, as she examined the signs of livor mortis, the settling of blood in the body after death.

"The child was on his back but had obviously been moved. The damage to the skull is in the front. That has to be the position he landed in."

"Did the parents say they had moved the body?"

"They probably don't know. It's instinctive to turn the person over, look them in the face."

Kenzie nodded. She recorded her thoughts and questions and proceeded. When she had finished with the gross examination, she moved on to the eyes, ears, and mouth. Unsurprisingly, all three showed traumatic changes. That would happen when plunging face-first into the pavement, even falling from just a few feet up. Kenzie took pictures and set aside one eyeball for microscopic examination.

She looked at the mouth, frowning. Dr. Wiltshire looked up at the screen as she took a few pictures and moved the camera in for a closer, enlarged view.

"Observations?" Dr. Wiltshire asked.

"No broken teeth. The blow was closer to the top of the head than the front of the face. But there is significant bruising and tearing of the frenula."

"There is," Dr. Wiltshire agreed.

Kenzie met his eyes, then returned to the autopsy. She examined the mouth injuries closely and considered the color of the bruising. Not bright red. Not sustained in the fall.

3

Kenzie would need to do a microscopic examination of the eyes to gather all the information she could. There was blood visible on gross examination, but she would need more magnification to make a full evaluation.

"X-rays?" Kenzie asked.

Dr. Wiltshire nodded. She didn't really need to ask; she knew what needed to be done. "What will you x-ray?" he prompted.

"Head, of course, we will need to see how extensive the skull fracture is. Neck and shoulders." She paused. "Ribs, front and back. From there… we'll see."

He nodded his agreement.

Kenzie proceeded as planned. Dr. Wiltshire took a break while she did the films, so he didn't have to worry about a lead shield. Kenzie could see him through the window to the observation room, swigging some pills down with a bottle of water. She eyed his splinted hand while waiting for the machine to perform each of the x-rays she needed. It appeared to be a temporary splint, not a full cast. Hopefully, that meant it was only a minor injury, a hairline fracture or two that would heal quickly and without further intervention. She hadn't been able to see how much swelling and bruising there was because of the way that it was wrapped, so she couldn't guess at the extent of his injuries.

When Dr. Wiltshire came back in, she queued up the x-rays and they reviewed each one. The most important ones in determining cause of death were, of course, the skull x-rays. The massive fracturing from the fall was certainly extensive enough to have caused the child's swift demise. But it didn't sit right with Kenzie. It didn't match up with some of the other observations that she had made.

The neck and shoulders were also consistent with a fall from a height, with the heaviest part of the child, the head, hitting the ground first.

Kenzie put up the rib x-rays without a word, and she and Dr. Wiltshire studied them.

"What do you see?" Dr. Wiltshire invited.

Kenzie sighed and shook her head. She used the mouse pointer to indicate the callus formations on the posterior of several ribs, bright white on the x-ray. "String of beads," she said. "That's how my professor described it in med school."

"Which indicates?"

"The child has been squeezed or shaken hard enough to fracture ribs. In the absence of any brittle bone or connective tissue disorder… abuse."

"Resulting in death?"

"No. The calluses are healing fractures. Meaning it happened at least a few weeks before death."

Dr. Wiltshire nodded. "Follow-up questions for the investigators?"

Kenzie considered, then recorded several questions for the police to follow up on. Whether the custody of the child had changed recently. Whether there were any previous investigations into abuse. How many doctor and emergency room visits he'd had, and for what. Whether he had any diagnosed disorders.

"And we'll need to take bone samples to review for disease," Kenzie said, anticipating his next question. "See whether there is another explanation for multiple rib fractures."

At least there wasn't any danger of a child being inappropriately apprehended by DCF for abuse when there was actually an underlying disorder, traumatizing the child and putting unnecessary stress on the family.

But they would need to be mindful of the political consequences of any questions or reports that included allegations of abuse. Cash Wade was not a man to be trifled with. A number of ruined careers lay in his wake.

Eventually, they reached the point at which dissection was necessary. Kenzie wished that it could have been avoided. If there had been no findings in the gross examination and x-rays, and everything was consistent with a fall, Kenzie could have chosen to dispense with a full autopsy, ruling it an accidental death and avoiding any further indignity to the body.

But that was not the case.

Kenzie was bothered by the head x-rays and her observations of the tissue around the fractured skull, so she started there instead of with the Y-incision. Dr. Wiltshire made no comment or correction.

Kenzie made her cuts and peeled back the skin and tissue covering the skull to examine it, then removed pieces of the shattered skull to examine the bone and the bleeding within the subdural layer.

Except there was no bleeding.

She took a series of pictures of the membranes around the brain. The shards of the skull created by the explosive impact had cut into the membranes, blood vessels, and brain tissue. Yet there was little blood.

Kenzie pressed her lips together tightly.

"There was no bleeding from the fall. The victim was dead *before* he fell from that balcony."

Dr. Wiltshire shook his head, but it was in regret, not disagreement. "I concur."

The revelation that Michael Wade had not been killed in the fall from the window was only the first part of the answer. There was still more work to be done. And much of the evidence might have been compromised by the fall.

Any bone breaks could be the result of the fall or might have been inflicted earlier. The damage to the frenulum, Kenzie had already noted, could not have been perimortem. Neither were the previously broken ribs. Though looking at the x-rays under magnification, Kenzie could identify recent hairline fractures. Not starting to heal yet. Possibly caused by the fall or possibly broken within the previous few days.

Before proceeding with the dissection of the torso, Kenzie took a closer look at the bruising inside Michael's mouth and also dissected one eyeball under magnification. She was straightening up and arching her sore back when she saw that a couple of police detectives were in the observation room. A male cop she recognized as Detective Tuttle, and a woman she didn't know. Dr. Wiltshire had undoubtedly called them when Kenzie had discovered the boy was already dead before he fell. Kenzie instructed the computer to turn on the speaker in the observation room.

"Did Dr. Wiltshire fill you in on everything?"

Tuttle stepped forward, closer to the mic in the observation room. He pressed the click-to-talk button and addressed her.

"He told us there was no bleeding from the skull fracture, so Michael was dead before he fell."

Kenzie nodded. She waited for anything more, but that was all the detective had to offer. Dr. Wiltshire had only given them the minimum they needed to know to get them there and give them a heads-up that it was now a homicide investigation. Michael hadn't climbed over the railing. Whoever had dropped him off the balcony had intended to cover up the actual cause of death, and that suggested homicide, not accident or natural causes.

"We have made a few other findings that you need to know about for your investigation."

"Go ahead."

Kenzie showed them the pictures of the torn and bruised frenulum. "This is Michael's frenulum. It is that little string of tissues that holds your lip to your upper gums. As you can see from the dark bruising, this happened several days ago, not today."

"What causes that kind of injury?"

"This is sometimes referred to as a bottle jamming injury. It can be caused by a bottle, pacifier, spoon, or other object being forced into the child's mouth. Usually by a frustrated caregiver trying to force feed or quiet them. It can also be caused by a hit or slap directly to the mouth."

"Not an accidental injury, then."

"It would be very rare for it to be an accidental injury. It is almost always indicative of abuse."

"But you don't know by whom."

"Obviously, I can't tell that from the bruise."

Kenzie showed them the x-rays, indicating the damage that was definitely caused by the fall, the healed or healing fractures that were not caused by the fall, and recent breaks that could not be determined to be one or the other.

"Have there been any previous investigations into abuse?" she asked.

"Not that we are aware of. We will look into it."

"Is that everything you have so far?" the female detective asked.

"Not yet. I've just been investigating the ocular injuries," Kenzie gestured to the organ she had been dissecting.

"Eye injuries?" the woman inquired.

"Right." Kenzie pulled up the photos she had taken so far and indicated areas of damage. "There are a number of retinal hemorrhages. Areas where the tiny blood vessels of the retina have bled. Experience tells us that this is usually caused by traumatic head injury."

Dr. Wiltshire had returned to autopsy, but did not interrupt, letting Kenzie deal with the presentation and answering any questions.

"Like the one sustained by the victim?"

"Not from the fall from the balcony. If the head injury did not bleed after the fall, then neither did the eyes. These injuries were sustained before death. They appear to be recent. It's possible that the drop from the balcony was meant to obscure another head injury. And if that was the intent… then so far, they have succeeded. I'll be doing a more thorough examination of the skull and brain to see what preexisting injuries I can identify. As well as the hemorrhages, you can also see some retinal tearing."

"That's quite serious," Tuttle suggested.

"Yes, retinal tearing can lead to blindness. The tears in this case are quite small. Still, retinal tearing in children is almost always associated with trauma, unlike in adults where it can be spontaneous, part of the natural aging of the eye."

"Caused by being hit in the head?"

"Hit in the head or shaken violently. It could be the result of injury sustained in sports or roughhousing, but in most cases…"

"It is indicative of child abuse," the female detective finished.

Kenzie nodded. She looked the woman over. "I don't think we have met before, Detective…?"

"Oh, sorry. Detective Baker."

"Baker. Yes, retinal hemorrhages and tearing are common signs of Shaken Baby Syndrome. But they can occur in older children, too, not just infants. It is easier to cause damage shaking an infant, because their heads are so heavy and they have little control or stabilization until they get a bit older."

"So did these happen when he was a baby or more recently?"

"The hemorrhages are recent. The tears do not show any sign of healing or scarring, so I assume they were both caused recently."

"And is that all you've got?" Baker inquired.

"Do you need more than that to begin your investigation?"

"No, no. I just don't want to race out of here if you still have more to tell us." Baker gave her a little smile to show that no offense had been intended.

"Okay. Yeah, that's all I've got for you so far. But as you can see, I'm not done with this autopsy. I imagine Michael still has a few more things to tell us. But it will probably be along the same lines... signs of recent child abuse as well as older, healed injuries. You can see from the bruising..." Kenzie brought up a few representative pictures, "that these injuries are different ages. This is not just one incident of a parent losing their temper."

Baker and Tuttle both nodded.

"We'll look into it further," Tuttle confirmed. He looked hesitant. "You have heard, I assume, that this is the child of..."

"Cash Wade," Kenzie filled in. "Yes, so I heard. But he is not immune from investigation. If he or his wife had something to do with this..."

"We'll find out. I just mean... you will need to be careful of what you say. Keep this very quiet, don't let anything leak out. If there are accusations or innuendo made in the media before the facts are established..."

"It won't leak from here."

"Good." Tuttle nodded. "I don't mean to make any accusations. Just to make sure you're aware of how sensitive the situation is and how easily it could get out."

"I'm sure that Mr. Wade's PR people will be feeding the story to the press with their own spin," Dr. Wiltshire said. "But that won't stop people from speculating. There will be accusations of abuse made without anything coming from this office. And unfortunately, we will not be in a position to refute anything that is said. All we will be able to say for the time being is that it is under investigation."

Tuttle looked like he would argue, but he just nodded again, keeping his lips pressed tightly together.

"Keep us informed as to what is happening in the investigation," Wiltshire requested. "Any circumstances we need to be aware of to interpret our findings. And if you have any questions regarding scenarios or the specific injuries we have found…"

"We'll keep in touch," Baker agreed.

She and Tuttle left the observation room, expressions grim.

4

It was past their usual dinnertime when Kenzie arrived home. She was tired from the physical work and emotional toll of the autopsy, glad to be home where she could rest and regenerate.

She had called Zachary to let him know she was on her way home, so she was a little disappointed to see that he hadn't started dinner preparations by the time she arrived. It must have shown on her face.

"I have a plan," Zachary assured her quickly. "But I didn't want to start too early. I figured you would want a shower and change before you eat. You usually do."

It was true. After a particularly grueling autopsy, she always felt sweaty and disgusting and wanted a nice hot shower to scald it all away.

"If you need something right away, I can bring you a drink," he offered.

Since she shouldn't drink alcohol on an empty stomach, that would be a fruit juice or soft drink. She could have a glass of wine later with dinner.

"Yeah, that all sounds good. Why don't you bring me a grapefruit juice?"

Zachary's relief at her reaction was obvious. "Will do!" he agreed.

Kenzie retired to the bedroom to drop off her purse and other items. She started the shower warming and began to undress. Zachary brought her a glass of grapefruit juice.

"Your drink, Miss."

"Perfect." Kenzie had a long sip, then set it on the dresser as she finished undressing.

"I don't know how you can drink the stuff," Zachary said, shaking his head. "I mean… I can force myself to, but I don't enjoy it."

"Well, considering your usual diet… I wouldn't expect you to."

While his palate was expanding, he still returned to childhood favorites when he was tired, stressed, or wanted to celebrate. Chicken and stars soup, macaroni and cheese, pizza, burgers. His love affair with garlic bread provided endless amusement.

Zachary watched Kenzie divest of her clothes appreciatively. But he didn't try to start anything. He knew by now that she needed the shower more than anything else and wouldn't want him to touch her.

"You'd better start on that dinner now."

"Yes, ma'am."

"A minute ago, it was Miss."

"Well…" he looked flummoxed for a minute. "It's ma'am when you're giving orders."

That made sense. He had probably been well-trained by foster mothers and social workers to show respect and "yes, ma'am" for all he was worth when he was told to do something.

"See you in a few minutes. I'll try not to be too long."

He probably had a good idea that it would be at least half an hour before she was out of the shower, which was why he hadn't started dinner before she arrived home. A nice long, hot shower was just what Kenzie needed.

When she dressed and returned to the kitchen, Kenzie found that Zachary had been hard at work. With his ADHD and PTSD-related executive dysfunction, coordinating the different parts of preparing a meal was challenging. She was lucky if he could get breakfast on the table without forgetting anything, or one main dish for supper.

But he had managed to get plates, cups, and cutlery on the table, a jug of water, a wine glass in case Kenzie also wanted a real drink, a salad with a choice of bottled dressings, and a couple of microwaved dinners from the freezer.

"Good job," Kenzie approved. "This looks great."

He draped a dishtowel over his shoulder like Pat Parker often did when working his culinary magic in the kitchen. "Did I forget anything? Anything else you want me to get?"

Kenzie took a careful look and shook her head. "No, I think you got it covered."

"And we can have ice cream for dessert."

"Ice cream sounds good."

Kenzie sat down and started to dish up. Zachary waited a moment to see if she would discover something she was missing and, when she did not, sat down across the table from her.

"So, how was the autopsy? Took longer than you expected?"

Kenzie rolled her shoulders. Everything had loosened up in the shower, and she felt much more relaxed. "It's not done yet," she told him. "Sometimes it takes a few days to get everything done."

"Because you're waiting on tests?"

"No, because we're taking extra care to be thorough. We can't take the chance of a case like this going sideways. Everything has to line up and be presented perfectly."

"A case like this? Because it is political?"

"It isn't political… but there is political pressure."

Zachary took a bite of his microwave dinner and chewed slowly. "How is that?"

"Because it is not a public figure who died, but someone in his family."

"So he will bring his position to bear, even though it isn't actually anything politically motivated?"

Kenzie nodded at the assessment. Zachary didn't ask who the deceased was or who he was related to. He knew that information would be confidential. When Kenzie discussed her cases with him, she never named names.

"Was it like… a kid with a drug overdose? Or a spouse?"

He would find out sooner or later. And Kenzie knew that he was careful not to repeat anything they discussed about the medical examiner's office.

"No. It is a child. A young child."

"Tragic. Lots of public sympathy," Zachary suggested.

"Yes. But there are going to be some problems with them portraying themselves as grieving parents. At least once our findings are published."

"They aren't the parents?" She could see that Zachary's mind immediately went to foster care or adoption, an affair, or a second marriage.

"I haven't checked into any of that. But... they lied about what happened. And the victim shows signs of abuse."

"Oh, boy. Well, that's going to be a problem."

"It's a very delicate situation."

"Yes, it is."

Zachary's eyes went hazy. He was no longer looking at Kenzie or imagining what kinds of problems they would encounter in the media. Instead, Kenzie was pretty sure he was back in his own childhood; abused in his own family, placed into foster care, and exposed to more abuse from caregivers, other foster children, institutional care, and probably a lot of other situations he had never told Kenzie about, and maybe never would.

Kenzie put her hand over his on the table. He flinched, but then kept his hand in place and gradually refocused on her.

"It's okay," Kenzie assured him. "Just stay with me."

5

———

"I'm okay," Zachary told her immediately, shaking his head as if to shake off the memories. "Sorry, I just spaced out for a minute there."

"It's okay to talk about it. I can see how this might disturb you."

"It's fine," Zachary said. "We both know that I have a past." He shrugged. "We don't need to go over all of that again. Tell me more about the case. What did you find in the autopsy?" He took a bite of his dinner, though he didn't look like he was enjoying it.

Kenzie outlined her findings so far, watching him carefully to see if anything would push him over the edge. She didn't need to go into anything in detail if it appeared to bother him. She could stop at any time and they could change the subject. He could tell her about what he had been working on that day, if he had any interesting cases in his PI business.

"So those things are pretty conclusive?" Zachary asked. "They aren't things that you would see on a child who was just hyperactive or clumsy?"

"Some of them, on their own. Bruises of different ages on shins, knees, and elbows, but not the stomach and back or around the arms. He could conceivably fall and hit his mouth against a piece of furniture. Toddlers do things like that. The ribs..." She shook her head. "Unless he has brittle bones, somebody squeezed him very hard."

"Not just the paramedics trying to resuscitate him, because they were healing."

"They didn't happen during CPR or the fall," Kenzie confirmed. "They happened some weeks ago."

"And everything else is different ages, so it's ongoing, not just one incident."

Kenzie nodded her agreement. "I'm not sure what we're going to find is the cause of death, but they tried to cover it up so, chances are, it wasn't just Sudden Cardiac Death or choking on a candy or toy. Whoever threw him over that balcony is involved in the abuse and complicit in his death."

Zachary continued to eat, chewing slowly. "What if it was natural, and they were only afraid that it was caused by something they had done to him?"

"I supposed that's a possibility. Or that they were afraid we would see evidence of the abuse that had occurred before his death and would jump to the conclusion that was what he died of. But I think either way, it suggests a guilty mind."

"Definitely trying to cover something up. Why else throw him off of a balcony?"

They both ate in silence for a few minutes. It was Zachary who spoke next, voicing what they had both been contemplating.

"There are other possible reasons. Rage, loss of control over something that the child did. Hate for him. Punishing the spouse by causing indignity to the child's body."

"Those... seem like a stretch. I hope."

"Yeah. I don't know why it feels better that it was just a logical decision to cover up a possible homicide. Like it's worse if it was an emotional reaction."

"I think... it's the depth of that emotion that is chilling. Having that much anger or hate for either the child or the spouse... that he would be willing to go to those lengths after his child—or a child in his household—had died..."

Zachary nodded. "That's a lot of anger."

Kenzie pondered it. "Right now, I'm going to proceed on the assumption that it was to obscure the evidence. Which means that I'll be looking very hard at the body to catch every clue."

"Yeah. It doesn't really make any difference to your autopsy what the motive was. You're dealing with the body on the table. It might matter to the cops investigating the case, but they'll develop their own theories and explore all possible avenues."

"We'll exchange information; each investigation will inform the other."

Zachary scraped up the last of his frozen dinner. Kenzie noted that he hadn't helped himself to any salad. But at least he was eating. She was watching his mental state and weight carefully as the days shortened. She knew his thoughts would be returning to Christmas, and his annual depression reasserting itself. It wasn't a big deal that he didn't eat the salad. He was still eating, and his weight was at a healthy level, his cheeks filled in rather than hollowed out. His dark eyes were bright and interested, despite the potentially traumatic subject matter.

"You never think about things like that happening in wealthy, upper-class families." Zachary pushed his empty dinner tray away from him an inch. "At least, I don't. I always associate abuse with the lower classes. The stress of too many mouths to feed and not enough money. People brought up in the cycle of poverty and abuse. Fostering kids just for supplemental income. Drinking and arguing getting out of control."

Kenzie smiled. "Rich people still have stresses too. They still drink and get into arguments. There are a lot of egos, power plays, high expectations."

"Huh. Yeah." He raised his eyes to hers. "But you never...?"

"No. My mom and dad never hit me or abused me in other ways. There were plenty of arguments when Dad was at home, but they didn't get out of control and never led to violence, as far as I know. They got along pretty well, as long as they weren't together for too long." Kenzie ended on an ironic note. She'd never really thought about the dynamic between her parents very deeply. It was just the environment she had grown up in and it seemed perfectly normal.

"So maybe your dad's work taking him away from home was a good thing."

"Yeah. It probably was. Most of the time when he was home, he was very loving and generous. I didn't hear many arguments between them. They were generally behind closed doors, voices lowered. When they were on display, they spoke to each other civilly, even lovey-dovey. I told you I didn't even know when they got divorced."

Zachary chuckled. "That's so crazy. I can't imagine."

"I was on my own by that time, halfway around the world, and they didn't want to bother me with it. I didn't notice any difference when I saw them. They were still fine with each other when I saw them together. I think their relationship now is probably better than it ever was when I was growing up and they were still married. Dad still has a space to park his car in the garage, a study in the house to work in when he is in town. I haven't asked about sleeping arrangements." Kenzie's cheeks got hot. She did not need to know whether her divorced parents slept together when Walter was in town. Or if they were sleeping with anyone else when they were apart. They were both healthy adults. She assumed they had interests other than lobbying and fundraising.

Zachary laughed at Kenzie's discomfort. "What was the point in getting divorced, then?"

She shrugged. "I suspect Mom wanted independence. Being able to manage her own affairs without worrying about the money she made going to Dad, or vice versa."

"But she runs his family foundation."

"Well… yes. But she always has. Since before I was born."

"You don't think that's strange?"

"Of course I do. But if it works for them, who am I to say anything about it?"

He shook his head in amazement. "What about your friends when you were growing up? In school or whatever. You must have seen signs of abuse in other families?"

6

Kenzie had to think about that one. Her first instinct was no, none of her friends had been dealing with abuse at home, against themselves or others in the home. If they had been, she would have noticed it. She would have reported it to her parents, a school counselor, or teacher. Of course.

But she knew the statistics. Upper class or not, the stats said that a number of the kids she had been going to school with were experiencing domestic violence. But she had always figured that if parents of that class didn't want to take care of kids, they had the money to hire someone to do it for them. There was no need to deal with the frustrations of child-rearing if they weren't cut out for it.

"I guess there had to be, but I don't remember seeing any red flags for abuse. I never thought that someone might be getting hurt…"

Zachary nodded. "Kids get pretty good at hiding it, avoiding questions and reports. Reassuring anyone who suspects that something might be going on."

"Still… you would think that I would have noticed something. Been uncomfortable. Seen bruises or other signs."

"Most abusers won't hit you in the face where bruises would be visible. Slaps, maybe, as long as you don't bruise too easily. But anything that might cause bruises or scars… under your clothes. Or learn how to hurt without leaving a mark."

Kenzie's heart ached when she thought of the experiences Zachary had been through. His childhood experience had been the complete opposite of her own. She'd always had food on the table, parents who were kind and generous and usually patient with her. And Amanda, her baby sister. Even though Amanda's kidney disease had put a lot of extra stress on the family, they had pulled together rather than being pushed apart, as many families in the same situation were.

Her mind shifted to the boy on her autopsy table. No bruises on his face. The torn frenulum was hidden from view, but clearly indicated violence, something being shoved into his mouth to keep him quiet. The damage she observed in the ocular exam and the burst eardrums suggested shaking and blows to the head. Broken ribs showed that he had been squeezed, someone crushing the breath out of him, probably to stop him from crying. Multiple restraint bruises and blows to the stomach and back. That poor boy had been through so much. And what Zachary had said was true; someone had gone to lengths to hide the violence, both before and after the boy's death.

"That's so awful," she told Zachary. "I can understand a parent who gets frustrated and loses it once. But not… systemic, ongoing abuse. Being careful enough to hide it means that they are making a choice. Instead of choosing not to take out their anger or frustration on the kid, they're choosing to hide it. To… get whatever satisfaction they get from letting go and keep anyone from finding out."

"Or pleasure," Zachary said.

"Hmm?"

"It doesn't always have anything to do with anger or frustration or being drunk. Sometimes it's just because they like to cause pain."

Kenzie nodded, swallowing. Was that true of someone in Michael Wade's orbit? They just liked to hurt little kids?

"There are tricks for hiding it," Zachary went on, continuing his previous line of thought. "So that friends at school or teachers don't notice it. Hiding bruises with long sleeves and pants, even when it's hot out. Makeup to cover it, though that's not as easy for a boy. Avoiding gym or any kind of sports or activity where you have to change."

Kenzie cast her mind back to school. There had been kids who wore jackets or long sleeves all year. Vermont might not get hot like the desert states, but it was warm enough that such things were uncomfortable. She had always rolled her eyes at kids, usually the less-popular students, who felt the need to hide under voluminous hoodies and layers of clothing and wouldn't look her in the eye.

"Oh, man. I was so blind."

Zachary nodded. "But even if you had known to look for those things… they aren't proof, are they? Even a teacher who is looking for them can't force a kid wearing long sleeves to roll them up to make sure he isn't covered with bruises, cuts, or cigarette burns. They can't call DCF and start an investigation just because the kid doesn't participate in gym. And the kids who are drowning… sleeping in class, drinking, repeat runaways… they're just seen as bad kids. Best to get them out of school so that they're not a negative influence on the others."

"Even now, when we're supposed to know better?"

He shrugged. "From what I've seen… yes. There may be some enlightened educators who can reach these kids, but most of them get jaded pretty fast when faced with the 'bad attitudes' of kids who don't trust anyone and lash out at those who try to help them."

"I guess. We figure that if they need help, they should be asking for it. They should be grateful and take the first hand that's extended to them."

"Yeah." Zachary toyed with his fork. "But a kid caught in the system or with a bad family… he knows he can't trust anyone, and that if he tries to get help, it's just going to backfire and generate more abuse."

Not that there was anything a toddler *could* do. By the time a child was old enough to find some trusted adult outside the family, it was too late. He'd already been trained to be quiet and not to trust anyone.

"Time for the ice cream," Kenzie declared.

Zachary looked relieved. He stood up and went to the freezer to get it out.

7

Kenzie went through her usual routine of processing all the emails, voicemails, and deliveries that had come in while she was gone. One day, maybe she would have a morgue of her own and be able to employ somebody to do those things for her but, for now, she *was* the person employed to do them. She had to keep everything in the office running smoothly. She was not expected to do more than assist with postmortems, not to do everything herself. But Dr. Wiltshire had left her a brief note indicating that she was to call him if she had any questions that needed to be answered and, in the meantime, to continue with her usual work and finish the autopsy of the Wade boy. Kenzie frowned, looking down at the messily scrawled note. It wasn't Dr. Wiltshire's usual precise script. But he had a broken hand, so he was either writing with the broken one, or with his non-dominant hand, neither of which was likely to produce neat penmanship.

She had performed autopsies, or portions of them, without Dr. Wilt-shire supervising her. Still, he didn't like her to do too much without his watching over things. He was responsible for any of the work she did, so he wanted to ensure it was done right.

It seemed odd that he would want her to proceed without him on a case that was so potentially explosive as the dissection of Cash Wade's son.

Kenzie continued with her administrative work, then finally called Dr. Wiltshire.

It took a few rings for him to answer and, when he did, Kenzie could hear a lot of background noise. Like he was in a garage or a department store.

"I guess you got caught up on another case?" Kenzie guessed. That would make sense, at least. He had a competing call that he had been required to attend.

"No. I have to see the surgeon about my hand," he dismissed. "What's up, Kenzie?"

"I just wasn't sure about proceeding on the Wade case. I can do it, of course, but… I thought you would want to be back here for it."

"I don't know when I will be in the office, so you'd better take care of it. I'm sorry."

"Oh, okay. Sure, of course. You can review my photos and notes before signing off on anything. I won't release the body until you've had the chance to look everything over carefully."

"Are you concerned that you got something wrong? Do you have a question that needs clarification?"

"No. I just thought you would still want to have a hand in." Kenzie winced at her own inadvertent pun. "I haven't even gotten back to it yet."

"Well, I'm available if there is something that concerns you. Something that you have questions on or want me to double check."

"Thanks. I had some questions about the original scene survey…?"

"Well… how detailed are these questions? The fact is it appeared to be an accident scene and we didn't do an extensive scene review."

"Things like how far the other rooms were from the balcony that he 'fell' from. Where is his bedroom? Whose room was it? What rooms are close? If he was dead before he went off the balcony, which we know to be the case, then there could be blood evidence or other trace that needs to be collected."

"I didn't go into the house. In fact… I wasn't present in person at the scene."

"Oh." Kenzie knew that he had to sign off before the body was removed. He hadn't sent Kenzie because she'd been out of town. Any of the death investigators could do it, of course, but Dr. Wiltshire was usually pretty particular about what he allowed.

"I had Ralph attend, and he took the footage and broadcast it to me on my iPad so that I could see what he did firsthand. The ME is allowed to attend virtually. I can't always get to every site in a timely manner in person."

"Right, of course, and this one looked like it was a pretty clear-cut accident."

"Exactly. We don't go into every death investigation expecting to find out that it was homicide. There are plenty that are attributable to natural causes, accidents, and suicide. And you can rule out suicide with a child so young."

"Right, of course. If he climbed or jumped, it wasn't because he intended to kill himself. Except he didn't climb or jump. And now we're looking at…"

She didn't use the word "murder." It could still be something else. Murder was a legal definition rather than a medical one. He could rule homicide, but it would be up to the police investigation to determine whether it was murder, manslaughter, or something else. Motive wasn't something that could usually be determined through an autopsy.

Dr. Wiltshire sighed heavily. Kenzie could hear pages going out over the hospital PA system. "You'd better go back there," he decided. "You'll need to find out the answers to your questions and take any samples or trace you identify."

Kenzie hadn't been expecting to visit the scene of Michael Wade's death when she had left home that morning. She had hoped to finish the autopsy with Dr. Wiltshire and had not prepared herself for investigating the scene of the death on her own. She asked for the police to assign someone to accompany her. There was no way she would just show up at the scene and expect to be let in, and she also did not want to walk into a homicide scene without some kind of protection. Of course the killer of a child would not necessarily pose any threat to Kenzie, but she wasn't going to walk into it blindfolded. And she also didn't need any accusations that she had planted evidence. She needed someone else there to confirm her story.

She expected to be assigned a young officer, someone they could spare to hang around with her for a while without being needed anywhere else.

But it was Detective Tuttle who showed up and told her he would be going over with her.

"Are you sure?" Kenzie asked uncertainly. "I could be a while out there. You probably have better things to do. You don't want to send someone junior?"

"I'd like to be there, see what you see, bounce ideas back and forth. The scene survey is a pretty important piece of the puzzle."

"Well, yes, it is," Kenzie agreed. That was why she had called Dr. Wiltshire about it when she hadn't been able to find what she wanted on the file. That was why she was going out there. Essential evidence had been missed when they had first arrived at the scene. Would it have been sanitized in the twenty-four hours since then? They couldn't take the risk of it getting any more degraded. Or lost. Or cleaned. "Okay. I just wanted to make sure that it wasn't a waste of your time."

"I can't imagine it would ever be a waste of my time to attend a scene with you, doctor."

Kenzie eyed him, trying to decide whether he was teasing, flirting, or just clumsy in his attempt at a compliment. He gave her a small smile and she still wasn't sure.

She grabbed her death kit and double-checked to ensure it contained everything she expected to need. If it turned out that a more extensive scene investigation was required, she would need to get techs out there with her.

8

Kenzie had grown up with the rich and powerful of Vermont. Her parents were not as ostentatious as many of the others she knew. They were more low-key, willing to work behind the scenes and not get a lot of recognition for the charitable donations and other work that they did. Walter Kirsch and Lisa Cole Kirsch were recognized as part of the ruling elite in Vermont politics, even if they did not hold governmental positions. There was power, and then there was power.

And there was rich, and then rich. Kenzie had grown up in luxury, given everything she needed, always with her own room and plenty of space to roam. She had nice clothes, good food and, when she was young, lots of playdates and parties. Her parents had been wise enough not to give her everything she wanted. She still had to do chores. So she had not been completely spoiled, but she certainly had not understood how the outside world worked back then. One of her responsibilities had been helping out with Amanda. The playdates and parties had ended when Amanda had been diagnosed with kidney disease. They had spent a lot of time in the hospital and taking care of her at home. The family's focus had turned intensely inward, and they had shut off the chatter of the world outside of their little circle. Until Kenzie had turned eighteen and donated her kidney to Amanda and, for a while, Amanda had been better. Kenzie had entered college life, had traveled, and had explored the big wide world outside of her family and Vermont to find her place.

The Wades, though, apparently had no clue what it meant to be understated or do their good works behind the scenes rather than in the spotlight. Their mansion put the Kirsch home to shame, and Kenzie knew that the Kirsch home was needlessly extravagant, especially with only her mother living there now. The Wade home was built like a Roman temple, with white marble and columns, a big white, shining block in the midst of the changing leaves of the grounds. There were fountains and greens and gardens, a gazebo that probably seated fifty, and no fewer than three swimming pools. It must take an army of staff to keep it looking so fresh and beautiful, like a painting of a house, with not a blade of grass out of place. Kenzie let out a whistle.

"I know, right?" Tuttle asked, shaking his head. "Can you believe that people actually live like this? And then have the gall to complain about how their lives aren't perfect?"

"Well… no one's life is perfect."

"But you can apparently get darn close."

Kenzie looked at the house and nodded. But within those perfect walls, a child had suffered over weeks or months and had died. The pure white stone hid the dark secrets within. It had not been a happy home for Michael Wade. Who knew what other suffering those beautiful halls hid.

"It would be nice if living in a home like this could actually make you happy," she told Tuttle.

He shrugged and drove down the long driveway that led to a circle in front of the house, then turned out of the ring to park in a small lot to the left of the house, out of sight. He had apparently been shown his place previously. Police were like staff. Helpful to have around when you needed them, but meant to be invisible when they were not.

She followed Tuttle to the door—the big front door, not a servants' entrance. He rang the doorbell. It was not long before the door was answered. Despite it being such a big house, someone kept close to the front door to ensure that visitors did not have to wait long. The person who answered the door appeared to be a housekeeper or personal assistant. A woman in a plain, understated skirt and blouse rather than the liveried butler Kenzie had anticipated. The woman's eyes flicked over them.

"Yes, how may I help you?"

"Detective Tuttle, ma'am. And this is Dr. Kirsch from the medical examiner's office."

"Yes?" She eyed Kenzie with disapproval.

"We have some things that we need to follow up on with regard to the young boy's death, ma'am. Some evidence that we need to gather that was not dealt with yesterday."

"They said yesterday that the scene was released. We could go back to normal. That woman and… was it you?"

"Yes, it was me. But some new facts have come to light that require our further investigation. I'm sorry to be a bother, but if we could come in and complete our business, we'll be as quiet as we can and get back out of your way again."

She pressed her lips together in disapproval. "Come in while I look into this."

She ushered them into a sitting room to wait, disappeared for some time, and eventually returned. She spoke to Kenzie rather than Tuttle. "I am Hilda Mathers. I am in charge of the household. If things are not kept running smoothly, that falls on me. Do you understand?"

"Yes," Kenzie agreed. If they were to mess something up or draw the ire of the lady and man of the house, it was Hilda who would take the blame. It was in her best interest to keep trouble out, not to grant Kenzie whatever she said she needed. "Like the detective said, we'll be as quick and quiet as possible. We don't want to interrupt the whole household. If we could see the child's room and the room he accidentally fell from, that may be all I need. If there is something else, we'll talk about it then."

"No one needed to see them yesterday. Just where the boy fell." Hilda gave a little shudder. "That poor boy. And his poor mother. So very tragic."

"It is," Kenzie agreed. "And we don't want to make it any worse for anyone by drawing this out longer than needed. They'll want us to finish the examination and the autopsy as quickly as possible, so they can lay him to rest."

"Yes, that's right."

"If you can help us to get this taken care of, I'm sure they'll be very appreciative."

"It's very unusual. We are not used to a *police presence* in the household."

"And you're not used to the tragic death of the young master, either. This whole thing is very usual."

"Yes," Hilda admitted. She took a deep breath and let it out slowly, then seemed to make her decision. "All right. I will take you there, but you cannot wander the house or disturb the servants. It's very important."

"We'll talk to you before we do anything else."

Hilda didn't appear to like that, but maybe she sensed that it was the best offer she was going to get. She nodded stiffly. "Follow me."

Kenzie and Tuttle followed. Hilda led them through back hallways used by the servants rather than the more public spaces where they might run into members of the household. They climbed a couple of flights of stairs to get to the third floor, which, according to the information Kenzie had been given, was the floor Michael had fallen—or been dropped— from. Hilda opened double white-paneled doors that slid into wall pockets, and gestured to the room.

"This is—was—Michael's room. The nursery."

"Thank you. We'll start here. And the room he crawled out the window from…?"

"Do you want me to show you now? Or when you are finished with this room?"

"Uh… now, if you don't mind. Then we don't have to bother you again until we are done."

"This way."

It wasn't simply across the hall or next door to the nursery. It was down two hallways, on a different side of the house. Hilda pointed inside the room, across to the balcony outside the sliding glass doors. She didn't look in the direction her finger was pointing, but looked studiously away from it. "There. That is where it happened."

Kenzie gave the room a cursory glance and nodded. "Okay. We'll start with the nursery and then in here. And we can reach you…?"

"On any of the house phones." Hilda indicated an ivory and gold antique-style telephone on one of the side tables. "Just dial one."

"We will."

She and Tuttle returned to the nursery and the housekeeper went her own way after one more disapproving look.

Kenzie and Tuttle shut the sliding doors so that no one walking by could see what was going on, and looked around the room.

"Anything in particular you are looking for?" Tuttle asked, donning gloves.

"Mainly anything that would indicate where or how he was hurt before being thrown off the balcony. He was killed somewhere in this house, presumably on this floor, in this room or the one with the balcony."

Tuttle nodded and began a slow walk around the room, looking at the neatly made bed, a rocking chair beside it, and the various toys and furniture around the room. The heavy drapes were closed and the room was dim. Kenzie switched on her ALS and shone it around the room, sweeping it quickly at first to see if any large areas had been soaked or spattered with bodily fluids, and then moving it more slowly in small arcs, especially around the rocking chair and the pillow of his bed. Tuttle looked at the taut sheets as Kenzie shone her light on them, looking for any spots that showed up under the light.

"The sheets have been changed," Tuttle said. "No way they looked that crisp after the kid slept on them, even after just one night."

Kenzie nodded her agreement. "I think you're right. We'll have to follow up with Hilda on where the other sheets went. This is why it is a problem to return to the crime scene after they have had time to clean things up."

"I know, but it didn't look like a homicide," Tuttle told her, irritation clear.

"Sorry, it wasn't meant as an accusation. It's just… an observation. We only have the evidence we have. That's not your fault."

He looked at her for a moment, then nodded. Kenzie ran the light over the sheets and pillow once more. "With a toddler, I'd expect spots of saliva and urine, at least. These sheets are practically new out of the package. Take the pillowcase off."

Tuttle obeyed and held the pillowcase out toward her. Kenzie shook her head. "I want to see if anything soaked into the pillow."

They examined the pillow. Several splotches showed up under the ALS. Kenzie nodded, satisfied. "They didn't change the pillow, just the pillowcase. Let's take that with us."

"It isn't blood."

"No," Kenzie agreed. "Probably saliva. But we may be able to tell if it was held over his face."

"Ah." Tuttle nodded and put the pillow into an evidence bag.

The room included a small fridge and space suitable for preparing a bottle or snack. There was also an en suite bathroom with a bathtub. Of course. Why would they take the boy halfway across the house for a bath? Kenzie shone her light around and didn't find anything too alarming. "Let's take samples from the trap. Both the sink and the tub." The garbage had been emptied and sat with a fresh white bag in it. The under-sink storage area—appropriately secured with child safety latches—included bleach and other run-of-the-mill cleaners. Dangerous when swallowed, but nothing unusual or alarming. The medicine cabinet over the sink contained cartoon bandages, several ointments and sprays, lotion, a children's melt-in-the-mouth painkiller, and, of course, a child's toothbrush and toothpaste.

"Let's document all of this. Take a few photos."

"Any reason to take the toothbrush?"

"Uh... yes, let's. If there is a significant amount of blood..."

He collected it in an evidence bag, handling it carefully to avoid damaging any fingerprints. "Could the mouth injury be caused by a toothbrush?"

"Yes, especially if he was resisting, trying to keep his mouth closed when... whoever was trying to brush his teeth tried to force it in."

Tuttle nodded his agreement.

"Anything else? In here or the nursery?"

"I'm not seeing any blood spatter using the ALS. Or any areas that have been bleached. I mean..." Kenzie shone it around the toilet's base, "you can see that bleach has been used here, but that's perfectly normal for a bathroom. Especially a little boy just learning to use the big potty."

"And then we're on to the other room."

Kenzie nodded. She was reluctant to move on to the room with the balcony, but she obviously had to.

9

"**W**ere you in here at all yesterday?" Kenzie asked, looking around the room.

"Briefly," Tuttle confirmed. "We were told that he had wandered in and climbed over the balcony rail, so we took a quick look around to ensure that everything matched their story." He shrugged. "There wasn't anything to refute it. Nothing that we found, anyway."

"What was it like?" Kenzie asked. "How did the household feel? Were there people in here?"

He considered her questions. "It was late morning. Everybody was a bit frantic, as you can well imagine. Wanting to do something when… it was too late to do anything. The glass doors were thrown all the way open…" He thought about it. "I don't think a child would open it all the way. More likely he just squeezed between them, and whoever came in here to see what had happened pushed them open the rest of the way. Went to the balcony, looked down…" Tuttle shook his head. "We didn't measure trajectories or anything. He fell close to the house, as would be expected in a fall. It is a long distance. A child falling onto concrete from up here, on his head… No one thought he had a chance."

"Did anyone attempt CPR?"

"I don't think so. None of the emergency responders. If one of the staff did, they neglected to mention it. It was clear from the condition of the body that there was no point. It was obvious he was too badly injured. The deformation in the skull…" He shrugged expressively.

Kenzie nodded. From the sparse notes on the file, it didn't sound like anyone had attempted any lifesaving measures, but it was essential to establish all of the facts as early as possible.

Kenzie shone her light on the handles of the balcony doors and along the carpet in front of them. No signs of blood there.

"We need fingerprints taken here," she indicated the handles, "and out there on the railing."

"Yes, ma'am," Tuttle agreed. "And we'll need elimination prints from anyone who might have touched them."

Of course they were always phrased as elimination prints, even when their purpose was to identify possible suspects. Everyone who had touched the door handles around the time of the boy's fall was a suspect.

"No one actually saw him fall, obviously," Kenzie suggested.

"No. No one claimed to."

If someone had, he would be lying, since things had not happened that way. If someone claimed to have seen him fall, then either he was the person who had dropped the body off the balcony, or they knew who did.

"Is there normally anyone back here that time of day?" Kenzie gazed through the doors at the big blue pool.

"I don't know how much they use the pools and how much they just lounge beside them," Tuttle said. "It didn't look like anyone had been in it. No water on the deck that I noticed. There are some lounge chairs with fresh towels beside them. It was late morning, so it's possible that someone had been in earlier, or that someone would be out getting a bit of sun. But no one said that they had been outside. We'll have to follow up on that a little more carefully."

"It's a bit chilly to be swimming."

"The pool is heated."

Of course it was. Kenzie could imagine jumping into the warm water on a brisk fall day. It would be perfect. Until she had to get out, of course, into the cool air again.

Had the killer considered putting Michael's body into the pool? But doing so would not hide the broken skull. They would still have to be able to explain that, and there was no way the boy could have hit the side of the pool with enough force while swimming or playing in the pool to do the damage he had sustained.

Kenzie left the window to look around the rest of the room. It was the sitting room of a suite, but did not appear to be in active use. Guest quarters, Kenzie guessed. Not in constant use. Would the door usually be left open so a child could wander in? Could Michael manage doorknobs? Did he wander a lot?

"Who was supposed to be caring for him?" she asked. "He must have been under someone's supervision."

"According to the statements we got yesterday, he was supposed to be sleeping in his room. No one was sitting watching him sleep."

"Late morning? Almost noon? Why was he still in bed? I don't know of any kids that sleep that late."

"Maybe he had gone down for a nap. Or maybe he was up late the night before."

"Maybe a nap," Kenzie conceded. He could have been up and around in the early morning, then worn himself out and been put down for a sleep. Toddlers that age still napped, didn't they? Amanda had napped even older than that, when she was five or six. In the afternoon, not the morning. But Amanda had been sick. Her energy had been low because of her kidney disease.

Kenzie shone her light all along the walls and carpets, looking for any sign of blood or anything else suspicious. But the room appeared to be spotless under the ALS as well. There were no toys that might indicate the boy had wandered in there on his own or often played there. If he had interrupted someone in the room and been killed there, then they had cleaned it up or covered it up well.

Thinking about the possibility of evidence being covered up, Kenzie checked the walls behind the paintings and the carpeting under a fancy silk rug, but they all appeared to be clean as well. She shook her head at Tuttle. "I don't think he was killed in here. There's no sign of it. We'll need to check the other rooms on the floor."

He grunted. "Why don't you go back to the nursery and call Hilda about seeing the rest while I take care of the fingerprints and check the balcony. You might find out who is available for further interviews as well. See if their statements today match their statements of yesterday. Ask any of the questions that have been prompted by your autopsy." He paused. "But don't ask any questions until I'm with you. Just see who is available."

Kenzie nodded her agreement. It would be essential for her to have a witness, and she was not a trained police interrogator. Tuttle would get her back on track if she messed something up.

She stopped at the windows again, looking out at the balcony. She wouldn't touch the doors to open them up until the fingerprint evidence had been gathered. But then she should make a careful examination of the balcony and see if there was any blood out there.

"If you want to leave the ALS here, I'll check after I print," Tuttle told her, guessing her line of thought.

"Okay, yeah. The floor of the balcony and the railing especially. Whoever threw him over the edge might have rested the body on the top rail before pushing it off. Bodies aren't as easy to move as you see on TV."

"No," he agreed. "Though a child that age does not weigh very much."

"Still awkward. Would either of the parents have been able to lift him over the railing?"

"Either one, I would think. Mrs. Wade is tall and doesn't look like a weakling. Cash is…" Tuttle shrugged. "I don't think any man would have a problem lifting that little boy over the railing. And Cash is built like a bull."

Kenzie nodded. "Okay. I'll go back to the nursery and let you do your thing here."

She left the ALS with him and went back to the nursery to have one more look at it and call Hilda for permission to search the rest of the rooms on the floor.

10

Hilda returned to the nursery at Kenzie's call, and considered her with a pinched expression.

"You said you would only be a few minutes. That you just needed to look at this room and the one with the balcony."

"We would like to look at the rest of the rooms on this floor. We need to gather evidence."

"You can't have the run of the entire house."

"This floor—"

"And when you are finished snooping through this floor, you will want to look at the other floors. This is a private home. Citizens have the right to privacy. You don't need anything in any of the other rooms. Mr. and Mrs. Wade's rooms. The child wandered into a room where he was not allowed and climbed over the rail. That is what happened. You can't make it into something else. You don't need access to any other rooms. Leave this family to their mourning."

Kenzie hadn't even heard any voices on the floor while she and Tuttle had been there. Either the Wades were somewhere else, or the sound-proofing in the house was very good.

"If you don't give permission for us to see those rooms, then we will need to get a warrant," Kenzie advised. "Because we do need to see them.

Getting a warrant will cause extra publicity in this case. There will be rumors. Is that what you want?"

There would soon be rumors and more people involved anyway, but Kenzie knew that Hilda did not want any of those things to happen and would do what she could to avoid them.

"I can't," Hilda said stoically, shaking her head. "I'm not allowed to give you permission to search any of the rest of the house."

"Then you'd better call them and explain the situation."

Hilda stared at Kenzie stubbornly but, eventually, she caved. "I will talk to them again. But you will not get permission."

Kenzie nodded her understanding.

"Where is the other one? The detective? He'd better not be snooping anywhere else."

"He's in the other room, gathering some evidence. He won't go anywhere else."

"He'd better not," Hilda affirmed. "Or there will be trouble. Mr. Wade knows the governor. The attorney general. The police commissioner. If either of you steps out of line…"

"Haven't we followed your instructions while we have been here?"

She glared at Kenzie for a moment, then nodded. "Good. See that you do. You stay here until I get back to you."

"I will."

With one more glare, Hilda left the room, her hand immediately going to her pocket to retrieve a cell phone. But she didn't use it while within Kenzie's sight and hearing.

While Hilda was gone, another woman appeared in the doorway of the nursery. She peered inside, a frown on her face, and saw Kenzie.

"Oh, there is someone in here. Who are you?"

"I'm Dr. Kirsch. With the medical examiner's office. We're just following up on…" Of course, anyone in the household knew what she was following up on. Kenzie made a little motion to indicate the nursery and what had happened the day before.

The diminutive woman's eyes welled with tears. She shook her head. "My poor little Michael. I just can't believe it. How could such a thing happen?"

"Come in," Kenzie motioned for her to enter, indicating the rocking chair beside the bed. Kenzie perched on the edge of the bed while the woman sat down. "Are you the…" Tuttle had said that the boy's mother was tall so, clearly, it wasn't this woman. And she was too old to be Michael's mother. Maybe a grandmother?

"I help take care of Michael. Or… I did."

"Oh, I'm sorry. This must be particularly hard on you, then."

She sniffled and dabbed at her nose with a tissue. "Yes. I just can't get over it. That poor little boy. He was the light of my life." She wiped her leaking eyes with her palm. "You might think I'm being dramatic saying that, since he wasn't my own child, but it's true. He was the bright spot in my life. A child brings so much joy and *life* into your life."

Kenzie nodded. She tried not to think about Amanda and how Kenzie had been a second mother to her and had helped raise her. When she had died… it had left a great hole in Kenzie's heart. She had never considered having a child of her own after that heartbreak. She didn't know how she could handle it if something were to happen to a biological child. She didn't know how she would be able to go on.

"I know what you mean," she said softly. "I'm so sorry for your loss."

The nanny nodded her head and sniffled some more. "My name is Sylvia Arnold." She held out a wet hand momentarily and then withdrew it, changing her mind. "I'm sorry; I should have introduced myself."

"That's okay. Can you tell me what you saw yesterday? What you observed personally?"

Sylvia looked uncertain. She shook her head. "It was such a shock. I came here to check on him." She looked around the room as if she might find something of importance or comfort. "He wasn't here. Usually, he stays here to play. But he wasn't. So I looked for him. When I realized what had happened, saw him out there by the pool…" Her eyes swam with tears and she shook her head in disbelief. "I couldn't make myself believe it. How could such a thing happen? That baby. That poor boy."

"What happened? Do you know?"

"He had climbed out over the balcony railing and fell… I couldn't believe it. I still can't. What would possess him to do that?"

"Was he… an active child? Did he take a lot of risks or not seem to understand when something was dangerous?"

"What child understands all of the dangers, even when they are told?

It's built into their nature. They need to experiment, push outside the boundaries, explore the world around them. That's what children do."

"It is," Kenzie agreed. "They have to separate from their parents at some point and find things out on their own. But he was still pretty young. Kids that age are not usually so daring."

She blubbered, wiping her nose and eyes. "You must think I'm so silly, he wasn't even my child, but I can't help it. I've been taking care of him since he was a baby. He was so special to me."

"Was someone supposed to be with him? What was he supposed to be doing?"

"I couldn't be with him. I had been given other tasks to do. They said… that he would be fine. He would be with one of the other staff members or his parents. They could all look after him. Everybody chipped in now and then. I couldn't be with him twenty-four hours a day. I still needed to sleep, have days off, run errands…"

"Of course you did. I'm not saying that you did anything wrong in letting someone take care of him. I'm just curious about what the arrangements were."

"I was to be helping out in the kitchen for a few hours. I thought everything would be fine."

"I heard he was sleeping, and this happened when he got out of bed without anyone realizing it."

"Sleeping?" Sylvia repeated, looking puzzled.

"Yes, I was told that he was asleep. That he had gotten out of his bed and gone into the other room and climbed out before anyone realized that he was up."

Sylvia nodded slowly. "He might have been down for a nap, maybe. He was up early in the morning. Maybe he was tired or was not feeling well."

"How was he the last time that you saw him?"

"He was fine. He seemed…"

"Happy?" Kenzie suggested, when Sylvia couldn't seem to come up with the right word to finish her sentence.

"Yes. Well… not, maybe not happy. He was a little stormy. He was like that sometimes. But I knew how to handle him. He just needed some attention. Maybe he was cutting a tooth."

"Right. So he was grumpy? Upset?"

"His cheeks were red... I would probably have given him a pain reliever, in case it was his teeth. That usually helped."

Kenzie wondered how often painkillers were required for injuries rather than teeth. Of course being hurt would make a child grumpy and harder to deal with. And from what she had seen, Michael was probably hurt a good amount of the time.

"Was he a moody child? What was he like?"

"He was colicky when he was young," Sylvia admitted. "He cried a lot and was hard to settle. His mother was at her wit's end. I would rock him." Sylvia rocked the chair. "Hold him for hours until he settled, and we both fell asleep here."

"Did they ever take him to a doctor to see if it was something physical? Something they could do something about? Maybe reflux medication or a different diet?"

She shrugged and shook her head. "It was just colic. You can't do anything about colic. Just wait for them to outgrow it."

Kenzie nodded slowly. Had Michael been colicky? Or had the abuse started way back then, and he was crying in pain? Or maybe both—he'd been colicky, which had precipitated the abuse.

"Did someone change the sheets on the bed yesterday?" Kenzie asked.

Sylvia shook her head. "Wednesday is the day the bedding is changed."

"Maybe he wet the bed? And it needed to be changed earlier?"

"He was dry when I got him out of bed."

"But then he apparently went back to bed. Maybe he had an accident during or after his nap. Maybe that's what woke him up."

Sylvia shrugged. "If he did, no one said anything to me about it. That wasn't normal for him. He was dry during the day. Sometimes, he still had accidents at night, but not during the day. He was very good."

"So you don't know who would have changed the sheets or why."

"No. What makes you think they were changed?"

"I could see that they were fresh, unused sheets. Still starched and ironed. They hadn't been slept in."

"I don't know. I don't think that could be true." She didn't offer any further explanation as to why someone might have seen fit to change the sheets on the bed after the child had died. They wouldn't be expecting anyone else to sleep in the bed anytime soon.

"Michael is the only child in the house, right?"

"Yes. Well, usually, he is the only child here. Sometimes a visitor… but no, he was the Wades' only child." She dabbed at her running nose. "His poor mother. What she must be going through right now."

Kenzie sighed. "I can only imagine. I remember how it was when my sister died. And she wasn't that young. She was sick for a long time, so we knew it was possible, but when it did happen, it was so sudden…"

"Really?" Sylvia leaned forward slightly, getting closer to Kenzie. "That must have been very hard for you."

Kenzie nodded. She rolled her eyes upward, trying to keep them from filling with tears. Bringing up her own loss during the discussion would not be helpful. Not to her, anyway. She needed to keep her emotions under control and not think about Amanda and that loss of years ago. She could separate from it. Compartmentalize it until she was somewhere safe to think about it again. Not in the middle of an investigation.

"So, if you were Michael's nanny, what are your plans now? Will you keep working here, doing something else? Maybe until there is another baby?"

"Oh, I don't think I could." Sylvia shook her head sadly. "I could not stay here and take another baby. I would be too afraid… that it would happen all over again."

Which was far more likely if she were talking about the abuse, rather than Michael going off the balcony. She couldn't bear to see another child abused. It would be too hard for her to handle.

"Was Michael happy here? Were they a happy family?"

"Of course, of course," Sylvia assured Kenzie without enthusiasm. "This was his home. Of course he was happy here. What child wouldn't be? He had toys, lots of room to run around, the pool. The staff was very good to him and Deanne would make cookies for him, even though Mrs. Wade said he didn't need them." She smiled conspiratorially at this memory. "Michael loved chocolate chip cookies."

"And I'll bet that Deanne made really good ones."

"Oh, yes. They are to d—they are so delicious. Just the right amount of sweetness, crispy on the outside and chewy inside." She gave the tips of her fingers a chef's kiss. "Perfect."

Kenzie leaned forward slightly to ask her question, hoping that she would not scare Sylvia away, but pull her in, where she felt safe to share confidences, as she just had

11

"Did Michael fall down a lot?"

Sylvia looked at her, frowning. "Fall down? No. This fall… it was just… no one could have foreseen that such a thing could happen. There was a railing. He would have had to climb over it."

"No, I mean just when he was walking or playing. He had a lot of bruises."

"A lot of bruises?" Her expression went stone-faced. Blank. "No, no, he didn't fall down a lot."

"Where did the bruises come from, then?"

"He did not have a lot of bruises."

"I'm the one performing the autopsy, Sylvia. I know exactly how many bruises he had, where they were on his body, and the approximate date he received them. Think about that."

Sylvia sat there frozen, thinking about what Kenzie had told her. The color slowly drained from her face, but she still tried to tell Kenzie that she was wrong.

"Those must have been from the fall. It was so awful. He must have been black and blue from falling that far."

"No, they weren't from the fall. He didn't bleed after the fall because he was dead. When the blood isn't circulating through your body

53

anymore, you don't bleed or bruise. And I told you that I could tell how old the bruises were. They weren't all received yesterday. They spread out over weeks."

"Well… he must have gotten them playing, I don't know. Some people bruise more easily than others."

"If you were the one who was taking care of Michael, then you must have seen that. How many bruises he had. You didn't bathe him?"

Sylvia looked torn between not making herself look any more guilty and lying and making herself look uncaring. She kept shaking her head. "Yes. Yes, of course I bathe him every night before bed. I did."

"Then you saw the bruises."

"Yes," Sylvia admitted reluctantly. "I told you they must be from playing."

"How would he get a bruise in the middle of his back while playing?"

"If he… fell backward out in the garden. Or walked into something backward. Children can be so silly, running backward and inventing all kinds of games."

"He had a lot of friends to play with, did he?"

"Well, no. There were not a lot of children visiting the Wades. He mostly played by himself or with one of the adult members of staff."

"And you think one of them hurt him like that?"

"No, no, I didn't say that!" She quickly tried to cover the suggestion. "He could have hurt himself playing alone."

"How did he get the bruises on his stomach?"

"He must have run into something."

"So he got a lot of bruises playing. Did you ever take him to the doctor to find out why he hurt himself so much? If there was something wrong with him? A brain tumor or blood disease?"

"No. That would be up to his parents, not to me."

"And when did they last take him to the doctor?"

"I don't know. Usually, they would have a doctor come here to check on him. But only if there was something that needed treatment. If it was just a bruise…" She shrugged helplessly with one shoulder. "Who would take a child to the doctor for that?"

"When was the last time he saw a doctor, do you remember? And if I could get the name of his pediatrician, that would be helpful. So I could follow up with him on Michael's medical history."

"I don't know. I can't give that to you. His mother would know."

"Was she ever concerned about the bruises?" When Sylvia opened her mouth to answer, Kenzie pressed on. "Or did she tell you to ignore them?"

Sylvia closed her mouth. She looked at Kenzie. "I think… I should not answer any more of your questions."

Tuttle appeared in the doorway of the nursery and looked in at them, one eyebrow raised in question at Kenzie.

It wasn't until then that she realized she had done exactly what she had promised not to do. She had interviewed the nanny by herself, without anyone recording or being able to verify what she had said. The nanny could claim that anything Kenzie reported was made up.

Not that she had provided any real information. There were hints that she was aware of the abuse and certainly someone that close to the child should have been aware and had a pretty good idea who was doing it.

"This is Detective Tuttle," Kenzie told Sylvia. She motioned for Tuttle to come closer. "And this is Sylvia, Michael's nanny. Sylvia, why don't you tell the detective about Michael and how you think he got those bruises?"

Sylvia was clearly terrified about talking to the detective. It was one thing to talk one-on-one to a sympathetic woman doctor. It was quite another to have to answer the questions of a burly police detective.

"I told you I don't know anything about it," she protested. "I don't know how Michael got any bruises. He was a child. He had accidents."

"That was a lot of accidents. Do you think he had a brain tumor or something that made him keep falling down or walking into things?"

"No. I don't know. He's just a little boy. I don't think there was anything wrong with him. He just got bruises."

"You realize," Tuttle said in a slow, thoughtful voice, "that whoever was hurting him could turn around and say it was you."

"I would never do anything to hurt him!"

"You're the one that was with him the most, aren't you, the one who was charged with his care? So if he was getting bruises while he was under your care, that must mean that you are the one who was hurting him."

"No! He didn't get hurt while I was taking care of him. I took good care of him."

"So he didn't fall down and walk into things when you were taking care of him?" Kenzie asked.

Sylvia considered the question, her eyes darting from one to the other. "No, No, he didn't get hurt when he was with me. Only when he was with… someone else."

"Who else?" Tuttle asked.

"I don't know. I couldn't tell you what happens when I am not here. Other people look after him. He doesn't tell me how he got hurt."

A toddler didn't tell her how he got hurt? Whoever was abusing him must have scared him pretty good. That was a hard lesson for someone so young to have learned already.

"You must have a pretty good idea," Tuttle pressed. "His mother? His father? Someone else on the staff?"

"What is going on here?" a loud voice demanded. "What do you think you're doing?"

12

They all looked up to see who it was. Kenzie knew without turning to look at the doorway who would be standing there. The belligerent, authoritative voice could only belong to one person. The master of the house. Crispin Wade. Always referred to as Cash.

He was a heavyset man, his body appearing to be solid muscle rather than fat. He was formidable. He seemed to fill the doorway. Sylvia was gasping, hand to her mouth, trying to stop her tears, sit up straight, and do whatever else she was supposed to do when the master entered the room. Stand and salute? Cash certainly seemed to have the presence to order everyone around, with the clear expectation of being obeyed.

"Ah, Mr. Wade." Tuttle didn't turn a hair. He had his own presence. He stood with his thumbs hooked in his pant pockets, making himself appear bigger and wider than he was. Not the same class as Cash, maybe, but enough to command respect. "Detective Tuttle. I believe we met yesterday."

"Yes," Cash agreed. "So what are you doing back here today? I thought you got everything you needed yesterday."

"Well, things are not as they appeared. Which means that we needed to come back today to collect more evidence. I appreciate your cooperation."

"That cooperation is over. You do not have permission to interview my staff. You've seen what you need to, and I would ask you to leave. You will not be welcomed back into this house again. Keep that in mind before you bother coming out here again. Stay on your own side of town."

Those were fighting words. Kenzie looked at Tuttle, concerned about how he would react to Cash's superiority. There was a red flush at Tuttle's throat, but he kept his expression neutral and didn't move a muscle to show any threat to Mr. Wade.

"We were hoping for your permission to search the other rooms on this floor."

"No."

"If you don't grant it, we will be back with a warrant. In fact, I won't actually leave. I'll sit in my car and wait for it to be delivered, and then I will search the other rooms."

"You can't do that."

"I can't leave the scene without ensuring I've obtained all the evidence. There is no other option."

"Get out of here. I know the governor!"

"Yes, sir. You're not the only one. But you don't think he's going to help to obstruct a police investigation, do you? What kind of a political leader would he be if he didn't look out for the most vulnerable in his state?"

"He will not allow you to make a spectacle of this household. We are personal friends."

"I'll have to get a warrant before a judge," Tuttle said meditatively. "And if it takes more than one judge to get a positive answer, I will shop it around until every judge in the county has seen it and either denied or granted me the right to search the rest of the rooms in your house. That will probably make a pretty good stir at the courthouse. People will start to ask questions. Will want to know what or where the warrant was for. It might be confidential, but word still gets around."

"You can't do that."

Tuttle shrugged. "We'll see."

"What are you looking for?"

"Evidence in the death of your son."

"You already did that yesterday. The boy fell from the balcony to the concrete below. It was a tragic accident. You have investigated. You have gathered evidence. And now it is time to close your investigation."

"We know what happened."

Tuttle said it quietly, but everyone in the room froze. Everyone in the adjoining rooms where servants worked and talked froze and listened.

"We just need to find out where," Tuttle said.

"You know where. We know what happened. Why are you stretching this out? We are mourning the loss of our son. This game you are playing is going to backfire in your face."

"Maybe," Tuttle agreed.

"I'm asking you to leave my house now. My property. Go back where you belong."

Tuttle nodded his agreement. He looked at Kenzie to make sure she was with him. They gathered their various evidence bags and were escorted out of the house.

Tuttle and Kenzie sat in the car and Tuttle proceeded to make several phone calls to try to get the warrant that they needed. Kenzie didn't want to be accused of hovering or eavesdropping, so she did her best to ignore him and look at her phone, checking her email and what else she could do remotely. She had not planned to be sitting in the car for hours.

But as it turned out, they would not be sitting there for hours. Tuttle got a call from his sergeant calling him back to the police station.

"Sir," Tuttle protested. "We need to search those other rooms. If we don't do it today, evidence could be destroyed. Some cleanup was already done since we were here yesterday. And I don't think that coming back a third time would get us in any more hot water than going back in today."

Kenzie could have told him there was no point in arguing with his boss about it. The decision had been made, and with Cash Wade's full weight behind it, there would be no talking his way into a warrant. The governor would make his calls. The attorney general. Maybe even the police commissioner. And they would all ensure that no warrant was granted or even applied for. If Tuttle didn't want to end up riding a desk for the rest of his career, he had better know when to back off.

He listened to what his sergeant had to say, his skin taking on a grayish tone. He said a few "yes sirs" and then terminated the call. He looked at Kenzie and shook his head.

"We're not getting it today."

"We're not getting it at all," Kenzie said.

"Maybe not." He pressed his lips together and cleared his throat, uncomfortable. "I hate politics."

"I know."

"I want to get this guy dead to rights. This guy probably beat his kid to death, and he's going to stand in front of me and threaten my case and get away with it? With everyone throwing their support behind him? How can we call it a justice system if it only applies to those who don't have any power? If there are two different sets of rules?"

"It's not justice," Kenzie agreed. "But maybe we'll be able to get him another way."

"You have a way?"

"I don't know yet. We have more evidence to process." She indicated the bags in the back seat, "and I need to finish the autopsy. I don't know what I will find yet. But I can tell you, I won't be finding that he climbed over the balcony rail and fell to his death in a tragic accident."

Tuttle licked his lips and nodded. "Yeah. When that is made public, the family will have to answer for it. One way or another."

"I just hope they don't try putting it on the nanny or some other innocent servant."

"You think the nanny is innocent?"

"I can tell you she is a lot more broken up about Michael's death than his father is. I haven't seen the mother, so I can't speak to what is going on with her, but Sylvia is about as grief-stricken as a person can be over an unexpected death."

"You think she'll talk?"

"I hope so."

"Okay. I guess it's time to get back to the office."

Kenzie nodded and sighed as they turned around and left the big white building behind them. She was glad that she hadn't grown up in a place like that. It might have damaged her irreparably. She had a pretty good idea that if she had grown up like that, her parents would have seen to it that she could not follow her passion to go into something like the medical examiner's office. She would have been given a choice between charities, maybe. The choice as to what highbrow politician she wanted to intern with. But she would not have been allowed to follow her heart.

13

Despite the fact that Kenzie had been thinking about Lisa and about her own growing-up years, and despite Cash blustering that he knew everyone of any importance and would be able to apply whatever political pressure was necessary to get his own way, Kenzie had not been expecting the call.

She was at the morgue long enough to get all the evidence and samples properly cataloged for processing. She was thinking about whether to take lunch before she restarted the autopsy, when her phone rang.

Kenzie pulled it out tiredly and looked at the face to see who was trying to reach her now. She swiped the call.

"Oh, hi, Mom."

"MacKenzie. How are you doing, dear?"

"I'm okay. Pretty busy at the office," Kenzie offered, hoping this would encourage Lisa to get to the point, since Kenzie had work to do. "Dr. Wiltshire is off, so I'm trying to hold down the fort."

"Well, you have certainly made yourself useful there. He puts a lot of trust in you."

"Yes, he does," Kenzie agreed, allowing herself a smile. She was proud of how she and Dr. Wiltshire worked together and how much trust he put in her. It was rewarding to see how much she had grown and learned since she had first started there, when it was purely an administrative position. She had hoped that it would grow into something where she could put her medical skills to use and get experience in the field so that she could qualify one day for real medical examiner work. Dr. Wiltshire had quickly advanced her so that she was doing more than she had ever hoped to in her job. One day maybe she would have her own morgue to run. "So I can't take too long to chat. How is everything?"

"Things are well. I am working on a fundraising drive for the Kidney Foundation, of course, and we are looking forward to Christmas to decide which campaigns to participate in or donate to. There are always so many worthy causes, but we can only help so many. And we're hoping to include some mental health advocacy or research causes this winter. How is Zachary?"

"He's good so far. I'm braced for his depressive cycle, but so far so good."

"Maybe it won't happen this year."

Kenzie shook her head. "Maybe."

"And your father is well. Have you talked to him lately?"

"Yes. Well, it's probably been longer than it should be. I'll make sure to give him a call." Kenzie paused, waiting to see if that was why her mother was calling. Just to tell her to talk to her father? Did that mean that something was going on with him, or just that Lisa wanted to ensure they continued to have a good relationship?

"I'm sure he'd be happy to hear from you. The two of you should go out for dinner the next time he is in town. Or the three of you—take Zachary with you. No need to leave him at home by himself!"

Except it would probably be doing Zachary a favor to keep him away from Walter, who wasn't his favorite person. They both tried to be positive about him and not discuss his negative qualities and their negative experiences with him. If Kenzie were going to keep up a good relationship with him, she had to let go of past hurts and misconduct. Walter was a good man who cared about his family. That was what she needed to focus on. It wasn't easy for either of them, and Kenzie knew that Zachary had a particularly difficult time forgiving Walter's offenses against Kenzie.

"Was there anything you needed, Mom? Papers to be signed or something…"

"I just thought it had been a while since we talked last, and I would try to get ahold of you. I'm sorry if I've caught you at a bad time."

"I do have a lot of work to do here."

"I understand you are working on that terribly tragic death in Congressman Wade's family. I can't tell you how shocked and saddened we were to hear what had happened to him."

Kenzie stiffened, her muscles tensing before she even had a chance to process what Lisa had said.

"I can't talk to you about active cases," Kenzie told her woodenly.

"No, of course not. I understand completely. But it has been all over the news. We were so sorry to hear of his loss. You remember how it was when we lost Amanda... nothing can prepare you for that. And they didn't have the warning that we did or the happy years that we had with Amanda. His son was so young. An unbelievable tragedy."

"Yes, it was," Kenzie agreed. "But you don't know the details, so I don't think you should talk about it as if you do."

"The poor family just wants to move on. To be able to put it behind them and grieve in private. It is so difficult when you are a public figure and everyone wants to know every detail of your life. They want to see how upset you are, to see and hear and intrude on all those private times. It is a very difficult situation."

"Yes, I'm sure it is," Kenzie agreed. She had not been the one in the spotlight when Amanda had died. She was just the sister, not the father or mother. She was a side story, and not a very interesting one. They wanted to see her mother cry. Lisa stood strong in front of the cameras and continued to pound the drum, raising money for the research that could have saved Amanda. Every question was pointed back toward the need for more research, for a cure.

Cash Wade, on the other hand, was not interested in fundraising, talking about domestic abuse, or naming something on his son's behalf. He was only interested in silencing everyone and putting it behind him so that he and his wife and their entourage could continue to enjoy the good life that he had established for himself.

"You'll be careful, won't you, dear?" Lisa prodded.

"Careful of what?"

"You know how things can get blown out of proportion. I just mean that something insignificant should not be turned into a circus. Into something that it is not. You know that the Wades are a fine, upstanding Vermont family. They have been in the state for almost as long as the Coles and Kirsches have."

Almost, Kenzie noted. Almost as long. So the Wades were "new money" Vermonters. Not part of the old guard. The congressman wanted to make himself a part of the old fabric, to hobnob with the old Vermonters and be seen as one of them. But he was still a bit too much *new money* to do so.

"You know that I don't make any determinations in the work that I do based on someone's position in the government or in Vermont society," Kenzie said sternly. "I am looking for the truth. Not a sound bite."

"Oh, I would never imply that you are just seeking publicity. But things can be taken the wrong way, and you don't want anything you say to be taken the wrong way. People like Cash Wade—" Kenzie noted that it was Cash now rather than Congressman, "—are very good at spinning things the way they want to. And very sensitive to anything that might be… exactly what they want to hear."

"The Medical Examiner's Office will publish its findings, whether Cash Wade likes it or not."

"I thought you would be a lot more sympathetic to an old friend than—"

"It doesn't matter who he is friends with," Kenzie insisted. "We will publish the truth. And right now, that is *not* something that Congressman Wade will want to read."

There was a small intake of breath. A little gasp that Kenzie would be so bold and would insinuate that Wade might have been in the wrong about something.

"What do you mean?"

"I've already disproved the story Cash Wade and his wife would like us to believe. So I wouldn't believe anything he and his cronies might whisper in your ear. Take everything they say with a grain of salt. Maybe a full teaspoon of salt. Because he is a liar. And we will not be supporting his lies in our final report."

"MacKenzie," Lisa reproved. "You can't go around saying things like that."

"I wouldn't say it to anyone else but you. We won't put it exactly that way in the report. But you should know the kind of person you are dealing with. Cash Wade is a bully and a liar, and if you think that anything he is saying about the loss of his son is true… you'd better wait until you see our press release."

"What are you saying?"

"I can't say more than that. I can't give you any specifics. But you should know that he is lying. His son did not climb over a balcony rail and fall to his death."

Lisa was silent. Kenzie could hear her breathing on the other end, still there but unsure what to say.

"You understand?" Kenzie asked.

"Yes, of course. You are very clear. And very sure of yourself."

"There is no doubt."

"And you won't have any mercy for an old friend?"

"No, Mom. I can't. I have to stay impartial. No matter what happens, I can't let family or friends affect the way I investigate and report on this child's death. I won't write anything that is not the absolute truth."

"And you can't… I don't know… excuse yourself from this case."

"No, I can't. We don't have a big office. It is Dr. Wiltshire and I and some other staff members that help with gathering evidence or dealing with transportation. And Dr. Wiltshire is out of commission with a broken hand, which will take weeks or months to heal enough for him to use again. So it's up to me to keep things moving and finish the autopsy on Michael Wade."

"I see. And there is no way to… soften your findings. To make it less… inflammatory."

"I haven't released anything yet. I don't see how you could ask me to be less of anything. We haven't said anything to the public. If anyone says that we have, they are lying. We will release our findings when the investigation is complete."

"Of course," Lisa agreed. "Well, good luck with that. I hope everything goes well and smoothly, and that you do not attract too much… negative attention. Let me know if you need anything."

"I will."

"I mean it, MacKenzie. Anything. Just call me. Understand?"

"Okay, Mom. Thanks. Take care of yourself and give Lola a kiss for me."

"I will, dear."

Lisa terminated the call.

Kenzie suspected Lisa would not actually give the dog a kiss on her behalf.

14

Kenzie moved Michael Wade's body back to autopsy and made sure that all of her equipment was ready before starting. She tapped the button on the floor and dictated the date and time and her own name. She paused for a moment, used to adding that Dr. Wiltshire was present as well, even if he wasn't attending to the same dissection as she was. He was usually in the room to discuss the case with and to take a second look at any findings.

It felt very strange to be starting without him.

But Kenzie eventually began, performing the Y-incision and exposing the viscera. She made initial observations, taking pictures of any areas of bleeding or bruising, trying to identify each individual injury on this boy who had been a punching bag for some adult in the home for the past weeks or months. Perhaps for all of his short life. It made her furious, but she had to keep her focus and remain objective and dispassionate. Even though she knew what had happened to him and who was likely responsible, she had to pretend she didn't. Imagine this was a new case that had just come across her table and she knew nothing about his history or what had happened to him. It was a puzzle to solve, that was all. She would find all the pieces and put them back together in a way that made sense.

She would expose the truth, just as she had exposed the internal organs for examination.

Kenzie removed each organ, making observations, weighing and measuring them, and probing them for any damage or unusual pathology. There were lacerations in the liver, and scarring where previous lacerations had healed on their own. The damage to his body went much deeper than the bruises on the surface.

After cracking the ribs, she was able to remove the lungs. She weighed them, looking at the number on the scale and frowning before making note of the numbers. She dissected them and made several slides to be examined later. She took samples of the fluids and made extensive notes.

She called Dr. Wiltshire, hoping to be able to discuss her findings with him. There was no answer. Had he been at the hospital all day waiting for a consult on his hand? She would have thought that his position would afford him some special treatment in getting a scheduled appointment at the head of the line rather than having to wait all day like a walk-in.

Kenzie continued with the postmortem, deciding it would be advisable to dissect the throat as well, looking for any internal bruising or damage that was not visible from the outside. She would need to be able to answer all questions about how Michael had died.

It was a long day. Kenzie never did manage to get ahold of Dr. Wiltshire. Hopefully, that was just because he was in the hospital and had his phone turned off while he had his consult. Maybe they would decide it didn't need surgery and would cast it right away. She hoped for the best possible outcome for him.

Zachary was at his computer when she got home, lost in some case. He looked up briefly when she walked in the door and said something unintelligible, then was once more immersed in whatever was on his screen.

Kenzie removed her shoes and outer clothing, and took her purse to her bedroom where she put it down. No comment from Zachary.

"What case are you working on?" she asked as she went to the fridge and poured herself a glass of water. There was no response. She might as well have been talking to the wall. "I'm going to have a shower. Then we'll pull something together for supper. Unless you want to order in."

Again, her comment was met with silence. Kenzie shook her head and retreated to her bedroom, where she stripped down and hopped into the warm shower. She let the hot water work on her sore muscles. Anyone who thought it wasn't hard work to move bodies around and spend half the day bent over an autopsy table, cutting through bone and tough sinews should try it for a day. It was no walk in the park.

And that was aside from the mental and emotional strain. Even though she had done her best to keep from getting invested in the case, not to worry about how things would turn out or who was responsible for the abuses she uncovered, she couldn't completely dissociate herself from the experience. She knew she had been working on a toddler. She knew those things should never happen to anyone, let alone an innocent child.

The shower felt good. Cheap therapy. Wash away all of the sweat and grit and bad feelings, and luxuriate in fresh, warm water, steam cleansing her pores and her lungs, and breathing in the aromatherapy of her shampoo, conditioner, and body wash. It was like a whole spa treatment, right in her own house.

She put on flannel jammies, even though it wasn't really late enough to be wearing jammies, and walked back out to the kitchen.

Zachary looked up from his computer, paying more attention to her this time. "Oh, you're home," he said, looking at her and then down at his computer, frowning. "I didn't—did I see you come in?"

"Well, you gave a lousy rendition of 'Hello, how was your day,'" Kenzie advised. "It seems like you were a little focused on your work."

He looked at his computer screen again. "I had no idea it was so late. Sorry, you've had a long day."

"It was," Kenzie admitted. "I hope they're not all like that for the next few weeks."

He stood up from the couch and stretched. Kenzie wondered how many hours he had been sitting there, lost in his investigation before she had gotten home. He needed to move more than he did. But the same was probably true of her.

"Why would they all be like this?" Zachary asked. He gave her a hug and a quick kiss. His body was warm and musky and she held on to him for a couple of seconds longer than he held her.

"Because Dr. Wiltshire is out of commission with a broken hand."

"Oh! Did I know that? I don't think you told me. Unless it was a whole conversation we had while I was working on this file..." He motioned to the computer, grimacing.

"I know better than to keep talking to you when you're hyperfocused. I told you about Dr. Wiltshire yesterday. That's why we had to come back."

"Oh yeah. Sorry. How badly is it broken?"

"Well, any break is bad for someone who works with their hands like we do."

Zachary nodded and looked down at his own hands. She wondered how many times he had broken a finger or another small bone in his hand due to abuse or fighting. He avoided fighting; he wasn't someone who immediately resorted to violence when faced with a threat. But it had only been a couple of months since he had broken knuckles fighting for his life and the lives of Bridget's twin girls before the police had been able to get there to effect a rescue and arrest the culprits.

"I don't know how badly it was broken," Kenzie said. "He didn't talk to me about it. I don't even know how he got it. But I hope he heals fast and I don't have to do all the work without him for the next few weeks."

"You'll need to get someone in there to help. A sub."

"Yeah." Kenzie wasn't sure how many people were available to do that kind of thing. Any medical doctor could do a postmortem, but she wasn't about to turn the lab over to anyone who didn't have extensive knowledge about forensic pathology and the standard procedures to follow. But maybe the hospital could loan them someone a couple of days a week. "That would be good."

Zachary looked at the fridge. Even without his opening the door, Kenzie could tell that he wasn't interested in anything he might find there today. Even if Kenzie were cooking, which she wouldn't be, he wasn't going to be tempted by anything remotely healthy. Whatever case he was working on stressed him enough that he was looking for comfort food. Junk, deep fried, dripping with cheese.

"You want to order pizza?" Kenzie suggested, before he could think of something even more unhealthy to eat.

He let out his breath and nodded. "That would be good."

At least they'd had salad the night before. Or Kenzie had, anyway. Kenzie sat down at the table. It felt good just to sit and relax for a few minutes. Zachary got one of the pizza flyers out of the drawer and made a call to order their dinner.

"We should have Tyrrell over one day," Zachary suggested. "Him and Robbie both."

Kenzie couldn't even begin to think of entertaining. Not after the day she'd had.

"Not today," Zachary clarified. "I just think that we should do it sometime. When you're not stressed out."

"I'm not stressed out, just tired."

Zachary eyed her. Kenzie thought about the autopsy and the call from Lisa and threats from Cash Wade.

"Well, maybe I am," she admitted. "There is a lot going on with this case."

"Is it the same one? The little boy?"

"Yes."

"I saw a story in the news today about a boy who died in an accident. In a fall."

"Probably the same one."

Zachary gave a low whistle. "There is going to be a big stink if you don't find the way they want you to."

"I know that already. And I know that I'm not going to say what they are hoping I will."

"And you don't have Dr. Wiltshire to fall back on."

Kenzie nodded. "Bingo."

"But he'll still look at what you've done. Approve it. Say that he agrees with your findings."

"Yeah. I would hope so. But it's going to be brutal, even with him backing me."

"What's he like? Did you meet him?"

"The father?" Kenzie asked. "He's... loud. Forceful. Not the kind of person you want to cross. He's already making all kinds of threats about the kinds of trouble he is going to cause, all of the people who he can talk to about getting me... I don't know, thrown off the case... forced to say what he wants me to say. I don't know exactly what he hopes to accomplish by calling anyone political to try to stop me. It isn't like I'm going to run for office."

"Who's he going to call?"

"He's already been making calls. Got Detective Tuttle blocked in requesting a warrant to search the rest of the house. And Lisa called this afternoon." Kenzie wrinkled her nose to express her displeasure at this development. "To tell me that I need to be careful not to rock the boat, and won't I make an exception for an old friend?"

"Cash Wade is an old friend of hers?"

"I guess. I didn't know there was any connection between them, but she says that his family has been in Vermont almost as long as hers."

"Which means...?" Zachary knew better than to speculate on the political world the Kirsches were a part of.

"Which means he is a new money Vermonter. Not as high on the social scale, but still significant. And maybe if he has *enough* money, he can buy the rest of what he needs."

"They always can."

"No, not always," Kenzie disagreed. "You need a combination of blood, breeding, money, and influence. All the money in the world won't buy you the rest."

15

"I can't believe that they were able to hide the abuse," Kenzie mused. "The people in the household must have known. Anyone that they did things with socially must have known. I know you told me about them making sure they didn't bruise his face and keeping him in long sleeves and pants when necessary, but they couldn't hide it from the nanny who bathed him. What about the children he played with? Swimming? They have three pools!"

Zachary shrugged. "He wouldn't necessarily have had suspicious injuries all the time. If he did, they could say he was sick and couldn't go swimming or have any playdates. They could tell people that he was sickly or had an immune disorder and couldn't go out to visit. They have a social life. They can go wherever they want to without him. And at home, it's just the staff. Just the nanny and anyone else who took care of him, if there was anyone. It could even be the nanny. People *do* hide it, Kenzie. No one wants to believe their friends are abusive. They'll look the other way and believe whatever excuses they are given."

"He must have been in terrible pain much of the time. And it doesn't seem like he saw any medical professionals. Maybe a doctor who came to see him at the mansion if he was sick, but they couldn't call him if the boy was bleeding internally or had any suspicious bruises."

"The rich pay them off. The poor… wait and see if the child survives. If not… dump or bury the body somewhere and never tell anyone what happened."

He stared off into space, and Kenzie didn't want to know what he was remembering. Whether he was thinking of something that had happened in his own family, or a foster family, or to someone like Ben Burton, who had hired him to find out what had happened in his past and discovered a tragedy he had kept locked away for far too many years.

"We should probably change the subject," Kenzie suggested.

Zachary nodded.

The pizza arrived, and they decided to be decadent and watch in front of the TV instead of visiting at the table. Dr. B, who led their couple's therapy, suggested they turn off all screens for supper and focus on each other. But they had already done that, discussing the difficulties Kenzie was having with her job, and they needed to just relax and not think about it anymore.

At bedtime, they exchanged massages, working on the knots in each other's muscles to help them relax for sleep. But Kenzie knew that Zachary was doing a much better job on her than she had done on him. Her massage of his muscles had been too short, and she had not really put the attention into it that she should. She hit the spots that she knew usually got sore when he was sitting on the couch hunched over his computer, but she had not really explored any other areas. She was so tired that giving him a massage made her *more* sore and took energy she didn't have. He could tell that she was tiring and had insisted it was her turn for a massage when really, she'd barely touched him.

Zachary, on the other hand, worked his way over Kenzie's back, neck, and limbs slowly, kneading at the sore and knotted muscles, rubbing fragrant lotion into her skin, and generally making her feel relaxed and safe and ready for sleep. She kept dozing off while he worked on her. Eventually, he put the bottle of lotion to the side, pulled the blankets over her, and lay beside her running his fingers through her curly hair and rubbing her scalp as she drifted off the final time.

Kenzie awoke a couple of hours later to an animal-like cry from

Zachary, followed by staccato, broken sleep-babble as he tried to reason with his demons. Kenzie fought her way through the sheets to put her arm around him.

"Zachary. Zach. It's okay. Wake up." She stroked his short, stubbly hair and neck, waiting for him to surface. "You're just dreaming, Zachary. Wake up. You're okay." She knew better than to grab his arm or shake him. Nothing that might make him fight back, thinking she was the enemy.

"*No!*" His body convulsed as if he'd been hit or had flinched to brace for a blow. Then softer, "No."

She thought that the second "no" was a conscious echo. Repeating himself and trying to orient himself to his surroundings and figure out what was happening.

"It was just a dream," Kenzie told him again. "You're safe. You're with me."

She knew she should say "Kenzie" instead of "me," because how was he supposed to know which "me" she was? Waking up out of a dream, he might think her to be Bridget, or his mother, or some other woman from the past. But calling herself by name felt awkward and a little silly.

"Kenz?"

"Yeah. You're okay. Do you want to tell me about it?"

He cleared his throat and moved around restlessly, looking around the room, re-establishing himself in space. This was where he belonged now, but he hadn't lived with her for long enough to automatically know where he was when he woke up. She knew he still thought he was in other places first. An old apartment, a place he had lived in with Bridget, maybe Bonnie Brown, an institution he had spent time in as a child.

"No, just a dream," he murmured.

"Yeah. Was it something from the past?"

"No."

She knew it wasn't the fire. She could usually tell when it was the fire. He was far more frantic, shouting to his family, curling up in a ball with his arms over his face, trying to hide from it, just as he had done as a ten-year-old.

"No," Zachary repeated. "Your case. I think it was just because of your case."

Michael Wade. It wasn't a shock that he would dream of the abused child. He had spent much of his childhood being abused and trying to protect the other children from abuse. If he had been in the same home as Michael, he would have tried to protect him. Hide him, step in front of the blows, distract the abuser with something else. A punishable offense that could not be ignored.

"I'm sorry."

"S'okay." Zachary felt for Kenzie and pulled her gently closer, tucking her against his body, his warm breath on her hair, arms around her protectively. "Not your fault." She snuggled into him, enjoying the closeness even though she had been jerked out of a sound sleep by his nightmare.

"You're one of the good guys," Zachary went on, his voice a low murmur, barely more than a whisper. "You'll protect him. Find out who did this and put him behind bars."

"I can't arrest anyone. But I'll give the police everything I can, and they'll get him. They'll take care of it. They won't let a child beater go free just because of his money."

Zachary gave a grunt of disapproval at the mention of the abuser going free. Kenzie stroked his jawline and neck, and rubbed the back of his head with its short stubble. He purred at that. Kenzie hoped that if she could keep it up long enough, he would drop back off and get a nice long night's sleep. She knew from experience that it was unlikely, but she could try.

"When will it happen?" Zachary asked. "When will you release your report and they will be able to arrest him?"

"I'm still waiting for some test results back. Going to go over some slides and samples tomorrow. Not a lot. Some tests can take months to get back, but I can release my initial findings before that. I'd really like to go over everything with Dr. Wiltshire first. And… I need to read over the parent and witness statements. I should have done that today, but I didn't have time to finish everything. I want to do this right. To make sure that all of my conclusions are rock-solid and no one can fight it."

"Yeah." Zachary stretched and relaxed, kissing the top of Kenzie's hair. "But be careful. You know guys like this. You don't want him gunning for you."

"I don't know how I'm going to stop him from being upset with me. He isn't going to like what I have to say. Hopefully, they'll be able to arrest him quickly. I'll coordinate with the police… make sure their investigation has run parallel to mine and come to the same conclusions. They know Michael was being abused. They don't doubt that."

"That's good." Zachary rubbed Kenzie's back.

She closed her eyes briefly, luxuriating under his touch and, without meaning to, drifted off to sleep again.

16

When Kenzie awoke in the morning, she was alone in the bed. Zachary always got up before she did, so that was not unusual. She hoped that he had been able to get back to sleep after the nightmare and hadn't been up since then.

She pulled on her housecoat and wandered into the living room, unsure whether she would find him asleep on the couch or hard at work. He was at his computer, tapping away. But not so lost in his work that he didn't notice her approach.

"Morning," he greeted. He squinted at her for a moment. "Have a nice sleep?"

"Yeah, it was good. How are you doing? Did you get back to sleep?"

He shrugged. "No. Couldn't settle back down again."

Which meant he had probably only gotten a couple of hours of sleep.

"You might want to take a sleep aid tonight, then," she said neutrally. If she told him he had to or really pushed for it, he would resist. It was better if he felt like he could make that decision for himself and her suggestion was only a thought to consider. He was the one who knew his brain, his meds, and his sleep requirements. As much as Kenzie wanted to insist, to dictate how he handled it and force him to take the meds she felt he needed, she couldn't do that. She needed to let him make his own choices.

And he'd been doing well at it. He was in a good place. So far.

One short night's sleep like that might throw him off the rails in December, when his traumatized brain was trying to figure out how he could survive the Christmas season, but now he was still in a good place, and he would handle it just fine. As long as she didn't keep bringing up child abuse cases that kept him awake at night.

She had seen terrible things before. She didn't need to take them home to Zachary.

"You want coffee?" Zachary asked.

"No, not yet. I'll get myself together first. Just wanted to say good morning."

Zachary nodded, smiled, and looked back down at his computer.

There were an unusually high number of messages on the office's voicemail system with queries or instructions about the Wade case. Lots of reporters and curious members of the public were hoping to learn more about the case. A few calls from government officials who "had an interest" in the case and wanted to know how things were going. A polite call from a funeral home saying that they had been authorized by the family to pick up Michael's remains and would she please call as soon as they were ready for transport.

There were no threats. No angry tirades from Cash Wade himself detailing what he would do to her if the autopsy results were not satisfactory. Apparently, that kind of thing was reserved for the confines of his home, when there was no one but his own staff to overhear. People he knew he could control.

Dr. Wiltshire had left a couple of messages with things that he hoped she would have time to follow up on, but which Kenzie highly doubted she would be able to get to. Where was he? She had assumed that he would still come in to deal with the desk work, at least, and to go over everything with her before she released her findings in the Wade case.

After taking care of the administrative functions that could not be avoided, Kenzie had Julie take over the reception desk and phones, and shut herself in the boardroom away from the constant ringing to review the statements on the Michael Wade case.

Cash Wade's statement was brief, and pretty much what she expected after speaking to the detectives and the nanny. He was in a different part of the mansion from Michael and, as far as he knew, Michael was sleeping in the nursery. The first that he knew something was wrong was the shrieking of the nanny. It was clear that it was more than just an argument with someone on the staff, but that something was really wrong.

He had hurried toward the sound, but then been distracted by the sound of staff members rushing downstairs and outside to the pool area. He had looked out a window and seen them gathering around something on the poolside deck. The screaming nanny forgotten, he followed to see what was going on. And that was when he had seen his son lying on the ground, unresponsive. Looking straight up, he could see the balcony overhead and knew that was where he had fallen from. He concluded that the nanny had not been watching the boy closely enough.

Which was a bit odd, because if he blamed the nanny, why was she still at the mansion? Why hadn't she been terminated on the spot? Even if he didn't blame her for his son's fall and death, it would still have made sense to let her go after his demise, since there were no other children for her to take care of.

But Kenzie had been under the impression that Sylvia also had other household duties. She had not introduced herself as the nanny, so maybe that was something she had only taken on as they had needed her to.

Still, Cash had not yelled at her for talking to Kenzie or being in the nursery. He had not made any bitter accusations about how his son would still be alive if she had only done her job. But maybe that was just Hollywood stuff. In real life, people didn't behave like they did in the movies. The scenes written for the silver screen were just that—scenes invented out of someone's imagination for the best dramatic effect. In real life, maybe someone like Cash kept his mouth shut and let the housekeeper or his lawyer deal with Sylvia's employment. Maybe he didn't even think about what her part in his son's death had been while he was trying to get the prying detective and assistant medical examiner out of his home.

Or he was waiting until they were out of the way to lay into her.

Or he didn't blame her at all.

Because he knew that she had not been the cause of Michael's death.

Maybe.

Kenzie went on to the mother's statement. Terri-Lyn Wade.

She also claimed to have been elsewhere in the building. Unlike Cash, who claimed he had been conducting business, she said she had been eating a late breakfast after her Pilates workout, which was her usual routine. Kenzie didn't judge her for starting her day so late. Before Kenzie had gone back to medical school, she'd followed a similar schedule, going to events in the evening, with plenty of socialization going on into the early morning hours, eventually crashing at home and sleeping until mid-morning or later. She didn't have a Pilates class, but she frequently didn't have her breakfast until many people were contemplating lunch.

Terri-Lyn had also been startled by Sylvia's screams. She had been on the main floor in the breakfast room, with windows at the front of the house rather than the back, so it wasn't until people started shouting and running toward the pool that she knew something had happened outside. She initially thought that the staff would take care of whatever had caused the disruption, but eventually decided that she'd better see what was causing all of the commotion.

A couple of staff members had blocked her way, not letting her go right up to her son, telling her she didn't want to see him like that and that there was nothing she could do. Cash would not allow her to get close, no matter how she begged. She didn't see his face before they zipped him into a body bag and took him from the house, and could only imagine the extent of damage that had been done by the fall.

Rather than blaming the nanny, she blamed herself for not going to check on Michael after her Pilates session and for the fact that he had been able to get through the sliding doors to the balcony. Rather than abdicating responsibility as Cash had, she blamed herself for things she probably had no control over. Whoever had used the balcony last and had not fastened the doors securely. Maybe a faulty door lock. The fact that Michael had been sleeping alone and she hadn't known that he had gotten out of bed on his own.

All of the things that she should have done or foreseen because she was the mother.

Even if there was no way she could have controlled ninety percent of them.

Her son was dead, and she blamed herself for it.

Kenzie smoothed the report pages as though they were crumpled or wrinkled, but they were not. She pictured the two parents. Cash she had met, so it was easy to put those words in his cultured, angry voice. Terri-

Lyn was more difficult because Kenzie had never met her. Was she a small, mousy woman who always let Cash push her around? A strong independent woman who did her own thing and was only married to Cash for convenience and money? Something in between? Kenzie had met all types in the upper echelons of the Vermont social structure.

Tuttle had said that she was tall and well-built. She had been doing Pilates so, in theory, she should have strong core strength. Not a little old lady. Not a shrinking violet, Kenzie suspected. Someone who could stand up to Cash when he got carried away with his orders and tried to control her life as well as the rest of the mansion.

Someone who felt a huge well of guilt for not having been there when her son went over the edge of the balcony. A mother who had wanted to protect and care for her son, but had not been able to.

Sylvia had implied that neither parent had the patience to deal with Michael when he had been a colicky baby and she had stepped in to hold him until he had cried himself to sleep. Maybe Terri-Lyn was not someone with much instinct for child rearing or who hadn't had the time to properly establish a bond with him. It could be challenging to bond with a child with colic or medical issues that kept them in constant pain or discomfort. They weren't the cute, cuddly bundles people expected, the baby you could hold or rock for hours just staring into his eyes. A baby who screamed, cried, and pushed or kicked against his caregiver was not easy to love.

Maybe Terri-Lyn recognized that she didn't have the proper mother-child bond with Michael, and that was what she felt the most guilty over.

That and the fact that she or her husband had been beating on him, eventually causing his death.

Maybe she felt guilty about that.

17

It was the nanny's screaming that had alerted everyone that something had happened, so she was clearly the one who had discovered his body after it had been dropped from the balcony. Kenzie moved on to her statement, which was quite a bit longer than either parent's.

Sylvia said she had been working in the kitchen, the same thing she had told Kenzie. She had taken a break and gone to look in on Michael to make sure that everything was okay. She didn't say who was supposed to be watching him during that time, if anyone. She had gone to the nursery and, not finding him there, had begun to conduct a room-by-room search.

She didn't say if she had called for anyone else to help her, or that she had alerted either parent to the fact that he was out of his room and she didn't know where he was. So maybe it was a fairly regular thing. Although Sylvia had told Kenzie that he would usually stay in his room to play.

She had reached a room with the door standing open and had entered to see if that was where Michael had gone. Looking around, she did not find him, but she felt a breeze and realized the balcony doors were open. She went to secure them, but it occurred to her that they were open wide enough to admit a child and checked to make sure that Michael was not on the balcony.

And that was when she had looked over the edge and seen Michael on the white concrete pool deck below her, splayed out and unmoving.

Her narrative ended abruptly. Kenzie imagined the screams that had drawn everyone in the household to the back of the house where Michael's body lay. Sylvia probably had little recollection of what had happened after she saw Michael there. Neither parent had said that she made it down to the main level or ran out to Michael's body. Perhaps she had collapsed, or someone had gone to her and comforted her, keeping her away from the body, just like they had prevented his mother from rushing out to see him like that.

More details had been added later. Bits and pieces of information that Kenzie imagined the detectives had managed to coax out of Sylvia and had her add to her statement.

"I did not see him climb over the rail. I did not see him fall."

"I heard a noise. That was why I went to find him."

What kind of a noise? Kenzie could imagine Tuttle prompting her. *Did you hear Michael playing? Crying?*

"Not Michael. Just a noise that made me think I should check on him and make sure he was okay."

Kenzie pondered this. What had Sylvia heard? She seemed to have refused to give the detectives any description of what kind of a noise it was. Footsteps? Voices? Toys being thrown? Something falling? Just "a noise."

Something that made her think she had better check on her young ward.

She said it was not a noise Michael had made, so maybe it was the parents. Maybe one of them had said something within her hearing that made her worry for Michael's safety. The boy had not just wandered out of the nursery and climbed over the balcony rail. He had been killed by someone before he had been dropped from the balcony. And that someone might have said something in Sylvia's hearing that tipped her off to the fact that Michael had been hurt again.

She was used to his getting hurt. She knew he would need painkillers. That she would need to rock and soothe him and try to keep him still so that the injury could start to heal on its own. She must know how badly he had been beaten in the past. She wasn't stupid.

So she had gone looking for him, only to find that she was too late and they had already killed him and disposed of his body in a way intended to obscure what had been done.

Kenzie heard a door open and looked up. It had not been the door of the conference room she was hiding out in, but one of the other doors in the suite. She waited for a moment, head cocked, trying to identify any other familiar signs to figure out whether it was George returning with a transport or Julie getting a cup of coffee from the kitchen.

But it didn't sound like it. She stood up from the table and left the boardroom to see who it was.

Dr. Wiltshire's door opened down the hall. Kenzie waited to see if he was going to the kitchen for a coffee and, when he didn't, she went to get him one anyway. Even though it was an inconvenience for him to be injured and to put everything on her, that wasn't exactly his fault, and she wanted him to be in a good mood.

She prepared his coffee and then went down the hall to his office. She entered through Dr. Wiltshire's open door, tapping on the door as she went by.

"I heard you come in."

He looked up quickly, startled even though she had knocked and been careful not to sneak up on him.

"Oh, Kenzie!"

She tilted her head and laughed. "I *do* work here."

She stepped forward and put the cup of coffee on his desk, switching at the last moment to putting it on her right, his left, so he could use his other hand. She looked at his right hand, still in a splint.

"What's the word? No cast needed?"

He sighed. "The splint is temporary. It needs extensive surgery and hardware if I am going to regain full function. They are trying to get a specialist lined up to do it. I'm not sure how long I will have to wait. Hopefully, just a day or two. And then the recovery period after that and physical therapy…" He shook his head, frustrated. "I would like to tell you that I'll be back on the circuit again in a month. But it could be as many as six. Assuming I get full function back again. Fine motor… it's vital for our work. I can't just be hacking and slashing. Even if I leave the sewing up to someone else, there is still so much more that I need full motor function for."

"Yeah," Kenzie agreed. With less dexterity, it would be difficult for Dr. Wiltshire to continue in his position. "You must have really done a number on it. What exactly did you do?"

"I'm embarrassed even to say. Suffice it to say that I do not have a future in the PGA. Or any other sport, for that matter. You would think I would have learned as a young man that sports are not my thing. But with what I do here, the coordination required, thoughtful planning, reflexes… I assumed that my work proved I had all of those things." He picked up his coffee with his left hand and sipped it carefully. "Sadly, there is still something vital that I lack."

Kenzie frowned at this response, which was really not an answer to her question at all. Dr. Wiltshire was avoiding answering. He had said it was embarrassing, and she supposed that was why. He didn't want to have to admit whatever had happened. Kenzie had experienced enough of those moments herself to be sympathetic. Stubbing her toe on something she knew was there. Possibly even the heel of her other foot. Tripping over a crack in the sidewalk or nothing at all. Walking into a closed door in the dark, thinking it was open. There was a long list of stupid accidents in her past too. Everybody had them, so why was Dr. Wiltshire so hesitant to admit his?

She'd heard him joke about playing golf before. Mostly about how his wife wanted him out of the house or wanted him to have a hobby before he retired so that he wouldn't think he could stay home all day with her. He had never actually claimed to be good at it.

But what could he have done to break his hand so badly while playing golf? Swung into a tree? Fallen down a slope and tried to catch himself? An accident with an electric cart?

"No need to look so serious," Dr. Wiltshire assured her. "At least your position here is assured, as there is no one else to take over the work at the moment."

"Will you be looking for someone to do some part-time work? When things pile up and two people are needed to handle the workload?"

It was a quiet time of year, but when December hit…

"I will see who I can find. I was already talking to the head of pathology at the hospital in Burlington, seeing who he could suggest."

"Good. Not that I want someone else to take over, but I don't want to be here twenty-four hours a day. I'll end up a zombie, and not the good kind."

He chuckled. "Fair enough. So, how are things coming on our big case?"

"Are you talking about Michael Wade?"

"Who else?"

"I just wanted to make sure. Because he's a small case and a big case."

Dr. Wiltshire stared at her, and Kenzie wondered whether her comment had been difficult to follow.

"A small boy," she explained. "But a big political situation."

"Right, of course," Wiltshire agreed. He took his glasses off and wiped them as if dust had prevented him from seeing her point. "Small but big. So what have we got?"

Kenzie pulled up a chair and settled in to discuss it more fully. "There are a number of things that I wanted to talk to you about."

"This may be a case where it is in our best interests to… leave things a bit vague."

Kenzie felt like she was the one staring at him now, in disbelief at what he was suggesting. "Leave them a bit vague? It's our job to provide as much clarity as possible. For the sake of the public and to give the police the best possible chance to catch the culprits in a case like this."

"I'm sure that there are some things that are… ambiguous. And perhaps it's best if they are just left that way. Digging down too far, we run the risk of accusing or even just implicating the wrong person. And that would be doing the family a huge disservice."

"Someone in that household was abusing him."

"So it would appear. But again… perhaps it was someone outside the home. Or someone who was only an occasional guest. And throwing shade on the family brings with it the danger of lawsuits. Defamation of character. False accusations."

Kenzie shook her head.

"There are… discrepancies in this case," Dr. Wiltshire tried approaching it from another direction. "Inconsistencies between what the witnesses report and what the body is telling us. We could simply state that there was disagreement between those things and the justice system would have to investigate and take it to its conclusion."

"But we know that the body is right. Not the witness statements. Someone could swear that they saw him walking around outside today, and it wouldn't make any difference because we know he wasn't. He's on a table in the cold room. That's the truth. And we need to be clear as to what the truth is. That is not in doubt. There's no *interpreting* the truth."

"I think it can be managed. If you'll bring me your first draft, I can go over it, or we could go over it together, and discuss the best way to word those *truths.*"

"I really don't think…"

"You and I both know that things are not cut and dried. There is often more than one cause of death or mitigating factor. We interpret what we find based on the clues at the scene and what the police find and communicate to us. Technologies change. We decide what tests are required or are not required. Our budget constraints require that we be conservative in how much time and money we spend on each case, pinching pennies like a grandma on a pension."

All of that was true, but Kenzie still didn't like what Dr. Wiltshire was suggesting that she do. Or what she thought he was asking her to do.

If Cash Wade was guilty of killing his heir, Kenzie wouldn't bury that fact.

She didn't have a lot of success going over her findings with Dr. Wiltshire.

He was distracted and complained about being unable to focus due to the painkillers he was on for his hand.

He agreed with each point she brought up, but then tried to spin it so that it was irrelevant or ambiguous in meaning. She had to assume that he either knew the Wade family or was receiving significant pressure from the people that Cash Wade had promised he would call. He had the influence he claimed to; Kenzie would give him that. Old money or new, the man had clout. He had clawed his way into Vermont society and had it by the throat.

Dr. Wiltshire left after just a couple of hours, signing off on whatever reports he could and apologizing that he didn't have the energy or focus to spend any longer with her.

"We'll go over this later," he promised. "Maybe put it to the side as 'undetermined' for now, and we'll revisit it when I feel better."

Kenzie just smiled at him. She didn't disagree with him aloud, but there was no way she was going to set the case aside or waffle on the cause of death. She had been raised by a couple of people who were adamant about standing by what they believed, and she wasn't going to cave to any pressure to do otherwise. She would uncover the truth and do whatever she could to ensure the culprit was caught and punished.

Since Dr. Wiltshire was gone and the phones and reception desk were already being covered, Kenzie decided that a field trip was in order. It was time she visited some of Vermont's hospitals.

The Roxboro hospital was small, but Kenzie knew from experience that it was staffed by competent and talented staff and that their emergency room was second to none of the city hospitals. When the wait time was long in Burlington or Montpelier, people would drive to Roxboro, knowing that they would get in and dealt with faster there, even considering the driving time.

A couple of people she had gone to medical school with had been posted to the hospital, so Kenzie made a couple of phone calls just to say hello and see if they were still there. And to casually mention that she would be by to pursue an inquiry.

When she spoke to the nurse at the triage desk in the emergency room, she smiled and nodded. "Dr. Pulman said that you might be stopping by and that I should help you out however I could."

"Well, that was very sweet of him," Kenzie said with a smile. "If there is someone I could talk to, I don't want to take you away from your duties here…"

Nurse Harris leaned over to look around Kenzie, emphasizing the fact that there was no one standing in line behind Kenzie and very few people sitting in the waiting room for their names to be called.

"I think you are safe."

Kenzie chuckled. "Okay. I don't want to cause problems. Dr. Pulman seems like a nice guy, but you never know what kind of a boss someone is…"

"He's not my boss," Nurse Harris said comfortably, "And my boss will not get after me for helping out the medical examiner's office when I am not inconveniencing any patients."

Kenzie nodded. She turned her phone around, showing it to Nurse Harris.

"Now, I know you get tons of people through here, so this is a long shot, but I wonder if you recognize this boy as having been a patient here before."

Nurse Harris looked at the picture for a moment, then nodded. "Yes. I recognize him."

19

Kenzie leaned in, surprised. "You know him? You're sure?"

She nodded again. "I've got a pretty good memory for faces. I know I've seen him here before." The corners of her mouth turned down. "What... what did he die from?"

Kenzie had done her best to make the picture look as if the boy were just sleeping, even going so far as to add a pink filter to brighten up his gray skin, but it was still obvious, to a nurse at least, that the boy was dead.

"I haven't released my findings yet. Would you pull up his records for me, please? His name is Michael Wade."

"Sure, of course." She turned to her computer and tapped in the name. She shook her head, frown lines appearing between her brows. "Hmm. W-A-D-E?"

"Yes."

"I do not see that name here anywhere. Is it possible that he was admitted under another name? Mother's name, stepfather's? A lot of kids have several different last names these days. It can be a bear to try to untangle them all."

"No." Kenzie hadn't seen Terri-Lyn Wade's maiden name mentioned anywhere. She was always Mrs. Wade or Terri-Lyn Wade. She couldn't imagine why Michael would be going by any other name.

"Well…" the nurse shook her head. "Do you think you could find out? I can't really pull up his file without a name."

"You would check ID, wouldn't you?"

"Yes, we check." Nurse Harris looked squinted her eyes up at the ceiling while she thought. "Oh… I wish I could remember more about the circumstances he was brought in under. He was brought in by his mother, or maybe his grandmother. He had fallen…" She pursed her lips and shook her head. "Or something had fallen on him. I think that was it. She was very upset. The mother. Said that she had only turned her back on him for a minute and then he had pulled something over on himself. You know how kids do. Climbing a tall piece of furniture or something."

Kenzie nodded. She tried to think of a way to find Michael's records if she was not registered under the right name.

"So he received treatment. Do you remember what day it was? How long ago?"

"No. A few months ago. I can't be much more specific than that."

"And he was brought in by his mother?"

"Umm…" the nurse stared off into space, thinking about it. "An older woman, so maybe stepmother or grandmother. It's so hard to know these days when you have women getting pregnant into their fifties or adopting or becoming parents to their partner's children. You just never know."

"Can you remember what she looked like? A tall, well-built woman?" Kenzie regretted that she had not seen Terri-Lyn Wade face-to-face, nor even looked up her picture online to see what she looked like. She could find a picture on her phone to show Nurse Harris. Kenzie hit the home button on her phone to search for it.

"No," the nurse said. "No, a little woman."

Kenzie stopped what she was doing and looked at her. "A little woman?"

"Well, you know, not *little*, little. Not like a dwarf. But quite short and small-boned."

"Dark hair?"

"Yes."

"And what did he call her? Did he call her Mom?"

"The little fellow wasn't calling anyone anything. He was quite badly hurt." The nurse nodded toward Kenzie's phone. "Not *that* badly, but it was pretty serious. We had to get him into surgery immediately."

Kenzie almost let herself tear up, thinking about what someone had done to that little boy. Pulled the furniture over on top of himself? She highly doubted that. It did happen, of course. Children died of crush injuries or head injuries from such accidents with regularity, despite the advice to parents to tether furniture to walls to prevent it. They didn't bother, or didn't know their kids were that mobile yet. Or thought that their children were too smart or mature to do something stupid like scaling a bookshelf to reach what they wanted.

But the injuries she had seen on Michael suggested ongoing abuse. Not just a single accident. Or one several months ago and one the previous Sunday.

"Funny about your question about checking ID, though," the nurse said thoughtfully. "She didn't have his birth certificate with her. We checked hers, of course, and set up his chart based on that."

"Arnold?" Kenzie suggested. "Could it have been set up under Michael Arnold?"

Nurse Harris typed the new name into her system and brightened. "Bingo. So he did go by her name."

"No." Kenzie shook her head. "She wasn't his mother. That was his nanny. Sylvia Arnold."

The nurse skimmed over the information on her screen, nodding in agreement. "Yes. That's the name of the woman who brought him in. The woman who said she was his mother." Harris paused, reading more that Kenzie could not see. "She said that she had no insurance. So we didn't need to collect that information. He had to be treated or he would probably not have made it. It was lucky she got him here when she did. She should have called an ambulance."

They probably wouldn't let her. They probably wouldn't let her call any authorities to the house. No paramedics, no police, no one who might have recognized the abuse and connected it to the Wade family. They didn't want anyone like that at the mansion. So Sylvia had done the only other thing she could, taking him away from there to a place where he was safe and could be treated for his injuries. Had his parents known about it? Had they allowed it? Or had she done it without their permission, knowing that Michael would die unless she did?

They hadn't fired her, so maybe they knew and approved of what she had done. Or maybe they didn't even know. She might have done it covertly, and if she was his primary caregiver, his absence from the home had gone unnoticed.

"Can you print that off for me? And anything else you have on file?"

"Of course." Nurse Harris started the print job and then paged through it on her screen. "It did look like what she had said. Something heavy fell on him. He had deep bruises, broken ribs, liver lac, fluid in his lungs. It was very serious."

"Could it have been caused by a person squeezing or crushing him?"

Harris looked at her for a moment, mouth open. "Well... I wouldn't have thought of that scenario. You would have to ask one of the doctors who dealt with his case, and he may not be able to remember enough after this long. We see a lot of cases."

"But you remembered him. Maybe he would too."

Harris nodded, but didn't look hopeful. "Michael was not a big child," she said, considering. "I don't think it would take a lot of force to do that kind of damage. But you should talk to someone in DCF with experience. *They* would have a better handle on that."

"I will look at some case studies as well," Kenzie told her. She was still waiting to hear from the police on whether there had been any DCF reports made concerning Michael Wade. She didn't want to be the one to call them. Not after Dr. Wiltshire had made such a big deal about avoiding any accusations of defamation. "Was he treated here for anything else? Or was that the only time he was brought in?"

"It wasn't the only time. That's probably why his face was familiar to me. Always brought in by Sylvia Arnold, no insurance, no birth certificate. It's not unusual for undocumenteds. But Arnold doesn't sound like an immigrant name." Harris rolled her eyes. "Not that you can tell by someone's name. But I mean, so many of them are Hispanic or else names you can barely pronounce. Arnold is so... American. And she didn't look foreign."

"No. She doesn't," Kenzie agreed. "I think she just didn't want him to be identified by his real name. That was why she could never bring a birth certificate or any insurance. She might not have been able to get him treated if she admitted she wasn't his mother."

"We would still have had to treat him. But it would have presented some additional problems. Thinking it was just an insurance problem, we didn't dig deeper than that. Was she... you don't think *she* was abusive, do you? I don't see how such a small woman could have caused those injuries."

"No, I don't think she was the one. She is the only one who seemed to care about him enough to get treatment."

And yet, it nagged at Kenzie. Sylvia had been the one to take Michael to the hospital to make sure that he didn't die, but she didn't care enough to stop the abuse. She hadn't taken the steps necessary to have him removed from the home. Once he was at the hospital, she could have told them that Michael was being abused by his parents or someone else in the household. She could have had him removed.

But she hadn't.

20

Kenzie went home early. She could continue working from her home office, making phone calls to the other hospitals in neighboring towns with the names Michael Wade and Michael Arnold to see if he had been treated in any other hospitals.

He had.

Sylvia kept taking him to hospitals with stories of accidents to have him treated, but she hadn't turned him over to DCF. It didn't appear that she had made any effort to stop the abuse. She just kept bringing Michael to hospitals, injured, worried about whether he would survive. She knew the bruises were not caused by clumsiness, falling down, or bumping into things, even if that was what someone had told her. She had recognized that Michael's injuries were serious.

"Kenz?"

Kenzie rubbed her eyes and sat back in her chair. She faced Zachary, but didn't look at him, her palms still resting over her eyes.

"Yeah. What time is it?"

"I thought you might want something to eat. I know you're working, but…"

"But I need to take care of myself," she finished for him. She removed her hands from her gritty eyes, recognizing that her body was telling her she'd been at it for too long. Zachary was absolutely right to interrupt her.

She looked at the system time on her computer. It was nearly nine o'clock.

She swore. "I had no idea it was that late. You should have said something earlier! You must be starving. Or did you already eat?"

Usually, Zachary was the one who got so lost in his work that he didn't know what time it was or that mealtimes had passed him by. She'd better not be picking up that habit. But she knew how hard it was to decide whether to break his concentration and bring him back to reality. She didn't like to stop him when he was immersed in something important.

"Do you want me to heat up some pasta for you?" Zachary suggested, without answering the question. "Or one of those rice bowls?"

"No. I can do that. I really do need to get off the computer. I can work on this tomorrow."

"I can heat something up. Really. I'll even take the plastic off when I'm supposed to. Put a warm cloth on your eyes or something for a few minutes while I do it."

Kenzie chuckled at him mothering her, just like she chided him when he was not taking care of himself properly. "Okay, I will. Work is put away. I'll eat whatever you heat up. And I'll take a few minutes to relax while you do it."

"Good." He nodded briskly. "I'll be five minutes."

What had he been doing all night? Had he been working on his own projects and also lost track of time, or had he been monitoring her, trying to decide when the best time was to interrupt her? Weighing just how important the work she was doing was against her need to relax and regenerate at the end of the day?

They sat at the table together twenty minutes later, eating and visiting, Kenzie still trying to put the concerns of the day aside so that she could relax properly. She told Zachary about Sylvia Arnold taking Michael to different hospitals, passing him off as her own son.

"I really can't understand her. If she cared at all about Michael—and she clearly did, or why would she be taking him to the hospital for treatment, probably behind her employer's back—if she cared about him, why didn't she report them to the authorities? They could have given him a safe home. Gotten him out of the place where he was being harmed."

Zachary nodded. "But the system itself has a lot of flaws. A much higher percentage of children die in foster care than with their own families."

"You can't tell me that she knew that. The perception of the foster care system, for those who are outside of it, is that it will provide children with a safe environment. Get them out of a dangerous one to where they can be safe. And for most kids, that's exactly what it does. I know that isn't your experience, but many kids only have one foster home, and they grow up there, safe and loved, until they are ready to be on their own."

"Or sent back to their biological families."

"Yes, I know that reunification is a big goal. But only when they believe it is safe. Only when the parents have gone through counseling and retraining and all of that stuff and are ready to take the child back again."

"I saw a lot of kids who bounced back and forth between foster care and their bio families. Social services… wasn't the best at determining that a parent was… reformed."

Kenzie thumped her fork down on the table with a bang that made Zachary jump. "I'm not talking about your experience. I'm saying that in *this* case, Michael at least would have had a chance of surviving if he had been removed and put in foster care. But no one did that. No one was willing to admit to the abuse they saw going on in that household every day and do something to protect Michael. No one did! They just let him die!"

Zachary stared down at his dinner, nodding. His face was blank, devoid of any emotion. She knew that her sharpness hurt him, but she wanted him to be as outraged about it as she was. She wanted him to see her perspective and to quit telling her it was an imperfect system. She already knew it was an imperfect system. But without it, Michael Wade had not stood a chance.

That little boy, hardly more than a baby, had not stood a chance because no one in the household was willing to step up, tell the truth, and get him out of there. They were all too worried about losing their jobs and any references from the Wade family. Maybe they were worried about the political fallout. Of being shunned and unable to get another job because of their political power.

But a child had died!

They should have stepped up. Everyone who knew about or suspected the abuse should have made a report and stayed on top of it until Michael was taken out of that home where he was tortured and killed.

Zachary's Adam's apple bobbed up and down as he swallowed. He moved mechanically, probably not tasting what he was eating.

He had hated foster care. He had been abused and institutionalized and had seen terrible things happen to other children. But he had survived. He had grown up and aged out of the system. And so had all of his siblings. It was true that they all had their difficulties and emotional problems. Some of that could be blamed on the system, and a lot of it came from the family they were taken away from. She couldn't allocate how much trauma had been caused by the foster system. And neither could Zachary.

"How was Dr. Wiltshire?" Zachary asked eventually, after a long silence that neither of them wanted to aggravate the other by breaking. "Did he make it in today? How did you say he hurt his hand?"

"He was in for a couple of hours. But… it was frustrating. He's on painkillers for his hand and I don't think he is thinking very clearly. He signed the paperwork he needed to and went home again."

"I hope he's not driving if he's in that bad of shape."

"I'm pretty sure he used a service. I didn't actually escort him out to the parking garage."

Zachary flinched. Kenzie felt bad for her mood and wished she could get past it. Zachary didn't deserve to be snapped at and to have to endure her grumping around all evening. But a lot had happened and Kenzie didn't know how to deal with it.

"He was telling me to be vague in the postmortem report," she explained, trying to give Zachary some basis for her irritation on the subject of Dr. Wiltshire, who he had thought would be a safe topic. "He is worried about political backlash and the Wades coming back at us with a lawsuit. He wants the manner of death to be left open. Requiring further police investigation. Let them take the flak for it."

Zachary looked at Kenzie, brows up in surprise. "Can you even do that?"

"Of course I *can*. Technically. Sometimes it is impossible to tell what killed someone, and you are left with saying that it is natural causes, even though you are pretty sure there was something hinky going on. If you think it might have been homicide, but don't have any proof, or only have a few clues that all point in different directions—maybe natural, or maybe an accident, or maybe homicide—then you can go back with 'undetermined.' But that is not the case here. I know that it was homicide. I can't say I don't know."

Zachary nodded slowly. "You can see his point, though. Maybe if you initially say it is undetermined and just let the police continue to investigate until they have overwhelming evidence that it was the father, then you avoid any accusations by the family that it was politically motivated or that you are incompetent or trying to slander him."

"But that isn't right."

"I know. I think he is just trying to make it easier on you."

"He's trying to make it easier on himself. He is the one who has to take responsibility for what I put in my report."

Zachary looked surprised at this. "Is he? Not you?"

"He's the medical examiner. I'm just an assistant. Anything that comes out of the Medical Examiner's Office is his responsibility."

"Of course. That makes sense. I had just never thought of it before. I thought that if you were doing the autopsies, then any complaints would come back to you."

"Sort of. But ultimately, to him."

Zachary scraped his dish for the last of the pasta sauce. "I know it wouldn't be right for you to say it was undetermined when you know it was homicide."

"But you still think I should."

"No." Frown lines appeared between Zachary's eyes as he looked at her. "Of course not. I would expect you to do what you knew was right."

Sometimes, the simplest things could just melt Kenzie's heart.

Lisa had warned her to be careful what she put in her report and how she handled the case. Dr. Wiltshire had suggested that she fudge her report. Both claimed to care for her well-being and wanted what was best for her. She had expected Zachary to fall in line behind them, agreeing that even though it didn't feel like the right thing to do, sometimes she might have to bow to the rich and powerful to succeed in life. Sometimes real life forced you to outgrow those ideals, and you just had to be grown up about it and let it go.

"Thanks," Kenzie told him sincerely. "It's really nice to hear you say that."

"I would never tell you to hide the truth."

They were truly matched on that one thing, if nothing else. They were worlds apart in other areas. But Zachary Goldman was also a truth-seeker and truth-teller. He might intentionally obscure the truth to protect someone else, as he had when he had rescued Madison and Luke, leading the criminal enterprise they escaped to believe they were both dead. He might hide his feelings and lie even to himself about what he was feeling. But put him on a case where the truth was inconvenient, dangerous, or political suicide, he would still pursue it to the ends of the earth.

Just as Kenzie would any of the cases on her table.

21

Kenzie had hoped that she would be able to sleep soundly after her long day. Her body and her mind were both tired, and she wanted nothing more than to just fall into bed and drift off into dreamland. Or, not to dreamland, but to nothingness. Not having to think about her work, feelings, or the tragedy of Michael Wade's death, but just to sleep.

And that hadn't happened. She had slept, but fitfully, with periods of restlessness in between, flipping back and forth as she tried to find a comfortable position and force herself to go back to sleep. The day's events and how she would write everything in her report kept pushing its way into her conscious mind. Her brain wouldn't let her push it off until the next day. She repeated phrases and tried to figure out the most clear, concise language to use to convey her findings and point the finger at Michael's father and the rest of the household.

There was plenty of guilt to go around.

She shouldn't have to feel guilty too. She wasn't the one who had been in the house, seen what was happening, and refused to do anything about it. By the time she was on the scene, Michael was dead; all she could do was try to see that justice was served on his behalf. That was her job. To speak for the dead.

"Kenzie."

Zachary's warm hand was on her shoulder, resting very lightly. Soft but solid, something anchoring her to the physical world.

"What?" She turned and looked at her phone to see if it was ringing, but there was no call and no alarm. "What's wrong?"

"You were dreaming. Sorry. I didn't know whether to wake you."

Having contemplated the same dilemma herself many times, she didn't blame him for waking her up. "Was I? Was I making noises?"

"Yeah. I was afraid… I didn't know if it was because of…"

It hadn't been a dream about the kidnapping. At least, Kenzie didn't think so. She couldn't remember much about it, but a few images still floated in her mind's eye.

"I think it was just the case. I can't let it go tonight."

"Do you want to read? Get up for a while and put something on TV?"

These activities sometimes helped her relax and get back to sleep on a bad night, but Kenzie was too tired to consider them tonight. "No. I really need to just sleep. I *was* asleep…"

And then he had woken her up. She didn't mean to accuse him or suggest that he had done something wrong, but it felt like she had barely dropped off. How was she supposed to get a good night's sleep when he woke her up at every disturbance?

"Sorry. You sounded upset. I didn't want you to be caught in that dream."

"I know." Kenzie snuggled up against his warm body, head on his chest, trying to reset. "It's okay. I just… I'm so tired."

"What can I do?" His arms encircled her and he rubbed her back in gentle circles. He kissed the top of her head.

Kenzie murmured something that wasn't really an answer, but told him to just keep doing what he was doing.

And he did.

Morning came too soon. Kenzie didn't wake up feeling relaxed and well-rested. All the burdens she had tried to put aside as she slept came rushing back to her. And now she couldn't keep pushing it off; she had to deal with it. She had to deal with the calls from the press and the various governmental offices who had absolutely nothing to do with the medical examiner's office but thought that they would give their input into her process and what she should be doing. She had to figure out how to write each finding in her postmortem report so that it was clear and unequivocal, and the police would have to act on it. Whether she or the office suffered a backlash from it or not, she didn't care. It had to be done anyway. Michael deserved the truth.

She put her coffee cup down on the table more forcefully than she had intended, and Zachary jumped and whipped his head around to look at her.

"Sorry," Kenzie told him without meeting his eyes. "Just slipped."

He shrugged and looked away from her again. "No problem."

They each asked the other how they had slept the night before, each of them knowing that the answer was that they'd slept like crap. But they made encouraging noises and said that they would sleep better tonight. Kenzie rubbed the middle of her forehead, knowing everything would not be resolved in a day. She would probably be sleeping restlessly for weeks, trying to get the report worded just right, and then dealing with the blowback, and whatever was in the papers, and having to deal with Dr. Wiltshire and his ire. He would probably be grumpy, strung out on painkillers, irritated she hadn't listened to him and followed his advice, angry that he couldn't work and had to wait and rehab his hand, worried that he would never regain the full use of his hand.

What had he done to it, anyway? Was there any soft tissue damage? Muscles? Nerves? If it was a crush injury, there could be all kinds of damage done to the connective structures. Damage that would prevent him from being able to use it properly even after the bones were healed nice and straight and strong.

"This afternoon?" Zachary was asking.

Kenzie let her fingers fall away from her face and looked at him. "Sorry, what did you say?"

"I just..." He looked awkward. "I just wanted to make sure that you remembered it's couple's therapy today. I know you've got a lot going on. Did you want to reschedule it? If you are too busy, I could just do a personal session today."

Couple's therapy. It was on Kenzie's calendar. She knew it was their week to attend Dr. Boyle's office together. Dr. Wiltshire knew that she took every second Wednesday afternoon off, and that was fine when he was around, but she hadn't thought about how her schedule might be affected while he was away from the office.

"Uh, yeah. That shouldn't be a problem. Julie will know that this is our week. I'll just double-check that she's okay with it. Dr. Wiltshire isn't there so, if something comes up… well, I'll let you know."

She had missed couple's therapy once, and that oversight had permanently affected his outlook, worried every time that Wednesday afternoon came around she was going to forget about it. It was such a small thing to have made such a significant impact, and she couldn't help but resent how he held that one mistake against her, even if he said he did not.

Did she and Dr. B hold it against Zachary that he had missed his own therapy appointments not just once, but multiple times? Sometimes because something was really wrong, and sometimes because it had just slipped his mind. And, of course, she always believed it was because something was seriously wrong, especially since her abduction, brief though it had been. The world no longer felt like a safe place and she worried that he had been abducted. A situation that was not improved by the fact that he *had* been abducted not so long ago to stop him from making trouble for a pharmaceutical research company that had been related to his case.

"Sounds good," Zachary said, his voice airy and casual. But she knew by his eyes that he was still worried. He wouldn't say anything else about it but, for the rest of the morning, until she left for work, he would be watching her and silently worrying that she would forget again.

They had talked it over, both during therapy and on their own, and had agreed that forgetting once did not mean that she had abandoned him or that he was less important to her than her work. No more than it meant that she was not important to him when he was distracted or followed a compulsion that took him somewhere other than where he was supposed to be.

They had talked it to death, and now it was all resolved. Except that he still watched her the same way and waited for her to do it again.

"You don't think Dr. Wiltshire will be in today?" Zachary asked.

"I don't know. I'm not counting on it. He was hoping to get into surgery in the next day or two if a specialist could fit him in, so I might have a message on my office voicemail telling me that he got in today and will be incommunicado for a day or two as he recovers. And that means I have to keep everything else moving forward. I still plan to be there, but I can't promise that something won't come up. I'll let you know if it does, and you can go ahead and have an individual session with Dr. B, and we'll do couple's next week."

He nodded. "Next week, things won't be as crazy."

Kenzie wasn't making any promises. Who knew where the case would go in the next week and what kind of craziness *might* jump out at her. "Could be a natural disaster," she pointed out.

"Could be a zombie apocalypse," Zachary deadpanned in the same tone of voice.

"Could be a train derailment."

"Could be the rapture," he suggested.

Kenzie shook her head and had a sip of her coffee. It was strong. She wondered if she or Zachary had switched it over to a stronger brew without realizing it. Or maybe he had done it intentionally, knowing that Kenzie hadn't slept well and figuring she would need a stronger kick to keep her going through the morning. "Hoo. That's strong. Wasn't expecting that."

"Is it okay?" he asked. "Do you want me to get you another cup? Less strong? Or stronger?" He smiled wickedly at the suggestion.

Kenzie made a face and shook her head. "No. This is just right."

"You want some sugar?"

"No." Kenzie took another sip of the potent brew and smiled to show she was fine with it.

The toaster popped and Zachary supplied her with toast and marmalade. And after a moment of staring at her blankly, a knife and tub of butter.

"Thank you."

Kenzie asked him about his day and the cases he was working on, the largest of which was an insurance fraud investigation. He was involving his sister Heather in the surveillance, which they were both enjoying immensely. When they had first met Heather, Kenzie hadn't had any idea how much like Zachary she was. She hid the trauma better and, being a woman, tended to do better at the social stuff than Zachary did. But they were both intensely interested in investigative work and solving puzzles, in bringing injustices to light, and had a mischievous sense of humor. Heather didn't have the same learning disabilities as Zachary and enjoyed organizing things in a way that was optimal for his ADHD brain, having raised two ADHD children of her own. They both had different strengths, but were interested in the same kinds of things.

Zachary cleared the table as Kenzie made the final preparations to go to work. Zachary kissed her goodbye before she exited to the garage.

"See you at couple's therapy this afternoon," he told her with a slightly strained smile.

Kenzie gritted her teeth. "I'll be there," she promised again. "Or I'll let you know."

22

Kenzie told Zachary that she was running late, but would be there. She needed to focus on finishing her report and couldn't keep texting him a countdown every two minutes.

She was only ten minutes late, and he had probably only been talking with Dr. Boyle for five minutes. And most of that would be introductory small talk. Dr. B checking in on how his life was going and if there were any new issues to be addressed in his personal sessions.

Their eyes turned to Kenzie as she hurried in the door, apologizing and out of breath. She didn't like to be out of breath or to have to apologize for her behavior. But she knew an apology was in order, even though she had been doing her best to arrive on time and the delays had not been her fault.

"I'm here, okay?" she snapped at Zachary when he turned accusatory eyes toward her. "I told you I would be. I didn't forget, and I'm here. It just took a few extra minutes."

Zachary didn't say anything at first. His eyes flicked toward Dr. B and then back to Kenzie. "Sure," he agreed. "No problem."

Kenzie sat down, blowing out her breath. "I'm sorry. I'm cranky and it's not your fault at all."

"You're under a lot of pressure right now," he said neutrally.

"Why don't you tell us what's going on right now that is stressing you out? Get it off your chest," Dr. Boyle suggested.

"Zachary already knows."

Dr. B just raised an eyebrow and waited.

"Okay. I'm getting a lot of political pressure on a case right now. From my mother, my boss, and various other political bigwigs who have nothing whatsoever to do with it. And my boss broke his hand, which means I need to do all the physical work. And he isn't even showing up for the paperwork and to discuss cases. I *need* him to be there, but he's been…"

She shook her head, knowing that Dr. Wiltshire was doing the best that he could and she would just have to be patient and understanding about the whole thing.

"He has to take care of personal stuff, and I guess I resent it that he's allowed to have a personal life and to deal with things like breaking his hand. It's silly, because of course he has to be allowed to have time off for illness and injuries."

Dr. Boyle smiled and nodded. "We understand that kind of thing intellectually, but our feelings are playing a whole different tennis game."

"Yeah. My emotions are all over the place. It isn't fair to anyone else that I'm feeling and behaving this way. But… I don't know how to change it."

"Why don't we break some of these feelings down a little. Your boss not being there feels like… what?"

Kenzie stared out the window behind Dr. B, trying to figure out what she felt and put it into words. "Like he's abandoned me, honestly. I know he didn't choose to hurt himself, but suddenly he's unavailable to me."

"Can you think of other times you have felt this way?"

"I'm not usually such a walking ball of prickly feelings. I'm a mess. I've always managed my feelings pretty well, so I don't know why I am so out of control this time."

"Have you always had to 'manage' your feelings?"

"I guess so. Everybody does, don't they?"

"What happens if you don't manage them? What if you just feel what you feel?"

"Well, you can *feel* whatever you like, but you can't walk around like a little storm cloud making everyone else miserable."

"Who do you think you heard that message from?"

Kenzie considered it. "I guess… from my mother. Maybe both of my parents. We've always been a little repressed," Kenzie joked, and gave a laugh. "My mother has always told me the *proper* way to behave in any social situation."

"But that isn't always a way that affirms your feelings."

"No. But you can separate your feelings about something from how you behave. People do it all the time. That's just… being civilized. Showing consideration for other people in society."

"So when you feel abandoned, how should you behave?"

Put that way, it sounded ridiculous to Kenzie. "I don't know how you should behave… I guess you just put the feelings aside while you're with other people and… serve and support them. My dad was away for a lot of my childhood and, when he came home, it was for my mom or because Amanda was sick and needed him. It wasn't for me."

"So you felt abandoned by him. Felt like you didn't matter. Your feelings didn't matter."

"I guess. And really… they didn't. As parents and as a family, we had to do what we had to do, no matter how any of us felt about it. None of us wanted Amanda to be sick, but that's what we got. And you just play the hand you're dealt."

"But you're still allowed to have feelings."

"As long as they don't get in the way."

Dr. B nodded. "And your boss being hurt and not coming into the office and dealing with his work feels like when your father was away, and only came back to deal with family problems. He wasn't there for emotional support when you needed it."

"But I'm not looking for emotional support from Dr. Wiltshire. He's not my father, and he isn't a father figure in my life." Kenzie paused, considering that. "At least, I don't think he is."

Dr. Boyle smiled. "Our feelings like to play tricks on us sometimes. You may never have intended to see him as a father figure, but he still is. Or he may not be, and you're just feeling extra pressure with your boss being gone that you want him to come back and take care of."

"Yeah. That's how I would describe it. I don't expect him to swoop in and 'there, there' me. I don't need any strokes or special praise. I just want him to do his job. So that I don't have to."

"When was the last time you talked to your father?"

Kenzie frowned, "Didn't we just establish that this wasn't about my father?"

"No. We're just discussing feelings. And they can change, or conflict, or hide other feelings. We want to look at the whole picture. Not just your work life and Dr. Wiltshire, but also your home life and your nuclear family growing up. These things all affect each other and, if things are off balance in one, they can cause problems in the other."

"I suppose." Kenzie looked over at Zachary. He knew quite a bit about her relationship with her father and how difficult it was, but he didn't volunteer anything or speak on her behalf. "It's… been a couple of weeks since I talked to Walter, I guess."

"And did he call you or did you call him?"

"He called me."

"When was the last time you called him?"

"I don't know. Maybe to wish him a happy birthday or something."

"You don't normally call him?"

"No, I don't. He's a busy guy. He isn't often free when I try to reach him, so I just let him call me when it works for him. Maybe that's being lazy, but it saves me a lot of aggravation."

"I would like to give you an assignment. I want you to call him during the upcoming week. Not for anything special. It's not an event. Just call him to chat for a few minutes. Would you accept that challenge?"

Kenzie squirmed. Usually, Dr. Boyle's suggestions were things for her and Zachary to do together. It was couple's therapy, after all. It was supposed to be about her relationship with Zachary, with Dr. B mediating, helping each to see the other's perspective. They were getting better at communication, learning how to talk to each other in language that was clear and didn't leave them with so many misunderstandings. They both came from such different backgrounds that it had taken time to build a solid foundation.

Kenzie really wasn't there for advice on her dad.

"I'll think about it. Maybe."

Dr. B nodded. "Don't make a big thing out of it, because it isn't. It's just one tiny thing that will take five minutes of your time and minimal effort. It's not a mountain to climb."

"Okay."

They were all silent for a few minutes. Kenzie shifted uncomfortably. She looked at Zachary, waiting to see if he had something to say, either about her being late and stressed out, or something about her relationship with her parents. He said nothing.

23

"How have things been going between the two of you?" Dr. B asked after a few minutes. "With things being so stressful at work, have you found that overflowing into your home life? How are the two of you managing?"

Kenzie didn't look at Zachary before answering this question. She stared out the window, taking a few deep breaths and trying to relax.

"I know that I have been more emotional. Less patient than I usually am. I've probably bitten Zachary's head off a few more times than I would have normally. But I also think… despite that, we're still communicating pretty well. We haven't gotten into any big arguments. I know that sometimes… I say things that hurt, and I regret that." She ventured a look at Zachary. "But Zachary's been very patient with me through it all. He hasn't lashed back at me. And he sure could have."

"That's good. Do you wish that you had more engagement from him? Are there things you want to discuss that you think he is avoiding? When you are impatient, is there a particular behavior you are looking for? Are you snapping about the same things?"

"No, I don't think so. I think it's just because I'm stressed. I get impatient because… he takes longer to do certain tasks than I would. Or he makes assumptions about how I want something done or about what I need, and it's wrong."

"Like?"

"When I'm just venting, and he wants to jump in and fix things or tell me what I'm doing wrong."

"That's a pretty common complaint between couples."

"I know. It's nothing. It doesn't mean there's anything wrong with our relationship. It's just normal couple's stuff. But *he* thinks I'm halfway to breaking up."

"No," Zachary protested, finally sitting up and taking part in the conversation, "I'm just trying to help out. To be a supportive spouse. And she's fine. She thinks she snaps all the time, but she doesn't. Not like…"

"Not like Bridget," Kenzie finished. "Well, I'm glad I don't sound like a screaming lunatic whenever he does something I don't like. But I wish that wasn't the standard. Zachary acts like I'm a saint, and I'm not."

"When does he act like you're a saint? When he's talking to friends?"

"No, it's not like that. Not to show me off. Just when it's the two of us, and he acts like I could do no wrong, which is clearly not true. I know I get impatient and hurt his feelings, but he won't admit it."

Dr. B looked at him. "How about it, Zachary? Is Kenzie perfect?"

He looked trapped. He looked at Kenzie and then at the therapist, his face getting pink. "There's no right answer to that question."

"It isn't a trick. No one is perfect. So is Kenzie perfect?"

"No." It seemed to pain Zachary to say so. He grimaced and shook his head. "She's great. She's a supportive partner. We do things together. She is interested in my work and I'm interested in hers. We have a good time together. We're communicating well…"

"But she's not perfect."

Zachary ran his fingers through his short hair and scrubbed at the back of his head, wincing.

He didn't answer.

"You see?" Kenzie said, and shrugged. "And, of course it is an impossible standard. He makes me feel like I can't do anything wrong or I will disappoint him. I won't be the perfect Kenzie anymore. I'll be… tarnished. Disappointing."

Zachary's brow furrowed. "No."

"You felt like you needed to be the perfect daughter growing up, didn't you?" Dr. B's eyes were alight with interest. "It's often true of the firstborn. You felt like there were a lot of expectations, and you had to meet them all."

"Sure. I guess. I tried to do what my parents wanted me to. Tried to listen when they told me my responsibilities or the right way to do something. And I did my best."

"But you weren't perfect."

"No." A shrug. Of course not.

"And when you made a mistake, they corrected you. They didn't tell you it was okay to fail. They asked you to do better. To live up to their standards, even if they weren't realistic."

"That's what parents do. They teach their kids the right way to do things."

"Yes. And they need to correct them when what they do is dangerous to themselves or others. But when they tried their best and failed, that's okay."

"I suppose."

Kenzie thought about little Michael. Had he been punished when he hadn't been able to do what his parents told him to? A toddler could not be expected to follow every instruction given to him. Probably not even half of them. They needed to try, and try, and try again to build their skills. They needed to be allowed to fail again, and again, and again.

But Michael had been punished harshly. Maybe for things he had done wrong, and maybe just for existing. For being there when his parents didn't want him around. For making a mess, as kids do. For making noise. For following them around. For wanting one more drink of water before bed.

"Kenzie?" Dr. Boyle asked quietly.

Kenzie wiped at the tears that suddenly wet her cheeks. "I don't know what this is all about," she said, embarrassed. "It isn't about this conversation," she gestured between herself and Dr. B. "It's... the case I'm working on. The abuse case."

Dr. B nodded sympathetically. "It's a terrible thing."

"I just can't understand it. I know that people get frustrated or angry when children can't or don't do what they're supposed to do. But... kids aren't just short adults. They have to learn and to try and make mistakes and try again. It isn't fair to expect them to be perfect."

"No, it isn't."

"Michael— this boy was just little. Barely two years old. And they just… how could they do that?"

Dr. Boyle didn't try to explain it. And that really wasn't what Kenzie was looking for. Dr. B probably dealt with parents who were in counseling. Children who had been damaged by abuse, as Zachary had. Families who were in conflict, maybe hurting each other. She saw it from both sides and knew what could happen when things got out of control.

"I'm sorry, Kenzie," the therapist said gently. "I truly am."

24

"I know this has been hard, Kenzie," Dr. Boyle said. She glanced toward the clock. "Our session is drawing to an end. You have an assignment, should you choose to accept it." She gave Kenzie a teasing smile. "Have you considered medication? If this case is triggering memories of your abduction or putting a lot of extra strain on you, you might want to consider it."

"No," Kenzie dismissed the possibility immediately. "I don't need medication." She was a doctor. If she needed medication, she would have sought it. But extra work was not something that could be medicated away.

"I have offered it before. It can be helpful in dealing with your traumatic memories. And it doesn't have to be permanent. Many people take an aid for a few months and then are able to continue without it. It isn't a lifetime commitment."

Zachary flashed a look at Kenzie. She was always getting after him to take his medications, even when he didn't think he needed them.

But she wasn't being hypocritical about it. Zachary needed medication to function every day, to sleep at night, and to help him with his compulsive behaviors. It wasn't the same as Kenzie dealing with a little extra stress.

"I don't need anything right now," Kenzie asserted.

118

"Okay. That's fine. The offer is open if you change your mind or find that things are getting worse and you get to the point where you need something. Don't feel embarrassed because you said no and then find that you do need something after all. You are a doctor, so you know it isn't a sign of weakness to need some pharmaceutical support if things get too bad. It doesn't make you any less perfect." She winked at Kenzie. "You don't have to give up the rest of your superpowers."

Kenzie laughed along with her. Not because it was that funny, but because she felt obligated. It was hard to admit that she wasn't perfect and that she was constantly chasing that perfection, even though she knew it was unachievable. She was a grown adult, and it was hard to admit that she still wanted or needed her parents' approval. She should have been long past that stage by now.

Dr. B met her eyes again, firm, holding the connection for a second longer than was comfortable. Kenzie tried to act as though she was much more "together" than she really was, keeping her eyes steady and not immediately looking away. Dr. B gave a nod and then turned to Zachary.

"I hope you don't feel neglected today. You are part of this dynamic too. Kenzie's stress and her feelings and what she is going through all affect your relationship and how you feel about yourself."

"I'm here to support Kenzie. What she's going through is important to me."

Kenzie felt like it was a little too pat. A careful, perfect, supportive answer, bare of any emotional baggage. Not the way he really felt. Like Kenzie's, his emotions could be a hot mess. Just because he appeared calm and collected, that didn't mean he was.

"Zachary," Dr. B's voice was reproving. "Are you 'fine'?"

Kenzie had to chuckle at that. One of the rules was that when one of them asked the other how they were, "fine" was not an acceptable answer. Or anything else that might be swapped in its place. No socially acceptable brush-off. Dr. B apparently didn't think he was being truthful about his emotions either.

Zachary opened his mouth to object, squirming in his seat. He looked at each of them, looking for the right response.

He might not have been the perfection-seeking child that Kenzie had. In fact, he'd been a hyperactive, impulsive, anxious child who was always screwing up and who his mother deemed incorrigible. She abandoned him because she didn't want to have to handle him and his siblings anymore. But he was still always seeking the approval of those close to him. Foster parents, his ex-wife Bridget, Kenzie, and his therapists. He was frantically trying to read them and figure out the right thing to say.

Because even though the poor guy had picked just the right thing to say, it had not rung true to either of them and they knew he was just trying to display the expected behavior.

"We talked about me too," he said. "I don't feel left out. I *do* want to help Kenzie."

"I believe that. But I think there's something else going on that you're not talking about. Now, we have about five minutes left. I can give you another five minutes over that if you need it. So... let's talk about what's bothering you."

Kenzie looked at him again. She hadn't realized that there was something else going on beneath the surface. He had fooled her.

"I'm not... there isn't really anything that I need to talk about. It can wait until next week."

"Yes, we can talk about it in your next session. And if you start today, even with just five minutes, you will have something to think of between now and then and maybe some strategies to try so that you can be that much further ahead when we meet again."

He stared at the carpet, fingers rubbing the arms of his chair anxiously. "I don't think it's anything. It's just that Kenzie's case... stirs some things up. Stuff starts rattling around in my brain." He shrugged. "Not really anything new. There's always something bouncing around in there."

"It's okay to say that this case is triggering for you, even though it has nothing to do with you."

"I'm not... hijacking Kenzie's issues."

"You're not," Kenzie and Dr. Boyle both said at the same time.

"It's just... like I said, stirring things up."

"Memories?"

"Not... clear ones. Mostly just feelings. I can't attach them to anything. And I know it is Kenzie's case, not mine. And not anything to do with my life."

He sounded frustrated. Kenzie could relate. She didn't want to be feeling what she was, either. She didn't want to be subject to emotions beyond her control. Illogical, inconvenient feelings.

"Okay. That's understandable. And you're doing a good job of trying not to butt in while Kenzie was discussing her feelings. But now the floor is open and you can talk about yours too."

Zachary shrugged, staring down. Kenzie could see the sweat on his face. While he appeared to be calm, the emotions were clearly having an effect on him. Dr. B had worked with him long enough to notice the tells. Kenzie had been oblivious to them, dealing with her own issues.

"Not really much to say. Anxious. Jumpy. Feeling like… I need to watch everyone. I might be in danger."

"Those are probably all pretty familiar feelings, considering your history."

"Yeah."

"You were able to identify that it was Kenzie's case that triggered them?"

Zachary considered. "I guess so. They started when she was talking about it."

"And they aren't attached to any particular memory? Something about a young child? You or one of your siblings, or one of the other children that you lived with?"

"There have been a lot," Zachary said helplessly. "Sometimes you see them hit. Sometimes… you just know that they were. Something telegraphs it, even if you can't put your finger on it. I don't remember any of the kids in the homes I was in dying, but I knew that could happen. I guess maybe as foster kids, we had talked about it; we knew of other cases where kids *had* died."

"And you were a witness to at least one death in institutional care as well."

"At Bonnie Brown. Yeah. But that wasn't the same. I mean… it was, because they hit her when she bit one of the guards… but she died later, not because of that."

"You don't know that," Kenzie interposed.

He looked at her. He had told her about Annie before. Reluctantly. She was one of the ghosts in his past. An autistic girl who had died in the children's center Zachary had sometimes been housed at. In the room next to his.

"You don't know that wasn't why she died," Kenzie pointed out. "She could have had internal bleeding or other injuries."

"They told her parents that she'd just died in her sleep. I knew that… they left her in handcuffs all night, so she asphyxiated."

"That's what you assume, and you might be right. But they might not have told the parents the truth, or all of it. Things were a lot less regulated then. They might have told her parents that she died in her sleep when they knew very well that it was because of internal injuries."

Zachary looked sick at the thought. Kenzie realized belatedly that she should have just kept this to herself. He had probably thought of Annie's death as peaceful, fading away in her sleep because she wasn't getting the oxygen she needed while restrained. He hadn't thought of her as being in pain and bleeding out in the cell beside his. He put his face in his hands. Kenzie bit her lip and looked at Dr. B. She hoped her apology was clear. She hadn't meant to make Zachary's pain worse.

"It was a long time ago," Dr. Boyle told Zachary. "And it's best to know the full truth, or as much of it as possible, even if it is upsetting."

"Uh-huh."

"But it wasn't Annie that you were thinking about specifically."

"No, just… all of them. All the kids that I knew, or didn't know."

"And yourself. You were not killed, but you were physically abused. You have those memories, even if no specific ones are coming to your mind. Your physical abuse probably goes back just as far as that of the child Kenzie is dealing with."

Zachary wiped away sweat or tears without pulling his hands all the way away from his face. "We always tried to protect the little ones. At home… in all the homes I was in. We always tried to keep them from getting their hands on the youngest children."

"But you weren't always able to. And early in your life, that child was you."

"Michael didn't have anyone to protect him." Zachary sniffled. Kenzie's eyes were burning again.

"No," Dr. B agreed, looking at Kenzie to see if she had anything to contribute. "He was the only child?"

Kenzie nodded. "Yes. And I hope they never have any others."

"They won't stop," Zachary said with assurance, probably thinking of his own parents rather than Cash and Terri-Lyn Wade. He didn't know them or what their plans were as far as more children were concerned. But he knew that Zachary's father had gone on to have several more children after Zachary and his full siblings had been taken into care. More victims of abuse. Who knew how many families and children the guy had around the state or surrounding area.

"Okay." Dr. B was using her "closing" voice now. Wrap up, summarize, and send them on their way until the next session. "We can discuss this more at your next session if you like. I think it's good if you each know what the other is going through right now. Do you agree?"

They looked at each other and nodded. Kenzie wasn't sure how she would handle Zachary's emotions on top of her own and everything else that was going on. Was she supposed to walk on eggshells around him? Not mention anything else about her case and investigation? That was what held the two of them together, their mutual interest in investigation and digging up the truth. If she couldn't talk to him openly because it was triggering his anxiety, what were they going to talk about?

Dr. B gave them both understanding smiles and sent them on their way. For the next week, they would have to map their way through the minefield themselves.

25

They had their usual ice cream after the session, a tasty tradition Kenzie had instituted to help Zachary feel good about their therapy sessions. A sweet association that would tell his brain to look forward to the sessions instead of dreading them.

But it turned out that it was just as important a tradition for Kenzie herself. And after today's session, she needed it more than ever before. They didn't discuss anything heavy over ice cream. They rarely did. But it was an essential part of reconnecting after the intense "inner work" that was part of their session.

Then Kenzie had more work to do. She couldn't afford to take off the entire afternoon and evening like she did when Dr. Wiltshire was in the office. She was too anxious about staying on top of everything while he was recovering.

She called Julie for messages and found that Dr. Wiltshire had not left any for her, though there was a slew of other messages. They would be in Kenzie's email when she logged in.

Kenzie had been putting off calling the Wades. After meeting Cash, she wasn't too eager to talk to his wife, but she would probably be much easier to deal with. Hopefully. A grieving mother might be impossible to get any information from. Still, at least she wouldn't be screaming at Kenzie like Cash. And if she did, what was easier than disconnecting the call? There was no danger of retaliation. Or physical retaliation, anyway. If she got another slew of phone calls from friends of the Wade family in high political positions, she would deal with that.

So, shut away in her home office, with the door shut so Zachary knew not to interrupt her, she called the number on the mother's witness statement. It rang a few times and she figured it would go to voicemail, then it was picked up.

There was a click and breathing, but no words.

"Hello?" Kenzie tried. "I'm looking for Terri-Lyn Wade."

More breathing and a sniffle. "Yes?"

"Is this Mrs. Wade?"

"Yeah. Who is this?"

Kenzie cleared her throat. "This is Dr. Kenzie Kirsch from the Medical Examiner's Office. I was hoping that you could answer some questions about your son."

"What?" There was a squeak of outrage in Mrs. Wade's voice. "You have no right to call me!"

"It's part of my job, actually. There are a number of unanswered questions, so I would like to get some details from you about your witness statement."

"No. No, I don't want to talk about it. This is cruel. You can't just call and interrogate me about my son's death like I'm a criminal."

A little unfair, since Kenzie had not asked a single question yet, let alone accused her of any wrongdoing.

"I don't think you're a criminal, ma'am. I'm sure you want this dealt with as quickly as possible, so I'm doing what I can to keep things moving forward."

"Well, I don't have any intention of answering any questions. You and the rest of the ghoulish doctors at the medical examiner's office can just leave me alone."

Kenzie frowned. She wasn't aware of anyone else from the office having called Terri-Lyn, so she wasn't sure why she would react to Kenzie's call this way.

"I just have a few questions."

"I'm not answering them."

"It would only take a few minutes, and I promise to be sensitive to your—"

"Cash said not to talk to anyone. He said that if anyone called me, I should ask for my lawyer. So that's what I'm doing. Lawyer, lawyer, lawyer. You can't ask me any other questions."

That wasn't quite how it worked, but Kenzie wasn't going to argue the finer points of the law with the woman over the phone.

"All right, Mrs. Wade. I'm sorry to have bothered you."

A few notes in Kenzie's ear notified her that the call had ended, so she didn't make a fool of herself talking to dead air. Kenzie was pretty sure that Terri-Lyn Wade had slammed the phone down.

She sat just looking at the phone for a few minutes.

There was no way she would call Cash to ask him about his statement. She had hoped that the questions she had about Terri-Lyn's statement would cover them both. But she didn't want him screaming at her.

While she was sitting there staring at her phone, she decided she might as well follow through on her assignment from Dr. Boyle and call her father. Dr. B had warned her not to make a big deal out of it and build it up to make it bigger and more onerous and difficult than it was; just make a casual call.

If Walter were busy, he wouldn't answer, and he would follow up with her another time. If he were free to take a call, then she was sure he would pick it up. He was a family man. He enjoyed his work, his calling as a lobbyist, but at the core of everything was his commitment to his family and making the world a better place for them. She tapped over to her favorites list and found his name. Another tap and the call was going through.

He was much quicker to answer than Terri-Lyn had been, which was satisfying. Kenzie would like to think that he was eager to talk to her.

"MacKenzie?"

"Hi, Dad."

"How are you? Is everything okay?"

Kenzie smiled and quirked her head. It was a telling question. She didn't call him often enough for him to consider it a normal occurrence, and he was worried that something was wrong.

"Yes, I just thought I'd touch base and see how you were."

"Ahh." He sounded like he was stretching out and settling in for a long conversation. "I'm delighted to hear from you. Things going okay with you and Zachary?"

"There are always bumps, but yes, we're doing just fine. Had the afternoon off to spend some time together." He didn't need to know that it was for therapy. It was technically true. And it was more important to their relationship than an afternoon museum date or going out for drinks.

"Excellent. Glad to hear that you're taking time together. You're like me; it is very easy for me to get caught up in my work and lose all track of how much time I'm actually spending at work instead of at home. One of the dangers of loving your work is that you're happy to spend too many hours doing it."

Kenzie agreed with his assessment of himself. She wasn't so sure it described her. She made sure that she spent time with Zachary. But it was true that she spent longer at the office than she was strictly required to. She worked longer hours than an office worker. But less than she had as a medical student.

"I suppose I might do that sometimes," she said tentatively.

He chuckled. "It's hard to admit. You're not supposed to prefer your work to the rest of your life. But who wants to spend time making dinner and cleaning the bathroom when you could be doing something more interesting, like pushing a bill through the legislature—or stopping one in its tracks."

"Or investigating an interesting medical puzzle," Kenzie contributed.

"Better than TV," Walter told her.

Kenzie laughed. It was. She often found herself getting bored with what was on TV. That didn't happen in the middle of an autopsy.

"Your mother told me about this case with the congressman's son. What a tragic loss."

"Yeah. It's a very sad case."

"Too bad you don't get to choose which cases you are involved with."

"Just pick the cheerful ones?" Kenzie suggested.

Walter's low, rumbling chuckle cheered her. "Okay, I suppose you probably don't have many of those," he admitted. "Though there are a few politicians I wouldn't be sad to see on your slab." He laughed again, at himself this time. "What a terribly inappropriate thing for me to say. A person can't go around making jokes like that. What if something actually did happen to one of my political opponents?"

"Would you be sad?"

"I would not," he asserted.

"Were you at Mom's?" Kenzie asked, circling back to his reference to Lisa.

"Yes. Spent a few days in Burlington for a conference recently. Had a very nice time visiting with her."

"You two have a good relationship."

"Best thing we ever did was get divorced. Though I wouldn't recommend it to anyone else," he warned seriously. "Things are okay with you and Zachary?"

"Yes."

"You haven't made the same mistakes that we did. We were too quick to rush into marriage, seal the deal because that was the expected thing. I don't think either of us was cut out for it. I don't regret that we got married. I wouldn't have had you and Amanda in my life if I hadn't, and I can't imagine my life without you."

Kenzie thought about the possibility of children in her and Zachary's life. She knew he would like children, but she had never been too keen on the idea herself. She had helped to raise Amanda. And then had lost her. She wasn't eager to do either one again. Zachary could enjoy his nieces and nephews and spend time with them. He could interact with them when he felt good, but they were not devastated when he had to be hospitalized or was not in good shape to see them.

"I'm glad that you made that mistake," Kenzie offered.

"Me too. But I'm glad that we straightened things out and dissolved the..." He hesitated, looking for the words that gave a sense of what he intended. "The onerous legal relationship and responsibilities dictated by the government. We are free now to have whatever relationship we want without it affecting our financial commitments or legacies."

Kenzie wondered if it also left them both free to pursue other relationships. She wasn't aware of any other serious relationships either of them had pursued. Neither of them had introduced her to any boyfriends or girlfriends. She was sure they must both have someone to take with them to charity and political events from time to time. But they were no longer limited by social convention to choose each other.

26

Kenzie found herself feeling more at ease at the office the next day. She was not surprised that Dr. Wiltshire wasn't there and was no longer expecting to hear from him each day. If he got back to her, he did; if he didn't, she would just deal with it. He was the one who would have to take responsibility for anything not done; that wouldn't fall to Kenzie. She felt reassured after talking to her dad, some of those feelings of anxiety and abandonment trickling away. Or maybe it was just because she had talked about them to Dr. B. Either way, she was glad to feel lighter and a bit more like herself.

She had a backlog of filing and other computer work after having Julie cover the desk for the last day and a half, so she spent extra time getting that done before it could become unmanageable.

The phone rang and she picked it up without more than a glance at the caller ID.

"Medical Examiner's Office."

"Is this… Dr. Kirsch?"

"Yes, how can I help you?"

"I want to talk to you."

Kenzie looked impatiently at the display on the phone. She saw WADE in front of the string of numerals and focused on the woman's voice. One of the other staff members in the Wade home? Someone who had finally decided to step forward!

"Uh, yes, of course," she agreed calmly. "Can I get your name?"

"This is Terri-Lyn."

Not a staff member, but Mrs. Wade herself. Kenzie tried to keep her breathing smooth and not give away the change in her attention level.

"Thank you for calling me back, Mrs. Wade. I'm glad to hear from you."

"It's Terri-Lyn."

"Okay, Terri-Lyn."

There was a pause. "Do you know who I am?"

"Yes. Terri-Lyn. Michael Wade's mother. We spoke briefly yesterday."

Another moment of silence. There must be a problem with the phone connection, with each of their voices being delayed a second or so, leaving too-long pauses when no one was talking.

"Yeah. You said you had some questions about my statement."

"Yes. If you just wait for a moment, I need to refer to my notes." Kenzie didn't want to miss any of the important notes she had written down. "Okay. You indicated that you were having breakfast when the... incident was discovered."

"Yes."

"And that you thought Michael was still sleeping at the time."

"Yes."

"But he had been up for some time."

Another pause as Kenzie's comment was relayed over the ether to Mrs. Wade. Then perhaps another second or two while Terri-Lyn considered how to respond to the comment. The seconds ticked by, making Kenzie wonder whether she had lost the connection at first.

"No. He was still in bed. He just got up and... went to the window without anyone knowing he'd gotten out of bed. If any of us had known that he was out of bed, we would have been able to stop him..."

"When had he eaten last?"

"Uh... the night before. Suppertime, I would guess."

"His stomach contents were partially digested. So if he had last eaten the night before, he died an hour or two after supper. If he died in the morning, when he was found below the balcony, he'd been up for a couple of hours and had already eaten breakfast."

"No, that can't be right."

"Those are the facts, Mrs. Wade. Either he died the night before, or he had been up for several hours before he died in the morning."

Kenzie already knew which it was. The death investigators who had retrieved the body had done their job competently and recorded the body temperature. It was still warm when they arrived. Not a child who had died the night before and then the body thrown off the balcony in the morning to disguise time of death.

He might have been killed an hour or more earlier than the family had reported, but not ten or more hours before.

"I… I don't understand it. I thought he was still in bed. Sylvia must have gotten him up. But why would she leave him alone?"

"You can understand why I have questions."

"Yes… I understand. It is confusing. I guess things get confused when something like this happens. There are always pieces that don't quite fit, aren't there?"

It was true. All of the clues didn't always point in the same direction in real life like they did in a movie, and there were often things left unexplained after an arrest and conviction. The human body was not always as predictable as she would have liked to believe.

But it was strange to hear someone outside of the medical profession or law enforcement express this thought. Most people who picked up all of their forensic knowledge from TV had expectations that far exceeded what could actually be done in real life. Or what was done when budget, time, and other resources were at a premium. There were not DNA or fingerprints at every scene. Or there was too much. Not every body that came through the medical examiner's office was dissected. People went unidentified and cases went unsolved. In many cases, the cause of death could not be determined from the body itself, and they needed more information from the police as to what had happened at the scene to make a determination.

"No, everything does not always fit," she agreed. "But in this case… I think the answer is quite simple. You and your husband would prefer to place yourselves as far from the scene as possible. You don't want to put yourselves in close proximity to him or to admit that he was up and active, and didn't just wander off for an instant and get himself into mischief."

"Whatever happened had nothing to do with me," Terri-Lyn objected. Effectively demonstrating Kenzie's point. "It must have been Cash. I wasn't around. I had been attending to other things all morning. I had my Pilates class and… other things."

"If you don't give me and the police the truth about what really happened, you just end up making yourself look bad."

There were prolonged sniffles on the other end of the line. Terri-Lyn's voice was breaking when she spoke again. Or she did a really good imitation of the grieving mother, now that she had been trapped. "I don't know what happened, MacKenzie, but it wasn't anything to do with me. I didn't hurt my son. I could never do that. You have to believe me."

"Someone *was* hurting him. There are a lot of unexplained injuries."

"I don't know what you're talking about. If there are other injuries… he must have hit something on the way down. He must not have fallen straight down from the balcony, but maybe… off to the side and he hit a tree or part of the house that stuck out…"

"I wish you would reconsider your answers. You must know that I can tell the difference between injuries obtained yesterday, or last week, or last month. And they don't look the same as injuries obtained at the time of death or shortly before."

A longer silence from Mrs. Wade. She continued to sniffle and breathe raggedly, at least keeping up appearances while she thought through the possibilities.

"I'm not even supposed to be talking to you," she said in a near whisper. "He told me not to, but I thought *you* would understand. That you would help me."

"I am trying to help you. My first responsibility is to the truth and finding out what happened to Michael. And I'm sure that's what you want to know too. It's a terrible thing to be left wondering for years afterward exactly what killed him." Kenzie thought about Zachary and the girl that had died at Bonnie Brown. Even now, decades later, he was still broken up over the thought that she had died of her injuries that night instead of just peacefully drifting off in her sleep. How would Mrs. Wade feel if Kenzie never identified the cause of death or fudged her report to hide it? Like Annie's parents and Zachary, she would wonder for years, and it would tear her up inside. "I know you want to find out the truth too," she told Terri-Lyn.

"It's Cash. I'll need to… I'll have to find a way to see you. He could overhear anything that I say at the house."

"We can work something out. If you come down to the medical examiner's office, we have a comfortable boardroom where we can sit down and discuss it."

"No. I can't come all the way there. It will need to be somewhere else. Somewhere he wouldn't know what I was doing. We could meet halfway, couldn't we? Get together for lunch so that he thinks it is just a friendly chat, not anything to do with Michael."

Kenzie doubted that she needed to pull a bunch of cloak-and-dagger tricks to avoid being seen by Cash Wade. Wouldn't he be off working? She was pretty sure that congressmen couldn't just lie around all day, but had to attend meetings in person. A lot of events, both political and charitable. Appearances that were just for visibility as well as those that were required to get things done.

"Yes, I guess we could meet for lunch," Kenzie agreed. "Today? Tomorrow?"

"I need to check my calendar…"

Kenzie shook her head, irritated. Terri-Lyn had known who she was calling and why, and Kenzie was sure she at least knew whether she was having lunch with anyone today or not, even if she didn't know her schedule for the rest of the week without looking.

"Do you think… a late lunch today?" Mrs. Wade suggested, pretending that she was looking at her busy schedule. She couldn't be expected to be anywhere but at home just days after her son had died. She could have canceled anything she wanted to.

"When and where?" Kenzie prompted sharply.

"Today at one-thirty… two o'clock…? I'll send you the address."

Two o'clock certainly was a late lunch. Kenzie wouldn't be able to wait that long without something to eat. She would have to grab something from the vending machine to hold her over for a few hours until she could get to the restaurant Terri-Lyn had picked out.

"All right," she agreed. "Send the address to my cell phone." Kenzie dictated the digits slowly to give Mrs. Wade time to write them down or enter them into her phone.

"Thank you," Terri-Lyn said distantly, and then the call was terminated. Kenzie looked at her desk phone in irritation. The woman could have at least had the courtesy to say goodbye, or to wait until Kenzie confirmed she had received the address.

She hung up the receiver and slid out her cell phone to look at it. No text. She laid it on her desk and worked on other things while she waited for the phone to light up with the arrival of the text. Mrs. Wade couldn't very well expect her to show up at a restaurant she never named or sent the address for.

The termination of the call had been very abrupt. Maybe Mr. Wade had walked in at that moment, and she'd had to end it before he could figure out what she was up to. And then she hadn't been able to send the address right away as she had planned.

A few hours passed, and Kenzie started to wonder whether something had happened to Mrs. Wade. If there was physical abuse going on in that household, then Michael might not have been the sole target. Cash might have no qualms about beating on his wife, especially if he guessed what she was up to.

That was when she really started to worry. Should she call the police and report it to them? She could fill Tuttle in and see if he wanted to go over to the Wade mansion to check on her.

She didn't really have any evidence that Mrs. Wade was in any danger, but she had to wonder. If Cash Wade had killed Michael, he wouldn't just sit around waiting for someone to find out about it. If he felt like his secret was threatened, he would take action.

27

It was a quarter to two when a text finally came through to Kenzie's phone with an address. Unknown caller. Kenzie navigated to the number to assign it Terri-Lyn Wade's name and found it to be a long stream of letters and numbers, clearly sent through some kind of anonymizer service. So Terri-Lyn did not want Kenzie to know her private cell phone number. She hadn't just blocked the number, maybe anticipating that, as someone involved in law enforcement, Kenzie might be able to see even a blocked number.

It was a relief to get the address and to know that Terri-Lyn was okay, whatever games she was playing. Domestic violence situations were fraught; it was difficult to know when things might explode. And things had definitely exploded at the Wade residence once already. Kenzie didn't want to be responsible for another because she had reached out to Terri-Lyn Wade as a witness and her husband found out about it.

Sending her the address so late meant that there was no way Kenzie would be able to get there by two. She had to wrap things up at her desk, make sure the phones were either covered or forwarded, hike to the underground parking to get her car, and then drive most of the way across town to reach the restaurant.

And Terri-Lyn hadn't even said what the name of the restaurant was, so Kenzie couldn't fix exactly where it was in her mind. She would have to use her GPS and look at the numbers on the buildings or signs.

Knowing that she would already be late and that it was Terri-Lyn's own fault for taking so long to get her the address, Kenzie didn't rush. What difference did it make if she were ten minutes late or half an hour late? Terri-Lyn would probably be late herself, knowing that social strata. She expected Kenzie to get there in a rush and then would blow in herself half an hour or an hour later, innocently surprised that her guest was angry and frustrated because of the wait.

The restaurant was not a restaurant, as it turned out. It was a private club. There wasn't even a name on the outside of the building. One of those places that the elite would refer to as "the club" and expect everyone to know what they were talking about. Or at least, expecting their peers to understand what they were talking about. And if they didn't, they were not social equals.

Kenzie walked into the reception area. Thick, plush carpets, dim lighting, and lots of black marble and brass accents. An older woman at the reception desk raised the glasses on a chain around her neck to her eyes to scrutinize Kenzie closely, emphasizing the fact that Kenzie had never been there and was not a member.

"Good afternoon. How can we help you today?" she asked politely.

"Dr. Kenzie Kirsch," Kenzie said firmly. She paused, waiting for the receptionist to think of the name and all the associations with the Kirsch and Cole Kirsch connections. "I'm here for a meeting with Terri-Lyn Wade?"

Maybe there wasn't even going to be a lunch. Since it was so late, Kenzie wouldn't be surprised if the lunch she had been invited to ended up being nothing more than coffee. A social necessity.

"Ah, you are Mrs. Wade's guest. We are delighted to have you, Dr. Kirsch. Mrs. Wade has booked the Wade family boardroom. Third floor, to your left when you get off the elevator." She nodded to the ancient-looking lift in the corner. Kenzie supposed people were supposed be impressed with its provenance, but instead she wondered how long it had been since it had been serviced and inspected. She looked at the grand staircase instead. A little more work to get to the third floor, but at least she knew she would make it to the top. She would leave the lift to the lifetime members, those with rooms named after their families and who were not physically able to make it up the stairs anymore.

"To the left of the stairs," the receptionist said, following Kenzie's gaze.

"Thank you."

"Have a lovely day, Miss—Dr. Kirsch."

Kenzie gave a curt nod and headed up the stairs. There was a big, wide staircase to the second floor, then it split into right and left arms heading up to the third floor. Kenzie took the left arm, through a reverse, and then turned left at the top of the stairs, hoping she was facing the correct direction.

The second door down from the stairs was dark wood with a brass plaque that read "Wade Boardroom." Kenzie sighed that she had made it to the right place.

Terri-Lyn had not, Kenzie suspected, chosen the boardroom that bore her husband's name in their private club simply because she wanted to have a private conversation with Kenzie away from any eavesdroppers, including her husband. She had wanted to signal to Kenzie just who she was, how rich and influential in their small Vermont community. Terri-Lyn Wade was no one to be trifled with. She and her husband's family were semi-royalty.

Kenzie wasn't sure of the etiquette when arriving at a private boardroom such as this, but Lisa had trained her to be polite and confident when dealing with the elite. She was one of them. Her parents' names had an immediate effect on any of Vermont's old money families. And if the new money had not heard of them, they had clearly not been moving in the right circles. Kenzie knocked on the door, a polite three raps, and then turned the handle and pushed it open.

She wasn't sure what to expect. Terri-Lyn and her husband as a surprise? Terri-Lyn and her lawyer? A boardroom table surrounded by Terri-Lyn, Wade, and a coterie of lawyers? What was the proper collective noun for lawyers? A bevy? A murmur?

But there was just one person seated at the table, head bent over a notebook so that her shining platinum and silver locks formed a curtain that prevented Kenzie from seeing her face for a second or two. Then the woman looked up.

Kenzie stared in shock, instantly recognizing her.

Kenzie did not know her as Terri-Lyn Wade, but Terri-Lyn Ellis, a girl she had known in school.

"Terri-Lyn?" she asked in disbelief.

The stranger with a familiar face stood up. She looked older than Kenzie. She was too young for the gray that streaked her hair. Most people Kenzie knew would have gone to great lengths to conceal such signs of aging, resorting to dyes and treatments to maintain their youthful appearance. But not Terri-Lyn; she carried her gray locks with an effortless grace, as if it were a deliberate fashion statement crafted by a skilled stylist. Kenzie had seen models with hair dyed gray. Twenty-somethings like silver foxes.

Terri-Lyn's face was also more wrinkled than Kenzie would have expected, more like Lisa's face than Kenzie's, even though they were the same age. It looked like she'd lived a very hard life, aging her prematurely.

"I thought it was you," Terri-Lyn said, taking Kenzie's hand in her slim one and pressing it slightly. "When I heard your name, I had to look you up, see if it really was you." She raised an eyebrow and shook her head. "How in heaven's name did you become a medical examiner?"

Kenzie laughed. Terri-Lyn made it sound like she had just stumbled into it, waking up one day after a night of drinking to find herself in the position by serendipity. "A lot of years of school and hard work," she said.

"But… why? Why would you become such a thing?"

"I enjoy it. It's very fulfilling."

Terri-Lyn continued to shake her head. She leaned toward Kenzie, put her hands on her shoulders, and bussed her cheeks with air kisses. Fake hugs and kisses.

"Sit down, please." Terri-Lyn resumed her seat and gestured to the room, palms up. "Well, what do you think? The Wade Boardroom."

"It's really something. Your husband must have made a pretty hefty donation to get his name on a door."

Terri-Lyn looked disappointed. Maybe Kenzie was supposed to refer to it as Terri-Lyn's name, not Cash's. Maybe the money had come from Terri-Lyn's family coffers.

As Kenzie remembered it, Terri-Lyn's family had old money, and plenty of it. She hadn't kept track of the Ellises over the years, but she had a vague notion that Terri-Lyn's father had passed away. Maybe her mother had too. Maybe she now controlled that wealth. But then, why not have the room named after her family? Or maybe Kenzie was supposed to assume that the room had been named after the Wade family based on influence alone, not any kind of monetary donation. But in Kenzie's experience, things like that didn't just happen without a large amount of money passing hands.

"Yes," Terri-Lyn agreed, her mouth downturned.

Kenzie pulled out a chair and sat down. There was coffee service on a sideboard, and various platters with tiny sandwiches and wraps, decoratively arranged fruits and vegetables, and a large bowl of salad accompanied by various salad dressing cruets. But apparently, they weren't eating yet.

"I didn't *think* you knew who I was," Terri-Lyn said. "When I called you on the phone, I said I was Terri-Lyn, but you just kept saying Mrs. Wade, and I didn't know if it was because you weren't allowed to call me Terri-Lyn, or someone was in the room with you, or… you just didn't know who I was."

"You could have said Terri-Lyn Ellis," Kenzie pointed out.

"Yeah… it's funny how I never use my maiden name anymore, even in circumstances like that."

Kenzie didn't think it was funny. It was downright weird. Why wouldn't Terri-Lyn introduce herself to an old friend by the name she had been using back then?

"Wow. I had no idea," she told Terri-Lyn. "I really didn't. I just thought you were doing that thing, asking someone to call you by your first name 'cause you're not comfortable with them using your last name. Or because you want to disarm them. I thought it was just 'call me Terri-Lyn.'"

"Right. I'm sorry for the confusion."

Kenzie stared at her old friend, trying to figure out where to begin. They clearly had a lot of ground to cover. "So… how are you doing? I had no idea that you had married Cash Wade."

"It was a thing," Terri-Lyn said vaguely. "I talked to your mother at the time. I think you were traveling. France or something."

Kenzie strained her memory. Had Lisa ever relayed that information? Had there been an invitation? Was it just assumed that Kenzie would not be able to be there, so her mother had answered on her behalf?

Lisa's more recent call came back to Kenzie now. *You won't have any mercy for an old friend?* Kenzie had thought that her mother had been talking about Cash, about how his family and the Coles had been friends, or the Wades and the Kirsches. She hadn't had a clue that Lisa had been talking about someone that *Kenzie* was friends with.

All the hours that Kenzie had spent on the Michael Wade case so far, and she'd had no idea that Michael's mother was her old school friend. She'd had no idea at all about her personal connection with the case.

28

Kenzie felt sick.

How could Terri-Lyn be involved in this? How could she know what her husband did and not do something to protect that little boy?

The Terri-Lyn she had known had been an idealist, interested in protesting against injustices, attending rallies, and helping to spearhead fundraisers for street kids and other similar causes. She hadn't exactly been radical, but she had been persuasive, talking people into helping out a cause that they probably wouldn't have looked at otherwise. Lisa had taught her step by step how to run a campaign and to ask people for money. Her own parents had not been interested in such things. They would open their wallets when necessary, making a splash in the news, but it had been Lisa who had taken Terri-Lyn under her wing and shown her what to do.

"I don't even remember hearing about you getting married," Kenzie confessed. "That was before Amanda died. And… a lot of the stuff around then is kind of wiped out by what happened afterward. I wasn't really myself… Then I decided to…"

"Change your whole life direction and become a medical examiner," Terri-Lyn finished.

"Well… that's not exactly how it happened. But I knew I wanted to go into medicine. I didn't know what I was going to do with it yet. I was interested in forensics. I had done a lot of the work on figuring out what Amanda had, even though it was too late…" Kenzie's throat constricted, hot and painful. She cleared her throat as if she just had a tickle, and paused for a moment to make sure she was okay before she resumed. "I was always interested in biology in school, and we were so involved in Amanda's treatment… I was often the liaison between Mom and the doctors. After she died, I was ready for a change in my life. Something with meaning."

Kenzie wondered if she had put her foot in her mouth by saying that. She didn't mean to imply that Terri-Lyn's life had no meaning. She was sure it did. Terri-Lyn had been involved in causes, and Kenzie was sure that hadn't stopped just because she got married.

"I mean… I felt like I didn't have any direction. I was just messing around before that. Sowing my wild oats, I guess. Travel, parties, going to the events Mom wanted me to attend."

Terri-Lyn nodded. "I remember how focused you were on your sister before we graduated. Everybody else is talking about prom dresses and limos and after parties, and you're like, 'the day I turn eighteen, I'm donating my kidney to Amanda,' because your parents vetoed it while you were still a minor."

It was the truth. Kenzie remembered that there had been graduation ceremonies and parties, and she knew she had been at her grad dance. Had probably even gone to it with one of the jocks, but it was all a blur. That hadn't been what was important to her. What had been important was saving Amanda's life. Finally escaping the chains that Walter and Lisa had put on her so that she could do the one thing that mattered.

"I don't know how my parents managed to hold out on my giving my kidney to Amanda. If it was me, I don't think I could have stopped the one thing I knew could cure my daughter. We all loved Amanda so much. How could they say no to that and make me wait for years before I could do it?"

"They just thought that was the right thing to do," Terri-Lyn said, her voice a little wistful. "One thing you could always count on was for your parents to do the right thing."

"Or what they thought was right," Kenzie corrected.

Terri-Lyn shrugged. "What's the difference?"

"Because they were wrong. I should have given my kidney to Amanda before that. We could have saved several years of extra pain and illness if I'd been allowed to give it to her when I wanted to. How can that be the right choice?"

"Because they didn't just have one daughter, they had two. They needed to protect you just as much as they needed to care for Amanda." Terri-Lyn looked stern. "Your parents adore you too, MacKenzie. You always act like Amanda was the only one who ever mattered, but they love you too."

"I know that. But it never… impacted on any decisions that I made."

Was that an awful thing to say? She hadn't depended on her parents' love. She hadn't considered it when she had decided to travel or go into medical school or any of the other things that she had decided to do in her life. She hadn't thought that those decisions had any impact on her parents. Of course they did; but Kenzie was supposed to separate from them and make independent decisions about the direction of her life, not just make the safe, prescribed decisions that her mother would have picked out for her.

Kenzie shook off the reminiscences. Enough of the stroll down memory lane. She didn't like where she knew it would lead. She gestured to the food on the sideboard.

"Can we eat now? I'm starving."

"Yeah, sure, of course," Terri-Lyn agreed. "Help yourself. That's why it's there."

"You're going to have some too, aren't you?"

"I don't have much of an appetite lately…" Terri-Lyn sighed and looked at what had been arranged. "Yes, of course I'll have something."

They both stood up and went over to the buffet. Kenzie selected a number of the small sandwiches and other items on offer. She could just imagine what Zachary would have said about those sandwiches if he'd been there. Or what he would think because, of course, he wouldn't speak his mind in front of Terri-Lyn.

"So tell me about your life," Kenzie said. "Since you seem to be familiar with mine, but I lost track of what you were doing. You got married when I was in France."

"Yes."

"That was a few years ago now." Before Amanda's death. Before medical school. How long? Ten years? "But you didn't have children right away,"

"No, we wanted Cash to get established first. It's a lot of work, a political career like he has. Well, your dad would know about that. He's the 'kingmaker' type. He works behind the scenes, but he knows what goes into it. I didn't think we needed the extra stress children would bring."

They finished serving themselves and returned to the table to eat. Kenzie hadn't asked anything else, but Terri-Lyn continued describing what had happened to her over the years.

"The first few years, things were pretty good. We were kind of wild and free, Cash was climbing the ladder quickly and there were a lot of fun events and appearances. I felt like I'd escaped my family and could finally be happy."

Kenzie frowned at that and ate her first tiny sandwich. She tried to remember what Terri-Lyn's family situation had been. Terri-Lyn had come to Kenzie's house a number of times, but Kenzie had only gone to Terri-Lyn's house once. Maybe twice. It had not been the type of place Kenzie wanted to spend a lot of time.

Terri-Lyn's family home had been nice enough as far as architecture went. Everything looked fine on the outside. It was a little smaller than the Kirsch home, but that was not unexpected or a problem. A lot of the kids lived in more modest homes than Kenzie did. She'd never said anything about them or said anything to indicate that she looked down at them.

But inside, it had been a different story. Not the decor which, like the outside of the house, was perfectly fine. But her parents had made Kenzie very uncomfortable. Even at the school and around other parents, they had never talked to one another in a civil tone. They would snipe and be sarcastic. On a good day. On a bad day, they would scream across the house at each other, yelling and throwing things.

Terri-Lyn was mortified by this behavior, of course. This was probably one reason that Kenzie didn't go over there more than she had. That and the fact that she was afraid of them. She had never seen anyone have a knock-down blowout fight and was terrified that they would kill each other in front of her.

They hadn't hit each other while she had been in the same room, although Kenzie suspected that they had in the next room, out of her sight. And once, she had seen Terri-Lyn's father slap her across the face.

And it had been over nothing. Terri-Lyn and Kenzie had been doing their homework on the dining room table. A group project, maybe. Any parent should have been delighted to see their child working diligently away. Terri-Lyn had been a mediocre student. She struggled in some areas, which affected her average, even though she was very good in a couple of subjects.

They had been making a poster together, carefully lettering each information panel.

"Terri-Lyn. Your mother needs the table for supper," her father had announced. "Put your stuff away."

"It's homework," Terri-Lyn protested. "If we put it all away, then we have to start out all over again. Can't we just eat in the kitchen tonight?"

"No. I'm not eating in the kitchen like a servant. Get your stuff moved out of the way."

Kenzie looked sideways at Terri-Lyn's father and started to put the felt markers and other supplies away.

"Dad!" Terri-Lyn protested, drawing it out. "That's not fair. I need to do my schoolwork."

"You can get it out again after supper. Better yet, do it in your bedroom so you aren't underfoot. I don't know why you set up here to start with."

"Mom said that—"

Mr. Ellis backhanded her across the face. Kenzie was so surprised and frightened she nearly wet her pants. She grabbed the papers and supplies she could and bolted out of the room.

Maybe Mr. Ellis had forgotten that she was there. Maybe he just hadn't cared, thinking that she wouldn't tell any tales or that he would be able to counter them if she did. Kenzie ran up the stairs to Terri-Lyn's room and shut the door.

After doing so, she realized she was trapped and should have run out the front door and gone home. If he came after her now, there was nowhere to go but out the window. She was examining the latch and the screen when the door behind her opened quietly, and Terri-Lyn entered. She was sniffling, but tried to pretend that nothing had happened out of the ordinary. Kenzie was on high alert, waiting for Mr. Ellis to come barreling after Terri-Lyn to hit her again, or to yell at the two of them. She'd seen plenty of after-school specials on TV, she knew how abusers would threaten their victims and everybody else not to talk *or else.*

But he didn't come. Only Terri-Lyn did. Her cheek was a hot red where she had been struck, but she didn't talk about that. She just brought up the rest of their schoolwork and put it in her room. "We'll finish up here after dinner," she informed Kenzie. "It's better. We can turn on our music and everything. It will be fun."

Kenzie nodded, looking around. She looked at her friend, waiting for the explanation, the excuses, the "This has never happened before." But it clearly had happened before. Terri-Lyn took it in stride and just tried to pretend that it was nothing. Everyone's parents embarrassed them sometimes. Terri-Lyn's father had just embarrassed her. Life went on.

Kenzie couldn't remember much more about that day. She had apparently gone back downstairs to the dining room to eat dinner with Terri-Lyn and her two parents who couldn't speak to each other civilly. She had made it through the meal and then returned to the bedroom to get their homework finished.

And they had never spoken about it.

29

Kenzie had told Zachary that she couldn't remember worrying about anyone at school being abused at home. Had she blocked out everything she had known about Terri-Lyn? Had she buried that memory of Terri-Lyn being hit by her father and just written it off as "one of those things"? Parental discipline. Like a spanking, except that Terri-Lyn had been older, so it had been across her face instead of her backside. Parents had the right to discipline their children.

She was sure there had been other signs that Terri-Lyn did not come from a happy home. She was always at Kenzie's house, talking to Lisa, but Kenzie hadn't really thought anything of it. Most of Kenzie's friends thought that her mom was cool. Lisa was pleasant and didn't treat them like little kids, but like grown adults who could reason and make decisions by themselves.

There had probably been other signs. Maybe bruises covered up with makeup so that Kenzie wasn't really sure they were there. Just a shadow she had seen for an instant, and then hadn't been sure there had really been anything there. A trick of the lighting. Terri-Lyn's attitude toward her parents had always been negative. It wasn't that she rolled her eyes, shook her head over their behavior to her friends, and whined about the things that all kids did—bedtimes or curfews that were too early. Family vacations. Strict standards of dress, makeup, or dating. Terri-Lyn's complaints had been more general, Harsher,

I hate them.

I would be happier if they were both just dead.

I would be happier living on the streets than with them.

Kenzie would exchange looks with the other girls and shrug. How did you argue with something like that? They could compete about whose parents were the strictest, but Terri-Lyn didn't participate. What would she say? "My dad beats the hell out of me"?

This all flashed through Kenzie's memory in an instant. Cash had taken Terri-Lyn away from all of that. She must have seen him as her savior. Someone had finally come along who said she didn't have to stay with them anymore, didn't have to put up with any more abuse. She had been happy with her new life.

"But things didn't last?" Kenzie guessed. "I guess sooner or later, you had to settle down to domestic life."

"I hate that word. Domestic. Who was domesticated? Me? Him? Why do people have to be domestic? Why can't they just do what makes them happy? Why do we always have to do things to please others?"

"Well…" Kenzie was uncomfortable with the suggestion. "We want people to see us a certain way. It doesn't mean we have to make everybody happy, but we have to choose… what kind of a person we want to be. I decided I didn't want to be a socialite like my mom. That never interested me. I wasn't interested in politics like my dad, either. I wanted something else. It took me a while to figure out what that was."

"Be glad you found it," Terri-Lyn said, toying with her food. She didn't look at all interested in actually eating anything. "I wish… I'd been able to pick the kind of life I wanted."

Kenzie studied her. "What kind of life would you have chosen?"

"I'd love to be… just a normal family. Like mom, dad, and kids, working at… a bank or an office. Normal hours, normal house. Kids come home from school and… I don't know. Everybody is happy and normal. Like at your house when we were growing up. Don't you want that? Kids, and parents who are home and do things with them…"

"Do you think that my dad worked normal hours?" Kenzie asked with a laugh, "That he was home all the time with us girls? He was away all the time. He'd come back for dinner and then he'd be off again for days. It seemed like weeks sometimes."

"Well, that would have been okay too."

"If you didn't have to see Cash for a few weeks?"

Terri-Lyn nodded and shrugged. "I wouldn't mind a break from him now and then. It's hard being his wife. I thought it would be so great. I thought we would be *that* couple, like your parents." She sighed. "Not like mine."

"Does he hit you?" Kenzie asked directly. Maybe she should have been more direct with Terri-Lyn when they were younger. Talked about the domestic violence rather than pretending that it wasn't happening. Maybe if she'd had some support, Terri-Lyn would have been able to avoid getting into the same kind of relationship again. Maybe she could have broken the cycle. How different would Terri-Lyn's life have been if Kenzie had reported what she had seen to a teacher all those years ago?

"Cash is fine most of the time," Terri-Lyn said. "Just sometimes, when he has too much to drink and too much pressure from his job… he needs a release valve. And if I'm all stressed too instead of helping him to unwind…"

"It isn't your fault if he hits you."

"Isn't it? You think you would let anyone say anything to you and it would never get you upset enough to hit someone? A man like Cash doesn't need a wife who always challenges what he says and second-guesses him. He needs someone who is supportive and looking for ways to help him and give him what he needs. Not harping on him like some shrew."

"He shouldn't hit you. Whether he is irritated or stressed or drinking or what. He doesn't have any right to hit you."

"I'm glad your life is perfect, MacKenzie. Not all of us can say the same."

"I'm not saying that my life is perfect. I have a lot of challenges and stresses of my own. But I don't take them out on my partner, and he doesn't take his out on me."

"Yet. How long have you two been together? It's still the honeymoon."

"A couple of years."

Terri-Lyn shrugged. "Like I said. Honeymoon. You haven't really been tested yet. Just wait and see. It doesn't stay like that."

Kenzie shook her head, thinking about her ups and downs with Zachary. Mental health issues, his depression, and his obsession with his ex-wife. Dangerous cases, beatings, and assaults that brought old, buried memories to the surface. Therapy sessions and wondering if he was dead. Being abducted herself and thinking she might never see him again.

They hadn't been tested? Most couples did not have to go through all of that.

"He was always better when I was pregnant," Terri-Lyn said. "I thought he would settle down if I could give him a son. Become more of a family man. Doting."

"Domesticated," Kenzie suggested.

Terri-Lyn laughed shortly. "Yeah."

"You were pregnant more than once?" Kenzie was pretty sure that Michael had been an only child.

"Yes. I had a couple of miscarriages. And then… a couple of terminations too. I didn't want to have a girl."

Kenzie felt the frown lines crease her forehead. "Why not? I thought you would like to have a little girl."

"Boys are better," Terri-Lyn said decisively. "That was what Cash wanted. A little boy to take after him. That he could do things with. What can you do with a girl? Girls are… too distracting. I would always have to watch her, make sure she stayed out of his way."

So Terri-Lyn had terminated any pregnancies that were not boys and then given Cash Wade the son he wanted. Or the son that Terri-Lyn believed he wanted.

"But things didn't turn out the way you had imagined?" Kenzie guessed.

Terri-Lyn looked at her, her eyes looking hollowed out and far away. "Things never turn out the way I imagine. It's like a curse. I'm just not supposed to be happy, I guess. Just enough to give me these brief glimpses… these ideas that I could be happy if I made all the right choices. But it doesn't matter how hard I try. Things never turn out the right way."

"Being pregnant didn't stop Cash from hitting you. And having a baby did not make him settle down and take responsibility for his actions."

"He's good to me," Terri-Lyn insisted, as if Kenzie had been the one to make the accusations and she had to defend her husband. "He's given me everything. Literally everything. I can have anything I want. Cars and pools and that house. It's like living in a dream. Only I always thought that when I had all of those things, the hitting would stop. I didn't think that things happened like that to people who were really wealthy and powerful. They didn't happen to *your* parents."

"No," Kenzie agreed. She hesitated about what to say. Terri-Lyn made it sound like abuse was just something that happened to people. That it could strike out of nowhere. Like it was a virus that some couples caught. "My parents *chose* not to behave that way. It had nothing to do with how much money or influence they had."

"It did," Terri-Lyn would not be deterred. "My dad said that if he had all of the opportunities that your dad did, he wouldn't have been that way. It was because of all of the stress he was under that he was the way he was."

"You don't think that my dad was under any stress? With a daughter who was dying of kidney disease?"

"She wasn't dying. She was on dialysis," Terri-Lyn said scornfully. "And then she got your kidney, so she was cured. That's not such a big deal."

Kenzie was flabbergasted. She stared at Terri-Lyn, trying to understand her viewpoint. Everything that Terri-Lyn's dad had said and done had twisted things up in her mind. He thought that if he had all of the advantages, he would be a different person. He told himself—and her— that he would have been able to control himself, or would never have gotten angry enough to hit his wife and children.

"Amanda *was* dying," she told Terri-Lyn. Terri-Lyn should have known that. She had been one of Kenzie's best friends. Before... whatever it was that had split them up. "A person can't live on dialysis forever. Sooner or later, the body gives up. It starts to fall apart. And even after she had my kidney... she was freer. She could get out to do the things that she had dreamed of. But she still had to take anti-rejection meds, go in for scans to ensure everything was functioning, and follow a careful diet and all of the other things that they told her would help her live longer. Transplanted organs still fail. They don't last forever. The kidney she had from me only lasted for a few years, and then she had to have another transplant. And that was what killed her."

"But she had good years in there. I'm just saying that your dad wasn't worrying about her all of the time. He could just go on with his life, do what he wanted, and not worry about his family. It wasn't like that with my dad. He didn't have any choice in his life. He had a good job, but it was never good enough. He had money, but it was never enough. There were always still more bills to be paid, and every time he thought he was catching up, one of us would buy something stupid. He wasn't made of money."

Kenzie could hear Mr. Ellis saying all of those things. Maybe she had heard him say them in real life, and maybe she could just imagine it from the complaints she had heard from him. But Terri-Lyn had bought into it and taken those same attitudes with her into her life with Cash. A man that she thought would have it all so he would never put his hands on her. Or had she always known that sooner or later, he would?

30

"We need to talk about Michael and what happened to him," Kenzie told Terri-Lyn.

A trip down memory lane was fine when you met an old friend under different circumstances. But she was there because of Michael, Terri-Lyn's son, who had died after months of physical abuse. It wasn't exactly a high school reunion.

"It was an accident," Terri-Lyn said. "A tragic accident. I don't know what he was doing climbing around like that. He wasn't usually that daring. But we tried to keep him safe. Childproofing. That room should have been locked. One of the staff must have left it open after cleaning it. No one could know that Michael would wake up and go exploring like that, would climb over the edge…" She trailed off, dabbing at her eyes.

Kenzie fixed Terri-Lyn with a firm stare. It felt familiar, Terri-Lyn telling stories or going off on a tangent and Kenzie having to be the one to demand the truth.

"Terri-Lyn. That's not what happened. I already told you that I know that isn't what happened. Michael was not killed in that fall."

"He was. There are a ton of witnesses. Everybody in the house can tell you that's what happened."

"As far as I know, only one person actually saw him fall. If there were others, they have not come forward. Everybody is just going with the story that they didn't know what had happened or that there was anything wrong until Sylvia screamed. And she screamed when she saw him on the ground. She didn't see him go over the edge."

Terri-Lyn's eyes welled with tears. "Don't be like that, MacKenzie. Please. I know you're probably still mad at me, but don't mess up this case because of something that happened years ago."

Kenzie shook her head and tried to read Terri-Lyn's expression. "What are you talking about? I am telling you what I know about your son's death. It doesn't have anything to do with… anything else."

"I always figured you knew. You just shut me and everyone else out and pretended you didn't care anymore. But that was high school, MacKenzie. Can't you let it go now?"

"Let what go?" Kenzie was baffled. She had no idea what Terri-Lyn was going on about. It was true that she had become more withdrawn during high school. She and her parents had been so focused on Amanda and keeping her happy and well until Kenzie was old enough to donate her kidney that Kenzie had neglected her friendships. But what did that have to do with anything?

"You know," Terri-Lyn prompted. "With Frankie Carter."

A flood of memories was attached to that name.

Kenzie had always thought it strange how people could forget about traumatic things and bury them so deeply that they didn't even remember what had happened. She knew that it was true, it happened, but she was always a little bit suspicious. Did they *really* forget completely? Maybe they just avoided thinking about it. She could begin to understand it with someone like Zachary, who had gone through such terrible things in his past. One trauma wiped out another. Children's brains were more malleable, and they simply couldn't live with all the memories and still function.

But she *had* forgotten about Frankie Carter. She hadn't thought about him in years. If Terri-Lyn thought she was making decisions based on what had happened with Frankie, she was sadly mistaken. The boy had not even crossed Kenzie's mind in over a decade.

"Frankie Carter. What does he have to do with anything?"

Terri-Lyn looked down, avoiding Kenzie's eyes. "You can't hold that against me after so long. I'm sorry for what happened, but it was just… a prank. Kids do things like that to each other. I guess I was a little jealous

of you. You always seemed to have everything that I wanted. But I just…
it was stupid what I did."

"What *you* did."

"Yes."

Kenzie had never known who was behind the "prank." She had thought that maybe it had been one of Frankie Carter's friends. Or one of the mean girls who didn't like Kenzie and her friends. She hesitated to call herself and her small circle of friends a clique, but that was probably how other people had seen them. They were always together, and Kenzie had to admit that it had been a closed society, excluding others she probably would have been compatible with. But they had drawn together and kept others out. Other girls who wanted into the circle of friends, who wanted to be noticed, who had felt slighted by one of them; any of them might have decided to turn the tables and pull a prank on Kenzie to put her in her place.

It had been Terri-Lyn? Terri-Lyn, one of *her* girls, one of her best friends? One of the girls who was supposed to have her back? Kenzie had always defended the other girls in their group. They had been a sisterhood when Kenzie hadn't actually been with her sister.

Kenzie swallowed, her throat tight. "That was you?"

"I'm sorry, MacKenzie. I really am. I didn't mean you to get hurt, just… I don't know. I wanted to see you fail at something. It was mean and I was a terrible friend. But please don't hold that against me. After all these years… you can let it go, can't you?"

"Terri-Lyn." Kenzie looked her directly in the eye. "I haven't even thought about that in years. It doesn't have anything to do with Michael's death."

"No, but you wouldn't be acting like this if… if we were still friends. You wouldn't be trying to put this on me, to say that it was my fault when it was just a horrible accident."

"I didn't even know until I walked into this room that *you* were Terri-Lyn Wade. I thought I was dealing with a stranger. I would approach this the same way even if you were someone I had never met before."

"But you do know me," Terri-Lyn grabbed Kenzie's hand and squeezed it, trying to convey the desperation behind her words. "You do know me, and you can't do this to me. You know that I wouldn't do anything to hurt anyone. You *know* me, and you know that I didn't have anything to do with Michael's death."

"I can't treat you any differently than any other witness."

For now, she would keep referring to Terri-Lyn as a witness rather than a suspect.

"I know that you can't in front of anyone else," Terri-Lyn said, holding on to Kenzie's hand tightly. "That's why we're meeting here, where no one else can hear what we have to say. A room I know isn't monitored or recorded by anyone."

Kenzie tried to pull gently out of Terri-Lyn's grasp, but the woman held on, not releasing her. "Kenzie, this is *me*. I know that in front of everyone else, you have to act like you believe the worst of me, and not even act like you know me. But we were kids together. You know I would not hurt my son."

Kenzie stopped arguing that she wouldn't treat Terri-Lyn any differently from anyone else. Terri-Lyn clearly wanted preferential treatment. As Lisa had suggested—for Kenzie to show mercy to an old friend. Had Terri-Lyn called Lisa? Had she planted that idea and been the cause of the phone call? She and Lisa had always been close.

"You know what happened to Michael," she told Terri-Lyn

"No, I don't know. Michael was just fine. He was sleeping. There was nothing wrong with him."

Had she looked in on her son and seen him lying on his bed, already dead? Is that why she was so convinced that he had been sound asleep? Had the killer left him there for a time, while figuring out how he would deal with the inconvenient body?

"You know that your husband abused him," Kenzie asserted. So far, Terri-Lyn hadn't actually admitted to that, though she had implied it.

"No," Terri-Lyn's mouth was a thin line as she pressed her lips together. "Cash might have been too rough with him sometimes… when he'd been drinking or was stressed out. Maybe he grabbed him or shook him when he was upset, but that's all. He wouldn't have done anything to hurt Michael on purpose."

"Your nanny knew. She took him to the hospital. If she knew that your son was that badly hurt, why didn't you? You were his mother!"

"Sylvia?" Terri-Lyn shook her head angrily. "She's always been jealous of me. She wanted Cash for herself. Didn't want another woman in his life. She's been a problem since the day we married."

Kenzie tried to understand why the older woman would be jealous of Terri-Lyn. She had a crush on the much younger man? She was old enough to be his mother. Kenzie had a flash of inspiration.

"Was Sylvia Cash's nanny?"

"Yes." Terri-Lyn nodded impatiently. "And she didn't want anyone else giving him any attention. She didn't want him to love anyone else. She's the one who told me to give him a son." Terri-Lyn's voice rose. "She said that he would settle down and be happy… that he would have a purpose, and he needed that…" She blinked, eyes shiny, but no tears fell. "But I think she just said that because *she* wanted a baby. *She* wanted Cash's son."

31

"Sylvia told you to give Cash a son?" Kenzie repeated, completely flummoxed at this revelation. "How did that even come up?"

"I was lonely. I was upset because... things weren't going well with Cash. We were having problems. And Sylvia was a shoulder to cry on. Someone who knew him and I could talk to her about him... she wouldn't be shocked by anything, because she knew him better than I did. She said that his father had been like that... wild... spending too many nights away from home... being... angry. I didn't know what else to do. It was something I *could* do, instead of just sitting around feeling sorry for myself and watching him drift further and further away."

"And she told you that having a baby would solve the problem."

"Yes. She said it had worked with Cash's father. He started coming home more, wanted to be around his family, settled down... I *wanted* that. She said it would work, and I thought she was thinking of me and how to make things better for me and Cash. But that wasn't it at all."

Kenzie shook her head.

"When Michael was born, she took over. He was so fussy and I was tired and didn't feel well. It was too hard for me to look after him all the time, and Sylvia swooped in and took over. She didn't even ask. She just said that was what she was doing. And I wasn't exactly eager to stop her. Having a baby is really hard."

Kenzie made sympathetic noises, encouraging Terri-Lyn to go on and tell her about what had happened.

"I had postpartum. That's what the doctor said. I couldn't do anything. I tried. But I didn't have any energy, and I was so… I just couldn't make myself move. I wanted to stay in bed. Just lie there and pretend that nothing had happened. That I didn't have a baby to take care of, or a family, or a household, or a husband."

"It was that bad?"

"Yeah. The doctor prescribed some stuff that eventually helped. I think. Things got better, anyway. I'm still not a hundred percent. I'm not back to the way I was before he was born. I'm working on my body, you know, doing the Pilates and everything to get it back into shape. But how do you shape up your… brain? It's not a muscle. You can't just exercise it and have it snap back to where it was before."

"Are you still seeing your doctor?"

"No. Just to get the prescription renewed. Why bother? He can't really do anything."

"You might try some therapy. It could help."

Terri-Lyn shrugged. "I've been through crap before. I guess I'll get through it again. But all this stuff…" She made a gesture that encompassed the room, but she wasn't talking about anything in the room. "You can't think I had anything to do with Michael's death. It was just an accident. Like I said from the start. Like everyone said from the start. I don't understand why you're making a big thing out of it. Michael just climbed over the balcony railing."

"You know that he didn't."

Terri-Lyn's mouth was a stubborn line. She let go of Kenzie's hand.

"So we're not friends anymore. You can't do anything to help me."

"Not the way you are talking about. I can't say that you and your family had nothing to do with it. If you want to help clear yourself and them, I need the facts. Not made-up stories. And if I show you any kind of bias, then everything will blow up. People will think I was bought off, pressured by the government, or persuaded by an old friend to look the other way. I can't do any of those things. I have to just do my job."

"Then why did you even come here?"

"Because that was the only way you would talk to me."

Terri-Lyn looked angry about this at first, but then she gave a little smile. "That is what I did, isn't it?"

"Yeah. And then you haven't answered any more of my questions. I'm no further ahead than I was."

"Well, I can tell you," Terri-Lyn leaned forward. "That neither of us had anything to do with it. So if you if you think that Michael was being abused and was killed by someone before he fell from that balcony… you should be looking in another direction. Maybe check out the person who was actually supposed to be taking care of him."

"Sylvia said that she had something else that she was working on, away from the nursery. That she wasn't with Michael twenty-four hours a day."

"Then where was she? And why wasn't she there when he fell?"

Both good questions.

"And Sylvia has been taking care of Michael since he was born?"

"Any time he wasn't with me. He had colic when he was little, and I couldn't handle it. All of that constant crying, for hours. I don't know how anyone can live through that. I seriously don't."

"I've heard it's pretty tough," Kenzie agreed. "And how often did Cash interact with Michael?" When she thought about Sylvia and Michael, Kenzie couldn't picture the nanny hitting him. And Michael *had* been hit. Those bruises had not been sustained in falls or walking into things. No connective tissue disorder or brain tumor had shown up in the autopsy to explain his sustaining such bruises through his own play.

"Cash didn't spend much time with him. He was too busy. Too important. When he saw Michael, he didn't want to play with him or do anything with him. He wanted to show him off or to pick him up for a minute and then put him down and not deal with him again two minutes later."

"He didn't have a lot of patience for Michael?"

"Who could? You don't have any kids, do you?"

Kenzie shook her head. "No."

"Well, they take a lot of work, and they're messy, and they don't care how you feel. They're selfish, greedy little energy hogs. And if you want one to be quiet, do you think they'll stay that way?" She shook her head. "Not on your life."

"Neither of you had much patience for him."

Terri-Lyn rolled her eyes. "No. The person who spent time with him was *Sylvia*," she insisted.

Kenzie hated to think that the little woman who had so clearly adored Michael could have been the one who hurt him. Still, she couldn't deny the possibility and keep looking in the opposite direction. Sylvia was the one who was Michael's primary caregiver. She was the one who had taken him to the emergency room, aware of his injuries and taking it upon herself to see that he was treated, possibly without his parents even knowing about it.

"All right," she conceded. "I'll look into it. Thank you for that information. And I *am* sorry, Terri-Lyn. I would never want to accuse you of anything, but I can't protect you either. I will do my best to figure out exactly what happened to Michael and see that justice is done."

Kenzie knew before even getting home that supper was going to be a bust. She would have to eat late, if she had anything at all. She hadn't exactly stuffed herself with the tiny sandwiches, fruit, and salad, but she wasn't feeling at all hungry.

"I'll just make myself a sandwich and we'll visit," Zachary promised. "You don't have to eat if you're not hungry."

That made Kenzie feel a bit guilty for all of the times she had forced him to eat when his medication had taken away his appetite and he was so nauseated. But she had done that for his benefit. He needed to eat in order to stay healthy, and he wouldn't eat unless she pushed him.

But luckily, he was off of those meds now and finding it much easier to eat and keep up his weight.

Kenzie didn't need to worry about losing weight because she didn't eat one evening.

She told Zachary about discovering that a witness she had contacted —she didn't give him any information on which case it was or that Terri-Lyn was possibly a suspect—was an old friend of hers from school. Zachary shook his head at the coincidence.

"That's why women should never change their names when they get married," he said. "It's impossible to keep track of people."

Kenzie snorted. "This from the private eye."

"Do you know how hard it can be to track down a woman who has changed her name with each of four marriages?" He rolled his eyes. "It's crazy. Why do they do that?"

"I don't know," Kenzie confessed. "I think that in a lot of cases, women like to take on a new identity. To start fresh. To be associated with their husband more closely. And that's not even talking about tradition and the taboo about single mothers and babies born out of wedlock. There is a lot of social tradition to deal with if you don't change your name."

"There are countries where the kids take both parents' names automatically. Or take the mother's."

"Or the parent's first name," Kenzie filled in. "Anderson. Jackson. Peterson. Can you imagine trying to track people down in those countries?"

"There must be tricks, but I wouldn't want to be doing it."

"Yeah. It would be pretty crazy. My mom has friends who do genealogy and say it is almost impossible in those countries."

"So you guys just lost touch over the years? Going in different directions?"

"Well, it was more than just that. I mean, part of it was my being involved with Amanda's care so much. I might not have had a long time with her, and I was waiting for when I could donate my kidney to her. It was really important to me to be with her. And other kids didn't understand that. Terri-Lyn says she wasn't dying, she was just on dialysis, and then she was cured with the transplant, but that doesn't even begin to describe the kind of life we were leading, watching her fail from day to day, hoping that she wouldn't get a virus or pneumonia that might end her life. Trying to be happy around her and act like it was all okay. It was really hard."

He nodded. "I can imagine."

"And then… I mean, it was high school and kids do crazy stuff. Stupid stuff. Some of the things that those girls did…"

Zachary raised his brows. "What? You didn't want to be involved in what they were up to?"

"No. It was… I didn't even know that it was Terri-Lyn at the time, but there was this boy I had a crush on. Frankie Carter. He was on the football team. Big jock. Big everything, he was really popular in school, had all of the girls swooning over him. I was no different than anyone else."

"I don't know about that."

"No, I wasn't anything special. And then... I started getting notes from this boy. Left in my locker, or people who approached me and said they were supposed to give them to me, or whatever. There was all of this cloak and dagger, very romantic; I'm sure my marks were trash at the time because my head was in the clouds, daydreaming about him. And writing in my notebooks; you know how girls do. *MacKenzie Carter. Mrs. MacKenzie Carter. Mrs. Carter. Frankie and MacKenzie. MacKenzie loves Frankie.* All of the lovesick teen girl stuff."

"Aww," he crooned, as if it were cute.

"And the notes were very exciting. Poems, little vignettes of how he had seen me the day before, doing something totally mundane, and had been dreaming about me since. And... spicier stuff. Suggestions. Talking about getting together. Talking about how... excited he was to meet me."

"But he wasn't the one writing the notes," Zachary guessed.

"No. I should have known, but I didn't see it. I was completely blind. Why would a jock like that be interested in me? And if he was, why wouldn't he just walk up and talk to me? He wasn't shy. I saw him talking to plenty of other girls. Being bold and stupid other times. He wasn't the kind of guy who walked around hiding behind a fringe of hair and blushing anytime a girl spoke to him. He was more than capable of walking up to any girl in the school and asking her out."

"But he didn't. And..."

"And so I started flirting with him more and more obviously, thinking that he was into it and he was the one writing me all of these notes. And saying things to him, little secrets that had been in the notes. Until one day..."

Zachary grimaced, anticipating it.

"I asked him if we could get together sometime. You know, privately. Since he'd been sending these notes saying that he wanted to..."

"And he had no clue."

"Nope. He had no idea who I even was. I thought he was joking at first when he asked who I was. Because we'd been connecting, in my mind. We had this emotional relationship already. And when he asked who I was, and said that he wasn't interested and would appreciate it if I would give him some space and stop acting so creepy around him…" Kenzie closed her eyes and shook her head, her cheeks warming up as she remembered the humiliation. "And, of course, it wasn't just the two of us alone when this finally blew up. It was in the cafeteria with half the student population watching. Or that's what it felt like, anyway."

"And it was your best friend who set this all up? This woman who is a witness in your case?"

Kenzie nodded. "What a mess. I never knew it was her. But maybe, on some level, I knew she had enjoyed it and liked seeing me put in my place. She didn't gloat, exactly, but maybe I sensed that she was a lot happier about it than she should have been."

"That's terrible." Zachary's voice was pained. He rubbed his forehead. "I know how cruel teenagers can be, sometimes without actually meaning to be. But that was carefully planned out and executed. She knew exactly what she was doing."

"Yeah. And maybe we drifted apart because she felt guilty about it."

"Or because she was jealous, the emotion that started it all in the first place," Zachary suggested. "Maybe she couldn't be around you, seeing all your successes."

"My successes?"

"Happy family. Good marks. Whatever else she was jealous about."

"Yeah, I guess so. I never knew there was all of this negativity going around. I just… I needed to be with my family and school was secondary to everything else. I didn't really care about it anymore."

"But to Terri-Lyn, the school community was still the most important thing in her life, and maybe seeing that it was not all-important to you anymore pushed her away."

"Anyway… by the time we graduated, I was already gone, emotionally. I remember a bit of the graduation stuff. Walking across the stage, the dance. I think I went to an after-party. But it wasn't a big deal to me."

She had left it all behind her with the rest of her childhood. Until suddenly, Terri-Lyn reappeared in Kenzie's life, the grieving mother of a homicide victim. If she really was grieving. It was hard to know exactly what Terri-Lyn's feelings toward Michael were. He was her child, and she had cared for him to some degree, but it was hard to tell how deep her feelings about him were. Some people felt things deeply, but showed little on the surface. Other parents made a huge fuss and pretended feelings of loss that they did not feel. It was difficult to tell from the outside,

They talked about other things, and Kenzie made sure they covered several other topics before returning to the Michael Wade case, so that Zachary wouldn't immediately know that was the case that her friend was involved in.

"What do you think about the possibility that the child might have been abused by the nanny?" Kenzie asked. "It's a twisted sort of relationship. She was nanny for the boy's father, talked the mother into getting pregnant, then kind of hijacked the kid's care while the mother was battling postpartum depression. The baby has colic, and the mother can't handle his care, but the nanny is already living in the house, so she jumps in and does what she does best. Taking care of babies."

Zachary shrugged. "Anyone can be an abuser. You can't tell just by looking at them. It isn't always a father or stepfather. There could be any relationship. Anyone close enough to hurt him or manipulate him."

"But she is devoted to him. She is the one who took him for medical treatment when no one else in the household did. And she's this little, tiny old lady. I really can't see her in the role of an abuser."

"Huh." Zachary gave a short laugh. "You don't have to be big and strong to abuse someone. She was still a lot bigger and stronger than a small child. And some of the women that I knew in care… Mrs. Phipps at Reachout…" He gave a shudder.

Kenzie had heard mention of the woman before. Usually in reference to her ability to beat and bully the teens in the group home she worked at.

"Just a little tiny woman," Zachary said. "Under five feet. And she was crip—handicapped. She had this leg that dragged, and she needed a cane to get around. I don't know what was wrong with it. Maybe a stroke, or maybe she was born that way. She could handle that cane like a ninja. You would think you were out of reach, and *whack* she'd bring it down across your knuckles. Or in the knee. Or jabbed straight in the spine. A few seconds, and she could have you curled up on the floor, which was right where she wanted you. Right where she could whale on you. A few whacks with that cane would have the strongest boy in the house begging for mercy."

"I can't imagine."

"She was wicked. It wasn't just to keep us in line. She enjoyed hurting and humiliating us."

"That must have been awful. I'm so sorry you had to deal with that."

He made a motion as if pushing it into the past. "Long time ago now. I've recovered. I'm just saying… she was maybe the smallest caregiver I ever had, and physically handicapped, but she was *vicious*. Terrifying."

Kenzie thought about this. Was that what Sylvia was like? A grieving, heartbroken caregiver to the rest of the world, but perhaps also the person who had caused Michael's visits to the hospital and his eventual death? It was still hard to believe, even with Zachary's story. She pictured his Mrs. Phipps as a wizened old witch with a hard face, her weapon of choice always close at hand. Not at all like the devoted nanny she saw in Sylvia Arnold.

<h1 style="text-align:center">33</h1>

It seemed like Kenzie was getting more and more behind at the medical examiner's office. She hoped that Dr. Wiltshire would stop in to sign the paperwork on his desk and maybe take a few things off her hands. In the meantime… she could only do what she could. Julie had spent a lot of time on reception lately, so she was off working one of her other jobs, leaving Kenzie to either man the phones and reception desk or to direct calls to the voicemail system and deal with other duties.

She decided she'd better stay at her desk and get some of the paperwork done. It was too easy to become buried in just a few days by the amount of paper that the medical examiner's office produced. She focused on clearing the voicemails, phone message slips, and emails that had accumulated to make sure that nothing got overlooked.

Detective Baker had left a couple of messages, so Kenzie called her back to see what she needed. She didn't want to be responsible for holding up the Wade investigation.

"Hello? Oh, Dr. Kirsch. How are things? I understand Dr. Wiltshire has left you in the lurch."

"Well, sort of. I'm doing what I can. What can I help you with?"

"You've had a couple of discussions with the folks at the Wade household."

"Yes. Mostly the nanny and Terri-Lyn. Mrs. Wade."

"Anything interesting?"

"I wouldn't know where to start… if you want to stop by here, we can go over it. I need to write down what I can, but I'm not sure what is relevant to the autopsy report and what you need to know. A lot of it doesn't directly impact the autopsy report, but you might want to explore further…"

"Okay. I'll take you up on that. And the other thing is, you might be interested to know that there *was* a DCF visit. Two of them, in fact."

Kenzie sucked in her breath. "I thought they came up clean."

"Well, they did initially. But it seems that some of the documentation got… misfiled."

"Intentionally?"

"Maybe?" Kenzie could picture Baker's shrug. "I wouldn't say that it was not a possibility. But of course, I don't have any proof that it was buried or interfered with."

"Just the name on the file should be enough proof of that," Kenzie said in disgust. "You wouldn't believe the amount of pressure I am getting to obfuscate in my report."

"Oh, wouldn't I?" Baker returned dryly.

Kenzie laughed. If there were anyone who was probably under more pressure than she was with regard to the investigation into Michael Wade's death, it would be the detectives.

"Maybe you would," she agreed. "What do you think? About your investigation so far, I mean. Was the additional evidence that Tuttle and I supplied of any help?"

"Most of it is still being processed. It is an interesting case. No lack of possible suspects. But unfortunately, the kind who can ruin your career if you point a finger in the wrong direction. Not that I'm in the habit of carelessly pointing out potential killers."

"Yeah. Can you shoot me a copy of the DCF reports?"

"Already on their way. If they aren't in your inbox yet, they should be soon. And I will try to get down to talk to you today or tomorrow to find out what you discovered in your conversations. Any high points?"

"Well… you should probably know that, unbeknownst to me, I actually know Mrs. Wade from way back. I didn't know that until yesterday, because I've only heard her called by her married name. So… it won't affect my autopsy report, but you should be aware of the possible accusations of bias. Obviously, we haven't kept in touch, so I don't think I can be accused of being a close friend. I haven't seen her in years and years."

"Understood," Baker agreed crisply. "In a place like Vermont, you can't really expect not to run into people you know from time to time. I know I have as well."

"Okay, good. I wanted to make sure that you knew right away."

"I'll make a note on file, including the date you disclosed it to me."

"Aside from that… well, pretty much what you would expect. Everybody denying that they know anything about what happened to Michael and pointing their fingers at each other."

"Trouble in paradise?"

"Mrs. Wade made it clear that all has not been well between her and her husband. But even more finger-pointing toward the nanny. I don't think there was any love lost between the two of them."

"Why didn't she fire her, then?"

"She was Mr. Wade's nanny."

"Oh. Ohhh…" Baker drew the syllable out thoughtfully. "Well, that *is* interesting, isn't it?"

"I doubt if Mrs. Wade would have been allowed to fire her. And I don't think she was prepared to. From what she said, she's not up to raising a young child on her own. She would have had to find someone else before firing Sylvia Arnold."

"Anything to it, do you think?"

"Maybe…" Kenzie didn't want to commit to anything. "I find it hard to picture her as an abuser or murderer, but my partner reminds me that it doesn't really matter what she looks like. Outer appearances can be deceiving."

"That they can," Baker agreed.

"Sylvia Arnold was the one who took Michael to the hospital when he was injured. She can't deny knowing about the abuse, even though she tried."

"Maybe it's time for us to have another chat with her."

Kenzie nodded her agreement, even though Baker couldn't see her. "Yeah, you might want to. I hate to think of her doing something to that little boy. She seemed so broken up about it. But we've all seen mothers weep over their kidnapped or murdered children, only to find a few weeks later that they were the perpetrators. Looking sympathetic doesn't mean anything."

"Some of the most horrific killers have been sweet-faced. Okay, I'll leave you to your work. Will stop by later."

Kenzie hung up the phone and went immediately to her inbox to scan for the DCF reports. They had just arrived. She printed copies and filed the electronic copies immediately, then started to skim-read as the reports came off the printer.

DCF had twice been called out to the Wade mansion. Considering the amount of influence Cash Wade wielded, it had taken some guts for someone within the household to make a report. Even though the details of such reports were supposed to be kept from the accused abusers, this kind of information often leaked out. So a reporter could never be sure that her identity would remain unknown. As such, Kenzie thought that she must have recognized that the abuse had become extreme, or she wouldn't have dared make the report.

The first call that had been investigated by DCF had been a report of suspected abuse. The subject child had significant bruises, cried a lot, and was often sick in bed. The case worker, a Moriah Wright, had apparently not been expecting the Wade mansion when she responded to the report. There were a lot of details in the report describing the property, both exterior and interior. This had clearly been a novelty for someone who was used to investigating homes with six children sleeping in a single-room apartment or a house on its way to being condemned for health code violations. She was used to reporting any red flags in the child's environment in detail, so she followed a similar process for the Wade mansion, listing everything she thought argued against a child being neglected or abused there. Poverty was a red flag for neglect and abuse. Extreme wealth was not.

She detailed meeting with each of the women who took care of Michael, Terri-Lyn Wade and Sylvia Arnold. She conducted the interviews separately. She was also introduced briefly to Michael. Wright reported that Michael appeared to be healthy and well-nourished. He was clean, dressed in clean, well-maintained clothes. His hair was combed. His face washed. No sores or rashes that would suggest he wasn't getting the vitamins he needed. She didn't report any bruises. When she asked for the opportunity to examine Michael more closely by having him raise his shirt and pant legs, the request was denied. Not much the social worker could do about it. Without concrete evidence to back the abuse allegation, she could not take him into custody and take him to a doctor herself.

The child's father was not available. He was out of town on business. The case worker reported that he was a congressman, though Kenzie wasn't sure what relevance that had. She supposed that if he were a construction worker or unemployed barfly, those would have been red flags. The case worker wanted to cover all of the bases so that she couldn't be accused of being biased or so blinded by the family's wealth that she hadn't done a thorough investigation.

Both of the women had denied there was any possibility of Cash Wade being abusive. Both described him as a loving, caring family man.

Wright had been shown to the nursery and reported on everything being clean and neat, with no apparent hazards to such a small child. She was told that he was supervised at all times and, during the interviews, he had been taken to the kitchen, where he was given a chocolate chip cookie and looked after by one of the kitchen staff until they were finished.

She reported that each of the women was cooperative and concerned about the allegations that had been made, but denied that there was any possible truth to the reports. Both women were well-dressed and well-groomed, presenting themselves well. They were calm and did not show any sign of deception or contradict themselves or each other. Both suggested that perhaps the report had been made by a former employee who wanted to get back at his ex-employers for perceived wrongs. Sometimes people did things like that, making false reports as a method of retaliation. Wright, of course, knew this to be true. She did not confirm or deny the identity or position of the person who had made the complaint.

The allegation was cataloged as "unsubstantiated" with no recommended follow-up.

The second report that sent a social worker to the Wade mansion suggested that Michael was abused and the victim of medical neglect. There was no indication whether the report had come from inside the mansion or was made by a former employee. Still, Kenzie assumed from the contents that it must have been made by someone on staff. How else would they have known to call when they did?

Upon arrival, the case worker, this time Delia Rose, found Michael Wade sick in bed.

He was pale and lethargic. Kenzie's stomach tightened as she read these details. She wrote down the date of the report to check later whether it matched up with any of the emergency room visits. Rose did not see any injuries on Michael's face that suggested abuse. Like Wright, her request to examine Michael more closely was denied. She was not allowed to pull down the blanket, pull up his shirt, and see whether there were blackening bruises or signs of internal bleeding. She was told he had the flu and would probably bounce back in a day or two.

There were bottles of water and a pediatric electrolyte solution on the bedside table, as well as saltine crackers and a bowl with remnants of what appeared to be porridge or pablum. They suggested that he was being properly taken care of during his illness. There were no medications in evidence. Kenzie didn't suppose that a social worker would look kindly on medicine left within reach of a child, no matter how sick he was. A bottle of syrupy children's Tylenol could be swallowed in a few seconds, leading to great harm.

When she touched him, Rose found Michael to be warm, but not burning up. If he had a fever, it was low grade, nothing to be concerned about. He didn't engage with her or answer questions, but he was only a toddler, and he was sick. Not someone that Rose expected to get more than a word or two out of.

Sylvia Arnold sat in the rocking chair beside the bed, where it was evident she had been spending a good deal of time. A wastepaper basket filled with crumpled balls of tissue and food wrappers suggested that she was spending all of her time there. The mother, Terri-Lyn Wade, had made a brief appearance, checking in on her son and talking to Sylvia and Rose for just a few minutes.

She indicated that Sylvia was watching over Michael most of the time, with Terri-Lyn or someone on the house staff taking over when Sylvia needed a break. Terri-Lyn said Sylvia had some medical or first aid training and was the best one for the job, but didn't go into detail. Sylvia didn't offer any credentials, just saying vaguely that she had experience with sick kids.

Rose suggested that the boy be taken to the doctor if he hadn't already seen one. Terri-Lyn indicated that a family doctor would make a house call if his condition worsened or was prolonged. If they had any concerns, outside medical treatment would be sought. No expense would be spared.

Rose obviously knew they had the money to follow through on these promises and would not hesitate to take him to the hospital due to lack of funds or insurance. There was no reason to suspect that they would avoid treatment. At the time, the best place for the boy was in bed in his own home. If things got worse, the hospital was not far away.

Rose recorded the second report as being unsubstantiated and, as with Wright, did not recommend any follow-up action.

35

The case workers seemed to have been diligent, recording the details of their visits and everything that they had observed while there. Kenzie had read a number of DCF reports, and nothing seemed amiss. She couldn't see any gaps that the case workers should have filled.

The only troubling factor was that they had not been allowed to examine Michael for injuries. As Zachary had told Kenzie, serial abusers frequently learned to avoid facial injuries or scarring on the arms or other places they might be seen. Michael's worst injuries had been focused on his torso, both belly and back, which the social workers would have been able to see if they'd been allowed to look. But the legislation said that bruises alone did not constitute evidence of serious bodily injury. There had not been any indications of abuse or risk factors noted in the SDM Risk Assessments the social workers had performed. So they hadn't insisted that Michael be examined by a medical professional.

Kenzie was not looking forward to the next step, but she knew she had to do it anyway. She dialed the number for DCF and asked for Moriah Wright. She introduced herself, planning to ease gently into the conversation. But Moriah's voice immediately choked up and the sniffles started.

"I saw the notice on that poor boy," she cried. "We get a notification when one of the kids we have visited... when something happens like that. I feel so awful. I don't know what to say. I've talked to my supervisor and gone over the investigation. She says I did everything right and couldn't be blamed for what happened. But... I'm not trying to get out of being blamed. I want... I want to know what I should have seen. What I could have done differently. Everything I saw said that he was being supervised appropriately. My boss says it's just one of those things. People can't be expected to watch their kids twenty-four hours a day, and sometimes these things just happen when they think that they're asleep or their backs are turned for a few minutes..."

"I'm afraid I have more bad news for you," Kenzie cautioned. She hated to push this sensitive woman further into despair. She would need to toughen up if she were going to pursue a career in social work. "The evidence shows that Michael Wade did not die in the fall from the balcony."

"Oh, dear... how long was he lying there before...?"

"No, he was dead before he fell from the balcony."

"How could he be...?" Wright's voice was mystified.

"Someone threw him off of the balcony after they killed him. To obscure the cause of death."

There was a sharp intake of breath from the social worker. Shocked out of her tears, for the moment at least. "He was killed? What happened to him?"

"I haven't issued my final autopsy report yet. But there were signs that he had been severely physically abused over the last few months. Bruises in various stages, broken bones, scarring. Investigation into emergency room admissions shows that he has been treated a number of times over the past year for potentially life-threatening injuries."

"No... I did a medical records search. We look for that kind of thing."

"He was admitted under the nanny's name. Michael Arnold rather than Michael Wade."

"Without a birth certificate or social?"

"It was an emergency situation. They checked the nanny's identification and used the name she gave them. There was no insurance claim, so they never took the further steps to verify it."

"How did you figure it out? You can't search under every potential name someone might have used."

"One of the ER nurses recognized him and described Sylvia Arnold as the mother. We tracked it back from there, and found the pattern."

Wright sniffled again. "What did I miss? How could I have known that he really was being abused? Everything seemed fine. There were *no* risk factors. No sign that he'd been injured."

"You never interviewed the father?"

"He wasn't there. They said he was often on the road with his work. He obviously wasn't one of the primary caregivers."

"But you have to check everyone in the home."

There was no answer for a moment. "Do you know how many people are in that home?" Wright asked. "There was more of a chance that the cook or chauffeur or a maid was hurting Michael. They were there every day, the father wasn't. I interviewed the people who had the most contact with him. The mother and the nanny."

"Did you know that the mom had postpartum?"

"No. No one ever mentioned that." Kenzie could tell from Wright's voice that she knew postpartum depression was a red flag for an over-whelmed caregiver. It didn't make them an abuser, but it did increase the risk.

"And that she was abused?"

"No. How did you know that? She told you?"

"I… am familiar with her from a number of years ago. Know a bit of her history."

"I didn't have any idea. She didn't disclose that in our interview."

Kenzie didn't imagine she did. And there had probably never been an investigation into abuse in Terri-Lyn's family of origin. Even if there were, the records would have been destroyed long ago.

"They didn't want you to examine him more closely because he was covered with bruises. You would have known immediately that he was being abused."

"I couldn't insist. There was nothing else to indicate that he was being abused. No evidence that the caller who reported them was telling the truth. Both caregivers seemed caring and engaged. The child was taken care of. I watched him with them… he seemed more partial toward the nanny, but that would be expected, if she is the one taking care of him most of the time. I didn't see any behavior that suggested he might be hurt."

"And I assume he wasn't verbal?"

"No. Pointing. Whispering a word in his nanny's ear. Nothing more than that. He didn't want to talk to me, or engage with me. Shy. He just wanted to go play so, when the cook came around and offered him a cookie to keep him out of the way during the interviews, he was happy to go."

"I'm sorry to be the bearer of such bad news," Kenzie told her. "And I agree with your supervisor. I don't think you did anything wrong. If you had insisted on a physical examination, the abuse would have been discovered. But bruises themselves are not conclusive. And if there hadn't been obvious bruises, DCF could have been sued, and Cash Wade is a very powerful man."

"Thanks. I do appreciate that."

"I wondered if there was anything that didn't make it into your report? That you thought about later, or noticed at the time but didn't think was important enough to be included in your report, or maybe something that you wished could have been investigated further, but wasn't."

"Well, I wished that I could have examined him more closely for bruises, obviously. But more to clear the Wades than to accuse them. Everything I saw seemed perfectly fine. I was sure there was nothing to worry about." She sniffled, and Kenzie heard an echo in her head. *Nothing to worry about.*

"Okay. If you think of anything after we hang up, please call me. I'd like to know before I issue my final report."

"Sure. I will."

"Ms. Wright..." Kenzie tried to capture Wright's attention again before she could hang up.

"Yes?"

"If you had to guess, which of them do you think was hurting him?"

Wright sighed. She hummed while she considered the question. "I don't really think I should say."

"I won't put it down anywhere. I'm just curious as to your impressions."

"Well... I would say the mother. She didn't seem as involved in his care. But then... it's usually the person who has the most contact with him, isn't it? And that would make it the nanny."

36

Kenzie expected the conversation with the second social worker, Delia Rose, to go much the same way. It took a few transfers to get to the woman's voicemail, so she left a message, not leaving very much information. She didn't want the worker to avoid her because she was calling from the medical examiner's office and thought she was about to get her hands slapped. Or to go into a tailspin like Wright because she thought she should have done something more to save Michael Wade. Both of them had been put in a difficult situation, unable to establish any pattern or evidence of abuse before the boy had been killed. It was a difficult situation for anyone, regardless of how experienced they were.

She heard a familiar footstep in the hall and looked up to see Dr. Wiltshire approaching. He gave her a wry smile as he walked up to the desk.

"The dead rise again," he said, with an embarrassed chuckle. Kenzie guessed he was feeling bad about leaving her in the lurch and not getting back to her on exactly what was going on and what his plans were.

"Well, I certainly hope not," Kenzie told him. "That could make our business quite challenging."

He laughed more openly at that. "If you could accompany me to my office, I'm still not very good at dressing and undressing with this contraption."

His arm and most of his hand were covered by an overcoat, so Kenzie couldn't see what kind of cast he had on now. She stood and followed him to the kitchen, where he set down his peace offering of a dozen donuts, and then to his office. She helped to pull his jacket off so that it didn't get caught on the external hardware. Dr. Wiltshire's hand and arm were enclosed in a high-tech-looking external fixation cage and cast combination. What little she could see of his fingers was black and blue. It looked like he'd been trampled by a horse.

"Ouch," Kenzie said expressively. "Exactly how did you do this?"

He looked at her, expression pinched. "I don't think full disclosure is required at this point."

Kenzie raised her brows. Whatever he had done to it, he had done a magnificent job.

"They think you'll be able to regain full functionality?"

The repairs had obviously been done by a skilled orthopedic surgeon. It wasn't just a slap-dash cast put on by an intern still getting his hours in.

"He is hopeful," Dr. Wiltshire said, looking critically at the fixation device as if it were the first time he was seeing it. "Luckily, there were no torn tendons or ligaments. Didn't seem to be any nerve damage." He grimaced. "All of the nerves seem to be functioning fully, from what I can tell." He rolled his eyes expressively.

"Is it in a lot of pain?"

"Not as much now as in the beginning. With all the bones held in place and the swelling going down, it is definitely improving. But it isn't a walk in the park."

"I guess not." Kenzie hung Dr. Wiltshire's jacket up on his coat rack. "So, are you just in for a few minutes to sign off on work?"

She wanted to set her expectations correctly and not expect him to be back full time if he were only going to be there for an hour and then take off again. It would also help her prioritize his tasks, ensuring they hit the most urgent and important cases first.

"I'm not sure yet how long I'll last. Between the pain of the injury and the wooziness caused by the painkillers, it has been hard to find just the right balance. I'll stick around for as long as possible, but if I'm seeing double from the painkillers, then I'm not much help to anyone around here."

"Okay. Understood. If you want to start on this pile here," Kenzie pointed to it. "That will cover off the most vital stuff."

He looked at the pile but didn't pick up a file. "We need to talk about the Wade case."

Kenzie nodded. "I am getting close to being able to issue my post-mortem report. But I'll definitely want you to look at it to ensure I haven't missed any key points or said anything that could be construed as... controversial."

He leaned back in his chair and rubbed the point on the bridge of his nose where his glasses sat. "The more convoluted and ambiguous, the better, on that file."

"I'm not going to bury the truth."

He sighed. "Of course not. I know that."

She sat down in the chair across from him. "So, what did you want to talk about?"

"Somebody is leaking."

In the morgue, that statement could have several very different meanings. Kenzie shook her head. She knew she had not said anything that had reached the news circuit. She had been very careful. Reporters had been calling her nonstop, but she had remained firm. She had been careful not to say anything of substance to anyone outside the medical examiner's office. One never knew what ears might be pricked nearby.

"I've been very careful. What has been released?"

"Starting a couple of hours ago, there have been several stories posted about Cash Wade's son being killed in an accident."

Kenzie nodded. Not surprising. A lot of people knew that. It had been bound to hit the press sooner or later. The Wade family had been lucky to keep it out of the media for the first few days.

"The publicity seems to go in two different directions. First, about whether there was any foul play. If the congressman himself was involved in the death or was there at the time."

Kenzie nodded. "Something I wouldn't mind knowing for sure myself. But I don't think anyone in that household will tell us. Maybe I'll be surprised and he will confess or Terri-Lyn will come forward to say what really happened. Or maybe we'll be able to get someone else for it. But right now, Cash is still a pretty good candidate."

"The other direction the publicity is taking is to question the competency of the medical examiner's office. Why do we still have the body? Why hasn't it been released along with the autopsy report? Is there some conspiracy? Some cover-up?" He shrugged. "You know how it is."

Kenzie nodded. "They're always impatient. But sometimes, it takes time. Especially when I am working on my own."

He grimaced. "Yes, I'm sorry about that. I have not been available. But you've done well to hold down the fort and I appreciate that. How close are you to being able to issue your report?"

"I just found out that there were DCF reports. So I'm dealing with that right now. I've talked to one of the social workers, and I'm waiting for a callback from one. I'd like to find out what impressions she had, if anything, about what was going on in that house."

"Of course. Such background is always helpful."

"And I had a long talk with the mother."

"Glad to hear it. She was rather evasive last I heard. How did that go?"

"Well, it turns out I know her from way back when I was in school."

"Medical school?"

"High school."

"Oh." He pursed his lips. "Well, that *was* a while ago now."

"I'm not quite as old as *that*," Kenzie laughed, "but… yes, it was a long time ago. Longer than I would like to admit. We were close friends once, but we drifted apart. I haven't even thought of her for years, let alone seen her. I didn't even know she was married. Or that she had married Cash Wade."

"I see. That doesn't sound like a problem for us. And did she give you any details of what happened that day?"

"I got some things to look into, but she didn't confess. It would be really nice to have a confession, you know."

He chuckled. "It would make things much easier. Well, you leave that to the police detectives. There is only so much investigating that you can do from your end. Leave the police work to them."

"I know. I will. And I've liaised with them and let them know everything I found. I'll give them a copy of the report before I release it. Make sure there's nothing else to be considered from their end."

He nodded his approval. "It sounds like you have everything under control. I assume any results I need to review are in this pile?" He indicated the high-priority pile that Kenzie had pointed him at.

"Yes. If you work on that one, it would really help me out."

"Leave me to it. I'll get done what I can."

"Let me get you a coffee. That should keep you focused," Kenzie offered.

"That would be brilliant. And there might be some donuts in the kitchen…?"

"I noticed that," Kenzie said dryly. "I'll bring you one."

37

Walking back toward her desk, Kenzie heard her phone ringing. It sounded somehow more urgent than usual. Talking to Dr. Wiltshire about the stories circulating in the news, she felt a stronger push to close the Wade case quickly. But at the same time, she couldn't do that before she was finished gathering the evidence, assembling it, and considering it carefully. She needed to know what had happened. Not just a guess, but certainty about the cause and manner of death, even if she couldn't point her finger at who the police should arrest.

She dashed the last few steps, though she slowed enough that her shoes would not skid on the tiled floor. She didn't want to go crashing into the desk because she couldn't stop. She grabbed the phone before it could go to voicemail.

"Medical Examiner's Office."

"Medical Examiner's Office?" a woman's voice repeated flatly. "I don't know if I have the right number. Someone asked me to call back? Do you have a Dr. Kirsch?"

"Speaking. Sorry about that. I was running for the phone." Kenzie puffed a little bit. "Whew. Who am I talking to?"

"Delia Rose. DCF. I gather if I'm talking to you, it is not good news."

"Unfortunately, no. Do you remember a child you investigated a report on named Michael Wade?"

"Yes. I remember him. Sick in bed. Had the flu. But that was weeks ago. He didn't die from that."

"No. And I suspect it wasn't the flu that caused him to be in bed when you went to see him."

"What do you think it was?"

"I think he had been beaten. He had a number of old injuries. There was a hospital visit around the time that you made the report. Lacerated liver. They said that he climbed a bookshelf and pulled it over on top of himself."

"A bookshelf. I don't remember seeing any freestanding bookshelves at that house. Everything was built in. Or antique. No bookshelves that I remember."

"Yeah, we don't think that's what really happened."

"No, I doubt it."

Neither of them said anything for a minute. Kenzie cleared her throat.

"So what do you want from me?" the social worker asked eventually. She was tough, ready to move on. Nothing like the tenderhearted Moriah Wright who had cried and blamed herself for Michael's death.

"I was just hoping for your impressions of the home. Things that might not have made it into the report. You have to put anything concrete in there, but your own feelings and instincts, even though they may be just as important, do not necessarily make it to paper."

"I figured there was something there." Kenzie pictured Rose as a square-jawed bulldog of a woman. Fierce. Someone who had seen the worst of humanity and was still sticking it out. "It was the second report, and you don't usually get two reports on a family unless something is going on. That doesn't mean you can prove it. And people do make reports just to be vindictive. But two calls on the same child within a few months of each other… and it wasn't someone who had any skin in the game. Not someone who wanted custody or was interested in one of the parties involved. Sometimes if a woman doesn't want her love interest's kid around, she'll make a little call to DCF to stir things up and make people suspicious…"

"But you didn't see that in this case."

"The reports came from two different parties. I figured there was probably a reason for that. Wouldn't you?"

Kenzie nodded, the phone to her ear. "Yes, I would be suspicious."

"The nanny was the primary caregiver. Mother not so interested. Father was not present when I visited, and I was told he was not there very often. I made a couple of phone calls to him. He answered me, but kept canceling appointments for me to go see him. Something important came up that he had to handle. Big corporate. Politics. He was oh-so-important. Like trying to nail down Jell-o."

Kenzie laughed at the expression. That described a lot of the lawyer and political types that she had dealt with in the past. They were slippery, that was for sure.

"But eventually, you managed to meet with him?"

"Eventually, I gave up. He wasn't at home. I talked to him several times. No red flags that I could find and another report had not been made since we had visited. Eventually… I just issued my report."

"And you didn't see anything in particular that worried you?"

"No. Nothing that I could put in a report. Father was absent, but responsive. If he wasn't there, he couldn't be hurting the kid. He was sick in bed, but appeared to be properly taken care of. All of the expected precautions were in place. He was well-nourished. Had someone beside the bed watching him, which honestly, most kids do not have when they are sick, even at that age. Parents will put them down in the crib and check back every so often to make sure they are still breathing and haven't developed a fever or a rash. Sleep is the best thing, and most parents do not have the resources to hover over the kid for a day or two without a break."

"Did you check out the bathroom attached to the nursery?"

"Nope. What was in the bathroom?"

"A lot of painkillers."

"Well, that's not that unusual. Kids get into things. Fall and hurt themselves. Teething and need something for their gums. Sore and irritable after vaccinations. The doctor suggests a certain painkiller, so the caregiver buys a bottle on the way home. They don't bother to check what they already have at home or ask the doctor if they can give him something else."

"Yeah. It's certainly not a smoking gun. But the child had multiple emergency room visits and the postmortem x-rays show a lot of previously broken bones."

"We didn't find any record of hospital visits. There was a family doctor, but he didn't see the boy very often. He hadn't had any occasion to notice anything suspicious."

"The nanny took him, admitted him under her name."

Rose made a disgusted noise. "So now you know there was abuse. No one covers up an emergency room visit unless there is something to hide. A pattern of injuries."

"Yeah."

"The nanny knew that he was being hurt. Did Mom?"

"I assume she did. Michael's injuries were quite severe, both when he had to go to the emergency room and at his death. I don't see how any parent could not be aware."

"She could be the abuser."

"Yes. That's one possibility."

"You favor someone else?"

"Not favor... but there are other possibilities. The father. The nanny."

"Was the father home at the time of his death? It didn't seem like he was around very often."

"Yes, he was. And I think... at least some of those trips away from home were fictional. I think he was home most of the time. At least during the evenings. I don't think he was really traveling or putting out fires or whatever he told you."

"Abusers lie," Rose admitted philosophically. "You can't expect people to tell you the truth. He's an accomplished liar if that was all made up."

"Politicians," Kenzie said with a shrug.

"Yeah. Professional liars."

38

It wasn't until evening that Kenzie had time to read what was in the news about the tragic death of Cash Wade's son. She figured by the time she finally got to it, things would be fairly well-developed. News traveled fast. Especially bad news. Speculation ran rampant and the juicier, the better.

She hoped that it wouldn't be too bad. But if Dr. Wiltshire had already seen it and was worried about it, then it wasn't just a whisper. As soon as she typed the name Cash Wade, the window filled with news stories, social network discussions, and every other form of news she could think of. The story had been picked up by print papers, radio, and TV.

"What's up?" Zachary asked, when he saw Kenzie leaning forward to sort through the headlines to figure out where to start.

"Cash Wade. He is all over the internet."

"Oh? What's going on?" Zachary typed it in on his own computer, and whistled, shaking his head. "Is Cash Wade a suspect in the death of his son? What is the ME covering up? Where was Cash when his son died? Tragic accident or foreseeable tragedy?"

"Yeah," Kenzie agreed. "Wow, this is really exploding."

"The conspiracy theories are taking off," Zachary observed, scrolling down farther and looking quickly through headlines. He might have difficulty digesting long-form articles—his learning disabilities caused him significant problems—but scanning through headlines and boxes filled with videos and conversation threads was right up his alley. He was a big-picture guy and would be quick to pick up on any patterns or anomalies. "Is it a government cover-up? Is Michael Wade really dead? Insider reports that his body never arrived at the ME's office."

"Really?" Kenzie laughed in disbelief. "I think they'd better find a better insider."

"Apparently, Dr. Wiltshire's broken arm is probably the result of him not complying with the orders to hush the whole thing up. Either that, or he fought off ninjas armed with nunchucks who broke in to steal the body."

"Broken hand," Kenzie corrected, chuckling. "He won't tell me how he broke it. I would think that if it was ninjas, he would have told me about it!"

"He's keeping things from you. It's a big conspiracy. They beat him into submission."

"Well, that's one secret he's kept very well."

Zachary was quiet for a few minutes as they paged through the different reports and clicked from one article to another.

"Not good for Cash," he murmured after a while. "Financial trouble. Infidelity. Rumors of government corruption."

"No wonder things were stressful at home. How long has this been going on?"

Zachary shrugged with one shoulder, looking at her for an instant and then back at his screen. "There's no telling if any of it is actually true. It could have been going on for months or years, or be a complete falsehood."

"True," Kenzie agreed. There were bound to be all kinds of rumors once people started to ask questions about whether Cash had been involved in his son's death. There would be all kinds of speculation that was utterly untrue from people who didn't even know him or his family. "Do you think you can sort out which rumors have some basis in fact?"

Zachary grinned. He was always happy to put his expertise to use in one of her cases. Just like he was happy to call on her when there was some insight she could provide for one of his. Their mutual interest in solving puzzles had been one of the things that had pulled them together.

Zachary wasn't one to shy away from the more graphic medical information that Kenzie could provide, and Kenzie had come to admire Zachary's investigative ability when it came to internet searches, background checks, finding patterns, and seeing the things that no one else did. His obsessive nature was a benefit in the investigative field.

"Sure," he agreed, "I can dig into this. But your police investigators will already be on top of it."

"I'm sure they will. But they're not you. And they won't share any information with me that they don't think directly relates to Michael's death."

Zachary nodded, his eyes intent on his screen as he rapidly typed in searches, popping open a new tab with each one. She probably shouldn't have given him an assignment in the evening. There would be no more conversation as he dove deep into the research project, and it might keep him awake far into the night. She should have waited until morning to ask.

39

Kenzie's phone rang and, knowing that Zachary's attention would be otherwise occupied for the rest of the evening, Kenzie looked at the screen to see who was calling. Walter. She sighed. Did she really want to talk to him again so soon? But she tried to take Dr. B's advice to heart and not make talking to him a big deal. She could have a short conversation without it taking too much energy, keep it light, and feel good about having regular contact with him. The less of an "event" it was, the better. She pasted a smile on her face and swiped to answer.

"Hi, Dad."

"MacKenzie. Glad to catch you, honey. I just wanted to check in and see how you were doing." His question trailed off on a tentative note.

"Fine, Dad. What's up?"

"I just know there has been a bunch of publicity around this case of yours. I imagine you're getting a lot of phone calls. And then the way it's blowing up on social media, you might be upset…"

Because they were accusing her of incompetence or being involved in a conspiracy or cover-up. That made sense. She could see how he would be worried about her.

"Oh, no. I'm fine. I don't invest too much energy into what the internet trolls are saying. You know how they say you can't please everyone all the time?"

"Sure."

"There are some people you can't please any of the time. They'll always find something wrong with what you are doing. And these trolls don't know anything about me. They're just making stuff up for their own entertainment. Who cares what they have to say?"

"Ah. Well, that's a healthy attitude to have. Good for you. Young people today can get so invested in their online image."

Kenzie was amused that he thought of her as a young person. But of course, in his mind, she was still a kid. His kid. She would never catch up to him and be a peer. She would always be less experienced and need to be protected and sheltered.

"I'm not one to worry about my online image," Kenzie assured him. "I stay in touch with close friends, but I don't live online."

"Well, I hope you'll have this case cleared up soon. It must be stressful for you."

"It shouldn't be too much longer. I have written most of what I need to. There are just a few missing pieces I would like to fill in. If we can."

She might never know the exact circumstances of Michael's death. As far as she knew, the police were still being blocked from getting a warrant to search the rest of the Wade household, even just the floor Michael had apparently been dropped from. That meant they might never have the full crime scene details that would help inform Kenzie's report. More unknowns than she would like.

But if the police could not get into the house again, or even if they could get into the house but everything had been sanitized, they could not identify exactly where Michael had been killed or gather any more forensic evidence. Kenzie would have to be satisfied with what she had.

"I assume there is a reason you haven't issued it yet?" Walter prodded. "I take it that means that it wasn't just a child falling from a balcony, as has been reported."

"You know I can't share any of that with you."

"Oh, no, of course not," he agreed heartily. "I wouldn't expect you to share any details with me. From your report not being issued, and the chatter online and offline, I'm deducing there is more to it than that.

Maybe someone in the household is lying. Maybe someone was complicit in his death. Just negligence, or more…?"

"Mmm." Kenzie didn't give him any indication of whether he was on the right track or not. It wasn't any of his business. He could speculate all he wanted to, but she wouldn't give him the information he wanted. If the congressman, governor, or one of Walter's other cronies had asked him to do damage assessment or control, they would have to be disappointed.

"Your mother reminded me that Cash is married to Terri-Lyn, that girl you used to go to school with. Michael was her son."

"Yes. That was a bit of a shock. I guess Mom knew right away, but I didn't even remember hearing anything about the wedding. I was out of the country. And Terri-Lyn and I had drifted apart."

She had never told either of her parents about the prank, and hadn't known it was Terri-Lyn. As far as they knew, Terri-Lyn's and Kenzie's estrangement was solely due to the fact that they no longer ran in the same circles. They had gone to school together and, when school had ended, they didn't have the same opportunities to see each other.

"I think we went to the wedding," Walter said vaguely. "Your mother and I."

"Did you? Well, that was nice of you. Was there anything else, Dad? Things are going okay with you?"

"Oh, yes. Certainly. Couldn't be better. Just thinking… I'm sure you want to get this case off your desk as soon as possible. Maybe it would be best to leave some questions unanswered. But that's just me worrying about my girl. You know how parents are."

"Sure. I've got to go. I think Zachary is calling me, so—"

"How *is* Zachary? I know it's getting later in the year, the days are getting shorter and that affects him."

"It isn't so much the shorter days as just Christmas itself. So far, he's doing great." She glanced over at Zachary, expecting that he would still be deep in his data, completely unaware of her conversation beside him. But he was watching her curiously.

"Are the two of you considering children? It's a big step, I know, but you're not getting any younger."

Kenzie opened her mouth, and no words came out. She was shocked that he had asked. Lisa sometimes hinted about grandchildren, but Walter usually stayed out of her private life.

"Uh…"

"I'm sorry, MacKenzie. I know that's taboo. I shouldn't be asking. It's totally up to you. I have just been thinking, with this case, about your friend Terri-Lyn having a child. I don't know whether it is something you are considering."

"I don't know, Dad. Not now."

"Okay." His voice took on a lighter note. "None of my business. I won't ask again."

He was a good man, and he cared about her, her relationship with Zachary, and her plans for the future. Even if it was irritating to have him poking his nose into her business and checking up on the Wade case, she knew he had her best interests at heart.

"Love you, Dad. Take care."

"You too, sweetie."

He hung up. Kenzie lowered her phone to her lap. Zachary was still watching her out of the corner of his eye.

"What's Walter up to?"

"I'm not sure whether it is personal interest or doing damage control for Congressman Wade. Or both mixed together. You know how he is. When he gets his teeth into something, he doesn't let it go."

"He was asking about me?" Zachary asked.

"Uh… yeah. He often does. Wants to make sure that everything is good between us. He wants me to be happy, and part of that is…"

"Me being happy," he finished. "Keeping you happy."

She shrugged. "They know about your depression. You've been open about that."

He nodded. As hard as it was to let people know how much he struggled, he was trying to push back against the stigma of mental illness by talking about it. Bringing it out into the light rather than making it a shameful secret.

"Yeah," he agreed quickly. "I just… it's a little disconcerting to hear people talking about me."

"I thought you were still focused on that," she nodded at his computer. "I should have put it on speaker and let the two of you talk to each other directly. I don't mean to treat you like… an object, like you're not even in the room."

"No, it's okay. Being open is being open. I wouldn't care if you were talking about me… getting a sunburn or not liking brussels sprouts. Why should talking about my depression be any different?"

"But I wouldn't talk about other medical issues with him. So there is a difference."

Zachary nodded, scratching his jaw thoughtfully. He looked back at his computer. "Something to think about. Maybe talk to Dr. B about what she thinks."

"If I've crossed a boundary line, it's okay to tell me. Then I know better for next time."

"I don't think so. Discomfort doesn't necessarily mean that you did anything wrong. It might just be something I need to get used to. Maybe because deep down I still feel like I have to cover it up. I don't know."

"Well… I'll try to be more sensitive about it. Let me know how you feel… when you figure it out."

He chuckled at himself, cheeks pink. "Yeah. One day I'll have this all sorted out."

"You *are* feeling pretty good right now, aren't you?" Kenzie asked. "I mean… maybe you're uncomfortable because I think you're fine when you're not. Or because I told someone that you were, and I was wrong."

"No. I'm pretty good right now," he echoed her words. "Watchful… because I don't know when it will hit. But still in a good place for now."

"Good. You can tell me if you're worried about it. Or if things start to… get dark."

"I will."

Kenzie swallowed, a hot lump in her throat. There was nothing like thinking of Zachary's pain to get her choked up. Each year, she hoped he would be able to manage the Christmas season better. With the last med change, maybe this would be the year.

40

Kenzie wanted to have another chat with the nanny. She knew a lot more now than she had the last time they had talked, and she wanted to confront Sylvia with some of the facts and hoped that she would break down and give Kenzie the scoop on what was going on in the household. If she were the one who had been abusing Michael, maybe she would confess. That was a long shot, but she still felt like she would get more information from Sylvia now that she had completed the autopsy and talked to Terri-Lyn.

She looked up Sylvia's number and tried reaching her cell phone. No answer. She continued with her administrative work, reviewing the papers Dr. Wiltshire had signed the day before. Each time she finished a batch of files or discrete task, she tried Sylvia's number again. After several calls, it became clear that Sylvia was not going to answer. She was probably avoiding Kenzie, either because of her own guilt or because she, like Terri-Lyn, didn't want to chance being overheard by Cash. Or by Terri-Lyn, for that matter.

Kenzie switched tactics and tried the main house number. It was answered after two rings.

"Wade residence," a woman's voice said sharply.

"This is Dr. Kirsch," Kenzie said. "Is Sylvia around? I'd like to speak with her for a few minutes."

There was silence for a moment. Then the woman spoke again. "This is Hilda," she said softly. "You want to talk to Sylvia?"

"Yes. She's not picking up her cell."

"She isn't," Hilda agreed. "I've been trying to reach her."

"*You* are trying to reach Sylvia? She isn't at the house, then?"

"No. I don't know where she is. She didn't tell anyone she was going out."

Kenzie thought she caught a trace of concern in Hilda's quiet voice. "Are you worried? When did she go out?"

"I don't know. Sometime last night, maybe? Or during the day yesterday? No one is sure. She didn't tell anyone. She just seems to have disappeared."

"Has that ever happened before?"

"Oh, no," Hilda was emphatic. "Sylvia has always been very responsible. She is the first one who will get after a new staff member for not keeping us informed on his schedule. We can't function efficiently if people don't communicate."

"Right," Kenzie agreed. "And Sylvia has always done that?"

"Yes, of course."

"What about when she took Michael to the hospital? Did she tell you what she was doing then?"

Hilda didn't answer at first. Then a faint, "What?"

"If she thought it was important to keep everyone informed about where she was and what she was doing, then you must have known what she had planned when she took Michael to the hospital."

"No. I don't know what you're talking about," Hilda said unconvincingly.

"Was Sylvia the one who hurt him?"

"Doctor… I don't know where you are getting any of this." Her voice turned crisp. "I'm afraid Sylvia isn't here at the moment. You'll have to call back another time."

"Is someone listening in?" Kenzie guessed.

"No. I have work to do. I don't have time to go on a wild goose chase."

"Are you really worried about Sylvia, or was that just made up?"

Hilda paused, and was nearly whispering when she answered. "Yes, of course I am. But there's nothing you can do about it."

"I can. I'll have someone over there to track her down right away. You're concerned about her welfare, right?"

"Well… yes. Of course. She's never done anything like this before."

"And she could be in trouble. She might have had a heart attack out there on the grounds in some isolated area no one walks through very often. You've checked her room to ensure she's not… passed out on her bed?"

"She's not in her room. I did check." Hilda cleared her throat nervously. "I don't go into other staff members' rooms. I've never intruded on Sylvia's life before. But… I was worried when she didn't answer her phone."

"Okay. Hang in there. I'll get someone out there right away."

Kenzie called Baker and found her and Tuttle together. A tap of Baker's speaker button and Kenzie was talking to them both. "We need a welfare check out at the Wade residence. Sylvia Arnold, the nanny, is missing."

"According to who?" Tuttle demanded sharply.

"Hilda, the housekeeper. I was trying to reach Sylvia on cell and, when that didn't work, I tried the house phone, and Hilda said that Sylvia is missing. She disappeared sometime yesterday or this morning. Hilda has been trying to get her too. But she isn't anywhere to be found. And she's never done that before. She's always told everyone else how they have to let them know if they're going out and for how long."

"She's not just a short-term employee," Baker said before Tuttle could speak. "She's been there for how long, Dr. Kirsch?"

"Since Cash was a baby. That puts it at what, forty years?"

"That does sound serious," Tuttle admitted.

"She could have had a heart attack and be somewhere on the grounds."

"Or she might have rabbited if she knows something about this case that she is not willing to tell."

"I think that's less likely," Kenzie said cautiously. "But I suppose it is possible. I just don't see her leaving after so long. She must be due some kind of pension, even if she decided to quit because there are no more children to look after."

"She must have done something else between Cash being a child and

Michael," Baker pointed out. "She didn't have to quit just because Michael is dead. There was other work for her to do."

Kenzie nodded her agreement. "She's right."

"We don't need to go ourselves," Tuttle reasoned. "We can send a patrol officer over for a welfare check."

"They won't let a patrol officer in the door and he wouldn't know how to insist," Kenzie warned. "When Cash or someone tells him that he can't come in and that Sylvia is fine, he'll back down. Besides, this could be your chance to get back into the house and look around."

"Hmm." Tuttle considered this. "We won't be able to do a thorough search like we could if we got the warrant. But we could at least get a peek at the nanny's room and any others close by or places Sylvia might normally have spent her time. If she was involved in Michael's death, there could be evidence in her room."

"That's what I'm thinking. You can at least see what is in plain sight. And if she isn't around and you are concerned there has been foul play, then…"

"Then we can get a warrant for a more thorough search of her rooms to collect trace evidence. Which, you never know, could lead us to some answers about Michael."

"Exactly," Kenzie agreed.

"Okay, we'll get on this. Thanks for the call."

"Any chance I could tag along?"

"Wait a moment."

There was a click, and Kenzie thought she had been put on hold so they could discuss it privately. After a few minutes, she heard Baker's voice again. "We'll meet you over there. If they object to you being there, we can't really justify it under a welfare check. But if they let all of us in without question, then you're there with permission."

"Okay," Kenzie agreed. It was as good as she was going to get, since she had no right to be there for a welfare check as a member of the medical examiner's office.

"So you might end up sitting in your car outside," Tuttle said, in case Kenzie hadn't understood the parameters. "If they say no, we're not going to try to get you in."

"I understand."

"Okay. See you there. We'll be out of here within ten minutes."

Kenzie glanced over her desk and figured she could also tidy up and be on her way in that amount of time. "See you there."

41

Hilda must have been watching for the police to arrive, because she opened the door without their having to knock. Her eyes flicked over Tuttle and Baker, and she apparently recognized them without their offering their names or badges again.

"Come in," she invited. She looked at Kenzie and, at first, blocked her from following the two detectives. "Why are *you* here?"

"I wanted to talk to Sylvia as part of my investigation. If she's here..."

"She isn't. I told you that."

Kenzie waited. She really didn't want to go back to her car while the detectives searched the property for some sign of the nanny.

Eventually, Hilda stepped back and motioned Kenzie in.

Kenzie nodded. "Thank you."

Hilda nodded. Her face was impassive, a calm, emotionless exterior cultivated over many years. But she gave Kenzie's arm a squeeze as she went by. "I really am worried about her."

"Yeah. Me too."

Hilda led the three of them to Sylvia's quarters. Rather than being on the second floor where most of the staff quarters were, her room was on the third floor with the family's rooms. The nanny slept close to her ward, naturally. They wouldn't want him disturbing his mother and father if he got up at night.

Her suite was therefore next door to Michael's now unoccupied room. Tuttle knocked on the door sharply and called Sylvia's name and, when she didn't answer, opened the door and entered.

Kenzie looked around. The room was warm and inviting. All of the personal touches that she would have expected from a woman who had been living in the household for decades. It was not the sterile room of a hotel. The suite was comprised of a sitting room and a bedroom, and boasted a full bathroom with a luxurious jetted tub. The sitting room contained a few comfortable pieces of furniture and built-in shelving that held classic books, as well as pictures of the children Sylvia had cared for, and a number of homemade trinkets fashioned by inexpert little hands. Bowls and picture frames, and a little set of pudgy barnyard animals made of lumpy clay.

After a brief look around, they headed into the bedroom. As Hilda had already looked, they knew they were not going to find Sylvia curled up in the bed, in either severe emotional distress or having something seriously wrong with her medically. Kenzie immediately checked the floor on the far side of the bed, which was not in sight of the door, to make sure she hadn't fallen off and been missed. There was no sign of her.

The bed looked comfortable, covered with a homemade quilt and several throw pillows with cross-stitched proverbs. It was neatly made, so chances were that Sylvia had not left or been taken in the middle of the night. Somehow, that didn't make Kenzie feel much better. There were more photos, with one of Michael prominently displayed on her bedside table.

She had an antique writing desk with pigeonholes, amply supplied with pretty notepaper and pens. Did she have a family of her own that she wrote to? She hadn't mentioned anyone, but that didn't mean she hadn't raised children of her own between Cash and Michael. There were pictures of more children Kenzie couldn't identify.

Baker opened the closet door. It was arranged neatly, though a couple of things had fallen off their hangers and not been picked back up. Baker pointed silently to a narrow space on the shelf that was unoccupied. Tuttle strolled over and had a look. He was the only one of them who could see the top of the shelf without a step stool.

"No dust," he said. "Something has been removed recently."

A suitcase? It was the right size and shape, and Kenzie didn't see any other luggage. A few large shoulder bags, but nothing for overnights. Nothing that might have held a couple of changes of clothing.

Kenzie stayed back, looking around, her eyes open for anything that might belong to Michael or indicate that he had been in Sylvia's room. But why would he be? There would be no reason for her to bring him into her rooms. They had everything he needed in the nursery, including the rocking chair where Sylvia sat watching him when he was sick.

The detectives went quickly through the room, looking for anything that was obviously missing, anything that was out of place, or might hint at foul play. The room was clean. If Michael or Sylvia had been hurt there, the perpetrator had left nothing behind to give him away. Maybe he had shed hairs or skin flakes. But without an obvious crime scene, there was no point in looking for microscopic evidence that could have been brought in on Sylvia's clothes or person from anywhere or anyone in the house. Cash's or Terri-Lyn's DNA in the room would mean nothing.

Once they had finished a cursory search of the rooms, the detectives spoke to Hilda, who hovered in the hallway waiting for them to finish.

"You want to come in, ma'am? Tell us if you notice anything missing?" Tuttle suggested.

Hilda walked in, both reluctant and curious. Peeking in before stepping over the threshold. "I don't go into Sylvia's rooms," she said. "So I wouldn't know if anything was missing or out of place."

"If you could just take a quick look around. You never know. Something might strike you."

She nodded and walked haltingly around the suite. Her cheeks were red, embarrassed to be there, obviously considering Sylvia's rooms forbidden territory.

"It all looks normal. Maybe a suitcase. I wouldn't know what was missing from her clothes. She wouldn't have left anything on the floor like that," she indicated the clothes that had fallen off the hangers in the closet. "Did you do that?"

"No. They were like that when we arrived."

"She wouldn't have left them like that."

"Bag them," Tuttle told Baker. "I doubt we'll get any trace from them, but you never know. There may be something significant about them."

Baker complied, putting each item of clothing into a separate paper bag and carefully labeling and signing each one.

"You think she just left?" Hilda asked, looking around and shaking her head. "She wouldn't have just left. Sylvia would not have left without a word."

"What if she was upset? What if something scared her or made her feel like she couldn't stay here?" Tuttle suggested.

"I just… no, I can't see it. She would never have done that. And…" Hilda looked awkward. "I know Michael wasn't here anymore, but she loved Mr. Wade too. Not romantically. Nothing like that. She raised him, though. She was his nanny his whole life, and she wouldn't leave him. I just can't see her doing that."

"What if she was afraid of him?" Baker asked.

"Why would she be afraid of him?"

None of them gave any explanation. Hilda looked around at the three of them. "Sylvia never had any reason to be afraid of Mr. Wade."

"He was never angry at her? I understand things have been pretty tense around here lately. Mr. Wade was under a lot of pressure." Baker's voice was quiet, non-accusatory. "It was only natural that he might have gotten angry if he was under pressure. People snap. Say things they shouldn't. Mr. Wade was a passionate person."

"Angry at Sylvia? I don't think I ever heard him say a cross word about her in all the time I've been here, and that's a long time. She said once what a hellion he'd been when he was younger, but that was when he was a teenager or young man. I doubt he'd ever raised his voice to her since then."

"Did she say how she had handled that? When he'd been a problem as a teen?"

Hilda shook her head. "I'm sure I don't know. I've seen her with teens. She has a way. She's firm, but unbending. They eventually listen."

"How *has* Mr. Wade been lately?" Tuttle asked, stepping closer to Hilda and looking down at her, being a little more intimidating than Kenzie thought was necessary. "If you listen to the news, he'd been going through a lot of stuff the last few months. I assume he had been… difficult to be around when things were not going well."

"I wouldn't talk about my employers, detective."

"Shouting? Violent?" Tuttle raised his voice as if demonstrating. "Was he aggressive? Toward you? Toward his wife? Michael?"

She stepped back from him. "He was not violent," she insisted.

"Did he fight with his wife?"

"Every man fights with his wife."

"Had it been getting worse? How did she react when she found out about his latest affair?"

"I don't know what you're talking about."

Tuttle spoke slowly and clearly as if she might not have understood him the first time. "When Mrs. Wade found out he'd been catting around again. She was upset, wasn't she? Did she threaten to leave him?"

"No. She wouldn't do that."

"Because she would lose her position if she did? Lose all of that money? And what about Michael? Would she lose him too, if they divorced?"

"They wouldn't divorce."

"Why? Because there was a prenup?"

"Of course there was a prenup. Everyone has a prenup. It would be stupid not to. But if he was the one who was having an affair, then he would be penalized, not her."

"So maybe she did threaten to leave him. To take all of that money. They've probably been stripping the paint off the walls with their arguments lately."

Hilda shook her head, but it wasn't very convincing. They *had* been arguing, Kenzie deduced. Maybe Terri-Lyn hadn't threatened to leave him, but they were arguing. And where had Michael been when they were fighting? And how did Sylvia fit into it all? What had happened to her? Had she left on her own?

"Does Sylvia have a car, Hilda?" Baker asked.

Hilda bit her lip. "No, she didn't drive anymore. There was no need for her to have one."

"How did she get around when she wanted to leave the property?"

"The chauffeur or someone else would take her. Or we would call for car service from town if no one else could take her."

"And did she call the car service yesterday or today?"

Hilda hesitated, then shook her head. So she had been concerned enough that she had already checked.

"She packed a bag but didn't call for a car service?" Tuttle challenged. "Where did she go? How did she get there?"

"I don't know."

"Did anyone drive her?"

"No… everybody says they did not."

"Are all of the cars accounted for? She didn't 'borrow' anyone else's?"

Hilda shook her head. "Of course not. She wouldn't do that. I told you, she didn't drive anymore. She wouldn't take someone else's car."

"Then how did she leave?"

"I don't know." Hilda's eyes were wide as she continued to shake her head at the questions. "I don't know where she could have gone."

Tuttle looked at Baker. "We'd better start a search of the grounds. Can you give us permission to search?" He addressed the question to Hilda.

"I'm just the housekeeper. I can't give you permission."

"Then get Mr. Wade or whoever can give us permission and find out. Impress upon him the seriousness of the situation. If he doesn't give us permission, we will be forced to get a warrant, and I will not go easy on him after being prevented from getting a warrant the past few days. If harm has come to Sylvia Arnold, and he impedes this investigation, there will be consequences. He won't be able to talk his way out of it this time."

Hilda nodded jerkily and left to find Mr. Wade. Kenzie braced herself for the explosion when he found out that the cops were back and trying to get permission to search the property yet again. And this time, it would be a broader search. The whole house. All of the outbuildings. All of the surrounding land where a woman or a body could be hidden.

42

Surprisingly, there was no explosion. And it wasn't because Cash Wade was away and therefore couldn't rage at them. Kenzie had been wondering whether they would be able to talk Terri-Lyn into a search if Cash were away. Terri-Lyn wouldn't care about Sylvia as much as Cash would. And there was also the possibility that she would refuse to do anything he hadn't directly sanctioned, forcing the police to get a warrant issued.

Instead, Mr. Wade arrived with quiet, measured tread on the thick plush carpeting. Rather than being furious that they had returned and were again demanding the right to do a further search, he looked worried. There was an N-shaped frown line between his brows.

"Hilda said that Sylvia is missing?" Cash asked, looking into her rooms from the hallway as if they might be mistaken and she was just sitting there waiting for him to show up. "How could she be missing?"

A look had flashed between Baker and Tuttle. "That's an excellent question, Mr. Wade," Baker said. Maybe they sensed he would be more amenable to dealing with a woman, more likely to be soft and sympathetic. "No one seems to know of any plans she had to leave. She didn't call a car service. No one drove her unless maybe *you* did it without anyone realizing it?"

"No. No, I haven't taken her anywhere. She didn't go out very often. No one took her?"

"No. Can you think of anywhere she may have gone?"

"Of course not. She wasn't given to traveling." He seemed stumped. He looked into her rooms again. "She didn't leave a note, maybe?"

"There was no note."

"Her suitcase is missing," Tuttle contributed. "Maybe she decided that in light of everything that has happened, she needed a vacation."

"A vacation?" He sounded incredulous. "No, of course not. *This* was her quiet space, where she went when she needed to get away from it all and relax. She could never be relaxed on a vacation away from her family. She only traveled when she needed to accompany us on a family vacation. That's the only time she ever used her suitcase. Where would she go?" he asked the room.

No one had an answer for him.

"This is crazy," Cash said, raising his voice. "She wouldn't leave me like that!"

Kenzie found it interesting that he didn't enter Sylvia's sitting room. Was it because he thought the police wouldn't let him? It was his own house, and it hadn't been declared a crime scene. Was it because he had been trained to respect his old nanny's private space and didn't dare chance her disapproval?

"Rather than wasting time speculating on where she might have gone," Tuttle said, "Don't you think we had better begin a search? If she's had a heart attack or a stroke, or fallen and broken her hip… she could be lying on the ground somewhere, just praying that someone will find her. Don't you think we'd better look sooner rather than later? We can float all the theories we want later. For now… I think we'd better act."

"Yes," Cash agreed, looking grimly determined. "Yes, by all means. Mobilize the forces. Begin the search." He looked around for someone else to help, maybe thinking that Hilda was still standing by waiting for instructions, but she had not returned after informing him of the situation. Not finding the help he was looking for, Cash pulled out his phone and hit one of his favorite contacts. "Bill. Sylvia is MIA. She might be hurt or… anything. We need to start a search. Get the men together, and start organizing them. The police will be down in a few minutes to give them instructions." He looked at Tuttle and Baker, one eyebrow raised in inquiry.

Tuttle nodded and pulled out his phone to call for backup. They would need a lot of people to search a property that big. It wasn't just the house they would have to worry about. Kenzie thought about wells, septic tanks, and creeks. What places might exist around the property that would make the perfect hiding place for the body of an old woman, especially one as small as Sylvia?

And that was assuming that someone hadn't taken her off the property in the trunk of his car. There were bound to have been a number of people that had come and gone in the last twenty-four hours. They didn't know for sure what time Sylvia had disappeared.

"We'll want dogs," she told Tuttle, as he started to issue orders for the support he would need. "This is a big place."

He nodded his agreement. They had their work cut out for them. He and Baker were not going to just walk around the basement or the back-yard and find her body hidden under a tarp. It was going to take a massive manhunt to find out what had happened to Sylvia Arnold.

Kenzie still secretly harbored the hope that they would find Sylvia alive. Maybe she had managed to talk her way into a lift into town. Maybe she had called for a ride-share service nobody thought she knew how to use. Maybe she'd had a medical emergency and was waiting desperately for someone to rescue her.

But Kenzie had a bad feeling that they would not find her in time.

It was probably already too late.

With Cash behind the search this time, there was no push-back from the police department or any of the political figures who had been making their influence known over the past few days. Quite the opposite. There was a constant stream of municipal and state police, as well as the FBI, local search and rescue, and every other organization that Kenzie could think of. She didn't envy Tuttle, trying to stay in control and coordinate everyone in the search.

She worried about evidence being trampled outside, about the woman's scent being contaminated by all of the searchers, but when the search dogs arrived a couple of hours later, they went straight to work.

They had already checked the septic tank and there were no wells, so two of Kenzie's predicted body dump sites had been eliminated.

But one of the outbuildings, an old bunkhouse that hadn't been used by the staff for years, had a root cellar with a loading passage behind the house. One of those mysterious doors set into the ground that Kenzie remembered seeing as a child in some old farmhouses. A bulkhead door.

"Medical Examiner's Office," Tuttle announced, as he escorted Kenzie through the small knot of law enforcement officers and staff. "Everyone step aside, please."

Kenzie could hear Cash bellowing like a bull, mourning the loss of his beloved nanny and threatening retribution on whoever had taken her from him. She hoped he had not seen her there, but had merely been given minimal details of what they had found.

That she was dead. That someone had hidden her body.

That they would find whoever it was and demand justice.

The keys to the lock on the door had probably been lost years before or the lock rusted shut. The killer had apparently made no attempt to unlock it, but had simply used a crowbar to pop it open.

Sylvia's small body lay at the bottom of the stairs, dumped unceremoniously through the doorway rather than carried down and set on the floor. Kenzie deduced she had been dumped by someone who didn't care about her. Someone who loved her would have taken her down the steps, stretched her out on the floor, arranged her head and her hands. She wouldn't just be splayed there, half on the floor and half on the stairs, with limbs flung in every direction.

Kenzie looked around the frame of the door before taking a step inside. She had the small scene-of-crime kit she kept in her car. Not as robust as what she would have brought if she had come from the office, but it was sufficient for what she needed to do before authorizing the removal of the body. Booties for her feet so that she wouldn't track in trace evidence embedded in the treads of her shoes. Purple gloves on her hands so she could touch the body. A stethoscope to confirm death if necessary.

Kenzie skirted the body at the bottom of the stairs and did her job stoically, walling off thoughts of the living, breathing woman she had talked to earlier in the week. The woman who had taken her precious charge to the emergency room. Who had sat and rocked beside the boy's bed when he had been hurt and sick, comforting him all night long.

She confirmed death. No heartbeat or respiration. Body cold and stiff, in full rigor. Kenzie bagged Sylvia's hands in case she had managed to scratch her attacker or get any evidence under her nails or between her fingers. She examined the woman for a fatal wound, and found no gunshot or knife wound. Whoever had killed her had been more subtle than that.

Had Sylvia seen it coming? Had she known her attacker? Known that she was going to die?

Kenzie went through the motions of taking a few pictures and looking for any trace evidence on or around the body. She gently lifted Sylvia's shoulder and head from either side to look at her upper back, neck, and head. No obvious injuries.

Was it possible that Sylvia had died naturally? Perhaps had a heart attack or stroke? And someone had been afraid of the police investigating a second death in the home and had hidden her body to cover it up? A second death to investigate would, Kenzie was sure, open up the rest of the house and grounds for a search for evidence in Sylvia's death and anything connecting the two. Kenzie's determination that Michael's death was a homicide rather than an accident would eliminate the possibility that the two deaths were coincidental.

Kenzie walked around the root cellar, looking around for anything else that had been disturbed or added to the scene. There was no weapon, no hastily scrawled note or other evidence that would point them in the direction of the killer.

Not yet. Kenzie would see about that when she looked at the body back at the morgue. She climbed the steps back out of the cellar and dialed Dr. Wiltshire's cell, hoping he would not be too groggy on painkillers to deal with her.

He had already heard the news from other quarters and answered on the first ring.

"Kenzie. I was told you were already at the scene."

"Yes. I've had a look around. I'm ready to authorize the removal of the body, but I wanted a second opinion." She kept her voice low. "With all of the political stuff surrounding this case, I want to make sure that everything I do is double and triple checked. I don't want any accusations that I've missed anything."

"Of course," he agreed.

"I'll send you some pictures, and you can tell me if you want me to walk you around the crime scene. Or the dump site, to be more accurate."

Dr. Wiltshire made an affirmative noise. Kenzie tapped her screen to gather up the photos she had taken and send them to Dr. Wiltshire. She heard the alert on his end as they were received and waited while he looked through them.

"Not much to see," he grunted.

"No. There isn't."

She gave him a few more seconds to look at them. "Is there anything else you want to see?"

"No. But let's do it anyway, just to cover all bases. Call me back on video chat, and we'll walk the crime scene together once."

"Okay."

Kenzie hung up, then called him back again immediately on video chat. She framed the root cellar door on her screen and, at Dr. Wiltshire's instruction, zoomed close to the damage made by the pry bar. Then she walked down the steps. "I don't think I'll lose the signal, but it may glitch a bit," she warned.

Dr. Wiltshire walked her through the steps she had already completed, making her confirm them or do them again. She turned on her flashlight to walk around the body and the perimeter of the cellar, then retrieved the Alternative Light Source from her death kit and did it again. Various molds fluoresced on the walls, but Kenzie could see no blood spatters or other bodily fluids.

"That's everything," Dr. Wiltshire confirmed. "I can't think of anything that you have missed. Go ahead and release the body for transportation and have the crime techs go over the scene with a fine-toothed comb. George is already on his way over."

Kenzie thanked Dr. Wiltshire for his help and returned to the surface. She nodded at Tuttle, who was maintaining control over the scene. "ME's office releases the body for removal and transport. Our truck should be here soon. The techs can start working."

Tuttle nodded. He looked around the small yard surrounding the bunkhouse. It was unmaintained and overgrown. Kenzie would not have known that there was another outbuilding here, but supposed that anyone who had been working in the house for any length of time would have known about it. She didn't see any litter or footprints left behind by the killer. They had been careful.

"I guess I'll see you at the autopsy," Tuttle said. "You'll hold off until I can get there?"

Kenzie looked at her watch. "It's possible I could fit it in this afternoon, but it would be a squeeze, and all the stars would have to align correctly. Let's not rush it. I'll start in the morning."

"Okay. Works for me. Don't know how long we'll be here. And we'll want to go over everything you have on her," he nodded toward the body, "from your investigation into Michael Wade's murder. Any statements she made, testimony of other witnesses, whatever. We want to make sure everything is shared."

Kenzie nodded.

She noticed that, for the first time, Tuttle had referred to Michael Wade's death as a murder.

43

Kenzie arrived home late, which she knew was not a good thing. It was Friday night. Date night. She had intended to be home in good time. She tried to even get off a little bit early Friday afternoons to make it seem more special for her and Zachary, more like a break, even though she usually worked at least a few hours on Saturday and didn't take the whole weekend off.

Dr. B had suggested that they get out of their comfort zones and visit different venues from where they would normally go to. They both tended to stay home to relax, to cuddle up in front of the TV, which was a fine choice of activities but did not provide as much opportunity for chatting, learning about each other, and opening up. As they visited museums, fairs, and other cultural and tourist sites, they would naturally have more things to discuss, they would broaden their world and have more questions for each other about what they liked or disliked and get to better understand their very different backgrounds.

They had talked about going to an art show today, followed by milkshakes or another treat to make sure they both enjoyed the evening, even if one or both of them hated the show. All this came crowding back to Kenzie as she removed her shoes and outerwear after returning home. She let out a long sigh. It would be hard to raise the energy to do that tonight. She was already wiped out. They would need to eat supper, then spend at least an hour at the art show, and she would probably fall asleep drinking her milkshake. Like one of those funny videos of a toddler face-planting in his mashed potatoes or commuters nodding off on the bus or train, heads tipped back, glasses askew, snores vibrating.

She heard Zachary close his laptop in the living room and the couch springs squeak as he stood up. He walked across the room and smiled at Kenzie as she hung up her jacket.

"Long day for you," he observed.

Kenzie rolled her eyes. "Man, was it ever," she agreed.

"You look beat."

"I am. But," she kept her tone light as if she weren't dreading it, "tonight is date night, and we have plans."

Zachary grimaced. He looked at her and then at the clock. "What if I used a veto tonight?" he asked. "I'm not sure I'm in the mood for an art show and you look ready to collapse. It's not actually supposed to be torture."

Kenzie chuckled. "No, that's not the intention," she agreed. "I *am* tired."

"I think it's too much tonight. If we feel like it, we could try again tomorrow night. Tonight, why don't we just stay home? I know we're supposed to get out to explore the world on date night, but we've been doing really well at that, and I don't think it would hurt our relationship to take a break from it just once."

"We'll get back on track again next week," Kenzie said.

Zachary looked relieved. "Okay. Why don't you have your shower and I'll order us something adventurous for dinner. We can play Truth or Dare to learn more about each other."

They had *never* played Truth or Dare. Kenzie was surprised that Zachary even knew the game. It was a friend or party thing, and he'd not had close friends growing up in foster care. She laughed. "I don't know about Truth or Dare, but I'll take the rest."

"Fair enough."

"And it's not your veto. I agree. It would just be too much tonight."

He nodded cheerfully. "Okay. Off you go. Wash away the day."

Kenzie gave him a salute and headed for the bedroom and en suite bath.

. . .

Zachary's "adventurous" dinner turned out to be pizza, one of their old standbys. Kenzie had to admit that she took comfort in the familiar cheese and garlic-laden fare. She felt like she had been stripped bare and wrung out that week. The difficulty of an autopsy on an abused child, finding out she knew the victim's mother, the political pressure, and then the murder of Sylvia had all added up to feel like an overwhelming burden.

But she did her best to put it all aside during her time with Zachary. She asked him about his work and tried to focus on him for a while, giving her more time to unwind before she talked to him about her day. She was feeling much better after her shower, more like a human being, but she was still pretty raw.

The good food and conversation helped.

"Do you think we could go visit Joss this Sunday?" Zachary asked. "Since we were interrupted last week? Or do you need to be at the office catching up on everything? I understand that you might need to put in more hours than usual. Or to take a break and not have to think about going out of town. Dr. Wiltshire being gone during all of this is stressful for you."

He'd been listening.

Kenzie shook her head. "I don't know how things are going to work out this weekend, so don't promise anyone anything. If it works out, we can buzz down there for the day, but not the whole weekend. If not, we'll just push it forward another week."

"Sure." Zachary took a big bite of his garlic cheese bread and asked a question Kenzie didn't catch.

"You want to try that again without a loaf of bread in your mouth?" Kenzie asked, laughing.

He chewed and swallowed, cheeks reddening. "Sorry. That was rude. That habit of grabbing the food I want before anyone else can get it reasserts itself..." He licked his lips and wiped a few crumbs away. "How is Dr. Wiltshire doing?"

"Well, hard to say. I'm not seeing very much of him. But he at least has had his hand surgery. It has an external fixation cage that looks very space-age. But he's still in a lot of pain, trying to balance the painkillers with their side effects so he can get a little bit of productive time in. I'm hoping that in another week, it will at least be healed enough that he can back off on the painkillers and be there to sign documents, approve things, and consult on cases. I can do the autopsies without him, but I'm very slow and have to keep looking things up to make sure I don't miss anything and that it is all well-documented. It's a lot faster with him directing me."

"You'll be releasing your report on Michael Wade soon?"

"Yes. That should cause another explosion in the media. More accusations, gossip, and conspiracy theories."

"There are some interesting rumors about *how* Dr. Wiltshire broke his hand."

Kenzie had another bite of pizza and contemplated this. "Are there. It's interesting because he hasn't told me exactly how he hurt himself. Of course he isn't required to tell anyone. It's his own business. But still… it is strange that he wouldn't. We work together. I'm a doctor. He knows he can trust me. I'm not going to make fun of him or something."

"Maybe the way he broke it was embarrassing."

"What, you mean like 'tripped over my dog' embarrassing, or 'fell off the bed during sex' embarrassing?"

Zachary laughed loudly at that. "Have you ever actually done either of those?"

"I've never broken my hand," Kenzie told him. Which, of course, did not answer the question and kept things interesting.

Zachary continued to chuckle. "Okay, well, I was hearing more along the lines of broken by a bookie he owed money to or slammed it in the car door because he was distracted by a girl walking by."

"He implied that it might have been a golfing accident. I'm not sure how you smash your hand while golfing, but I guess if you swing into a tree or get in someone's way, it would be possible…"

"You can break bones doing anything," Zachary said authoritatively.

"I suppose so. I honestly don't even know if he plays golf. He jokes around about it sometimes, but he hasn't mentioned participating in a tournament, going out with buddies, or coming back on a Monday and telling me about a good score he got on Sunday. Just jokes about how his wife needs him to have a hobby that will keep him from spending too much time at home when he retires."

"Well, golf is one of those hobbies that will eat up hours of time."

Kenzie agreed. "I don't even know for sure if he is married, or if that's just a line he gives me, like a comedian doing stand-up."

She thought about Sylvia's room; all of the pictures around it of Cash, Michael, and other children she had apparently taken care of, whether they were her own, Cash's siblings or cousins, or another family altogether. She might have left the Wade family's service after Cash was too old for a nanny and rejoined them later when Michael was born.

But Terri-Lyn had said that Sylvia had recommended she get pregnant, so she had already been in place before Michael was conceived.

"Dr. Wiltshire doesn't have any pictures of his wife or children on his desk or in his office."

Zachary pursed his lips, thinking about it. "Certainly not a requirement, but it does make me wonder. Does he mention his wife by name? Or any children?"

"No, he always says 'my wife' or 'Mrs. Wiltshire'."

"I would wonder about that too."

He looked like he wanted to say something, but didn't open his mouth and ask. Which, for Zachary, showed great restraint, as he normally blurted whatever came to mind.

"What?"

"I heard that there was some more activity at the Wade residence today. I wondered whether you were involved in that. Or whether you heard anything about it."

"How did you know about that? I don't think a statement has been released."

"No, but I was doing some research on him. You know, checking to see what is true from all the rumors swirling around. And then the story broke that there were all kinds of police at the estate. More than when Michael died. And mentions of other vehicles, including a white van."

Kenzie nodded slowly. George had used the unmarked van for transport, rather than the one painted with the logo for the Medical Examiner's office, trying to be discreet in the transportation of the body. But Zachary suspected the significance of that vehicle. Maybe others had too.

"Yeah. I was back there today."

"And not to investigate Michael's case."

"Well, it is probably related. But no, we weren't back there because of Michael this time."

"Figured."

Kenzie leaned back in her chair and stretched. She should exercise some restraint if she were going to avoid putting on more weight. She was determined to take off what she had put on lately, but that wasn't as easy to do as it seemed like it should be. Especially on stressful days when one of them decided they needed to order comfort food.

"This other death was not Cash Wade," Zachary said, "Or we definitely would have heard about it."

"No. It wasn't Cash."

She gave him a warning look, letting him know she wasn't about to play twenty questions about who it was and the accompanying details. Not when there was so much speculation in the media. Once she had done the autopsy and had something to say, she would release it publicly, and she and Zachary could discuss it.

"He is in a lot of trouble," Zachary commented.

"He is? Because of the rumors?"

"No. Financial is way up there. You wouldn't think it would be a problem for him to support himself with all the wealth he inherited. Or will inherit one day."

"*Will* inherit? I thought that his parents and grandparents were all dead."

"But a lot of what he has was left in trust. So he can only access a certain amount or use it for a certain purpose. That makes it a little bit harder."

"How much financial trouble is he in?"

"There is speculation that he will file for bankruptcy by the end of the year."

"And you think that is true? Not just his detractors trying to make people think he has a problem?"

"His credit rating is pretty bad. He's been defaulting on a lot of loans and payments."

Kenzie shook her head. "I never understood how the wealthy could end up in such trouble. If you have that kind of money, you should be able to pay the bills. If you can't, you need to find a way to cut the bills down."

"Can't disagree with you there. I always thought that if you had enough money to live on, you were set. But from what I have seen… no one is ever satisfied with what they have. They always want to spend more than they have. They're always trying to make more. Win more. Make these deals that are too complicated to understand, to get around paying taxes."

Kenzie nodded.

"Why didn't you end up like that?" Zachary asked curiously. "Your family is very wealthy. You could have lived a life of leisure. Lived like your mom, just going to events and being seen, raising money for causes other than herself. You could have done anything, really, and you decided to be a medical examiner. To work for a living and pay for everything yourself," he gestured to the contents of her modest home, "rather than paying with family money. You could have something much nicer than this and not have to work."

"That didn't really appeal to me. I did it for a while after school… just drifted and went where I felt like going, with the people I felt like going with. But none of them were serious relationships. It wasn't a very fulfilling life."

"And you'd rather be living like this? Working long hours around stinking corpses? Exhausting yourself with a new case because you want to… uncover the truth."

Kenzie smiled widely. "Yes. Exactly."

"You're amazing." He pushed his plate away as well, signaling that he was finished with his meal. "Bridget was just the opposite… working class stock, but she wanted to be rich. She wanted to be elite. Someone like your mom. So she cultivated those friendships…"

"And Gordon."

"And Gordon. He's the one who fulfilled those dreams for her. She was well on her way, just by knowing the right people. She knew what she wanted. And she was willing to… do whatever it took to get it."

Including dumping Zachary when she realized he would not be a part of that picture. He wouldn't fit into that lifestyle, no matter how hard she tried to train him. She had thought that she could take an impressionable, broken man and shape him into what she wanted him to be.

She had not understood that Zachary's depression, PTSD, learning disabilities, and all of his other issues could not just be smoothed over and that he could not be forced to be a different person from who he was. There would always be friction, and he would never fit into the society she had imagined for him.

44

I t was Saturday morning, and no one was sleeping in with their families or getting a few holes in on the golf course. Kenzie performed the autopsy, with George on hand to help her with anything physical. Baker and Tuttle watched from the observation room.

The body was fresh, so there wasn't too much of an odor, and the big exhaust fans whisked that away quickly, with fresh air being pumped into the room continuously. A lot nicer than a lot of morgues where the air circulation was neglected. They had tables that were easy to raise and lower with a press of the foot, voice-controlled computer systems. The observation room allowed law enforcement to observe without being underfoot. Their mics were muted unless they needed to ask a question, so Kenzie didn't have to listen to an endless discussion of the previous night's game or a new love interest. She could stay focused on the job at hand and tune everything else out.

She started, as usual, with a gross examination of the body, top to toe, front and back, noting the patient's height, weight, age, build, identifying marks, and anything else appropriate, followed by a catalog of external injuries. Sylvia's body was unremarkable. She was in good shape for a woman of her age. No surgery scars. Nothing to indicate that she'd had heart surgery. Although angioplasty would not leave any scarring on the chest. Kenzie carefully checked the usual incision sites for an angioplasty catheter and found none.

There were a few bruises on the body, but nothing of particular concern. Older people often bruised easily, and bruises on knees, shins, and forearms were very common. Kenzie didn't see any that would have suggested restraint or a fight.

She examined the eyes and ears carefully.

"Some minor petechial hemorrhages in the eyes," Kenzie observed, focusing the camera to take a few pictures for the file and for the detectives to see. "While this can be a marker for asphyxiation, it is not always present in asphyxiation cases and can also be caused by things like coughing, crying, or vomiting. We all observed Mrs. Arnold crying recently."

Nothing that caught her interest in the ears. They looked healthy. No recently ruptured eardrums. No significant scarring.

Kenzie studied the throat with the magnifying glass and under the alternative light source. She couldn't see any bruising. She had hoped there would be, providing her with a quick answer. She took x-rays of the head, throat, and torso, looking for any sign of violence. Despite the lack of bruising, she had still thought she might find a broken hyoid. At first, nothing was notable on the x-rays, then Kenzie spotted a hairline fracture.

"Here on the sternum," she pointed out the fracture line to George, who moved the mouse point around and clicked several times to mark it. "Fractured sternum can occur when someone is given CPR. We know that none of the police at the scene gave her CPR. She was already long dead by the time she was found. Did the killer try to revive her with CPR? Was it an accident rather than homicide and someone hid the body afterward simply because they were afraid they would be blamed or it would bring the family more bad press?"

There was no answer. She wasn't actually expecting one, she was just posing questions that came to her as she proceeded with the autopsy. She examined the ribs closely, figuring that if the sternum was broken, it wouldn't be unexpected for one or two ribs to be as well. She found one more hairline fracture on a rib, which George marked on the x-ray for her.

"Nothing of concern on the skull or neck in the x-rays, so I am going to go to the torso next, see what kind of damage there may be around those fractures. Looking for bruising, which we can date, or any damage to the soft tissues or organs."

She performed the Y-incision and opened up the chest and abdominal cavity. "There is some bruising, but it is minimal. Perimortem. Likely occurred very close to the time of death."

"But not the cause of death," Baker checked from the observation room.

"I haven't yet established cause of death, so I can't comment on whether it is related."

She continued with a dissection of the heart and then removal of the lungs. She noted the weight of the lungs on her autopsy report with a sigh.

"Lungs are quite heavy."

No one asked what that meant. Kenzie proceeded with a closer examination of the lungs, carefully dissecting them and noting anomalies. As she took sections for the microscopic examination, she looked toward the observation room.

"As with Michael Wade, the lungs are congested with fluid, slightly frothy. It is a clear sign of asphyxiation."

"So, does that mean homicide?" Tuttle asked.

"Asphyxiation can be caused by many things. It doesn't mean that the manner of death is homicide. But considering the fractured bones and the similarities between Michael's autopsy and Sylvia's, it is very suspicious. I'll see what else shows up in the autopsy and will review my work and confirm my findings with Dr. Wiltshire, but I believe that both will be homicide, death due to asphyxiation."

"Same cause of death for both," Tuttle said. "Pretty likely the same person, then."

"It seems unlikely that Sylvia's death was a copy of Michael's, since my findings have not yet been released. No one but the killer would know how he was killed."

"Or a witness," Baker added.

Kenzie nodded. "Yes, or a witness to Michael's murder."

"If the killer was Sylvia, someone could have exacted retribution on her, killing her in the same way."

"I suppose they could," Kenzie agreed.

"Is there anything you can tell us about the killer based on Mrs.

Arnold's autopsy?" Tuttle asked. "Size of hands, strength needed, exactly how she was asphyxiated? Are we talking about a plastic bag over her head? Or something else?"

"From the broken ribs—and in Michael's case, previously broken and healed ribs—I believe that it was mechanical asphyxiation. They were prevented from being able to take a breath. In Michael's case, that would be quite easy. Any of us here would have the strength to asphyxiate a child that small. Hold him tightly against you, arms wrapped around him in a hug, and squeeze until he is unable to breathe."

Both of the detectives considered this, saying nothing at first. Kenzie could picture it herself. A bear hug. Squeezing the child until he stopped crying. Until he stopped breathing. Until, at last, it was too late to revive him.

"And doing the same to an older woman?" Baker asked. "I guess it would take considerably more strength to squeeze a tough old broad like Sylvia to death. She would have fought back. Hard. I don't think the bear hug would work as well for her. You'd need to be able to control the limbs, or risk getting scratched up while she tries to get herself out."

"With Sylvia, it was probably a little different. Either positional asphyxia, such as laying her prone while she was in handcuffs—" The way that Zachary had said that Annie had been killed in the children's center he had been held in. "—or, more likely, in my opinion, by pressure on her chest while she was lying supine."

"Lying on her back?" Baker clarified.

"Yes. Lying on her back with a weight on her chest. Someone sitting or kneeling on her."

That would account for the broken sternum and rib. Minimal bruising at the time of death, since death had been pretty quick, shutting off the body's circulatory system before the bruising could develop. No sign of a ligature or hands around the throat. No bruising around the mouth.

"So, how heavy would you have to be to do that?" Tuttle questioned.

"Not big. Just heavy enough to prevent her from breathing or throwing you off. She is a small, elderly woman; pretty much any adult could have done it."

"Great. Nice of you to narrow it down for us," he said sourly.

Kenzie smiled and shook her head. It wasn't her job to do all of the work for them. She could only do so much to find the killer. They had to take it the rest of the way.

Kenzie sorted through the evidence that had come in with Sylvia's body. The clothing she had been wearing. Some mashed receipts and change. They had not yet found her wallet. Kenzie looked at each of the receipts, but none were recent. Just slips of paper that Sylvia had left in her pockets. Incidental purchases when she had gone into town. A bottle of Tylenol from the pharmacy. A small bottle of milk. A package of candies.

Where had the killer disposed of her purse, with her wallet, phone, and other items that might help point in the direction of the killer? Where had he disposed of the suitcase? It was all together, Kenzie supposed, dumped in a river or ravine, buried under two feet of rich Vermont soil.

Cash's granddaddy had once farmed on that property. That was obvious from the extra outbuildings and abandoned equipment Kenzie had seen in the unkept areas past the rolling velvet lawns and blemish-free fruit trees.

But Cash had been raised as a child of wealth. He hadn't had to work the land like his grandfather and great-grandfather. Instead, he was inside, staring at computers, communicating with his business partners over the phone and email. Maybe not the type of work best suited to a man of his physical prowess and temperament.

He had taken his frustrations out on his wife and son. As the pressure had built, so had the abuse. Escalating until Sylvia had needed to step in and see that Michael, at least, got the care he needed. Had she treated Terri-Lyn as well? Bound up her wounds, given her Tylenol, and sponged her brow?

Kenzie suspected not. Terri-Lyn wasn't exactly well-disposed toward Cash's old nanny. She had not spoken warmly of how the woman had helped and cared for her. She had complained instead about how Sylvia had taken Michael when Terri-Lyn had been unable to care for him due to her postpartum and Michael's colic. A perfect storm. A situation dangerous enough that Sylvia had stepped in to take charge of the infant to make sure that his needs were met and his mother had time to recover. Rocking the colicky baby long into the night.

Had Cash known how much danger his child had been in at that point, or had he been like so many men, blind to how his wife was struggling, succumbing to her depression, drowning in her own black emotions?

Maybe he had. Maybe he had been the one to tell Sylvia that she needed to take charge of Michael. The very thing that Sylvia had been hoping for when she had told Terri-Lyn to get pregnant to heal the marriage.

That, as it turned out, had been a mistake.

45

The police detectives had observed the autopsy, and Kenzie, in turn, sat in on the police interviews with Terri-Lyn and Cash, separate of course. Kenzie observed from a monitoring room, watching the action on the cameras. Never face-to-face with the interviewees. It might be unusual for a medical examiner to sit in on a police interview, but she was the one who could tell the police whether what the witnesses said was believable from a medical standpoint. And she had once been friends with Terri-Lyn Wade. She probably couldn't tell the police anything about Terri-Lyn now that they couldn't deduce themselves, but it was always possible that something Terri-Lyn said could trigger a memory that would somehow be relevant or helpful.

This was no casual interview asking the witnesses if they had seen or heard anything that the police might be interested in. It was not a careful, gentle consultation with grieving parents who also happened to be politically connected to everyone at the top of crime enforcement in Vermont. Terri-Lyn was brought into the small interview room and looked around in dismay at the small table and chairs fashioned from metal tubing with a plastic seat and back screwed on, the disgusting green walls, and the bright lighting that washed out her complexion. It probably smelled as bad as it looked, and the plastic cup of water placed on the table before her had not come from a bottle and didn't sparkle. If she were expecting to be pampered in a lavish boardroom, with her whims being met by a cop playing the role of dedicated servant, she was sadly disappointed.

Terri-Lyn looked at Tuttle in disbelief, as if waiting for him to figure out that he had brought her to the wrong room. He gestured to one of the chairs. "Have a seat."

Terri-Lyn's nose wrinkled as she looked at it. Maybe she was wondering whether it had been disinfected lately. But lacking any authority here, she eventually sat down gingerly. It wasn't like she was going to catch anything from sitting in the chair used by other criminals. There were several layers of cloth between any bacteria that remained there and her pampered skin.

"I don't know why I'm here," Terri-Lyn offered, without waiting for the questions to begin. "I don't know what happened to Sylvia."

"That's fine, ma'am," Tuttle agreed. He picked up a cup of coffee that had been left on the table, took a sip, swished it around his mouth, and swallowed. "We just want to go over where you were for the twenty-four hours preceding the discovery of Mrs. Arnold's body and the circumstances surrounding your son's death one more time."

"I've already said everything I plan to on that."

"Yes, ma'am. Can you tell me your activities from Thursday afternoon through Friday morning?"

"I already told you that on Friday. I was at home. I didn't go out. I am in mourning for my son, you know. I don't need to be seen in public with all of the… well-wishers. People who want to console me. I really don't want that right now. I just want to be at home, protected, where I can… mourn the loss of my child."

"What part of the house were you in?"

"All day?"

"I don't imagine you go into every room of the house daily. Especially those areas that are set aside for the staff. You were not near Mrs. Arnold's room, for example?"

"Certainly not. Why would I be?"

"So, if someone said they saw you there?"

"They would be lying," Terri-Lyn said icily. "I wouldn't have any reason to be near Sylvia's room. If I needed her—and I didn't—I would just call her and she would come to me."

"Of course," Tuttle agreed. He looked at Baker, then back at Terri-Lyn again. "So, which rooms did you say you were in?"

"I don't know. My bedroom suite. The dining room. The gym. The pool. The morning room." She shook her head. "I can't be expected to remember exactly what I did every minute of the day."

"Of course not, ma'am. But everything that you can remember is extremely helpful. We can start to build a picture of what was happening in the house at various times. Do you remember the last time you saw Mrs. Arnold?"

"The last time? No, of course not. I don't have anything to do with her. She was Cash—Michael's nanny, not mine. That was her job and, since Michael wasn't there anymore, I had no reason to have anything to do with her."

"But you didn't fire her? Let her go since her services were no longer needed?"

"No. She could still perform other functions around the house. Cash said it would be cruel to let her go, an old woman, when she wouldn't be able to get a job anywhere else. We could pay her a pension, or continue to employ her to do work around the house. I would rather have someone actually doing work. Not just sitting around, getting paid for being alive."

"That was very thoughtful of your husband."

"He has known her for a long time. He cared about her deeply."

"Did that bother you?"

"Bother me? Why would it?"

"Because she was taking your place in his universe. She was looking after his son. He knew and loved her long before you ever became a part of his world. Some women would resent that."

"She didn't take my place." Terri-Lyn's nose wrinkled. "What a thought. That old woman? She was good at what she did, but Cash didn't see her as some… love interest."

"But she was a mother figure to him."

Terri-Lyn looked for a way to argue, then shook her head and said nothing.

Tuttle let the silence draw out for an uncomfortable length of time.

"So you don't know the last time you saw Mrs. Arnold alive?" Baker asked.

"No. I have no idea. I doubt if I saw her at all on Thursday."

"What was she doing?"

"How would I know? Sitting in her room. Reading a book. Writing letters. Whatever old women do when they have nothing else to do."

"Did she like to read?"

"I don't know."

"Like to write? Keep a journal?" Baker prodded.

"How would I know? I don't socialize with her. I have no idea what she does in her spare time."

"You know she writes letters, so you must have seen her do that. Maybe seen her sitting at her writing desk composing letters to her friends."

"I don't know. Maybe I saw her once."

46

Tuttle leaned forward. "Did you and Mrs. Arnold get along?"

"We got along just fine. She was the employee and usually Cash dealt with her. I spoke to her when I needed to." She shrugged. "That wasn't very often."

"You didn't confide in her?"

Terri-Lyn snorted. "Of course not."

"You didn't tell her about the difficulties in your marriage? She didn't suggest things would improve if you bore Cash a son?"

Terri-Lyn's jaw clenched. "She might have said something to that effect once. If she did, it was unsolicited."

"Was it. And *did* having a son improve your marital relationship?"

"No." Terri-Lyn's tone was bitter. "It was a ridiculous suggestion. Children put a strain on marriage. They don't help it."

Tuttle and Baker both nodded sympathetically. "Having kids is hard work," Baker empathized. "Men have no idea what it's like to go through pregnancy and then to try to raise a screaming, flailing baby. They think it's easy, that everything just falls into place. But there was no place for a baby in your marriage, was there?"

"Michael was a difficult child right from the time he was born. There were complications. He had colic. Then all of the teething and growing pains and whatever else. He was always crying or fussing over something and wouldn't listen to a word I said."

"It's a difficult age," Tuttle said. "They want to be able to do everything they see people around them doing, but they are not capable. It must be very frustrating for them."

"For them? Try for me! Constantly demanding attention. Wouldn't do what I said. Give Daddy a hug. Stay in your bed. He wouldn't do anything I said and had the attention span of a gnat. There was something wrong with him. That was probably what killed him, if it really wasn't the fall from the balcony. He probably had something wrong with him, but the doctors never found it. Maybe something was wrong in his brain."

"But you must have had good times together, too," Baker suggested. "Playing games. Sharing a popsicle together. And babies look like little angels when they are sleeping. Sweet cherubs."

"Cherubs?" Terri-Lyn scoffed. "When they finally wind down at the end of the day, like a mechanical toy, it's such a feeling of relief. I wished he would be quiet and sleep all of the time."

"And now he will," Tuttle said.

"You're taking it the wrong way. You know that isn't what I meant."

"He was an inconvenience to you. Nothing more. You were glad when he died."

"I was not. Ask your cops. I cried. I have been *deep* in mourning."

Nothing seemed further from the truth. Terri-Lyn didn't appear to have given her son a moment of thought in the last week. She had better things to do.

"Tell us again what you were doing when Michael died." Baker said, "How you realized something had happened."

"I was eating breakfast. I'd had a headache and slept in. Then Sylvia started screaming. I couldn't believe she would do that when I had a headache. She knew how much the noise bothered it. I thought she was screaming at the gardener or something. It went on for a few minutes before I realized it was something to do with Michael. And then… when I went outside, no one would let me close. I was nearly hysterical."

"That must have been very difficult for you," the police detective murmured.

"It was. You can't imagine what it is like to lose a child."

For a moment, Kenzie thought Baker was going to make up a story about having lost a child herself, but then her expression changed slightly. "Cash was there ahead of you? So he saw what had happened?"

"He didn't see it happen. But he was over there. Where Michael was. He saw him on the ground. For me, I never saw him after the fall. I need closure. I need to see him again to make myself understand that he's really dead."

"Didn't you say in your earlier statement that you had been doing Pilates?" Tuttle asked.

"Yes." She shrugged. "I had been. Before I sat down to eat breakfast."

"You do Pilates with a migraine? I thought you had been in bed, asleep, because all of the noise and light bothered it."

Terri-Lyn shook her head. "I know I just have to push through. I can't neglect my training program. Even now... the body-mind connection is essential, you know. If you want to feel good, you need to *feel* good."

Kenzie had no idea what Terri-Lyn was going on about.

But Tuttle had picked up on an inconsistency in her story. And it was not the only one.

"Why don't you tell us the real story about how Michael got hurt," Baker said, putting her hand over Terri-Lyn's on the table as if to comfort her. "You must want to get it off your chest. The body-mind connection *is* strong. The way that you must feel now, knowing that what happened to Michael was partially your fault... you must just feel sick about it."

"I didn't do anything to hurt him. What are you talking about?"

"The bruises and other injuries that he had. I know how frustrating it is as a caregiver. Especially with a demanding baby like Michael. Sometimes you just want him to shut up. To give you a little peace and quiet. And if you've got a migraine... well, you're not really responsible then, are you? It's extenuating circumstances."

"I didn't hurt him," Terri-Lyn maintained. "And *you* know that. These games that you're playing. You just want to lay this at my door instead of Cash's because of his position. It's much easier to get rid of the wife and then play up how sad it is. He lost his child because of what his wife did. He lost his wife, the love of his life, poor Cash. Poor, poor Cash."

"Are you saying that Cash hurt him?"

"I'm not saying anything. But if you look at the two of us, you know which one it was. Look at his size. His history. You think he was patient with Michael?" She blew out her breath explosively. "He didn't want a son. He couldn't stand having kids around. He thought it was a good idea. A good look for him. But *he is the drunk. He is the loser,* not me. Your precious congressman is a failure. He can't control his drinking. Can't keep it in his pants. Can't manage money. How bright do you have to be not to spend the *millions* that your grandfather left you? Millions, and he fritters it all away. We are on the brink of bankruptcy because he doesn't understand how to do a single thing. He is just a puppet. An empty suit."

"He hit Michael?"

"He hit me enough times! You ask anyone in the household and they'll tell you it's true. He gave me a black eye. He was always pushing and smacking me around, especially when he was drunk."

"And Michael?"

She rolled her eyes and shook her head, unable to understand why they weren't more concerned about her plight than they were about Michael's. "Yes, he hit Michael. If you talked to your coroner, you know that. Cash hit him. Wouldn't leave him alone. He liked to have someone to take things out on. She should have told you that. She should have told you that *I am the victim here.* I can't believe she doesn't care one bit about her best friend at school. She should have helped me."

"You're talking about Dr. Kirsch?"

"Yes! MacKenzie. She shows up at the house, blundering around, asking questions, getting Cash all wound up. And she doesn't have any idea what kind of a mess she made of things. Everybody is saying that she's protecting Cash now and is afraid to issue her report because it will implicate him. Well, she *should* implicate him! He was the one beating on me. He was the one who had no self-control. Just like my father. *He* is the one you should be looking at, not me. And I should be the congressman. Congresswoman. You think he knew what he was doing? He just followed the instructions. They told him everything to do. What to sign. Where to be. When to smile. A trained dog could have done the job. But he's got to screw it up *thinking* and trying too hard to make all these changes and decisions. He should have just shut up and smiled."

The two detectives were nodding along, looking sympathetic. Terri-Lyn was revealing a lot more about herself than she would have if they had gone in with a hard-nosed cop attitude. And Kenzie was sure that she was right about Cash. He was the one who had been hurting Michael. He was the one who could have most easily dumped Michael's body over the railing.

"What made Sylvia go looking for Michael that day?" Baker asked. "She said that she heard a sound. She must have known that he was out of bed. What do you think she heard?"

"What she heard? How would I know?" Terri-Lyn demanded.

"Do you blame her for not supervising Michael?"

Terri-Lyn considered this for a moment, then nodded. "Of course, how could I not? I know that is cruel. She loved Ca—Michael and would have done anything to protect him. But he was my son, not hers. She was supposed to be watching him. If Cash hurt him… Sylvia should have been watching him. She shouldn't have let him anywhere near him, not at that hour of the morning."

"Why not?"

"Cash was working. He had important things to do. He wouldn't have wanted Michael around, getting in the way underfoot. She should have kept him in the nursery or given him lunch in the kitchen. Michael shouldn't have been around Cash."

It was interesting to see Terri-Lyn's story start to unravel. She had played the guilt-stricken mother when she had made her initial statement. Her fault for not supervising Michael. Her fault for not knowing that he was out of bed. Now, it was Sylvia's fault, or Cash's.

Had Sylvia cleaned up after Cash? Would she have done that if she knew he had killed the boy? She had obviously loved Cash just as much as Michael. Had the whole thing been staged? Cash drops the body from the balcony. Sylvia is in place on the main floor and starts to scream?

But Kenzie had a hard time believing that could be true. Would Sylvia really have covered for Cash?

She had with her visits to the emergency room. She had made up stories of how Michael had been hurt. Given him a new identity. Given him medicine and sat up with him without saying a word about the man who had beaten him.

What was one more time?

For her grown-up little boy?

47

They took a break between Terri-Lyn's and Cash's interviews. Kenzie met in the break room with Tuttle and Baker as they refreshed their coffee cups.

"What do you think?" Baker asked Kenzie.

"Terri-Lyn's pretty happy to throw Cash to the dogs. I guess she's had enough of him."

Tuttle nodded, his face twisting into a sneer. "I've had women like that in the interrogation room before. She won't back down; I'll tell you that."

"She didn't seem really impressed with *you*," Baker told Kenzie, taking a sip of her too-hot coffee and wincing. "I think you were supposed to save her from all this."

"I'm not sure how I could have done that, even if I had been inclined to." Kenzie shook her head.

"Well, it's a good thing that you're not inclined to, because this case will be all over the news for a long time, and everybody's actions will be examined under a microscope." Baker forced another sip of the coffee and winced a second time.

"In Terri-Lyn's defense, she didn't grow up in the best family," Kenzie allowed. "I didn't see the red flags then but, looking back... I can see them now. I think her father was probably pretty abusive."

Tuttle nodded. "That's pretty much expected with a woman like this. Stuck in an abusive relationship with her spouse, possibly a co-abuser, an abusive dad is almost guaranteed. Sometimes mom. Sometimes it comes from somewhere else, but home life is the most common. If you really want to mess a kid up, just beat the hell out of them every so often. There doesn't have to be any logic to it. Best if there isn't and they can never see it coming."

"Did Sylvia keep a journal?" Kenzie asked curiously. "Or was that just a bluff?"

"It's possible she did," Baker said cautiously. "She didn't really have other people into her rooms; she cleaned it herself. It was her private sanctum. So it's hard to tell what is missing and how she spent her spare time if it isn't reflected in what is already in the room. We know that she has kept journals in the past, and we know that she wrote letters from the writing desk and pretty notepapers she kept on hand. The housekeeper and cook said she often had letters to post when one of them was going into town."

"Anyone in particular? Did she have family?"

"She had three kids. We're trying to get in touch with them. From her phone logs, she didn't keep in close touch with them. Maybe she wrote them letters, but she didn't call them, text, send emails." She shrugged. "That's not surprising. She was not really a tech person. A lot of people in her generation don't ever get into it, though some like to use Facebook to keep track of grandchildren."

Kenzie remembered the photos of other children in Sylvia's rooms. Probably her own children, then, raised during the years between Cash and Michael. "Did she still work for the Wades while she raised her own family?"

"Sounds like it. Not as a nanny, but the family employed her in other ways, just like Terri-Lyn said. Cash did not want to let her go."

"I wonder if her kids would have any insight on Cash, then. They might have heard things from Sylvia over the years. How she had raised him, what he was like when he was a boy. They would know what he was like as a young man when they were growing up in the house; they might have some interesting stories about him."

"Might do," Tuttle agreed. "We'll be sure to ask them when we break the news." He shook his head. "I can't understand them cutting all ties with her when she was getting so old. They had to know she didn't have a lot of years left."

Kenzie sighed. She closed her eyes briefly, thinking about her own parents. "You always think you have time, even if you don't. I've been trying to get closer to my parents, and it's tough. They live in a different world than I do. I have all of the day-to-day stuff that seems so important and immediate. My work. My relationship with my partner and his health issues. Visiting his family out of town. I do some work for my dad's charitable foundation, which is run by my mom, so I could just say that is my connection with them, but it isn't the same. That's business, and I deal with foundation staff, not usually dealing with my parents on a personal level."

Kenzie shrugged and rubbed her eyes. She went on.

"And I come from a pretty good family and have a pretty good relationship with them. I don't know what Sylvia's relationship was like with her kids. She seems like the motherly type, really close to the kids she was a nanny for. But… it's possible that it was different with her own kids. That they were secondary to her relationship with Cash, or were always being compared with what he had been like as a kid."

"Ugh, can you imagine that?" Baker asked, nodding. " 'This rich young brat that I raised was so much more promising than you. I love him so much.' That could definitely be off-putting for her natural kids."

"You're interviewing him next? How is he managing? He was pretty concerned on Friday when Sylvia turned up missing."

Kenzie had not seen him after being called to the root cellar. She had been very engaged in dealing with the body and had not seen him or talked to him after that. She had heard him wailing outside the crime scene when Sylvia's body was discovered.

"Not sure how he is. Today is the first day that he would consider coming in. I think he's taken it pretty hard. She was a mother figure to him. Gotta be tough."

They spoke for a few more minutes, and then Kenzie returned to the monitoring room to watch the next interview on the screen.

Cash showed none of his wife's concern with the setting of the interview. He seemed utterly blind to his surroundings. He sat at the table without being asked and leaned forward, elbows on the table, to talk to the detectives. He seemed intense, determined to get to the bottom of things. After Terri-Lyn's tirade about how incompetent he was in his family life and job, Kenzie had been expecting Cash to be somewhat tentative, in need of direction, and perhaps bumbling through questions, not sure why he was being interrogated as he was. But he gave an air of being absolutely sure why he was there and ready to engage with the detectives.

Yet there were a few clues that he wasn't quite himself. When she had seen him before, he had been clean-shaven, but there was a blur of blue-black whiskers on his cheeks today. His eyes were red-rimmed. When Baker put a cup of water in front of him, as she had with Terri-Lyn, he immediately drained it and pushed it back to her in a mute request for more. Baker left the room for a moment to get a refill and placed it before him again. He nodded and took one mouthful, then looked at them expectantly.

"You know why you're here," Tuttle said in a businesslike way, as if he were following a written board agenda. "We would like to review your movements in the twenty-four hours before Mrs. Arnold was found, and also to review the circumstances of your son's death."

"I was home. I've been home since Michael's... accident. I couldn't be expected to make personal appearances after that. I've taken a few meetings by video chat but stayed home, close to my wife."

"How is she taking it?" Tuttle asked with apparent concern.

"Well, you've seen her. I imagine you are as good a judge of how people react to a death as anyone."

"I saw her today, but I didn't see how she has been managing it for the last week. Things can change a lot in that time. How has she been?"

"It was very upsetting," Cash said. "It isn't like Michael died in his sleep or from the measles or some virus. The accident was very disturbing, even if she didn't have to see his body afterward. And then all of the stuff that has been going around about the medical examiner's report." Cash's lips thinned as he pressed them together. "A report that hasn't even been released yet."

"The medical examiner's office is working on it and promises to have it in shortly. But you already have a pretty good idea what it will say."

"That woman coroner said he didn't die in the fall. She has no idea what she's talking about."

"All of her work will be reviewed by the chief medical examiner. But I'm afraid that from what we're hearing... Michael was killed before he fell from the balcony. Before he was *thrown off* of the balcony."

"If he was thrown off, his body would have landed further out," Cash pointed out.

"If someone threw him further from the house," Baker agreed. "But someone who knew about trajectories might have known better and just let him drop straight down from the rail."

Cash snorted at this. "The criminal element is not exactly well known for being intelligent. All that stuff on TV about criminal geniuses is just prime-time entertainment fodder."

Baker gave a soft laugh. "I'll admit that most of our cases are exactly what they look like on the face and few of the criminals that we deal with have made more than a cursory attempt to hide what they did. It doesn't usually take hours of investigating to identify a suspect or to recognize what someone has attempted to cover up."

Cash sat back, folding his arms across his chest. His knees jiggled impatiently. He looked ready to jump out of his chair but was forcing himself to stay contained.

"In this case, for instance," Tuttle said. "It didn't take us long to figure out that the boy was dropped off the balcony to obscure his real cause of death. And it didn't work out that way, because it was quite simple for the assistant to the medical examiner to figure out the cause of death."

Cash cleared his throat and shifted. He looked around the room, eyes going to the walls, the light, the furniture, and the posts on the wall, as if he were taking in each thing for the first time, realizing where he was. Waking up to the predicament that he was in.

"I'm under a lot of stress right now," he said without any prompting. "Things are heating up in the media, and that puts a lot of pressure on me. You know you can't believe even half of what they are saying online."

"Of course," Baker agreed. "But there are a few points that we can verify for ourselves. For example, it isn't very difficult to look at your credit report."

"I have money. I don't know why everyone says I have spent it all. That's not true."

"But you haven't been making rent or utility payments on all of your properties. One of your subsidiaries did not make payroll and needed to borrow money to do so. You have defaulted on some fairly hefty business loans."

"I had a deal that did not go through. It has affected cash flow temporarily. It will be straightened out."

"That's not what your credit report says."

"A credit report isn't all-knowing. It is just a bunch of numbers and predictive analysis. You might as well ask your two-year-old to predict the future."

They were all silent for a moment, Cash's use of "your two-year-old" in such a casual way ringing in their ears.

"A credit report is just bull," Cash amended. "It is a bunch of numbers that don't have any bearing on each other or your case. What does it matter to you or anyone else whether I defaulted on a loan? Or changed a company name. Or stayed in a hotel one night when I was in town because I didn't want to wake my wife up going into the house late at night."

"Don't you have spare rooms at the mansion that you could have used?" Tuttle challenged.

"There are all kinds of rooms, but they don't come with the same amenities. I had no intention of waking the house staff up to attend to my needs when it was just as easy to go to a hotel where everything is ready for me."

Including a pretty young girl he enjoyed spending time with, if the rumors on the internet were true. Zachary believed that one was. As well as the rumors about his being forced to declare bankruptcy soon. He acted like everything was fine, but he was used to showing people a calm, confident demeanor.

"We have talked to a Miss Michelle Bentley," Baker offered. "Perhaps you would like to consider that before telling us that you only went to the hotel because they have fluffy towels and complimentary toothpaste if you forget your own."

Cash ground his teeth, glaring at her. Baker didn't push. She just sat there waiting for him to correct himself or to move on to something else.

"My personal life is none of your affair," Cash insisted. "Neither are my financial affairs."

"They both have a bearing on our investigation."

"How?"

"You weren't getting along with your wife. Going to someone else instead. You have a prenup, and you know that the fact that you were cheating on her means that she will benefit from the prenup, and you lose out. You are already having money problems, and that would ruin you."

"And what does that have to do with anything?"

"Men who are losing everything sometimes find ways to take their families out of the picture. It bothers them so much to be a disappointment to their families that they would rather kill them than to have them see their failings."

"That's ridiculous."

"An annihilator would rather see his whole family dead than admit that he has failed them. Or failed to reach whatever financial goal he thought he should have achieved. They have a wildly distorted idea of what they can accomplish in life, and when they cannot reach that goal, they feel the need to..." Baker shook her head, looking for the appropriate metaphor. "To burn everything down," she said finally.

"I haven't burned everything down."

"You're losing it."

"I am not losing it!" he raised his voice, shouting the words back at her.

Baker just smirked. "Really."

"You're trying to provoke me," he accused.

"You are not acting like the calm, collected congressman you were trying to portray when you first walked into this room."

"My son just died. And the woman who raised me. How do you think that makes me feel?"

"I think you killed both of them."

The astonishment on Cash's face was comical. Surely he had seen that coming? He had seen that was where they were going, what they were hoping to prove.

"I did not kill either one of them!"

"Prove it."

"Michael's body was found outside, nowhere near where I was. By Sylvia. How does that make me guilty of Michael's death?"

"You were in the house and dropped his body over the rail. You may think that you go unobserved in that house, that everyone just works in the background and doesn't see your comings and goings, but that isn't true. People see you. They pay attention to where you are at all times. So they can tell us a lot more about where you were and what you were doing than you think."

"I didn't do anything to hurt him."

"Oh, didn't you?" Tuttle exploded so unexpectedly that Cash jerked back from him, raising his hand to his face protectively. "You hit that boy," Tuttle accused. "Don't even try telling me that you didn't hurt him. Do you know how many people can testify to that fact?"

"How I choose to discipline my son has nothing to do with you. And nothing to do with his death. I did not kill him."

"Discipline. Is that what you call it when you beat the hell out of a toddler for interrupting you? For getting underfoot?" Baker challenged.

"That's a misconstruing of the circumstances—"

"That is *exactly* what happened. You know it, and I know it, so you might as well not even try."

Cash folded his arms again, glaring at her. But he didn't deny it.

Maybe there were too many witnesses and he was trying to think his way out of the trap he found himself in.

"Do you know how often your nanny had to take that boy to the emergency room to ensure he didn't die from the injuries you inflicted on him? But this time, she couldn't get there in time to save him. She was too late. So the two of you concocted a plan to make it look like he was killed in an accident instead of being beaten to death. You would drop the boy over the railing. She would scream and attract everyone's attention. You would all play the part of hurt, grieving parents, and no one would be the wiser. That's how you thought it would all play out. You weren't planning on the medical examiner being able to tell that he had been dead before he was dropped."

"I may have lost my temper once or twice—"

"And sent him to the emergency room with broken bones, a lacerated liver, or internal bleeding," Tuttle finished grimly.

"No. I never caused that kind of damage. Never."

"We have the hospital records, Mr. Wade. He *was* hurt that badly. Just how hard do you think you can hit a kid without causing major damage?"

He shook his head insistently. "I am not that kind of person. I just… I just was under a lot of stress. He always wanted attention. He was always crying and demanding attention. He didn't know when to stay out of my way."

"Like… all of the time?" Baker suggested.

"You don't know what you're talking about. I loved my son. I loved to do things with him, to spend time with him. But sometimes he wanted to do something with me and I had work to do. Or I was… having a discussion with his mother. He just didn't know when to stop and leave me alone."

"He was barely more than a baby. You can't expect him to be able to predict human behavior. You can't expect a child that old to know when to leave you alone or to follow instructions. Both you and your wife seem to have this… blind spot where your son is concerned. It's like you think he was an adult rather than a baby. Like he chose to annoy you and was being disobedient when he couldn't do what you expected him to. He was a toddler. Can't you understand that?"

Cash put his hands over his face, trying to compose himself. "Look… I admit that I had hit him once or twice. I just got so… frustrated and angry. I've always had a temper. That's not my fault. But you can't judge me by that. I didn't kill him. I would never do that." He removed his hands and stared earnestly at the two of them, trying to convince them by his sincerity that he was innocent.

Baker looked at Tuttle. They didn't say anything for a minute, but were clearly communicating with each other. Baker stood up.

"Mr. Wade, remind me of your real name?"

"I go by Cash on everything."

"Is it Christian?"

"Crispin."

"Crispin Wade, you are under arrest for the murder of your son. I assume you will want to consult with your attorney—"

Cash covered his face again. "No, no, no! I told you, I didn't want him to die. I just… couldn't stop it."

"Mr. Wade, you need to call your lawyer. Anything that you say to us now is on the record and is going to be used against you—"

"I should have stopped. I shouldn't have let it go so far. But it wasn't my fault." Kenzie thought from the snuffling and sobbing Cash was making behind his hands that he was crying now, finally letting himself go. "How could I let that happen my son? I never thought it would go that far."

"Are you prepared to make a statement? A full and honest confession could mean a lighter sentence. People understand how difficult parenting can be, especially when you have a high-needs child and a lot of stress in your life," Baker was echoing back what she had heard Cash say, trying to prompt him to go on and tell them more details.

"I can't. I just… you wouldn't understand. You think that I'm responsible and… I guess I am, but…"

"It's time to get it off your chest," Tuttle said firmly. "But let's get a waiver signed first. Then you can explain the whole thing to us. You'll feel so much better when you do."

Baker laid her hand comfortingly on Cash's shoulder. "Come on, Mr. Wade. Try to pull yourself together. We need this signed, and then you can explain what happened. I'm sure that once we understand what took place…"

She trailed off, not promising him anything in particular. A hint of sympathy and the possibility that they could be understanding and forgive a misstep if he just explained what had happened. It was very subtle.

It took a few minutes of encouragement to get Cash back under control. He went through half a box of tissues and several spells of self-recriminations that didn't lead anywhere. They managed to get him to stop crying and positioned the Miranda waiver in front of him, encouraging him to sign it and then tell them all about what had happened.

It looked like the show was over. It was only a matter of time before they got a complete confession from Cash Wade and prosecuted him for his son's death. With his power and influence, Kenzie knew he might only get manslaughter. They would say that he had been in extreme emotional distress, that he hadn't known what he had been doing, and hadn't been able to stop himself from killing his son once he had started. But there was one problem with that.

Cash had not beaten his son to death.

49

Kenzie suspected that the house staff had a much better idea of what was going on than anyone was willing to admit. They were trained to be discreet. They had been keeping the family's secrets for too long. Kenzie didn't know if there were any others who, like Sylvia, had been there since Cash was a child. He had been cosseted and protected when he should have been forced to take responsibility for his own behavior. As a grown man, he was still trying to blame his own behavior on someone else.

A learned pattern that had been in place for many years and everyone in the household had been taught to toe the line. Cash was a golden child. The wealthy, brilliant, up-and-coming heir to the throne. Not someone who had to follow the same rules as everyone else.

What Kenzie knew was that Michael had not been beaten to death. The old bruises certainly showed a pattern of abuse. His injuries had landed him in the hospital in the past. But there was a difference between hitting and asphyxiation. Nothing Cash had said hinted at asphyxiation.

Kenzie used a quiet interview room to put a video call in to Hilda, the housekeeper. The woman had a number of problems getting on to the live video chat, pecking randomly at the screen and peering at it closely so that Kenzie got an excellent view of her nostrils. But eventually, they were face to face, Hilda sitting down with her phone propped up on the table.

In the kitchen, from what Kenzie could see. She would have preferred somewhere more private, but it was essential to keep Hilda feeling comfortable and not confronted, so she let it go.

"Hilda, we need to know more about what happened the day Michael died," Kenzie told her. "There are too many different stories, too many inconsistencies. And I think you and the rest of the staff know much more about it than you have told us up until now. I know that you are used to keeping family matters quiet, but… Michael and Sylvia were family."

Hilda was already dabbing her eyes and nose with a tissue, which she balled up in her hand. "I have known Sylvia for thirty years. Had known her. Now she's gone. But I know her. She would have told us to keep quiet and not cause anyone in the family trouble. She *was* family. More than any of us. She always saw Cash as a son. Her firstborn son. Even if she never carried him, she was the one who raised that boy, who took care of all of his cuts and scrapes, nourished him."

"I know. It must have been really hard for her to see what he had become. To see him being so abusive toward his own son."

Hilda shook her head. "I never saw anything," she proclaimed. "I never saw him hit the boy."

"But he did. He's admitted that to the police. And I can tell you… Michael was black and blue with bruises. Maybe you already knew that. Maybe you helped Sylvia when she bathed him or saw him running around in his diaper. He was covered with bruises."

"Maybe he had one of those diseases that makes you get bruises from the littlest things…"

"He didn't," Kenzie said flatly. "Those bruises were real. Evidence of severe abuse."

Hilda dabbed at her eyes. "I always hoped… we tried to keep Michael in the nursery, away from them, so that he wouldn't get hurt. But you can't control a toddler." She said it fondly. Someone who knew a lot more about childhood development than Cash Wade. They couldn't force him to stay and play in the nursery when he wanted to be with his mom or dad. There were probably prohibitions against locking him in or forcing him to do anything physically. Certain boundaries that a servant was not allowed to cross.

"You knew that he was being hurt."

Hilda didn't admit it or deny it.

"You knew that Sylvia took him to the hospital? Not just once, but multiple times. Because she knew he would die if she didn't."

Hilda looked away from the phone screen. The cook passed behind her. Other conversations were going on around her. Too quiet for Kenzie to hear, but there were still a lot of people aware of the conversation. Cash would not be happy if word of this got back to him.

"You knew about the hospital visits," Kenzie said, wording it strongly.

There was a very slight nod from Hilda.

"You knew that his father hit him."

"But—"

"Sylvia tried to intervene, to make sure that he got medical treatment, to save his life."

Hilda swallowed and nodded, a bit more firmly this time. "Yes. Of course. We were all concerned, but Sylvia most of all. She was the closest to him, physically and emotionally. She was his caregiver."

"Who paid for those hospital visits?"

"What?"

"Hospital visits are not cheap, especially where lifesaving surgery is required. And Sylvia never used insurance because that would tip the hospital off regarding Michael's identity. Sylvia didn't have that kind of money. So who paid for it?"

"I suppose… Mr. Wade."

"You suppose? Or you know?"

There were several seconds of silence while Hilda considered this.

"The truth will come out," Kenzie said. "Whether you say what happened or not. There are financial records. Bank transfers, deposits, payments. She wasn't paying for major surgery from the petty cash in her wallet. That money was used for things like more baby Tylenol to keep him quiet. For milk and other treats to settle him down when he had to sit and wait in the emergency room. Who paid the hospital bills?"

"Mr. Wade."

"So he can't deny that he knew about them."

"No," Hilda admitted.

"He knew how badly Michael was hurt."

"I… I guess."

"What did Sylvia hear that day?"

"What do you mean?" Hilda's brows drew down in puzzlement, confused by Kenzie's change in direction.

"Sylvia's statement said she had been working in another part of the house. She had not been with Michael. But she heard something that made her go check on him. So what did she hear?"

"I don't know."

"Was she working in the kitchen? Maybe I should ask the cook what Sylvia heard."

"She heard…" Hilda swallowed hard again and licked her lips. She looked around the kitchen, but no one supplied her with a water bottle or another drink, and she didn't seem inclined to ask anyone else into the conversation.

Kenzie was expecting to hear that she heard a scream or cry from Michael. She knew the sound of her baby's voice and dropped whatever she was doing to go to him. But she was too late to stop Cash from doing what he had. And then she couldn't make herself do anything to implicate her "oldest son" in the child's death.

Finally Hilda spoke.

"She heard an argument."

50

Kenzie felt cold. "What argument?"

"It was…" Hilda was having a difficult time speaking, putting the words together to tell Kenzie what had happened. She looked around her again. Kenzie could no longer detect any background conversations on the video chat. The other staff members were silent, waiting for Hilda to tell her story. None of them seemed to be trying to stop her, which Kenzie thought a good sign. Maybe more of them wanted to talk about it, for the story to go public so they didn't have to shoulder the silent burden alone.

"Mr. Wade and his wife," Hilda finally managed to get out.

"Did you hear the argument too?"

"I… yes. He was… very loud."

"What did he say?"

There was a long pause while Hilda thought about this, gathering her thoughts or trying to figure out all of the implications of telling someone in law enforcement what had actually happened. The story would contradict her earlier statement. At least Kenzie assumed it would. It had been left out of her account, even if she hadn't covered it with lies. And it would contradict the statements of other staff members, Sylvia, Cash, and Terri-Lyn. They had all carefully left the argument out of their accounts.

While Hilda was gathering her thoughts, Kenzie tried to picture what had happened. How had an argument resulted in Michael's death? She first envisioned the boy trying to get his father's attention while they were fighting and getting hit and thrown out of the way for being in the wrong place at the wrong time. But as she had already reminded everyone involved, Michael had not died from a blow.

"Mr. Cash, he said…"

"What did you do?" Cash screamed. "What have you done?"

His wife's replies were more difficult to make out, her quieter, higher voice not carrying through the walls and floors as easily. Cash's bellow was like that of an enraged bull. No one in the house could have failed to hear it.

"He's your son! He's only a child!"

Terri-Lyn railed at him, screams of anger and self-defense. "It's your fault!"

A crash sounded as someone's body hit the furniture or a heavy piece of furniture was thrown over.

"You said it wouldn't happen again!"

"You're never here!" Terri-Lyn screamed, "You're always off with that woman! You don't even care about your business, your home, how I will live when it's all over! You think I will be content to be your ex-wife while you marry that piece of fluff?"

"He was my son! My only son!"

"You're taking everything away from me. You thought I would just stand by while you ripped my life to shreds? And while you're gone, he's here. Whining at me. Pawing at me. Always underfoot."

"No, no, no…"

"Don't act all righteous to me!" Her voice shrilled. "You're no better than me. You come home drunk or mad because of some deal that slipped through your fingers, and you whale on him! You think I carried that thing inside me for almost ten months to see him used as a punching bag? I gave you my body! I went through pain you'll never imagine. To bear a wailing, screaming whelp who only ever shuts up for *her*!"

"You're the devil! You have no human feelings!"

More crashes, the two of them having a knock-down blowout fight.

"Because you're always sorry afterward? You think it's different if you apologize and fuss and grovel and give him a new toy? You're better than me because you feel sorry? You still hurt him!"

"I never sent him to the hospital."

"And I did? What did I ever do? Besides loving him too much? I held him. I could hold him and quiet him as well as *she* could."

"No…" Cash's voice broke off in despair. "You promised me. You got down on your knees and promised me it would never happen again. You're not a mother. You're a monster!"

"This is the end," Terri-Lyn promised. "This is the end of *your* life."

They could hear her walking down the hallway. Half-running, loud footsteps. A door opening and the familiar sound of the sliding doors being opened. There was a last moment scuffling, Cash following her, wrestling with her, trying to beat her into submission as he had before. And then a wail from him, unlike anything any of them had ever heard before.

And a noise outside. The solid thunk of something hitting the pavement.

Hilda suddenly became aware of Sylvia running through the room, sobbing in anguish. Hilda was paralyzed, unsure what to do or who to call.

Then Sylvia started screaming. The heartbreaking shrieks of a mother whose child was ripped out of her hands for the final time.

Hilda was numb as she heard Cash descend the stairs to the main floor and make his way to the poolside area. She caught a glimpse of his face as he walked by the open door. Gray skin, wide eyes, his mouth twisted into an open grimace. As he reached his son's body, others in the household were released from their game of statues and went out to assist or comfort him.

It was ten minutes before Terri-Lyn came down, dressed in a red kimono dressing gown. Her face nothing like Cash's. Quietly triumphant, superior, the horrible specter of the angel of death. She went to the back door, but not out onto the pavement where her husband knelt over the rag doll body of his son, his keening cry a faint echo of Sylvia's, the one person who had truly loved the boy and never done him harm.

And then the act began.

. . .

Kenzie's eyes moved from Hilda's face on the tablet screen to the detectives on the other side of the table, out of Hilda's view.

They were all familiar with violence. They saw it, or the results of it, on an almost daily basis. But they were not immune to it. The story of what had really happened at the mansion that day rang in their ears and was as much a part of them now as it would be of Hilda for the rest of her life.

They all shared in it now.

"It was Terri-Lyn who killed Michael?" Kenzie asked, trying to keep her voice as steady and non-judgmental as possible. "His own mother?" She remembered hearing Ben Burton's story from Zachary, similarly horrific. Mothers were held up as the example of perfect love and devotion, the highest, purest form of love. And then there were women like Ben Burton's mother. Like Terri-Lyn. Who took back the life they had given.

"She wasn't his mother," Hilda said in a disgusted tone. "It takes more to be a mother than simply to bear a child. She was never what she should have been. They gave her excuses. She was depressed. She was overwhelmed because he was so colicky, so needy, and he was her first child."

"She never bonded with him."

"Could she? The woman is as cold as an iceberg. Who would expect her to bond with anyone, much less a screaming, squalling newborn?"

"What happened?"

"You would have to ask her that. She was alone. She wasn't supposed to be left alone with him. We all knew it could happen again. One day, she would succeed in silencing him permanently."

"She squeezed him to stop him from crying?" Kenzie asked, and she had to wipe the corners of her eyes, which were suddenly leaking hot tears, ruining her professional persona.

Hilda nodded stoically. Her tears dried as Kenzie took on the burden herself. "She never could stand him crying. She would shake or squeeze him until… he stopped."

51

Kenzie was watching the camera screen once again. Tuttle and Baker began by Mirandizing Terri-Lyn, pushing a waiver into place in front of her and instructing her to sign it if she understood everything she had been told.

Terri-Lyn looked from Baker to Tuttle, and back at Baker again, trying to decide which of the cops was more sympathetic to her story.

"What is all this? Why are you telling me this now?"

Baker spoke in a calm, even voice. Not pleasant, exactly, but removed, unemotional. "We want to make sure that you understand your rights before we ask you anything else about what happened the morning Michael died."

"I already told you—"

"A crock of lies," Tuttle snapped. "Of course you did. And now, it is time to own up and talk about what really happened. The time for cover-up has come to an end. You need to switch tracks now. We know what happened to Michael. How you killed him and dropped him off of the balcony, and pretended that it was an accident. All while telling your husband what a low life he was."

"Well… he is that," Terri-Lyn pointed out.

"No doubt," Baker agreed. "But so are you. Now tell us about what happened to Michael. The real story this time. There's no point in making us drag it out of you. Let's talk about what you did and why."

Terri-Lyn looked at Baker coldly.

"Why? I don't know who is talking to you, but if they are telling stories about me, I guess you know why already. He was ruining me."

It wasn't clear, to begin with, which "he" she was talking about.

"I didn't marry a poor man," Terri-Lyn said, a sneer distorting her mouth and nose. "I married a rich man, a rich, powerful man who was predicted to be the future governor of Vermont. This is the man I put my trust in. All of my hopes. Do you know what kind of home life I had? Did perfect little MacKenzie bother telling you anything about it? I wasn't going to live the rest of my life that way. I wasn't going to be a no one, smacked around by a no one, living and dying in obscurity. I wanted people to know who I am. Who I married. I was finished with being a nobody."

"And you hoped Cash would keep you on top of Vermont society. Everyone would know him and, in turn, know who you were. And in the beginning, it seemed like everything was going according to your plan."

Terri-Lyn favored Baker with a glare. A look that said, "Who do you think is telling this story?"

"Big wedding, big splash," Baker went on. "All of your friends and high society folks there. Congratulating you, giving you gifts. You get back to the mansion, and it's the honeymoon period. Everything is still going great. Maybe you notice a few chinks in Cash's armor, but you're willing to overlook those because everything is going great, and everybody else thinks he is fabulous."

Terri-Lyn licked her lips, maybe thinking about those early days. The whirlwind of society gossip that Kenzie had missed because she had been overseas. The splashy headlines. The first flush of married life, riding a roller coaster.

"How long did it last?" Baker asked. "How long was it before he hit you the first time? A week? A month? Maybe even a year? And then one day, when you thought everything was going great, he smacks you. Drunk, probably. You can excuse it once because he was drunk."

"How did I ever think I was going to get away from it?" Terri-Lyn demanded. "Did I think the rest of the world was any different?" She considered the question seriously. "Of course on TV, all families are perfect, even the defective ones. They still all love each other and take care of each other. MacKenzie's family, some of my other school friends… I didn't think they were like that. So it seemed like I should be able to land a man who wouldn't hit me, wouldn't stay out drinking, wouldn't turn into a ba— like him."

"But it turned out that you just picked out a higher-class jerk."

"Yeah. And not only that, but one who couldn't hold on to what he had. All of that money from his grandfather, the political appointments, all of that *promise*. He couldn't hold on to any of it on his own. It was all slipping through his fingers like water. And he was letting it go, spending his time with escorts and call girls when he had a job to do. Drinking and doping and beating on me. I wanted a man who wouldn't beat on me!"

But she'd stayed with him anyway. She hadn't been able to abandon ship. Even if she had figured it out in those first few months, she had stayed with him for years, and things didn't get better.

"I just wanted him to settle down, to stay at home, to be that stable, steady person for me… I didn't even care about the money or position anymore. I just wanted him to come home and take care of me." Terri-Lyn rubbed her forehead. "I thought I could at least have that."

The detectives nodded, making encouraging noises.

"Sylvia told me that if I had a baby, he would come back. He'd settle down and be a daddy and we could all be a family. That was how it had been with Cash's father. He had settled down when Cash was born. He'd stopped going out so much and had stayed home to play with him and take care of him. So it would be the same for Cash. When he saw his son, he would come back to me."

"But it didn't solve everything," Tuttle said flatly.

"It didn't make anything better. I was sick, I was in pain, and couldn't do anything, even after the baby was born. It was like someone had taken my body and replaced it with a different one, and nothing worked anymore. My body went flabby and weak and I couldn't get out of bed. I couldn't take care of a screaming baby all day long. How could anyone?"

"Babies with colic are a challenge to anyone," Baker sympathized. "I can't imagine how difficult that must have been with your postpartum depression."

"I was relieved when Sylvia took him. I needed my sleep, just for one night. I couldn't keep doing it. Couldn't keep feeding him and changing the stinking diapers and just… didn't have the energy to listen to one more scream. I don't know how I could have kept going if she hadn't taken him. I probably would have rolled over on him in my sleep. I was so exhausted I just wouldn't wake up. And then he would be gone."

She said it philosophically. She had, if Kenzie were right, put a lot of thought into it. She obviously knew that this sometimes happened when mothers kept their babies in bed and were too tired to wake up if something happened. She knew she could use it as an excuse. That it was just a tragic accident. Something that had been outside her control, being an exhausted mom having to deal with a shrieking, colicky baby who screamed all the time. And that would be a permanent solution. She would never have to worry about him again.

Had this idea festered with Terri-Lyn over the ensuing weeks and months? And then one day, she had just followed through, taking her son away from Cash.

"So Sylvia saved Michael. And rescued you from having to look after him all the time. It sounds like you were really having a hard time with him."

"I appreciated it at first. In the beginning, I couldn't think of anything I wanted more. Just for the screaming creature to be gone and to lie in my bed and sleep for as long as I needed to."

"You needed recovery time. It doesn't sound like you got it until then."

"No. I didn't." Terri-Lyn looked at Baker, her head cocked to the side, looking like a curious bird. "But then… after a while… I realized that she had him all the time. That she had stolen him from me. She was raising him like he was her son. He wanted her. She would rock him all night long." Her eyes got big in wonderment at this accomplishment. "This old woman, and she just rocked, and rocked, and rocked… and he slept for her. I don't know when she slept. How she got the rest that she needed. There I was, a woman in my prime, and I couldn't understand how she could do it."

"You started to resent her?"

"Yes. She was a witch. A thief. She had stolen my son from me and was trying to steal Cash too."

"How was she doing that?"

"Because Cash could go see Michael when he was with her. Meet him or pat him on the head or hold him for a few minutes, and everything was right. And Cash loved her already because she was his nanny too. She'd already stolen his heart years before. When she spoke up, when she wanted something from him, he always listened. Whatever she wanted, she could have."

"Was there anything romantic between the two of them?" Tuttle asked.

Terri-Lyn's face twisted. "Gross. No. There wasn't anything between them, not like that. But it didn't matter. He had other women to satisfy those needs. So what did he need me for anymore? I was just the wife, the arm candy, and rarely even that anymore. He was leaving me more and more, instead of staying with me like Sylvia said he would."

"So you resented him, and you resented her. And you had to do something about it."

"I had to take Michael back. At least some of the time. I had to act like I was happy to be the mommy, that I liked to be with him, that I got something fulfilling out of it."

"But you still didn't form a bond with him." Tuttle leaned forward in his seat.

Terri-Lyn shook her head, scowling. "I don't know what this bond is that they talk about. I never felt it. I don't think Michael ever felt it. He was my baby, and I tried to keep anyone from finding out that I wasn't all gooey over him like the other moms. And sometimes, Cash would come see him while he was with me, so I got what I wanted. But not often enough. And sometimes he didn't even want to see Michael. He just wanted him out of the way, and the kid was so annoying. When he was an infant, at least I could put him in a seat or a crib, and leave him there to sort himself out. Shut the door and ignore his screaming. But when he got older, more mobile, that doesn't work anymore."

"No," Baker agreed. "So you turned to other solutions…"

"It was Cash who hit him. I never hit him. He was just trying to toughen him up. Trying to get him to stop crying all the time. To listen to what his daddy told him to do. But he didn't. He was too little still. And Sylvia would get in the way, offer to take him away." Terri-Lyn rolled her eyes. "I couldn't stand that woman. What right did she think she had to my baby? Just because she rocked him a few times when he was colicky? She was the hired help, not Michael's mother."

"What did you do to stop Michael from crying?"

"I would just hold him." Terri-Lyn put her hands in front of her, curled as if she were holding Michael in front of her, hands around his torso with his legs dangling. "And I would give him a little shake." She demonstrated with a firm jerk. "And I would tell him no. No, Michael. Be quiet. No crying. No."

"And that worked?"

"Sometimes it did."

"And when that didn't work the first time, would you do it again?"

"Yes," Terri-Lyn said through gritted teeth. She demonstrated giving the baby a couple of firm shakes. Nothing that looked very violent. Her eyes were intent, drilling into the face of the imaginary baby. Firm. Telling him with her facial expression that he needed to stop. "Stop crying. Stop crying! Stop crying!"

She went still. She looked at the two police detectives. "It didn't hurt him. I wasn't doing this," she shook the imaginary child violently back and forth, so they could all imagine the baby's head flopping forward and back, brain bouncing around in his skull, causing the damage known among medical examiners as Shaken Baby Syndrome. "I wouldn't do that."

"What would you do if he still didn't listen?"

She folded her arms, looking stubborn. "Call Sylvia. Tell her to take care of him."

"Oh, I see. Even though you didn't like her?"

"Yes. She was the only one who could quiet him."

"Why don't you tell us what happened the day Michael died?" Baker said, reaching out like she was going to touch Terri-Lyn to comfort her, and then pulling her hand back so that she didn't actually touch her. "There seems to be a lot of confusion, a lot of different stories about what happened."

52

"It wasn't any different than any other day," Terri-Lyn insisted. Though surely she understood that it had ended up being very, very different from all of the days before it. But if she was only playing a part, acting like a loving, concerned mother, then maybe it was no different living her life without Michael than it had been living her life with him somewhere else in the house, out of the way so she didn't have to think about him or her failure to keep Cash in line.

"I have to get up and do my Pilates. That might seem like it isn't important, but it is. I had to build up my core strength. I had to rebuild my whole body after Michael was born. It was so awful, feeling like some alien body had been swapped in place of mine. I had always thought I would be a strong woman, that nothing could change that. If I wanted to be in a good space, physically and mentally, then I needed to do my exercise routine."

"Of course," Baker agreed.

"And then… it was a Sunday morning, you know, like it is today. That meant that Cash didn't have to work. We could have a lazy morning, just like the families on TV or in comic books. You know how they lay around, reading or smoking a pipe. I wanted that picture in my head. I got Michael from Sylvia and gave her some jobs to do in the kitchen and such. Told her that I needed her to take care of them. And I took Michael to where Cash was, sitting at his desk going over some papers. I tried to talk to him but he wouldn't talk to me! Told me to go back to my rooms with the boy, and he'd come see him later."

She looked around vaguely at the interrogation room. But not seeing the room, Kenzie didn't think. Remembering what had happened that day. Picturing it in her mind. Trying to construct the scenario she had wanted, and what she had ended up with.

"I stayed in his rooms. Not his office, but in his sitting room. Michael wanted to play. Wanted to go back to the nursery. I told him no, made him sit, to be quiet like he was at church. I remember my daddy smacking me if I ever got out of line at church. Kids can be trained to behave the way you want them to. If you try hard enough, make them stop and pay attention."

"So he was just sitting quietly on his own?" Baker asked.

"On my lap. He wouldn't sit on his own. He would be moving around all over the place and fooling around. I could hold him on my lap and make him be still when I told him to."

"How did you do that?"

"Just held him still."

"And squeezed," Tuttle suggested.

Terri-Lyn didn't answer.

"If he didn't sit still, you squeezed him, didn't you? Or if he was making noise? If he wasn't the perfect, quiet child, you wrapped your arms around him and squeezed him tighter and tighter until he stopped."

"He always stopped," Terri-Lyn informed him proudly, as if this demonstrated her stellar parenting skills. "I would hold him tight, and he knew it was time to stop squirming and sit still with Mommy."

While she literally squeezed the breath out of him, constricting so tightly that she broke ribs on multiple occasions.

"And then what happened?"

Terri-Lyn looked at Baker blankly, her eyes dark holes. "What do you mean?"

"When Cash finished his work and came out to see his son, what did he say?"

"There were... words exchanged. He realized that he had pushed it too far this time. That he had taken too long on his stupid work and gave

up on his chance to see his son. Fathers who neglect their children…
shouldn't be allowed to see them."

"He saw that you had hurt Michael again. After you promised you
wouldn't."

"No. Cash was the one who hurt him. He took him away from me.
He was the one who threw Michael over the balcony. What kind of father
does that? You see what kind of person he is? He should be locked up."

Hear, hear. Kenzie agreed. Both of them should be locked up.

"Maybe the kind of father who wants to protect his wife," Tuttle
pointed out. "The kind who wants to keep her from being suspected of
having done something terrible to the child. When he took Michael from
you and found that you hadn't just hurt him, but killed him, he did it to
cover for you. To make his death look like a tragic accident."

"He should have thought about me before," Terri-Lyn's mouth formed
a pout. "He should have done something about it when he still could."

It was, all in all, an exhausting day. Kenzie found it difficult to deal with
the emotion of the deaths rather than just the clinical details. The police
had to deal with a lot more of that stuff than she did. She was grateful
that most days she could retreat into the data and just be concerned with
solving the puzzle of what had caused a person's death rather than who
had done it and how and why.

Zachary had texted her a couple of times during the day to let her
know that he was out on a job, doing some surveillance of an insurance
claimant suspected of fraud. Giving her a little update every now and
then.

Suspect on the move

False alarm. Checked the mailbox

No movement for six hours

There were definitely worse things than watching police interviews.
She didn't know how he could sit for so long—and longer—without ever
even laying eyes on a suspect. He would be tired when he got home too.

They both headed home at about the same time. Zachary had planned
it that way, of course, so they could spend dinner and the evening
together. He was very good at scheduling around their together time if he
possibly could.

He beat her home and she found him downloading his camera shots onto his laptop when she arrived. He hugged her, smelling of stale sweat after sitting in a car for so much of the day. His sandpaper cheek rubbed against hers. But rather than being irritated by these evidences of his long workday, she was comforted by the *realness* of their life together. His familiar appearance, smell, and feel all provided a texture to her life that she would miss if he were gone.

She thought of how her father had been so absent from her life as a child, gone while the senate was in session, traveling to meet with clients, to press the flesh and to convince people to support his causes. She'd always been happy when he came home and spent time with them. But she had wanted him to be there more often. To be more of a part of their day-to-day life.

Zachary buried his face in the soft skin of her throat, collarbone, and shoulder, taking a deep breath to inhale her scent and scraping the sensitive area with his whiskers.

"Hey!" Kenzie pushed him away. "Cut that out! You're going to give me a friction burn!"

He laughed, kissing her and making goosebumps run down her neck and arms. Then he withdrew and kissed her on the forehead.

"How was your day?"

"Mmm." Kenzie squeezed him tightly. "Let's just say… I'm glad I don't work with psychopaths every day."

Zachary chuckled. "I think we can all be thankful for that."

"Other than the people who *do* work with psychopaths every day."

"Yes, other than them," Zachary agreed.

They moved to the kitchen together without discussing it, even though neither had yet had the time to shower off the sweat and grit of the day. Zachary poured himself a glass of water and looked questioningly at Kenzie. She opened the freezer and pulled out a pint of chocolate chunk fudge ice cream to see how much was left. She really only needed a bite or two. Just something to take the edge off the day.

They sat down at the table. Kenzie told Zachary about the interviews with Cash and Terri-Lyn, trying to impart to him the morass of emotions she had felt in watching them. Her helplessness over what had already been done, her anger at two parents who had put their own needs and feelings ahead of the little boy they were supposed to love, cherish, and protect. But he had been an inconvenience for them. A pawn that had eventually outlived its usefulness.

"And then there was the nanny," Kenzie sighed.

"What did you find out about her? Do you know for sure… which one of them killed her? How it happened?"

"I figured going into it that it was the same person as had killed Michael. Both were asphyxiation by mechanical compression, so the chances that they were done by two different people was… pretty remote."

"Did you know the mother killed him rather than the father?"

"I was really hoping that it was the father, to tell the truth. I didn't want it to be her."

Zachary nodded his understanding. "We never want to hear that a woman, a mother, could do something like that. It's… somehow it's more horrific when it is a mother than a father or stepparent. We expect all mothers to have that innate love…" Zachary swallowed hard and took a drink. Thinking, Kenzie supposed, about his own mother, abusive and negligent, who had labeled him incorrigible and abandoned them all when Zachary was ten. Another prime example of a mother who did not meet society's standards for selfless, unfailing love.

"And it's hard on us when they don't," Kenzie agreed, filling the void in the conversation. She didn't tell him it was all that much worse because she knew the mother. Had once known her closely, thought of her like a sister, a soulmate. But Terri-Lyn was not the girl she had been in the early grades. The change had already started in high school when she had realized how different her family was from Kenzie's and the families of other kids at school who still had both parents at home. When she had decided to punish Kenzie for having the perfect family by humiliating her in front of the school.

She hadn't conquered that jealous streak and that need to get retribution by taking something precious away from the person she was angry with.

"Did she confess to killing the nanny as well? Or give enough information that they'll be able to hang it on her?"

Kenzie let a chunk of frozen chocolate melt in her mouth.

"I wondered how she had gotten the nanny out there to the place in the woods where the body was dumped. The nanny was small, but even a small body is difficult to move very far without a gurney or a wheelbarrow, and there wasn't any sign that someone had pushed or pulled anything with wheels through there. It would have been pretty hard to. The ground is bumpy and overgrown."

Zachary nodded. "If there is anyone who knows about the difficulties of moving a dead body, it would be you."

"It's always best to use the tools you have. We don't lug them around in our arms or over our shoulders."

Zachary snorted at the image.

"So, how did she get her out there?"

"She didn't have to. The nanny took regular walks around the property to stay in shape. No Pilates for her."

"And the mother met her out there."

"Yeah. Waited for her or confronted her there, and then had it out about Ca—about the father and about what the mother had done. Everyone knew or had a pretty good idea of what had happened. They knew that Terri-Lyn was responsible, even if they didn't know all the details. They were loyal employees and didn't talk about it in their statements to the police. Everybody stuck to the line that they didn't know anything was wrong until they heard the nanny screaming."

"But the mother didn't think that the nanny was going to stay quiet? Figured that she was going to go to the police?"

"She couldn't say why she had gone to talk to the nanny, but I think she must have planned to kill her from the start. What else would she go out there for? It wasn't part of her normal routine. It wasn't to plead with the nanny to stay quiet. That wasn't her style. She said it was an accident."

"An accident?" Zachary repeated. "How exactly was it an accident? The nanny tripped? Had a heart attack?"

"I think that's what she hoped to convince the detectives of. But she ended up giving them a pretty full confession. She stopped the nanny on her morning constitutional…"

53

"What are you doing here?" Sylvia demanded, her eyes darting around the woods as she evaluated escape routes. "Isn't it enough that you killed Michael and ruined your husband? Why are you still here? Why didn't you leave? You should get as far away from this place as possible. Leave us alone."

"Why should I go?" Terri-Lyn challenged, her dark eyes defiant. "This is my home. Cash is the one who is responsible for Michael's death and, if they arrest him for it, do you think I'm going to do anything to save him? Do you think I would align myself with him after all he has done? I'm done pretending to be his loving, devoted wife. I'll tell the media just who he is. Not the loving family man he has portrayed himself as. He is a failure. A drunk. He has no redeeming qualities."

"You've never appreciated him," the smaller woman sneered. "You have no idea what he could have become if you'd been the person you pretended to be. If he'd had the love and support of a wife instead of a cold, hard-hearted woman who only cares for herself. You could have supported him. Lifted him up. Understood that no man is perfect and turned a blind eye to his mistakes. But instead, you have to tear him down, weaken him, drive him away. Before you came here… things were going well for him. He was a rising star. Now…"

"Now he is nothing," Terri-Lyn said with satisfaction. "He's ruined."

"I could say that *you* are too."

Terri-Lyn took a step closer to the older woman, getting into her personal space, making sure she towered over her, physically intimidating.

"You don't scare me," Sylvia said coldly, though she looked around like she was waiting for someone to show up and rescue her. "If I tell what I know, you'll go to prison for the rest of your life. So why don't you leave? So that Cash doesn't have to deal with *that* humiliation as well."

"What do you think will happen if I talk?" Terri-Lyn challenged. "If I tell them what Cash did. What he did over and over again, beating me, beating Michael. The medical examiner already knows. She's seen the bruises. All the police need is confirmation as to who did it. And I have enough pictures of my bruised body to show that he wasn't picky about who he hit."

"They wouldn't put him in prison. Not a man of his stature and reputation."

"I would make sure they did! And even if they didn't, do you think he'd ever be allowed in politics again? He'd be ruined for life. In fact, maybe that's better. Ruin his reputation. Make him walk around for the rest of his life like a ghost, with everyone knowing what kind of person he really is."

Sylvia swore and shoved Terri-Lyn, forcing her to take a couple of steps back to keep her balance. Sylvia was a tough old bird, surprisingly strong, considering she didn't follow any of the programs Terri-Lyn thought necessary for building strength. But Terri-Lyn was strong too. And she had been training. Had been trying to get back that hard, lithe body she'd had before getting pregnant. She shoved Sylvia back, driving her back farther and farther with each push. Sylvia flailed at Terri-Lyn, trying to stop her and force her back.

Terri-Lyn gave one more hard shove, this time making Sylvia trip and fall over backward. Terri-Lyn threw herself on top of the woman and pinned her wrists in place so that she couldn't move. Sylvia struggled, but Terri-Lyn held her still. She felt again what it was like to hold Michael in her arms, forcing him to be still, to submit to her will and her strength, to listen to her like a child was supposed to. When she used to go to church, they talked about children being submissive and obeying their parents, but as far as Terri-Lyn had seen, that was not the way children behaved. Not in modern days, anyway.

Sylvia squirmed, trying to escape Terri-Lyn's iron grip. But Terri-Lyn wasn't letting her go. This was the woman who had stolen Cash from her. Sylvia had stolen his heart, had made it so that Cash had nothing else to give to Terri-Lyn. And she was the one who had stolen Michael too, alienating his affection so that he didn't even want to be around his own mother and was always asking if he could go see Nanny when Terri-Lyn wanted him to be with her.

Sylvia was stronger than the baby, that was for sure. There were a couple of times when Terri-Lyn thought that Sylvia was going to throw her off. But she squirmed and writhed and twisted her hips and Terri-Lyn hung on, like a fisher who had caught a marlin or a shark. If she could just hold on long enough, she knew that Sylvia would give in. She worked her way up to kneel on Sylvia's chest, all of her weight on that one point. She watched Sylvia's face turn white and then blue, gasping and begging, her mouth opening and closing like the dying fish that she was, until, at last, she was still.

Even then, she waited, wary of a trick. Gradually, Terri-Lyn relaxed her muscles, released her grip on Sylvia's wrists, and eventually got to her feet and stared down at the old witch. She was a witch, just like the one on The Wizard of Oz that got crushed beneath the house. Because she had been evil. She had tried to take away all of the happiness that Terri-Lyn had earned. And now, she was banished. Terri-Lyn didn't have to worry about the old witch and what she might say anymore.

Zachary shook his head, looking almost as shell-shocked as Kenzie felt. Terri-Lyn hated Sylvia with such venom. This woman who had raised her husband and who had rescued Terri-Lyn when her son's care had been too much for her and helped to keep him safe. The woman who had, as far as Kenzie had seen, been the most caring and compassionate person in the Wade mansion.

Yet Terri-Lyn had seen her as a threat. As someone who had usurped her role and was trying to take away the things that she valued most. Not her husband and son, but her prestige and social position, her money, her place in the mansion. Those were things that Terri-Lyn would not give up on.

"People do evil things," Zachary offered in a subdued tone.

"Yeah. You never really know what is going on in someone else's mind. I wouldn't have thought she was anything like that. Abused, yes, but someone who would intentionally kill two other people? Her own child? I never would have thought it of her."

"You think she is a psychopath, like you said earlier?"

Kenzie shrugged. "There's no actual clinical definition of a psychopath. But yes… I think that with how she was brought up, she decided that her comfort and success were all that mattered. It didn't matter what anyone else in the family needed or did; she needed to look out for herself and never let anyone in again."

Kenzie stared off into space, thinking about it. She had another bite of ice cream.

"So, is she the only one who is being charged?" Zachary asked. "If the father didn't actually contribute to the boy's death…"

"He was certainly responsible, on some levels, for what happened. And for covering it up. He was arrested, but I think the murder charges will go away, and he'll get a pile of child abuse charges, as well as obstruction and accessory. And spousal abuse too, for that matter. He might not have killed Michael, but he could have. And he certainly contributed to the circumstances of Michael's death. From what the staff said, and the evidence of the previous rib fractures Michael suffered, it's obvious that she had done this before. Holding him so tightly that she broke his ribs and he passed out. They had been lucky to be able to revive him before. This time… she was more determined, or he took too long to get to her."

"You would think that if he knew she had done it before, he would have seen to it that she was never alone with the boy. That any time she was upset, somebody should stay with her or take him away. If they had reported the earlier incidents, she would have been in jail and this would not have happened."

"For that to happen, they would have to admit that the family was not perfect. And what are the chances they would lock him up for his part in the abuse as well? That had to be why he stayed quiet."

"That, or he really didn't care."

Zachary reached across the table to touch Kenzie's hand. A quick flutter of a touch to show that he cared about her and what she was feeling after having dealt with the psychopaths.

"What do you want to do tonight? It's Sunday, which is usually your rest day, but you'll have to get up and return to work in the morning. So these last few hours…"

"I don't know. Shower, eat, and relax." Kenzie looked at the clock on the wall. "Did you want to chat with Lorne and Pat, since we weren't able to get back down there this weekend?"

"Yeah. But they'll understand if you're busy with something else. If you need to nap or just want to veg out watching TV… it's been a tough day for you."

"Yeah. Well, after this," she took another bite of chocolate ice cream, "I'm going to shower. If you want to call after that, I'll see how I feel. I might eat while we chat, or just take some time to myself and not think about all of this. I'll just see."

Zachary nodded. "Sounds like a plan."

54

Kenzie picked at leftovers from the fridge while Zachary started the video chat with Lorne Peterson and Pat Parker. She wanted more ice cream. Or pizza. Or something equally bad for her. But she was trying to eat a salad and some vegetables left over from other meals. She was feeling virtuous about not having ordered in. But she wasn't actually happy with what she was eating.

Zachary was telling the two men the general shape of their week and how things had gone since they'd had to leave the Sunday brunch so abruptly. The big case that Kenzie had been working on, though Lorne and Pat did not want too many details about Kenzie's cases. Zachary had a PBJ sandwich on the plate beside his computer, which certainly looked better than salad.

"Tell them about *your* case," Kenzie told Zachary. "It sounded pretty exciting."

Zachary looked at her, brows drawn down in a frown. "What?"

"Your surveillance," Kenzie prodded. "That sounded really interesting."

He took another second to realize that she was teasing and grinned. "Oh yeah, sitting around in my car for hours on end, hoping to catch some glimpse of someone lifting a child or doing gardening or one of the things that she said she couldn't do due to the accident. That's very exciting."

"And did you?" Pat asked.

"Did I what?"

"Catch her doing something she wasn't supposed to be able to do?"

"No."

They all laughed at his dour tone.

"Sometimes, our jobs suck," Zachary told Kenzie.

"Yeah, sometimes they really do. Lorne, I was wondering… when you and your wife were fostering, how many kids did you have?"

She looked around the corner of Zachary's screen to see his face for a moment.

"Oh, usually two or three at a time."

"But how many did you have in total? Do you know?"

"Oh, no. I lost track. It's possible that Lilith would know. She was the record keeper and administrator, not me. I just tried to keep things going smoothly. Provide whatever assistance I could give when I wasn't at work."

Kenzie nodded.

"Why do you ask?" Lorne asked. "You're not looking into foster care, are you?"

"No." Kenzie had to admit that the thought did cross her mind occasionally, knowing that many people found it fulfilling, and it was an important service to the community. But she also knew how difficult it would be. Zachary had been highly traumatized when he had gone into foster care and had been so high needs that he had never had a family who could take care of him for long. She knew it would mean giving up much of their time with each other. And if she ended up with a child like Terri-Lyn, with no conscience to speak of, she knew she couldn't handle that. "No, no. I was just thinking about this case. If either the victim or his killer had gone into foster care… maybe there would have been a chance for them. When I think of the number of kids that you helped… I'm very proud of you."

Lorne Peterson's face turned very pink. "Well, thank you, Kenzie. It wasn't really my doing. It was really Lilith who was in charge of the whole thing. But I did what I could."

"And I know that you did a good job, or Zachary wouldn't still be in touch with you. I know you were a good foster dad even if he was only in your home for a couple of weeks because of the way he has kept in touch with you for all of these years."

Zachary nodded his agreement. Lorne wiped sweat from his face, looking embarrassed and proud at the same time. Pat gave him a quick hug around the shoulders. "He's one special guy," he agreed.

"If you ever wanted to talk about foster care, feel free to ask," Lorne said. "I've been out of the loop for a long time, so things have changed, but the basics are still the same, and I know people who are still 'in the business,' so to speak."

"Okay, thanks," Kenzie agreed. "It's not something I'm planning on."

He nodded and didn't push it. Zachary gave Kenzie a sideways look. He would just have to trust her that it wasn't something she was asking about because she wanted to start fostering children. She wasn't even sure she wanted to have children of her own. Her parents would be delighted if she decided to provide them with some grandbabies, but providing grandchildren or even having someone to carry on the family name were not good reasons for having children. If she chose to have children, it would be because she wanted them. Being pushed into it, or encouraged to have children for the wrong reason, as Terri-Lyn had been, couldn't happen. There was nothing wrong with them just enjoying Zachary's nieces and nephews and the children of friends.

Dr. Wiltshire had been in over the weekend and had reviewed Kenzie's postmortem results and the attendant exhibits, so the official medical examiner's reports were issued hard on the heels of the news that both Cash Wade and his wife Terri-Lyn had been arrested in connection with the abuse of Michael Wade, his death, and Sylvia Arnold's death.

That was a lot for the media to handle, and it seemed like everywhere Kenzie went, she saw headlines and news reports on the deaths. She saw her autopsy reports summarized in five-word sound bites that were usually inaccurate and definitely overhyped. The cause of death itself, asphyxiation, was not as sexy as a drug overdose or shooting, so they had to find other ways to grab people's interest, usually by getting things completely backward, at least in the headline.

With the autopsies complete, the bodies could be released. Cash Wade was already out on bail, so Kenzie left a message for him about

Michael's body being available for pickup by his funeral home. She wasn't sure who to contact about Sylvia Arnold's body. Despite the fact that Sylvia had been so devoted to Cash, Kenzie suspected that he would not be managing her transportation and funeral arrangements. She looked through Sylvia's phone, which had been reviewed by the police detectives, and was not needed for the prosecutions of Terri-Lyn or Cash.

Baker had told her there were three children and that Sylvia didn't keep in very close touch with them by phone. But their numbers were in the contact list, so Kenzie grabbed the number for Caden, the child she seemed to be in touch with the most often, and called him up. She explained about needing someone to claim Sylvia's remains. It always felt awkward to her to call up total strangers and to try to get them to pick up their deceased loved ones' remains. In many cases, the family members had been estranged for a long time and didn't know how to handle her call.

Caden spoke to her briefly and seemed like a nice, polite young man. He had heard the news of his mother's death and seen the headlines about Cash Wade and his wife and all the publicity swirling around them.

"Can I come there to talk to you?" he asked Kenzie. "I just… this is hard to do over the phone."

"Sure, of course," Kenzie assured him. "And your siblings, if they want to come in. But you don't have to if you don't want to. You can communicate with your funeral home and I'll deal with them. As long as the proper paperwork is signed, I don't actually need you to come in person. A lot of people don't."

"I'd just like to come in and do it face to face."

Kenzie agreed. She gave Caden her contact information and the hours she would be there and hoped she wouldn't be in autopsy when he came by. She had a couple that she needed to attend to. She needed to take care not to get behind while Dr. Wiltshire was out of commission. If she got behind, catching up again would not be easy.

By the time Caden came in, she had forgotten all about him and was immersed in her work. She looked up, smiling, when she heard footsteps coming toward her. For a moment, she was startled, thinking he was Cash Wade, but there was only a passing resemblance. He introduced himself and shook her hand. Sylvia had raised him well.

"If we could sit down together somewhere," Caden suggested, "you could show me everything I need to do to get this done."

Kenzie pulled out a form for him. "It's actually very simple. If you'll fill this out—"

He looked at the form, shaking his head. Kenzie stopped, frowning. There was no way to do an end run around the paperwork. If he wanted his mother's remains released, he would have to complete everything.

"Could we sit down?" Caden repeated.

Kenzie nodded and escorted him into the boardroom, where they sat down at the table and she again showed him the form. "It's not a lot of work, just this one form, and then I can get the ball rolling. Do you know the funeral home you want to use?"

"Yeah. I think so. But I need a hand with this, if you don't mind."

"Uh, sure. I'm happy to help." Kenzie slid the paper in front of him, right side up, and pointed out the sections. "This is your mother's information up here, her name and birth date—"

"I'm dyslexic," he told her. "It would be a lot easier if you could tell me what you need and write it down for me. Otherwise, it will take me a really long time to fill this out, and it will probably be all wrong and you'd need to do it over again afterward."

"Oh! Of course." Kenzie relaxed once she understood the problem. "My partner is dyslexic too. I know he loathes forms. Everything so densely written, and then he has trouble writing as well, so he always takes twice as long as he thinks he should to fill it out so that it is legible."

"I'd be happy with twice as long," Caden laughed. "Maybe ten times as long. It's not that I can't, but it will be much easier to get it right the first time if we just go through it together."

"Sure."

She read the questions to him, explained them when necessary, and then wrote down the information he dictated back to her. He had most of the dates and information in his head, which Kenzie thought was pretty impressive. Most family members she dealt with did not know their parent's information by heart. But with the difficulty Caden had looking information up and writing it down, he compensated by memorizing what he needed to know. He was charming and polite, and Kenzie enjoyed the short interchange as she filled in his answers.

"There. That's got it. You just need to sign at the bottom." She made an X by the signature box and turned it around for him. Caden held the pen awkwardly in a left-handed grip and twisted his body to write in a position that was almost upside down to scribble his illegible signature diagonally across the box.

"Great," Kenzie approved. The form didn't need to be machine read. The signature didn't have to fit neatly inside the box. "That should do it, then. I'll let the funeral home know that we have all the paperwork and they can pick up her remains at any time."

"Thanks for helping me out with that." He gave her a warm smile. "I always dread filling out forms. And do you have... any personal effects?"

"We can just send those along with the remains, if you want."

"No, I wanted to get them today, if possible."

"Yeah. We can do that. Give me a minute and I'll bring them to you."

There wasn't much for him to collect. Kenzie grabbed the bag labeled with Sylvia's name and returned to the boardroom to hand it to him. He looked through it, frowning.

"No wallet or purse?"

"No. The police haven't found them. It's a pretty large property, it would be easy to drop them or hide them in the woods somewhere and they would be very difficult to find. Or toss them in the septic tank or some abandoned building. I'm sorry."

He shrugged. "It's okay. Not your fault." He pulled out Sylvia's phone and apparently knew her passcode. He tapped through the apps, pulling up the photos app to thumb through the most recent pictures. He shook his head. "Should have known it would all be Cash and Michael." He grimaced. "Her other family."

"She seemed to be very devoted to them," Kenzie agreed. "It's rare to see such strong employer-employee bonds. But I understand she knew Mr. Wade from the time he was a little boy."

"Yes. Knew him way before any of us were ever thought of," Caden agreed. "We grew up on the property, knowing Cash and the household staff. It just seemed natural to us that she would live with him and that he would be such a big part of her life. That was all we had ever known. But when we got old enough to go out into the world on our own... it was a bit of a shock to realize that the rest of the world didn't have that kind of long-term, close relationship between employers and employees."

Kenzie chuckled. "I guess that would be a bit of a shock when that's how you grew up."

"He wasn't just her employer. He was her everything. She was so excited when Michael was born. Another Wade baby."

"From everything I have heard, she was a really good caregiver to him too. He had colic and… there were a number of issues. But she took good care of him. She was very patient and loving."

He nodded, swiping through some more pictures on the phone. "Yeah, she was a good mom, too. We always felt like the household was our extended family. Everyone knew who we were, would help us, give us a cookie, whatever."

"That's nice. How did your dad feel about it? It must have been strange for him to live there. Or was he part of the staff as well?"

Caden lowered the phone. "We never knew who our dad was. Or who *they* were. It was just Mom."

"Oh." Kenzie studied him for a moment, wondering if there was more, then pushed the questions away. It was none of her business.

Her job was done. Her time with Sylvia Arnold had come to an end.

55

The message was from an unknown caller. A blocked number, burner phone, or even an ancient payphone still in service. Kenzie tapped it, figuring it would probably be a cop.

"She wasn't a saint, you know." Terri-Lyn's voice was sharp and bitter. "Everyone in the media is acting like Sylvia was this wonderful person who was the perfect mother and nanny. But you didn't live with her. You didn't see what was really going on."

There was a long period of silence, and Kenzie thought the message was going to cut off there. She'd heard that Terri-Lyn, too, was out on bail. It was amazing how much easier it was for a rich person to get out on bail than a poor one. Even a confessed murderer like Terri-Lyn.

"You should have listened to me, MacKenzie," Terri-Lynn carried on. "You should have listened to your mother and helped me instead of railroading me like you did. One day, you're going to be sorry you did that."

Kenzie's finger hovered over the red End Call button, but she could see from the time code that the message wasn't yet over.

"I did the only thing I could. I was driven to it. Instead of people being sorry for what I had to go through, they're calling me a monster. A murderer. Worse." She sniffled and gulped, crying for herself. "You would have done the same thing. You don't know what they were like, Sylvia and Cash. Don't spend any time feeling sorry for them. One day it will all come out, and you'll be sorry you didn't stand by me. You just wait and see."

There was another period of silence, and this time the message cut off.

Kenzie sat staring at the phone. A knot of anxiety twisted in her stomach.

She knew that she had done everything properly, had dug as deeply as she could, and searched out all of the evidence that both bodies had to offer. As she had told Zachary, she hadn't wanted it to be Terri-Lyn.

It was out of her hands and up to the police and prosecutor to put the case together.

Wherever Terri-Lyn went and whatever term she had to serve, it wasn't Kenzie's fault.

And no amount of time would bring Michael back.

SHATTERED TO DEATH

*That those who are broken
may be mended*

1

K enzie was just dropping off to sleep when her phone rang, making both her and Zachary jump.

Zachary instantly sat up and reached for his phone, even though it wasn't his ringtone. He pulled back after touching it, realizing by then that it wasn't his phone that was ringing. It took longer for Kenzie to rouse herself to some semblance of logical thought and to reach for her phone. Her phone was usually on silent mode so that it would not disturb Zachary at night. In theory, Kenzie would awaken to the phone's vibration on the side table and be able to silence it and leave the bedroom to take the call without waking Zachary. In reality, he was usually the one who awoke to the vibration and had to shake Kenzie awake to see whether it was an important call.

But tonight, she was on call and had turned the ringer on and set her volume to high so she couldn't miss a call-out. Dr. Wiltshire had attended two calls in person the night before, so it was his turn to sleep while Kenzie dealt with any calls.

It wasn't like a call-out was an emergency. It could wait a couple of hours if she didn't answer the phone immediately. It wasn't like her patients were going anywhere or would be more dead when she got there.

She liked to get to a scene as early as possible to take temperature readings and talk about the circumstances with the person who had discovered the body and any other witnesses. While most calls that the ME's office got were routine, she wanted to be on top of it if it were a potential homicide, when details like an accurate time of death could become very important. A whole case could hinge on who was or wasn't around during the relevant window.

Kenzie blinked hard and picked up her phone. "Medical Examiner's Office," she answered, after confirming that the call had been routed through the ME's office line.

"We need the medical examiner to attend a scene." The voice on the other end was male. Calm and official. But there was something in the tone of his voice that alerted Kenzie that he was nervous or excited. A slight change in pitch? His breaths coming faster than she would have expected. She couldn't put her finger on precisely what made him sound young and inexperienced, despite the definite adult timbre of his voice.

"Can I get the details?" Kenzie asked. "Address and what happened?"

It wasn't a law enforcement officer; she was pretty sure of that. They had their own particular official tone. Much more forceful and confident. Expectation, but also a hint of the routine, of a resignation that the ME might not get there for several hours and they would be left standing around the body waiting for someone to show up.

"Persons Residential Care," the voice on the other end of the phone informed her, following up with the address. He didn't answer the "What happened?"

"Got it," Kenzie agreed. "Can you tell me the circumstances of the death? I'd like to know whether I can get by with the death kit I have with me or whether I need to pick up additional equipment from the office."

"Well… I don't know. He just died."

"He just died?" Kenzie repeated. "In a medical facility?"

"Yes. I don't know what happened. Someone should come."

"I'll be there. No sign of violence? What was the patient in care for?"

"Psychiatric."

His answers were not particularly helpful and, from the muffled sounds in the background, Kenzie assumed that he was covering the mouthpiece and speaking to someone else, or someone else was talking to him and he didn't want Kenzie to hear everything being said.

"I'll be there shortly," she promised.

He hung up without any thanks or goodbye.

"Everything okay?" Zachary demanded as soon as Kenzie lowered her phone. He ran a hand over his dark buzz-cut and blinked.

"Sure. Just got a call-out." She shrugged. "We both knew it could happen."

"People ought to pick a more convenient time to die," Zachary suggested playfully.

"They should," Kenzie agreed with a smile. She sighed and got out of bed, putting her phone back on the side table while she stripped off her pajamas and quickly pulled on clothes more appropriate for a scene of death attendance.

"Murder?" Zachary asked.

"No. Medical facility." She didn't tell him anything more than that. Not like she could; so far, she was completely in the dark about what had happened.

Kenzie glanced out the window. *In the dark* was right. The sun had been down for hours. People *did* choose inconvenient times to die.

"I could drive you," Zachary suggested. He had done that once or twice before, especially if he thought she was too tired to drive or needed him there for another reason.

But there was no need for him to be around in this case. No indication that it was anything other than a patient dying in his sleep. It was not an uncommon occurrence in a psychiatric facility.

"No, you stay home and get your sleep," Kenzie told Zachary, even though she knew there was no way he would sleep while she was gone. He would get up and work on his laptop or watch TV. Or just pace. "I don't know how long I will be, but I'm fine. No need for both of us to be out."

"I'd be happy to come along…"

"Not necessary. Thanks for the offer, though."

Zachary sighed. Kenzie knew that he would have preferred to go with her, but she didn't know how long she would be and didn't want him sitting around in the car waiting for her to finish her routine tasks at the scene.

Though it wasn't like he minded spending time sitting in the car. In fact, he chose to sit in it for hours on end when he was on a surveillance job. That was the life of a PI, sometimes. More often than not, he was assigned to keep an eye on someone to learn their schedule, where they worked, whether they were having an affair, or whether they were able to do more than they had told their insurance company after an accident. People actually lied to their insurance companies. Who would have guessed?

"Sorry," she told him. "I doubt I'll be too long. I should be back tonight."

"You'd better be. I don't like you stepping out on me for these stiffs."

Kenzie grinned. She finished getting dressed and ducked into the bathroom to check her hair and try to tame the wild, dark curls into something more professional. She put on a coating of her trademark red lipstick, though she knew no one but she would appreciate it, considering the circumstances. She picked up her phone and handbag as she walked back through the bedroom and got on her way.

2

———————

Kenzie knew generally where Persons was, but hadn't been there before. Or she might have attended there once as a medical student, but couldn't remember much about it. Maybe when she was writing a paper and needed to interview someone? It was several years in the past, and the sleepless nights of medical school had blurred the memories.

She gave her baby, a beautiful, cherry-red convertible, time to warm up before backing out of the garage and getting on the road. She was soon outside the town limits, getting away from the glaring streetlights and sparse traffic. It took a few minutes for her eyes to adjust to the dark of the country road, and then she could see stars sprinkled across the black canvas of the night, thousands of twinkling pinpricks, and a sliver of a bright moon.

She had that awake-alert feeling that she got when she was taking care of an emergency when she would normally have been sleeping. She remembered the early morning starts to vacations when she had been young, sometimes having to go to the airport in the wee hours to catch an international flight. Sleeping with her head resting on her mother's shoulder while they sat in the chairs of the waiting area for boarding to begin. But not sleeping. Staring at the dark windows and watching the preparations covertly, looking as though she were asleep, but with an alertness running through her body, her brain primed to take everything in.

The care facility was not far away. Just away from the hustle and bustle of the town. Somewhere quiet for people to recover. To take a break from their stressful, pressured lives and regenerate, get healthy before returning to the homes and families waiting for them.

Kenzie pulled into the parking lot and couldn't identify any particular parking space that she should take. It was quiet; just a few cars from the night staff were there. And a long black hearse backed into one of the staff stalls near the doors. Kenzie pulled up to the big double doors and shut off the engine.

A security guard walked out to meet her as she grabbed her death kit and walked toward the doors. He held up his hand to stop her and send her back. "I'm sorry. You can't park there. And it turns out your services are not needed. You were called in error. Just a mistake."

Kenzie frowned at him. "I'm sorry?"

"You're from the ME's office, right? I'm sorry. You aren't actually supposed to be here."

"I was called about a death."

"Yes, that was wrong. You shouldn't have been. Someone who didn't know proper procedures…"

Kenzie shook her head, brushing aside his hand as he reached out to block her and send her back.

"I'm sorry, but once I am called to a scene, I have to attend."

"But you weren't supposed to be."

"Actually, I was. The ME's office is required to attend any deaths occurring at a psychiatric facility."

"There's no need." He blocked her more aggressively.

Kenzie looked him in the eye. "Look. I've told you that I'm required by law to attend. There's nothing I can do about it. There's nothing you can do to change my mind. I can call the cops to get them to remove you so I can get to the scene. Is that what I need to do?"

He hesitated, wavering.

"Events have been set into motion," Kenzie reiterated. "I need to follow a certain procedure. Will you let me in, or do I have to call for backup?"

He lowered his hand slowly. "Well, I don't see why you have to be so stubborn about it…"

"It's the procedure I have to follow. If it's just an unattended death, someone who died in his sleep, then my time here will be very short. I'll be in and out with no fuss or bother. But you can't stop me from attending, or there will be consequences. You don't want to get arrested for impeding an investigation, do you?"

"You're not even the police," the guard grumbled, but he stepped back and grudgingly let Kenzie pass.

Kenzie preceded him into the building, but she did not have any idea where to find the body once she got there. She looked around. There was no one waiting inside to escort her to her patient. The security guard trailed her in.

"Can you point me in the right direction?" Kenzie asked. "Or should I just wander around looking for a body?"

"Down the hall and to the right," he grumbled. Then he apparently decided he should do more than just give her directions. "I'll show you."

Once they were down the first hallway, Kenzie could hear voices. Casual, routine voices, doctors or nurses talking to each other as they completed their duties. The security guard led her around another corner, and then she could see where people were gathered in the hall, pulled in by the specter of death.

There were a couple of young men in dress pants and white shirts wheeling a gurney into a patient's room. Kenzie hadn't seen an ambulance nearby. And ambulance attendants did not wear white shirts.

But she *had* seen a hearse.

"Excuse me!" Kenzie hurried forward as the two men bent over in the cramped space, preparing to lift the body onto the gurney. "Don't touch that body. Get back."

They stopped and looked at her, frowning. A doctor standing outside the room, gray hair and a dark mustache, prominent creases between his eyes, turned to her.

"Who are you?"

"Dr. Kenzie Kirsch. Assistant to the Medical Examiner."

"What are you doing here?"

Kenzie motioned to the body on the floor. "Looking after him."

"You're not needed here. This is a doctor-attended death. No need for the medical examiner to be involved."

"Well, I was called, and I am required to be called for all deaths in a psychiatric facility. And you," Kenzie motioned again to the funeral home workers. "You can go. Leave me your card. I'll call you when we finish with the body."

The two men looked at each other, not sure what to do.

"You're not taking this body," Kenzie said firmly.

"Look, Dr. Kirsch," the doctor spoke to her again. "This is all just a misunderstanding. I'm sorry. You should not have been called. Just let the funeral home take care of the body, and you go home and get your sleep."

"I need to fulfill my obligations. There is a strict procedure to be followed. I'm sure you've seen it all before. It shouldn't take me too long."

There was no blood on the floor, no apparent injuries. The man had clearly not been shot or stabbed. Kenzie looked down at him, her mind already running through checklists. What she would need to see, what pictures she would take. What she would tell Carlos or whoever came from the office to transport the body, what she would tell death investigators if she needed someone else there to help collect evidence.

"This is ridiculous," the doctor complained.

"Well, it doesn't hurt you. It's just one extra step before the deceased is sent on to the funeral home. We make sure that there are no concerns, and then the family gets the body," Kenzie assured him. Of course, the doctor was old enough to know all of this anyway. He was obviously not inexperienced. He knew the way it all worked.

The doctor threw up his hands in frustration, defeated. "Fine. Do what you have to do. But it is over my objection. You don't need to be here. It is just a waste of time."

"Well, better a waste of time than having to exhume a body later on down the line!" Kenzie told him cheerfully.

The funeral home attendants backed off to let Kenzie do her examination. One of them hemmed and hawed for a minute, then handed her a business card, and he and his associate took their gurney and departed. The doctor shook his head.

"Everything would have been taken care of in five minutes. Now I'm going to still have a dead body here in two hours. Before long, we'll have patients getting up and finding one of their number dead on the floor."

Kenzie rolled her eyes as she performed the first checks on the body to ensure the patient was properly deceased. She would have the body out of there well before patients started getting up in the morning. Unless both of the ME office trucks broke down, and if that were the case, she knew of a hearse that could probably be pressed into service…

She rested her fingertips lightly on the man's arm. "How long has he been here, Dr.….?"

He hesitated, then supplied his name. "Dr. Alvarez. He can't have been there for very long. He was asleep. Must have just gotten up… maybe he wasn't feeling well and went to get help, or something for indigestion, and just keeled over."

Kenzie shook her head. "He's in full rigor."

"That can't be right."

"How long did you wait before calling someone?"

"It takes a while for people to get here," he said cautiously. "Maybe… an hour?"

It had been less than an hour since Kenzie had been called, but she knew that it hadn't been Dr. Alvarez who had called her. He had an accent and an older voice. More of an attitude, almost a bullying manner. The man who had called her on the phone had been softer spoken, younger, probably not very experienced in dealing with unexpected deaths. And that someone had called her after Dr. Alvarez had called the funeral home.

"It's been more than an hour," Kenzie disagreed. "Full rigor. That takes a significant amount of time."

But something wasn't right, because the body was still quite warm to the touch. And it shouldn't be if he had been lying on the floor for long enough for full rigor set in. Kenzie took a couple of temperature readings, writing them down and noting the time and the stage of rigor mortis. When time of death indicators did not match the witness stories or each other, there was good reason to be careful. Measure everything twice. Note everything down with dates, times, and pictures. Interview all witnesses to get their stories before they started to change.

"He hasn't been lying there for hours," Alvarez objected.

Kenzie just shook her head. She knew he was wrong or lying to her. Or there was something very strange going on with her newest patient.

3

Kenzie continued to examine the body, a little bit at a time, head to toe, front and back. Much more carefully than she would typically inspect the body at the scene when there didn't appear to be any sign of illness or violence. She usually saved her detailed examination for the postmortem. But she didn't like what was happening at this scene already, which meant that she doubled down and did more than she had to.

The patient was a Black man, tall and thin, with the high cheekbones and very dark skin of a Nigerian. He was wearing what appeared to be institution-issued pajamas. Not the skimpy johnny worn at a hospital, open in the rear, but pants and a button-up shirt in matching lightweight blue-gray cotton. Such dark skin made it difficult to appreciate any bruises. She would have to use an alternative light source at the morgue, which would help make them a little more visible. She thought there might be bruising on the forearms and a swelling on the back of his head. There were no lacerations, nothing that appeared to be caused by a weapon. He could have hit his head anywhere. Falling out of bed. Looking for something that had fallen under a table and sitting up before he was clear of it. It might have happened before he was admitted to the facility.

"What can you tell me about the decedent?" she asked Dr. Alvarez. "Name, medical history?"

"This is Leander Isah. Bipolar. Began experiencing symptoms as an older teen. He has been in and out of institutions since then."

"Do you have his medication protocol?"

"It will be on the computer, of course."

"I would like to get a copy of that. And anything else you can provide about his treatment and medical history, when he was admitted, anything unusual that may have happened the last few days."

Alvarez looked at her silently, not agreeing or disagreeing. Kenzie wondered if he were going to be a problem. Or maybe she would be dealing with another doctor or the director of the facility.

"This was a natural death," Alvarez told her.

"It may have been," Kenzie said neutrally.

The frown lines between his brows deepened, as if Kenzie agreeing with him was more of a concern than her disagreeing.

Other people watched from doorways and the nursing station partway down the hall. Kenzie glanced up at the approach of a young man in blue scrubs. He was very handsome, very young. New on the job. He was trying to see or listen to what they were saying without being too obvious about it. Finding a reason to come a little farther down the hall to gather more intelligence about what was happening. Because he knew some-thing, or just because he was interested in the gossip?

"Did you know Mr. Isah?" Kenzie asked him without raising her voice.

Alvarez looked perplexed at her question, then realized she was talking to someone else and turned his head to see. The nurse swallowed and looked at Alvarez before answering. Alvarez gave a curt nod to grant him permission to answer.

"I have treated him," he admitted.

"What was he on? Do you know his med protocol?"

The man scratched his neck, thinking about it, then shook his head. "I'm not sure. SSRIs. A mood stabilizer, but I don't remember which one. I think maybe… an antipsychotic? It will all be on the computer."

Kenzie nodded her agreement. "How about night meds? A sedative? Sleep aid?"

"Yes, most of them take a sleep aid."

Kenzie knew that when Zachary was admitted to the hospital psych ward, they usually insisted on his taking a sleep aid at night, even though he didn't like to. Sleep was essential to good mental health. And, she suspected, very important to the mental health of the nurses and other members of the staff, who liked things to be quiet and uneventful at night. It wasn't good if patients were up wandering around and getting involved in altercations.

"Did he wander at night? Was it unusual to see him out of bed?"

The nurse didn't say anything, looking again at Dr. Alvarez.

"What's your name?" Kenzie asked.

"Nurse Craig, ma'am."

"Nurse Craig. You were usually here at night?"

"Not always…" He looked around as if searching for a calendar or clock that would give him the answer. He looked back at Kenzie. "Uh… yeah, I guess I was usually here at night."

"And you knew Mr. Isah? He had been here before, or he had been here for long enough this time that you were familiar with him?"

"Yes."

"And did he usually get up and wander at night? Is it unusual that he was out of his bed?"

Nurse Craig cast one more look at Dr. Alvarez and then nodded. "Yes, I don't think I had seen him out of bed many times before. Maybe once. Not like some of the wanderers."

"How was he today? Were there any issues?"

A long silence. Kenzie busied herself with examining the body and didn't stare at Nurse Craig, but waited for him to decide to talk.

"He was agitated earlier. Earlier in the day."

"Over something in particular?"

"No. He was just… yelling a lot. Upset at the people around him. Acting like everyone was getting in his way."

"What is he normally like?"

"Very quiet."

"He doesn't yell?"

"No. Not like some of the patients."

Kenzie smiled and nodded. She remembered what it was like working in a hospital. People yelling for attention all the time. All her time being taken up by a few patients, and then she didn't have as much time for the quieter, more compliant patients. Time that they needed.

"Did something happen to upset him? Or had his meds been changed? Any change at all in health or care protocol the last few days?"

"Uh…" Craig looked at Alvarez. "You'd have to check with his doctors on any changes in their orders…"

"Anything?" Kenzie asked Alvarez, rather than arguing that the nurses probably knew all the patients' meds better than the doctors. The doctors would have to check his chart. The nurses would probably know at a glance if something had changed or was wrong.

"I'll have to look at his treatment protocol," Alvarez said vaguely. "Though I'm sure it had nothing to do with Mr. Isah's death."

"If you don't know what it was, how can you know if it had anything to do with his death?"

He favored her with a glare but didn't try to argue. Kenzie had dealt with doctors like him before. Big egos. Thought they were superior to everyone else and couldn't possibly make a mistake. Usually, it was the surgeons, but Kenzie was sure that psychiatrists were not immune.

"What do you know about what happened here today?" She asked Alvarez. "Rigor mortis says that Mr. Isah has been dead for some time."

As with the bruises, his complexion made it harder to see the livor mortis, where the blood in his body had settled due to gravity after his death. Kenzie could see faint shadows, but they were hard to make out and it would be easier with the ALS. She hadn't brought the portable light source with her in the death kit, not expecting to need it at a hospital death scene.

So she couldn't say for sure that his body had been moved after death, but she was pretty sure that it had. His positioning didn't feel right, though she had nothing to back it up yet. Her subconscious had noted something that hadn't yet made it to her conscious mind. She made a mental note to follow up on the livor mortis during the autopsy.

She stepped back from the body to take a few pictures, recording his position.

"Will *you* be doing the postmortem?" Alvarez asked, looking down his nose at Kenzie. "Or will that be handled by someone more senior?"

"I will be handling it," Kenzie said steadily. "So if there is anything that you want me to know before I start, you should tell me."

He pressed his lips together, sniffed, and shook his head.

Kenzie looked at Nurse Craig. "I want to talk to you alone. And anyone else who was involved in Mr. Isah's care."

"For a death by natural causes?" Alvarez challenged. "Why would you need to do that?"

"I need to make a full inquiry into anything that I believe needs investigation. And this case is starting off very strangely. You trying to keep me from the scene. The body being in full rigor but still warm. Your insistence that it was natural causes when we don't yet know anything of his meds or physical condition. He should have been asleep in his bed, not up. All of those things are setting off alarms for me."

"That's ridiculous."

He didn't say *what* was ridiculous or how Kenzie might have misinterpreted the circumstances. Just went straight for a complaint that her investigation was ridiculous. Nice.

4

Kenzie called Carlos and got him out of bed to come to the scene for transport. She didn't want to leave the body alone while she was conducting her interview with Nurse Craig and anyone else there who she might need to talk to. There was enough going on that was out of the ordinary that she didn't want to risk her death scene being "sanitized" by someone while she was out of sight. When Carlos got there, she took him to the side and explained as much as she could in whispers. He nodded seriously and didn't make any complaint about how boring it was to babysit a dead body while she interviewed the staff.

"Is there somewhere we could meet privately?" Kenzie asked Nurse Craig.

They both glanced at Alvarez for his objection, but he kept his mouth shut. Kenzie wanted to interview him too, but she had a feeling he wouldn't tell her any more than he already had. He would be a problem. She would just have to work around him. Hopefully, the doctors that were on during the day shift would be more helpful.

Nurse Craig led her to a family visit room and motioned to one of the soft chairs. He stood with his hand on the door, trying to decide whether to close it or to keep it open. He looked at Kenzie, brows raised.

"Closed," Kenzie suggested.

He gave a nod and closed the door. "Sorry, I don't mean to be stupid," he said, flushing a little. "Some women don't like to be shut alone in a room with a man… I didn't want to make you uncomfortable."

"Thank you, that was very thoughtful." Kenzie motioned for him to take the seat adjacent to her. She exhaled, took a deep breath, and let it out again. "Okay. This is all a bit of a mess, isn't it?"

He shrugged as he sat down, as if he didn't know what she was talking about.

"Information is being withheld. Evidence is being covered up or altered. I take it Dr. Alvarez has already told you to be careful of what you say, maybe to tell me a fake story to put me off the trail, but that wouldn't be a good idea. I would suggest that you *don't* do that."

"A fake story!" He tried, but failed, to sound outraged. It just came out as a weak, token protest. Kenzie was sure he wanted to share what had really happened. That's why he had been hanging around and had gotten close enough to involve himself in the conversation.

"I'm glad you're going to tell me the truth," Kenzie said. "That will make it much easier."

"Well, yeah. I wouldn't tell you a story."

"But you might neglect to tell me the full truth."

He grimaced. "I honestly don't know what happened here tonight. Like I said, Leander was agitated earlier. He was having a bad day. I don't know if it was a bad reaction to medication or something else. But whenever I saw him, he was upset, complaining, trying to get someone's attention to tell them his story. But nothing would settle him down. He wasn't normally like that."

"Has he had a recent med change?"

He hesitated for just a second, then dove into it. "He was in a drug trial."

"Oh. So he was on an experimental drug."

Craig nodded seriously. "An… experimental treatment," he agreed. "I don't know what drug or drugs were involved. They don't tell us. And they don't tell us who was participating, but it was pretty obvious which patients were in the trial."

"Because of their behavior?"

"Because their treatment schedules changed. Their meds, when they had therapy, which doctors were around for therapy at that time, stuff like that. I wasn't told which patients were on the drug and which were on a placebo… but it was obvious."

"Good? Bad?"

"I don't know."

Kenzie cocked her head. "You don't know?"

"Well… with therapy and medications, it can be hard to know, sometimes. Sometimes therapy… shakes something loose and, even though it makes the patient upset and unhappy for a few days, it was something that they needed to get out in the open and deal with. And sometimes quiet behavior just means… withdrawal. Shutting down. Deeper depression."

Kenzie nodded slowly. "You're right. That makes sense."

She thought about Zachary and his memories resurfacing when triggered by an adverse event. It made his life hell, and he complained about not being able to repress the memories as he used to, to just shove them down and forget about them again. Dr. B said that it was his brain's way of healing. Getting the memories out instead of keeping them inside to fester. It meant he was stronger and more equipped to deal with them now than he had been as a child or teenager. Even though Zachary would have preferred everything to go back to the way it was if he had a choice, it was better to heal. To deal with those memories in a positive, permanent way.

"So Isah was on this new experimental protocol. Changes to his meds and therapy schedule, who he was having therapy sessions with. Have I got that right?"

Craig nodded. He glanced toward the closed door to reassure himself that they could not be overheard by anyone. "This is private patient information, and we've also signed confidentiality agreements about any experimental studies that are going on. Even though I don't really know anything, I don't know if I should even be telling you that there *is* an experimental protocol."

"You are required by law to disclose information to me in the course of my investigation. It's not the same as when you have a living patient. Even then, if you knew that a patient was on a drug that had a negative interaction with another drug they were going to treat him with, you would be expected to disclose that information as early as possible."

Craig nodded slowly, but obviously was not entirely reassured.

"I appreciate that you have been eager to help," Kenzie told him. "I wish that everyone would be as helpful as you."

Rather than looking pleased at her compliment, Craig looked shame-faced. Kenzie tried to meet his eyes and figure out what was going on that he felt so embarrassed about, but he didn't look at her. He just stared down at the swirling, muted colors of the carpet.

"Did Isah have friends among the other patients? Anyone that he hung around with? Talked to?"

"No, not really. They all keep to themselves, mostly. They have group therapy meetings, but they don't... play cards together and that kind of thing, not really. People come and go, and some of them know each other from when they have been here before or at other institutions together. But no... really close friendships."

"Can you tell me what happened to Mr. Isah? How he died? How he was discovered?"

"I had other patients to deal with. Dr. Alvarez and the others were taking care of Leander."

"Dr. Alvarez and the others? What were they all doing?"

"I don't know. I wasn't there. I know he had been agitated, and... Dr. Alvarez was trying to calm him down. He had been violent toward the staff earlier, in the cafeteria, and they are very strict about that kind of thing here. A lot of places, they look the other way when patients are physically abusive of the staff, but at Persons... they don't tolerate it."

"How had Leander been violent?" Kenzie asked, adopting Craig's usage of the patient's first name.

"Just... pushing people away. Striking out. It wasn't... directed or angry. Just... you know how someone is when they don't want anyone to touch them. Defensive. Overstimulated."

"Sure." Kenzie nodded. "I can understand that. So what did they do about it if they have a low tolerance for any kind of staff abuse? They threatened to have him transferred somewhere else, maybe? Kick him out of the program?"

"They called the cops." At Kenzie's look, Craig went on quickly, trying to fill in all the details before Kenzie could complain or express her disbelief. "I don't think they charged him with anything. It was a threat... showing him they were willing to act. And they have private security here, and they all kind of look alike, the actual police and the private cops. For someone like Leander… I don't think he knew the difference. He thought that the cops were always watching him. And if he didn't shape up, they would hurt him."

Kenzie nodded slowly.

"They could put him in jail for assault," Craig said. "But they wouldn't hurt him."

"But he hadn't had a good experience with police in the past," Kenzie guessed.

"He was from Africa. Who knows what kind of police force they had in the country he came from. Probably all corrupt. You hear that about them over there. And the police here… they're no picnic either. Not when you're a Black person with mental illness."

Kenzie could well imagine. She'd seen it on TV. Isah would be taken for a gang banger, an addict, a homeless person. The kind of person society did not want out in public, but were eager to put behind bars. The police would be conditioned to react to him as a violent offender rather than as a man needing help and extra patience and care.

5

So what happened?" Kenzie asked. "When the police came? I take it that didn't help to settle him down."

"I don't know," Craig said, shaking his head. "I wasn't there when it happened. I was taking care of another patient. There was a ruckus. I knew something was going on. It was loud at first. But then he quieted down. I figured it probably took a needle to do it. He wasn't going to be quiet just because the police came. Probably made it worse."

"You think he was given a sedative?"

"Probably. They should have done that earlier rather than calling the police. There wasn't any way calling the police would make anything better."

"So, by the time you finished with your other patient, everything was quiet again?"

Craig nodded. His eyes skittered to the side.

"What did the other staff members say about it?"

"Nothing. Everyone was just quiet. The doctor said that he was asleep and to just leave him be, let him sleep it off."

"Was that Dr. Alvarez?"

"No, before he came on shift. Dr. Miller."

"So he didn't think that Leander needed any monitoring?"

"No. Said to just stay out of there."

"And you did?"

Craig looked at her, frowning. "I do what I'm told."

"Had Leander been sedated like that before?"

"Yes, sure… just the day before."

"And there hadn't been any complications? So you figured everything would be fine?"

"It seemed like everything was okay. He'd been okay before, and the doctor said not to disturb him, so I didn't."

"You don't have a policy about patients having to be monitored when they have been sedated? Every fifteen minutes or every hour?"

"Well… yeah. If the doctor doesn't say not to."

"But he said not to, so you didn't."

He shrugged uncomfortably. "I do what I'm told," he repeated.

"When did you know that something was wrong, then?"

"When…" He swallowed hard. "When Dr. Alvarez told me to call the funeral home."

"And you decided to call me."

His eyes didn't meet hers. "I just called the funeral home, like I was told. That's what we do when there is a death. The doctor decides if anyone needs to be notified, and the family says which funeral home they want to use, and we call them to pick him up."

Kenzie had known as soon as she heard Nurse Craig's voice that he had been the one who had called her.

"You wouldn't take it upon yourself to call the ME's office unless you thought something was wrong," she said.

"No," Craig agreed.

"It's a good thing you did call me. If there was something suspicious about his death, no one would ever have known. He would have been embalmed and buried or cremated without anyone ever looking into it."

"Seemed like… something that should be reported."

Kenzie nodded. "Any death in a psychiatric facility is supposed to go through the ME's office. And any death that is suspicious in any way."

"It wasn't really suspicious, though, was it?" Craig asked, his brow furrowing again. "I mean, patients do die. And when they're on as many meds as psychiatric patients are…"

"If it was a drug interaction, that should be investigated."

He shrugged. "I suppose. But there are a lot of deaths in hospitals that are not suspicious…"

Kenzie nodded. "Of course. But the laws regarding psychiatric facilities are stricter than those for a hospital. And you had a feeling about this one. And you should follow that feeling. I think you did the right thing, whether they agree or not."

He nodded slowly, but still looked unsure of whether she was right. He had stepped outside the bounds of what he had been told to do and was afraid he would lose his job over it. Afraid that he had gone too far and should have just kept his head down and listened.

"You did the right thing," Kenzie told him firmly.

"What do you think it was? You think it was a drug interaction?"

"I don't know. We'll do a tox screen. We'll need to know what drug trial they were doing. It could be a lot of things. Sometimes the cause remains unknown in a case like this. Sudden cardiac death."

"Excited delirium?" Craig asked.

Kenzie grimaced. "I won't attribute a death to excited delirium," she said. "There is enough controversy over whether that is really a thing or is just a way of covering up deaths in custody."

"You don't think it is real?"

Kenzie pursed her lips, considering her answer. She didn't want to step on anyone's toes. She didn't want to be accused of slandering anyone who had ever attributed a death to excited delirium or to say that it was just another way of saying that cops had been too violent with a detainee.

"I think that 'excited delirium' is unproven and has been applied much too broadly in the past. I think that there are actual physical reasons that someone dies in custody. Not just that the detainee was… overly excited or upset. I don't think there is a psychological state of excitement that kills someone without any other cause."

Craig didn't seem pleased by her answer. "But it does happen that way sometimes."

Kenzie shook her head, pressing her lips together. "I don't have the years of experience that Dr. Wiltshire has. I'll discuss it with him. Maybe he has seen cases where it is warranted. But the cases I have seen in medical school or the media… there has been a lot more going on than a patient just being overly excited or upset."

"I've seen it happen."

"Then maybe those cases should be reviewed by an ME as well. Have they been?"

He shook his head, clamming up.

Kenzie wondered just how many other cases there had been and if they had all been at Persons. Craig didn't look old enough to have worked at too many other places.

There was another nurse on duty. Michelle Hernandez seemed to be a very cheerful, bright-eyed young woman. Her oval face and black-framed glasses gave her an open and pleasant appearance. Kenzie wondered about two young nurses both being put on the night shift. It seemed like the presence of an older nurse would have been beneficial. The young nurses were equipped to handle most of the stuff they would see from one night to the next, when patients were mostly just sleeping. But occasionally, events such as Isah's death needed the steadying hand of a more mature, experienced nurse.

Hernandez seemed more curious than upset by the events of the night.

"So you're really a medical examiner?" she asked Kenzie eagerly. "Don't you get tired of dealing with bodies and wish you had a live patient now and then?"

Kenzie laughed. "I am an assistant to the medical examiner. And… no, I don't really wish that any of my patients were alive. That might be a little awkward, you know…" she teased.

Hernandez seemed not to follow her meaning for a moment, then giggled. "I didn't mean if any of the people you are supposed to autopsy were alive. I mean… don't you wish you had a real, live person to treat sometimes? Maybe a hybrid practice, where you see live patients for other things? I think… it would be really boring and depressing to only deal with dead bodies all the time."

"It isn't, actually. I find it quite interesting. I guess that I do get a little depressed by it sometimes… when a child is killed, or something else upsetting. But I try to distance myself from those things. Just view it as a puzzle that needs to be solved. I can't totally divorce my feelings from a case, but I try to look at each one as objectively as possible and not to take the stress home with me."

Would Zachary agree she didn't take her job stress home with her? Kenzie knew that she sometimes couldn't help it. Some cases *did* get to her. Or the outside pressures to make a certain finding or release her findings within a certain timeframe because of political issues.

But she had *tried* not to take the stress home with her, that was true. She hadn't said that she was always successful.

"I think I would find it really hard," Hernandez confided.

"Well, you might not be suited for pathology. If you picked your profession because you like to help people and be part of the healing process, then you're not going to find a lot of fulfillment in dealing with patients who are already deceased. But I got into it more because… I like to solve a puzzle and to dig down and find the truth. I'm more about… helping the survivors to accept what happened and seeing justice done."

Hernandez smiled sunnily, giving a nod of understanding. "That makes sense. It's more… like you're a cop than like a doctor."

Kenzie shrugged. "I am a doctor and not a cop… but yes, it is a lot more about solving crimes and protecting the public than any other job as a doctor. But not all the deaths that I investigate are homicides. There are plenty that are natural causes, accidental death, or suicide. And sometimes what I discover might help researchers to understand the processes that result in death… and maybe help to treat diseases in different ways in the future."

"That's so interesting."

Kenzie thought that they had exhausted the topic. Hernandez had been the one to introduce it, but she seemed to be done with it now. Kenzie readjusted her position, leaning toward Hernandez, trying to suggest by her body language that they were in this together, helping each other out. Kenzie was someone Hernandez could trust.

"How well did you know the patient who died tonight? Mr. Isah."

"Not real well. He hadn't been here for a long time. But I'm often on day shifts, so I probably knew him better than Anthony."

At Kenzie's puzzled look, she clarified. "Nurse Craig. Anthony."

"Ah. of course. He didn't mention his first name. So he's on nights more often, and you're on days more often? Or evenly split between the two?"

"I just take nights now and then. When I need a bit more money or pay rent, or someone calls out sick and they need someone to cover."

"I see. And how had Isah been? Have there been any changes in his behavior lately?"

Hernandez stared past Kenzie, thinking about it. "He's bipolar, so it is hard to say what is 'normal' in his case. Sometimes he is down, very quiet, in a depressive phase, and sometimes he is more…" She trailed off, searching for words.

"Happy? Outgoing?" Kenzie suggested.

"No… um… irritable. Intense. Maybe bordering on paranoia sometimes."

Kenzie nodded. "I see. And lately, he has been in a more manic state? More irritable and paranoid?"

"Yeah. Really… I haven't seen him that bad before. If I didn't know better, I would have thought he was off his meds. But he was still taking them. Sometimes a medication stops working without warning, and I think that might have been the case with Leander."

"You don't think that it was something they had added to his protocol? Maybe an experimental drug?"

"Oh… we're not told when they are put into those programs. We're not supposed to know. So that we can be more objective. If we are told that a patient is on a new drug, we might see symptoms or changes where there aren't any. Like the placebo effect."

"Anthony said that he thought Leander was part of the drug trial."

"Well… he might have been. I don't know for sure. But I hadn't seen him so agitated before."

Kenzie nodded. "I'll get his medical records, and we'll see what they show."

"I hope it isn't anything to do with the trial," Hernandez said, her face a picture of concern. "Research into effective treatments for psychiatric illnesses is so important. If it gets out that there was a death related to the trial…" She shook her head. "That would be really bad. We need the research."

"I hope it wasn't either," Kenzie agreed. "We'll just have to see what shows up in the postmortem."

There wasn't any point in staying around waiting for the other staff members to arrive. That was still several hours away. So Kenzie had Carlos take Mr. Isah to the morgue, and she headed home.

There was still a chance of several hours of sleep before she had to be at the office. Kenzie found herself pretty wired after the events at Persons. Still, she knew that if she didn't get a few hours of sleep, she would eventually hit a wall at work and not be able to get all the way through her day. So she returned home.

There were lights on in the house, so chances were that Zachary was still awake. He should have gone back to bed, but he rarely got more than a few hours of sleep and probably didn't think there would be any harm in waiting for Kenzie for a while to see if she got home in good time.

Still, Kenzie was quiet unlocking the door and stepping into the kitchen from the garage. It was possible Zachary had fallen asleep while working on something, leaving the lights on. She peeked into the living room, where she had seen the lamp on, and Zachary looked up from his laptop.

"Hey. How did it go?"

Kenzie divested her outer clothing and purse. "Hard to say. It was an interesting experience, I'll say that. I've never had anyone try to send me away from a scene before."

"Send you away?"

"Send me back… say that I wasn't needed."

Zachary looked comically puzzled. "Because… no one was dead?" he suggested.

"Oh, someone was dead. In fact, the funeral home got there ahead of me, and I had to chase them off. Another thing I've never had to do before."

"You *did* have an interesting night." He patted the couch next to him. "Come tell me about it."

Kenzie hesitated.

"Or did you want to go back to bed?" Zachary asked. "You probably need the sleep."

"Well, I do, but I'm too wired to sleep right away. Need some time to unwind first."

"Here? Or did you want to get changed? Stretch out in bed?"

"Yeah, bed would be nice," Kenzie admitted. She didn't want to wait until she was too tired to change and didn't want to lie down in bed with her work clothes on. She would need to shower and change in the morning anyway. She wasn't saving any time by already being dressed. She looked at the clock on the wall. It wasn't that late. She could still get a few hours in.

Zachary closed his laptop and stood up from the couch. "Let's go back to bed, then."

In a few minutes, they were cuddled together in bed. Kenzie knew she wouldn't fall asleep any time soon, but at least she was comfortable and in the right place. When the adrenaline wore off and her circadian rhythm reasserted itself, she could just drift off.

"So," Zachary prompted. "Why exactly did they try to chase you off? If there was a dead body, you couldn't just go home, could you? They can't just send it to the funeral home without your sign-off."

"Well, depending on the circumstances, they can. The ME's office doesn't investigate every single death in the state. Only the ones that we deem necessary. If someone dies under their doctor's care, and the doctor doesn't have any concerns, then he can sign the death certificate and the family is free to make all the necessary arrangements."

"Okay," Zachary was nodding. "Makes sense. Is that what happened? The doctor decided he just wanted to sign the death certificate himself?"

"Yes. Only, I had already been called to the scene. And the protocol says that once we've been called to a death, we have to follow through. They can't just change their minds and say they don't want us to look at it anymore."

"Then why did they?"

"It was an interesting case… It was one of the other staff members who thought that it should be looked at more carefully. So when the doctor told him to call the funeral home, he did, but first he called me."

"Sneaky," Zachary approved. "Good thing you got there before the funeral home had taken the body away."

"Well, I wouldn't have had to go far to find it again. They wouldn't have been able to have it cremated before I had an order to get it back again. But it's always better to examine the body in situ. See the scene. Anything else that is of note."

"Did the doctor know who had called you?"

"I'm not sure. The nurse who called didn't want me to say anything about it in front of the others. But they must have figured out what was happening because they knew who I was when I got there. The security guard tried to send me home and so did the doctor. Maybe they didn't know who had made the call, or the nurse pretended it was a mistake and he thought he was supposed to call me. I don't know. Everything is still pretty mixed up."

"Sounds like it. So what was this death? It was at a hospital?"

"Private psychiatric care."

He stiffened slightly. Usually if Zachary needed help during a depressive cycle, he went to the psych ward at the public hospital. But he had recently had an experience with a private hospital, and it had not been positive. Kenzie didn't think he would choose to go to a private psych hospital any time in the near future.

"Not that one," Kenzie assured him.

He let out a breath. "Good. Glad to hear that."

She could tell he was thinking it over. Whether she had ever been called out to that facility. Whether she ever would be. How close he had come to being the next body on the medical examiner's table. But they would probably have done the same as Persons. Called for the funeral home rather than the medical examiner. Or maybe even conveniently lost the body. Or arranged for the funeral home transporters to lose it. How many cases were slipping through the cracks because the doctors simply didn't want the medical examiner checking up on their work?

Any doctor could request that the medical examiner review a case. But they could also make cases that the medical examiner should have reviewed disappear.

"So can a doctor do that whenever he wants?" Zachary asked, his brain going down the same path as Kenzie's. "What's to stop him from bypassing the medical examiner on cases that should be going to you? Cases that are clearly malpractice or homicide?"

"There are certain cases that are mandated by law. The medical examiner must review them, and the doctor can't just sign the death certificate himself. Sudden deaths, unattended deaths, anything violent or the least bit suspicious—and deaths in a psychiatric facility. There is a list of cases that always have to go to the medical examiner."

"And what's to stop them from just calling the funeral home in those cases?"

Kenzie shrugged. "Medical ethics. If they *have* any. And I imagine if the funeral home director got suspicious or spoke up about cases coming to him that should be going through the medical examiner's office. I've never actually heard of it happening, so I'm not sure what the checks and balances are... they assume that doctors are professional and won't take the risk. But of course... you hear about doctors being accused of every other human frailty, so what is to stop them from breaching their professional ethics?"

"It could be quite a scam."

"Could be... but I don't think it is something that is happening all the time. I haven't heard about it before. I think I would have... maybe gotten a memo to watch out for this or a warning that it was going on."

Zachary nodded. He rubbed Kenzie's back in soothing, slow circles. "Did it look like an interesting case? If the nurse thought it was something you needed to look into, it wasn't just a routine death."

"I don't know yet. No obvious sign of what he died from. We'll see what shows up when I have him on the table. It wasn't an obviously violent case. But he might have been in a drug trial, so I have to be concerned about whatever drug he was on and whether it could have contributed to his death. And there was police involvement earlier in the day."

"The police. Why?"

Kenzie spoke slowly, trying to figure out the best way to tell him about it. She was worried that it might be too close to a death that he had witnessed as a child in custody. Annie. The girl in the cell next to Zachary's. It burned her up just thinking of how he had been treated as a child and teenager. Being housed in isolation in the children's center because he could not comply with the rules. Imprisoned for being a kid with ADHD and PTSD that no one cared about.

"Kenz?"

"He'd been having trouble earlier. Agitated and violent. They had called the police to deal with him."

"Did they take him into custody?"

"No, doesn't sound like it. I think they ended up just leaving. But trying to deal with psychiatric patients by bullying and threatening them…" Kenzie shook her head.

"You can't bully someone into being neurotypical," Zachary contributed.

"No. That's exactly right. It's unfair and just not the right way to deal with people. I get it about holding people responsible for their own behavior, but when the person is clearly mentally ill and cannot comply with your rules… I think you need to find another way to deal with it. Calling the cops to deal with someone manic when you haven't tried every other possible solution…"

"They must have their own isolation rooms. Soft restraints. Something."

"Yeah. I didn't look around, but they seemed like they were fully equipped. They had their own security as well. And if he was unmanageable there, maybe they should have transferred him to the hospital. They could treat him there."

"You don't know how he died?"

Kenzie thought about it for a minute. "No. There are still too many possibilities. Without having conducted an autopsy, I can't really guess. It might have been medication, or heart disease, or an altercation earlier in the day. He could even have been in restraints and ended up hurting himself trying to escape."

7

At some point in the night, Kenzie had fallen asleep. She couldn't remember finishing her conversation with Zachary, so she had probably dropped off in the middle of it and slept soundly until her alarm went off in the morning. She turned it off and closed her eyes, falling quickly asleep again. She could go in a little late. Mr. Isah wasn't going to get any deader. Anything else that was waiting on her desk or computer could wait.

She had felt worn to the bone since Dr. Wiltshire had been gone. She tried not to take too much on, to keep to a reasonable schedule. It wouldn't do anyone any good if she burned out and couldn't do anything. Better to go slowly and fall a little behind for a while than to end up sick and unable to do anything or to face her work again.

She wasn't sure how much time had passed before Zachary was shaking her shoulder gently to wake her up.

"Kenzie. Sorry. Do you want to keep sleeping? I didn't know if I should wake you up. How long do you want to sleep?"

"Mmm." Kenzie stretched her muscles and rubbed her eyes. She wasn't ready to get up yet. And if she had to look at the time and answer his questions about when to get up, she would no longer be able to sleep.

"Your phone has been ringing," Zachary told her. "It's on silent."

"It's been ringing?"

"Yeah."

Kenzie swore under her breath. Who was so desperate to reach her? Why couldn't they wait until she was ready to get to the office and dig into her work? Did it really matter what time it was when she performed the autopsy?

She reached for the phone but couldn't find it. Zachary picked it up, detached the charge cord, and put it into her hand. Kenzie didn't recognize the number, but the same one was repeated several times.

With a groan, Kenzie pushed herself up into a sitting position. She rubbed her eyes and looked around. It was late but, as she had told herself earlier, she could start a little late after being out at a call the night before. She had that flexibility.

The number wasn't blocked, so it wasn't the governor or some other high-powered government official who wanted to know what was going on with a case. It wasn't Dr. Wiltshire; she knew his number, unless he'd had to change it for some reason. So who was harassing her so early and couldn't wait for her to get in?

Zachary put a glass of water on Kenzie's side table and left the room. He could be such a thoughtful guy when he wasn't distracted—or completely lost in his own world. Kenzie had a few swallows of water and cleared her throat before tapping the number to dial back her persistent caller.

He apparently recognized her number or had already added it to his contacts directory. He had a calm, pleasant tone, despite the fact that he had been calling her relentlessly. "Ah, Dr. Kirsch, thank you for getting back to me."

"I didn't check my voicemail. I just saw that you have been calling me. Who is this?"

"This is Dr. Cook."

Kenzie shook her head, the name not ringing any bells. "From Persons?" she guessed.

"Uh... no. I have been assigned to the Medical Examiner's Office. To assist while Dr. Wiltshire is healing."

"Oh! I wasn't told that someone had been assigned. I'm sorry. When will you be starting?"

"Today. That is, I would be... if I could. The office has not been opened, and I'm afraid I haven't yet been provided with keys."

"You're there now?"

"Yes."

Kenzie swore. "Sorry, like I said, I had no idea that you had even been assigned, let alone that you were starting today. I was out on a call late last night, so I slept in this morning." Kenzie ran her fingers through her curly hair, mussed and knotted from sleep. "I won't be able to get in for… about an hour. There's a coffee shop on the main floor of the building that is quite nice. Why don't you relax there for a while, and I'll meet you and give you the tour?"

"I have already discovered it and have been working on Wi-Fi. Although, of course, it has nothing to do with the Medical Examiner's Office. Just personal stuff."

"Okay. Hang out there, and I'll get in as quickly as possible."

After disconnecting, Kenzie got out of bed and went to look for Zachary.

"Would you believe that they got me a substitute pathologist without even telling me? And the guy's been waiting there since…" Kenzie looked at the call log on her phone. "Seven-thirty, the eager beaver. They had to do it on a day that I slept in, didn't they?"

"Of course," Zachary agreed. "So, are you heading straight in?"

"Not without a shower and coffee, I'm not. He's hanging out at Boys in Brew, so he's fine until I get there. He isn't just standing around waiting."

"Do you want me to get your toast and coffee? Or are you just going to get something at Brew?"

"I'll start with a coffee here… and pick something else up when I get there."

Zachary nodded. "I'll get it going."

He stood up right away, so Kenzie didn't have to worry about whether he would remember to get the coffee started or would get lost in his work and forget all about it. She could hear him setting up the machine for another carafe as she returned to her room.

Kenzie looked around Boys in Brew when she arrived. It was populated mainly by cops going on or off duty, with a few visitors or rougher-looking customers who had just been released from interviews or an overnight stay at the jail. In the corner was a young man with a button-up shirt and a lab jacket typing industriously on his laptop. He looked up from his work, apparently feeling her eyes on him, and smiled. He started to close his computer to prepare to join her. She waved him down.

"Just give me a minute to grab some breakfast. Do you want another coffee? A Danish or muffin?"

"Oh, I've had enough this morning. I didn't want to just freeload on the WIFI, so I've been working my way through more coffee and breakfast than I would normally have."

"Okay. I'll be with you in a minute. Finish what you were doing. No need to stop mid-sentence."

He raised the lid of his half-closed laptop again. Kenzie watched him while she waited in line and then waited for the barista to prepare her breakfast order.

Dr. Cook looked way too young and way too handsome to be a medical examiner or even just an assistant medical examiner. Kenzie had gone back to school several years after graduating, so she had been older than most of her classmates. She was used to doctors who looked younger than she was. But Dr. Cook seemed too young to even have a degree, let alone a doctorate. His hair was neatly styled, a little long on top and short in the back. His eyes were a clear blue that Kenzie suspected was boosted by a pair of colored contacts. Did anyone have such bright blue eyes naturally? He looked like he had walked off the set of *The Young and the Restless* rather than being an actual medical doctor.

The barista caught Kenzie's attention and handed her the breakfast order. Dr. Cook finished what he was doing and joined her.

"Sorry to keep you waiting," Kenzie apologized. "Like I said, I was out late to a scene last night and had no idea that you would be here this morning, or I would have arrived much earlier."

"No problem, doctor."

"Call me Kenzie."

He nodded, but didn't.

Kenzie led him to the security desk in front of the elevator, where he showed the guard his newly minted security pass and introduced himself.

"Did they give you a parking space?" Kenzie asked. "You can get in from the parking garage as well. You don't have to go all the way around."

"I don't think I'm senior enough to qualify for a parking space. I'm just temporary."

Kenzie shrugged. She didn't have any say in it. She knew that the parking garage was not full. There were plenty of spaces available. But how they were assigned was up to the police department and building management. Kenzie was just glad to have one herself. She wouldn't want to have to park her baby on the street.

"Are you new in Roxboro?" Kenzie asked Dr. Cook. "I don't think we've run into each other before."

"Yes, I'm out of Burlington. I've taken a long-term room at the hotel so that I'm not commuting back and forth. There's no point in wasting all that time and gas. I'll be here for a few weeks… however long it takes Dr. Wiltshire to get back on his feet. Or on his hands again. And then I'll head back to Burlington and see where they want to assign me next."

"Is that by choice? Or are you looking for something permanent?"

"I'm happy to be temping for a while. Figure out what I want to do. What I enjoy the most."

"And you're a pathologist?"

"Yes. I'm fully qualified for the position."

"Good. I didn't know how strict they are with their qualifications. If they would assign us someone from general practice or obstetrics or something. Officially, all that is required is to be a medical doctor."

"I've done my fair share of postmortems and death investigation reports."

"That's great." Kenzie was glad that she wouldn't have to train him. She still found herself in the position of apprenticing to Dr. Wiltshire, learning from him. While she had now done a few autopsies completely on her own, she preferred to have someone experienced she could ask questions of or bounce ideas off of.

"I'm here to assist you, not to cause you more work," Dr. Cook told her.

"Glad to hear it."

Kenzie gave him a quick tour of the office, past her reception desk at the outside of the suite where she answered phones and dealt with the public, to the meeting rooms, kitchen/breakroom, morgue, autopsy, and Dr. Wiltshire's office, from which she assumed Dr. Cook would be working until Dr. Wiltshire was back and fully functional. For the time being, Dr. Wiltshire was only coming in occasionally to consult with Kenzie and to sign off on various reports and documentation. Now that his hand was healing, he had dialed back on the painkillers and could focus longer than he had been initially. However, he still wasn't up to full days, even just doing paperwork.

"Okay." Dr. Cook put his laptop bag down in Dr. Wiltshire's office and hung his outer gear on the coat rack. "So where do you need me first? It looks like you have a fair bit of paperwork out there."

"It's not bad. I'm mostly caught up. An office like this goes through a *lot* of paper! I will want to do the Isah autopsy today. He is the body I was called in on last night. I want to make sure..." Kenzie trailed off, thinking about how to voice her concern. "I'm a little worried that there may be a problem at the private facility that he died at. Just a gut feeling..."

But it wasn't her gut. It was the fact that Nurse Craig had felt the need to go around his boss to bring the death to the attention of the medical examiner's office. It was the police involvement, experimental medications and protocols, and Isah's escalating violence. It was Dr. Alvarez's apparent attempt to cover up what had happened to Leander Isah and hurry the body to the funeral home without any examination.

But Dr. Cook didn't need to know all the details. She didn't want him to be biased by her feelings, but to approach the postmortem with the fresh eyes of an outsider. She shouldn't even have told him she had any concerns; that had just slipped out.

"Then we shall start with the autopsy," Dr. Cook agreed.

"If you can familiarize yourself with the morgue and get his body prepped for me, I'll just make sure there isn't anything urgent on voice-mail or email."

Dr. Cook agreed and returned to the morgue, impressing Kenzie by not getting turned around. He acted like he knew exactly what he was doing.

8

When Kenzie was finished processing the emails and voicemails that had arrived overnight to ensure that there was nothing more urgent than the new arrival, she returned to the autopsy to find that Dr. Cook had taken care of everything as she had asked. He had retrieved the right body, which George had already processed and cleaned up. He had it waiting on the autopsy table Kenzie usually used, which was pre-set to the right height for her to work comfortably. Or as comfortably as possible. If she had a longer post-mortem or several of them to do, she could get quite sore standing, reaching, cutting, and manipulating a body for that long. But that was just one of the things that a medical examiner had to be prepared for.

Leander Isah's clothing and the evidence bags containing any trace evidence collected for processing were arranged on the side counter should Kenzie need to examine anything more closely. The appropriate file was opened and on the computer screens, ready for her. Dr. Cook was clearly familiar with both the software and proper procedure, a time saver for Kenzie. She had been worried that she might have to walk him through everything, despite his being a pathologist and claiming that he had the experience necessary to do the job he had been assigned. When dealing with government bureaucracies, one never knew how much the people making the decisions on up the line understood what really happened in the ME's office and what their needs were.

"This all looks great, thank you," Kenzie told Dr. Cook.

"Is there anything else?"

"Nope, it looks like you've got everything ready. Dr. Wiltshire and I often work on separate postmortems at the same time so that we can consult each other on what we are doing. Mostly so that I can ask him questions or he can catch anything that I might miss or not be aware of. But I think we should do one together to start with. Then there are a couple of routine posts I haven't gotten to yet. We have a bit of a backlog because of Dr. Wiltshire's injury."

"That's why I'm here. You don't want me to start one of those while you do this one?"

"No. Let's do one together to get used to each other's processes."

Cook nodded his agreement. Kenzie washed up and donned the appropriate gloves and garb. Dr. Cook was ready to begin. Kenzie tapped the button on the floor for the recorder and announced the date and time, decedent's name and file number, and her own name. Cook announced his name, providing her with his first name, Jeffrey. She thought it suited him.

Kenzie began with the gross examination, talking to Dr. Cook as she began. A little self-conscious at first since it was the first time they had worked together.

"I didn't have an ALS at the death scene last night, so I want to use it today to identify any bruising. The victim has very dark skin, so it's hard to see any contusions under white light."

Dr. Cook murmured his agreement. Kenzie positioned the lights over the body and slowly worked her way down, head to toe, front and back.

"Victim has restraint bruises on the forearms. Some lighter bruises on the upper arms, possibly from being held down, but it is hard to tell for sure because they are faint." Kenzie measured and took pictures of the bruises. "Livor mortis in the chest makes it difficult to ascertain whether there is any peri-mortem bruising. When I arrived on the scene, the victim was on his back, but the livor mortis in the chest indicates he was prone, not supine, for some time after his death."

Kenzie paused in her examination of the body for bruises to tell Dr. Cook about the advanced rigor mortis, which suggested that the man had been dead for several hours before she had arrived, in contrast to the elevated body temperature, which indicated that death had been quite recent.

"Does that make any sense?"

Cook nodded slowly. "There have been some studies done… try a search for hyperthermia and rigor mortis or postmortem caloricity. It seems counterintuitive, but a high body temperature actually speeds rigor mortis and livor mortis. You would think that a warm body would develop rigor more slowly, that it would be something that only sets in as the body cools, but algor mortis—the cooling of the body—is not actually what causes the stiffening of the body or the settling of the blood. A higher body temperature *speeds* rigor. The full cycle of rigor mortis, from stiffening to release, can occur in just six hours instead of twenty-four." Cook lifted one of Isah's arms to demonstrate the rigor had already released.

"So what does that do to our time of death calculation?"

"Screws it up royally," Cook admitted. "Full rigor in three hours or less. It is impossible to tell anything from the body temperature if you don't know what temperature you are starting from. With such quick rigor, you know you are starting with a higher-than-normal temperature, but you don't know what that temperature was, so you don't have a starting point."

"So he had a fever."

Cook nodded. "Something raised his body temperature. Whether it was illness or something else, we don't yet know."

"We'll check for common viruses and white blood cell count," Kenzie determined, and gave the voice commands to add those tests to the appropriate section in the postmortem document on the monitor so she wouldn't forget them.

She looked at Cook. "Anything else? To do with the rigor mortis or hyperthermia?"

"Tox screens."

Kenzie nodded. They were already on the default checklist, so she didn't need to add them. Several drugs were known to raise body temperature. Maybe it was surprising that Kenzie hadn't encountered this problem before. How many drug addict autopsies had she done without realizing that a high body temperature could throw off all the Time of Death calculations?

"It's not particularly common," Cook told her, reading her face. "If you don't know that hyperthermia was present, you must work on the assumption that it was not."

"Right. Okay. Continuing with the contusions." Kenzie went on. No abdominal bruising. There was some faint bruising on the upper thighs and, when Kenzie rolled the body over, around the buttocks. Kenzie's eyes met Cook's. She dictated her findings to the computer, again taking pictures and measurements, and continued with the gross examination.

After reaching the victim's toes and the soles of his feet, Kenzie returned once more to his head where, at the scene, she had noticed a bump. She took pictures and measurements and probed the swelling with careful fingers.

"X-rays. We're going to want skull and chest at a minimum."

"Throat?" Cook suggested.

Kenzie looked back at Isah's throat, where she had found no bruising. She raised her brows at Cook, wondering what he had seen that she hadn't.

"The other bruises would indicate a pattern of restraint and assault. Even though we can't see anything on the throat, we should be extra careful to identify any hairline fractures to the hyoid or other structures. When death occurs very quickly from strangulation or blocking the blood flow to the brain, there may be very little bruising on the throat. TV would have you believe you will always have a ligature mark or finger bruises around the throat, but that is not the case. There may be no visible bruising. Especially in a patient with as much skin pigment as your victim."

Kenzie nodded. "Any other X-rays you would recommend?"

"Maybe knuckles, in case we have any boxer's fractures."

In case he had fought back against someone who had attacked him and broken his knuckles on their face.

"Okay."

Kenzie started to set up for the X-ray series that would be required and put on a lead apron. Rather than bother with the lead barrier himself, Dr. Cook left the autopsy and watched Kenzie from the observation room, getting a couple of bottles of water from the small fridge while he was there.

He returned once Kenzie was finished taking the X-rays, and they scrutinized each series on the monitors.

"No skull fracture," Kenzie observed. "I didn't think that the bump on the head was that serious."

"Might want to do more imaging to check for hematomas."

Kenzie nodded. It was still possible that there had been bleeding inside the brain, even without a skull fracture. The brain bounced around inside the skull, structures tearing, blood building up between the membranes, between the brain and the skull, or deeper within the brain. It didn't look like the head trauma was that bad, but even a whiplash with no impact could cause the brain to bounce around enough to start a bleed.

Kenzie magnified the X-rays of the throat several times, and they both searched it for any fractures on the hyoid bone, but it seemed to be undamaged.

"Here, though…" Kenzie turned to the chest series. Isah's sternum was clearly fractured, as were a couple of upper ribs. "CPR breaks?" she suggested to Cook.

"Possibly."

"But I don't see any bruising or swelling around them." Kenzie's brow furrowed as she looked at them as closely as possible.

"We can check more easily when you open him up."

Kenzie nodded.

There were no fresh fractures on the knuckles. But there were many bright white patches showing calcification from previous breaks.

"He must be a fighter," Kenzie suggested. But the man's very thin build did not suggest a street fighter or MMA fighter. He did not have the muscles she would expect on someone who fought professionally.

Cook shook his head. "I don't think so." He took over manipulating the images, zooming in and examining each finger individually. "These aren't boxer fractures."

"An old crush injury, maybe?" Cook was right; there were a lot of breaks, but they were not on or around the knuckles where she would expect them to be. But maybe something heavy had fallen on his hands.

Or they had been slammed in a door. Perhaps a heavy garage door rather than a car or house door.

"No. I've seen something like this before in cases of torture. All of these individual breaks in every finger. In an accident, a crush, or single impact, there is an epicenter where there are more breaks, shattering, and then fewer breaks as you move outward from the impact. Not methodical breaks across each finger like this."

Kenzie shook her head slowly, fighting a brief moment of nausea at the idea of torture, of each finger being methodically broken individually. "Poor guy."

"Yes," Cook agreed. "Where did he come from?"

"I don't know for sure. I don't have all his history. One of the nurses said that he was from Africa and had experienced police violence over there. Still, he didn't say which country it was. Africa is a pretty big place."

"And they have some pretty brutal police forces. I don't know whether they do that or not," he nodded to the X-rays of Isah's hand, "but several countries are well known for their level of police violence."

9

Kenzie looked at the clock.

"I'm going to need to take a break before we continue. Clear my head, use the bathroom, check the mail. Make sure that Julie got down to cover the phones."

Cook nodded. "Sure. Half an hour? An hour?"

"Probably just half an hour."

"What can I do for you while you're working on that?"

"Uh… I guess familiarize yourself with the files on Dr. Wiltshire's desk. Most of them are just reports ready to be released, but I don't want to do that without someone else looking at them first. Catch any possible errors, let me know if you think there is something else that should have been checked or discussed. Just backstop me."

"Sure. I can do that. I'm going to get another coffee, even though I don't need one." He gave her a model-perfect smile. "Can I get you one?"

"I can do that—"

"You had more things on your list than I have on mine. I'll do the coffee."

Kenzie shrugged and shook her head, stopping herself from objecting further. She was used to being the one to get Dr. Wiltshire his coffee and see to all the other administrative duties. It seemed backward to have Dr. Cook, her senior in experience, doing it. But he was there to support her in whatever ways she needed help while Dr. Wiltshire was unavailable. So if he volunteered to make the coffee, then she should let him make it.

"Of course," she said finally. "That would be great."

"Good. I'll bring it to you at the front desk?"

"Yeah."

He nodded his agreement and began to strip off his gloves and other protective gear. Kenzie did the same and walked out to her desk to check on Julie and the mail.

She worked rapidly through the mail and the forms that had been submitted in her in basket while catching up with Julie and seeing how long she would be able to help. Julie worked on contract with several law enforcement agencies in the building, so her time was not all Kenzie's. She had been covering more hours since Dr. Wiltshire's accident, but couldn't be there all the time. Kenzie covered the phones some of the time and forwarded them to voicemail the rest of the time. People were used to dealing with electronic communications and could fill out most of the forms they needed online, so they didn't need someone in the reception area all the time.

Dr. Cook walked out with a couple of cups of coffee, gave one to Kenzie, and offered the other to Julie.

"We haven't met, so I'm not sure how you like it. I'm Dr. Cook."

Julie smiled and giggled, took the coffee from him, and then shook his hand. "Julie. Nice to meet you."

"Dr. Cook has been assigned to help us with the backlog created by Dr. Wiltshire's injury," Kenzie told Julie, even though she already knew this much.

Julie smiled and nodded, her eyes shining as she looked the young Dr. Cook over. When Dr. Cook went back to the kitchen to get his own coffee and retire to Dr. Wiltshire's office, Julie looked at Kenzie, her eyebrows up and bright eyes snapping with excitement.

"He is so cute! Why didn't you warn me?" She patted at her hair as if he'd caught her right after getting out of bed or the shower.

"I didn't know I needed to," Kenzie laughed. "Don't you have a boyfriend?"

"Well, technically…"

Kenzie knew that Julie was practically engaged to the guy. She chuckled. "I'm going to call him and tell him you're making eyes at the new doctor."

Julie snorted. "Yeah, let him know that he'd better up his game if he wants to keep me."

"Well, no making eyes at Dr. Cook and distracting him from his job. He's supposed to be reading reports and helping with autopsies, not chasing after the admin staff."

"Who's making eyes? I'm making *plans*."

Kenzie sipped her coffee and went back to the mail, chuckling.

Kenzie was glad she had taken a break as she returned to the autopsy with fresh eyes and a refreshed outlook. It could take an effort not to be swept into the misfortunes that had brought victims to her table. She tended to take some cases a little too personally. As if she had been responsible for letting the tragedy take place in the first place.

Now, she'd had a chance to distance herself again and was ready to proceed. She suited up again.

"Anything else you think we should check before opening him up?" she asked Dr. Cook.

"I'd take some swabs of bodily fluids before going any further. Always best to get what you can before beginning the internal examination and potentially causing contamination."

Kenzie agreed and began with the various swabs and fluids they would need to test before opening the thoracic cavity. Each sample was carefully labeled and double-checked before going on to the next one. Cook didn't make her feel like he was hovering over her, waiting impatiently for her to get done, so Kenzie felt comfortable taking her time to ensure everything was double and triple checked. Better to get it right the first time.

Eventually, they were ready to begin with the Y-incision.

"Would you like to?" Kenzie asked, gesturing to the body. "You must be getting bored just watching."

Not to mention that she was interested in seeing his technique and making sure he was just as capable of doing a postmortem as he seemed to be at everything else.

Dr. Cook raised one brow. "Are you sure? You're doing just fine yourself. You said you just wanted the supervision."

"No reason both of us can't work it together."

"As long as you don't think I'm interfering in your case…"

"No. I'd just as soon have you participate."

He nodded and picked up a scalpel. "Besides, then you get a chance to see what I'm made of."

"Well, that too," Kenzie admitted. "But you haven't done anything to make me think that you're not fully capable. I don't think you're going to break down or go into hysterics."

"Or throw up?"

Kenzie shrugged. "Everyone throws up sometime. Just don't do it on the body."

He grinned and proceeded with a very neat and professional Y-incision. They both examined the sternum and fractured ribs, bringing the camera in close and magnifying the area.

"There's no bleeding," Kenzie pointed out.

"None at all," Cook agreed. "I would say that the resuscitation attempt occurred quite some time after death."

Kenzie made a note of their findings. She resisted the impulse to sigh. How long had Mr. Isah's body lain undiscovered before someone had realized he was deceased and attempted to resuscitate him?

It at least matched up with Nurse Craig's claim that he was told to just leave Isah alone to sleep off the sedation. No one had checked on him. No one knew he had died until it was far too late to do anything about it.

But at least that pointed toward natural or accidental causes rather than homicide. No one had been in with him. It had, at least on initial examination, not been a violent death.

"Do you have his medical records?" Dr. Cook asked.

"Still waiting for the facility to send me what they have. There was the suggestion that he might be involved in an experimental treatment."

"Oh? What sort of treatment?"

"I'm not sure. The nurse said he didn't know anything, and the doctor was difficult. The staff wasn't supposed to know who was in the trial. But there had been changes in his daily schedule and some observable changes in behavior."

"Good or bad changes?"

"More agitated. Sensitive about people in close proximity. It sounds negative, but might actually be a positive sign."

"Right," Dr. Cook agreed.

He motioned for Kenzie to take over and, without discussion, they began the dissection of the organs, trading off every so often so that they both had the chance to participate.

"Organs are congested with blood," Cook noticed.

"Yeah. Asphyxiation, do you think?"

"No froth in the lungs. I would suggest sudden cardiac death, perhaps due to a reaction to a medication or allergy. Perhaps a congenital disorder. We can run DNA for known mutations. Long QT syndrome and others."

Kenzie wouldn't mind if it turned out to be a natural death. She could just send the body to the funeral home without having to involve the police or worry about whether the culprit would ever be brought to justice.

10

So, how did everything turn out?" Zachary asked. "How is the substitute for Dr. Wiltshire?"

"He seems to be pretty good. I was worried at first about him being so young, but I don't think he's quite as young as he looks. Either that, or he was a prodigy and started medical school early. He has a good solid base, more experience than I have."

"Just a youngster?"

"Looks like some teen heartthrob."

"Oh, boy." Zachary put his hand over his heart and feigned concern. "Do I have reason to be jealous?"

"Yeah, I think you'd better be. Although Julie will probably get his phone number before me. She was pretty taken with him."

"Don't you already have his phone number?"

"Oh… that's right. I do. Well, then, you might have to settle for Julie, instead."

Zachary chuckled. "Well, I suppose if I have to settle for the younger woman… Wait, isn't she engaged?"

"Practically. But she said that she wants to keep her options open. I don't know if you could keep up with her, though, old man."

"I can barely keep up with you. I don't know how I would manage with anyone younger."

Kenzie laughed.

The screen on Zachary's phone flickered to life, and his eyes darted over to it.

"I'm going to change," Kenzie offered, "then we can get started on dinner."

"Sure."

But when Kenzie returned a few minutes later, Zachary's gaze was tightly focused on the phone in his hands, and he didn't even look up at her. Kenzie walked into the kitchen and started to bang around noisily, waiting for him to notice that she was back and could use some help getting dinner on the table. But there was no response from him.

She could march back into the living room, shake him out of his trance, and insist that he put away his phone and help her out. But that would result in their both being tense and upset and with Zachary making apologies, yet still distracted by his unfinished text conversation, making it difficult for him to get anything done or to engage with her at supper.

On the other hand, if she let him finish what he was doing on the phone then, even if he didn't help her prepare dinner, he would at least be able to hold a conversation with her while they ate. She could tell him a little about her autopsy, and he could tell her about whatever case he had spent most of his time on. They were each puzzle-solvers, interested in hearing about each other's investigations and trying to anticipate how things would turn out.

Unlike most of the people Kenzie knew, Zachary was not squeamish about autopsy discussions, even at the table. Even, occasionally, with pictures that would have turned most people off their feed. Maybe Zachary had spent so much of his time nauseated on his previous med cocktail that he had become accustomed to it.

She continued to work on dinner, and it was some time before Zachary wandered from the living room to the kitchen, his eyes still on his phone. Kenzie turned her body toward him and waited for him to say something.

"Kenz... It's Rhys."

Kenzie's stomach knotted. Rhys was a Black teen that Zachary had befriended during an investigation a couple of years earlier. A mostly non-speaking boy with lots of trauma in his past. He and Zachary shared some of the same sorrows and challenges. They had become friends despite the disparity in their ages.

He and Rhys communicated primarily through a messaging app on the phone since a spoken conversation was out of the question. Even Rhys's messages, communicated primarily in gifs and short phrases or single words, could be difficult to follow sometimes. Another puzzle-solving opportunity.

"Is he okay?" Kenzie asked, assuming from Zachary's tone that he was not. Something had to be wrong for him to use that cautious, concerned tone.

"He's been… the last few days, it has seemed like something was off. It just didn't feel right."

Kenzie nodded, encouraging him to go on.

"Then last night…"

Kenzie swallowed and waited. Then last night, what…? She hoped Zachary wasn't about to drop a bombshell about Rhys having committed suicide or something else equally horrible.

"Stanley Green saw him out at night, wandering. Alone in the dark."

Kenzie turned away for a moment to stir the pot and smooth out the expression on her face, then turned back to Zachary.

"He was okay, then? How did Stanley find him?"

Stanley was an old friend of Rhys's aunt. They had once expected to be married, but she had been abusive and Stanley had eventually withdrawn from her and her family, breaking things off. It wasn't until after her death that he had returned, deciding to be a male figure in Rhys's life, to try to fill a hole that had been left years before when Rhys's grandfather, who had been raising him, had been murdered.

"He was out on the streets near Stanley's house. I think… he must have gone to him for help. Wanted to talk to him. Or wanted some kind of help."

"What did he say? What did he want?"

"He didn't say. He was uncommunicative." Zachary held up his phone. Kenzie had assumed that it had been Rhys that he had been texting with, but she had been wrong. "They've been waiting most of the day in the emergency room, and he's just been admitted. But Vera and Stanley don't know what's wrong. Why he went looking for Stanley, and why he's stopped communicating altogether."

Kenzie's chest felt tight when she thought of Rhys shutting off the dribble of communication he had managed to keep going the last few years. It had been a challenging way for them all to live, but Rhys had seemed okay most of the time. He had seemed like a normal teenager, just one with communication problems. No teenager was completely happy. And Rhys had dealt with enough tragic and traumatic things that no one expected him to be happy and outgoing.

But losing that last bit of communication, having him go back to where he had been after his grandfather had been killed and everything in his life had been permanently changed, would be devastating for Vera, his grandmother. And for Zachary, who felt things deeply and had become very attached to his quiet young friend.

"I'm so sorry. Does Vera want you to go to the hospital?"

"No… I wouldn't be able to see him. And once she's finished with the admission, she'll go home. There's no point in her camping out at the hospital when she won't be able to see him."

"At her house, then? She probably wants to talk."

"It's Stanley who was texting me. I'm not sure what Vera will want. I'm sure Stanley will go there to keep her company…"

Kenzie looked helplessly at Zachary, unable to guess what he wanted from her.

"I just…" Zachary shook his head. "I don't know."

Kenzie opened her arms, and Zachary was immediately holding her, pressing himself against her, hanging on for dear life. Kenzie squeezed him, then just held him firmly, trying to communicate all her love and care to him. He was lost, struggling to find his way through this new challenge.

Zachary was sniffling, trying to hold back tears. Kenzie didn't tell him everything was fine or it would all turn out okay. That was unknowable. Rhys had lived a difficult life, and adolescence, with its hormones, bullies, and stresses, had been hard enough for Kenzie, raised by two loving parents and not dealing with the losses and abuse Rhys had suffered. His mental health was already tenuous, and something seemed to have put him over the edge.

Kenzie held on to Zachary. She pressed her cheek against his. "It's good that he was seeking help. That he was reaching out to Stanley. I think that's a good sign. A sign that he hasn't just cut himself off from the world. If his mutism has gotten worse, it's not necessarily because he chose not to communicate, but because whatever he wants to communicate is such a big deal for him."

Zachary nodded.

"He *wants* help, Zachary. He reached out to someone."

"Yeah." Zachary's voice was hoarse, almost breaking. "But why not me? What did he need? Why didn't he message one of us? He knows we'd do anything to help him."

"I don't know. Maybe it is something that he thinks Stanley can help him with better than you or me. Or Vera. You can offer him many things, but you're not a Black man, and maybe that's the perspective he needs right now. Or maybe... he feels like Stanley could protect him from something or give him some kind of opportunity that you and I can't."

"Do you think he'll be okay?"

"He's in the best place for him right now. You know the psych ward at the hospital. That's where you would want to go, isn't it? When you are having problems and know you need professional help, that's where you feel the most comfortable."

Zachary nodded. "Yeah. The staff is really good."

"You know they are. You've been there and experienced it. You know that they'll help him. They know what they're doing and are compassionate and professional."

"Yeah."

Of course, Zachary had also had a bad experience there with a nurse who wasn't so nice or professional. But Nurse Debbie was no longer there. She was behind bars for the crimes she had committed. Rhys wouldn't have to deal with her whispering lies in his ears.

"We can call later and see how he's doing. Vera can put you on his list so that the staff can talk to you. Once he's ready for visitors, we can go see him. You know it isn't the end of the world. He just needs to be somewhere safe right now."

Zachary cleared his throat. "He can't be out wandering the streets."

"Exactly. Even though he was trying to get help, that's not a safe way to get it. There are so many people who would take advantage of someone like him. I'm glad Stanley found him and that they took him to the hospital."

"Yeah."

Zachary finally pulled back from Kenzie. They both breathed, looking at each other, and then Zachary looked away, overwhelmed by the intensity of his emotions.

"I'll set the table."

Kenzie's first instinct was to tell him that he didn't need to do anything; she would take care of it and all he had to do was sit down and eat with her.

But it would be better if he had something to do to keep him busy. He was doing something with his hands and being helpful and productive. Sitting around in silent contemplation would not improve his outlook.

Kenzie turned back to the stove while he went to the cupboard and started to pull out the dishes to set the table.

He was back and forth between the table and cupboards too many times. It irritated Kenzie, but it wasn't Zachary's fault that he couldn't remember everything he needed the first time or that he might be intentionally dragging out the job so that it took as long as possible. She would have preferred that he went back into the living room and watched TV for a few minutes until dinner was ready, but that was what was best for her, not best for him. And he was the one who needed the support right now.

11

You think Rhys will get better?" Zachary asked tentatively.

Kenzie didn't answer right away, building time into her answer so that he would know she wasn't just responding off the cuff or brushing off his question as unimportant. It was a question that deserved due consideration and an answer that was thought out instead of just a programmed social response.

"I do think he'll get better," she said. "He has been doing pretty well this year. And he has lots of loving people in his circle that want to help him. He didn't try to harm himself. As far as we know, he hasn't been experiencing any new symptoms. This is probably… surfacing trauma that he hasn't dealt with yet. Something that he needs to have some counseling on. Maybe get a med change. Sometimes, a patient stops responding to a treatment. He's getting older, bigger, and is dealing with hormonal changes. I think they'll stabilize him fairly quickly, and he'll be able to go home."

Zachary adjusted and readjusted the table place settings. "Is that right?" he asked anxiously. "I know the forks are supposed to go on the left, but today, it just doesn't look right."

"Of course it doesn't look right," Kenzie told him slowly, "because it's left."

Zachary didn't respond for a minute, then looked at her in disbelief. "Are you teasing me?"

Kenzie shrugged and nodded. "I suppose I am."

"Don't you know that you're not supposed to tease someone when they are upset?"

"Why not?" Kenzie challenged. "It seems to me you could use a bit of cheering up. Something to laugh about."

He snorted. "I don't believe it. Do you have no social graces?"

But the corners of his mouth were turning up slightly now. His eyes took on a little life instead of being locked in that dark place Rhys's sudden decline had taken him.

"You're the kind of person who tells jokes at a funeral, aren't you?" he challenged.

"Or in the morgue. Yep. Sometimes, people can start out a little stiff. They need someone to loosen them up a bit."

He chuckled. "We should call you Morticia, like that woman on *The Addams Family.*"

"I always did like her." Kenzie started to remove pots from the stove and to transfer them to serving bowls. "And the little girl. Wednesday. She's a blast."

Zachary blew out a breath, his shoulders lowering a bit as some of the tension released. "You know my favorite character?"

Kenzie looked at him, then back at her work. "That's easy. Thing."

"Have I told you that before? How did you know?"

"Because he can be anywhere, do anything without being tied down to a body or brain. He doesn't have to deal with unwanted emotions. Is practically invisible. But very... *handy.*"

Zachary groaned. He took the serving bowls from her to put them on the table, and even remembered to get out serving spoons for them.

Kenzie kept an eye on Zachary throughout the evening. It was clear that he was still thinking about Rhys and wondering if everything would work out okay. But he tried to act as though his attention was on her and it was just a regular evening, with nothing on his mind. She was torn between encouraging him to discuss it with her—to get it off his chest and be honest about his feelings—and trying to keep him distracted and not focused on it, worried that his own mood might spiral downward.

It was that time of year. She had already been watching him for any signs that he was entering his usual depressive cycle, which would culminate on Christmas Eve, the anniversary of the fire that had changed his life forever. It would start to manifest sometime during the fall, and ramp up from there. But maybe on his new med protocol, they would be able to manage it better this year, and it would not end with a stay in the hospital psych ward to keep him from harming himself. They could have a quiet Christmas Eve at home, enjoying a few simple traditions that did not include candles or trees, and on Christmas morning, the crisis would pass.

He had promised to tell her when he started to go down that tunnel again so she could support him. They could discuss with his doctors whether increasing his medication doses was warranted and the best way to get through it with as few problems as possible. But it was possible that he wouldn't recognize when the depression started. Or that he would choose not to tell her, unwilling to bring her down or admit his vulnerability.

She had seen some subtle changes in the last couple of weeks and was worried that the crisis with Rhys would bring his symptoms on in full force much sooner than they would if he didn't have to deal with the extra stress, focused on his friend's pain and trauma.

"You can stop looking at me like that," Zachary said, not turning his face to look at her. He must have seen her look in his direction in his peripheral vision. She didn't see how he could have.

Kenzie pretended she had been looking past him at something else or staring into space. She readjusted her head and her gaze slightly. "What? Oh, was I looking at you? I was just thinking…"

"I'm fine," he snapped. "I'm not the one who had to go to the hospital."

"No, you're not," Kenzie agreed. "I'm sorry if you're feeling stressed about it."

"I'm not. You don't need to worry."

"Okay," Kenzie agreed lightly. "No worries, then."

He did turn his head to look at her for a moment, searching her expression, then turned back toward the TV again. Kenzie tried to focus on what they were watching and not worry about him. He was far too attuned to her feelings and would know if she were brooding.

Kenzie's phone rang. She looked down at it and saw Walter's name on the screen. She stood up from the couch and flashed the screen at Zachary so he would know that it was a personal call and not a work call, then retreated to the bedroom so she could talk to him privately and without distractions. She swiped the call while she was in the hallway, then answered it after she closed the bedroom door.

"Hi, Dad."

She sat down on the bed and made herself comfortable.

"MacKenzie! I'm glad I reached you. How are you doing?"

"I'm good. How about you?"

"In the pink. I was hoping that you wouldn't be stuck in the morgue this late."

"No. It would have to be an emergency for me to be there now. Something really urgent because of political implications or a mass casualty event."

"You get called out to murder scenes sometimes."

"Yes. You're right. Or a call-out. But then I would be at the site, not at the morgue. So, how have you been keeping yourself?"

"Nothing unusual." He gave her a few details of bills he was lobbying for or against. Nothing that really interested Kenzie. It was hard for her to see the importance of many of the bills presented at the legislature. So many of them were unsuccessful because they had no merit. If she couldn't immediately see how one of them might impact her own life, it was difficult to be concerned. She wasn't like Walter, who would dig deep down to sort out the possible areas that a seemingly benign bill could impact in the future. He was the passionate lobbyist, and she kind of felt like he would address anything that was of any concern. so she didn't have to worry about it herself.

Even though she knew that they weren't always on the same page on important issues.

She still felt like he would do everything necessary to protect his family.

"But, enough of that," Walter wrapped up. "You're not interested in politics."

"It all sounds very interesting," Kenzie told him. It was important to support him and to show interest in what concerned him, even if she didn't see the point most of the time. He was important to her. Therefore, what he was concerned about was important to her, too. "What are your plans for Christmas this year? Are you going to be around?"

There was a pause.

Kenzie had been thinking about Zachary and how she would need to tailor their holiday season around his needs. And how that would change, depending on whether he was at home or hospitalized.

She hadn't been thinking about Walter's mysterious disappearance on Christmas Day the year before.

According to him, he had simply gone into hiding when a certain Russian oligarch had been looking for him. While he considered whether to support the Russian's cause as he had initially promised. Realizing that the man he was helping was a mobster responsible for all kinds of atrocities against his fellow human beings, Walter had initially backed out of the deal. Until the Russians had coerced his cooperation by kidnapping Kenzie.

She suspected that he had not been in hiding over Christmas, as he had said, but had actually been abducted himself. However, the Russians had been unable to gain his cooperation until they had pushed the right button by threatening Kenzie's health and safety.

"I just meant… I wondered whether you were going somewhere special, or spending some time at Mom's, or…"

"I like to keep things pretty quiet for Christmas, so I doubt I'll be jetting off to Paris or Hawaii," Walter said, his voice smooth and not showing any signs of distress over her question. "I will probably at least stop in to see Lisa on Christmas Day. We usually spend a little time together that day."

Kenzie made a noise of agreement. As a family, they hadn't done anything big for Christmas since the death of Kenzie's younger sister, Amanda. But her parents did usually spend the day together, even though they had been divorced for years. Kenzie was determined to be a better daughter and spend at least a few hours with the two of them this year. As long as Zachary's health would allow it.

"That sounds good. I hope I'll be able to stop in and see the two of you."

"Make sure your mother knows. You don't want her to be working at the soup kitchen or another function when you happen to drop in. Coordinate your schedules if you can."

"I'll give her a call," Kenzie agreed. "I don't know exactly what we'll be able to do, and if it will just be me or both of us, but…"

"How is Zachary?" Walter asked. "Is he worse? Is that why you're thinking about it?"

"No, he's doing pretty good. He's on a good med cocktail right now, but I know he could start having worsening symptoms any time in the next few weeks."

"It must be difficult to anticipate that."

"Yeah. I am trying not to think about it too much. We don't know what will happen. We know he will likely hit a depressive cycle, but maybe the meds will control it better this year. He hasn't had to be hospitalized every year, even when he hasn't been taking meds regularly. So as long as…" Kenzie trailed off, thinking about Rhys.

"What?" Walter asked after a moment when she didn't finish. "There is something?"

"No. Yes. It's just that today, one of his friends, a young man he has been trying to help, was admitted to the hospital. He's had some kind of episode… I don't know how long it will take him to get over the bump in the road. It could be quick and he's out in a few days with a med adjustment, or it could be something that takes a long time to address. And of course…"

"And of course, you're worried about how Zachary will react to it. Whether it will bring him down."

Kenzie nodded and sighed. "Yes. I shouldn't worry so much about outside influences. It's more about how he's been doing up until now, and how the meds are working. Things like Rhys having problems don't necessarily trigger depression in him. It's just that the depression is already there, and other things might aggravate it… But I'm talking out of school, because he says he is okay, and I shouldn't be second-guessing him. Zachary is good. We're both just dealing with something upsetting. We are resilient, and it doesn't directly affect us."

"It's hard seeing friends go through difficult times."

"Yes. And this kid had been through so much already. Lots of trauma when he was younger. He deserves a break."

"Maybe they'll sort him out at the hospital. He'll be able to deal with someone there who knows how to handle him better."

"Yes. Maybe. We have a lot of good doctors here, and I should assume that they will be successful and that he'll be back on his feet and better than ever."

"I hope they do. For his sake and for yours."

"And his family's. His grandmother cares for him, and she could really use a break, too. Can you imagine raising a teenager at this stage of your life?"

"Oof," Walter grunted. "That would be pretty difficult. At this age, I expect to be free to go where I want to go and do what I want to do. Not to have to keep track of a teenager and make sure he is safe and stays on track. Especially one who is mentally… vulnerable. I would be worried all the time, wouldn't you?"

Kenzie had to admit that she would be. She wasn't sure how people could raise children without going mad with worry. How could parents let them out the door, knowing what kind of crazies and influences were out there? How did they raise children to be emotionally resilient, independent, and savvy? How could they let their kids be themselves and explore the world without having a nervous breakdown?

"I think it would be really hard," she agreed. "I can't even imagine dealing with a teenager *now*. They have… so many needs."

Walter chuckled. "And when the time comes, you just step up and do what you can, knowing that you're going to make mistakes because you're not perfect, and neither are they. You're going to set rules they don't like, and argue, and have to discipline them. But they're also very rewarding." His voice was warm. "Teenagers can also be wonderful creatures, full of vitality and a fresh worldview. Passionate, fun-loving, and excited by the world around them."

"Really?" Kenzie thought back. She didn't think that she had been all those things. She had tried to follow her parents' rules and to help take care of Amanda when she was sick and to think about the future and how she was going to make her mark on the world when the time came and she was free of the constraints of parents. But she'd been so bogged down with responsibility and worry over Amanda, she hadn't really gotten on her own path until years later, after Amanda's death. Then, she had suddenly realized that she wasn't where she wanted to be in life. Things had to change.

"You were a serious kid," Walter admitted. "Maybe you didn't have as much fun as your classmates. You were too focused on Amanda's health and her future… whatever it was."

"And then I gave her my kidney and thought that was all I would ever have to do and I was free to go and do whatever I wanted to."

"And didn't know what it was you wanted to do."

Kenzie laughed. "How did you know that?"

"I watched you struggle. We both did. You'd had lots of responsibility in your life, right up to giving Amanda a piece of yourself. Then she was cured, as long as the kidney functioned, and you didn't really have any idea where you wanted to go. All those parties and social events were meaningless."

He had understood Kenzie much better than she had thought. She had felt that she was on her own and that no one saw what was going on with her. She thought that the struggle had all been in her own head and that she looked like every other young adult venturing into the world and finding herself amidst the parties and plays, the friendships and suddenly serious adult relationships.

And maybe her struggle had been invisible to the rest of the world, but it had not gone unnoticed by her parents.

"Well, thanks for being there, Dad. I always knew you guys supported me in whatever I decided to do."

No matter how much they disagreed on politics and causes, Kenzie had always known that her parents would do anything she asked.

12

Kenzie worked her way through the lab results that had appeared in her email inbox and various other pieces of correspondence, some of which required her action, and some which did not. It was hard to keep up with everything when she had an increased role in performing postmortems and managing the medical examiner's office. But with Dr. Cook there to take some of the overflow, she should be able to relax a little. Start taking her Sundays off again. Get home in good time for dinner instead of being late half the time and forced to rely on frozen dinners, leftovers, or takeout every day of the week. It wasn't good for her to be overworked and overfed. Both came with negative consequences.

Kenzie opened a report from the toxicology lab and read the bolded words several times before they sank in. She looked at the name and checked that everything was right.

"A drug trial, my foot!" Kenzie exclaimed as she entered Dr. Wiltshire's office, now temporarily Dr. Cook's office. "Look at that!"

She threw the printed copy of the initial toxicology screen down on the desk in front of Dr. Cook. He raised his brows and picked up the paper, wondering what she was blowing up about. He pursed his lips as he read the scant details.

"MDMA," he said.

"Methylenedioxymethamphetamine. MDMA. Freakin' ecstasy!" Kenzie blew up. "They gave him ecstasy!"

Dr. Cook made a calming motion with his hands. "MDMA has a long history of use in psychotherapy. It has been used off and on for decades."

"How does giving patients a rave drug, a psychedelic, count as therapy? How does that help anyone?"

"You're going to need to calm down before you talk to anyone at Persons about it. You need to approach it quietly and calmly, or they won't tell you anything. Have a seat."

He nodded toward the visitor chair that Kenzie usually sat in when she spoke with Dr. Wiltshire. She didn't feel like sitting. She felt like going out and punching someone in the nose. What were they doing, dosing psychiatric patients with ecstasy? They were causing more problems than they would ever solve. She forced herself to sit down and tried to listen to what Dr. Cook had to say.

There were, of course, legitimate uses for many drugs that were abused. Just look at fentanyl. It was causing terrible problems on the street. Yet it was a very effective painkiller at the proper doses and could help patients immensely.

But fentanyl was not ecstasy. It was an opiate. A painkiller. People might abuse it, but it was developed to treat pain and worked in cases where nothing else did.

"MDMA can be helpful in working with traumatized and defensive patients," Dr. Cook explained. "It helps to open people up so that they can talk about their feelings, about the traumas they have been through. There are indications that it could be a very effective way of treating PTSD if used wisely."

Kenzie thought about Isah's broken fingers. Every single digit broken in multiple places. Trauma? No one could deny that the man had been through a traumatic experience. Whatever torture he had endured before coming to the United States, whether at the hands of the police or some other faction, was enough to cause anyone long-lasting trauma symptoms.

She took a deep breath and tried to control her emotional reaction to the discovery. To hold off judgment until she fully understood from Dr. Cook exactly how MDMA might have been used legitimately in Isah's treatment.

"Okay. So how does that work? Is it approved? You can't just give your patients whatever you like. MDMA is a controlled substance."

"There are ongoing trials. The doctor would have to be part of one of those studies to use it legitimately."

"And is Persons in an approved clinical trial?"

He shrugged. "I assume that will be part of your investigation. If you want me to make some phone calls, I can find out. If you think that is the best use of my time."

Kenzie rubbed the center of her forehead. "I've heard of drug trials for marijuana. Of course it has some medical uses. And there were LSD trials years ago. I thought they had all proven that psychedelics are too dangerous and don't have any therapeutic value. All this nonsense about 'opening minds' ended up failing on all counts, damaging people further. Those trials were all shut down, the doctors who performed them disgraced."

Cook seemed unperturbed by any of this. Kenzie didn't understand why he wasn't just as upset as she was. Someone had overdosed their patient on MDMA. They had killed a man, and she and Cook were calmly discussing ancient drug trials.

"I don't know if that is a fair representation of the LSD studies," Cook said. "They weren't exactly discredited, but there was a lot of negativity surrounding them. And maybe too many people willing to experiment, whether they really had a psychiatric disorder that could be treated with lysergic acid or not. It was more the cultural view of LSD with the war on drugs than hallucinogenics not being effective in treatment."

Kenzie rolled her eyes. "You're younger than I am. It isn't exactly like you can remember that."

"No," he smiled. "I wrote a paper on it."

"Oh, really. Does that mean you are pro-hallucinogenic? You believe that it is an appropriate and effective treatment?"

"Some of the studies have been very positive. I have seen cases where LSD or MDMA has changed someone's life. It has been called miraculous. People who have suffered from anxiety or trauma for years, crippled by it, plagued with nightmares, flashbacks, and the inability to move forward in their lives. Suddenly, after a few treatment sessions, they can get out, to move past the fear. To start to live normal lives again."

"Are these controlled trials? Or off-the-books experiments?"

"There has been a plethora of both." He shrugged and smiled in agreement with Kenzie's cynicism. "With Nixon's War on Drugs, any use of LSD, mushrooms, or MDMA for treatment had to go underground. It wasn't tolerated. There is good reason to keep drugs off the street, not to let kids and addicts experiment with them, mix them, overdose, and get into trouble. The War on Drugs was a good thing. And a bad one. There are a lot of people suffering from trauma now who don't have to. They could be treated effectively if they knew about it and got into a program."

"So you think that they were treating Isah legitimately."

"I have no idea. Do you?"

"I know that the nurse said he was part of a trial therapy. And that his behavior had changed."

"So you said. If you believe that the MDMA had anything to do with his death, then you will need to investigate it further."

"You don't think it did?" Kenzie challenged.

She wondered briefly if she were overreacting. If she were jumping to conclusions. But there was a connection between ecstasy and hyperthermia. She knew that much. Isah did have MDMA in his system and her death scene observations had shown that he was hyperthermic. It didn't take a huge rise in body temperature to kill a person. There was a clear line from MDMA to death by hyperthermia.

"What else was in the tox screen?" He looked down at the paper she had thrown at him. "No LSD. No street drugs. Just MDMA."

"It's only a preliminary result. There is still more testing to be done. They roll any positive results to us as fast as they come in. We don't know yet what other drugs might have been in his system."

"Well, this will help guide you in pursuing other testing. Was the MDMA pure? Was it mixed with something else that might have caused a reaction? Was it part of a trial being held at Persons or smuggled in or passed to him by another patient? Did he take it on his own, believing that it would help? Was he trying to commit suicide?"

Many questions needed to be pursued before Kenzie jumped to conclusions about what had happened to Isah. Maybe the MDMA had been a contributing factor, but only one of several. Or maybe it had been the only factor, and the staff at Persons were being reckless in their experiments. There had certainly been indications that they were trying to cover something up. Maybe she had just found out why.

13

Kenzie sat down across from Paul Casey, the director of Persons.

"So, explain to me what you are here about today," Casey told Kenzie, frowning and looking around his messy desk as if the answer might be there. He was a large man, spending too much time sitting at a desk. His short dark hair framed his round face, gray at the temples, and he had a small mustache over his lip. His clothes were rumpled-looking even though it was early in the day. As if he had slept in the brown leather couch in his office the previous night instead of at home in bed.

"I'm following up on the death of Leander Isah."

"So you said."

"We are waiting for the medical records you were going to send us."

"It will be sent. I don't see any particular urgency, considering he is already dead."

"We need them to conduct our investigation properly."

"Yes. I'll get them over to you."

He looked at the door, like it was time for Kenzie to leave. But she was just getting started. "Mr. Casey—it is *mister*, not doctor?"

"Yes." He looked irritated by this inquiry. "I am not a medical doctor. I have some background in medicine, but I am an administrator, not someone with my boots on the ground. Do I need to have a doctorate to have this conversation?"

"No, I just want to know for sure who I'm talking to. We need certain things to ascertain how Mr. Isah died. I know it is inconvenient for you, and maybe you think we don't need these records, but we do. It is my responsibility to investigate deaths like his and to find out what happened."

"Deaths like this? Mr. Isah was ill. He was under the care of a medical doctor. It is my understanding that the medical examiner does not investigate cases where the deceased was under the care of a medical doctor."

"We can. If we are called in, or in certain other cases, such as a death at a prison or a mental institution."

"You can't tell me that you have to autopsy every person who dies in a mental institution."

"I'm saying that we have to investigate it, yes. There won't necessarily be an autopsy required for every case. Still, we need to see what the circumstances are, investigate, and decide whether we need to do a postmortem."

"Every death," he repeated.

"Have you had other deaths here that have not been reported?" Kenzie asked suspiciously. It certainly sounded like it.

"No." He closed his mouth and shook his head. "Leander's death was the first we've had to deal with. That is why I was not familiar with the requirement."

"There haven't been any other deaths at this institution?"

Casey was sweating. He wiped his forehead with a limp-looking sleeve. "We are a fairly new facility."

"Where did you work before this?"

"I was at a clinic in Burlington."

"In charge of it? Like here?"

"Yes. Well, there was someone else over my head, but I was mostly in charge of how things were run. I do have experience in the industry."

"And was that clinic a mental institution?"

"Why?"

Kenzie favored him with a glare. She was the investigator. He was the one who was supposed to be answering the questions. And she was starting to suspect that he was not telling the truth. Not a word of it.

"Was it or was it not?"

"It wasn't *just* a mental institution. We did family counseling. Other outpatient services. Whatever we needed to do to serve that community."

"What community? Burlington?"

"Yes, but... I meant serving families who were... concerned with mental health."

"Who had people in their families who were being treated."

"But it wasn't all inpatient. Plenty of work was being done for walk-ins, families of patients, the school system, and all those touch points in the community..."

"And housing mentally ill patients."

"Yes. That was one of our services as well."

"So it is a mental institution. And we should have been investigating any deaths there, too. Were there any deaths while you were there?"

"No. It's not that common. Our patients are generally not physically ill. If they were, they would be treated at a hospital or medical clinic somewhere."

Kenzie wrote down a few notes. She would need to follow up on Casey's history and see just how many patients had died at the institutions he had run. It was pretty hard to keep track of any statistics if the bodies never came through the medical examiner's office. If they were sending them all directly to funeral homes, saying that they had died of natural causes, how would the funeral homes know any differently? How would the medical examiner ever hear about them? How could they keep on top of any problems in the system?

But she didn't want to back Casey so far into a corner that he wouldn't answer any of her questions. She didn't want him dummying up and going to his lawyer for advice. So she didn't ask him the names of the other institutions he had been at lately. It would be easy enough to find his employment history through other means and find out where he had been. If she couldn't find it easily herself, she could ask the police to find out for her. Or even Zachary. It wouldn't be hard for a private investigator to find out.

"So, now you know," Kenzie said, giving Casey a reassuring smile. "When there is a death here, it's like a death in custody at the prison or police station; we need to review it just to make sure that everything is being run properly and there aren't any concerns. I'm sure you won't have any trouble complying with that rule in the future."

"Of course not," Casey assured her. "We run a tight ship here. We follow all relevant laws and ensure that our patients receive the top medical care they deserve."

"It's a very important service," Kenzie told him. "Mental health is one of my passions as well. One of the things that my family foundation is putting money into, and that I am interested in for personal reasons as well. I think we need to do a lot more for the mentally ill than we do. Providing services like you are here."

Casey puffed out his chest proudly. Kenzie had learned from her father that she could rarely go wrong by complimenting people, even if it was over the top. People drank it in, felt that they deserved it, even if it wasn't sincere. It was a lot easier to deal with people if you complimented them. Preferably more than once.

"I see this as one of the most vital services in the community," Casey told her. "We have done a lot to improve our physical health over the last hundred years. Figured out a lot of things about how the human body works and made a lot of advancements in treatment and in extending life expectancy by decades. But what have we done by way of treating the mentally ill? We might have moved away from barbaric shock treatments, straitjackets, and people locked away in institutions for the rest of their lives, kept away from the public where they might upset people. But where are we on curing schizophrenia? Or even just finding effective treatments? Where are the drugs that are *effective* against depression, bipolar, anxiety, dementia, autism, ADHD? That don't just mask it, shave the peaks and valleys, or slow the progression?"

"Or PTSD," Kenzie suggested. "That should be treatable. And so many people suffer from it. And children with complex PTSD. We know what causes it, why can't we reverse the process? Why can't we do anything for these people?"

Casey leaned forward in his seat, nodding eagerly. "The number of PTSD cases has skyrocketed with lockdowns, school shootings, and the child pornography trade on the internet. Abuse is rampant. Children and spouses have no safe place to go. And when they escape it… It isn't over. They still suffer for years and decades afterward. Can you imagine all the pain?"

Kenzie adjusted her body language to mirror his. "And when people have these symptoms, this problem in their lives, what do we give them? Antidepressants and various kinds of talk therapy? Why is there so little we can do?"

"Persons is at the forefront of treatment of PTSD," Casey told her. "There are some fresh new—and older, proven—therapies that can help. You would be amazed at some of the miraculous recoveries we have seen. I think that PTSD is the perfect condition for us to target. It isn't congenital. It isn't genetic. It isn't caused by a virus or bacteria and is not progressive. It has been caused by a discrete event or series of events, and should be reversible. And in fact, we have proven that it can be reversed. *Permanently* reversed."

"That's amazing. And this is just through talk therapy? Behavioral stuff or EMDR?"

"No. And not antidepressants, either. The cutting edge in trauma recovery is hallucinogens."

Kenzie raised her eyebrows in a parody of surprise, hoping she wasn't overdoing it. "Hallucinogens? What do they have to do with trauma?"

"All of those gurus in the sixties and seventies who preached using psychedelics to alter your consciousness and open your mind were absolutely right. These altered states of consciousness and removing fears and anxieties are vital to treating PTSD. Combining these drugs with exposure therapy and helping patients to be able to talk about their trauma is life changing. People who couldn't even put into words what had happened to them, or couldn't even recall it, are able to face their traumas and move on from them."

Kenzie nodded slowly. "That's amazing. I had no idea. So, do you use LSD? Mushrooms?"

"Both are possibilities, and we find that different things may work for different people. But LSD is tricky and is hard to get approval for. The drug of choice is known as MDMA, which you may know as—"

"Ecstasy," Kenzie filled in. "But isn't that dangerous?"

"In a clinical setting? No, everything is carefully controlled, and we start with very small doses. It would be dangerous for people to experiment with it on their own, especially getting MDMA off the street, cut with who-knows-what other garbage, if it even is really MDMA and not some substitute. But in a carefully controlled treatment program, it is one of the most important tools in our arsenal."

"Huh." Kenzie nodded, hoping she looked impressed. "Isn't it amazing how some of these old cures and treatments come back around again in slightly different forms? I've heard that mushrooms were used by indigenous tribes for their psychoactive properties."

"Absolutely. It can be very helpful to look at how certain illnesses were treated by shamans and healers in all different societies. The ancient oral traditions of these cultures are steeped with all kinds of knowledge that we can tap into. Modern man is not necessarily smarter than primitive man."

"So you're using these methods now? Here at Persons?"

He nodded, then his eyes flickered with the sudden consciousness that he should be cautious about what he told her. That their life-changing therapies could have something to do with Isah's death. Or that they might be blamed. He stilled and looked at her, trying to decide if he had already said too much or if she were really interested in his responses.

"With MDMA and psilocybin?" Kenzie persisted.

"We really can't divulge anything about our patients' treatment plans. That is highly confidential, as are any drug trials or new treatments."

"But I do need to know this information as it relates to Mr. Isah. You are required by law to provide the medical examiner's office with the information we require to investigate his death."

"We cannot disclose any details of drug trials. Including who the participants are or were. Breaking the study controls will mean the trials cannot be used."

"And if you need to start new ones, I'm sure you will. It was suggested to me by one of the staff members that Mr. Isah was a subject in one of these trials. His therapy schedule had changed, and his behavior had been altered. I understand he was increasingly violent toward the staff, and there was an altercation the day he died."

"I don't think anyone in this facility had enough information to determine whether Leander was in one of the experimental programs. And violence is not a common reaction to MDMA."

"Maybe not, but agitation, anxiety, and panic attacks are not unheard of."

"At higher doses," Casey dismissed. "Not in the controlled doses that we use in our trials."

"So you would have investigated any deviations from the norm, anything that was not a known side effect of MDMA and the treatment program you were using."

"All of the patients, their reactions, and the program itself are being carefully monitored. We have plenty of protections in place. It is of the utmost importance to us that our patients are treated safely and that if there are any problems, they are addressed immediately. We'll have a team meeting, go over any problems, and come up with solutions before it goes any further. We are a small, agile company. We can make the necessary adjustments quickly."

"Even to a trial protocol? There must be things that you cannot just change on the fly. Controls and procedures that are in place."

"Still, if we felt that a patient's health was in danger, either because they were on the protocol or because they were not, then we would address that. We won't put our patients' lives in danger."

Kenzie nodded sagely as if satisfied by this. She had a lot more questions to be answered, but it was probably time to get the police there to ask. They were the ones who were trained in interrogation and investigation procedures. As a representative of the medical examiner's office, Kenzie was authorized to ask questions that pertained to the postmortem and investigation into Leander Isah's death, but she needed to get the police involved before going too far afield. And she didn't want to take the chance of spooking Casey into destroying records or convincing other members of the staff to cover things up.

"It's good to see that you put such a high priority on patients' safety," Kenzie told Casey. "So many places now seem to put profit above everything else. But I know that you are not like that."

14

This is Dr. Richards," Casey introduced a blond woman in a lab jacket to Kenzie. "She was the doctor in charge of Leander's care. She can answer some of your more specific questions about his background and treatment. And I'll check the status of those records you needed."

Kenzie got the feeling that he was more likely to stall on giving her Isah's medical records and information on the trial protocols they were running and Isah's involvement in the program. She really hoped that he would not go so far as to destroy information. One reason that she needed to get the police involved as quickly as possible. Kenzie was the best person to ask the medical questions, but the cops could go in with a subpoena and a search warrant and get their hands on the information she needed.

"Thank you," she murmured. "That would be very helpful."

Casey left Kenzie with Dr. Richards, glad, Kenzie was sure, that he was quit of her, for a little while at least. He had not been happy having to deal with her questions. He would be even less pleased about the police when they arrived.

Kenzie turned her attention to Dr. Richards, who took Kenzie to a family visiting room where she could sit in a comfortable chair and sip a bottle of water while they pretended to be cordial to each other.

The first thing Kenzie had noticed about Dr. Richards was her mass of blond, curly hair. Sitting facing each other, Kenzie found the woman's face even more striking. She was beautiful, perhaps more believable as a model than in the role of doctor. Even, well-proportioned features, expertly applied makeup, and doll-like "bedroom eyes" that Kenzie was sure Richards used to her full advantage if she were ever pulled over by the cops for speeding or had to convince a store clerk to allow her to return a product that was not normally returnable.

And how did it affect her relationship with her patients? She would be alluring or threatening to men, depending on how secure they were. Or maybe both alluring and a threat at the same time. And women... Dr. Richards had probably been dealing with the jealousy of the women around her all her adult life.

She wasn't young like Dr. Cook. Older than Kenzie, perhaps heading toward fifty or even sixty. It was hard to tell with the makeup and the youthful curls arranged around her face. She had a lot of fine lines around her eyes and mouth. The hair was probably bleached and dyed, professionally highlighted to look sun-kissed. Kenzie was sure she did not get that much time out in the sun with a busy doctor's practice. A sweet floral scent floated around Kenzie when Dr. Richards sat down.

"So you are with the medical examiner's office," Dr. Richards said, sounding surprised and interested. "You are certainly not what I would have thought of on hearing your profession."

"You don't look particularly like a doctor in a mental institution either," Kenzie pointed out.

Richards laughed softly. "You know, I suppose you're right. We are both used to dealing with people's prejudices and preconceptions about what someone who lurks in the morgue or spends her days in the halls of the cuckoo's nest should look like. We've both kind of... broken the mold."

Kenzie had to admit, despite having to fight people's biases against women doctors and against their idea of what a woman in the medical profession or in the morgue should look like, that she had to fight the same biases in herself when she looked at Richards. Dr. Richards wasn't the blocky-faced, bullying, sexless woman that might be portrayed on a TV show. Just as Kenzie was no Morticia Addams.

"Funny how we have certain expectations," Kenzie agreed.

"Amazing. Society expects that two women as attractive as you and I wouldn't have two brain cells to rub together, forget actually getting through medical school and having a successful practice." Richards raised her hands, palms up, and shrugged. "Yet here we are. Tell me about your job."

"What do you want to know?" Kenzie returned, surprised by the question. She was there to talk to Richards about her treatment of Leander Isah, but Richards was leading with Kenzie's role. "I investigate suspicious or sudden deaths. See whether there has been any foul play or if the death could have been prevented. As I was telling Mr. Casey, any death in a mental institution is treated the same as a death in custody in the prison or police station, so we are required to investigate Mr.—Leander's death. To nail down the cause and manner of death."

Richards was nodding. "Of course. I understand that. It sounds like a very interesting job."

"Most people find it pretty morbid, but I enjoy solving a puzzle, seeing how our bodies work—or don't work, as the case may be. Human bodies are much more resilient than we give them credit for. Many of us are walking around with genetic mutations or tumors that we will never know about, pain that we can't identify the source of, organs or blood vessels in the wrong locations..." Kenzie shook her head. "And yet we survive and thrive."

"Until we don't," Richards offered dryly.

"Yep. And then it is my job to identify which of those things—or some outside event—caused your death. It's fascinating work."

Richards leaned back in her chair, smiling and nodding. "So, tell me what you have discovered about our Leander. I was shocked to hear of his passing. I know he wasn't in the best of health, but I certainly didn't expect him to die."

"I am still investigating, which is why I am here looking for records and the opportunity to talk to you and anyone else involved in his care. I was quite surprised to discover that he had MDMA in his bloodstream."

Dr. Richards chuckled at this. "Most people don't know about the use of hallucinogenics in the treatment of mental health conditions. Or if they have heard about it, they believe it was abandoned back in the seventies. And, of course, it was for a time. Or went underground. When legitimate treatments are vilified, it can set medicine back by decades. But we are now in the position where people are more open to these methods of treatment again. I think that the use of medical marijuana has helped. People can see that something once considered a tool of the devil has many legitimate medical uses, from glaucoma to nausea, pain control, and anxiety. It makes them more open to the possibility that other chemicals they consider 'bad drugs' can be used for good."

"Like healing trauma victims."

"Exactly."

"What can you tell me about Mr. Isah and his treatment?"

"Well, we have to be careful there for several reasons. Of course there is doctor-patient confidentiality..."

"Which is not an issue any longer."

"And we have also all signed nondisclosure agreements with regard to certain treatment programs."

"Because they are experimental? Or for other reasons?"

"As we've just covered... society has certain negative opinions about some of the available treatments. Even if these are well-established ways to treat trauma patients and help remove inhibitions, they are looked at with a certain amount of skepticism. We have to be able to control the dialogue, to make sure that they are presented the right way so that people can understand how they are being used and how helpful they are."

"I don't see how that stops you from talking to me about the treatments Mr. Isah was receiving."

"Well, I might need to talk to our corporate attorney about whether I can do that under the terms of the NDA."

"The NDA can't tell you to do something illegal, and withholding vital information about a death from the medical examiner is a breach of the law."

Dr. Richards frowned, but she did not argue the point.

"What can I tell you about Leander...? He has had mental health issues for many years, with symptoms initially emerging when he was a teenager, which is pretty typical. He had a lot of negative encounters with doctors and law enforcement in his native country. They are not well-known for treating the mentally ill with any compassion or understanding. He came here as a refugee after proving torture and demonstrating his life was at risk. He's lucky he got in before they tightened up immigration. If he tried now… with his mental illness diagnoses, I don't think he would get in, no matter what shape he was in."

Kenzie shook her head. "How terrible."

"It was. And it is still something that happens all over the world. We are lucky here, and yet I'm sure you know that even in the most progressive countries, there is still a lot of prejudice against the mentally ill. Lots of abuse, people who target vulnerable populations. Many of our homeless are the mentally ill who simply have nowhere to go. Nowhere safe. Most of those on the streets will be incarcerated at some point. We opened the doors to release people from the asylums and pushed them into the prison system instead."

"Had Leander been incarcerated?"

"Nothing of any length. Mostly just the types of misdemeanors that the homeless and mentally ill are charged with—loitering, vagrancy, disturbing the peace, public intoxication or urination." She gave a little shrug. "Where are they supposed to go? What are they supposed to do?"

"And he could afford to come to Persons?" Kenzie asked, making a motion that encompassed the institution. "How did he get placement in a private institution?"

"He was able to access it through a grant. There are foundations and government programs that provide 'scholarships' for those who can't afford it to get better medical treatment than they would be able to access through the public hospitals. Or specific treatment programs that are not offered through the public system."

"I assume the government doesn't support or provide any hallucinogenic treatments."

"They will," Richards said with certainty. "The number of people suffering from PTSD and other trauma-related illnesses will make it impossible to ignore the fact that there is a solution out there. People will not allow the government to blithely push aside a treatment that is so effective for so many people. It may take time, but they will have to accept it sooner or later."

Kenzie suspected she was probably right. The population wasn't likely to accept it if word got out that hallucinogenics were more effective than any other treatment. People would be self-medicating. The government would be forced to step in and start regulating the industry and making sure it was available to more than just an elite few.

"How was Leander responding to the hallucinogenic program?"

Richards didn't answer at first, pondering the question. "I think he was doing very well here. I know we all hoped to see positive results very soon. The treatments were having an effect on him."

"Good or bad?"

"It can be very difficult to process trauma. Very tough on the sufferer. Painful, dealing with flashbacks and anxiety, feeling like you're right in the midst of it again. That's one reason we recommend hallucinogenics. It allows the person to get out of themselves, to dissociate from the negative feelings, and view the trauma from the outside. To get desensitized. But it is a process. Patients don't always have positive experiences to begin with. They are re-exposing themselves to a trauma, which stirs up many negative feelings. Leander was… not yet able to separate from those feelings."

"So it was making things worse for him."

"No." Richards shook her head. "That would be misconstruing what was happening with him. Even though he was dealing with negative emotions, he was progressing well. We would have been able to cure him. I'm sure of it."

15

Kenzie wasn't sure she had made any progress on the investigation into Isah's death. While she did have confirmation that he had been part of an MDMA treatment trial, she still didn't have his medical records and sensed that everyone at Persons was holding back information and doing everything they could to keep her from discovering what was actually going on in the place.

Was it just MDMA? There wasn't really any reason to cover that up if it was an approved trial. Maybe they had decided to use other hallucinogenics that were not on the books? LSD or a dangerous psychedelic like PCP? On the drive back to the morgue, she called the tox lab and asked them to look for any other hallucinogenics that might not be on their standard panel, just to be sure.

She hesitated about calling homicide, but knew that she would have to. Especially since the staff at Persons were not cooperating with her requests for information. Once she returned to the office, she called Dr. Wiltshire, hoping that discussing it with him would help clear up her conflicting feelings about it.

The phone rang several times, and she thought it would go to voicemail. He could be out doing something else. Or sleeping. She was glad he was weaning off the heavy painkillers he had been on when he first broke his hand and in the days leading up to and immediately following the surgery. She needed him to be awake and alert when she talked to him.

"Kenzie."

"Oh!" Kenzie was startled by Dr. Wiltshire's voice, when she had already decided that he wasn't going to answer and the call would go directly to voicemail. "Hello, doctor. It's good to hear your voice."

"And yours," he agreed warmly. "What can I do for you today? I hear you've got a substitute now so, hopefully, you can catch up on some of the things that have fallen behind."

"Yes, we got a Dr. Cook. Do you know him?"

"We've met. He's young. Devastatingly handsome?"

Kenzie couldn't help giggling at the description. "Well… yes. Glad I wasn't the only one who noticed. He seems to be competent."

"Top of his class all the way, from what I understand."

"Was he? Wow, good for him."

Kenzie had done well but had not been at the top of her class. Not very often, anyway.

"So, what can I do for you today, Kenzie? You have something you need me to sign off on?"

"No. Nothing that's ready to go yet and, once it is, Dr. Cook can do it. But… I don't know; I wanted to talk through a case with you and see what you think. I think I will have to call in homicide, but I was hoping to avoid that."

"Okay, tell me what you know."

Kenzie related what she knew about the private hospital trying to send the deceased directly to the funeral home without letting the medical examiner review the case first, about the various findings in the post-mortem and the MDMA trial. And the facility's refusal or at least resistance to handing over the medical files she asked for.

"Hmm." Dr. Wiltshire cleared his throat. "Well, the resistance from the care center is certainly concerning. We should have all the details of how the deceased was treated before his death. There may be other things that we need to check before releasing the body."

"Yes. And I wonder about talking to some of the other patients about how the care is, what they are doing in this therapy, and so on? To ensure that everything is aboveboard and that they aren't fudging on the trial results or covering up if Isah's death was somehow related to the trials."

"Not a bad idea. Probably best to go in with a detective so that there are witnesses and someone is there to help you out if you experience more resistance from the staff."

"I should call them in." Kenzie wasn't really asking the question. She just wanted Dr. Wiltshire to confirm that was what she should be doing. She already knew it.

"Sooner is better than later. You don't want to wait until evidence has been destroyed, either inadvertently or intentionally. You have been at the facility twice now. They might decide it is time to take measures."

"That's what I was thinking, too." It would be stupid of the clinic, of course. They were better off cooperating with Kenzie and the police, even if something they had done had contributed to Leander's death. The destruction of medical records would be evidence of a guilty mind. As long as they didn't tamper with anything, they could keep saying they didn't believe that anything they had done had resulted in Leander's death. They could keep saying that they had made all the right choices and wouldn't have changed anything. But as soon as they started the coverup, they were shooting themselves in the foot.

"Give them a call," Dr. Wiltshire advised. "Read them in on all the results to date and your feelings about the resistance and the medical staff there. They know you're not someone to raise alarm bells for no reason."

"Okay," Kenzie agreed with a sigh. As much as she didn't want to, she knew that it was the right thing to do. She couldn't even explain why she was so uncertain about making the call that she knew needed to be made. Maybe it was because she knew how they would react to the hallucinogenic trials. Even worse than she had. And if the results were really as promising as the doctors said they were, Kenzie didn't want to take the chance that an investigation could get them shut down and a treatment that might be life-changing for people like Zachary and Rhys could be put out of their reach.

Dr. Cook was hanging around when Kenzie terminated the call with Dr. Wiltshire. He raised his brows at Kenzie.

"Everything okay?"

"Sure. I just wanted to run things by Dr. Wiltshire and to see what he thought about the Isah case."

"You called Dr. Wiltshire on that case?"

"Yes."

"I am the other doctor on that postmortem. Don't you think you should talk to me instead?"

"Oh…" Kenzie blew her breath out. "I didn't really think about that. Sorry, I'm not used to having you here yet."

Though Dr. Wiltshire hadn't suggested she take it back to Dr. Cook. He could have, but he had been willing to consult on the case instead.

"What did he say?"

"That I should go ahead and talk to the police, get them involved, so we can get the documents we need before they are potentially destroyed."

"You think that you need to bring them in?"

"Yes. I knew that I needed to… I hoped he would say no, that I'm just seeing shadows where there aren't any. But he didn't oblige."

Dr. Cook was quiet for a minute. He looked at Kenzie. "What do you think of your Dr. Wiltshire?"

"He's a great doctor. I've learned a lot from him. And he's very personable and compassionate, as well. I think those are important traits in a medical examiner."

"Otherwise, they come off like Igor?"

"Or Frankenstein. Yes. You don't want to come off as unfeeling or taking pleasure in other people's tragedy."

"And how about… his personal life? That doesn't impact his job?"

Kenzie frowned at him. "What do you mean, his personal life?"

"His… hobbies. What he does in his off hours."

"I don't really know anything about it. He's married, or at least jokes about his wife a lot. May or may not play golf." She shrugged. "He's here when he should be, puts in a lot of hours, He's pretty productive, runs this morgue efficiently."

She wasn't quite sure what Dr. Cook was talking about. Did he know something about Dr. Wiltshire's private life that Kenzie didn't?

Dr. Cook looked like he would walk away without any further comment.

"Hang on!" Kenzie insisted. "What are you talking about? You don't ask a question like that and then walk away! Spill."

He hesitated, half turned away from her. "I've heard rumors. They're probably not true. You're the one who knows him personally. That trumps things that I might have heard."

"You've heard what rumors?"

There was another pause before Cook decided to answer.

"I've heard that he gambles."

"Gambles? Really?" Kenzie shook her head. "I've never seen any sign of that."

"Then like I say, it's probably just unfounded rumor. People who are jealous and want to see him brought down a notch or two."

But Kenzie's mind was already off and running. Was that how Dr. Wiltshire's hand had gotten broken? He owed some bookie or loan shark a lot of money and it was a warning to pay up? It had been a pretty brutal warning, if that were the case, and could have permanently retired him. Dr. Wiltshire had needed a specialist to reconstruct his hand. Judging by the complexity of the external fixators, the damage had been very extensive. Was it all because he was behind on his debts?

She tried to think of whether there had been any other signs that Dr. Wiltshire might be a closet gambler, but couldn't think of any. He was never away from the morgue unexpectedly and hadn't shown any sign of sudden windfalls or financial difficulty. He didn't talk about sports, cards, or betting. He spoke of his wife and gave every indication that he just lived a quiet, uneventful life, doing yard work or playing golf when he was not working.

"I really can't see it," she affirmed. "I don't know who started that rumor, but I've worked with him for a few years, and I don't think he does. I really don't think he does."

Or maybe that was just what she wanted to believe.

16

When Kenzie arrived home, she could hear Zachary talking to someone on the phone, and he did not come to the garage entrance to the kitchen to greet her as he usually did. She took off her outdoor clothing quietly so as not to startle or disturb him, and stood in the kitchen, straining her ears to hear every word or nuance to figure out who it was. A client? Someone he was investigating or one of the resources that he used? One of his brothers or sisters? There were a lot of people that he emailed or talked to throughout the day. Still, he usually dealt with them earlier, not into the supper hour when Kenzie should be arriving home.

Zachary spoke quietly, just a few words here and there as he listened to the caller. But Kenzie had a pretty good idea who it was by the time he had finished. When he disconnected, she stood in the doorway to the living room, looking at him.

"Was that Vera?"

Rhys's grandmother. Zachary nodded. "Yeah, she wanted to give me a rundown on how he's doing. I wish I could be there…"

Kenzie nodded sympathetically. Zachary was used to being the one in the hospital, and it was probably frustrating that he had no control over the situation. It was in Vera's hands, and he couldn't even talk to Rhys unless she approved of it and ensured that Rhys had access to his phone or someone who could communicate his messages. And that assumed that Rhys wanted to communicate and was able to. Was his silence the previous day just an aberration? Caused by missing his medications or his body not responding to them the same way anymore? Or was it something more serious that would take longer to resolve?

"What did Vera have to say? How is he?"

"No change since they admitted him. He still isn't communicating. Very withdrawn. What could have caused such a drastic change? I don't understand it."

"We don't know. The doctors will investigate and try to counsel him, try to figure out what happened, if anything. It may be random… we just don't know. I assume since it has been a day, they have checked for anything emergent, like a stroke or seizure. It's not unusual to see sudden changes in teenagers. A lot is changing, physiologically."

"But they don't usually stop communicating."

"Well…" Kenzie couldn't help smiling. "Actually, a lot of parents complain about how their teens have stopped communicating. But that's more of a relationship thing, kids developing independence from their parents, focusing on peer group and their place in the new communities around them."

"They don't just stop talking altogether."

"No. Though Rhys didn't communicate that much before now. Maybe this is his brain's attempt to go to the next stage, moving away from dependence on his caregiver to more independence." Kenzie shook her head. "I don't think that's what it is. But it's something to think about."

"I'd like—" Zachary started, then stopped, shaking his head. Kenzie waited to see if he were going to finish his thought or reword it and, when he didn't, encouraged him gently.

"You'd like what?"

"You're busy. You've had a long day. It's not a good time to make last-minute plans."

"Sometimes life happens, and we have to adapt. No one was expecting Rhys to crater like this. It's no different than if he was in an accident or came down with some physical ailment. We can't wait for a better time to deal with it. It's happening now. We adapt to it."

"Okay… I was just thinking… that we should get together with Stanley. I don't know why… whether it's because he needs support, or because

I need to hear for myself what's been going on with Rhys, or just… because it's the only way I can feel closer to Rhys right now. I just feel like we should."

"Okay. You want to call him? Do you want to invite him here? Go out for dinner?"

"I'll call, I guess. You're okay with doing something if he agrees? It just seems like too much of an imposition on you."

"It's not. I want to do what I can to support Rhys too. And to support his support network. I don't know whether we can do anything that helps. But we can be there. We can ask."

Zachary nodded, but didn't make any immediate move to pick up his phone and make the call. Maybe he knew Stanley would still be at work and didn't want to bother him there, or perhaps he was just trying to process the conversation before taking the next step. Kenzie considered her next move.

"I think I'll change. You can let me know what he says."

Zachary didn't need the pressure of her hovering over him, waiting for him to make the call. She would normally shower and change into her jammies or start making supper, but if they were going out to dinner with Stanley or having him over, neither was really appropriate. So she would just give Zachary some room and change out of her work clothes and wait to see what was decided.

After changing, she pulled out her laptop, checked her email, and fiddled around without getting anything done. After a few minutes, Zachary tapped on the door, then opened it and peeked in. Kenzie nodded at him.

"He's agreed to go out for dinner," Zachary said. "Is that okay?"

"I said it was."

Arrangements were made and, an hour later, the three of them were sitting at the bar where Zachary had met with Stanley once before, back when he'd been working on the murder of Robin Salter. Zachary looked around as if refamiliarizing himself with the place, and Stanley gave a little laugh.

"It was a pretty messed-up case," he said. "That family… not exactly the most functional one."

"No," Kenzie agreed. There had been a lot of big problems with Rhys's mother and aunt, and things had not ended well for either one of them.

And Rhys was probably damaged forever by the traumas they had both inflicted on him.

Or maybe not. Maybe there was a chance that someday Rhys would be able to be treated with whatever therapy came out of the trials being conducted at Persons and in other psychiatric practices across the country and around the world. Maybe one day, it would be unimaginable to them that once upon a time, childhood trauma had been something people had been forced to carry around for the rest of their lives, whether they could deal with it or not.

"But you really stepped up," Zachary said. "You've been a real role model for Rhys. Someone that he looks up to and admires."

Stanley was embarrassed by the praise. He rolled his eyes and didn't address the compliment directly. "I really felt like he needed someone. And when he was younger… well, I thought we would be family. I would marry Robin, and even though Gloria didn't have a man in her life, I could be a positive male role model for Rhys as his uncle." He sighed and wiped his forehead, eyes far away. "Then I had to leave because of Robin's instability and abuse. But I always regretted that I couldn't fill a role in Rhys's life. I was glad to become a part of his life again after Robin died."

"Well, you've done well," Kenzie affirmed. "Like Zachary said."

Stanley sipped a bottle of beer, looking away from them and shrugging a little as if protesting that it was nothing.

"So tell us about last night, what happened with Rhys," Kenzie suggested.

Stanley nodded. He stared off into space. "There isn't much to tell. I think Zachary already knows the whole story. I had gone out for some pizza and, on my way home, I saw this boy on the street… and it looked like Rhys. I thought it couldn't be, but as I got closer, I got more and more sure, instead of realizing that it wasn't him, like I expected. So I pulled over and told him to get in. Took him home and asked him what had happened, what was wrong. I didn't expect any long explanation. You know how our Rhys is…"

They nodded in agreement, both having dealt with Rhys's communication difficulties in the past. Kenzie would have expected a few gestures, a gif or two on Rhys's phone, maybe a typed word or two. No actual speech, but they had all become accustomed to Rhys communicating in his own way.

"He didn't try to respond to me in any way. He had obeyed when I told him to get into the car and he came with me into my apartment, but he acted like he was in a fog, like he couldn't even understand what I was saying, let alone know how to communicate back to me. No gestures, no voice, no phone. Just… nothing. Like he wasn't even there."

"Dissociated?" Kenzie asked.

Stanley raised one hand palms-up in an "I don't know" gesture. "One of the doctors said something about a dissociative fugue, so maybe. But I thought those things were pretty quick. A few minutes, and it would pass."

"Well, no. A dissociative episode can be very quick, just a few seconds, so that people around you don't even notice. But a fugue state can last weeks, even months."

Zachary made a noise of protest. "Don't tell me that!"

"It doesn't mean that's what Rhys is experiencing or that it will last for very long. I'm just saying… that type of state *could* last a long time. But he's safe where he is. Everyone knows where he is and that he is safe. They'll keep him there until they can be sure he'll be safe when he's released."

"I don't think they've even diagnosed anything yet," Stanley said. "That's just one of the phrases they were throwing around. They said there were a lot of possibilities."

"Of course," Kenzie agreed. "It's too early to know for sure what has caused this or what the diagnosis or prognosis will be."

"How has he been the past few weeks?" Zachary asked. "I have talked to him a few times on the phone, but I haven't seen him face to face. Is this… something that has been coming for a while, or was it completely out of the blue?"

Stanley rubbed his chin. "I didn't see it coming. But… he has been having trouble in other areas. And he's been quite emotional. So… I guess I'm not surprised that something broke. But I don't really know what caused it."

17

Zachary scratched the back of his neck, looking at Kenzie and then back at Stanley. Kenzie tried to think of a way to help reduce his anxiety.

"I worry," Zachary said slowly. "I mean… he's had to deal with so much already, and he's been strong and been able to get through it. But there's still Luke, and I don't like the two of them being involved."

"But Luke has been fighting against the traffickers," Kenzie pointed out. "He's been working with Joss against them. He isn't working with them anymore."

"I know… and I gotta give him that. But he could always go back. I know it's a hard temptation to resist. The drugs and the lifestyle and doing what he knows. And even if he continues to fight the traffickers, what if they figured out his connection with Rhys and targeted him because of what Luke is doing? Or even if… they identified Rhys as a target another way? Through other kids at school who are in the business? Or because he's alone by himself wandering the streets?"

Kenzie put her hand over his on the table. "I know that there are a lot of hazards and things to worry about. But Rhys is safe right now. He's in a safe place. We need to focus on what's going on with him now rather than what could happen in the future. You are catastrophizing. Imagining the worst that could happen. And it's not even related to what's going on with him right now."

Zachary blinked at her and shook his head as if she had missed the whole point. "I *am* thinking about what's going on right now. Rhys is out on the street alone at night, looking for Stanley, and he's so traumatized he can't communicate? It's Tirza all over again."

The name didn't mean anything to Kenzie. She glanced at Stanley and saw the same blank expression on his face.

"Who's Tirza?" she asked.

Zachary made a noise of disgust, as if she should have known immediately. "The autistic girl at Summit who was snatched from school and trafficked. They let her go after a few days because her mother did a big media blitz, confronting the police for ignoring what she was telling them about Tirza and saying that she had just run off with some boy. But she insisted it was a kidnapping and made things too hot for the traffickers, so they dumped her. *She* was found wandering on the street. Unable to communicate with anyone because she was too traumatized and she normally uses an AAC to help her communicate."

Kenzie saw the parallel immediately. How similar the two cases were and his concern that Rhys might have escaped or been dumped by similar traffickers after a night of abuse. They both looked at Stanley. Rhys hadn't been able to communicate so, of course, Stanley couldn't answer their questions about what had happened to Rhys that night. And the doctors wouldn't tell them anything. But there might be other signs. Stanley might have guessed.

"Do you think… something like that might have happened to Rhys?" Kenzie asked Stanley. "I know there's no way for you to know, but did it look like he was just out walking on his own, or like something might have happened to him? Some violence…?"

Stanley shook his head slowly. "Well, I can't be sure, but… I mean, they wouldn't just dump him after a few hours, would they? I mean… he didn't look scuffed up or… torn clothing… anything like that. Physically, he seemed pretty much the same as ever. It was just…" Stanley swallowed. "He seemed so far gone." He licked dry lips and then took a swallow of beer. His eyes glittered, but he shed no tears.

Kenzie turned her attention back to Zachary, trying to take the pressure off of Stanley to let him recover. "I think Stanley would have been able to see the signs if he'd been kidnapped, assaulted, and trafficked. And I agree; I don't think that traffickers would just take him for a few hours and then dump him."

"There are plenty of other predators who would," Zachary argued.

Kenzie nodded, conceding the point. "But it didn't look like there had been any physical violence. So hopefully… that wasn't the problem." She sighed. "But I don't understand what he was doing out there, looking for Stanley. And why no one knew he was gone until Stanley saw him wandering the streets. He should have been at home. Vera wouldn't let him go out late like that."

"She doesn't always know where he is," Zachary said with a quick shake of his head. "There have been other times when he's shown up to see me, and I know she didn't allow it or know he was there. Sometimes, he takes off during school, and they must not do callouts when students miss classes. Or not every teacher takes attendance, and he knows which ones he can scam. At night… I didn't know he was going out at night, but he probably just waits until she's asleep, and she never knows he's gone. If Luke could sneak out on Joss, who's pretty savvy and, I would guess, doesn't sleep well, then it would be easy for Rhys to sneak out on an old woman who takes out her hearing aids for bed and might take a sleep aid."

Kenzie had to admit that there had been a few times when her parents hadn't known where she had been as a teenager, and would have been horrified if they had known. She hadn't been that wild, but she had tested the limits and experimented, like any child growing up and trying to separate from her parents and become independent. Zachary was right; it probably would not be hard to sneak out on Vera.

"And what happened? Where did he go? What did he do? Did something happen while he was out, so he went to find Stanley? Or did he sneak out because he needed to see Stanley?"

They both looked at him. Stanley's eyes were no longer filled with tears. He frowned and shook his head. "I wish I knew. I've never known him to do that before and, when we connected, he didn't communicate anything to me."

"What things did you normally talk about?" Zachary asked. "You were a father figure to him. Did he talk to you about school? Challenges he was going through? Complain about Vera's cooking?"

Stanley snorted. "He never complained about her cooking," he said with a forced laugh. "That boy might have been as skinny as a rail, but he sucked the food down like a vacuum cleaner."

Kenzie and Zachary both laughed. They had seen it too.

"Never really said much about school, either," Stanley continued. "If it was too hard, or he was being bullied by a student or harassed by a teacher. I remember how bad school was for me, and I was a big kid and could defend myself and speak just fine. I can only imagine what it was like for a kid like Rhys."

Zachary rubbed his eyes. Sitting beside him rather than across from him, Kenzie could see behind his hands rather than being blocked by them. She couldn't see much in profile, but she could see his grimace.

"Have a drink," she suggested, worried about flashbacks to his own painful school experiences.

Zachary picked up the glass of ice water before him and took a couple of swallows. He nodded at Kenzie. She took deep, measured breaths, hoping that he would match his breathing to hers and be able to stay in control of his emotions.

"What did you talk about, then?" Kenzie asked Stanley.

"I don't know. We hung out. Watched sports, did some guy stuff together. We didn't spend a lot of time talking. I asked him how he was, but we didn't discuss feelings or what was happening at school."

A safe relationship. Non-demanding.

"Did he talk about Luke and Aster?" Zachary asked. "Anything about what they had gone through?"

Stanley shook his head. "I only know of their existence by talking to you. Rhys never mentioned them."

And he hadn't gone to Luke. If something had happened to trigger Rhys's episode, it had been something that had sent him to a father figure, not the boy he was attracted to.

"And Vera… she doesn't know about his interest in Luke?" Kenzie asked.

Stanley shook his head, but Zachary made a face that suggested he disagreed. "She hasn't said anything about it, and he hasn't told her," he said carefully, "but that isn't the same as not knowing."

"You think she knew?" Stanley said doubtfully. "I think she would have said something."

"She has said a couple of things that made me wonder. I think she has her suspicions, even if she isn't sure. She didn't want him to be bullied at school if people saw him and I out together…"

"Oh." He hadn't mentioned that to Kenzie before. She thought about it. "When did she say that? I didn't realize."

"It was way back… a year… almost two. With all the publicity after…" He cleared his throat. "After Teddy Archuro."

"That was before Rhys even met Luke, wasn't it?"

Zachary shrugged. "Yes. Vera's raised Rhys from the time he was a baby. She's probably had plenty of occasions to notice who he tends to be attracted to."

"But he hasn't told her? They haven't discussed it?"

"Not as far as I know. He has wanted it to be kept quiet from her. I've been careful not to allude to it. I've seen what can happen when kids are outed before they are ready or when their caregivers are unwilling to accept it. I don't want him to be kicked out and have to fend for himself."

"Vera wouldn't do that. She loves him too much."

"She's religious. She's quoted Bible verses to me before. When parents are wrestling between moral values they have spent a whole lifetime learning, and their children's choices… too often, their response is to split with the kid."

Zachary's intuitions about such things were usually pretty accurate, so Kenzie didn't argue. Maybe he was right and, if Vera were faced with a crisis, she would choose her religious beliefs over her grandson, though Kenzie had a hard time believing it.

"Do you think it might have leaked out at school?" Stanley asked. "Kids can be pretty good at picking these things up."

"It's possible," Zachary said. "They might have guessed, or he might have done something to give himself away. Maybe there is someone at school that he likes, and it has ended up causing problems. Only…"

Kenzie waited to hear what the counterargument was.

"Why would he go to Stanley?" Zachary said with a shrug. "If he'd never talked to you about it before," he looked at Stanley, "and you're not gay. Then why would he come to you to talk about it?"

Stanley shook his head. "I've tried to be careful of what I say around him. You know…" His cheeks and throat were turning a dusky red. "Not saying anything disparaging or using slang words for them. So maybe he knows that I'm a safe person. But…" He shook his head. "It isn't something we have ever gotten into. I hope he knows he could come to me about anything, but I'm not exactly the person most kids would choose to confess their deepest secrets and attractions to."

Kenzie looked at Zachary. "You're wondering why he didn't go to you?"

"Well, I guess," he admitted. "I'm trying not to be all egotistical about being the person Rhys would go to for help or to talk about it. I've helped him with other things in the past. I already know about him being attracted to Luke. We've talked about mental health issues. He knows that I have admitted myself to the hospital before. So why wouldn't he talk to me if he was having problems with bullying, being gay, or being depressed or having other health issues? Why Stanley instead?"

18

Kenzie could hear Zachary on the phone again as she got ready for bed. She had expected him to be tired and getting ready for bed too, but he seemed restless and wound up. He didn't usually make late phone calls unless it was urgent, and he didn't seem to have any particularly urgent cases.

She waited until she thought he was off the phone before entering the bedroom and potentially distracting him. She peeked around the door to make sure he was off.

"Sorry," Zachary apologized. He massaged his forehead tenderly. "I just… had to make sure."

Kenzie moved into the room. "Had to make sure of what?"

"I just called the hospital. Asked whether I could talk to Rhys."

Kenzie looked at the clock. "It's late. He'll be down for the night. They'll have him on a sleep aid to make sure that he takes the time he needs to recover."

"I know. He is. I mean, they wouldn't tell me that because of privacy, but of course he is. And even if he wasn't asleep, they probably wouldn't let him talk on the phone. And even if they let him, and I was on his approved caller list, he wouldn't be able to because he's not communicating right now. I was just hoping for… something. Just a bit of reassurance."

Kenzie nodded. "Did you get it?"

She fully expected the answer to be no.

"Actually…" Zachary gave a small smile. "Do you remember Nurse Val from when I was in?"

"Sure. I remember Nurse Val. Very nice lady. Helpful."

"Yeah. So I got her. And she said, 'You know we always take good care of you when you're here, Zachary. We give you something if your anxiety gets too bad, and we make sure someone is with you or checking on you every fifteen minutes if we have concerns. We always respect your privacy, but we let your family and friends know that you are okay and we are taking good care of you.'"

Kenzie breathed out. "So Rhys has been given something for his anxiety and they are keeping him under close supervision."

Zachary nodded. "Yeah. I just wanted to know that he was okay. And I shouldn't even have to ask because, like Nurse Val says, they've always taken good care of me there. I know they are professionals and I know what the routines and procedures are. I just needed to hear it."

In the morning, Kenzie got an early call from Detective Elena Garcia, who had apparently been assigned the Isah case.

"Dr. Kirsch, it's good to talk to you again. I'm going up to Persons and, from what I understand, you have been involved in this case from the start. Do you want to go with me? You can fill me in on all the details on the way there, and be around while I conduct a few interviews; let me know if you see anything I don't?"

Kenzie knew from a past case that Zachary had been involved in that Garcia took an unusual approach to her investigations and seemed to enjoy involving non-law enforcement officers, something that most of the detectives Kenzie knew wouldn't have even countenanced.

But it was to her advantage. This time, at least.

"Sure, I'd love to help out," Kenzie agreed. "I have already talked to a couple of people, though, so I probably shouldn't be around when you do it. They wouldn't want to talk in front of me in case something they said conflicted with what they had told me before."

"Right. I've read your interview notes and know who you've talked to and the broad strokes of those investigations. I think you're right, and I won't have you sit in on those re-interviews. But I'd like to talk to some patients over there and get a feel for what is happening. I don't like the idea of this drug trial. Certain drugs are restricted for a reason."

"I don't know what to think of the trial right now, to be honest. In concept, I can understand why they would want to do it and how success could change the whole landscape of how we treat these conditions. But there is also such a potential for misuse and abuse…"

"It's something that can only be used in hospitals, right?" Garcia asked.

"Mmm. I don't know what the guidelines are, but I don't think it is restricted to hospital use. I suspect that it could be used in an outpatient model too. Maybe not with take-home meds, but a doctor or nurse who would see to their administration and stick around for a few minutes to make sure that there was no reaction."

"I've seen what these drugs can do to people. You probably have too, on your table. Why they would mess around with them, I don't under-stand. It's too dangerous."

"We prescribe other drugs that are dangerous when taken as a recre-ational drug or used the wrong way. Amphetamines. Fentanyl. Ketamine. Digitalis."

"And the opiate epidemic should be warning enough for us."

Kenzie shrugged, almost dropping the phone from her shoulder. While she didn't agree with Garcia on this point, there was no point in arguing about it. That was outside of the scope of the case. And neither of their opinions would have any effect on whether opiates were deemed too dangerous to be used in a medical setting.

"What time do you want me there?"

"I could come pick you up now if that's convenient. Spend however long we need to at Persons, and then I can drop you back at home to get your car and go wherever else you need to."

"That doesn't make much sense if you're conducting interviews that I'm not attending. Either I end up hanging around with nothing to do while you do those interviews, or you have to run me home and then go back. I'll just meet you there."

"Okay, fair enough. I can be out there in about half an hour. What is your schedule like?"

"I could make it in about the same. After I have my coffee."

Garcia laughed. "Already had mine. Okay, I'll see you out there shortly."

Kenzie had not thought it possible that the staff at Persons could look at her with more disapproval than they had on the previous occasions. But they were clearly not happy about the police now being involved, as well as the intrusive medical examiner's office. Garcia waited impatiently for the person who would approve her talking to some of the patients and explain to her where the medical records were and why they hadn't been copied or released to the medical examiner's office yet.

The blond receptionist clearly had her nose out of joint and didn't want to let them talk to anyone, but Garcia pushed back pretty hard, and the woman was eventually cowed into calling Dr. Richards to ask what to do about the police investigation.

Dr. Richards entered the reception area, her forehead creased in consternation. She shook her head, her blond curls bouncing gently.

"I'm sorry, Detective, uh…?"

"Detective Elena Garcia," the detective announced crisply. "What exactly is the delay?"

"Er… what delay? I don't understand what you're doing here."

"We are here to continue with the investigation into Mr. Leander Isah's death."

"I'm sure the medical examiner's office will tell you that they have fully investigated that case and are about ready to issue their findings," Dr. Richards said, nodding in Kenzie's direction. "We have been fully cooperative. But we are now getting into the situation where your investigation is interfering with our operations and could compromise patient care."

Garcia looked at Kenzie, who shook her head. "We're still waiting on the medical records we requested several days ago."

Richards brushed these concerns away with a motion. "They're in the works. And you aren't going to find anything different from what we already told you. There really isn't any reason to get them other than the completeness of the records. You're barely even going to look at them."

"We have significant concerns about how this case has been handled thus far," Garcia said. "Dr. Kirsch's findings thus far are quite concerning."

"We have explained the treatment that Leander was undergoing. And his history. The traumas that he had suffered in the past necessitated quite intense treatment. And I'm sure Dr. Kirsch can tell you that those who have survived torture often suffer from significant physical and emotional impairments. They unfortunately have a significantly shortened lifespan."

"You're saying that it was the torture that caused Mr. Isah's death?"

"I'm not saying that. I'm just pointing out that it is not unusual for a patient with that sort of history to die… unexpectedly. It may have been a stroke or seizure, some kind of infection or old shrapnel still in his body…"

"I don't believe that any of that is the case," Kenzie said evenly.

"Still, torture has many physical and psychological effects. I can't be expected to tell them all to you now…"

"What would help," Kenzie said evenly, "would be his medical records."

Richards blew out her breath explosively. "They are in the works."

"They better be in my briefcase before I leave here today," Garcia told her.

The two women glared at each other, neither willing to back down. But Garcia had the law on her side, including a subpoena for the records. There wasn't much that Richards could do unless she wanted to end up in a jail cell for contempt. The longer she delayed, the better the chances were of her being incarcerated. Garcia did not want to give them any longer to destroy records.

"And you will note that we have also asked for all security video for the forty-eight hours before Mr. Isah's death. And it had better all be there. Missing time or cameras would be a problem."

"We need to protect our patients' privacy—"

"And we need to protect your patients from you. If all the proper safety protocols were followed, you should not have to worry about the recordings."

"What about the other patients?"

"What about them? You're afraid of their faces being on video? We're not going to send footage or patients' faces to the media, you know."

"Our patients frequently come from very wealthy and influential Vermont families. Even if your officers see their faces, happen to mention the names to their wives…"

"That will not happen."

"So you say. But how can I be sure of that?"

"You don't need to be sure. You only need to follow the law, which says that you must turn that information over to me."

19

They had finally been given a patient consultation room in which to interview a few of the patients in Isah's ward to see if they had seen or heard anything the night that Isah had died or in the days leading up to his death.

A woman was brought in, dressed in the blue scrubs that most of the patients wore. She had long dark hair, which hung in curtains around her face. She kept her head bowed and didn't look at them.

"What's your name?" Garcia asked gently, even though she had already been provided with it.

An easy question to get the woman started, to help her to share in a way that wasn't painful or threatening.

"Janice Martin." Her voice was low and subdued, almost too quiet to hear. Like she wanted to just fade away from them.

"Janice. My name is Detective El Garcia, and this is Dr. Kirsch. It's nice to meet you."

Janice nodded, but her eyes were far away and she didn't look at either of them.

"Do you know why we wanted to talk to you today, Janice?"

"Because of Leander."

"Yes, that's right. Your room is right next to Leander's, is that right?"

She nodded.

"So you see him coming and going, or if there are people coming and going to his room."

"Not all the time," Janice objected. "We aren't allowed to stay in our rooms all day."

"Oh, you're not?" Garcia leaned forward, looking interested. She had probably thought of it as a hospital where people stayed in bed all day. But that wasn't the way it worked in a psychiatric treatment center. People were encouraged to be up and around, socializing, participating in activities, group therapy, personal therapy, and so on.

"No," Janice shook her head. "You're not allowed to just withdraw from the world." She said it wistfully, as if that were exactly what she wanted to do.

"Oh, I see. They want to keep you… present," Garcia said. "An active participant."

Janice nodded, moving forward and back a little with the nods, like she was in a rocking chair. She put her feet up on the seat of the chair so that her knees were folded in front of her chest. She wrapped her arms around them, curling herself into a ball. Demonstrating very effectively how she wanted to just withdraw from the world.

"So did you see Leander the day before he died?"

"Yeah, I guess."

"Did you see when he went to bed?"

"I might not have been in my room then."

There was a period of silence while Garcia considered this answer. "Do you know when Leander went to bed?"

"I don't know when he went to sleep."

"Was he up and around during the afternoon before he died? He wasn't sick in bed?"

"No."

"No…?" Garcia prompted, realizing she had asked two questions and wasn't sure which one Janice intended to answer.

"He wasn't sick in bed."

"Good. So he was apparently feeling well enough during the day to participate in activities."

Janice's shoulders lifted and fell.

"Did he have therapy? What was his schedule, do you know?"

"Yes. He had therapy in the afternoon. With Dr. Miller."

"Good. He went to his appointment?"

"Yes. You have to. You can't say no."

"And when he got back from therapy, what did he do then?"

Janice stared down, not answering for a long time. Then finally she spoke again. "He wanted to go to his room."

They waited for more information. Kenzie studied Janice's pale face. It was difficult to read anything from her flat affect. Withdrawn, not wanting to engage with them or talk to them about Leander and whatever had happened the day he had died. Because she didn't know? Because it was too painful? Was she afraid?

"And did they let him go to his room?" Garcia asked.

"No, they said he wasn't allowed until bedtime, that he needed to do other things." Janice shook her head. "Write a letter. Socialize with other patients. Engage with the world." She let out a sigh. Obviously, she didn't like doing any of these things any more than Leander did. Or maybe she was projecting her feelings onto Leander.

"So what did Leander choose to do?"

"He didn't want to. He said he wanted to go to his room, kept trying to go back there. Sometimes after therapy… you just want to sleep. They should let you sleep. It's hard."

"What kind of therapy had Leander been doing?" Kenzie asked. "Do you know? Was he doing CBT? EMDR?"

Janice looked at Kenzie. "Are you a real doctor?"

Kenzie smiled. "I'm a pathologist, actually. Not a therapist. I don't know as much about psychotherapy as I should, but I know some of the therapies that are used. I understand that Leander was in a program for his PTSD."

Janice nodded but didn't offer any details.

"Was it to do with the drug therapy?" Kenzie prodded. "Had they given him the trial meds?"

Janice looked around uncomfortably, as if trying to find a way out of the room and away from their questions.

"What other patients do is none of your business," she told Kenzie flatly. "You keep your eyes on your own page and worry about the work you have to do. Everyone is entitled to privacy in their treatment program."

She was clearly repeating the words that had been told to her more than one time. The party line. Stay focused on your own therapy and don't worry about anyone else's.

"But you probably know more about other patients' therapy than they thought. One of the nurses said that he knew which patients were in the experimental program, because their therapy schedules had changed. And some of them, like Leander, were acting differently than they had been before."

Janice nodded her agreement.

"So you noticed the changes too?" Garcia asked.

Janice shrugged. "We all know everything," she said. "Everybody sees where everyone else goes. Everything they do. You can't help knowing."

"And what kind of therapy was Leander doing?"

"He was in the trial drug program."

"And do you think he was in the control group or getting the actual drug?"

"Getting the drug. If he was getting the placebo… he wouldn't have been like that. He wasn't like that before."

"Like what?"

"So… agitated. He was upset all the time. But especially after a session." Janice swallowed and licked her lips.

Kenzie glanced around reflexively for a mini fridge or somewhere she could fill a glass of water for Janice, but there didn't seem to be anything. They should have had something available. A lot of psychoactive meds caused dry mouth. Kenzie was quick to spot the signs and was always filling glasses of water or handing Zachary water bottles if she noticed he was swallowing or licking his lips a lot. Or moving his tongue around his mouth, trying to generate some saliva.

"They have two kinds of sessions," Janice explained, her voice small. Doing what she knew was forbidden and talking about someone else's treatment. "Sessions where he got the drug, and sessions that were just talk. They alternated."

"Ah." Garcia made a note of this. "And this session was drug or talk?"

"Drug."

"How could you tell the difference?"

"His eyes were different. Big pupils. And other things. Sweating and anxious. They say it makes you more social, makes you want to be around people more, and that it makes you feel good. But not everyone was like that. And it didn't last for a long time. You would be happy and fun for a while, and then… when it wore off, you feel sad or mad, and some people really paranoid. Leander was never very happy or social."

"What time was his therapy?"

Janice frowned, thinking about it. "I don't know what time… hmm… after breakfast, and then he wouldn't be back until after lunch."

Kenzie raised her brows. She looked at Garcia, making sure that she saw this was significant. "That's a long session."

Janice nodded.

"When you have a therapy session, is it that long?"

"No. Half an hour or an hour. But Leander was always gone for a long time."

"Was everyone who was doing the experimental therapy gone for that long?"

"No. Different lengths. Maybe there were different dosages or drugs…" She shook her head. "We weren't supposed to talk about it."

"I know," Kenzie agreed. "But this is an investigation into what the doctors were doing. And if something was going on that shouldn't have been, and Leander was hurt during the process, then you need to tell us so that we can find out what was going on and who was responsible."

"Leander just died," Janice said. "It wasn't anyone's fault. He had a bad heart."

"Is that what the doctors told you?"

"Yes."

"That he had a bad heart?"

"Yes."

That was interesting. Kenzie looked at Garcia to make sure she wrote this down. "We don't have his medical records yet. I guess that will be one of the notes in the file we receive."

Janice nodded her agreement. She looked around. "I shouldn't be here. I should be doing arts and crafts right now."

"That sounds interesting. Do you like arts and crafts?"

"Sure." Janice looked directly at Kenzie for the first time, getting a little more animated. "I've always liked to make things with my hands. I'm good at it."

"What are you working on right now? Or do you do something new each session?"

"I'm working on a sculpture. It's clay. We don't get marble or anything like that. It would be too expensive."

"I guess so. And pretty heavy, too. I don't know what it's like to work with marble, but I imagine it would be difficult."

"Yeah. So we only have clay, but it is versatile. I'm working on this bird… it is an eagle, on a branch, just lifting its wings to take off."

Maybe representing Janice's wish to be able to lift herself up and fly out of there, away from their negative feelings and able to feel the wind through her hair. Or feathers. Whatever the reason, it was the only thing that had brought light into Janice's eyes during the interview.

"That sounds awesome. Inspiring. I'd like to see it."

"Maybe before you go. I should go now, though. Or I'll miss my chance." Janice stood up.

"We were hoping to find out a little more about the timeline," Garcia objected, motioning for Janice to sit again. "Leander got out of his session after lunch, which still leaves several hours before lights-out time and when he was discovered. Can you tell us about what happened during that time?"

"No." Janice looked around restlessly. "He kept trying to go back to his room. They wouldn't let him. He… put his head down on one of the tables and went to sleep, but they wouldn't let him sleep. We're supposed to follow a proper sleep schedule. Sleeping at the wrong times can mess up your circadian rhythm. See? I even remembered what it is called this time."

"He was trying to go to sleep?" Kenzie asked. "I thought he was agitated."

Janice made an impatient sound. "He didn't want anyone near him. He wanted to be alone. He wanted them to stay away from him and he wanted to go to sleep."

"Oh, I see." Kenzie wasn't sure she did, but she could look up some information later. Zachary had more experience with mental health issues than she did. Maybe he could explain the seemingly opposite symptoms to her.

She remembered how he had been after the assault by Archuro. He had switched from being unable to sleep more than a few hours at night to sleeping all the time, throughout the day and night. It was his brain's way of trying to heal from the trauma. Pulling away from the world.

Cocooning to protect himself. He had not wanted to talk to anyone about what had happened. Not to Kenzie, his therapist, or his foster father. He had avoided and canceled therapy sessions. Dr. B had probably been horrified to hear what he had been through, and that he had withdrawn and not talked to her about it when he needed to the most.

Maybe that was how Leander had felt. That even though he should have been talking to someone about the feelings that the treatment was stirring up, he only wanted to avoid the issue and hide from the world.

20

————————

The next patient they had in was David Gentle. The man looked nothing like his name would have implied. He was of average height, but with the back and shoulders of an ox, easily the size of two men. He looked like someone who could eat Zachary for breakfast. From his face, he was not a gentle giant, either. He scowled at the police detective and medical examiner, not happy to be there, already looking bullish and resistant.

Kenzie found herself immediately checking for escape routes and contemplating how to defend herself if he exploded. The orderly who brought him in did not stay with him as Kenzie thought he might. Kenzie knew that Garcia was trained in handling criminals who might get violent, but that didn't make her feel much better. Garcia wasn't there with a gun, taser, and baton on her belt. She was in plain clothes and, trained or not, she was much smaller and lighter than Gentle. Kenzie wasn't sure how much help she would be in a fight.

"You are David Gentle?"

"Yeah."

"You were told why you were here?"

"You want to talk about Leander."

"Yes. I'm Detective Garcia, and this is Dr. Kirsch. How well did you know Leander?"

He looked around, restless, apparently not liking being enclosed by these four walls. "I didn't know him. I don't know anyone here that well. We're not here to make friends."

"But you got to know people while you were both staying here together," Kenzie suggested, knowing how it had worked with Zachary. "Even if they aren't the type of people you would normally have befriended, when you're housed together for a few weeks or months, you get to know the others. Their personalities and behaviors. And sometimes… things that you have in common."

He grunted and didn't agree or disagree with this assessment.

"So you learned things about Leander, even if you were not friends," Garcia agreed. "What kind of person he was, how he spent his day, what his schedule was."

He shrugged his massive shoulders. Kenzie thought he looked like a huge turtle trying to retract his head into his shell. He continued to scowl at them as if they had personally offended him by expecting him to come and talk to them.

"What did you think of Leander?" Garcia prodded.

"I thought he was weak," Gentle grunted. "Physically and mentally. Frail. Like a puff of wind would blow him over. He needed to toughen up. Parents don't do their kids any favors by protecting them from every bit of opposition. They need to learn how to stick up for themselves and face things that are hard." He blew his breath out in a hard puff, clearing his throat with an animalistic growl.

Kenzie thought of what she knew of Leander. Gentle was wrong about his having an easy life. Run-ins with the police in a country where they were not nearly as nice as in the US. Torture and his mental illness. He'd had a difficult time, at least from his teen years. Before that, who knew? Did he have both parents? Had they been victims or abusers? Kenzie had little doubt that he'd had to fend for himself from early on in life.

"Did you talk with him very much?" Garcia inquired.

"No, we didn't talk. I told you he wasn't my friend."

"Can you tell me where you might have seen him during the twenty-four hours before he died?" Garcia suggested. "Can you tell me what his schedule was, when he was in his room, and when he was occupied with therapy?"

"What am I, his social secretary?" Gentle slapped his hand down on the table. Not hard, trying to intimidate them, but impatient. "This is ridiculous. I don't know anything about him."

"Was he in his room the whole time?"

"No. We weren't allowed to be in our rooms the whole day."

"So you weren't in your room the whole time either."

"No." He favored Garcia with a glare that said he thought she was an idiot for asking when he had just said they weren't allowed to stay in their rooms.

"So if you were not both in your rooms all day, you must have seen each other at some point."

"Maybe." He rolled his eyes.

"Did you take meals with him?"

Gentle considered the question. "Suppose so. I don't think he was there for lunch."

"Why not?"

"In therapy."

"Is that normal? To miss meals because of therapy?"

"If it's a long session." He shook his head and looked over their heads. "Sometimes they went long."

"Were you doing the same kind of therapy as Leander was?"

He eyed Garcia. "I don't know. I guess we were all doing pretty much the same thing."

"Were you both in the experimental program?"

His face tightened, jaw muscles clenching. Kenzie could practically hear his teeth grinding together.

"It's none of my business what else anyone else is doing."

"Are you in the experimental program?"

He looked around as if hoping to find a way to avoid the question. He looked back at Garcia. "Yes."

"What do you think of the program?" Kenzie asked gently, hoping that a less adversarial approach might help Gentle to relax and give them something useful.

"I don't know," he said after considering for a moment. "Sometimes it is good and sometimes not."

"What is good about it?"

"It… changes the way I feel." He shook his head, brows drawn down in concentration. "It… calms me down. Opens me up." He rubbed his hands on his pants, drying sweaty palms or trying to calm himself down without the drugs. "It's… different."

"So it lets you talk about yourself? Your feelings and things that might have happened in the past?"

He shook his head, mouth tightening.

"It can be hard to talk about the past," Kenzie prompted, watching his face for any changes. She didn't want to provoke him, but to nail down what was going on in those sessions as best she could. A man like Gentle could be very difficult to reach. He had so many layers of protection. His physical mass and strength, his intelligence, his anger, and other emotional barriers.

"Who *wants* to talk about the past?" he snapped. "The past is the past. I don't know why all of you psych types always want to talk about the past. It isn't like you can change it."

"No," Kenzie agreed. "But it can still affect how we think and act in the present, and sometimes that needs to be changed."

"What do you know about it?" he demanded. "Nothin' ever happened to you."

"I don't know what happened to you. I grew up in a pretty nice family, good circumstances. But my sister died, and that was really hard. And I have had… things happen to me as an adult that were… very difficult and upsetting."

"Maybe you should take some of their drugs and see if it helps you."

Kenzie nodded. "Maybe I should. Do you think it would help?"

"I would leave here. If it wasn't for the drugs."

"But if you leave, you can't be part of the program anymore."

"Yeah, that's right. It's good. I think… it's good to be able to turn the defensive part of your brain off. Sometimes. And then… just be open."

"But you said there were parts of the program you didn't like, too," Garcia said. "You said you didn't really know what you thought about it."

He looked at her, maybe a little less angry now, thinking about being opened up in therapy, about how good it was to be able to talk about his traumas in an open, nondefensive way.

"There are things I don't like. Things I don't remember."

Alarm bells rang in Kenzie's head. She leaned toward Gentle, studying his face.

"What things that you don't remember?" Garcia prodded.

"A lot of things. I remember the drugs opening me up... being away from my body. Looking at things in a way I never did before. But... sometimes it can be for hours, and I don't remember all of that. I only remember... a few minutes. And then... it's hours later, and I don't know what happened. Where I was, what I did." He shook his head. "Things happened that I don't remember."

Kenzie nodded slowly. She had heard that MDMA could leave memory blanks. And maybe that was a good part of the therapy, not bad. He couldn't remember if he'd had a traumatic session. He could get the memories out in the open, but not have to suffer from reliving them. But there were problems with the memory gaps, too. Things could happen when someone was in a suggestible state. It made him vulnerable. And if he couldn't remember it afterward to make an accusation, then there could be abuses going on that were never brought to light.

"It's good to feel different sometimes," Gentle said, "Not so... raw and angry. Being able to get out of my head sometimes is good. It's... hard in there."

"Yeah, I can imagine," Garcia acknowledged.

"But then there are times..." It took some time for Gentle to think about his answer and string the words together to describe what he wanted to say. "Sometimes you don't get that good feeling. Sometimes... it can be really bad. Really... freaky."

"A bad trip?" Garcia asked.

"Yeah. Yeah, I guess you could put it that way. I don't know, I never took illegal drugs, you know. Maybe that's what it's like. But I would see things, feel things, the whole world out of kilter. Like you were on a different planet or in a different time. And bad things happened. Really awful, terrible things."

"Like what?"

"I don't know. I could see things happening to me. Other doctors, experiments. And bugs and snakes. I knew those weren't real, but they were..." He shuddered. "I never knew whether it was going to be good or bad. I want to stay and have the good sessions, the ones that open me up, but the bad trips and then other times that I can't remember... I don't want that. No one would want that."

21

The interview with David Gentle had gone better than Kenzie had expected, but it was still a big relief when he walked out of the room and she could breathe freely again. Garcia eyed Kenzie as she took a long drink of water.

"That was an interesting one."

"Yeah. I was a little worried about him."

"I could see that. You don't trust me to handle it?"

"Of course I do… but he was a big guy. Obviously very strong. And you…"

"Not as big or muscular. But I assure you, I could have handled things if he had gotten violent."

Kenzie still had her doubts about that, but she kept them to herself. "I'm sure you could have. But society has trained us to believe that women are weaker… potential prey to men like him. So it is a conditioned reaction, no matter what I believe logically."

Garcia nodded. "I get that."

The final patient that they were to interview arrived with the orderly. A woman, slim, with dark, slightly tangled hair. Her face was closer in shade to Garcia's than Kenzie's, but she couldn't be sure whether the patient was Hispanic as well, or just tanned. She had a permanently wrinkled brow and bags under her eyes like she hadn't slept in days. Kenzie was sure the facility would have given her a sleep aid if she weren't sleeping well. Sleep was vital for good mental health.

The orderly had her sit down and, instead of leaving the room, just retreated to the door, shut it, and stood there like they were in a prison. Kenzie looked at him and then at Garcia to see what she thought of this.

"Is there a reason you need to stay with her?" Garcia challenged.

"She could be a danger to herself or others."

Garcia and Kenzie looked at the woman, who seemed so far away that it was hard to imagine she could be a danger to anyone.

"Hi," Garcia said, getting closer to the patient and trying to meet her eyes. "I'm Detective Garcia. What was your name?"

The woman didn't answer. Did she speak? Was she even aware of their existence or the questions posed to her? It was hard to imagine that she could be a very good witness to anything. She would have no idea when Isah had been in his room. She might not even know who he was.

Garcia opened her mouth to try again when the woman said faintly, "Cara."

"Cara? What's your last name?"

She didn't enlighten them on that point, even though Garcia gave her an extra long time to answer.

"Can you tell us her last name?" Garcia asked the orderly.

"Anderson."

"Cara Anderson." Garcia wrote it down in her notepad. "Thank you for your assistance. And is she… does she talk? I mean, there's no point in me trying to interview her if she isn't even verbal. Is there a better way to communicate with her?"

"She can talk," the orderly told her, but offered no other advice.

"Cara." Garcia continued to try to make eye contact with the woman who was obviously having none of it. "How are you today?"

Maybe it was Paul Casey's idea of a joke. Giving them a patient to interview who clearly could not be interviewed. The woman was practically catatonic.

Kenzie's mind wandered to Rhys, and she wondered if he were making any progress. Had they changed around his medications? Increased the dosages? Was his anxiety being addressed through therapy? From what Nurse Val had said, he was being closely monitored, someone either staying with him or checking in again every fifteen minutes. That suggested they were pretty concerned with him and taking the necessary precautions. But how long would it go on? They wouldn't keep someone in his room for days on end.

Cara's eyes flicked over to Garcia after a few minutes. "Who are you?"

"I'm Detective Garcia. And this is Kenzie Kirsch."

Cara's eyes did not move to Kenzie.

"Do you know why we are here, Cara?"

"Why am *I* here," Cara countered.

"Well… to help you with the problems that you've been having," Garcia offered vaguely. "They take good care of you here, don't they?"

"I need to go."

"Go where?"

Cara looked around the room, frowning. "I am not supposed to be *here.*"

"You are being treated. This is the right place for you to be. And I am here to interview you about what happened to Leander. You know Leander, right?"

"Leander." Cara looked around, but he wasn't there. She gave no sign of whether she was upset or disappointed by this or preferred not to have him there. But Kenzie thought there was a slight lift in her voice. Someone who liked Leander. Maybe that was why Paul Casey had picked her out to interview with them.

"Is Leander your friend?" Garcia asked.

"I'm not sure." Cara swallowed and looked around. She started to rise from her chair, then sat back down again. "Is he here? He was hurt."

"Yes, he was hurt," Garcia agreed. "Did you see how he got hurt?"

Cara shook her head. "He was very upset. He was telling them to leave him alone. He wanted to go to his room. They wouldn't let him."

"Yes, that's what Janice said too."

"They should just leave him alone. They shouldn't hurt him."

"Do you think someone hurt him?"

"He was on the floor." Her eyes were big and round.

Had she seen him after he had died? Or even before?

"Do you know what time he was on the floor?" Garcia prompted.

"No." Cara's head shook back and forth.

"Do you know what day it was? Was it the day he died?"

"They should leave him alone. He wasn't hurting anyone. Why do they act like he is when he just wants to be left alone?"

"Why did they say?"

Cara sat quietly, thinking about it.

"Was there a reason they wouldn't leave him alone?" Garcia tried again.

Cara rubbed the deep creases between her eyebrows. "It's so hard to remember."

"Are you on the experimental therapy too?"

A slight shake of her head, but Kenzie wasn't sure whether it had been intended as an answer or was just a random movement.

"Cara? Do they have you on the drug for the experimental program?" Garcia persisted.

"No!" Cara's voice was suddenly loud, accusatory. "That's not my program!"

They were all riveted on her, waiting to see if she were going to escalate. Maybe the orderly was right and she could be dangerous, and he hadn't just come to watch the entertainment of their trying to talk to a non-communicative patient. Cara didn't stand up or get confrontational. She didn't appear to be angry. Maybe just erratic. The occasional burst of pique, and then it was instantly gone again.

"How did Leander feel about the experimental drugs?" Garcia asked. "Did he like it?"

"No." Cara picked at the fabric of her hospital clothes. "He wanted out. He didn't want to take it."

Garcia looked at Kenzie questioningly. Kenzie studied Cara. "If Leander didn't want to take it, then why was he still in the program?"

Cara stared up at the ceiling. "He wasn't allowed to decide."

"If a patient doesn't want treatment, he is allowed to refuse," Kenzie pointed out.

"No. We can't." Cara looked at Kenzie for the first time and shook her head. "You're a doctor. You know that."

"Why aren't you allowed to refuse?"

"Someone else says so."

"Who says?"

She shrugged. "Whoever. Your mother. Brother. Doctor." Her shoulders lifted again. "Whoever."

Kenzie looked over at Garcia. "My best guess is someone holding medical power of attorney. If a patient is judged not to be competent to make their own medical decisions."

"That makes sense. These people are—" Garcia looked at Cara and reworded. "These patients may not be capable of making those kinds of decisions for themselves."

"But if he wanted out of the program, they should have taken him out. He was the one who knew what it was doing to him. Why was he kept in the program?"

"I guess we'll find that out when we get his medical files. Who made medical decisions on his behalf and what they had to say about it. I can understand that sometimes patients might need treatments they don't want, but… it seems to me that with an experimental program, there are more risks. More reasons to avoid the treatment until it has been fully approved and deemed safe. Let someone else be the guinea pig."

Kenzie nodded. "If things were not going well for him, and all the accounts we've had so far are that he was reacting negatively to the therapy, then why didn't they pull him out when he asked them to? It seems like the right thing to do."

Garcia nodded. "But if they really believed in the program and thought that it was doing him good… maybe they could see benefits that the other patients and Mr. Isah himself did not."

"Maybe," Kenzie agreed. It was hard to know what anyone was thinking or feeling. Leander might have objected to all forms of treatment. He might have just wanted to go home. And he couldn't. He still had to be treated. He wasn't ready for the outside world yet.

"They shouldn't have hurt him," Cara repeated. "They shouldn't have put him down on the floor."

22

The video recordings Garcia had demanded and Isah's medical records were in a box ready for them when they were finished interviewing the witnesses. Garcia looked through the box doubtfully. "This is all of the video recorded in the forty-eight hours before Mr. Isah's death?"

The earnest receptionist raised her hands in a pleading gesture. "That was what I was given. I'm sure it's everything that you asked for. I don't have any way of knowing personally if that is all of the video or not."

"And are these all of Mr. Isah's medical records? History, current treatment protocol, everything?"

"Yes, that's everything."

Garcia showed the files to Kenzie. "They seem pretty slim to me."

"Everything is digital. We've printed out everything we can, and it's all in there."

"You have digital records that are not printed?"

"I don't know. We printed everything…"

"Everything you *could*."

"Yes."

"What about the stuff you couldn't print? Where is it?"

"It's… in the system."

"Why don't you copy it onto a USB drive for Dr. Kirsch."

"I… don't think I can do that."

"We've subpoenaed all of the information."

"I know. But I don't think… I don't think the system allows you to make a USB copy. They don't want people taking information off the system. Just walking off with it."

"There must be a way to make a backup copy."

"I guess."

"Your system is backed up every day, isn't it?"

"Yes."

"Then make us a backup."

"I don't know how to do that. We'd have to get one of the techs in to do it. I've got no idea how."

Garcia rolled her eyes at Kenzie. Kenzie shook her head.

"Get your tech guys in here," Garcia told the woman sharply. "I will be back for the backup tomorrow. It better be ready."

"I'll… I'll courier it to you," the receptionist squeaked helpfully.

"Good. Then I won't have to come back here again. Because I'm not going to be happy if I have to come back here."

She nodded vigorously. "I completely understand that. I'll get it together. I promise. I'll find out how to do it."

Garcia nodded. She lugged the box full of recordings and files out with her. Kenzie laughed as they left the building. "I thought that poor woman was going to wet her pants. You weren't very nice to her."

"I'm done being nice. I'm nice the first time I ask for something. You keep stringing me along, and I'm not going to put up with it for long."

"I guess that's how you get things done."

Garcia nodded. She grabbed the bundle of files from the box before putting it into her car. "I will give those to you. Review them and fill me in on anything I need to know. So far… I don't necessarily like what these people are doing, but it doesn't seem to be anything criminal or that directly caused Mr. Isah's death. But I'm not the one who is qualified to make that judgment. I look forward to hearing from you."

"Thanks." Kenzie took the files from her. She thought that Garcia was right; the files did seem a little light. They might cover the basics, but Kenzie suspected that there was a lot more information the hospital could have given them about Mr. Isah.

She headed back to the office to read through them and find out what more she could.

Kenzie looked up from the files, her eyes sore and gritty, to see who was calling her on her cell phone. She was ready to close her eyes and take a break so, when she saw that it was Lisa Cole Kirsch, she picked up the phone and swiped to answer the call.

"Hi, Mom."

"MacKenzie. How are you doing, dear? I'm sorry for calling you in the middle of the workday. I know you are probably swamped right now…"

"No, it's okay. I need a short break. How are you?"

"I am just fine. Enjoying the lovely autumn weather. I don't like the winter, but when the leaves start changing color, there is nowhere I would rather be than Vermont."

"A lot of people would agree with you. It is very nice right now."

The autumn weather could be wet and miserable, so Kenzie, too, had been enjoying the fact that it hadn't yet turned. She should spend more time outside. Zachary had made a goal to spend more time outside getting some exercise and fresh air and pursuing his photography hobby —a change from taking pictures of adulterous couples, accident reconstructions, and insurance scammers—and he had done very well at following through and getting more sun and exercise during the year. Which was a pretty big accomplishment for someone with ADHD, whose natural inclination would have been to put it off or forget about it.

"And Zachary, how is he?"

"He's doing pretty well. I was just thinking about how much he's been enjoying the weather this year. He's been spending a lot of time outside, and I should be following his example."

"We should *all* be following his example," Lisa agreed with a laugh. "Good for him. And his mental health? I would imagine it has improved with being outside more."

"He's had a pretty good year. It's that time now, though… As it gets closer to winter, I worry about him. The days are already getting shorter, and I'm sure he's thinking about Christmas and how he's going to manage it this year, even if they haven't started talking about it on TV yet."

"I hope he has a better time of it this year. He was in the hospital for a long time last year."

"Yes, he was. But they got him stabilized on this new med protocol, and it's been pretty good all year. So, fingers crossed that it continues to hold out and we don't have to make any big adjustments. And that if he does spend time in the hospital this year, it won't be as long. He doesn't have to be hospitalized every year so, hopefully, this will be one of his better years."

"I certainly hope so," Lisa agreed.

Hopefully, it would be better for all of them. They had all been through the wringer the previous year, even if it wasn't something they wanted to discuss.

"And Walter was telling me about your young friend…?" Lisa suggested. "That has just been admitted?"

"Yes." Kenzie sighed. She hadn't heard an update on Rhys's condition yet and hoped he was doing all right. "Rhys. He's had a pretty tough time in life. I don't know whether the trauma has resurfaced for some reason, or something new is going on, bullying or hormones maybe, but he is having a difficult time. I'm hoping his stay won't be long, that they can deal with these new issues."

"Rhys. That isn't a very common name. What's his last name?"

"Salter. Do you know him?" Kenzie couldn't imagine Lisa would have had the opportunity to run into Rhys anywhere. It was just idle curiosity, or she knew someone else by the same name and wanted to make sure that it wasn't him.

"Salter. No. I don't think I know anyone by that name."

Kenzie was glad this was not followed by, "Wasn't that the name of the woman who was murdered?" She didn't want to have to explain that.

"Well, I certainly hope he gets the help he needs," Lisa continued. "I am increasingly convinced that we need to put more time and money into these issues. There are so many people who are suffering so badly from mental illness. You don't know it until you start looking around, asking questions, and really listening to the answers."

"Mental illness does need more attention," Kenzie agreed. "It's not a very sexy cause, but people desperately need the funding. Depression kills just as many people as some of the other causes you campaign for. We can't ignore it just because we can't see it as easily as a wheelchair or dial-ysis machine."

"You know that we are now," Lisa said. "The foundation is putting a lot more money into mental illness in the last couple of years. It has really come to the forefront now. We can't ignore it."

"Yeah. Thanks." Kenzie always choked up a little when Lisa started talking about how much money the Kirsch family foundation was putting toward mental illness campaigns. She knew it was because of Zachary, and she loved her parents for caring enough about Kenzie and her partner's happiness to make such significant changes to their funding.

"I have sent you some documents to be signed. Have you had a chance to look at them yet?"

"No, I'm sorry, Mom. Things have been crazy, and I am behind where I should be. I know I promised to pay more attention to it, so I'll get to it as soon as I can. With Dr. Wiltshire breaking his hand, things have been a little crazy lately. Can you get a second signature from someone else this time?"

"Of course. But do try to stay on top of your emails. And read through the new funding requests. We need to keep things moving forward. There are a lot of people who need that money a lot more than we do, you know."

Kenzie smiled. "I know, Mom. We just have to keep giving it away."

Lisa laughed. "We'll do our best."

23

More than one person had asked Kenzie about Zachary's mental health recently. Kenzie could not escape the fact that his depression was not going to just go away. The usual seasonal depression was bound to hit him any time now. The last couple of years, it had hit earlier, so she knew they were living on borrowed time.

With the worry over Rhys's hospitalization, Zachary was bound to be worrying and thinking about his own mental health.

She didn't ask him how he was doing. He had promised to tell her about any major downturns. She knew that the year before, he had kept her informed about how he was feeling, even though he'd been disappointed with himself and had not wanted to let her know how much he was struggling. She didn't want to make things more stressful by hovering over him, waiting for something to happen.

But it was already on her mind and, when she woke up a couple of hours after lying down to find Zachary's side of the bed empty, she felt a familiar tightness in her stomach. That feeling of dread that his health had taken a turn for the worst, and he had begun the descent. She feared not just for his happiness, but for his life. He had attempted suicide in the past, and his behavior the previous year, when he started having suicidal thoughts again, had been very scary.

Kenzie got out of bed. She pulled on her housecoat, slid her feet into her slippers, and shuffled out to the living room.

If Zachary were working at his computer, that was a good sign. As long as he wasn't watching some horrible video over and over again, trying to solve a murder case. And if he had started to work on his computer and then fallen asleep on the couch while he worked, that was a good sign, because it meant that he had fallen asleep spontaneously instead of having to take a sleep aid or sit up awake all through the night because his brain just wouldn't shut down or he was worried that he would never wake up.

But he wasn't in the living room working at his laptop or slumped over asleep. He was pacing.

Kenzie caught him as he paced from the kitchen into the living room, then turned around to go back. He saw her and stopped.

"Hey," Kenzie said softly. "How are you doing?"

"Oh. Just restless. Sorry, I didn't mean to wake you up."

"You didn't wake me up. I just woke up on my own and you weren't there. So I thought I would check on you."

"You should go back to sleep. You have work in the morning."

"So do you. What's up? Are you worried about something?"

He tried to stay where he was, but eventually gave in and paced back into the kitchen.

"I don't know. Just restless, really. My brain is going, but... it's jumping from one thing to another. As soon as I tell it to stop thinking about one thing and try to switch to something else... then it starts grinding away on something else. I really just want it to stop."

"But there's no off switch."

They had talked about it before. Kenzie knew how frustrated he got with his brain and his inability to just shut off when he wanted to. Kenzie knew that it was hard enough for her to let go of a problem and relax for the evening or night so that she could sleep, but it was much worse for Zachary. Kenzie could usually do a bit of meditation or get a few minutes of exercise, think about something else that she enjoyed, and her brain would usually settle down enough to relax for the evening and sleep at night. But the same was not true for Zachary. When his brain got in a rut, it *really* got in a rut, and he could be going over the same argument in his head or fighting the same obsession for days without relief.

"Maybe it's time to take something to help you sleep," she suggested.

Not a hard push. A hard push, and Zachary would get upset about her trying to force him to do what she thought was right. It was his body and brain, not hers, and she wasn't his doctor. It was up to him to decide whether to take something to help him sleep, and he would resist it for as long as he could. All Kenzie could do was to make the suggestion. If he were unable to sleep for several days, he would probably end up in the hospital again. But she couldn't jump directly to that just because he was having one restless night.

"It's pretty late to take anything tonight," Zachary said, marching restlessly across the room, back and forth. "If I take something now, I won't be able to get up before noon."

An exaggeration, but Kenzie understood his concern. There was a point at which it became inadvisable to take anything, because he needed to be able to get up and get back to work in the morning. He had to take high doses of strong medication for it to work, and they always made him groggy and made getting up and getting his brain operating again difficult.

"You slept last night?" she checked.

"Yes, I did. This is the first night I've been up… and I'll probably still get an hour or two in." Zachary looked at his spot on the couch as if wishing he had already fallen asleep there. "I just need to wait… until my body is tired enough to tell my brain to shut off…"

"Are you worrying about Rhys?"

He stopped momentarily and looked at her, then resumed pacing. "Yes."

"I'm worried about him too. I hope that we'll hear he's doing better soon."

Zachary nodded jerkily. "Poor kid. I just want to be there to help him through this, and that's the one thing I can't do. I can't be there with him when he's in the hospital."

"I know. It's hard."

He looked at her and nodded, acknowledging that she knew what it was like to have a loved one in the psych ward and not to be able to do anything for him.

"I left a message for Vera during the day, but she hasn't gotten back to me. I don't know if that means that things have gotten worse, and she doesn't want to tell me."

"It probably just means that she's spending a lot of time at the hospital, and then going to bed as soon as she gets home."

He considered that, his steps slowing a little. "Yeah. Maybe."

"She needs more sleep than you do, especially going through a stressful time like this. She's probably sleeping ten hours a day. Between that and meals and visiting at the hospital…"

"If she's visiting. If she's allowed to see him."

"She's his guardian. They can't stop her from seeing him."

"The psych ward has rules…"

"I know. But she can insist."

"She wouldn't. If they told her not to, she wouldn't go. And what if Rhys didn't want to see her?"

"Why wouldn't he? He loves his grandma."

"I know, but… it's different when you're feeling so bad, and you don't want anyone to see you like that and don't want to have to talk about how you're feeling. And I'm okay with talking, normally. I don't have the trouble with communicating that Rhys does. It might just seem too hard."

Kenzie sighed. "I supposed so. But I hope not. I hope he's okay with her just visiting and talking to him or holding his hand."

Zachary stopped pacing and closed his eyes briefly, maybe picturing it, trying to see how that felt. He nodded, letting out his breath in a long, controlled stream. Maybe that image helped. He could picture Rhys being comforted and in a safe place, sleeping tonight and having someone there to take care of him and his grandma visiting again in the morning to see him through the dark tunnel.

Kenzie took a step toward Zachary and brought her hands apart, offering a hug. Zachary took a step toward her. They both closed the distance and held each other for a few minutes.

"Come back to bed?" Kenzie suggested.

"I'm too restless. I'll keep you awake."

"Just come and cuddle for a few minutes, then. I need you."

She thought he needed the physical comfort more than she did, but if she said *he* needed it, he would just resist. If she said that she needed him, it was different. He would do whatever he could to comfort her and fulfill her needs.

"Okay," he agreed, as she knew he would. "But I don't know how long I'll stay. I might leave as soon as you're asleep. If I can't lie still, I don't want to disrupt your sleep."

Kenzie nodded. She took him by the hand and led him back to the bedroom.

24

One of Kenzie's problems with Dr. Cook substituting for Dr. Wiltshire was the time he arrived at the office. Not because he started late, but the opposite. He was there too early. With Dr. Wiltshire, she had time to get to the office and work her way through the voicemails and emails that had arrived overnight to make sure that there wasn't anything urgent that needed to be taken care of and to get the majority of the reports printed and digital filing done. And then there was checking on any bodies that had arrived overnight to make sure that everything had been checked in properly, assigned a file number, and assigned a position in the queue. And she needed to check which funeral homes were planning to transport the bodies they were finished with.

But Dr. Cook arrived too early and messed up the workflow. Sometimes, he had reviewed the voicemails in the main mailbox before she got there, which was irritating. With Dr. Wiltshire, she just passed on any messages that he needed to deal with. She handled the rest and made sure that everything was logged and filed. She didn't like Dr. Cook changing things around, even though, of course, he was entitled to and, as Dr. Wiltshire's substitute, he was really her superior rather than her helper, even if that was how he chose to frame it. She couldn't order him around or tell him to stop trying to be helpful.

"Dr. Kirsch," Cook sounded grave, and Kenzie wondered what was going on. "I'm glad you're here. If you could come to my office…"

Kenzie motioned to her desk. "I have a lot of stuff to clear first thing."

"I've taken care of it. Please come with me."

Kenzie did, of course, once she had removed her outer clothing and stowed it away.

"Is something wrong?" she asked as she sat in the visitor chair in front of Dr. Wiltshire's—or Dr. Cook's—desk.

"I picked up a disturbing voicemail this morning. Let me play it for you."

"We get crank calls sometimes," Kenzie told him. "Stupid kids fooling around, people who are worried about zombies or mentally ill people who think they are dead."

Dr. Cook looked at her for a moment, mouth open, then shook his head. He picked up Dr. Wiltshire's desk phone and put it on speaker while he dialed into the voicemail box and then accessed it. He played a saved message.

"Why don't you just stay in your office and do your job there?" A flat computer voice read. "Stay where you belong instead of trying to stop good people from doing good things. Just do your damn autopsies and stay out of everyone else's business. Your friends will benefit by you staying out of the way. You do your job and let us do ours."

Kenzie closed her eyes. It was too early in the day to be dealing with voicemail threats.

"Uh…" She rubbed the orbital bones around her eyes, looking for something to say. "Yeah, sometimes we get stuff like that. It's just people blowing off steam. It isn't anything."

"Do you know who this is?"

"Someone at Persons, I would guess." At his questioning look, she clarified. "Persons Residential Care. That's where Leander Isah was."

"And why would they be making telephone threats?"

"Because they don't like the fact that they are being investigated in the context of his death. Whether or not they have done anything to endanger Isah or any other patients, I can't tell you why, but they have been resistant from the beginning, from the minute I showed up there for the scene review. It's been challenging to get the records that we needed from them. It took Detective Garcia going there with a subpoena yesterday before they finally released anything. And even then, the files seem a little… light. Sanitized."

"How do you know it is them?"

"I guess I don't for sure. The police will have to check the incoming line and see where the call came from. But that's the only one that I'm doing anything on outside of the office. So if they want me to stay in the office and not investigate elsewhere, that is the case they are talking about."

Cook nodded. He steepled his hands together and thought about it. "We'll need to bring the police in on it."

"Detective Garcia is already on the case. I'll let her know. And we can send her a copy of the voicemail. Not that it will help, since they used text-to-speech to synthesize the voice."

"Sounds that way," he agreed. "But as you say, they may be able to trace where the call came from. We might get lucky with it pointing directly back to Persons."

"Not that it is such a big deal. It's certainly not the first irate call we've gotten from someone we were investigating."

"Hmm." He didn't seem willing to let it go. "What did that mean? Your friends will benefit by you staying away?"

"I… don't know," Kenzie admitted. "Just blowing smoke, I would guess. I don't have any friends involved in the case. Maybe they're talking about the patients we interviewed yesterday. Calling them my friends would be a stretch, but you know how people talk sometimes. Doctors' offices, especially therapists, use the 'royal we' when talking to patients. I could see them referring to the patients as friends to make it sound more supportive and less clinical."

"Your friends will benefit by you staying away," Cook repeated, trying it out. His tone was skeptical, but he nodded. "It could be, but why *your* friends instead of *our* friends?"

"Because I spent time with them yesterday… so now they're my friends too."

"Do you really think so?"

Kenzie shrugged. "I have no clue. It was just an idea."

"You have friends who are in psychiatric care? Who might benefit from the types of programs that Persons is running?"

Kenzie's stomach tightened. "Oh..."

Cook studied her face. "So you do. Who?"

"Well... my partner, for one. He is okay right now, but he has been hospitalized for... psychiatric care in the past. And... a boy that we know. A teenager. He was just admitted to the hospital. He's having some kind of crisis. Both of them have very traumatic pasts... the type of thing that Persons is treating with this MDMA program of theirs."

Cook nodded slowly. "So... maybe if you backed off, they could help you with those friends. Seeing that they got treatment. This new, experimental treatment that isn't available anywhere else."

"Maybe that is what they were talking about. Though I don't know that. It's as good a theory as any. And I don't see how they would know anything about Zachary or... either of them. They would have to be guessing that I am close to someone who had mental illness and could benefit from their program or the type of program they are doing."

"Considering the statistics, everyone has a friend who could benefit from psychiatric care."

"I guess so," Kenzie admitted. "It's a pretty good bet that everyone knows someone who is struggling with their mental health. Although something like PTSD is not quite as common as just depression or anxiety."

Cook waved a hand. "Still pretty common in today's world. With kids going through lock-down drills at school and war and terrorist threats, human trafficking, child abuse... I'm sure you probably have other friends with it that you haven't even thought of yet."

"I guess."

"Okay. I'll pass this on to the police."

"I have Detective Garcia's information, and I can just email it to her."

"Make sure you do it right away. Don't sit on it."

Kenzie nodded. "Sure. Thanks for taking it seriously. We've had threats before and... it can be disconcerting."

"I'm sure nothing will come of it. They didn't exactly threaten to come after you and your family. They just said they're doing important work and don't want you to interfere with it. But I want to be sure it is handled."

"Yeah, I agree, better safe than sorry."

Kenzie stood up, not sure whether she had been dismissed yet.

"Your partner," Cook said, "what's going on there?"

Kenzie hesitated. "What do you mean?"

"I mean… well, I wouldn't ask for any private medical information, of course, but… how is his health? Is this something that concerns you?"

"I told you, he's good right now." Kenzie wavered. "Well… I mean, he had a bad night. Worrying about our other friend that I mentioned. But overall, he's doing okay right now."

If it weren't the beginning of his depressive cycle. Kenzie was braced for it. For how thin and gaunt he would get. The loss of him from her life, as his thoughts and attention were turned inward, leaving her on the outside, all by herself.

"I hope," she added honestly. Zachary promoted openness about his mental illness, trying to be a part of the solution in overcoming the stigma. "He will hit a depressive cycle sometime in the next few weeks. That is his usual pattern. Then he will improve again after Christmas."

"That's pretty exact."

"Like I said, he had a lot of childhood trauma. Beginning with a fire on Christmas Eve. Or rather, culminating with a fire on Christmas Eve. So he has a connection with that date. It isn't exactly Seasonal Affective Disorder because it isn't triggered by the change in the weather or the days getting shorter. It is cyclical, but because of his history."

"I see. And he's had this for how long?" He held up his hand, stopping Kenzie from answering. "This is personal. I'm sorry. I shouldn't be asking. I was only curious, but it is none of my business and he isn't even here to say whether you can talk to me about it or not. I'm sorry."

"No, it's okay. He has said before that he wants to be open and transparent about it and that the more people talk about mental illness, the more normalized it can become. He was ten at the time. So this has been going on for many years."

"Good grief. It's depressing just to think about it. The poor guy."

Kenzie nodded. "And until now, I would have said that it will likely be a pattern that continues for years to come. We're doing our best with medications and therapy, but PTSD can be pretty hard to overcome, and it's become so ingrained."

"But hallucinogen-mediated trauma therapy might offer some relief."

Kenzie shrugged. "It could," she admitted. "I haven't discussed it with him but, as you can imagine, I have been thinking about it."

"Well, maybe things will work out well for Persons. And if not, they are not the only place offering this treatment. There will be other opportunities to get into it."

25

Kenzie called Detective Garcia about the voicemail and forwarded a copy to her by email.

"It's really nothing," she told the detective, "I'm sure you get much worse threats all the time. I'd put money on it being someone at Persons. And, of course, someone we talked to, which is why they used the computer voice. It was someone whose voice we would have recognized."

"Undoubtedly," Garcia agreed crisply, her accent stronger for that one word. "I'll make some waves. They can't threaten law enforcement and get away with it. I don't suppose you've had a chance to review the medical records yet, have you?"

"I've been through them once. I'll need to study them carefully at least one more time. Make sure that I pick up everything I can. But on the surface, there isn't anything that points to cause of death. No matter what they told Janice Martin, he did not have a bad heart."

"Oh, let me write that down." Garcia shuffled papers for a moment, and then Kenzie could hear computer keys being tapped. Garcia had pretty good speed. "Okay, got it. Anything else in the medical records that I should know about?"

"I'm not sure the files are complete. Like you said, they were pretty slim. Some abbreviated stuff on his medical history. They wanted to

420

ensure that we got the stuff on torture because people who have been tortured have shorter lifespans and, sometimes, we never really know what killed them. We don't know enough about how the body works to understand all the ways that torture can damage it. There may be stuff right down past the cellular level that we don't understand. The way that neurons communicate with each other. Mitochondrial function. Remapping the brain."

"But you know for sure that there is stuff missing? Or you're guessing that there must be?"

"Well, for one thing, there are no consents."

"What kind of consents?"

"Consents to treatment. Especially for the experimental program. That kind of thing usually involves all kinds of paperwork—waivers, consents, long lists of the potential risks. They don't want to get sued if things don't go well. They need informed consent. And I don't see it anywhere."

"Would that be something that Isah had signed? Or his guardian?"

"Hard to say. If it was me, I'd get both. Was he competent? Was he not competent? I'd want to get his signature to prove that he consented to it, and to get his medical attorney's signature to make sure that they approved it. There are a lot of ethical problems with experimenting on people with serious psychiatric illnesses."

She could tell Garcia was thinking this through. "Because you have to experiment and test it out on psychiatric patients to find something that works, but if they have serious issues, how can they consent to it?"

"Exactly," Kenzie agreed. "We have a bad history of experimenting on people without their permission or guardians' informed consent, so we need to cover all our bases. But it is still an ethically gray area. Psychiatric patients, children, pregnant women, the elderly. They are all vulnerable populations. We want to have the proper medications to treat them, but we don't want to experiment on them. Or we do, but we're not allowed."

"Not speaking for yourself, of course," Garcia said dryly.

"None of my patients need to give consent. They're all dead. About as safe as you can get."

Garcia laughed.

"Although, we do try to respect things like last wishes, religious constraints, that sort of thing. If we know of a prohibition, we'll try to work around it if we can."

"So even after they're dead, you still have to deal with the nut jobs."

"Uh…"

Kenzie wasn't sure how to approach Garcia calling religious people nut jobs. Garcia hadn't meant it that way, she was sure. She was thinking of the more extreme cases that sometimes made the news, with people shrieking to the cameras about their religious rights being violated.

"Okay, not nut jobs," Garcia said irritably, understanding Kenzie's silence. "I just mean… hysterical families. People who are always threatening to sue. They are so… reactionary and don't really think things through."

"There can be issues," Kenzie said. "We do our best to respect people's beliefs, but we can't always do things the way they would like." She'd had more than one experience with a crazed relative who thought she wasn't handling things as she should. Or crazed members of the public. Things *could* get a little crazy sometimes.

"So, consents are one thing you are missing," Garcia said, reminding her where they had segued from. "Anything else?"

"Well, the receptionist talked about the electronic assets that she hadn't been able to give us. There should be recordings of the sessions. From what I see of the protocols on the paperwork we have, all the sessions were supposed to be video recorded. And there is nothing like that in what I got. Not even photographs or audio recordings. So that's going to be a big thing if we want to see just what they were up to. If we can watch a recording of how Isah reacted during his session that day, what kind of shape he was in and if he was agitated like the witnesses suggest…"

"They recorded all the sessions? Isn't that a breach of privacy?"

"Not if the patient knew they were being taped, and it was for clinical purposes. It's a good record for the people running the drug trials. Provides you with a lot more information than just a page of written notes."

"I told them I would go back today. So I definitely will. That will be the mother lode."

Kenzie nodded her agreement. "Yeah. It will be very helpful to see what he looked like that last day. Skin color, respiration, what his emotional state was. All of that."

"And if he was being restrained," Garcia suggested.

"Yes. It would be helpful to know that, too."

"I have a couple of other questions," Garcia said. "If you have a few minutes to humor me."

Kenzie looked at the system time on her computer. She would probably advance the Isah case more by answering Garcia's question than anything else she could do. "Yeah, sure."

"First, talking about consent and competence and all of that..."

"Uh-huh."

"Our interviews yesterday."

"Yeah?" Kenzie started to think about where Garcia was going on this before she got around to asking the question. They had interviewed psych patients. They would not be reliable witnesses if ever called to testify in court. But they had gone into the interviews knowing that. Knowing they were not interviewing experts, but people who might be able to give them a small insight here and there into the life or the mind of Leander Isah.

"Obviously, they are not good witnesses," Garcia confirmed. "But if we had to use something that one of them said, we could, right? I mean, just because they are psychiatric patients, that doesn't mean that they don't know when someone enters or leaves their room. They can tell time or know that it was after lunch or before supper, or that everyone had just been given their meds."

"I guess, yes. It would be up to you to figure out how much to ask them and how to present it to the jury. Because they will be seen as... well, crazy."

"Fair enough," Garcia agreed. "How about the drugs?"

"The drugs?" Kenzie echoed. She thought about each of the patients they had interviewed. Janice, David, and Cara. They had all seemed to be coherent and anchored to the present. They seemed to understand what she was talking about. But they were on psychoactive drugs. And possibly hallucinogenics. Kenzie blew out her breath through pursed lips, whistling slightly. "Well... I hadn't really thought about that."

"Cara Anderson was definitely high," Garcia said. "Did you see her eyes? I think she had just come from therapy. Should we even have been interviewing her in that state? As far as I could tell, they all knew what was going on. But that Cara, she was pretty far gone."

"I don't think it was all the effects of the drugs, but yes, I think it would be hard to separate the effects of the drugs and her psychosis and to say that she knew what she was talking about when she said this or that."

"She said Isah did not want to be in the drug trials. That he wanted out."

"Maybe you can find someone else who will say the same thing. From a more… stable perspective."

Garcia sighed. "That's what I was afraid of. There aren't going to be a lot of people who can verify that statement. And most of the people who can, who would be good witnesses, are the people who don't want to talk to us."

"The doctors rather than the patients."

"*They* are not going to tell us that Isah wanted out of the drug trials," Garcia said flatly.

Kenzie grimaced. "Yeah, it might be hard to find anyone who will say that on the record."

"The second question," Garcia said, "is even less pleasant than that one."

26

Kenzie took a deep breath and held it for a moment.

"Okay. What do you want to ask me?"

"I've been doing some research on these MDMA trials. I know some stuff about it from dealing with raves and kids on X."

"Uh-huh?"

"The kids think that rave drugs are harmless, that nothing will come of them taking them. They're just good fun. Get a good buzz or have an out-of-body experience, and the next day, you're back to school or work with no adverse effects. But I know the stuff can kill you."

"Yeah," Kenzie nodded. "If you get too much and your body overheats… it can cook you alive. Your brain can't operate at those temperatures." Her mind went to Isah's hyperthermic state when he had died.

"Ecstasy also makes the users… well, more sexually outgoing," Garcia said delicately.

Kenzie cleared her throat. "Yes. Increased libido and sensitivity are associated with MDMA. Though it also causes sexual dysfunction."

"One thing that I found was that a number of these trials had been shut down or disqualified because the supposed therapists running them were taking advantage of their patients'… sexual openness."

Kenzie tried to hold back her disgust that someone who claimed to be a medical practitioner trying to heal someone would do something so reprehensible. She sipped her water, trying to swallow the lump in her throat.

"Unfortunately… I did find evidence in the autopsy that Mr. Isah had been sexually active. There was bruising that would indicate that it was either rough or non-consensual." She had another swallow of water. "We took swabs and sent them for analysis. But there was no semen present. If his assailant was a male, he was wearing a condom."

"When were you going to tell me that little tidbit?"

"When I release my findings. Along with everything else."

"But you didn't think it was worth mentioning before this? As part of my investigation into Persons, for example?"

"I didn't get the lab reports until this morning. Until then, I was hoping that it would not be a dead end. That I would be able to give you more information than just that he appeared to have been assaulted sometime in the days before his death. I was really hoping there would be DNA."

"No such luck," Garcia said philosophically, as if she had been expecting this all along. And maybe she had. That would have made it only too easy. Only Isah's rapist had not necessarily had anything to do with his death. It definitely meant that Persons had to be thoroughly investigated by the proper authorities. But the two incidents did not necessarily tie together, other than by the fact that Isah had been the victim in both cases. "Okay. So that's a dead end. We'll inform the feds and have them start an investigation into the possibility of a sexual predator operating around vulnerable people at Persons."

"That was your last question?" Kenzie asked.

"That's it. For now. I'll head over there later today and get a copy of the electronic assets, which hopefully includes the recordings of the therapy sessions."

"I got a call back from Vera today," Zachary offered during dinner that evening.

Kenzie breathed a sigh of relief to hear that, especially since Zachary's voice was upbeat rather than depressed or flat. "That's good to hear. Has she been spending a lot of time at the hospital?"

"I'm not sure how many hours she has spent there. They're going to put Rhys into a different facility, one that is better for treating kids with trauma issues."

"That's good news! Is it inpatient or outpatient?"

"Inpatient. At least in the beginning. They'll also have transition programs to help return him to outpatient care once he's shown an improvement."

Kenzie nodded. "I didn't think the city had anything like that. How did Vera say he was doing?"

"She was… worn out. He's not good. It's been an emotional few days for her. It was completely unexpected. She was blindsided. But they're keeping a close watch on him, doing everything they can to get him the help he needs."

"Were there any signs that something was going on at school? Bullying or abuse of any kind?"

"It sounds like there might have been something," Zachary admitted. "They'll need to investigate it more carefully… dig into it when he's able to talk again. Or… communicate, anyway. When he can tell them what was going on with school."

Kenzie remembered Cara Anderson, her eyes so far away, in the same room as Kenzie and yet Kenzie hadn't even been sure that Cara knew she was there until she had finally started answering their questions. It was heartbreaking to think of Rhys like that. He had blossomed so much in the time that they had known him, growing into a prankster who loved to tease Zachary, especially about his relationship with Kenzie, and who Kenzie knew cared deeply about his friends. What had happened to make him withdraw so completely?

"What did Vera know about school?" Kenzie asked. "Had Rhys's grades dropped?"

"She said that there had been some fights at school. Nothing big, just… some scuffles. School locker room. Cafeteria. Not actually during classes. Of course." Zachary chewed vigorously to get his salad down. Kenzie knew he didn't enjoy it. He tried to eat whatever she served, but vegetables were always a challenge. "Who would do something in front of a teacher? Nothing blatant, anyway. Maybe a little verbal abuse. Maybe touching or poking him when the teacher was turned around. But they wouldn't be able to beat him up or do anything too obvious. Not right in class."

"And Vera didn't know what those scuffles were about?"

"No. When the school administrators brought them up, they suggested it was just horseplay. Friends getting too into it, not knowing when to stop or when someone's feelings were hurt."

Kenzie rolled her eyes. "Am I glad that I'm not in school anymore. Teenagers are vicious creatures."

"Yes, they are," Zachary agreed. "The biggest incident, I guess, was when he blew up at the resource room teacher when she was trying to help him with something. That got an immediate call home to grandma and one-day suspension."

"What happened? And what did Rhys tell Vera? Did he have any explanation?"

"According to the school, to the resource room teacher, he had been stubborn, angry. In a mood. She noticed that something was bothering him before anything actually happened. She tried to distract him from whatever it was with the work rather than demanding to know what was going on."

"Sounds reasonable," Kenzie approved. She picked up a carrot stick and munched it while Zachary continued with the description.

"She had him working on math, which is one of his better subjects. She put her hand on his shoulder to check his work, and he blew up."

Kenzie held her breath. "Physically? Verbally?"

"Jumped up, knocked her away from him, and shouted at her not to touch him." Zachary sounded sympathetic rather than judging of this behavior. Kenzie wondered, though, what had triggered Rhys's violent reaction. He had undoubtedly been in the resource room and dealt with the resource teacher many times. It sounded like she knew him well, and he would have been used to her presence and the way that she worked, the way she would lay her hand on his shoulder when she was ready to look at his work. So what had triggered the reaction this time? Was he off his meds or on something illicit? Steroids to build up his muscles or alcohol intended to help him to relax and loosen up?

"What explanation did Rhys give? To the teacher or Vera?"

"The teacher thought she had just startled him. She said it wasn't his fault. When Vera tried to talk to Rhys about it, he just kept pushing her away." Zachary caught Kenzie's look. "Emotionally. Not physically. He would wave her off and shake his head and growl at her. Go to his room and shut the door. Signaling that he wanted space and didn't want to talk about it."

Kenzie picked at her salad. While she enjoyed it more than Zachary did, she still wasn't really big on green salads herself. Even though she knew she needed them.

"I hit a teacher once," Zachary offered.

"You did? Why? What happened?"

She couldn't imagine Zachary hitting anyone without being heavily provoked. He was the victim of abuse. Not the perpetrator.

"It was when I was first in foster care," Zachary said, mulling it over. "I think… I was still with the Petersons. Mr. Peterson and his wife, Lilith. Back before." He shrugged expressively.

Back before Lilith had become aware of Lorne's affair with Patrick Parker, and they had immediately been disqualified as foster parents. The Petersons had been the first family Zachary had gone to in foster care. Straight from the hospital, Kenzie assumed, though he didn't talk much about that time and she wasn't sure what rehab and care he had been through during that time.

"I fell asleep in class," Zachary explained. He rubbed his forehead, trying to remember the details. "I think… that was when I'd had a reaction to my meds and ended up in the hospital, and then I still had to go to school, even though I'd been awake half the night. So I fell asleep. And the teacher… smacked my desk with the ruler to wake me up. I guess I just reacted. Thought I was being attacked and defended myself before I was even awake." He swallowed and shook his head. "I remember how I felt. The horror when I realized that I had punched her, right in the stomach. I thought they were going to kill me. I thought that they would lock me up and throw away the key. I knew you weren't allowed to hit adults. Especially teachers. I ran… and hid…"

"You were ten?"

Zachary nodded. "I think so. Maybe just turned eleven, I don't remember. That's when Mrs. Peterson said I couldn't live with them anymore." Zachary poked at the food that remained on his plate, his face clearly reflecting the pain and sorrow he had felt when he learned he was being moved from the home. "She figured if I would attack a grown woman, that she and the other children in the home were not safe. It didn't matter that I didn't mean to do it. I could just as easily make a mistake and hit one of the other kids."

Kenzie reached across the table to pat his hand. "You never would."

"I never hit any kid in my family. Unless they hit me first and I had to defend myself."

"You had the right to defend yourself. And it wasn't your fault that you hit the teacher, either. She should have known better than to do something like that. I remember the crack it would make when a teacher smacked a ruler down on a desk. It was like a gunshot. Meant to frighten and intimidate."

Zachary frowned. "You think she meant to scare me?"

"Why else would she do that? If all she wanted to do was to wake you up, she could say your name or nudge your shoulder. She wanted to scare the pants off you and to humiliate you in front of the rest of the class."

He considered this. "I don't know about that. Do you really think so?"

"Would you ever do something like that to a kid? To Mason, maybe?" Mason was Tyrrell's son, Zachary's nephew, a kid who kept his parents hopping with a raging case of ADHD. He very much reminded Zachary of himself as a child. Kenzie knew how hard Mason was on his parents. Not because he was a bad kid or tried to upset them, but because he just couldn't moderate his behavior and was constantly getting into things that he shouldn't or doing things he should have known better than to do. And he was also a very sensitive little boy who would cry over his daddy not showing up for a visit or being shouted at when he stepped over the line, as he invariably did multiple times a day.

Zachary shook his head immediately. "I would never do something like that to Mason. He can't help the way he is and, if he was sick and fell asleep, I'd just let him be."

"And if you had to wake him up, you wouldn't do it like that, would you?"

"Well, no. But I understand Mason. I know what it's like to be in his head. Most people… don't know what it's like. They think he's just being bad, acting out, trying to get attention. So they get frustrated, and when they see a way to call him out on his behavior, to try to teach him a lesson…" Understanding flooded into Zachary's features as he connected this to his teacher's behavior when she had woken him up. "It was. It was a way to get the better of me, call me out in front of my friends."

Kenzie nodded. "Yeah. It was."

"Well, the joke's on her," he said flatly.

"Oh, how is the joke on her?"

"Because I didn't have any friends."

Kenzie shook her head. She didn't laugh. It was tragic, not funny. "You must have had a few."

"I was only there for a few weeks. I think… maybe there was one kid who liked me. And we weren't friends. He just… needed someone to stand by him."

That sounded like a story for another day. She didn't want to focus too much on Zachary's stories from the past. They were likely to make him depressed, and she didn't want that. She wanted to keep his spirits up as much as possible.

"So where was it that Rhys got transferred to?" she asked. "The place that has this program for traumatized kids?"

"I wrote it down," Zachary offered. He had known that she would ask. And maybe hoped to be able to see Rhys before too long if the program would allow it. He pulled out his phone and tapped and scrolled to find it. "Here it is. Persons Residential Care."

27

Kenzie stared at Zachary in shock.

"What?" she demanded, aware that her voice was screeching. "They're transferring him to Persons?"

Zachary nodded, his eyes wide as he took in her reaction. "Yeah. What—what's wrong? You know them?"

"I'm investigating a case involving them right now!"

"Investigating a case…" Zachary repeated. "You mean that there was a death there."

Kenzie nodded. She looked around, trying to figure out what to do. Who to call. How to make sure that this didn't happen. "Yes, there was, and there's no way I want Rhys going there."

"But it sounded like… Vera said that… I thought this was a really good opportunity. She was going on about the program, how there isn't anything like it in the state and Rhys was lucky to get into it. She's really excited about it. They told her that it could really help him. They've had miraculous results."

Kenzie shook her head. "No, no, no. We don't want him getting into that program. You don't. Trust me."

"Well… what are we going to do? They've already started the process." Zachary touched his phone to wake up the display and looked at the time. "He's probably there now, just getting settled."

"We have to put a stop to it. She doesn't have to go ahead with it, even if she's already signed all the paperwork. She can withdraw her consent at any time."

Zachary nodded. "Okay. Then we need to get her on the phone." He tapped the screen again, unlocked it this time, and tapped to find Vera's number and call her back. He put it on speakerphone as it started to ring.

Kenzie held her breath, unable to believe the coincidence. Vulnerable Rhys going to Persons? Being put into the hands of a predator? At least she knew what was going on. At least she was in a position to put a stop to the process before Rhys got hurt. If she hadn't known… She shuddered at the thought of them all supporting Vera and telling her that she was doing the right thing, with Rhys suffering abuse at the hands of his therapists, drugged and confused about what was going on.

The phone had rung quite a few times before Vera picked it up. "Hello?"

"Vera, it's Zachary. And I have Kenzie here with me."

"Oh, thank you for calling. It's nice that you're concerned with Rhys and how he is doing. I already told you everything… We're just in the middle of things right now, so…"

"Vera," Kenzie interrupted, "you can't put Rhys into that program."

There was silence for a moment, and Kenzie thought Vera had already hung up. "He's already been approved for the program," Vera said, her tone confused. "I don't know what you mean."

"It's not right for him." Kenzie didn't want to say too much and tell Vera that there had been a death at the institution or that she believed there might be abuse taking place in the sessions or after the sessions were over, while the patient was still under the influence of the drugs. She didn't want to get sued for anything she said to Vera. "There are… some questions about the program and whether it might be harmful to the patients. I really don't think you want to put Rhys into it."

"We've already talked to the doctors about it. They gave me a list of possible risks, but I don't think there is anything to worry about. The benefits far outweigh any of the risks that they talked about."

"I doubt they have been open with you about all the risks. What did they tell you about the program? What are they going to do?"

"It's the only one in the state that's open to minors," Vera said promptly. "If I want to get him into one, it has to be this one, because otherwise he has to wait until he's an adult. And we don't want to wait until he's an adult. We need to work on this now. Try to reach him... to get him back on track again."

"What kind of therapy is it?" Kenzie pressed.

"There is… a drug-mediated therapy," Vera said, talking slowly in order to remember and recite what she had been told. "That just helps him to relax so that he can be open to what the therapist is saying, and be able to talk to them. Or communicate with them. You know."

"That drug—" Kenzie started.

"And there were some other therapies that they do. I don't remember all the initials. Different kinds of behavioral therapies. I think he has done some of them before. It seemed like they helped for a while, so maybe he just needs a 'refresher.' They're always finding new things, you know, ways to make it work better, and they say they are at the cutting edge. They can do a lot more for him now than they could when he was little. They were very positive and said that they were sure they would be able to help him."

"The drug they are using is not approved," Kenzie told her. "There could be side effects. Or other problems. Conflicts with the meds he's already on or a preexisting condition…"

"They said that. But they said they would be doing a full review of what he is on now and a physical, to make sure there was nothing to worry about. They said that was a risk that they could limit. They're doing really good work, Kenzie. They had a lot of success stories that they were telling me about. Kids who hadn't improved with anything else, but they were cured with this new therapy."

"It isn't safe," Kenzie repeated. "There are a lot of questions and concerns. I don't want Rhys to be put into that program. It is too dangerous."

"He's already all signed up," Vera said firmly. "I appreciate your concern, Kenzie, but it isn't up to you. It is up to me."

"I know, but you haven't been given all the information. They're sugar-coating it for you. Telling you all the good possibilities without telling you what damage you could be doing. Is the drug MDMA? Is that what they're doing?"

"It was a very long name," Vera said. "I don't recall. They said it is a very safe drug. It was developed in 1912, and has been safely used since then."

"Do you know what this is? Have you ever heard of ecstasy?"

"Yes. I know that a lot of legitimate drugs get used as street drugs," Vera told her in a clipped tone. "People sell painkillers and amphetamines and a lot of other legitimate drugs on the streets. That doesn't make them bad. They said it isn't addictive, and it will be strictly controlled. They won't make any mistakes. They know how much is safe to use for a teenager like Rhys."

"It hasn't been approved for psychiatric use, only for testing. If you want Rhys to take this therapy, you should at least wait until it is approved," Kenzie said desperately.

"If I wait, then we will miss this window of opportunity. It could be years before the authorities get around to recognizing it as a legitimate treatment. Rhys needs something now, Kenzie. You haven't seen him. He can't wait. We need to bring him back now, before he falls deeper into this… this hole."

"If I could tell you more about the dangers, I would," Kenzie said. "Maybe you could look it up online and get an idea of what some of the other risks are. Don't rely on them to tell you everything, because they won't. It's really not a safe therapy."

"I trust the doctors who are running it. They seem to be very experienced with it and very competent. I'm sure they know what they are doing and that Rhys isn't at any risk."

"Which doctor is running the program?"

"A Dr. Richards. She is really a lovely woman. We had a long talk, and she told me all about her experience and that she would personally be in charge of Rhys's case. She said she was so impressed with Rhys and the work that he's done so far, and she wanted to help him to succeed in life. If she can get him talking again…"

"There isn't any guarantee that this program will do that—"

"I know there is no guarantee. But if we could get Rhys back, if there is any possibility of getting the old Rhys back… Do you know what I would give to be able to have a conversation with him again? Not just gestures and phone pictures and some written words, but an actual spoken conversation…?"

They had really preyed on Vera. Kenzie thought that the chances of getting Rhys talking normally again were slim to none. It had been years since the initial trauma. Nothing that they had done thus far had been able to bring the old Rhys back. Kenzie remembered the pictures of the grinning, happy boy in Vera's photo album. Rhys before his grandfather had been killed. That carefree boy was gone for good. No amount of therapy could take away the memories of what had happened to him and the troubles he had gone through since. But Dr. Richards had worked away on Vera, promising results that far outstripped what they were likely to accomplish with the hallucinogenic therapy. There was no guarantee that the treatment would work. And every possibility that it could result in abuse and further damage. Or even result in his death.

"Vera. You could lose him. You might never get that little boy back, but you have Rhys now, and if this messes him up worse or kills him…"

"I've already lost him," Vera told her. "You haven't seen him, Kenzie. You don't know what it's like. He's gone to a place where I can't reach him. He won't talk to me or even look at me. I don't know if he can even hear me. He needs this, Kenzie. Don't try to talk me out of it."

Kenzie opened her mouth, looking for something to say. Then the call ended on Zachary's screen and the display dimmed.

She looked at Zachary. He shook his head.

"How do I convince her?" Kenzie asked. "They can't put him into that program."

"It sounds like it's too late. I don't think you're going to be able to convince her."

28

Neither of them slept very well that night. Kenzie didn't know what to do. She kept going over the conversation in her mind, but couldn't come to a conclusion as to what she could have said or done differently. She needed to see Vera face to face. To talk to her more openly about what had happened at Persons. But she knew that if she did, she would be opening herself up to a lawsuit. Even if she were vindicated, there would still be a black spot next to her name, and who knew if she would be able to continue in her position in the medical examiner's office? If it came out that she had given Vera confidential information while trying to convince her to take Rhys out of the MDMA therapy, Kenzie couldn't see her employment continuing for long.

She was sitting with a cup of coffee in the morning before work. She was up too early because she hadn't been able to go back to sleep. She'd only gotten a couple of restless hours in, if that. She was barely functioning. She couldn't face her usual toast and marmalade for breakfast, so she would be running on caffeine and adrenaline. And by the afternoon, that would be gone, and she would be crashing.

She considered calling Dr. Cook and telling him she would not be in. It was a Saturday, and she wasn't required to work, though she usually put in a few hours anyway. But she didn't want to take the chance of messing up because she wasn't properly focused. Her work required great accuracy and attention. She couldn't afford for results to be misfiled or to miss an important clue in a postmortem, allowing a killer to go free.

Her phone rang. It was Dr. Wiltshire. Kenzie was surprised. She picked it up and swiped to accept the call.

"Kenzie," Dr. Wiltshire's voice sounded strange. "You're on the morning news."

"What?" Kenzie went into the living room, where Zachary was sitting with his computer. She turned on the TV. "Why would I be on the news?"

She couldn't think of anything she had done recently that could have made interesting news. Her work was interesting, but most people were not interested in pathology. Those who did had CSI on TV, which was much faster paced than anything Kenzie worked on. And it wasn't like she had talked to any reporters or was working on anything high profile.

"It's looping," Dr. Wiltshire said. "They'll rerun your segment in just a few seconds."

The "up next" banner running along the bottom of the screen said, "Medical Examiner investigates violent death in Persons Residential Care."

"I never talked to anyone about the investigation," Kenzie told Dr. Wiltshire. Though he should have known that without her saying so. They had worked together long enough for him to know that she wouldn't go babbling about a case to the press.

The segment began. Zachary looked up from his computer as the reporter announced that the medical examiner's office was investigating a death that had taken place in a private psychiatric clinic the previous Monday. A picture of Leander Isah was shown. Not one that Kenzie had ever seen. He looked younger in it by perhaps ten years. Were they trying to make him more appealing to the public by presenting him as younger than he was? To outrage viewers even more? Or had it been that long since he had seen his family, and that was the best picture they had of him?

The reporter gave some background context for Persons and Isah himself, talking about the torture he had endured as a young man and his immigration to America. Pulling at those heartstrings. Getting them invested. Everyone watching already knew it was a death investigation, but they were prepared to be shocked and outraged even with that fore-knowledge.

"Mr. Isah came to this country hoping for a better life. He was admitted to Persons Residential Care with the promise that they could improve his life and help him move on from those things that had happened to him as a young man. His stay at the home was sponsored by an anonymous donor. He could not have afforded it himself and neither could his family or friends. They were all hopeful that this was the opportunity they had all been praying for. A chance to get better."

Kenzie was too angry to grieve Leander's passing. She had done that privately already. She was angry at whoever was making a big show of a family's private grief in the media, trying to profit from it. She was angry at Persons for putting Isah in danger and offering therapies that hadn't been properly tested. Angry at the anonymous donor who had made it possible for him to live there and receive the treatments that had contributed to his death. She was angry at everybody involved. It wasn't fair that he had to go through it.

After feeding the audience a little more schmaltz about Isah and his situation, the reporter continued with the story.

"We have received exclusive footage from the final night of Mr. Isah's life. Let's have a look at that."

The reporter turned to look over her shoulder at what was probably a blank green screen as the channel rolled the footage of Persons Residential Care behind her and then switched to full screen.

No sound accompanied the video, and it had that jerky quality that Kenzie knew meant it was from a surveillance camera that used a lower frame rate to limit the file size. She saw Isah sitting in an area with tables and chairs. The dining room during mealtimes. Multipurpose room when meals were not being served. Patients could play games, put together puzzles, or visit with friends or family members. Similar to the setup that Kenzie had seen when visiting Zachary in the hospital psych ward. Isah was sitting with his head down on the table. The other patients they had interviewed had said that he was tired and wanted to go back to his room. He'd had a very long session.

A very long drug session, Janice had told them. The session had probably included both the administration of the MDMA and talk therapy. Then that was alternated with sessions that were just talk, without any drugs. Patients would have to learn to communicate and experience their feelings and memories without the drug too. To integrate with the rest of the world without a hallucinogen.

An orderly walked up to Isah and slapped him on the back. Encouraging him to get up and not fall asleep at the table, Kenzie assumed. Isah startled, throwing his arms out in alarm. The camera caught the orderly's profile as he laughed at this response. He punched Isah in the shoulder. Probably not hard. Just another encouragement to get up and engage with the rest of the residents. He wasn't allowed to go to sleep, it would mess up his circadian rhythm and make it harder to sleep at night. Though Kenzie assumed Isah would be given a sleeping pill if needed. The psych ward was pretty free with them. They wanted the patients to be able to get the sleep that they needed. It made things easier on the night staff, and patients who had slept well would be better behaved during the day. Sleepless patients were not stable.

When Isah did not get up, the orderly stepped away at first. No need to get into a fight over it, Kenzie assumed. One of the doctors or nurses might have an easier time convincing him he needed to get up.

But the orderly returned with a helper. They stood there, just a few feet apart. Both orderlies talking animatedly with Isah, while he tried to shut them out and put his head back down again. They got in his face. They poked and prodded him. The bigger of the two hauled him to his feet. Kenzie was struck by how thin and frail Isah seemed. She had noted his height and weight during the autopsy, of course. He was underweight. But she hadn't really thought that much of it because Zachary often lost a considerable amount of weight during his depressive cycle, which he then had to gain back when he was feeling like himself again. And the men from some of those African countries were very slim. Isah's forehead gleamed with sweat and his clothes looked limp and damp.

Isah fought back against the two orderlies. Several doctors and nurses hurried in and tried to break up the skirmish. The lack of sound to go with the video made it seem like it was happening in a vacuum. A void that swallowed up every noise.

They all latched on to Isah. Two people, then five, then Kenzie wasn't sure anymore. She could no longer see Isah as he was swarmed. He struggled as the staff held on to every limb. They took him to the floor and pinned him down. Kenzie held her breath, watching them, waiting for them to jab a needle into him or haul him off to an isolation room to calm him down.

When they finally backed off, satisfied that he was cooperating or that they had punished him enough, Kenzie expected him to remain there, motionless. She'd seen enough videos on the news of just that thing in recent months. Police detaining criminals and holding them down for too long. Squeezing every last breath out of them.

But Isah moved sluggishly when they backed off. The two original orderlies lifted him to his feet. Isah was breathing heavily. He staggered like a drunk, but was clearly alive as they took him out of the camera's range. Kenzie breathed a sigh of relief. She knew that he still ended up dying, of course, but she was glad not to have to witness his death herself.

The altercation matched what the witnesses had said, but that wasn't the end of it. Nurse Craig had told her that they had called the police because Isah had fought back, which had then caused another skirmish. Only then had Isah been sedated and been allowed to go to sleep, never to waken again.

"Within hours, Leander Isah was dead," the reporter announced solemnly. "The medical examiner's investigation began at the scene on Friday night. Why have her findings not been issued yet? It seems pretty clear from this video that Isah was injured during this altercation and that those injuries led to his death. But where is the medical examiner in all of this?" They showed Kenzie's professional headshot. The one that used to be on the ME's website, before it had attracted too much unwanted attention.

"I hate it when they show that picture," Kenzie grumbled to no one in particular. There was a reason that it wasn't on the website anymore. They didn't want the weirdos and psychos to be able to track her down so easily.

The reporter went on about Kenzie being unable to be reached for comment and Dr. Cook announcing that they had nothing to say about a death still under investigation, and that the ME's report would be issued in due course.

A non-story. Meant to get a lot of people angry and demanding answers. But of course they would not be satisfied with what she put in her report. Not when the reporter had said that Isah was injured. They would be more interested in making up conspiracy stories to explain what they and the reporter had decided were the real facts of the case.

Of course, in this case, they might be right. The clinic was going to a lot of trouble to cover up what had happened to Leander. Missing consents, video of the session, and treatment notes. Kenzie was glad that the footage had been leaked. Too much was being kept quiet. It was too easy to silence the vulnerable patients. Even if they were able to tell the truth, the staff would just say that they were lying.

"Where did they get the video footage?" Dr. Wiltshire asked.

Kenzie shook her head slowly. "I don't know. That's the first I've seen of it. Detective Garcia got the surveillance video yesterday, so I guess it came from her office."

"You're saying that the police leaked it?"

Kenzie stiffened at his tone. "I'm not *accusing* anyone. I'm just answering your question. I haven't seen the video before. I don't know how I could have leaked it if it was never even in my possession."

"There is going to be a big stink over this. The police and our bosses do not like stuff like this getting out. Especially on an active case."

"No," Kenzie agreed evenly.

"This is not the first thing we've had leak from the medical examiner's office."

"I don't know how I or anyone else in our office could have leaked something that we never possessed in the first place. You'll have to talk to the police department, see what they did with it. It must be someone from their office. Like I said, I don't even have that footage. Pretty hard for me to send it to anyone."

"They did mention you by name. They know you are working on the case."

"Since that's my job, it's pretty obvious. Dozens of people could have told them you were off on medical leave and I was the only one doing autopsies."

Dr. Wiltshire sighed. "You're right," he said. "I'm sorry, I'm not even there, and I'm acting like I know what's going on. I guess maybe I feel guilty for not being on top of everything. Though you know I wasn't always on top of everything when I was there..."

"I don't think that's fair," Kenzie said. "You always seemed to have things under control. No one can do everything. I can't keep up with everything with you gone. Dr. Cook and I are doing what we can to keep up, but it's not like having you there. It's going to be a long, hard haul with you gone. Are they giving you any idea when you will be able to do procedures again?"

"The bones are healing as they should, but it isn't a quick process, especially at my age. And then I imagine I'll need to do a lot of dexterity exercises before I feel ready to jump back into it."

"Well, at least if you slip, the patients aren't going to complain."

He chuckled. "No. So, what should I know about this case? Things do not look good after seeing that video."

Kenzie agreed and brought him up to speed with what she knew.

29

It was a while before Kenzie got off the phone with Dr. Wiltshire. She had retreated to her bedroom so that she was out of Zachary's way and not revealing any confidential information. When she finally disconnected from the call and returned to the kitchen, looking for something to eat, Zachary closed his laptop and joined her.

"Vera called."

"Oh." Kenzie was cautious, assuming the worst. "What's up? Is Rhys okay?"

He nodded, but his eyes were grave. "No change, I don't think. But Vera saw the coverage about Persons this morning and is a *little* upset about it."

Kenzie let out one bleak bark of laughter. "*Now* she's concerned about it."

"She didn't know why you were trying to discourage her from the program before. Now she knows it was because you are investigating a homicide there."

Kenzie nodded. "Right. So does that mean she's pulling Rhys from the program?"

"No."

Kenzie looked at him. Zachary didn't say anything while he got

444

himself a yogurt cup from the fridge. He sat down, removed the top, then got up again to get a spoon from the drawer. He looked at Kenzie.

"Vera's not going to pull Rhys from the MDMA program?"

"No. She's upset, but not enough to pull him out. She said that one patient dying doesn't mean the whole place is rotten and that it wasn't anything to do with the MDMA program. It was obviously because of them piling on and restraining Isah like they did. Not anything to do with the drug. She still thinks that the trauma therapy is worth the risk. The chances of Rhys improving, maybe going back to normal, versus the chances that something could happen to him and he could die like Isah... she thinks it is worth the risk. The chances of something happening to him like that is so remote... she doesn't think it is even worth considering."

"So she's upset about it happening at the facility that Rhys is going to, but she doesn't think that there is any danger to Rhys."

Zachary nodded. "Yes."

"Oh..." Kenzie ran her fingers through her hair, trying to decide how to handle this. Vera wasn't asking her to do anything. It wasn't Kenzie's responsibility. But she and Zachary felt very close to Rhys, and she couldn't just let it go without going to bat for him at least one more time. "I want to do *something!* Is there any way we could go see him? Are they allowing visitors?"

"There's nothing that says we can't try."

Kenzie studied him, trying to read his face. "Yeah? Does that mean you're okay with going over there? Even if the chances are low that we will be able to see him?"

"Of course."

His response was so quick and certain that Kenzie had to laugh. "Well, okay. I guess I know how you feel about it." She wanted to ask a second time to make sure that he really, really understood that it might just be a wasted trip, but Zachary wasn't a child. He understood the time it would take to drive out there, jump through the bureaucratic hoops, and then drive back home again. He knew the time it would take out of his schedule and that their chances of doing anything productive were slim. Chances were, they wouldn't see Rhys, no one would tell them how he was doing, and they would be run out on a rail, wasting several hours of the day. "Okay," Kenzie said again. "Let's go, then."

Zachary indicated his yogurt cup. "Breakfast."

"You can eat it in the car."

"No, *you* need to eat something for breakfast. I'll be done by the time you're ready to go out the door."

That *was* why Kenzie had returned to the kitchen. It was late for her to eat breakfast, and her body was waking up and telling her to do something about it. If she didn't grab something at home before they went out, she would end up buying a donut or something equally unhealthy on the way there.

"Grab me a granola bar. I'll eat on the way too."

Zachary raised his brows at this suggestion. He knew how adamant she was about not eating in her car. But just this once… Kenzie had the uneasy feeling that she should not wait. She should get over to Persons as soon as possible.

"I'm just going to get my purse. Grab me a granola bar," Kenzie repeated.

Zachary stood up to obey, and Kenzie retrieved her purse from the bedroom. She put on her outdoor gear and shoved the granola bar into a pocket before getting her shoes on. Once in the car, she let the engine run to heat the car a bit before leaving. She pulled the granola bar out and started to remove the wrapper. She became aware of how much the wrapper was crinkling and looked over at Zachary. The grimace on his face told her that it was, in fact, triggering his misophonia. She tried to remove the wrapper quickly to reduce the time he had to listen to the noise, which meant that she spilled greasy crumbs into her lap. And onto the car's upholstery.

"Argh. Going to have to get it detailed," she complained, brushing the crumbs away the best she could. She didn't have a plate for the granola bar. Now that it was out of the protective sleeve and catch-all wrapper, she would get more crumbs on her clothing and car as she ate.

But she would need to vacuum it out anyway. Whether she had to vacuum out a sprinkling of crumbs or half a granola bar's worth, it would be pretty much the same amount of effort. She put the car into reverse and backed out of the garage.

. . .

"They're not going to let us see him," Kenzie said with certainty when they were halfway there. Leaving the city streets behind, driving through the countryside to the facility, which felt both isolated and close by at the same time. "They haven't been at all cooperative with my investigation of Mr. Isah's death, and they're certainly not going to be any happier after seeing that video leaked to the public. Especially with my name all over it as if I were the one who had released it."

"They must know that they gave it to El—Detective Garcia, not you."

"Sure, but they'll assume she gave it to me."

"Nothing you can do about what they think. I know they might not let us in. We talked about that."

Usually, he was the one who obsessed over a problem. Kenzie felt like someone else had taken over her brain and she could not control how it was working—or not working—anymore. She wanted to argue with Zachary, to explain to him how she was sure that they would not be able to see Rhys. To argue him to the ground about it.

But she was the one who didn't want to be disappointed. She wanted to see Rhys and to know that he was okay. That the facility hadn't just eaten him whole. That he was being treated with kindness and respect, not shoved around and abused the way that Leander had been. There were too many similarities between the two. Maybe they were just superficial—both very slim, black men. Both had dealt with terrible traumas and been institutionalized in the past. Both wanted desperately to be free of the trauma and the ways that it had held them back in their lives.

She had not been able to save Leander. He had died before she had even met him. It was her responsibility to reveal the cause and manner of his death, to bring the truth to light.

And she had to do what she could to save Rhys from harm and further trauma.

She hadn't told Zachary or Vera about the sexual abuse. She couldn't bring herself to. They knew that Rhys was vulnerable. Zachary had brought it up many times before in connection with Luke's history of trafficking young men and women. They all knew that when a person was unable to speak up, it made them a target. Like Tirza. The perfect victim was one who couldn't point the finger at his abuser.

Kenzie managed to keep quiet and not raise her doubts again before they got to Persons.

There were several media vans parked just outside the property, reporters and their equipment, hoping to find a way in. Being kept outside the property line because it was a private clinic. Kenzie drove in through the open gate with a guard standing next to it, eyeballing all the cars. She found a visitor parking space and eased her baby into it.

At the front desk, Kenzie didn't speak, but let Zachary take the lead. She hid partially behind him while he told the receptionist confidently that he was there to see Rhys Salter.

The receptionist looked at him with an uncertain expression. They probably discouraged visitors, even if they didn't outright ban them. The woman tapped Rhys's name into the system and read what appeared on her screen.

"Rhys has just arrived. The program doesn't usually allow any visitors in the first couple of weeks."

"His grandma asked us to check in. To make sure that everything is okay and he is settled in."

"If there were any problems, she would have been informed."

Zachary nodded and waited. She made a gesture as if expecting him to leave, but he didn't.

"Is he in a therapy session right now?" he asked and, when she opened her mouth to answer that he was, so Zachary would have to leave, he quickly inserted, "I'll wait until he's done."

"We don't have the space for visitors to wait here for hours."

Zachary looked at the small grouping of chairs. "Oh, this is just fine. We'll stay here until he's ready."

She was trying to be polite, but Zachary didn't seem to be getting the message. "You can't wait here," she said flatly.

Zachary motioned Kenzie over to the chairs, and they both sat down. Kenzie looked at Zachary speculatively. "Do you really think you can get us in?"

He nodded, keeping an eye on the woman as he talked to Kenzie in a low tone. "If she'd made a big deal, a scene, or just called security, then I wouldn't be as sure. But they're trying to avoid the appearance of anything improper. After the media attention this morning, they need to look squeaky clean. And there are going to be a lot of people in today to check up on their loved ones."

"They need to reassure everyone that everything is fine and the death of Mr. Isah was just a one-off."

"And the assault," Zachary reminded her. "If it was just a death, it wouldn't be as big of a deal. People do die in hospitals and psychiatric care. But the assault is what frightens people. He wasn't doing anything except sitting at a table with his head down, and they attacked him for no reason."

"Well, they had their reasons. But they won't get very far with people telling them that Isah wasn't allowed to just rest after a therapy session. He had to be involved in socializing with others or taking part in other activities. Intervening with him physically—and so violently—is over the top. People will not just accept it."

"You hope not." Zachary's eyes were far away. "But I didn't think they would accept shocking autistic kids for behaving like they had autism, either."

Kenzie had to concede the point. Zachary had believed that exposing what was going on at Summit would have enraged people so much that the place would be shut down, or, at the very least, would be prevented from using electrical shocks in their therapy any longer. But the public did not rise up against them and insist that they be shut down. A couple of years later, they were still operating.

Dread crawled in Kenzie's gut. Surely she wouldn't run into the same problems with Persons. Surely, the public wouldn't accept that it was okay to use drugs and other practices that could result in the patients' deaths in their desperate search for a cure.

30

The receptionist kept throwing glances in Zachary's and Kenzie's direction, and Kenzie knew that she was anxious about having to deal with them. She didn't like them sitting in her waiting area, patiently waiting for something she couldn't grant them. She wanted them out of there, someone else's responsibility.

Eventually, Dr. Richards entered the reception area and looked around. Kenzie nudged Zachary. He looked up, and his eyes widened at the sight of the white-jacketed, golden-haired bombshell. He looked at Kenzie.

"The lovely Dr. Richards," Kenzie murmured.

"Wow."

At Kenzie's reproving look, he fumbled for a better response.

"I mean… how does she have enough time to put that much care into her hair and makeup when she's working as a doctor?" Zachary said. "I mean… granted, this is a private clinic, but they still keep their staff busy, don't they?"

Kenzie chuckled. "Good save. Looks like she's coming over here."

Dr. Richards looked at Kenzie for a moment before deciding to approach her. She looked hesitant. Not what she wanted to be doing.

"Uh, Dr. Kirsch, isn't it?" she asked. "You're the one who wanted to see Rhys Salter?"

"Yes. Zachary and I." Kenzie nodded at him. "We are close friends and I'm sure you can understand that after the publicity this morning… we had some concerns."

"Well, of course, everything in the media has been blown out of proportion." Dr. Richards hesitated, then tilted her head slightly to indicate they should join her somewhere more private. Kenzie and Zachary stood and followed her. She led them to a meeting room, not her office, and motioned for them to sit.

"I'm sorry. I'm sure you understand that things are a little disrupted here this morning. We are not used to dealing with so many inquiries and requests to see patients." She waited for Zachary and Kenzie to make themselves comfortable, though that was impossible in the cheap, hard-seated stacking chairs. "As I say, the media is really blowing this situation out of proportion. You already know, Dr. Kirsch, that the footage you saw on the TV this morning had nothing to do with Mr. Isah's death. He was alive and well following that incident where he was… safely restrained. He went back to his room and was perfectly fine."

"And then he died."

"Yes… But I'm sure you already know that his death had nothing to do with that minor scuffle. Really…" she rolled her eyes, "it looked much worse than it was. People expect trouble these days, after seeing so many police actions go awry, that is where their minds immediately go. But our staff are well trained in proper restraint and de-escalation. What you saw was really nothing. There was no risk of Mr. Isah being hurt."

"Well, that isn't what we are here for," Kenzie told her. "We're here to see Rhys. He was just transferred yesterday, and we would like to see that he is settled and has everything he needs. We want to see him and talk to him."

"There's no need to take on such a confrontational tone," Dr. Richards said repressively.

Kenzie would show her what a confrontational tone really sounded like if she continued to stall and block them from seeing Rhys. Kenzie forced a smile and a light tone. "Good. Are you going to bring Rhys in here, or will we be going to his room?"

She and Dr. Richards stared at each other, a showdown. Kenzie was not someone who would be put off by an administrator mouthing meaningless reassurances. Nor was she going to back down because of Dr.

Richards's physical appearance. She was there for one thing, and that was perfectly reasonable. Zachary had already assured her that if they pushed, the hospital would give in rather than having to face any more negative publicity.

Eventually, Dr. Richards took a deep breath and let it out again. "It would probably cause the least disruption if I take you to him," she relented. "I would ask that you just speak with him briefly to satisfy yourself that he is in good condition and then leave quietly so we can continue treating him. I don't want him to get agitated, which he may do if he has visitors. It is difficult for him to be here, leaving everyone he loves on the outside, and we don't want to remind him about what he is missing. We want him to be comfortable and rested so that he will not be resistant when we begin his therapy."

"What therapy are you planning? Are you talking about giving him MDMA?"

Richards's lips pressed tightly together, drawing a thin, flat line that was not particularly flattering. "Since you are a doctor, I know you understand doctor-patient confidentiality. You are not Rhys's guardians. Even if you were, there are certain things that I would not be able to tell you, to preserve his confidentiality and his trust in me."

"You are not prevented from talking to his grandma about what therapy he is undergoing. In fact, you would be negligent in not giving her all the details about any therapy he was undergoing."

"Nevertheless…" Dr. Richards stared steadily at Kenzie. "You are not his guardian. Mrs. Salter has been informed about what therapies Rhys will be undergoing. If she has not communicated those to you, it is not up to me to tell you anything about them."

"You are doing hallucinogenic therapy. That's what she said."

Dr. Richards shrugged, still giving nothing away. If Kenzie were just guessing, then Richards would not be tricked into telling her.

"When are you starting?" Kenzie asked, hoping that they would be able to push it off as much as possible. "I assume you'll wait until he has been here long enough to establish a relationship of trust. It wouldn't be good to jump into something scary like that without first ensuring he could trust you not to do anything detrimental to his health."

No comment from Dr. Richards.

Kenzie shook her head, exasperated. "Okay. Let's go see Rhys." She stood up.

Zachary scooted his chair back noisily and stood as well. Dr. Richards nodded and led them out of the room. "Again, I would ask you to keep this brief and low-key. It is not the time for a long, involved meeting. You don't want to make Rhys homesick."

Kenzie didn't make any promises.

Dr. Richards didn't push it further. Maybe she recognized that she had already done as much damage control as possible. Now, she needed to shut up and let the visit progress. She needed things to seem as routine as possible so that Kenzie didn't overreact and report to the media that there were even bigger problems at Persons than she had initially thought.

She led them into the wing where Kenzie had initially attended when she had found Mr. Isah on the floor that first day. It was a sobering thought, and Kenzie grew even more tense about the visit to Rhys. What if they found him motionless on the floor or on his bed? Or hanging from a light fixture?

31

She needn't have been so worried. When they arrived in Rhys's small, bare room, they found him lying on his side on the bed, facing the doorway. At first, Kenzie thought he was asleep, but his eyes were not closed. He stared out at the empty hallway dully, and did not look at all interested when Kenzie and Zachary appeared there. She was used to him being animated and interested whenever she saw him. He was always friendly, teasing Zachary, giving them a few big smiles, even if the rest of the time, his face fell into a long, hangdog frown. He was not a happy boy, but he could still enjoy a visit from his friends.

But this time, he did not. Kenzie wondered whether he was even aware of their entering the room and greeting him.

They both said hello, and, not receiving any response from him, turned their gazes toward Richards, who had stationed herself inside the door and appeared to intend to stay there.

"We would like some privacy," Kenzie said firmly.

"I need to make sure that everything is going well…" Richards countered.

"You didn't have anyone in the room before we came. Now, there is someone here visiting with and supervising him. You don't need to be here, eavesdropping on our conversation."

"I am here for Rhys's protection. You are not his guardians. It would not be wise for me to leave you alone with him without knowing your intentions."

"You know our intentions. To talk to him and make sure that he is okay. And I'm not going to do that with you hovering over us. If you aren't sure if it would be okay with his guardian, then you can call her."

Richards didn't move.

"Do you need her number?" Zachary asked politely, pulling his phone out.

"I do not," Richards snapped. She withdrew from the room, leaving them alone there. The door to the cell-like room was still open, with staff walking by occasionally to keep an eye on things and ensure that all residents were well and safe.

Zachary moved over to the bed, in front of Kenzie. She held back her irritation at her view of Rhys being cut off. But it was really Zachary who was Rhys's friend, not Kenzie, so it was appropriate that he should be the one to move closer and try to engage with Rhys. There were no visitor chairs in the room. No furniture other than the bed, and a little closet alcove that was empty. Rhys did not have any personal items there. No phone, no change of clothing, no pictures.

Zachary crouched on the floor in front of Rhys, about an arm's reach away.

"Hey, Rhys. It's Zachary. How's it going?"

He waited for what seemed like a long time. The seconds drew out with no response. Rhys didn't acknowledge his presence and didn't answer him. He was much like Cara had been at first, acting as if he were completely oblivious to their presence, even with Zachary right there in front of his face.

"I guess you're having a pretty tough time," Zachary said quietly. "Vera said that you've been having some trouble at school. Maybe dealing with some teasing or bullying? It's so tough to be a teenager. You feel like you can't be in control of anything in your life. And when things go wrong… there's nothing you can do about it. You can feel so helpless and hopeless."

He paused again. He shifted his position, moving from a crouch on his feet to kneeling in front of Rhys. Not very comfortable on the hard floor.

"Vera said that you had trouble with the resource room teacher too,"

Zachary offered. "Did she do something to you? Was she giving you a hard time?" He paused. "Was she bullying you or touching you?"

Something in Rhys's face shifted infinitesimally. Kenzie couldn't have said what exactly it was. She still couldn't tell if Rhys were actually seeing Zachary or not. His attitude didn't change. He didn't answer Zachary, but he had reacted, however tiny that reaction had been.

"Teachers do that sometimes," Zachary said, watching Rhys closely. "Even though they know they're not supposed to. It's not your fault if she did. Any more than it would be your fault if she hit you."

No movement, no response.

"How are you feeling about being here?" Zachary put his hand on the bed. He didn't touch Rhys. The gesture seemed to be one of solidarity and comfort, even though he didn't make contact. "I know how hard it is to admit that you need help. To have to go to the hospital or another place like this to get treatment. It feels like a failure, even if everyone tells you that it isn't, that it was something outside of your control." Zachary rubbed his temple. "I always feel like… I should be able to control what goes on in my own head. How can I not be responsible for what happens in my own head? But they're right. It isn't something that I can control. All I can do is try to get help when I need it. Let someone else in."

He knelt there, staring at Rhys for a few minutes in silence. A staff member walked by in the hallway, looking in at them and then continuing on his way.

"Did they tell you about the therapy they're going to do here?"

Kenzie could feel Rhys listening to Zachary now, attentive to every word. Nothing had changed in his position or in his face that Kenzie could tell. She could just feel that he was listening to Zachary. She no longer had any question about whether he could see them and knew that they were there.

"It's something called hallucinogenic mediated therapy," Zachary told Rhys. "Do you know about the LSD trials they did back in the seventies? Well, it's sort of like that, except with a different drug, MDMA. They use it to put your mind in a more receptive state. To open you up to new experiences and make it easier to talk about your feelings and what happened in the past."

Zachary broke eye contact with Rhys for a moment to look at Kenzie. She wasn't sure whether he was hoping that she would jump in at this juncture to talk to him about the therapy process he was facing. But there wasn't much more Kenzie could tell Rhys about it than Zachary had already said. She hadn't been through one of the sessions herself. Hopefully, Garcia had gotten the videos of the therapy sessions with the other patients at Persons, and Kenzie would get a chance to review a few of them. Then she would have a better idea about what to tell Rhys about it. By then, he might have already gone through a session or two. She wished she could shorten the process and prepare him for it now.

Rhys's hand moved, and he caught Zachary by the wrist. Zachary immediately looked back into Rhys's face, smiling reassuringly.

"Hey, bud. I'm still here. I'm not going anywhere."

He didn't say anything, just looking at Rhys. Kenzie breathed, waiting to see whether Rhys would say a word or make a gesture to let them know what he was thinking. He was good at finding nonverbal ways to communicate what he wanted to tell them. But she didn't see his phone anywhere in the room. Had they taken it away from him? Stored it somewhere safe so that it couldn't be taken from his room? Or was it at home with Vera?

"It's okay," Zachary assured him. "This is probably pretty scary, isn't it?"

No sound or further movement from Rhys. Kenzie believed he understood what Zachary was saying to him.

At the very least, Rhys had reached out to make physical contact.

"You went to Stanley Green," Zachary said, eyes intent on Rhys. He shifted his position again, to sit on the floor, slightly below Rhys's level, relieving his knees. But he didn't appear to be comfortable in this position either. Kenzie doubted whether the bare floor felt very good on Zachary's tailbone, which he had broken, not for the first time, the previous year. While he appeared to have healed up from that accident without any significant effects, Kenzie did see that flash of pain every now and then when he sat down the wrong way or had been sitting for too long in a hard chair. He changed his hand position to squeeze Rhys's hand for a moment, then let it go again. "Did you go to Stanley for help? Were you having a problem that you thought he could help with? Or you just didn't know where to go for help?"

Rhys didn't give any sign of why he had gone to Stanley. Or if maybe he had just been in that part of town and it had been a coincidence that Stanley had seen him out walking. It seemed too much of a stretch that it might have just been a coincidence. He had to have been going to Stanley for something.

"Did something happen, Rhys?" Zachary gazed into Rhys's eyes. Trying to read him without any verbal communication. "Did someone hurt you? Kidnap you or abuse you…?" Zachary's eyes again went to Kenzie. This time, probably to make sure he hadn't managed to trigger her by mentioning kidnapping. The word still made Kenzie's heart race and her gut clench, but she was stressed already and didn't think that her response to the word was significant enough for Zachary to see it.

Rhys pulled his hand back from Zachary. They weren't touching, and it was a definite withdrawal. Zachary looked back at him.

"It's okay," he reassured the boy. "Whatever happened, it's okay. We'll help you get through it. Okay? I'm not going to force you to talk about it. You know that. I can wait. Handle it however you want to. But you're safe here. You're safe here from whatever might have happened to you out there."

You're safe here.

Kenzie wished she could be sure Zachary was right. She wanted to reassure Rhys that everything was okay and that he would be safe at Persons and could take his time to tell his own story. But she had her doubts about just how safe it was.

32

Eventually, Zachary was all talked out. He wasn't getting any more information from Rhys about what had happened to him and why he had been out wandering in the streets so late at night. And why he had lost his ability or will to communicate. Kenzie felt worn out just from watching the interplay between Zachary and Rhys, looking for the tiniest indications of what Rhys was thinking or feeling. She was sure that it must have been even more exhausting for Zachary, and probably for Rhys, too, who seemed to be tired now, at the brink of sleep. His eyes kept blinking, slower and slower, glazing over in the pauses between Zachary's comments. Eventually, they both knew that it was time to go.

The staff had been keeping an eye on them and, when they exited Rhys's room, an orderly or male nurse hustled over.

"All done? I'm not sure how you can have such a long visit with someone who does not want to communicate!"

Zachary looked at him. "What makes you think that Rhys doesn't want to communicate?"

His name tag gave his name as John. He rolled his eyes. "Well, the fact that he doesn't try. No words, signs, writing, nothing. He's just completely blocking everyone out."

Zachary shook his head. "Maybe he's blocking *you* out."

"Everyone else, too," John insisted. "You're nothing special. I know he didn't say a word to you while you were in there. If you're going to try to tell me that he was communicating with you telepathically, you're just as disturbed as he is."

"I am," Zachary confirmed. "Maybe even more so."

John looked momentarily confused, his brows drawing together. He looked at Zachary to see whether he was serious, then looked over at Kenzie, waiting for her to laugh or to give him some sign as to whether Zachary was teasing. Kenzie shrugged her shoulders, not bothering to give him any information.

"Would you mind showing us around a little?" Kenzie asked. "I was going to get a tour the last time I was here, but we ended up going too long with our interviews and had to get home."

"Uh, I haven't been authorized to do that."

"I'm not asking about anything confidential or private. Just… the arts and crafts room, where the MDMA or talk therapy are held, if they aren't in use right now. Any common areas, I'm not asking for trade secrets."

John looked around for one of the doctors or administrators who could tell him whether this was kosher, but there didn't seem to be anyone senior around to tell him. Kenzie gave him her most charming smile.

"Oh, come on, John. Are you telling me that the arts and crafts room is a secret? That there is something there I can't be allowed to see?"

His neck was a little red. Kenzie cajoled, pleased to see that she was having an effect on him. "Please? I would really like to see some of the other areas. It doesn't have to be anything to do with any studies or treatment options. You must tour prospective patients or families through here from time to time, as they are considering whether it is where they want their loved one to be admitted."

He shrugged uncomfortably. "Well, yes."

"Then I don't see the problem in giving us the tour. As you know, our loved one, Rhys Salter, has just been admitted. And if you want more reason, maybe Zachary here would consider Persons the next time he needs a med review or supervision."

John looked at Zachary, brows down, then back at Kenzie, not quite believing what she was saying. He knew that she was just trying to get him to give them a tour and didn't think that she was serious about Zachary, even though she said it in a perfectly serious tone. People didn't talk about their mental illness that way, or about their potential need to be hospitalized for it again in the future.

"Uh, what…?"

"I have seasonal depression," Zachary said. "Some years, I end up needing to be admitted for a few weeks. Or longer, if there is a change made to my cocktail or something that needs more intense therapy."

"You do?"

Zachary nodded. He raised his brows. The orderly cocked his head, brows drawing down, and shook his head slightly. "No…"

"I sometimes need extra support," Zachary said. "Isn't that what you're here for?"

"Of course." He nodded his agreement. Then he gave a shrug. "Fine, I'll take you around, but it will be a short tour. There's a lot going on today, what with…" He didn't finish.

"The media attention this morning?" Kenzie asked.

"Yeah." He rolled his eyes. "I don't know what that chick at the ME's office is doing, leaking that video to the press. Just what does she think she's going to accomplish? All she's going to do is ensure that there are fewer options available for people who really need them."

Zachary looked at Kenzie, smothering a laugh.

"Maybe it wasn't the ME's office," Kenzie said.

"It was." He was sure of himself. "She's been making all kinds of trouble here, coming around, interviewing people, making a pest of herself. Got everybody wound up over it."

"You think she's intentionally making trouble?"

He considered for a minute, then grimaced. "I don't know. I mean… I can see how it looks bad, but sometimes, the only way to get a patient under control is to intervene physically. I don't mean like that was normal, what you see on the recording, but you can't hear what's going on, you can't see what happened the rest of the day. The guy was trouble. He was all over the place, unpredictable. He needed to be shown that there are consequences. You can't just diss the staff and refuse to cooperate and think that everybody is going to serve you hand and foot. We're not here to make the patients happy. We're here to make them better."

Kenzie nodded as if this all made perfect sense to her.

John looked at Zachary. "Like I said, that's not usual. It isn't like we go around beating up patients or physically restraining people who aren't doing anything. You wouldn't be like that. You would be cooperative and understand that sometimes there are rules that you don't like, or you have to wait, or that it takes time to get meds adjusted. You wouldn't be like that."

Zachary nodded. "He was causing a lot of trouble?"

"He'd be like that, quiet, looking like he wasn't going to be a problem for anyone, and wait until everyone's attention was somewhere else. And then he'd suddenly explode, causing all kinds of trouble. It was deliberate. You couldn't leave him alone, couldn't assume that because he was quiet, he was going to stay that way. All it would take was one patient going over to talk to him, someone getting into his space, and he would go ballistic. You can't tell from the video how crazy he would get. Everybody had to help get him under control right away, or we wouldn't be able to."

They walked in silence for a couple of minutes. John led them into a room that was clearly the arts room. Shelves lined with half-finished sculptures and tools, vertically filed portfolios and paintings, easels, paints, jars of paintbrushes, with some textiles work at the far side of the room, away from the paints.

"Oh, this is cool." Kenzie walked around the room, looking at the works in progress. "It's always so neat to see what everybody is working on. Did you ever do anything like this?" she asked Zachary. "Were you ever anywhere they had an art therapy program?"

He shrugged. "When I was a teenager, I remember a couple of programs. But nothing like that in the city psych ward. They just don't have the funding. If they try to kick off an arts program, it's just like… pencils and reams of copy paper. As cheap as possible. Pretty hard to get inspired with anything like that."

"Yeah, that would be hard."

"I'm not artistic," he confessed. "My drawings are just about as good as my handwriting."

Which was to say, unrecognizable to anyone but him. Unless he really spent the time and attention on it, like he did when filling out a form. But the personal notes he made to himself in his notebooks were dauntingly messy.

"You can be artistic in other ways. You have your photography."

"That's not really… well, yeah, I guess it is. Some of the stuff I see other photographers putting on display is very artistic, so I guess it *can* be artistic…"

"Yours is, too. I love having a peek at what you are looking at when you show it to Lorne. You never show it to me because you don't think it's good or that I would be interested, but I am. I think your photography is really good."

He blushed. Kenzie laughed. They headed for the door to exit the art room. Kenzie glanced down at a garbage can she passed, with the remains of a broken sculpture in it. It looked like it had been really detailed, and she stopped to look at the feather pattern on a wing and to try to reconstruct the sculpture in her mind. A bird lifting its wings to take flight, or alighting on a fence post. She took a couple more steps before she heard Janice Martin's voice in her head.

An eagle, on a branch, just lifting up its wings to take off.

She stopped and looked at the sculpture in the garbage again. Had Janice's sculpture been broken accidentally? Had someone done it on purpose? Did she know about it?

Kenzie got an uneasy feeling, dread creeping up on her again.

33

"What is it?" Zachary asked, instantly zeroing in on Kenzie and the worry that must have been written all over her face. "Are you okay?"

"Yeah. It's just…" Kenzie couldn't tear herself away from the broken sculpture and the worried anticipation making her heart race and her breathing quick and shallow. She looked at the orderly. "John… where is Janice Martin? Can you take me to her room?"

He scowled and shook his head. "No. I told you we can't be bothering the patients. I agreed to show you some of the common areas and, if she is out doing something, you can see her, but—"

"I need to see her. Now."

"You can't," he said flatly. "Now, let's stop with all the demands. It's time for you to go. We have too much else to do to be worrying about your questions. Okay? Enough is enough."

"I want to see Dr. Richards."

He widened his eyes at her. "I just told you—"

"Get her for me. Have her paged. Something. I need to talk to her."

"Dr. Richards is very busy." He looked at his wristwatch. "She'll be starting a session soon and will be tied up for a couple of hours—"

Kenzie looked around. She started trying random doors, knowing that they were not in the housing wing, but intent on causing enough disruption that he would have to listen to her and call one of the doctors or security.

"Ma'am," John said in exasperation, trying to stop her. But Zachary stepped in between them and, while he was far from being an imposing figure, he was like the short basketball guard who was *always* in your face. The orderly could not get past him to deal with Kenzie unless he really got physical, and he didn't want to do that. Not after the media leak that morning. "Ma'am!"

"Get me one of the doctors," Kenzie insisted. "I need to see Janice Martin. If I don't see her, I will call the police."

"The police? For what? We aren't required to show you anything or anyone."

Kenzie pulled out her Medical Examiner's Office badge. "You see that? I'm law enforcement. And you need to show me Janice Martin's room or let me talk to someone over your head in administration. Have you got that?"

He looked at the badge, confused and stunned. "What the...?"

She pressed it toward him. "Medical Examiner's Office. And you know I have an active investigation going on here. So you need to listen to what I'm telling you."

"But you..." His neck and face flushed a deep red, remembering how he had mocked her and called her out, not realizing who he was talking to.

Kenzie waved this away. "I don't care what you said about me. I already knew what people were saying. It was on the morning news. Janice Martin's room. Now."

He shook his head and staggered away from them, not saying whether he was taking her where she had asked him to or back to an administration office. She followed him anyway. Either one would help. They turned into the housing wing, and he started to work his way down the hall, sticking his head into the doorways of the rooms that stood open to see which was which. There were no nameplates outside the doors, probably for privacy purposes, so a staff member had to either remember each occupant or look inside to see who was there. John was clearly flustered. He probably knew which one was hers when he wasn't.

"Here," he motioned to a closed door, "she's probably having a nap or is out at a therapy appointment."

With complete disregard for the patient's privacy, Kenzie grabbed the door handle and pushed the door open. The door stuck and there was resistance as she pushed it open. On the other side, with part of a sheet looped around a corner of the door, Janice hung.

34

John shouted a curse when he realized why Kenzie had to put her shoulder to the door to get it open. He shoved her to the side while he tried to reach up to unhook the loop of the sheet and get Janice down. Zachary grabbed Janice by the legs and lifted her, muscles straining with the effort. Kenzie did the best she could to help the two of them get her down and, once Janice's body was on the floor, Kenzie immediately took charge, checking for a pulse and starting chest compressions.

"Get help," she told John. He darted out to the hall and raised the alarm, calling out code words to get the attention of any nearby staff. An alarm rang. Too late for Janice, Kenzie knew. She kept up the chest compressions, knowing how unlikely it was that she'd be able to bring the woman back. She didn't have any equipment with her. No epinephrine. No heart monitor. Not even a stethoscope. But the woman was still warm, and Kenzie kept at it so she could at least tell Janice's family that she had done everything she could.

Zachary stood back, white-faced, staring down at Janice's body and Kenzie in her fruitless labor.

John returned to the room with others. Too many people for the tiny room. They squeezed through the half-closed door to gawk at Kenzie and make unproductive recommendations.

"We've called an ambulance," John said. "They won't take long to get here, even though we're outside the city. We're actually pretty close to the fire station."

"It's too late," Kenzie told him.

He stared at her blankly. "But you're doing CPR."

"It's too late. It's not going to do anything. By the time they get here…" Kenzie trailed off, looking down at Janice Martin's red face and the bruises around her neck where the sheet had been tied. She sat back on her heels, stopping the compressions.

"Aren't you required to continue until the EMTs get here?" Zachary asked. "I thought that once you had started, you had to keep it up until…"

Kenzie shook her head. "I'm calling it. I'm a doctor. I declare someone dead or confirm death every time I go to a scene." She looked at her watch and pulled out her phone. She started a voice recording and, announcing the date and her name, started dictating to the phone. After making her initial observations, she turned off the recording. "I need everyone out of the room. You need to clear out until any forensic evidence has been gathered. I'll call in a couple of death investigators to help me out and arrange for transport."

"What's going on?" A woman's voice cut above the babel of the onlookers, and Dr. Richards forced her way in as others were exiting. She looked down at Kenzie and at Janice's body, and her face turned gray. She swore and stepped back as if she had been slapped. "Janice! No!"

Kenzie nodded. "She was hanging when we opened the door. I'm sorry. It's too late for us to do anything for her."

Dr. Richards sank down to sit on the bed, swearing. Kenzie nodded to her and spoke to Zachary. "Can you help the doctor out? She looks a little faint. But she shouldn't be touching anything in here, potentially contaminating the scene. Just out into the hallway. She can wait there."

Zachary nodded. He took Dr. Richards by the arm and coaxed her up and then out of the room, murmuring to her.

Kenzie called the staff from the medical examiner's office who would be needed, then turned her attention to who else would need to be involved. She dialed Detective Garcia's number.

"Dr. Kirsch," Garcia read the caller ID before answering her phone.

"Nice to hear from you. Did you call to discuss that impromptu press release with the video this morning?"

"What?" Kenzie was momentarily distracted from her purpose for calling. "How could I have been the one to leak that video? I didn't even have it."

"Nice try. I sent it to you. You might think that it was something the public should be informed about, but we have to follow certain protocols, and doing what you did to leak it like that could cause damage to our case. I know that you want to know as badly as I do what happened to Mr. Isah and see that the perpetrators are brought to justice, so—"

"I didn't get the video," Kenzie said flatly. "When did you send it?"

"Last night." computer keys tapped briefly. "And… I do have a read receipt, so obviously, you opened it."

"Obviously *someone* opened it," Kenzie corrected. "I didn't. I haven't even looked at my email from yesterday yet."

There was a pause as Garcia considered this. She apparently decided she couldn't prove who had opened the email and read it. "Who else would have had access to it? Assuming that it was not someone who hacked your email system."

"Well… Dr. Wiltshire is not in the office. He has remote access to his own email, but I don't know whether he would be able to figure out how to retrieve mine. It is the main department email, so I assume he has all those details. All the lab work comes back to that address, so I guess he could if he needed to retrieve something while he was away. The substitute ME, Dr. Cook. Julie, who handles phones and such when I'm away sometimes. She temps for others in the building. I don't know if you use her?"

"Julie? Sure, I know who she is. I can't imagine her trying something like that. She'd lose all the clients she temps for."

"Yeah. I don't know. I don't think anyone else in the office can access it easily. And I don't leave the computer turned on if Julie and I are away, so no one like the cleaners or death investigators who are there after hours."

"That's a fair number of people who could access it."

"Yeah. And I imagine anyone on your end could access it, too."

Garcia made a growling sound and swore in Spanish under her breath.

Kenzie didn't really want to know what she was saying. She was not happy, that was for sure.

"When I find out who leaked it, heads are going to roll," Garcia threatened. "Things like this could really mess up a case."

"At least your name wasn't attached to it. The reporter didn't say that I was the one who leaked the video, but they certainly talked like I was, mentioning that I was the one at the ME's office investigating the death."

"They certainly left people with the impression that the video came from you," Garcia admitted. "I figured it had too, since you were the person I sent it to."

"The only person?"

"No, of course not. I shared it with others who are involved in some way with the investigation. And I saved it to the electronic workspace on our servers so that anyone involved in the investigation can access it."

"That's a lot of people who could have accessed it."

"Yes, it is. And who knows how many of them would be outraged enough to leak it to the press to influence public opinion." Garcia sighed.

"So… I didn't call you because of the video."

"No?" The snap re-entered Garcia's voice. "What's up?"

"I'm at Persons right now—"

"What the hell are you doing there again? I thought you were going to stay away from the place. You've been threatened once already. You shouldn't be there talking to anyone without a police escort to keep an eye on things and attest to anything the witnesses say."

"I was here to see a friend. But while I was here… there's been another death."

"What?"

"Janice Martin, one of the patients you and I talked to."

"She's dead? What happened?"

"You should come over, or send someone from your team. It appears to be suicide."

"I was planning a nice quiet catch-up day today," Garcia grumbled. "What did she have to go and do that for? Why today?"

"Sorry. Wasn't in my plans either."

"I'll be over soon. Don't do anything until I get there."

"I've called my office, so they'll be here shortly too. Help with collecting any evidence and processing the scene."

"What happened? What did she do?"
"Hanged."
"Okay. I'll be there as soon as I can."

35

When Garcia arrived, Kenzie walked her through what had happened, as far as she knew.

"You remember the sculpture she talked about making? The one she was so proud of? When I saw it in the art room garbage, I just had a feeling. I knew that she wouldn't throw it out unless…"

"Unless she was despondent and never planning to come back."

"Yeah. So I insisted on looking in on her. But I was pretty sure…"

"It was a good call."

Garcia looked at the body and swore under her breath. "Two deaths in a facility this size in a week. That's gotta be a record."

"I doubt it. Sometimes, one death can trigger another, especially in someone already having suicidal ideations. And deaths in a facility like this… I have to say, they're not rare. You take a lot of people who are depressed or bipolar, having breaks with reality, or tortured with traumatic memories, and you can imagine… they're not the most stable population."

"But while they're here, they are supposed to be monitored, aren't they? Someone is supposed to be checking on them regularly. Janice said herself that the patients aren't allowed to just stay in their rooms all day. They have to be out where there are other people around." Garcia glared at the door, still only partially open because of Janice's body on the floor behind it. "Why do they even have doors? Wouldn't it make more sense to have rooms with no doors? So that the people who are supposed to be supervising them can see what is going on? I mean, how do you stop this?" Garcia gestured. "How do you stop people from finding new ways to kill themselves?"

"People have the right to privacy, I guess. They aren't in prison. They need to be able to change and sleep in private. They lose a lot of autonomy in a place like this, and what little they have left is precious." Kenzie pressed her lips shut, thinking about Zachary. How much more she knew about how a place like Persons operated and how it felt to live there from her talks with him about his experiences, when he was willing to share them.

Garcia nodded. "And any death in a psychiatric facility must be reported, right? So you would know how often people die here and from what."

"Well, you would think so. That's the law. But when I first came here to review Isah's death scene, a funeral home was already trying to collect the body. They seem to be in the habit of just calling the funeral home instead of the medical examiner's office. They are required by law to report it to us, but they haven't been. In some jurisdictions, anyone who dies within two days of being released from a mental facility is supposed to be reported, but how many of those do you think get reported?"

"I'm guessing not very many?"

"From what I was able to find—zero are reported under that statute. A few are reported as homicides or suspicious because of the circumstances, but none are investigated or tracked just because they were psychiatric patients who were released too soon."

"Wouldn't it be obvious if they were suicides?"

"Some suicides are obvious. Like this." Kenzie pointed to Janice's body. "But what about suicide by cop or by provoking someone else to harm them? Or the person who steps into traffic or falls from a mountain trail? Or a drowning victim? They might be classified as accidental or undetermined, but if they aren't connected with a psychiatric history…"

"I guess." Garcia thought about this. "So is it just Persons that is not reporting deaths, or all of these types of facilities?"

"Vermont law says that all deaths in mental institutions must be reported, but the psych ward in a public hospital would be a gray area, and that's probably where most of the deaths are. They probably make a judgment call. And there are only a few other psychiatric facilities like this. I don't know what their practices are. I did some calling around to the funeral homes to find out how many pick-ups they have made from Persons in the last year…"

"And?" Garcia looked at Kenzie expectantly.

"There are a lot more than you would anticipate. I would say it is… concerning."

Garcia did not appear to be happy about this. She rubbed her forehead. "Tell me I don't have to open a homicide file for each one."

"You'll have to look at them on an individual basis. I only have a rough list so far. I'll have to take it to Dr. Wiltshire and find out what he wants to do. What *do* we do? Exhume every one of them? What about the ones that have been cremated or shipped out of state? I would assume that at least half are natural or accidental. That's a lot of time to spend on cases that aren't going to lead anywhere."

"But then you wouldn't know how many were related to these drug-induced therapy sessions. The drugs alone can kill them, let alone the effects they might have on a person's mental health. I mean, we're talking about something that's supposed to make them *better*, but I know there has been trouble with some antidepressants that actually make people suicidal when they weren't before."

"Most of those warnings are attached to SSRIs," Kenzie advised. "But while I was waiting for you, I did look up MDMA and suicide."

"And?"

Kenzie hesitated. Garcia put her hands on her hips and gave Kenzie a stern look.

"These are just raw numbers. I haven't dug down into the analysis, and it was a study of teens using recreational drugs, not a study on people in MDMA therapy."

"Okay. Caveat noted. What did you find?"

"The rates of suicide in kids who use MDMA is twice as high as those who use other drugs and not MDMA."

Garcia whistled. "That sounds significant."

"And the rate of suicide is nine times higher in kids using MDMA than that of kids who are not using any recreational drugs."

"Nine times?" Garcia stared at her. "So, you take a kid with no history of drug abuse, and you put them on MDMA for this trauma therapy; you think that kid is now nine times as likely to commit suicide as he would have been?"

Kenzie looked for a way around it. She thought about Rhys. *Nine times more likely to commit suicide after using MDMA?*

She couldn't let that go. She had to call Vera about it again, even if Vera was angry at her for sticking her nose somewhere it wasn't wanted.

She nodded at Garcia. "Like I said, I haven't analyzed the study or its results. But the raw numbers... yes, that's what it looks like."

Garcia looked down at Janice's body. "These people are playing with fire. No, with Semtex!" She swore.

"Those stats wouldn't necessarily carry through to a clinical setting," Kenzie said cautiously. "Where they're using carefully controlled doses, staying with the patient while they are feeling the effects of the drug, and monitoring them carefully afterward, the rates shouldn't be that high. There have been very promising results in using MDMA to treat PTSD."

"I'm beginning to wonder if that's just pumped-up advertising copy. How do you know they aren't just seeing the placebo effect? Or making it up?"

Kenzie shrugged helplessly. She couldn't exactly argue against being paranoid about the results and seriously considering just how much they were being manipulated. They were dealing with two deaths. She had an idea of how many more deaths had not been reported, and it was mind-boggling.

36

Kenzie had planned to follow Janice's body to the morgue to start on the autopsy immediately. But when she stepped out into the hallway and saw Zachary's face, she changed her mind. It would make little difference to Janice's family whether she did the autopsy Saturday afternoon or Monday morning. But it would definitely make a difference to Zachary.

And to Kenzie herself, if she were honest. She knew she was running on adrenaline, and it wasn't a good idea to perform any medical procedure, even an autopsy, in that state. She didn't want to miss anything or make any mistakes. She didn't know whether Dr. Cook would want to come in to supervise or assist in an autopsy on a Saturday when there was no need for it to be done that quickly. Kenzie hadn't slept the night before; she'd had an emotionally draining visit with Rhys, and then she'd had to deal with discovering Janice's suicide, her initial attempt at CPR, and all the emotional fallout that came from her discussion with Detective Garcia about the other Persons deaths and suicides connected with MDMA use.

"Are you going to the morgue?" Zachary asked, anticipating Kenzie's plans.

She squeezed his arm. "No. Let's go home."

Zachary raised his brows. "Really? Are you sure?"

Kenzie nodded. "Yeah. It isn't urgent. We know what happened. I don't have a big backlog. I can do it Monday."

"If you're sure," he said doubtfully. "Isn't there going to be a big backlash from the media? They're camped out outside. They see the ambulance, police cars, and ME's van; they'll figure out that there was another death and will want details."

"The ambulance left again right away since there wasn't anything for them to do. I had them bring the unmarked van for transport." Kenzie nodded to Carlos. "Can you transport without parading the gurney past the media out there?"

Carlos nodded. "Yeah. We're parked in back, and there is a loading bay. Won't be a problem."

"Good. And Detective Garcia won't have come in a marked car. If we're lucky, the reporters won't have anything to report. Nothing to tip them off to there being another death. And if there is…" Kenzie sighed and shrugged. "If they figure it out and write headlines about it… then what? I can't control what they write. I'm not the one who leaked the video. I didn't have anything to do with that."

Zachary paused to consider the situation before nodding his agreement. "Works for me," he agreed. "I just wanted to make sure that it was what you wanted to do and it wasn't… because of me."

Kenzie guessed she hadn't masked her reaction to Zachary's state very well. "It's not just you."

Kenzie was concerned about him, though. Zachary was quiet on the way home. He didn't ask her questions about Janice's death or anything she had discovered or discussed with Detective Garcia when he had been out of the room. He didn't mention the visit with Rhys or his concerns about the boy's fragile mental health. Kenzie could think of little else. She could only imagine how Zachary's obsessive brain was managing it.

She watched him for clues as to how to help when they arrived home. Zachary paced back and forth through the house, apparently unable to settle down in front of the computer or TV, where he normally would have been on a Saturday afternoon when he took time off to relax.

"Do you want to do something together?" Kenzie suggested. "Or… have a shower or go for a walk?"

Zachary looked at her, continuing to pace. "I don't know. I have all this heat building up inside me. I don't want to explode. I want to do something with it. But there's nothing to do."

"Maybe a nice brisk walk? Try to burn off the energy that way?"

"Maybe," he agreed, but didn't make any immediate move to do so.

"Do you want to talk to Dr. Boyle?"

He immediately scowled. "There's nothing wrong with me. I'm fine, Kenzie. It was just an intense morning."

"I know it was. For me too. I didn't say anything was wrong or that you were going off the rails. I just thought you might want someone to talk to about it. You can talk to me, but if you want to talk to someone else, someone outside of it, you could try Dr. Boyle." Kenzie looked at the time. "Or your OA group meets in an hour. You could go to a session there."

"This isn't anything to do with obsessive behavior."

"Not exactly, no. But it might be what you need to keep from slipping into that territory." She didn't suggest he might be heading toward a covert visit to Bridget's house. He hadn't done that since the Godfrey case had been resolved. But there were other obsessive behaviors that could get worse if they were the only way to calm his brain. "I think the group is open to discussing anything that might be stressing you out. Get it off your chest and out into the open."

"I don't need a meeting." His tone was resentful, and Kenzie didn't pursue it. She hadn't intended to make him feel worse. She had meant to be helpful. Apparently, she had failed at that.

"Okay. I think I will decompress watching cat videos on my computer." Kenzie motioned toward the bedroom, where she would curl up with her computer and a glass of wine. "So I'm interruptible if you decide you want to do something. Go out or watch a movie or chat. Whatever you want. If you don't want to, that's okay too. I shouldn't make suggestions when you didn't ask for them."

Zachary's shoulders relaxed a little. "No, it's okay. I don't know what I want myself. I'm just all wound up. I'll figure it out."

Kenzie stopped herself from suggesting that he might want to take one of his antianxiety pills. He was aware of his options and could decide for himself.

                                    37

K enzie and Zachary managed to fumble their way through the
weekend without stepping on each other's toes too much.
Sunday was better than Saturday, with a quick trip to see the
Petersons' for family dinner. The highway driving and seeing his family
always helped Zachary to de-stress. He and Lorne Peterson exchanged
their recent photography, heads together for a couple of hours while
Kenzie and Patrick Parker drifted on to other topics. Nothing about work.
Lorne and Pat did not have the same appreciation for postmortem procedures as Zachary did. Few people did. And Kenzie didn't want to bring up
anything that would stress Zachary out more. She didn't make any
mention of Rhys or the cases at Persons. She was sure that Lorne and Pat
would have seen the leaked video from the previous day, but they also had
enough experience with Zachary not to bring up institutional living or
violence, leaving it to him to bring up if he wanted to talk about it.

On her way to the medical examiner's office on Monday, Kenzie was
thinking about the leaked video. Had it come from someone at the office?
Or from the police department? She certainly hoped that it was the police
department, where there were a lot more suspects to choose from and she
didn't have to think that it might be someone she worked closely with.

"You want to get to the Martin autopsy right away?" Dr. Cook asked
on her arrival, as he brought her out a fresh cup of coffee.

Kenzie accepted it gratefully. "Yeah. As soon as we can. But I need to clear the weekend's email first, check for messages, and ensure everything is organized for the week."

"I've already been through most of it. Nothing too pressing. We might as well get to the autopsy before the media starts to ask questions about a second death at Persons. You know it won't take them long."

Kenzie tried to keep her expression neutral and not show Cook how irritated she was that he had been trying to do her job instead of sticking to his own. He was just trying to help. He thought he was doing a good job by clearing the decks before they started. Had he been the one who opened the video email from Garcia and leaked it to the press? Or left it up on his computer so that someone else saw it and decided to act on it?

She also needed to work on her report on the Isah case. She had most of the information that she needed, but she had wanted to watch the video recordings from Persons before finishing her report to make sure that there wasn't anything else that she hadn't been aware of.

Now that she had seen the altercation before Isah's death, she had to consider how that fit into the situation. And there would be more video from Garcia that Kenzie hadn't watched yet. Whoever had leaked the video to the media had only released the most upsetting one, but it wasn't the only video that was available. Other angles and other segments taken before and after that might provide more context and information about what had happened to Isah. She particularly wanted to see what happened after the staff had dogpiled onto Isah and then led him off. Then what...? He had been alive after being restrained, but had something that happened during that episode caused another problem that Kenzie hadn't noticed in the initial autopsy? And what had happened when they had called the police in, and then had to sedate him? She might need to go over the postmortem once more after watching the rest of the video recordings. Just to make sure she hadn't missed anything.

"Dr. Kirsch?"

Kenzie looked at Dr. Cook. "I would like to get both out on the table. Janice Martin and Leander Isah. If we have both up simultaneously, we may notice similarities that we wouldn't otherwise."

"Good idea. Do you want me to prep while you ensure everything else is covered?"

"Uh, sure. Just don't get started without me."

"I won't."

He was a good guy. Bright, respectful, and a good worker. But Kenzie was still uneasy about him. She didn't like having his fingerprints all over everything. Particularly not in the domains that had been solely her purview. Dr. Wiltshire had always expected Kenzie to take responsibility for the general emails, voicemails, service requests, filing, and other administrative work. She had her own procedures and didn't like someone else messing with them. That was how things got missed or misfiled.

She shook off her misgivings and put her nose to the grindstone. She wouldn't get anything done by worrying about what Dr. Cook, who was supposed to be her superior, was doing. Kenzie sat down at her computer with the fresh cup of coffee and went through what had accumulated over the weekend.

She even checked the archived and deleted emails before moving on, making sure that Dr. Cook had not deleted anything from the main inbox without telling her, thinking that she would be grateful for his taking charge of it.

Once she was satisfied that Dr. Cook was correct and nothing needed her urgent attention, she joined him in the autopsy. The two bodies were laid out on the tables, everything in order for Kenzie to start.

"Let's just do a quick refresher on Isah first," Kenzie suggested. She brought up his file on the computer and skimmed through the notes, transcribed recordings, imaging, and lab reports that had come back so far. She pulled back the drape and glanced over the work that she had done on Mr. Isah. Had she missed anything? Was there anything she needed to look at now that she knew about the violent restraint? She reviewed the bruising that she had already recorded. She had noted restraint bruises on his arms already. And there was the cracked sternum. Evidence that someone had tried to perform CPR, or had he been hurt in the skirmish?

Kenzie searched for the word *sternum* in her notes and reviewed what she and Dr. Cook had earlier concluded. There was no swelling, bleeding, or bruising around the broken sternum and ribs. He had already been dead when it was fractured. Just as Janice had been when Kenzie had started CPR on her. No blood flow.

"Okay." Kenzie nodded. "Let's start with Janice, then. That is, Miss Martin."

She tapped the record button on the floor with her foot and dictated the usual setup information. Patient name and file number, date, Kenzie's and Dr. Cook's names. Kenzie began with the gross examination. She dictated Janice's vital information. Age, height, weight. She took pictures of the bruises left on her neck. Then she stopped and looked at Dr. Cook.

"We have a problem."

3 8

Elena Garcia sat down in the observation room. She looked at Kenzie, Dr. Cook, and the two bodies before looking up at the monitors.

"Okay, Dr. Kirsch. I wasn't expecting a call from you so quickly. And it looks like you haven't even started Janice Martin's autopsy yet. Is there something on Mr. Isah's autopsy that has come to light now that you've had a chance to examine the videos?"

"So far, the only video I've watched is the one shown on the news. Was there anything else I should be aware of?"

Garcia shrugged. "Nothing too worrisome. Mr. Isah was still alive after the altercation with the staff. If he was injured in that encounter, I'm sure you'll tell me about it."

"No. Nothing that we could see. I'll review the additional video later. How about his therapy sessions? Anything unusual there? An allergic reaction to the drugs that may have worsened over the next few hours?"

"I'm going to be picking it up this afternoon. I'll let you know when I've got it. Maybe we can find a more secure way to transfer it to you. Since we seem to have a security problem."

Kenzie nodded. "Yeah. Password protect and tell me separately. You can text it to me."

"Sounds like a plan. Anything else I should be watching for when I review them? A reaction to the drugs that seems concerning? Agitation or excitement? Anything going on that hasn't been disclosed."

"That's about it. Do you have the full experimental protocol so that you know what was supposed to happen? Anything on the doses they were using? What if someone wanted out of the trial? Reasons for withdrawal? What government guidelines did they have to work within?"

"I still don't have the full documentation."

"It should be on the file of every person involved in the trial," Kenzie said irritably, shaking her head. "Okay. Let me know when you get a copy."

Garcia indicated the monitors. "So what are we seeing here. Why haven't you started the autopsy?"

"The first step in a postmortem—after we have collected any trace evidence and prepared the body—is the gross examination."

Garcia nodded her understanding.

"What do you see?" Kenzie asked, falling into Dr. Wiltshire's usual Socratic method.

Garcia looked at the monitors as if there might be some small, hidden thing she should pick up on, but shook her head. "I see the bruises on her neck, from hanging. Red flushed face and swollen features."

"Focus on the bruises on her neck."

Garcia looked at the monitors. "Okay…"

Kenzie moved Janice's head this way and that, allowing Garcia to see the bruising all the way around.

"How would you describe the location of the bruising?"

"Around her neck."

"More specifically?"

Garcia struggled. "In a ring around her neck?"

"Yes." Kenzie nodded. "Now, when someone is hung, where is the force of the ligature? How does the ligature lie against the throat?"

Garcia opened her mouth, staring at the monitors. "Gravity pulls the body down, so most of the force is at the front of the neck, with little pressure on the back. And the ligature would be positioned upward?" She ended the suggestion with her tone going up in a question.

"Exactly," Kenzie agreed. "A bruise like this, on the same level all the way around the neck, with no break in the bruising at the back of the neck and no upward angle, suggests strangulation by a second party rather than hanging."

"And then hanged to make it look like suicide rather than homicide."

Kenzie nodded. "This was homicide, not suicide."

"You're sure?"

Kenzie looked at Dr. Cook. She still needed to do some further routine tests and to write her report, but it was clear that Janice Martin had been strangled. He nodded his agreement.

"Yes," Kenzie told Garcia. "This bruise is not consistent with hanging. Someone killed her and then hanged her after death."

"Pretty bold to be able to do that right in the middle of the day in a psychiatric institution where the patients are supposed to be closely monitored."

"Very bold," Kenzie agreed. "Or a conspiracy. He might have had someone watching his back, looking out for any witnesses."

"Right. And a murder after Mr. Isah's death…? What *is* your finding in Mr. Isah's death?"

"I'm still gathering information. It isn't quite as obvious as this." Kenzie pointed at the bruises.

"So that's it, you're not going to actually do an autopsy on Martin?"

"You don't always need to do a full dissection to find cause of death. In fact, we avoid doing a full dissection unless we absolutely need to. I'll do a few non-invasive tests. Some blood, hair, and tissue samples. Just to get a clearer picture of the state of her health prior to death. But I can tell you it wasn't a poisoning."

Garcia laughed tersely. "Fair enough. Well, I'll leave you to it, then. We will question the appropriate parties at Persons and I'll get you the session videos and testing protocol, if I get them today."

"What did you think of Dr. Richards?" Kenzie asked Zachary as they ate supper. She saw the confusion flash across his face and realized the question had come out of nowhere. "Sorry. I was just thinking."

What she had been thinking of was who might have been involved in a conspiracy to silence Janice Martin and ensure that she couldn't tell them anything more about Isah or the experiments going on at Persons. Of course Dr. Richards had to be one of the suspects. She was very involved with the therapy and with Janice. She had been the first staff member to respond to the orderly's shout for help, which meant she had been nearby. Maybe waiting for the alarm to be raised.

"If someone was murdered, rather than having committed suicide," Kenzie suggested to Zachary, making it a theoretical question rather than telling him anything directly about the case.

His eyes were bright and interested, and he watched her closely for more information.

"And if you had to look at other people in the institution who might have been involved… what do you think of someone like Dr. Richards. She could have been involved, but… she doesn't seem like the type, if you know what I mean."

"Because she's female?" Zachary suggested.

"No… well, maybe partly. But I've dealt with female killers before. I know they exist."

Zachary sipped his water, looking at her, his eyes thoughtful. "We have been programmed to believe that beautiful women are good and wholesome. That someone who acts pleasantly and smiles is good, and someone who is ugly, rough, dirty, or talks rudely or in a way that suggests he is uneducated is bad or dangerous."

As much as Kenzie wanted to deny it, she really couldn't. That was the way the world seemed to work. It was reinforced on TV shows and movies, by women in positions of power who were compelled to portray themselves as beautiful, young, professional women, despite how old and craggy their male counterparts were allowed to be.

Kenzie's own initial reaction to Dr. Richards's beauty was telling. She had difficulty believing that such a beautiful woman could be a doctor. Doctors had to work at all hours of the day, sometimes for incredibly long periods. Young doctors had to work a lot harder and longer than older doctors. They looked tired and careworn. Not bright and fresh and beautiful, looking like they had just come from a hair salon. Dr. Richards seemed like too much of a bombshell to be taken seriously.

Even though Kenzie had known a bombshell or two who had been incredibly successful professional women.

"So when I think of someone like Dr. Richards and my instinct is that it couldn't possibly be her, you think that's just my reaction to her looks, and not a gut instinct based on what I've learned about her over the past week."

Zachary shrugged widely, smiling. "I can't tell you which it is. But it sounds like you know."

Kenzie speared a few beans and ate them.

"And what is *your* gut instinct about someone like Dr. Richards?" she asked Zachary, interested in hearing his perspective. He'd solved his share of murders and dealt with his share of murderers of all persuasions.

Zachary rubbed the back of his neck. "Well…" he rubbed his arms as if trying to scrub something off of them. "I think of a young blond woman who had me completely fooled. Until the… err… *shocking* revelation that she was a sadist who had been deeply involved in several criminal enterprises and had been a participant in the murder."

Kenzie remembered the aide at the special needs school who had turned out to be an abuser. She nodded, remembering how innocent the woman had been able to portray herself as. A victim, even. She had been very good at manipulating people. An expert.

Was Dr. Richards another master manipulator? Someone who used her beauty and apparent youth to influence those around her?

"She's probably perfectly innocent," Zachary said, "but I happen to be a little leery of beautiful blonds working at institutions where they could do great harm."

39

Kenzie had tried several times to reach Vera on the phone to talk to her about Rhys and his admission to Persons. But when she tried in the evening, Vera was probably already settling into bed and not interested in taking any calls. During the day, she had likely spent a good amount of time at Persons, visiting with Rhys and staying close to make sure he was okay. Though she hadn't been there when Kenzie and Zachary had visited on Saturday.

Maybe she was just avoiding Kenzie and didn't want to talk to her. She wasn't under any obligation to, after all, and if she didn't like what Kenzie was saying, why answer the phone?

But Kenzie hoped that she was just busy.

She decided to try calling Vera from the office before taking her lunch break, hoping it would be a better time. Or that Vera would give in and answer Kenzie because she kept calling. Even if it were just to tell her to back off and leave her alone.

"Hello?"

Kenzie was glad to hear Vera's voice. She didn't sound like she knew who was calling, so maybe she hadn't looked at her caller ID before answering the phone. Kenzie put as much warmth into her voice as she could.

"Hi, Vera. It's Kenzie."

"Oh, yes. I'm sorry. You left me a message before, but my voicemail isn't working… Rhys always helped me to retrieve the messages and I can't figure out how to do it without him. I guess this old dog better learn some new tricks." She sighed. "I can't rely on him to do everything for me."

"I'm sorry about that. I didn't want to pester you with phone calls, but I didn't realize you were having problems picking up messages."

"It isn't anything you have to worry about. How have you been? I saw on the visitor log that you and Zachary were by to visit Rhys. You don't know how much I appreciate it. He doesn't have a lot of friends or outside support, and I know how hard it is to visit him now while he is… so unresponsive."

"We're glad to do it. We want to make sure he is okay." Kenzie made a mental note that she and Zachary should go by to see Rhys again, to ensure they visited him at least once a week while he was away from home. Vera needed all the support she could get, and it had to be lonely and frustrating to be the only one visiting Rhys. "Has there been any change? How is he today?"

"About the same. He will have his first treatment this afternoon. They are hoping that he'll be more responsive after that."

Kenzie swallowed. She hated the thought of Rhys doing the MDMA therapy when Persons had already demonstrated that they were, at the very least, having problems with the follow-up supervision required afterward. While it might be a legitimate therapy when handled correctly, she wasn't confident in their ability to keep Rhys safe.

"I wanted to talk to you about that. Do you think you could put off the drug therapy for a day or two while considering the risks? Or maybe get him transferred? I don't know if you heard that there has been another death over there?"

She wasn't sure how Vera could have missed it, but anything was possible. They surely wouldn't be advertising it over at Persons. If Vera didn't listen to the news on a regular basis, it could have escaped her notice.

"I heard about that," Vera admitted. "A suicide. Terribly tragic. But they said that is what happens when you don't catch someone in time. They need to start the therapy early, and not wait so long. I don't want to put off Rhys's treatment, Kenzie. I don't want him to end up like that poor girl."

"It wasn't waiting too long that killed her," Kenzie assured Vera. "I can tell you that with authority. It had nothing to do with her waiting too long for drug therapy. If that's what they're telling you, it's just a pressure tactic."

"You know that he needs something. We can't just let him sit there like he is now. He is so lost in his world that half the time he doesn't even know if there's someone in the same room. I can't bear to see him drifting away like this. It hurts too much."

Kenzie's chest ached at the thought of Rhys sitting there day after day, for almost a week now, without any progress. Without any sign that he wanted to speak or was trying to reach out to them. Withdrawn inside himself.

"I want him back too. I want a therapy that will change things and bring him back to us. But this experimental treatment is not the answer. And Persons... I would rather he was anywhere right now instead of Persons."

There was silence from Vera for a few breaths. "Why do you say that?" Vera asked finally. "It was a godsend that we were able to get Rhys into this program. I don't understand why you are so against it."

"I can't say a lot about it. But I really don't like him being there. I think if you could get him transferred back to the hospital..."

"The hospital can't do anything for him," Vera snapped. "They already said as much. They have no idea what to do for Rhys. And how many years have they had the chance to figure it out and help him? He was there for months when he was a little boy, and that is no place for a child. The juvenile place they put him in after that was no better. You don't know what it's like, Kenzie, but I've already been through all the other options."

Vera was desperate to find the one thing that would turn things around for Rhys. But Kenzie didn't think Persons was the answer. Not with the deaths that she was aware of. Not just Isah and Martin, but the other names Kenzie had collected when she had made calls to the funeral homes in town. They had a problem.

"I know you wouldn't intentionally put him in danger..."

"Of course not. This is the best place for him, Kenzie, and I won't turn around and put him back into the hospital psych ward. That may be the best place for Zachary when he has his depression, but it is not the place for a boy like Rhys. He's better off at home than there, and I can't look after his needs. I'm an old woman and I'm tired. I've raised my family. I love Rhys dearly, but he's more than I can handle when he is this sick."

"I know. And… we would be happy to help in any way we can. With time, finances, whatever we can provide."

"I'm not asking for charity. We got a grant for him to be admitted to Persons, where the trauma therapy program is. And he needs trauma therapy. In all the time since my poor Clarence was killed, Rhys hasn't had anyone who has really been able to help him to understand and accept what happened." There were sniffles from Vera, which caused a lump in Kenzie's own throat. "He's never talked about what happened that day. What he saw. What Robin did. I thought… that it would be best if he just forgot and that he would be able to go on and have a normal life. You don't remember things that happened to you so young. We kept it quiet for so long, that trying to bring it up now and get him to talk about it… he just can't. We ruined it. We failed him."

"You did what you thought was best for Rhys," Kenzie assured Vera. Though she wasn't sure that was actually true. Vera had done what she thought was best for her daughter, not her grandson. She had tried to protect her from the consequences of her actions. To cover it up, bury it. Rhys had been the victim of that cover-up as much as he had as the sole witness of the murder.

"We've been given one more chance to fix it," Vera insisted. "This is our one chance at a therapy that isn't offered anywhere else, that might address the old trauma. They have so many stories of the patients it has worked for. Miraculous recoveries."

Maybe too miraculous. Kenzie was suspicious of any strong sell tactics from Persons or any other institution. Why were they pushing it so hard?

A private institution like Persons was sometimes set up for charitable reasons or because the owner really believed in what they were doing and wanted to provide a service that just wasn't being offered in public institutions. But that wasn't the vibe she got from Persons. They hadn't professed their faith in the MDMA treatment program and how they believed they were going to change the face of trauma treatment around the world. They had hidden it, pretended that it wasn't happening.

They were in it for the profit. The fact that there were even grants available for the program meant that there was big money behind it. A big pharma company, maybe, hoping to patent a new form of MDMA or a better delivery system. Or an institution that was packaging the entire program to sell it to hospitals and treatment centers all across the country and around the world.

"I know that they have told you a lot of great success stories," Kenzie told Vera. "But you don't even know if those are legitimate stories. And it worries me that they are pushing it so hard. I want Rhys to be treated just as much as you do, but with a legitimate, proven therapy. With something that I know has been tested and proven effective."

"They say that it has been. But they need more patients to provide the numbers. They've been able to prove it in cases that were not as serious, but they need participants like Rhys, who were more severely affected. And especially because he's so young. They don't get a lot of teenagers in a study like this, and they need to prove that it is effective for teens and young people too. They need kids like him in the study if it is going to be used to help them."

That sounded closer to the truth of why they were funding Rhys's treatment and pushing so hard for Vera to put him through the MDMA program. Rhys was a goldmine as a test subject, checking all the boxes for teen patients, severe psychiatric illness, serious childhood trauma, and minority race. They wanted to be able to say that it had been tested on all those demographics.

"They want him for their own purposes," Kenzie told Vera. "They don't care about him as much as they do about selling their system or their product."

"But they can't use him to sell it if it isn't successful," Vera pointed out. "They need good results. It's just as important to them that it be successful as it is to me."

"They'll twist the results to show whatever they want. It doesn't matter whether one individual succeeds or fails. It's the numbers they need. And your permission to put Rhys's face on their literature. A token young Black man."

Silence from Vera. Kenzie had probably pushed it too far. She had offended Vera with her suggestion, and she wouldn't listen to any other arguments.

"I did give them permission to use Rhys's picture," Vera conceded eventually. "They were so convincing. So passionate. And Rhys needs this so badly."

"I know. But I think it is too dangerous. Especially at Persons Residential Care."

40

Kenzie needed to get away from her desk to clear her head. She was bad about working through her lunch hour most days, relying on the sorry vending machine sandwiches down the hallway, which was not a healthy choice. She knew she needed to get up and move around when she had been sitting all morning, but she usually excused herself because sometimes she was standing for an autopsy, so her job wasn't *all* sitting. And the sandwiches… if they were not unhealthy for her body, they definitely were for her emotional state. She needed something that would make her feel alive. Thick brown bread and stuffed full of sprouts, tomatoes, and other veggies. She headed for *It's a Wrap*, a sandwich shop that did some really nice wraps, rolls, and regular sandwiches. They would satisfy her need for something that looked virtuous but tasted good too.

Her phone buzzed in her pocket, and Kenzie pulled it out, thinking it was a text message, probably from Zachary. They sometimes touched base over lunch if things were not too busy. Kenzie liked to know what Zachary was working on and that he was in good spirits. Especially as it was getting later in the fall and she was starting to see what she thought might be warning signs that he had started to slide back into depression.

But it wasn't a text message. It was a voicemail, left by Detective Garcia while Kenzie had been on the phone with Vera. She remembered now that she had seen the call ring through and had meant to call Garcia back when she got through with the call with Vera. But she had been so out of sorts when she had finished the call that she hadn't done it immediately and it had slipped her mind.

Why couldn't Vera just trust Kenzie enough to take Rhys out of Persons? She knew what Kenzie's job was. Kenzie had mentioned the deaths at Persons, so Vera knew that Kenzie was investigating them, even if she hadn't seen the leaked video of Isah's altercation with the staff. Vera knew that Kenzie was looking into one or both deaths at persons, so why didn't she just *listen* when Kenzie told her that there was a problem and Persons was a bad place for Rhys to be? That the MDMA program was too risky to bet Rhys's life on.

On the other hand, Kenzie had to admit that she could see Vera's point. What kind of quality of life did Rhys have if they did nothing? He had no life right now. All he did was stare at the wall. And even if he recovered from this episode and returned to the way he had been before showing up on the street in some kind of fugue, what kind of a life was that? If he had been given the choice of staying the way that he was or the possibility of dealing with his traumatic past and being able to speak to communicate like the rest of the kids he went to school with, wouldn't he have taken it, even knowing that there were risks?

Maybe he would be willing to take the chance of having a reaction to the drug, resulting in permanent physical disability or death, but what about the rest? What if it made his traumatic memories worse? Introduced flashbacks and bad trips? What about the risk of abuse by one of the therapists? Would he really choose to be exposed to possible predators while in a drug-induced, vulnerable state?

She couldn't see him agreeing to all the risks. But Vera was his guardian, and she was allowed to make that choice, to put him into a situation that could be dangerous to him physically, emotionally, and psychologically. Kenzie shook her head, scowling, and stepped forward to cross the street.

"Careful!" a bystander warned sharply, grabbing Kenzie's arm. Kenzie froze, and a heavy dump truck went barreling by in front of her.

Kenzie put her hand over her heart. "Whew! Thanks!"

"I could see he wasn't going to stop," a tall man with silver-framed glasses said, peering at her as if to make sure she really was unharmed.

"The light was red when he went through, but you have to watch. Don't be looking at your phone while you're crossing the street.

Kenzie looked down and saw that the phone was still in her hand, though she had not listened to the message from Detective Garcia.

"I wasn't, actually, but I was distracted by my thoughts. Thank you for grabbing me!" She laughed. "I don't normally thank strangers for grabbing me in the street, but in this case, I'll make an exception."

He laughed as well, and they crossed the street together now that it was safe.

"Can I buy you lunch?" the man asked.

Kenzie shook her head. "I should be buying you lunch, to tell the truth! As a thank you for saving my life. But actually… I'm just going to grab something quick and then get back to the morgue."

He gave her a confused look. Kenzie laughed.

"I work there," she explained. "I promise I'm not a zombie."

"Well…" he feigned relief at this, wiping his brow. "I'm glad to hear that. Maybe I could call you sometime…?"

Kenzie shook her head. As grateful as she was that this man had kept her from being flattened by a dump truck, she wasn't interested in pursuing any kind of relationship with him, even if it was just friendship.

"Umm… I'm sorry, no. I'm not interested. I'm… in a relationship."

"And that keeps you from talking to people?"

"Sorry," Kenzie brushed him off again. She looked around and decided to change her destination. The way the man's body was positioned, he was almost certainly going to *It's a Wrap* himself, and Kenzie didn't want to have to prolong the discussion any longer. "Thank you again. I've got to run."

She turned and walked the other way down the street. The man stood there, scowling after her. Kenzie grimaced to herself and hoped that she wouldn't run into him anywhere else in the next few days. Some people just didn't understand the word "no," and she didn't want to keep bumping into him. She would go back to vending machine sandwiches for the next few days, until she had given it enough time that she wouldn't be worried about his looking for her on the street.

She rounded a corner and found a hole-in-the-wall burger joint she had never been to. Crossing her fingers that the food there would at least be edible, Kenzie entered. It was a nice, clean, open cafe. Dark after being out in the bright sunshine outside but, after she blinked a few times, her eyes adjusted so that she could read the chalk menu board. They did not have a wide selection. Kenzie smiled at the woman behind the counter. A young woman, her hair pulled back and secured in a ponytail.

"A single burger and fries."

"You want a drink to make that a meal?"

"Uh, sure." Kenzie looked around. "Fountain drinks?"

"Over there." The woman pointed. "Self-service." She handed Kenzie a cup. "You go ahead and get the drink while I grab you a burger."

There were people there ahead of Kenzie, chatting and picking up their orders, and people coming in behind her. It seemed like the place was popular. That was a good sign.

The burgers looked and smelled fantastic. So much for getting an ultra-healthy sandwich for lunch. But Kenzie had barely escaped death. What was one burger now and then? She needed the iron in the beef anyway.

With the burger and fries in a bag and the cup all clutched in one hand, Kenzie remembered again about the message from Detective Garcia as she headed back toward the office. She used her other hand to dig out the phone. She thumbed through her screens again to find the voicemail, then pressed play and held it to her ear.

"Dr. Kirsch," Garcia's words were clipped. She sounded somehow more Hispanic on the phone. Or maybe it was the urgency in her tone. "I have received the therapy videos from Persons. Well, not everything, obviously, but I have video of Isah's latest sessions, and you are going to want to view them."

Kenzie stopped at the corner and waited for the light to change to allow her to cross safely. This time, she *was* paying attention to her phone when her attention should be on the traffic. She pulled it away slightly while she looked around, then put it up to her ear again.

"I'll send you an email with a link," Garcia promised on the voicemail. "But they will be password protected."

There was a hand on Kenzie's shoulder. She pulled away sharply while listening to the end of the message, irritated, knowing immediately that it would be the same man, getting after her for not paying attention to the traffic and putting herself in danger yet again.

"The password is—"

Before Kenzie could finish turning to glare at the man for daring to touch her again, it was too late. A second hand landed on her back, and both shoved suddenly and violently.

Kenzie was not braced for such a thing, and even if she had been, it was a hard, strong shove. She had an instant to register that it couldn't be the man who had held her back before, but she was staggering away from him, trying to stay on her feet. The momentum of his shove took her off the curb and out into the street. Kenzie knew the light hadn't changed yet and tried desperately to stop herself and get out of the traffic lane.

There was a scream, the screech of tires from more than one vehicle, and an impact.

41

Zachary was focused on the insurance reconstruction case to see what needed to be done, shutting everything else out. He knew his phone had buzzed a few times, but he ignored it.

The phone started to ring. Not just the vibration that he was expecting with the sound being switched off. A ring that meant that someone on his important caller list was calling through his do-not-disturb function. And yet, it wasn't one of the programmed sounds that would tell him who it was. Zachary looked over at it.

Blocked caller ID.

He rolled his eyes. Who was trying to reach him? For his phone to be ringing, the caller had to have dialed him two or three times in a row, not allowing any time in between. The behavior of someone who really needed to reach him and was going to keep trying until he got through.

He picked it up and swiped the onscreen slider to answer the call. "Zachary here."

"Zachary, thank goodness I finally got through to you!"

Zachary took only an instant to identify the voice. "Mario?"

Mario Bowman had helped him out in the past, and Zachary counted him as a real friend. A cop who knew how to make things happen, who could be counted on if Zachary needed help getting through to the right person on a case, who knew how to grease the wheels so that things happened.

"Yeah. You had your phone turned off, or what? Never mind. It's Kenzie. She's been in an accident."

Zachary's grip tightened on the phone. "What?"

"Motor vehicle versus pedestrian. Get over to the hospital."

"I will." Zachary swallowed. "Is she okay?"

"I don't know many details yet. She's injured. Rushed to the hospital in an ambulance. Cops on the scene are still getting the story. But I wasn't about to wait until they actually have something to say."

"Okay, thanks, Mario. I owe you."

"Are you driving yourself? Maybe you should take a taxi, Zach. I don't want you to be in an accident too."

"No, I'll be fine." Zachary wasn't going to wait around for someone to pick him up. He needed to be with Kenzie. He couldn't wait one minute. He disconnected the call and put his phone in his pocket.

He was hyperfocused on the drive, weaving his way through traffic and taking shortcuts through alleys, every little thing that could shave a second off the trip. He tried not to think of anything that Mario had said, but the words kept ringing through his head. *Rushed to the hospital. Vehicle versus pedestrian.* It was bad. A pedestrian had no protection from a car. A ton of metal racing toward an unprotected human at sixty miles an hour.

It was bad. Would she even be alive when he got to the hospital? Would she be in surgery? Would they take him off to a private room to break the news to him, confessing that she had died or that they didn't know if she were going to make it?

He didn't know how he would manage without her. What had started as a casual date and friendly relationship had developed into something far more for him.

He had known he loved Kenzie but didn't realize how much until that moment. How could he possibly live without her now? They had been weaving their lives together, fixing all the problems, building up their communication, learning about each other a little more each day.

He didn't know if he could live without her.

He pulled into one of the empty stalls designated for the emergency room. He ran into the hospital, seeing and hearing nothing around him until he reached the inquiries desk.

"Kenzie Kirsch," he said urgently, "she was coming in by ambulance. Is she here? Is she okay?"

The woman gave him a tolerant smile. She moved slowly, ridiculously slowly, like she was putting on an act for a comedy skit. Zachary wanted to shout at her to hurry up.

"Please," he said urgently as she typed something into his computer. "Kenzie Kirsch. K-I-R-S-C-H."

"I think I know how to spell *Kirsch*, considering we have a whole wing named that."

Zachary opened his mouth, and nothing came out. Despite his urgency to discover what had happened to Kenzie, he was stunned by this information. He knew that the Kirsch family foundation was very generous with its donations, and that they were primarily in the area of medical research because of the fact that Amanda had died from kidney disease, which they hoped to find a cure for. And he knew they had recently been giving more money in mental-illness-related causes too.

But he had no idea that a wing of the hospital was named after them. Was that a new development, or had it happened years ago and Kenzie had just never mentioned it?

"Kenzie. MacKenzie, actually, but she goes by Kenzie."

"If you'll sit in the chairs over there," she motioned toward the waiting area, "someone will come talk to you."

"Is she okay? Is she alive?" Zachary was immediately panicked that she hadn't told him anything about Kenzie's condition. Was that because it was too late? Over and over again, his brain replayed a scene of a grave-looking doctor breaking the news that Kenzie had already passed.

"Someone will talk to you," she repeated firmly.

Zachary stood looking at her, waiting for more information. She looked back at him, not giving in. Eventually, Zachary dragged himself over to the waiting room chairs. But he couldn't sit down. He paced back and forth, his guts tied in knots. He was falling to pieces. He knew he should be strong for Kenzie, but he didn't even know if she were still alive.

"Sir, you need to sit down." A Black security guard stepped in front of him, blocking his path. Zachary looked at the broad chest and broader gut, the high-vis X that made him look like a crossing guard, and the utility belt with a walkie-talkie jammed into a holster. He turned around and paced back the other way. The security guard followed him, persistent. "Sir. Sir! You need to sit down if you're going to wait in here. You're disrupting the other patients and visitors."

Zachary looked around at the people who were waiting in the chairs. Most were ignoring him while they tapped on their phones. A few were watching with keen interest. But he didn't see anyone who was alarmed by the fact that he was pacing.

"Disrupting them? I'll sit down when someone lets me know how my girlfriend is doing. She was hit by a car! I don't know if she is even alive!"

"I'm sorry to hear that, sir, but you need to respect the others who are using the waiting room the way it is intended." He rested his hand on his walkie-talkie, as if he might have to call someone, and that would show Zachary.

"There's nothing that says I can't pace. I'm not taking up any extra chairs, so there's room for everyone to sit down."

"*I* say you can't pace," the power-hungry security guard said in a tough tone. Who did he think he was, Dirty Harry? "Now you can sit down, or you can leave. I don't think you want to be arrested, do you?"

"Arrested for pacing?"

"For trespassing, after I kick you out," he said with a satisfied smirk.

"I can hear him out there!"

Zachary turned his head as a familiar voice emerged from one of the curtained examination areas.

"Just go get him."

"Kenzie!" Zachary bolted toward the voice. "Kenzie?"

The guard chased after him, grabbing at his sleeve and missing, too out of shape to keep up with Zachary's sudden footrace.

"Where are you? Kenzie?" Zachary pulled open a couple of empty curtained areas before a doctor or nurse in green scrubs opened one of the curtains and stuck his head out.

"Are you Zachary?"

He dashed over to the cubicle. "Kenzie?" He pushed through the curtain and found Kenzie sitting on a bed. She was wearing her regular clothes, not a hospital gown. He didn't see any blood. No IV or bandages. She looked just like she did every day when she got home from work. Maybe a little frazzled, but she was often that way after work too.

42

Kenzie looked at Zachary and shook her head. "Look what the cat dragged in."

Zachary's wild eyes met hers, confused. "What?"

"You look like someone dragged you out of bed and roughed you up. What was going on out there? You fighting with security?"

"Nobody would say what had happened to you. They said I had to wait. The guard said I couldn't pace and had to sit down in a chair or he would kick me out. What's *wrong* with people?"

He got close enough to take her hands in his and look her over, eyes searching for any injuries. "Mario said you got hit by a car."

"Yeah, I did." Kenzie indicated the tear in the knee of her pants. "Scraped my knee. It hit the brakes before it hit me. It was mostly stopped. I think I fell because of the push, not the car."

"The push?"

"Someone pushed me. I stumbled onto the road." Kenzie shook her head. "I was off-balance and couldn't stop. There were cars, people screaming. I think I hit my knees before the car's bumper hit me. It happened so fast, and I hit my head."

Kenzie probed in her curly hair for the tender bump. "It's not bad. Just a small contusion. They want to do an x-ray, but you know they won't find anything in there, right?"

Zachary didn't smile at the joke. He was still confused and off-balance. Kenzie could understand the sentiments.

"I'm okay, Zach. I promise. I blacked out for an instant when I hit my head. That's why they insisted that I come in to get checked out. Otherwise, I would just have gone back to the office. But it couldn't have been more than a few seconds. It didn't seem like any time passed for me. I hit my head and then I was opening my eyes, getting up." Kenzie looked at the doctor who had come to talk to her before she'd heard Zachary arguing with the guard in the waiting area. "You don't think it's anything serious, do you?" She said it in a tone that told him what the answer was supposed to be. She wasn't asking whether she might have any serious damage. She was telling him to confirm to Zachary that she was just fine. Because she was.

"People get knocked on the head all the time," the doctor assured Zachary. "Nine times out of ten, it's nothing. They are told to go home and get some rest for a few days. We'll do some imaging to ensure there is no skull fracture, no blood pooling inside or significant swelling. Then I'm sure we'll be sending Dr. Kirsch home with you."

Zachary nodded, his eyes searching the doctor's face for the truth of the matter.

"Were you asleep?" the doctor asked sympathetically.

Zachary looked baffled by the question. He shook his head, then looked at himself. He seemed to realize for the first time that his feet were bare. He tugged at his pants with a drawstring waist. Not pajamas, but something he wore around the house when he didn't have to go out anywhere and just wanted to be comfortable. He ran his fingers over his head to pat down the hair that was standing straight up. He kept it cut very short so that it was low maintenance, and Kenzie had never seen it all sticking out like a porcupine before.

"Oh." Zachary started to get red. "No, but I just ran out of the house. I didn't think about anything. I just had to get here. They said Kenzie was hit by a car, and I thought the worst..."

She could only imagine how bad he'd thought it was. He was a master catastrophizer, an expert at jumping directly to the worst possible outcome. He'd thought Kenzie's next stop would be her own autopsy table.

"I'm okay," she reassured him. "More embarrassed than anything.

People must have thought I was crazy, jumping out into the street in the middle of traffic like that. But somebody..." She frowned, trying to remember each second leading up to the accident. "Somebody pushed me. Intentionally."

"They pushed you?" Zachary repeated. He didn't say it in a tone of disbelief, like the cop who had first responded to the scene had. He immediately believed that was exactly what happened and was trying to work it all out. "It wasn't just someone who bumped into you? Did you see who it was?"

"No. I was just... There was a hand on my shoulder and then and my back, and they shoved with both hands. Not an accident," Kenzie told the doctor, who was listening with diagnostic interest. *Concussion? Paranoia? Was Kenzie someone who normally told tall tales or made everything bigger than it was? Or was it a symptom?*

Zachary could read the physician just as well as Kenzie. He shook his head. "If she says she was pushed, then she was pushed."

"There was probably a crowd. People get jostled. For someone to push you out into the street like that... they had to know that you could be killed. I can't see anyone taking that chance."

Zachary's and Kenzie's eyes met as they both tried to work through the problem of who would want to kill her. Kenzie looked away. It wasn't something they could discuss in front of the doctor. She had already said enough to make him suspicious about her mental state. That wouldn't do. She wanted to go home for the night, not to have to stay at the hospital for observation. She hoped that Zachary would understand why she wasn't pursuing it.

"So once I get the x-rays done, I'll be able to go home," she told him.

The doctor didn't immediately nod, as she hoped he would. He motioned for Zachary to move back from Kenzie, which he did. Then he shone his light in Kenzie's eyes and ran her through a basic neurological check and asked her about her symptoms. "Any dizziness? Double vision?"

"No." Kenzie poked at the bump on her head again. "Just a throbbing headache."

"Yeah. Follow my finger with your eyes. Any nausea?"

"No. In fact, I'm starving." Kenzie looked around her. She was still feeling a little shaken and out of sorts. She knew what had happened, but there had been so much confusion at the scene of the accident, she wasn't sure who she had talked to or what had been done. "I had gone out to get lunch… but I don't know what happened to it."

At the doctor's questioning look, she explained further.

"I was holding my lunch when I… got hit. I don't know what happened to it. So I didn't get a chance to eat."

"Oh." He chuckled. "Well, why don't you have your partner go down to the cafeteria to get you something while we finish this examination." His eyes turned to Zachary. "Now that you know she's all right."

Zachary nodded, confirming that he wouldn't cause any further disruption. He looked again at his bare feet and pants and patted at the pockets, which were suspiciously limp. "I don't think I brought my wallet," he said, getting red. "I just flew out of the house without thinking about anything."

Kenzie smiled reassuringly. "You can probably tap your phone. If you're worried about it, my purse is around here somewhere…"

The doctor indicated it under the edge of the bed, but didn't pick it up. Zachary retrieved it so that Kenzie didn't have to bend over, and handed it to her. Kenzie unzipped the closure, chuckling to herself about the doctor's and Zachary's reluctance to touch it themselves. Was it memories of their mothers insisting on handbag privacy that made men afraid to touch a woman's purse or to open it? Or was it the possible risk of seeing or touching a feminine product? It was funny to see this unusual respect for a patient's or partner's privacy in action.

Kenzie found her wallet and pulled out her bank card, which she handed to Zachary. "There you go."

"What did you want me to get for you?"

"You know what I like. I did have a burger. Though I meant to get a healthier sandwich when I went out. But…" Kenzie trailed off. She didn't want to tell Zachary in front of the doctor about the man who had stopped her from stepping into traffic and then wanted to go out with her. Had he been the one who had pushed her? A complete stranger who she had spurned? Or was it just a random act by someone else? Or was it something more sinister?

Zachary looked at her with concern, waiting for her to finish her sentence. Kenzie shook her head. "I'll tell you about it later. But just… anything, really. I'm starving. I would take anything."

He nodded his agreement. "Okay. I'll try not to be too long."

43

It took too long to get home after the accident. Everything at the hospital always seemed to take much longer than it should. Kenzie knew she was impatient to get home, which skewed her sense of time and how long it was taking. Still, it really was ridiculous to have to wait for hours for an x-ray to be reviewed when they had the imaging almost immediately. And Kenzie knew all the post-concussion protocol. She shouldn't have to wait for the doctor to tell her everything she should and shouldn't do during the next few days.

She was as patient as possible, but Zachary was a bulldog, harassing the nurses and staff to keep things moving forward. If it had been for himself, she knew he would have been quiet and compliant and would never complain about the service he was receiving. But it was different when it was something to do with Kenzie. He was willing to step up and be a pain in the neck so they would get rid of him as soon as possible. Was that something he had learned while he'd been with Bridget? Or had he always been that way, used to looking after his younger siblings and ensuring that their needs were provided for or, later, for the other children in foster care with him whose needs might be ignored or neglected?

When it was time to go home and Kenzie had finally been completely checked out and taken to the door in a wheelchair, they ran into another small snag.

"You don't have your wallet," Kenzie remembered. "I should drive."

"I can drive without it once."

"If you get pulled over, you could be in big trouble for driving without a license."

"I have a license."

"But you have to have it with you."

"It wouldn't make that much of a difference. And I'm not going to get pulled over. I'll drive slow."

"I should do it, just to be sure," Kenzie told him firmly, expecting him to give in.

"You shouldn't be driving."

"They didn't say I couldn't drive."

"They said that you have a mild concussion. You're not supposed to drive when you're concussed."

"And you know this from personal experience?" Kenzie challenged.

"Yes."

"And did it stop you from driving?"

Zachary opened his mouth and didn't answer, looking trapped. A red flush crept up his throat and into his ears and face. "Well, you would have told me not to," he pointed out lamely.

Which, of course, was completely true. She wouldn't have let him drive concussed. Kenzie rolled her eyes, which wasn't the best choice given how her head was already feeling. "Okay, fine," she conceded. "But you have to be careful. I don't want you getting a bunch of tickets and fines because you don't have your wallet with you."

"When was the last time you saw me get pulled over?"

Despite the way Zachary drove, fast and often reckless, in Kenzie's opinion, she had never known him to get pulled over by the police. He seemed to have been touched by the good luck fairy and got away with it.

"Drive slowly," she insisted.

Zachary nodded. He offered his hand to Kenzie as she stood up from the wheelchair. She waved him off. "I'm fine. I really am. It's nothing more than a headache."

"You need to take care of yourself."

"I am."

He took her by the arm anyway, and they walked more slowly than they normally would to Zachary's car, which he'd had to move a few hours earlier out of the emergency room space to a space in a more distant parking lot. Zachary had offered to drive around to the door to pick Kenzie up, but she had declined. It wouldn't hurt her to get a little exercise and fresh air to clear her head. She pretended they were just out for a stroll together on a date. Maybe in a park or somewhere romantic. It took a bit of imagination, but Kenzie had learned from Dr. Boyle to reframe experiences and get what pleasure she could out of them. Better to enjoy the positive than to focus on the negatives.

"So, tell me what happened," Zachary told Kenzie once she was settled on the couch with a small bowl of ice cream, which he insisted would make her feel better. She hadn't objected. That was the kind of medical care she could buy into.

She shrugged uncomfortably at his question. "It's a bit mixed up. I mean, I remember everything that happened, but I'm not sure what it all means."

He nodded. "Just go through what you remember and we'll try to sort it out. It's like that sometimes with accidents, everything can get jumbled."

Kenzie related her walk to the burger joint, including the man who had prevented her from crossing the street when the dump truck ran the red, and how he had persisted in trying to get to know her better.

"Do you think that's who pushed you?" Zachary asked. "He was irritated because he'd saved you from the traffic and then you didn't respond to his advances, so he pushes you out into traffic to let fate have its way with you?"

"It makes a twisted kind of sense. But I don't think so. I don't think it's anything to do with him. I just…" She frowned and shook her head, trying to remember each thought and perception separately and in sequence. "I remember thinking just as I was pushed that it *wasn't* him. I don't know if I saw him or if I realized that the hands were too high or low or the wrong size. I don't remember what it was."

Zachary nodded. "Maybe you caught a glimpse of his face or clothing. Something that told you it wasn't him. Did you have an idea of who it *was*? Did you recognize it as being someone else? Even just a flash of recognition?"

"No… I don't think so. But I don't know. It all happened so fast."

"Was it a man?"

Kenzie pursed her lips and closed her eyes, trying to picture it and to remember each instant before she had gone staggering out into traffic. And after that. She turned to see who had pushed her.

"I think so. I'm pretty sure it was. But what does that tell me? That doesn't get me any closer to identifying who it was or why someone would do that."

"Have you had any threats lately?"

"No." Kenzie frowned, thinking about it. "Well… maybe."

"Maybe?" Zachary raised his brows, studying her.

"Well… there was a sort of a threat left on the medical examiner's office main phone number. But it didn't use my name and didn't threaten anything; just said… to mind my own business or something along those lines. That my friends would benefit from me keeping quiet."

Zachary looked as mystified by this as Kenzie had been when Dr. Cook had played the message for her. What was it supposed to mean?

"Was it… a foreign accent? Someone who spoke English as a second language?" Zachary suggested.

"No. I mean, I have no way of knowing. It was a computerized voice. Text-to-speech. So they could have any kind of accent or be any gender. There's no way to know."

"Right. It just sounds backward. They should say that if you want to protect your family from harm, you'll listen to them, but instead, they say if you want your family to benefit…?"

Kenzie nodded. "Dr. Cook and I wondered if they might be referring to Rhys and to you."

Zachary looked at her blankly, shaking his head slightly in confusion.

"As people who might have need of psychiatric services."

"Because you think this message was from…"

"Well, with what's going on right now, we just assumed it was coming from someone at Persons. Because of the timing. I had just been out there and, if someone was upset by my investigation…"

"Ah…" Zachary nodded, filling in the blanks. "Okay. You go to Persons and get the body of the man who died there."

"Isah."

"Isah. And then you go back to interview people about what happened leading up to his death."

Kenzie nodded her agreement. "Talked to some of the staff and the patients, tried to figure out what exactly had happened leading up to Isah's death."

"And that was when you got the call?"

Kenzie nodded. "That night, I think."

"So you think that whoever left that message might have been the person who pushed you into traffic?"

Kenzie appreciated that he didn't say "the person you think pushed you into traffic" or "who allegedly pushed you into traffic." He believed her from the start without any concrete evidence.

"I don't know. Honestly, like I said, there wasn't any threat of violence in the phone call, so I don't think so. But there's no way to know for sure."

"How did the person who left that message know you had friends who might need psychiatric care?"

"Dr. Cook asked about that too. I don't know. It isn't like Vermont is a big state. You hear things about other people, know things about them because you happened to work at the same place together or go to the same restaurant or any of those sorts of things. Or maybe they just assumed that I had friends who needed psychiatric care. I mean… doesn't everyone?"

"More or less," Zachary admitted. "We don't always know what services our friends have need of, but mental health challenges are so prevalent…"

"Yeah, that's kind of what I thought. Not that someone knew about you specifically, but knew that I would know someone who needed services."

"Did you talk to anyone at Persons about me or Rhys?"

Kenzie shook her head. She didn't think she had, but it was hard to remember what had happened on what days. Even without a concussion, it was easy for the days to run together and get muddled. "No. At least, I don't think so."

"Your instinct says it was someone at Persons, so you are probably right about that. Did you let the police know?"

"Yes. I informed Detective Garcia. So she went with me the next time and we stuck together."

"What was her assessment of… the threat level?"

"Neither of us took it very seriously."

"Well, maybe you should call Garcia and let her know what happened."

Kenzie didn't like to come off as hysterical. She did her best to present herself as a level-headed, intelligent professional. Any time she had to present something that was out of the ordinary or sounded like a bizarre coincidence, it made her uncomfortable, like she had failed somehow.

"Do you think that it's related?"

"There was a threatening call, and then someone committed violence against you. I think you have to treat it as if it is related. Deal with it as a serious threat. What if whoever it was escalates the next time?"

Kenzie's stomach and chest tightened. She didn't want to think of the possibilities. She didn't want to think about the violence that they had been targeted with in the past.

Zachary was right. She needed to let Garcia know.

<h1 style="text-align:center">44</h1>

D r. Kirsch," Garcia's voice was sharp and irritated. "I was beginning to worry that something had happened to you. Where have you been?"

"Uh… I was in the hospital, actually. They always make you shut off your cell phone. What's going on?"

"I left you a message this morning about the therapy videos. I thought that you would call me right back."

"You did…?" Kenzie rubbed the bump on her head, wincing. "I think… did I listen to that message?" She tried to remember what she had been doing before the accident. "I might have, I'm sorry. It's all scrambled."

"What happened to you? Are you okay? Why were you in the hospital?"

"I was hit by a car."

She heard Garcia's sharp intake of breath and curse. "Are you okay? I had no idea."

"Yeah, I'm okay, just a bump. Well, a mild concussion, but I'm sure that will disappear within a few days. My dad always said I have a hard head."

"When you say you were hit by a car, do you mean that someone hit your car with their car, or…?"

"No. I was a pedestrian. The car had stopped or just about stopped when it hit me, so it wasn't too bad, but I was knocked out, and I'm having some trouble remembering everything that happened right before the accident. I forgot that you had left a message. I think I was supposed to call you, but I don't remember why."

"I called to tell you I had gotten video from Isah's latest therapy sessions. I sent them to you with a link, and there is a password to open them so no one else can except you. Try to outsmart our leak."

"I'll get out my laptop and take a look. I'm at home," Kenzie added lamely. Like Garcia couldn't figure that part out herself.

"Are you sure you should be? If you're injured, you need to wait until you've recovered..."

"It really isn't that bad. Just a small bump. Minor concussion. The thing is... I was talking to Zachary about it, and he asked whether I'd had any threats lately..."

It took Garcia only an instant to connect the accident and Zachary's comment with the telephone threat. "And you had received one. Do you think it's related?"

"It feels like it could be related, or it could be completely separate. The phone caller didn't make any threats of violence. If he had, then maybe I would say they are connected for sure. But he never said he was going to do anything to me. He didn't use my name and he didn't make any overt threats. The stuff that was vaguely threatening... was about my friends being able to get help. Which I still think was a weird thing to say in a phone threat."

"You thought the phone threat was related to Persons. Have you had any further thoughts on if there was someone at Persons that it might have related to? Anything anyone has said to you since to clarify the situation?"

"Not really."

"Okay... well, I don't think I need to tell you not to go there on your own. If you're going to go by there to talk to anyone, call me first. You are not a cop, and you shouldn't be acting like one. And even cops need backup."

"I'm not planning to go back... Well, that's not exactly true, because I plan to go back to visit with Rhys in a few days."

"Talk to me first. Even if you have a legitimate, non-threatening reason to be there, someone could still take it as snooping and decide to come after you."

"Okay. I'll let you know, I guess."

"You need to watch those videos," Garcia said grimly. "I wouldn't normally push it. I'd tell you to stay home and rest and relax. The videos will still be there when you get back and are ready to take on your usual workload. But in this case… I think you need to see them."

"Do you want me to call you back after I've viewed them?"

"You will," Garcia said, and disconnected.

Kenzie hung up, thinking that was an odd response. But she was concussed, so maybe she wasn't thinking straight or had missed some kind of signal.

Zachary looked at her as she stood up. "Are you okay? Can I get you something?"

"I don't need to be babied. I'm okay. Garcia had sent me some videos this morning that she wants me to look at."

"She can't wait?"

"No. She said I'll want to look at them right away." She looked at Zachary. "They're videos of one of my patients."

He nodded. "Okay. Well… let me know if I can help with something. I'm happy to do it."

"Anything?"

Zachary didn't balk and wonder what horrible task she might be about to assign him. "Anything," he repeated.

Kenzie smiled. "Just a Tylenol and a glass of water?"

"Your wish is my command. Is it bad? Do you need something stronger?"

"I think the Tylenol will be enough."

"Okay. I'll bring it in to you."

Kenzie retrieved her laptop and sat down on the bed with it. She had a home office, which she and Zachary shared but, more often, they chose to work elsewhere in the house where they felt more comfortable. Kenzie's preferred station was on the bed. Her posture was probably horrible, but it was comfortable for her.

As she opened her email and went to her phone to find the password Garcia had left in the voicemail message, Zachary brought in a couple of Tylenol tablets. He put them on Kenzie's bedside table with a glass of water. He nodded and left her alone without trying to engage her in conversation. She was working, and he knew what it was like to get distracted by someone else when he was trying to work.

It seemed to take forever to log in to the email server, find Garcia's email, download the video files, and then enter the password to open them. Kenzie didn't know if it was her perception of time that was messed up, or if she was having more trouble than she realized performing these simple tasks with a concussion. Maybe it was just slow.

Eventually, she pressed play on the first of the videos.

She saw Dr. Miller, one of the doctors who had been there the night when she picked up Leander's body. He welcomed Leander into the treatment room and had him sit on the couch. Leander appeared to be anxious and jittery as he watched Dr. Miller prepare an injection.

"You seem nervous," Dr. Miller said in a calm, even voice. "Is there anything particular that is bothering you?"

"I don't want to do this," Leander said.

"Well, we both know that this is what is best for you. You want to get better, don't you? This is how you're going to get better. With treatment. Sometimes treatment is difficult, like debriding a burn. But you need to clear the old, dead stuff out of the way so that new growth can occur. All the old trauma is like scar tissue that we need to remove so that you can heal properly."

Leander didn't argue the point. He sat there watching as Dr. Miller swabbed a spot on his arm, then injected him. Kenzie was anxious watching the doctor pushing the plunger slowly, smoothly injecting the clear fluid into Leander's vein. Her own heart started to race, and she watched Leander for signs that it was affecting him.

"That wasn't so bad, was it?" Dr. Miller asked.

Leander was staring off into space. "That's not the part that hurts."

They continued with small talk, though Leander didn't seem too engaged with the conversation. But gradually, his body language and behavior changed. He leaned toward Dr. Miller when he talked. He held his gaze longer and moved in closer. Dr. Miller began to guide the conversation toward Leander's traumatic past.

"Do you remember what we talked about last time?"

Leander shook his head. "No."

"We talked about when you were arrested back home in Africa. Do you remember that?"

"I don't want to talk about that."

"That's why we're here, Leander. It's time for you to think about these things and to talk about them so that you will be able to get better and move on. You don't want to spend your whole life in Persons, do you?"

"The rest of my life?"

"The rest of your life," Miller agreed.

"No. I don't want to be here the rest of my life."

Kenzie closed her eyes briefly. In fact, Leander would spend the rest of his life in Persons. He had probably assumed that his lifespan would be much longer.

Leander wiped his forehead, which was beading with sweat. His body temperature rising with the MDMA. Had Miller given him too much?

"Talk to me about when you were arrested. Do you remember?"

"Yes, of course I do."

"Tell me about what happened. You can look at it from the outside now. You don't need to worry about how it will impact you or anyone else. You can view it like a movie. As if it was something that happened to someone else."

"They took me away."

"Yes. They took you away from your home and family. Where did they take you?"

"The prison… it was a terrible, dark place."

Kenzie leaned forward, listening, as Leander described the prison in great detail. The cell where he had been confined, small and dirty, with no amenities, not even a mattress or blankets. He talked about the sound of water dripping constantly, the rats and the flies that afflicted them. She couldn't have imagined all the details, all the horrors that Leander had suffered through just by being confined in the prison. She knew that there was worse to come.

"They questioned me," Leander related in an emotion-filled voice. "They took me out of there and would take me to another room. Not always the same one. Different rooms for different… kinds of interrogations." He swallowed and looked around for a drink, licking his lips.

Dr. Miller got him a bottle of water, cracked the lid, and gave it to him.

"Water," Leander said, holding the bottle up to the light and turning it around so that it bent and reflected the light in different patterns. "They wouldn't give me water. Not until the end. Not until I was going back to my cell. I longed for my cell. Somewhere safe."

Kenzie shuddered at the thought of such a terrible place being his only asylum. The place that he looked forward to going back to. Leander chugged several gulps of water and wiped his mouth with the back of his arm.

"What else did they do to you?" Dr. Miller prompted, putting his hand on Leander's arm.

Leander had difficulty, but went on describing the horrors and torture that they had inflicted on him. It was hard to listen to. Kenzie took a break to take her Tylenol and water, considering leaving the video playing while she went and did something else for a few minutes. She didn't want to end up with PTSD from watching the video discussing the tortures.

But Garcia had told her to watch it, so there had to be something there that was relevant to Leander's death investigation. Kenzie glanced at the date of the therapy session she was watching and saw that it was a few days before Isah's death. She was not going to see him choke on his water and die on the screen in front of her.

Garcia had watched it. Kenzie could watch it, too. She could pause it whenever she needed to. Mute it. She had options. Unlike Leander, who was caught in the middle of it. Even when he resisted telling Dr. Miller something, Miller would continue to press and insist until Leander provided more detail about what he wanted. Kenzie watched the session, wondering whether Miller was even a licensed therapist. He seemed to be asking a lot of questions and pushing his patient a lot more than Dr. B ever would. But Kenzie didn't have a lot of experience with other therapists. They would, of course, all have different techniques and different levels of comfort with various techniques.

Miller was, Kenzie assumed, certified to deal with trauma patients and had probably been through all kinds of training to do with the administration of MDMA under the auspices of the pharmaceutical company that was running the trials. They would have a strict protocol about what was expected so that all the clinics they dealt with would have similar, reproducible results.

As Leander talked about what he had been through, Kenzie noticed that Dr. Miller was rubbing first Leander's arm and then his thigh, sitting closer to him on the couch, until their bodies were touching. She could barely breathe as she watched the therapist inflict more and more intimate positions and touches. Leander did not appear to object to the contact. There were a few times when he stopped the doctor or pushed him away briefly, but the man simply resumed, and Leander appeared to be responsive to the affections.

But that was due to the MDMA. As Garcia and Kenzie had discussed before, sexual arousal and sensitivity were commonly reported effects of MDMA. That didn't mean it was what Leander wanted or that he would have been okay with what Dr. Miller was doing if he had not been high.

Leander started hallucinating, describing auditory and visual hallucinations he perceived rather than the torture Miller was asking him about. He began to get agitated and afraid of the hallucinations, clutching at Miller and begging for his help and protection. Miller answered with calm reassurances, stroking Leander and giving him more physical affection.

Then they moved off camera. There was still audio, but not a lot of what Leander was saying made sense anymore, and it was punctuated by grunts and thumps and other noises Kenzie didn't care to identify.

It was clear that Miller had gone far past what was appropriate in the therapist-patient relationship. Kenzie was sickened by what she saw and heard. It was no wonder Leander had objected to the therapy and said that he wanted out. For someone who had been tortured while in prison in police custody, in various physical, psychological, and sexual ways, to then be re-traumatized in what was supposed to be a therapy session was unthinkable.

Even though she and Garcia had discussed Kenzie's findings that Isah had probably been sexually assaulted, Kenzie had not expected this. Had not been expecting to see and hear it with her own eyes and ears. Kenzie was used to dealing with bodies, grieving family members, and people who didn't know how to react to the death of a loved one. The violence her patients had been subjected to was over. They were past being hurt. She didn't have to see and hear it herself.

She did not watch the other two videos Garcia had sent.

45

Kenzie sat on the bed for a few minutes, thinking about what she had seen and what to do next. She didn't want to watch anything else. She didn't want to think about what she had observed. But Garcia was expecting her to call back, and she had been right that she and Kenzie would have to talk once Kenzie had seen what the videos showed of the therapy session.

Kenzie needed to analyze it clinically. Not to think about the man or the betrayal of the patient's trust. But to think about how it had impacted his health and may or may not have contributed to his death. Because that was all that was on her plate. She couldn't do anything about the regulation of the doctors at Persons or about criminal charges being laid. That was outside her purview.

She took a deep breath and hit the button on her phone to call Garcia back.

Garcia answered with a sigh. Not angry, as she had been the last couple of times that she and Kenzie had spoken on the phone. But resigned. Subdued.

"Kenzie."

"I wish you hadn't sent that to me," Kenzie told her.

"I can understand your feelings about them. Did you watch all three?"

520

Kenzie didn't try to cover up the fact that she had not. "No. One was all I could stomach. I assume they are all relatively the same."

"Yes. But with Isah's agitation level increasing each time and more drugs needing to be administered. I don't know if the doctor was giving him multiple doses of MDMA or if he was giving him something else to take the edge off. A sedative, benzos, something like that. I guess… we'll either find out from the doctor, or by whatever other medical professionals review those tapes."

"He had benzodiazepines in his blood. We were told that he had been sedated after the cafeteria incident and the visit from the police."

"Right. I guess at least one person knew exactly why he was getting so worked up."

Kenzie shook her head. "It's sickening."

"Yes. We were forewarned… but I still wasn't prepared for what I saw," Garcia admitted. She'd had longer to get used to it than Kenzie had. And she had probably watched them multiple times, talked to different people about them, and maybe passed them on to the special investigations unit, the medical board, and the management of Persons. It would be a lot of work.

"I don't know what else to say about it," Kenzie said. "It does not have a big impact on the death investigation. I could see that the MDMA was affecting him physically, not just psychologically. You saw him sweating?"

"Yes. Quite a bit, especially toward the end."

"That is the best evidence of your cause of death. The bloodwork I got back today shows that he was on SSRIs as well. His serotonin levels were astronomical. The combination of MDMA and an SSRI can cause Serotonin Syndrome, which can be lethal. His body was overheating and, at some point, his heart stopped. When I arrived there, some time after his death, the body was still too warm."

"What about the altercation before his death. Putting him prone and dogpiling on top of him. Did he smother?"

"He was still walking and breathing after that, though probably neither one very well. The surveillance pictures are too distant and low resolution to see if he was sweating or how dilated his eyes were. Using the session tapes you sent me as a reference point, he was probably still high after he came out of those sessions. MDMA can last for several hours. Janice said that sometimes his sessions were quite long, I guess Dr Miller liked to take advantage of that nice long high."

Garcia grunted.

"The combination of the drugs, the PTSD and agitation, the altercation with the staff, and possibly having his breathing cut off briefly at that point… he would have been in bad shape. They took him back to his room. I don't know if he was in restraints when he died, but he had been restrained sometime before his death."

"Straitjacket? Padded room?"

"Wrist restraints at least. Maybe the police had him in cuffs while they talked to him to try to scare him straight. But he got so upset that they had to give him a sedative to calm him down. He wanted to go back to his room and go to sleep, so maybe that's what they let him do. I hope…" Kenzie's voice caught in her throat. She didn't know why she was getting so emotional about what Isah's last few moments had looked like. Did a few minutes of peace in his room before he died make up for everything else they had done to him?

"I hope so too," Garcia murmured. "I hope that for however long it was before he died, he had a little measure of peace. He didn't deserve to be treated that way."

Kenzie nodded and swallowed. She went on, holding herself as distant from it as she could and speaking around a lump in her throat.

"His heart gave out. I don't know whether they found him on his bed or on the floor. Whoever found him or someone who joined them shortly after that tried to do CPR. Broke his sternum and a couple of ribs. They probably thought that he had just recently stopped breathing because of how warm he was. But he'd already been gone for a while when CPR was attempted. There was no bleeding, bruising, or swelling around the ribs and sternum."

"And then they called the funeral home to pick him up," Garcia offered.

"Yeah. And almost got away with it. Would have if the nurse hadn't decided that the medical examiner needed to be involved."

"Thank goodness for that nurse."

. . .

There was a knock on the door, and Kenzie looked at it, reorienting herself to time and place. She had closed her eyes for a minute to try to set aside the disturbing images and information. It was stressful just knowing what had been happening to Isah, and she had found herself wanting to turn off the world and retreat into sleep. Apparently, that was exactly what she had done.

"Come on in," Kenzie told Zachary. "I'm off the phone."

He opened the door and poked his head in. "Everything okay? It's been a while and I just wanted to make sure you didn't need anything."

"I guess I fell asleep."

"Oh. I didn't mean to wake you up. You can go back to sleep if you want to. Do you want me to close the blinds?"

"I'd better not go to bed this early, or I'll wake up at two o'clock and won't be able to go back to sleep."

He grinned. "Then we can have a party together."

Zachary was frequently up in the early morning hours, either unable to get to sleep or, having slept a couple of hours, unable to go back to sleep.

Kenzie yawned, deciding to cover her mouth halfway through. "Sorry. How are *you* sleeping these days? Are you getting enough?"

"According to the experts, no, but it's enough for me to function during the day."

"And it's enough that it doesn't affect your mental health?"

"It doesn't make me more depressed. Just a little foggy sometimes if I'm really short on sleep."

"I remember that day last year when you hadn't slept for three days. That definitely affected you emotionally."

"That, yeah." Zachary waved it off with a motion of his hand. "I haven't had anything like that this year. I'm okay."

"You tell me and take a sleeping pill if that happens again."

He shrugged and nodded. "So you're getting up now?"

"Yeah. Let's have a late supper. I think I need something other than ice cream."

Zachary chuckled. "Heresy! You need some pizza to go with it?"

"Actually, I think I've got a frozen one. That might be a good idea."

Kenzie got up from the bed, her head throbbing a little but, all things considered, it wasn't too bad. The nap had probably done her good.

Putting a frozen pizza in the oven wasn't exactly a two-person job, so she did it herself, then joined Zachary again in the living room.

46

After a few minutes, Kenzie became aware that Zachary was studying her and wondered whether he had said something she had missed. She turned to face him directly.

"Are you okay?" Zachary asked. "Is it just the concussion? You seem… far away."

Zachary was usually the one dissociating, retreating from Kenzie when things got to be too much for him emotionally. Kenzie touched the bump on her head.

"No… I think…" She tried to think about what to tell him about what was on her mind. "I got some videos from Detective Garcia about what's going on at Persons. And… it's pretty disturbing stuff."

Zachary nodded seriously. "You want to tell me about it?"

"I really can't. It would be too inflammatory if it leaked out. Not that you would leak it. I'm just saying that I have to be really careful what I say. And honestly… you don't want to hear it. It would be too triggering."

"Okay." He touched the back of her neck and stroked a few tendrils of hair. "So what can I do to help?"

"I'm worried about Rhys." Kenzie swallowed. "He was supposed to have his first MDMA therapy today. I know that he's probably fine after just one session… just because something bad happened to another patient, that doesn't mean that the same thing would happen to Rhys. But... I just want to know he's okay."

"I can call Vera."

"I don't know if she'll even answer. She was not happy with me trying to talk her out of Rhys doing the MDMA therapy. She sees it as the only option, the only thing that might help him. She doesn't understand the risks and I couldn't tell her everything. I think we'd better stay out of it, or she'll say we can't see him. It might be worth it for me to be banned, if it gets her to reconsider the therapy. But I wouldn't want you to be blocked from seeing him too. I think he needs you."

Zachary frowned as he considered this. Kenzie knew he was going to argue the point.

But he tried a different direction instead. "How about Stanley? I could call him and see if he's heard anything."

"Yeah. That might work. He'll want to know how Rhys is doing too."

Zachary nodded his agreement. He took a minute to look at the contacts on his phone and find Stanley's number. It was late enough that Stanley would be off work, but not late enough for him to be in bed.

"Stanley, it's Zachary. I was just calling to see—"

He had put the phone on speaker, and Stanley cut in before he could even finish the explanation.

"He's not doing great," Stanley said. "The doctors say it will pass and they don't think it was enough to cause any damage. It was just a bad reaction, not an overdose."

Kenzie stopped breathing.

"What happened?" Zachary asked. "I knew he was supposed to have therapy this afternoon, but I didn't hear how things went. I was hoping you had heard."

"Vera didn't call you?" Stanley paused to consider this new information, then decided it was okay to give Zachary the information anyway. Rhys would have wanted his friend to know what was happening, so Kenzie thought it was the right choice.

"Well, like I said, he had a bad reaction to the drug. They're not saying that he was allergic or that it was an overdose. It's not life-threatening."

"What kind of reaction?" Kenzie asked, leaning toward the phone and hoping he would be able to hear her and wouldn't be put off by her involvement in the call.

"He's hallucinating... a bad trip, I guess, like on LSD. Seeing and hearing things. Not... not quite in this world."

Kenzie made a noise of understanding. "That can happen. Some people are quite sensitive to the hallucinogenic properties. Or it was a bad batch of MDMA, but that shouldn't be the case when we're talking about pharmaceutical grade."

"The doctors are telling Vera that it will wear off and he'll be fine and back to normal in a few hours."

"Okay, good. Is he still at Persons? Are they going to go ahead with another session right away?"

"No. They called for an ambulance. He's back in the city hospital. I don't know if he is still in emergency or in psych. But it's too late for visiting hours."

"They probably wouldn't let us see him anyway if he's in a crisis," Zachary said. "Unless he was asking for us and they thought it would help to calm him down."

Kenzie rubbed her eyes, thinking about it. "Do you know anything else about the session? How long it was? Who was leading it? Which doctor?"

Zachary's concerned gaze turned toward Kenzie, but she didn't meet his eyes.

"I don't know," Stanley confessed. "And I don't know whether Vera does either. Those kinds of things... aren't necessarily things they would tell us. It never occurred to me to ask, and I doubt she thought of any of those things. Does it make any difference?"

Kenzie tried to think of how to explain.

"Kenzie has been involved in an investigation at Persons," Zachary advised before she had a chance to get her thoughts in order. "So she knows some details about who is involved in what."

Stanley cleared his throat. "Vera told me that you didn't want him taking the therapy. I guess now we know why."

A bad trip was the least of Kenzie's concerns about Rhys. If it hadn't been caused by an overdose, Stanley was probably right and wouldn't cause any permanent or lasting damage. And might just be enough to convince Vera and Rhys not to continue with the drug therapy.

"You could try calling Persons to see if they would give you any details," Zachary suggested to Kenzie. "They could at least tell you who was treating him. You're a doctor, and you have the right to ask questions that are related to your investigation."

"It would be a stretch to connect Rhys with my investigations," Kenzie pointed out.

"I don't know what was in the stuff that Garcia sent you today, but Isah's death was related to the same kind of therapy as Rhys was being given, wasn't it? Seems like there's enough of a connection there."

Stanley spoke up again, his voice uncertain. "You think this therapy Rhys is doing is connected with a death?"

"I can't say anything about it," Kenzie told him. "I haven't released my findings to the public yet."

"I had no idea it was that dangerous."

"It shouldn't be," Kenzie said carefully. "Not in a controlled therapeutic setting."

"I'll tell Vera to give you a call," Stanley said. "If you know about this drug and this therapy, then she should talk to you about it before she does anything else."

"She doesn't *have* to call me," Kenzie said. "But I'd certainly be happy to talk to her about it. She should talk to someone who knows the real risks. Not just whatever Persons is telling her."

"I'll make sure she does," Stanley promised.

Kenzie was glad he was taking the line without any encouragement from her. She didn't want to push her advice on Vera, but she wanted to ensure that Rhys got the best possible treatment in a safe environment.

Persons was not safe, and Kenzie was glad he was out of there.

They said their goodbyes to Stanley and turned their attention to a call to Persons.

47

Kenzie didn't have much hope that she would be able to find out anything by calling Persons. Even if they were open to talking to her about her investigations, they would be circling the wagons now. They wouldn't want to give her any more ammunition. They wouldn't admit any connection with Rhys or agree that she had the right to ask about him. In a world that was so strict about patient privacy regulations, she wasn't likely to get anywhere asking about him.

She spoke as officially as possible when she reached Persons's after-hours receptionist or answering service. She made her voice as pompous and confident as possible.

"I need to talk to Rhys Salter's treating physician."

"I'm sorry, we don't have access to that information," the woman protested. "You'll have to call back during office hours."

"Rhys was brought to the hospital after an overdose at your facility," Kenzie said sharply. "I think that you can find that information for me. I need to talk to the doctor who treated him."

"I… I'm not sure about that. Is it urgent? Dr. Richards can give you a call back in the morning…"

"Was Dr. Richards the treating physician?"

"Well, I don't know. She's one of the doctors over here, the one that manages treatment plans and patient records…"

"Do you have an after-hours number for her?"

The receptionist protested a bit, but clearly did have an after-hours number that could be given out in case of an emergency, and she reluctantly passed it on to Kenzie. Kenzie thanked her politely and tried the number.

After dialing it, she wondered whether she should have blocked her phone number so that Dr. Richards wouldn't know it was her. She didn't exactly have high expectations that Richards would want to hear from her. But the call was answered almost immediately, so maybe Dr. Richards hadn't even bothered to look at the caller ID before answering the call.

"Nancy Richards."

"Dr. Richards, it's Kenzie Kirsch. From—"

"From the medical examiner's office. Yes, of course, Dr. Kirsch. I couldn't exactly forget you, could I?"

Kenzie grimaced. It wasn't exactly a ringing endorsement. Dr. Richards did not sound terribly excited to be talking to her.

"I'm sorry for calling you at home, Dr. Richards—that is, are you at home?"

"Yes, I'm at home. What can I do for you, Dr. Kirsch? It must be urgent, or the service would not have given you my number."

"It's about Rhys Salter."

"Yes?"

"You know who he is?"

"Yes."

"I understand that he was rushed from Persons to the hospital today after an overdose or bad reaction to MDMA."

"Unless he died, and I was assured he was doing all right, I don't see how that is any of your business."

"Rhys is a personal friend. I was there to visit him on Saturday when Janice died."

"You were there, weren't you?" Dr. Richards said vaguely. "Yes, I remember that. But still, I am not sure I understand what you expect from me."

"Well, I want to know which doctor was treating him and what happened."

"As the medical examiner?" Dr. Richards challenged.

"As a representative of the medical examiner's office, I am sworn to protect the public good. After what I have seen of the therapy sessions conducted for Mr. Isah as part of my investigation into his death, I have to confess that I would not be happy to find out that Dr. Miller was allowed to treat anyone else, especially a vulnerable teen."

Dr. Richards didn't respond. A long silence drew out between them.

"I don't know what you're talking about," Dr. Richards said finally. "But Dr. Miller was not involved in Rhys's therapy. So if that answers your question…"

"Who was? I would like to talk to the person who treated him today to find out what happened."

"You are not entitled to that information. The family has not indicated they want anything to be conveyed to you."

Kenzie again let the silence speak for her. It had worked once; she hoped it would work a second time.

"I was the one who treated Rhys," Dr. Richards said finally. "Does that satisfy your questions?"

"You were the one who did therapy with him this afternoon?" Kenzie asked.

Even though she knew that Dr. Richards still had to be high on the list of people suspected of Janice's murder, Kenzie felt relieved for the first time since seeing the video of Dr. Miller and Isah. Her muscles loosened and her pounding heart slowed.

A woman could still be an abuser or even a murderer. She and Zachary had seen it in other cases. But she couldn't help feeling relief that Dr. Richards was the one who had treated Rhys. She could see the two of them together. She thought that Rhys would feel safe with Dr. Richards. The woman gave off a vibe of compassion and concern. Rhys would have been unlikely to have seen her as a threat, even considering that a beautiful young woman had committed murder in his own family. As she and Zachary had discussed previously, people were naturally drawn toward attractive women. It was hard to see them as unkind or predatory.

"Yes," Dr. Richards confirmed. "I gave him a low dose of the drug and we sat together to see how it would make him feel. Unfortunately, it did not give him a good feeling. He was agitated and began to experience very vivid hallucinations. Even though MDMA is a hallucinogenic, most of our patients do not have any negative experiences with a low, well-managed dose. It just makes them feel more open and accepting. It makes it easier for them to access their emotions and share them. To reach some of the old memories and traumas and actually address them for the first time."

"What happened with Rhys? How bad was it?"

"It was a safe dose, Dr. Kirsch. And I don't believe that the reaction he had to it was allergic. I think he is probably just hypersensitive. That those parts of his brain are just easily triggered."

"But you had him transported to the hospital."

"With everything that has happened lately... I wasn't taking any chances. I did not want anything to happen to the boy. I figured he was fine and would just come down naturally, but I wasn't going to gamble on it. I'm sure he'll be just fine, and he'll be able to come back tonight or tomorrow."

Not if Kenzie could help it.

"That's a big relief," she told Dr. Richards. "I appreciate you taking the time with me. I'll check on him in the morning. But for now... I can rest more easily, knowing that it isn't serious."

48

Kenzie was finished with phone calls. She could spend a little time with Zachary before bed, de-stressing and decompressing, and then she would be able to get to sleep. She would feel a lot better in the morning. At least, Kenzie hoped she would. She didn't want to think about how her bumps and bruises might feel the next day.

But her phone buzzed as she prepared to get up and find Zachary to tell him what she had been able to discover about Rhys. Kenzie looked down at it in irritation. She wasn't sure who was trying to catch her, but it was a little late in the day for any more work calls. If it was a callout to a site, she would have to decline and see if Dr. Cook could attend. She hoped that her concussion symptoms would recede enough by morning that she would be able to drive and do her job without any problems. A good night's sleep, and she would be feeling better.

But when she looked at the face of her phone, she saw her father looking back at her. A requested video call. Kenzie settled back down on the bed with her back against the pillows and answered the call.

"Dad. Hi."

"MacKenzie. I hope it isn't too late?"

"I'm up for a bit longer yet. How are you doing?"

"Just as good as ever. You? And… Zachary?"

Kenzie rubbed her forehead with a fist. "Just tired."

"You do too much. If you're tired, why don't you get ready for bed now?"

"I've been working. I need some time to unwind. You know how that is. If I tried to go to bed right now, I would just toss and turn and be too hyped up to sleep. I'll take the time to relax first so that I can get a good sleep when I'm ready to go to bed."

"Of course. And Zachary, how is he?"

"Umm… He's doing pretty well. As far as I can tell, he's still doing all right. That can change in short order, but it seems like he's in a good place right now."

Walter nodded, smiling pleasantly. Kenzie studied him, trying to figure out if he was playing with her. Why had he called? Just to ask how she was? She knew that smile, and it wasn't genuine. He had something on his mind, or he wanted something from her.

"What's up, Dad?"

"Nothing. I know I don't call often enough. Though part of that is on you… you don't either. The phone works both ways."

"Yeah." Kenzie knew she didn't call him as often as she should. "I know that. Sorry." She rubbed her eyes, trying to relax and enjoy the conversation with him. But she couldn't if she thought there was something else going on. Something else that he wasn't telling her. Seemed like the story of her life. The Kirsches, however close they were, tended to keep things from each other. They were reserved and tried not to let things get too emotional or personal.

"Are you still working on that case at Persons?"

Kenzie was surprised by the question. But it had been in the news. Of course Walter had found out about it. He was always up on the news that might impact him personally or professionally.

"I haven't been out there since Saturday. I don't expect to be. Unless it is to visit a friend of ours who is a patient there. I should be releasing my findings on the current cases shortly. Maybe tomorrow."

"Good to hear. They don't need all the negative publicity."

Kenzie raised a brow at this. She wasn't aware of any interest that Walter had in Persons. Not that he would tell her if he did. He might know someone on the board there, or be working on a campaign that affected them. Or have done so sometime in the past. Walter liked to stay aware of everything in his universe: past, present, and future.

"They are pioneering some important therapies," Walter offered. "Treatments that could change the face of psychiatric medicine. Do you know how many people in the world—even just in Vermont—would benefit from their trauma therapy?"

"I can't say I have been very impressed with what I have seen so far," she told Walter. "I know they are making some really big claims about how they will change the world, but you can't believe everything you hear."

Walter should know more than anyone about the way scammers worked. About the claims made and promise shown, which fell apart on close inspection.

"Really." Walter frowned. "I don't like to hear that. What's going on that concerns you?"

"I can't talk about it, since it's in connection with my work at the medical examiner's office. But you know you can't believe everything people tell you. Get the evidence to back it up. All the miracle cures claimed by Persons are just that. They are snake oil salesmen."

Walter leaned toward the phone as if it would help him understand Kenzie better.

"What is snake oil?"

"Anything about their trauma therapy. The hallucinogenic drug-mediated therapy. You have no idea how dangerous it is. You want to know why these are not authorized treatments? It is because of all the risks, with very little chance of success."

"In your opinion."

Kenzie scowled at the phone screen. "In my opinion," she agreed. "Whatever *that's* worth to you."

"MacKenzie!" Walter looked taken aback by her comment. Hurt.

But he really had no right to be upset. He was the one who had decided not to take his daughter's word for it. His highly trained medical examiner daughter. Why had he called her if he wasn't going to take her word for it when she answered him?

He peered at her through the camera. "Are you okay?" he asked. "You don't seem like yourself today."

Kenzie sighed. She smoothed her curls, trying to get herself together, but careful not to touch the painful bump. "I'm okay," she told him. "But I'm not quite myself today, you're right."

"Anything I can do? Is it just because you have too much work? I know they got a substitute for your careless Dr. Wiltshire, but is it enough? If you need more, you should tell them that."

"It isn't that. And Dr. Wiltshire isn't careless." She shook her head. "Where do you get that?"

He shrugged. "I hear things. If it isn't the job, then what is it? You said that Zachary was okay. Is that the truth?"

"Zachary is fine. It isn't work. It isn't Zachary. I… have a minor concussion. I had a small traffic accident and hit my head."

"What? Why didn't you tell me this? Does your mother know?"

"No, I didn't call her either. It just happened today. I got home not long ago. So I haven't been holding anything back…"

Although if he had not called, she'd had no intention of calling either of her parents to let them know that she had bonked her head.

"What happened?"

"I was…" Kenzie tried to think of how much to tell him. What to hold back. How she could minimize it as much as possible so that her parents didn't smother her with their concern. "I was crossing the street, and I was bumped by a car. It was stopping; it just… hadn't completely come to a halt. I fell, skinned my knee, bumped my head. That's all. Don't worry. I've had all the tests you could think of. Nothing broken, no brain bleeds or anything like that. The doctors have confirmed there is nothing to worry about and sent me home."

"Is Zachary there? He's not out on a stakeout, is he? You have someone there with you?"

"Yes. Zachary is here, and he's waiting on me hand and foot. He's doing everything that you would do if you were here."

Walter frowned, considering this. Like he was looking for something that he could do for Kenzie that Zachary couldn't. But all he could have done was throw money at her, and that wouldn't have made her more comfortable or taken away the bump on her head. Zachary would see to it that all her physical needs were met.

"And you're going to take it easy for a few days? Give your brain a chance to heal before you jump right back into things?"

"It's not that bad. It's a headache and a bit of fogginess. That's all. I'm sure that after a good night's sleep, it won't even be that bad."

"Call your mother."

"Dad… why don't you call her for me? I need to relax. My head is really hurting from having to talk on the phone. Just give her my love and tell her I'm taking care of myself and that I will spend the rest of the night relaxing with Zachary."

Walter brightened at being given an assignment. And it was probably what he would have done anyway. "I will do that," he confirmed. "But you need to call her tomorrow to tell her I wasn't just blowing smoke. She doesn't always believe me, you know."

"I wouldn't either," Kenzie agreed. "If she wants to text me to ask if I'm really okay, I'll text her back to confirm. But only once."

"I'll make sure she knows."

"Thanks, Dad. Thanks for looking after everything."

49

They would probably not have been able to get in to see Rhys, but the fact that Kenzie was a medical doctor meant that they could talk their way past the nurses who were trying to keep any unauthorized personnel away from the boy. Zachary had called Vera to ask to be added to Rhys's authorized visitor list. The combination of that permission and Kenzie being a doctor got them in when probably the only other person who would have been able to see him was Vera. She said that she would visit Rhys later in the day. She was obviously exhausted from what she had been through with him already, and she needed the extra sleep afforded her because she knew that Kenzie and Zachary would be by to see Rhys.

Kenzie didn't recognize the nurse who led them to Rhys's room. She didn't know whether or not she was one of the nurses that Zachary knew. She would have to ask him later. She paused before taking them in to see Rhys.

"We have someone sitting with him. He's quite agitated. We have him on something to counteract the MDMA and keep the symptoms to a minimum, but he's still in quite a bit of distress. I just want to warn you before you go in. It's not pretty. And there's not anything you can do about it. He'll get through it… eventually. As long as there is no permanent damage, and there *shouldn't* be with the dosage he was given."

"All of the MDMA should be out of his system by now, shouldn't it?" Kenzie asked.

"It lasts longer for some. We do have other examples of MDMA-induced psychopathy lasting several days, but it should gradually fade."

"You think it will?" Zachary asked, concerned.

"Yes. It just takes some time. I wouldn't recommend that he continue this therapy."

"Well, no!" Kenzie agreed. "That would be pretty stupid. I just hope Vera agrees. She was really hopeful that this would work. It might take several conversations to convince her to pull back again."

The nurse nodded and unlocked the door for them. Zachary and Kenzie entered the hospital room. Rhys was sitting on the bed, half reclined, and jumped up when he saw them. The male nurse sitting in a chair next to the bed stood up quickly, ready to insert himself between Rhys and the visitors.

"Zach!" Rhys exclaimed, reaching for him.

Zachary reached out both arms and Rhys embraced him and held him tightly, pounding on his back.

Kenzie didn't think she'd ever heard Rhys use Zachary's name aloud before. He didn't often use his voice and, when he did, it was often used to address Vera to express some need. Just a word or two as he could squeeze them out. Just one phrase seemed to exhaust him. Rhys pulled back from Zachary and held his arms apart slightly as if he didn't know whether Kenzie would want a hug or not. "Kenzie."

Kenzie raised a brow at Zachary, surprised. "Hey, Rhys, how are you doing?" Kenzie held her arms out and Rhys closed in and hugged her, too. Not a tight one like he had given Zachary, but softer, a gentle squeeze, and then he pulled back again quickly.

He headed toward the nurse, arms held out for a hug, and the man shook his head and pushed him back slightly. "No, Rhys. That's fine."

Rhys turned around again. There wasn't anywhere else in the tiny room to go, so he eventually sat on the edge of the bed, looking from Kenzie to Zachary, his eyes wide.

"Crazy," he said. "Everything crazy." He held up his hands to indicate the room around him, wiggling his fingers in a movement that suggested shimmering or magic.

Kenzie had never heard him use his voice so much. They were used to relying on gestures and text messages of GIFs to communicate with Rhys. It was strange to hear his voice.

"Are you seeing things on the walls?" Kenzie asked. It was a common hallucination.

Rhys nodded. He stood up, looked for somewhere to go, and sat again. "Time to go, time to go," he singsonged.

Kenzie looked at Zachary again in disbelief. They had not been expecting such wildly divergent behavior. Rhys was like a different person.

"How have you been doing, Rhys?" Zachary asked. "Are you okay?"

"The spiders," Rhys said nonsensically. "In the eighties. Pray for me. Pray for me." He pressed his hands together and bowed his head in mock prayer. Zachary put his hand on Rhys's arm, but the boy pulled away sharply. He started to bounce his head up and down, making loud shrieking noises and scratching his arms.

"It's okay," the nurse told him. "You're safe here. There are no spiders. We will protect you."

Rhys's cries subsided to whimpers. "The eighties," he repeated. "Why? Why?"

"You're safe," Kenzie repeated the nurse's words. "It's just from the drug, Rhys. It isn't real. It's from the drug."

Rhys rubbed at the tears on his face. He shook his head and made a pulsing sound in his throat that was half sob and half song. "They're hungry."

"Nothing is going to hurt you." Zachary held his arm gently. "You're in the hospital. Everything will be okay soon. This will all pass, and you'll feel like yourself again."

"He's hungry." Rhys switched suddenly to another voice. "Stop it. *Just stop it!*"

Kenzie was alarmed at the rapid changes. She wasn't used to dealing with psychiatric patients, but was sure that jumping from one disturbing thought to another so quickly wasn't usual. Did the second voice mean that Rhys was dealing with a separate personality? Or was he remembering something or someone from the past? She felt like they should be able to explain each thing that Rhys said, to find the logical reason behind it and deduce what he was seeing or hearing. But that wasn't the way it worked. The brain did not work logically when it was in this state.

"That's what Robin said," Zachary said in a low voice intended for

Kenzie's ears rather than Rhys's. "When she would get overly upset by something, maybe a noise she didn't like, she would say that."

Zachary nodded toward Rhys and didn't repeat the words, "Just stop it."

"After Clarence's murder, that was the only thing Rhys would say. And then… he stopped saying anything at all."

Kenzie's heart squeezed when she pictured that little boy and the trauma he had been through. All that he'd had to suffer when he was young, bottled up inside him all through the years. Unable to talk about it or to share his pain.

Maybe there was something to the MDMA therapy. Even though Rhys had reacted badly to it, it had loosened his tongue, made it so that he could speak more than he'd ever been able to since he was a small child, made it so that he could tell them something about the trauma.

"Did you see Gloria kill Grandpa Clarence, Rhys?" Kenzie asked softly.

Zachary looked alarmed that she would suggest this to Rhys. To put it to him so baldly.

"Just stop it!" Rhys said it more loudly, a harpy's shriek. Then he cowered as if someone had shouted at him rather than his being the shouter.

"Is that what Gloria said?"

Rhys sniffled, the tears running down his face again.

"It wasn't your fault," Kenzie told Rhys. As a bystander, he was bound to feel guilty about what happened. That he hadn't been able to stop the murder of his grandfather, even if there had been nothing he could do about it.

For years, he had lived with that knowledge, knowing that Gloria had been the culprit and had never been caught and punished for her actions. And who knew how she had treated him, living in the same house? She might have abused and threatened him every night with all kinds of terrible things.

He stood up and went to Kenzie, hugging her again. Kenzie hugged him briefly, then separated herself from him, not wanting anything inappropriate to develop.

"What Gloria did wasn't your fault."

Rhys rocked back and forth on his heels. "Just stop it. Shut up. Just stop it now." His voice was thready, distressed.

"You're allowed to talk now. You can talk about it as much as you need to. No one is going to stop you."

"Just stop it."

"Were you doing something that Gloria didn't like?"

Rhys put his hands over his ears. "The spiders," he said, returning to the previous hallucination. He wiggled his fingers around his face, drawing the room as he looked around it, as if he'd been sprinkling magic pixie dust around. The spiders and other things he could see came and went over the next hour as they listened to him babble and watched him go from the frightening images around him, back to Grandpa Clarence's murder, and around and around.

It was exhausting. Eventually, they had to leave. Kenzie needed to get to work, and Zachary had his cases to work on, she was sure. In the space of an hour, Rhys had probably said more than he had in the previous ten years. Kenzie's heart ached for him. She didn't know what to expect. After the drugs wore off, would he go silent again? Would he be able to talk about the murder? Would it have done him any good to talk about it as he had?

It was no wonder Vera had needed the extra time to sleep.

Kenzie and Zachary just looked at each other, neither sure what to say.

50

It was strange to go to the office so late in the morning. But Kenzie hadn't wanted to leave the visit until the end of the day. She had wanted to see Rhys as early as possible to reassure herself that he was okay and everything would be all right with him.

She just hoped that it was true. She actually wasn't that reassured. Rhys was clearly still feeling the effects of the MDMA even after it should have fully cleared his system. She worried that he wouldn't go back to normal again as Richards had suggested. What if he was in that agitated, hallucinating state permanently? There was drug-induced psychosis. Drug-induced schizophrenia. People had been damaged by exposure to hallucinogens in the past, though usually LSD was identified as the culprit.

"I probably won't be able to get off for couple's therapy this afternoon," she warned Zachary. "Plan to just have an individual session. I'll probably need the time to catch up at the office after missing yesterday afternoon and again this morning."

"Okay," Zachary nodded, looking relieved by her words. Too often, he got wound up worrying whether she would make it to their session because she had missed it once. Since then, he had deemed her unreliable at getting to sessions, even though she had never missed again.

Since she had told him she would likely not be there, he didn't have to spend the whole day obsessing about it. He could just assume that she wouldn't be and that he would go on his own. Apparently, it was a relief for him to shed that burden.

"How are you doing?" Dr. Cook asked as soon as Kenzie walked in the door. He studied her face and then her body, looking for any sign of injury. He had probably expected her to be black and blue after hearing that she had been hit by a car, even though she had assured him on the phone that she was perfectly fine, aside from a skinned knee and very mild concussion.

"I'm fine. Still a little fuzzy today, so I'll need to be careful what I do, but I'm fine to put in a few hours." She decided not to build up his expectations either. She would offer a few hours and, if she were able to work beyond that, he would be impressed. If she had to go home to recuperate, then she had at least not promised a full day's work.

"Be careful," Cook warned. "You probably should have taken a few days off until you were clear of the concussion. Does it hurt?"

Kenzie nodded. "I've taken a Tylenol this morning but don't want to take anything that will just make me more foggy. So… a bit of a headache, especially if I get up too quickly or bend over to pick something up. And the bump itself is still tender." She reached up and touched the bump on her head, which she thought had already reduced in size. Even her own light touch made her wince. "But other than that, the worst injury is a skinned knee."

She didn't lift her pant leg to show him the large burn dressing that covered the skinned area and the bruise and swelling around it. It was such a minor issue compared to what could have happened with a car-on-pedestrian accident. She was lucky to be alive and so unscathed.

"Don't bend over to pick anything up then," Cook advised. "Call me and I'll pick it up."

Kenzie laughed. "How about I just don't drop anything?"

"Well, that works too. Do you want me to run you through the latest developments?"

Kenzie nodded her agreement and Cook detailed the latest arrivals and results, and anything else Kenzie needed to follow up on.

"Tox screens came back on your Janice Martin."

Kenzie nodded. "MDMA?"

"Among other things."

"Oh?" Kenzie clicked her mouse to navigate to the Janice Martin file and have a look.

"She had sedatives in her bloodstream. And the hair analysis was interesting."

Hair analysis showed what Janice had been using in the months prior to her death. A timeline of what she had taken when. "Oh?" Kenzie found the results and clicked on the report. She skimmed it as Cook summarized.

"Quite a history of LSD and PCP use as well as the MDMA. In about the same timeframe."

"So they weren't just using MDMA."

"Doesn't look that way. She has no history of using either before she started the MDMA."

Kenzie shook her head. "And those drugs were not approved for this trial." She had the trial protocols that Garcia had sent her close at hand. "MDMA was the only drug approved for the trial, and any other medications the patient was on had to be recorded and closely monitored to ensure that there were no contraindications."

"Sounds like they are playing pretty fast and loose over at that place,"

"Yeah. They really are. This trial seems like it was just a smokescreen for all the abuses they could think of. This Dr. Miller was a real…" Kenzie paused, trying to think of a less offensive word than the one on the tip of her tongue. "A real low life. The guy knew he was on camera, and even that didn't stop him!"

Dr. Cook looked at Kenzie, one brow cocked questioningly. He hadn't watched the videos of the therapy sessions. She hadn't even given him the password to do so. Without knowing who had leaked the video of Isah's altercation with the staff, Kenzie wasn't about to trust Cook or anyone else with sensitive information.

She puffed out her cheeks and blew out a breath. "Unethical and abusive behavior," she summarized for him. "Detective Garcia is already looking at it, going to file criminal charges."

"Good. Don't need doctors like that giving the rest of the profession a bad name."

Dr. Cook eventually decided that he had caught Kenzie up on everything he needed to and was just hovering, and retreated to his office. Kenzie looked over the messages that had piled up in her inbox and voicemail and started reviewing and filing them as appropriate. Something niggled at the back of her mind. Something she had forgotten? Something that she was supposed to do?

She was partway through the processing when she realized she had not yet called Lisa. She had promised Walter that she would, and she had better follow through if she didn't want both of them on her case. Even forgetting something temporarily right now would be bad; they would think it was a symptom of her concussion and that she was being affected by the injury more than she was willing to admit.

Kenzie decided that a ten-minute break was in order. She got herself a fresh cup of coffee and dialed Lisa's number. She called from her desk phone, because it would signal to Lisa that she was at work. Which meant two things: that she could not talk for too long and that the injury was only minor, as evidenced by the fact that she could still work.

"MacKenzie," Lisa greeted, as though it had been months since they had talked, and she was amazed that Kenzie had finally taken the time. "How are you, my dear? Your father told me about your accident."

"Yes, I'm sorry I made him my errand boy rather than calling you myself, but I was tired, and he needed something to do."

Lisa laughed appreciatively. "That man does need to be kept busy."

Kenzie chuckled. "I hope you didn't mind too much."

"No, dear. I was glad to know what was happening so I didn't have to hear about it from another source. It doesn't look good when you don't know that your own daughter has been in a car accident."

"No, I guess not. I would have told you today anyway, but…"

"Would you?" Kenzie's mother's voice was teasing, yet a reprimand at the same time. How many times had Kenzie failed to report important developments to her in the past? There were probably too many to count. "Anyway, let's not worry about what could have happened. It didn't, and I am glad we found out immediately. Even if I can't do anything for you, I still appreciate knowing."

"Thanks, Mom." Kenzie was warmed by her mother's concern. They might not have the closest relationship that a mother and daughter could have, but they were both working on it. And as long as they were working on it, there was hope for a better, closer relationship in the future.

"And everything is okay with Zachary?" Lisa inquired. "How is he handling you being injured?"

Kenzie thought back to how he had shown up at the hospital—shoeless, hair sticking out like a porcupine, his wallet left at home.

"Well, he was pretty panicked when he heard about it, but he's been good. Once he saw that I was okay, he settled down. He's been spoiling me at home, you'll be happy to hear, and drove me in to work this morning. He's taking good care of me."

"Good. And it hasn't triggered his... issues?"

"No." Kenzie said it with assurance and then frowned, thinking about Zachary and wondering whether it were true. Just because she hadn't seen it, that didn't mean that Zachary hadn't been masking any evidence of his trauma. He wouldn't want her to know if he were having trouble, and wouldn't want to put that extra stress on her. But she needed to know. She needed to have some idea where his head was. "From what I can tell, he is still doing all right."

"Good. And... how is your young friend? Rhys?"

Kenzie frowned. She tried to remember what she had told Lisa about Rhys before. She must have told her about Rhys being admitted to the hospital. But so much had been going on that she couldn't recall their exact conversation.

"Rhys... well, that's a long story. He was transferred to Persons Residential Care and ended up back at the city hospital after a... reaction to a drug. We were just visiting him this morning before I came in to work, and... he's not in good shape. I was hoping that things would be a lot better than they were."

"I'm sorry to hear that. Is there anything that we can do?"

"No. I don't think so. It's just a matter of time. Seeing if everything goes back to normal after a few days. Some of these therapies can be very tricky. I don't know if... this one that is being offered at Persons is risky. I wasn't happy with it from the start."

"I thought..." Lisa trailed off for a moment. "I thought trauma therapy was what he needed."

"It is. But this is an experimental treatment, and I'm not convinced that the drugs they are trialing are the best solution. I think they are too risky."

"I see. He won't be going back to Persons, then?"

"I hope not. And if he does, I hope it will be for generally accepted, approved therapies, not anything experimental."

"You are comfortable with the staff there?"

"No… I am not. Kenzie rubbed her forehead. "Mom, this is really getting into stuff I can't discuss with you. Stuff that has come up with work and anything related to Rhys's care… I can't really share them with you. I'm ethically bound to keep them confidential."

"But you are not happy with Persons. You don't want Rhys to go back there?"

"No. I'm hoping to be able to talk his grandmother out of it. I didn't want him in this trial to start with, but she insisted because they offered her some kind of grant or scholarship and talked up this trauma recovery program like it was a miracle cure. But that isn't what it is. It's… playing with people's brains when we don't know what we're doing."

"I see." Kenzie got the feeling that Lisa was writing notes to herself in the pauses, but wasn't sure what she would be taking note of.

Kenzie looked at the timer on the phone to see how long the call had been. "Well, I need to get back to work now, Mom. But I wanted to make sure that you knew I am okay. You don't need to worry about anything."

Lisa said her goodbyes, and they terminated the call.

51

Once she had finished processing everything in her inbox and voicemail, Kenzie had a list of calls she needed to make. Results that needed to be passed on to various parties, calls to families of victims, some information to pass on to Dr. Wiltshire, and so on.

She dialed the number for Detective Garcia, wondering whether she would be able to reach her. Garcia might be out on another call or deeply embroiled in her investigations. But Garcia answered right away.

"Dr. Kirsch. Good to hear from you."

"I have some information for you on the Janice Martin file. I'll send it to you by email, but I thought I would give you a heads-up."

"Of course. Let me just grab a pen. Okay, what do you have?"

"At the same time as the MDMA trial was going on, Janice was taking—or being given—other psychedelics as well. Both LSD and PCP were being used as well."

"LSD and PCP? You're kidding me. Those were approved for use in these trials, were they?"

"No," Kenzie agreed. "They weren't. And any trials that they were approved for use in would be highly regulated."

"I am *not* impressed with the regulation of the trials at Persons. Where was the oversight? Who was watching over these people? We

549

expect our laws to protect the vulnerable, not leave them open to every kind of abuse."

"Yeah," Kenzie agreed. "I'm really not happy with what I have seen over at Persons. They don't seem to have any trouble operating completely outside of the law."

"And you expect that *your* voice would carry some weight with them."

"As a representative of the medical examiner?" Kenzie asked, a little confused. "Yes. I expect them to at least respect my authority. But they don't seem to take kindly to any kind of oversight, do they?"

"I meant your family name," Garcia said. "Boy, I'm really impressed with all the work your family does in the medical field. I see your name everywhere."

Kenzie nodded. She was used to that. People often recognized her name from the foundation's charitable works and Lisa Cole Kirsch herself.

"My parents do a lot in the state. It's mostly run by my mother. My dad and I watch in awe and sign where we are told to."

"You're involved in the family foundation?"

"Only peripherally."

"And you don't find that conflicts with your medical examiner work?"

"No. Why would it?"

Though Kenzie knew she had already run into conflicts once when she had, without realizing it, signed a document that made it look as though she had a bias or conflict of interest. She had to be careful not to let that happen again.

Garcia's voice was cautious. "Well, funding psychiatric stuff at the hospital and at Persons and then having to investigate them."

Kenzie stared at the screen of her phone as if that might enlighten her as to what Garcia was talking about. How much was the concussion muddying up her thinking? She couldn't even follow what Garcia was saying.

"Pardon me?"

"I'm talking about your family foundation being involved in the funding of Persons."

"I… no, I didn't realize they had anything to do with Persons."

"Well, I can tell you from the paperwork we have been processing over there the last couple of days that they are."

Kenzie's mind immediately returned to the discussion she had just had with Lisa. Kenzie had told her that she didn't trust the staff at Persons or the trial protocol. She had thought it was strange that Lisa should be so interested in Rhys's care or how he was doing. She had thought that it was just because Lisa wanted to keep up with what was going on in Kenzie's life and what was important to her. She'd had no idea that the foundation was involved with Persons.

"They have made a large donation quite recently," Garcia informed her.

Kenzie rubbed the space between her brows. "Oh, this is not good."

"I assumed that you already knew about it and that you had… recused yourself or whatever it is that you must do in a case like this. I assumed the medical examiner's office already knew all the details about your family's involvement. I mean," Garcia's voice was conciliatory, "you aren't directly involved. Just because your family has given Persons a donation, that doesn't mean they are involved in the drug trials or the abuses that are going on there."

"But it suggests that we support what they're doing, which isn't true. I don't want anyone to think that I am involved in this in any way. Why didn't they tell me the foundation was involved in Persons?"

"They wouldn't have known you had anything to do with it as a medical examiner."

"Not in the beginning, maybe. But they certainly would have as soon as that video was leaked. And when my mother talked to me about it this morning."

"Ah. Well. You might want to talk to them about it, then. But I assume stuff like this happens all the time. They put money into so many different causes—the hospital and everything too—that there might be points at which they discover that they have invested in something they don't want to be associated with in the future."

"She was just asking me a few minutes ago about the staff at Persons. If I trusted them."

"And I guess you told her no."

"You bet I did."

"So maybe now she's trying to figure out how to get out of it. There was a contract for ongoing funding. I guess they'll take that to their lawyer and figure out how to get out of it."

The thought of ongoing funding going from the Kirsch family foundation into Persons was untenable.

"I'd better call them and find out what's going on. Or drive out to see her. Only I've got a ton of work to get done here. Maybe I should insist that she come here to see me. They're the ones who put money into it without telling me about it. I'm supposed to know all the recipients."

But she had to admit that she would only have been able to name two or three of them off the top of her head. And she hadn't really looked very carefully at the lists she had been given of institutions and programs that had received money from the foundation. She had never done any kind of due diligence to ensure that none of them had ever been associated with investigations by the medical examiner's office, or any of the medical regulators that she should be aware of.

But how could she be sure that none of the institutions they had dealt with had been involved in any investigations in the past? Or wouldn't be in the future? Just because someone died at an institution and the medical examiner's office had to look into it, that didn't mean they had done anything wrong. People died, which wasn't necessarily the fault of the hospital or medical facility providing them care.

"I guess... I'm going to need to investigate this some more," Kenzie told Garcia, flummoxed. "Thanks for giving me a heads-up."

"You're welcome. And how are you doing? Everybody in the building must have heard about your accident. No one spreads gossip like the boys in blue."

"Yes... well... it was just one of those things. The cars that were coming saw me far enough ahead of time to stop before they reached me. Almost."

"You could have been flattened. You don't know who it was? You never saw?"

"I don't know. Like I said in my report, a guy was talking to me earlier, and it could have been him, but I don't think it was. I thought before I got hit that it wasn't him. It was someone else. But I don't remember if I saw or felt something that told me it was someone else. It happened so fast. I felt the shove, and then I was out in traffic, trying to stop myself from falling. It was only a few seconds, if that. And I guess... no one else saw him, could say what had happened?"

"The investigating officer questioned as many witnesses as possible, but some people had already left the scene. No one saw the shove."

"It figures. I think it was just one of those random things."

"You mean you don't think it was related to Persons."

"Right. I don't think they had anything to do with it. It was just a random thing. Why would anyone at Persons come out here, to where I work, to shove me into traffic? What good would that do anyone?"

"Well, you did get a threatening voicemail as well. Why would they leave that? It was before I got the video of the therapy sessions, so we can assume that they didn't want those recordings to be seen by anyone."

"But you were the one going after those recordings, not me. I needed them as part of my investigation but, if they wanted to stop someone, wouldn't it be you?"

"Maybe I don't go wandering close enough to the road. Maybe they came here to talk to me or put a stop to my investigation and then saw you. Thought they would take the opportunity."

"I suppose," Kenzie admitted. "But it's hard to imagine. If you were one of the doctors there, and had either been involved in the abuse or knew that it was going on, wouldn't you want to get away? Just hit the road and keep on running so no one could follow you? Why stay here? Where you could be caught?"

Garcia laughed. "People are stupid. Or they think that the police are stupid. They don't think that they will be caught. You can bet that Dr. Miller never thought he would be caught."

"When he knew that the therapy sessions were being recorded?" Kenzie demanded. "How stupid do you have to be to let yourself be recorded abusing a patient?"

"Pretty stupid. Isn't that what I just said?"

"So you've arrested him?" Kenzie asked. "He's behind bars?"

"He is for now. I imagine he will make bail, and then whether he stays around to see the trial through or not…"

"I'm glad you got him."

"Me too. As soon as we saw what was on those recordings, we were on our way to arrest him." Garcia waited a few beats. "But you were attacked before I got to him. Do you think that it could have been Dr. Miller?"

Kenzie considered. She pictured the worried-looking doctor she had seen at Persons. The predator she had seen on the recording. She hadn't seen her attacker. She had only talked to Dr. Miller once, and the attacker had been behind her. How could she be expected to be able to see what had happened behind her back?

"Aren't there any… traffic cams or storefront cams that caught it? I just didn't see him."

"Nothing that caught that part of the road, unfortunately. You hear how there are cameras everywhere, but sometimes they just aren't where you want them to be. But you keep saying *him*. How do you know it was a man?"

Kenzie shook her head impatiently. She was just saying "him" because it was easier than "him or her." She didn't really know. But when she thought about it, she was pretty sure that it had been a man. Was that just her bias? That she thought that anyone who performed that kind of violence would be a man? Was it the size of his hands? The strength of the push? She couldn't remember either one particularly well, but her subconscious mind might have been more aware of it than she was.

"I just… think it was a man."

"Why?"

"Because… I just do. I don't know why. But you can't assume that is true."

"Could it have been Dr. Richards?"

Kenzie's immediate reaction was laughter. Of course it had not been Dr. Richards. But why not? What was it that made her react that way? She pictured the lovely Dr. Richards. Her finely lined face, her large blond curls, all looking like she had just stepped out of a salon. Smelling like jasmine and roses.

Kenzie stubbed her finger down on the desk as if to pin this thought before it could get away from her.

"Dr. Richards wears perfume."

"Ah," Kenzie could hear Garcia's smile in her voice. "The other senses kick into gear. So your attacker was not wearing perfume."

"No… unless the wind was blowing it away from me. And even then… she uses a good amount. I think I would still be able to smell it."

"Good," Garcia approved. "What *did* your attacker smell like?"

Kenzie closed her eyes to immerse herself in the scene again, but her head was throbbing and it was hard to concentrate.

"I don't know. There were other people there. Other smells from the street and my lunch. I don't know what he smelled like, but I know it wasn't like Dr. Richards's perfume."

"Well, that's one person eliminated. Of course, it doesn't mean she couldn't send someone else, but at least we know she wasn't at the scene when it happened."

"Do you really think I was attacked by someone at Persons?"

"I don't know. It's a definite possibility."

"You're pulling all their records and looking at everyone else. So if there was anyone else there who was involved in the abuse of the patients or anything else, then you'll know about it."

"I hope so. We didn't warn them that we were coming for everything, but…"

"But they could have started destroying evidence as soon as Mr. Isah died and the ME's office refused to stay out of it."

Garcia chuckled. "Yes. That's right. They've had over a week now. Hopefully, they don't know how to permanently delete anything from their computers. The electronics guys are looking at them."

"Are they still operating? Without their computers?"

"They can get by with clipboards and paper records if they have to for a few days. And computers are easy to buy. I doubt if we caused anything more than a hiccup interrupting their services."

"You don't think that anyone else was involved in the assaults, though, do you?"

"Where were they when the assaults were happening? When patients complained? Who was supervising Dr. Miller? What kind of background checks did they run? Does he even have a current medical license? There are lots of things to look at. At the very least, they failed to supervise Miller's work properly. They never reviewed the therapy recordings. What's the point in recording them if you never look at them? Or if they looked at them, then why didn't they do anything about it?"

Kenzie nodded her agreement. Somebody should have known what was going on. There should have been plenty of red flags.

52

O h, hi, Kenzie."

Kenzie looked up to see Julie, the young woman who often stood in for her at the front desk and phone reception when Kenzie had to be in autopsy or somewhere else.

"Hi, Julie." Kenzie looked at her desk and then at her calendar, trying to identify why Julie was there.

"I know I'm early. You usually don't need me until the afternoon. But I figured you might be behind or want to leave early because of..." Julie tapped her own head. "You might not be feeling very well. I had an open block, so if you want me to start now, I can."

"Actually..." Kenzie looked at the papers and notes she had scattered in front of her. Some written while she was reviewing her in boxes and some while talking to Detective Garcia. She had been tired before arriving at the office, and working through the rest of the day as planned seemed like an impossible task. "That would be so great, Julie. You're sure it's not a problem?"

"Would I be here if it was? I am at your disposal. Whether you want to stay here and get something else done, or go home or to your couple's therapy, whatever you want."

"Good. Yeah. I'm going to gather all of this up," Kenzie gathered the random notes into a pile, "And make sure that I process everything and get everything into my task list. Thank you. You're a lifesaver."

"Happy to help." Julie gave her a sunny smile.

Since Julie was there regularly, she already knew all the procedures and where everything was, and she was ready to slip into Kenzie's seat as soon as she vacated it. Kenzie took her papers to the boardroom and sat down to go through them.

She hadn't talked to Vera since they had been in to visit Rhys. She had expected Vera to call her by now to see how the visit had gone or to talk to her about what she thought the best approach would be to help Rhys.

Kenzie hoped that she hadn't gotten to the hospital to find Rhys in worse shape than he had been the day before. It was possible for a patient in an agitated state to have medical complications or to do something to harm himself when he didn't have the capacity to realize the damage that he could do. Kenzie's stomach knotted as she thought about all the things that could have happened to prevent Vera from calling her to chat briefly about Rhys's situation.

Of course, the other possibility was that even though she had given Kenzie and Zachary permission to visit Rhys, she still didn't want to talk to Kenzie about his treatment. It was, after all, her business and not Kenzie's, and they had differed on key points.

Only now Vera knew that Kenzie had been right about the risks of the MDMA therapy. That it might not be the miracle cure that she was hoping for, but had the potential to do permanent damage.

Kenzie called Vera's number, unsure whether she would answer the phone. If she were at the hospital with Rhys, as Kenzie expected her to be, then it might be turned off. Or she might just not want to talk.

"Hello?"

"Vera, it's Kenzie. How are you? I was just thinking about you and Rhys and wondering how things were going."

She didn't ask whether anything had changed, leaving it up to Vera to provide as much information as she wanted to.

"He's sleeping," Vera said. "He hasn't slept since the therapy session and was getting more agitated. The nurse thought it might be because he was too tired."

"That can certainly make things worse," Kenzie agreed. "Good sleep is really important for good mental health."

"I don't know when he slept last. I don't think that they were making sure that he was sleeping when he was at Persons. He went under pretty quickly once they gave him a sedative."

"Hopefully, he'll feel a lot better when he wakes up."

"Yes," Vera agreed. She blew out her breath. "Oh, my. I never thought that I would hear Rhys chatter on like that again. He talked when he was a little boy. He was a little chatterbox. But I've gotten so used to him being silent, except for the times he would get a word or two out. Having him talk like that…" she trailed off. "Did he talk the whole time you were visiting him?"

"Yes," Kenzie agreed with a laugh. "Yes, he did. And I know what you mean about it being disconcerting. Though it must be a hundred times more startling for you; you have lived with his silence for years. Zachary and I have only been occasional visitors."

"I don't think I realized… I knew that Clarence's death was traumatic for him. That was when he stopped talking. But I thought…" The seconds ticked by while Vera struggled to put her thoughts into words. "I thought that it had made a hole. That all those memories of what had happened around the time of his death were gone and that his brain was trying to reconstruct things in a way that was acceptable to him. I knew he had difficulty speaking and communicating, but I thought that was… because of the drugs and therapy he'd had when they sent him to the first place. That it had changed his brain chemistry. That *they* were the ones who had caused it, not us."

Kenzie didn't know what to say. She murmured something that sounded soothing but didn't make much sense. She was thinking along the same lines as Vera was. Whatever had happened that night had been far more damaging than anyone in Rhys's family or treatment team had ever thought.

It wasn't gone. It wasn't buried far under the surface. On the contrary, it was always in the forefront of Rhys's mind, bubbling up again and again. The feelings, sounds, and sensations of that day repeated over and over.

At least, they did when he was under the influence of MDMA. Whether that was how Rhys felt all the time, Kenzie couldn't be sure. But she knew now that what had happened that day long ago was not gone and forgotten, leaving a void behind. It was there in Rhys's brain, looming up, ever-present.

"I guess… it was long past time for Rhys to talk about it," Vera said finally. "I don't know why it took until now for me to realize. But he needs to talk about it. However we can get him to do that."

Hopefully, Rhys wouldn't stop trying to talk about it when he was no longer feeling the effects of the MDMA.

"I think you're right," Kenzie agreed. "I think it would be really good to get him into a situation where he's encouraged to talk about it."

"Yes," Vera sighed. Kenzie knew she probably didn't want to talk about Clarence's death and her own daughter's guilt.

"Vera… I wanted to ask you about something. This is sort of a change of topic, so I'm sorry. I don't mean to imply that this is unimportant. Just that there's something else I need to know, too."

"Yes?"

"You mentioned that Rhys had gotten some kind of grant to get into that program at Persons. Where did that come from? Was that something you had applied for?"

"Oh, no. We were approached by someone. They said that he had been specially selected for the program, that they thought he would benefit from it, and that there was a special bursary—like a scholarship— to cover it."

"Who was it? Was it someone from the hospital? From Persons?"

"No, a charity that handles things like this. But he said they preferred to stay anonymous in cases like this one. They didn't want to put undue attention on Rhys."

Kenzie called both Lisa and Walter and got voicemail for both of them. It wasn't unusual for her to have to leave a message for Walter. He was often busy with his lobbying. In meetings, behind closed doors, wining and dining influencers; he kept pretty busy. He would call her back when he was free, probably in the evening when he finished his dinner appointment.

Lisa was usually more available during the day, only unavailable when she was out at evening fundraiser events. If she were at a ladies' luncheon, or out with friends, or organizing an event, she would usually pause to answer the phone when she saw that it was Kenzie calling. It was unusual, but not unheard of, for Kenzie not to be able to reach either one of them.

There was a tap at the boardroom door, and Dr. Cook stuck his head in. He peered at the papers spread out in front of Kenzie.

"Everything okay, Dr. Kirsch?"

"Yes… but I'm not sure I'm being very productive today. I'm distracted and this headache…"

"Why don't you go home? You already have someone covering reception. And you normally have this afternoon off, don't you?"

"Yes. But I figured I would work through today because I missed yesterday afternoon…"

"You didn't miss yesterday afternoon because you were taking a vacation or playing hooky. You missed because you were hit by a car. And I think you need to take a day or two to recover from it. We don't have anything that is so urgent that you need to work injured. You will recover faster if you take the time to heal than if you try to push through and wear yourself out."

Kenzie waffled on it. She had an ideal in her mind of what she wanted to do, and then the practicality of Dr. Cook's advice. She knew she wasn't at her best. Not just because of the head injury, but also because of her distraction with Rhys's problems and the questions running through her mind about the threads that connected the three cases—the deaths of Leander Isah and Janice Martin, and Rhys's therapy at Persons. It was all connected, and those connections worried her. Their implications pressed darkly on the back of her mind.

"Go home," Dr. Cook said firmly. "Julie and I will hold down the fort. But I won't start any postmortems without you. You won't be out of the loop. I'll catch up on signing reports and reviewing your work on the Isah and Martin deaths so that I'll be up to speed when you get back and are ready to discuss them."

Kenzie sighed. "Are you sure?"

"Why push it? If you try to work while you have a concussion, you will make mistakes. We don't want any mistakes. Better to wait."

"We'll get behind."

"We'll be fine. We can get someone else in if we need another pair of hands. But we don't have a brain to replace yours. You're the one who knows where everything is, the files, the procedures, the history. We'll need that when you get back. Nice and fresh and ready to go."

"Okay." Kenzie gathered her papers together. "But only because you insisted."

"I did," he agreed.

Zachary was surprised when he looked up to see who had arrived and saw that it was Kenzie. His face brightened, but he looked confused and concerned at the same time.

"Is everything okay? I didn't think you would be able to make it today? Don't get me wrong, I am glad you did, but… is everything okay?"

"Yes. Dr. Cook said to go home to recuperate. He would hold down the fort."

"And that worked?"

"He insisted."

"He insisted," Zachary repeated meditatively. "I'll have to remember to try that sometime."

Kenzie laughed. She knew that she was stubborn and didn't always listen to good advice when it was given to her, or listen to Zachary's cautions or other things that she didn't want to hear. She hadn't gotten into the position she was in by being a shy, retreating wallflower.

Kenzie took the chair next to Zachary's in the waiting room. He reached over and rubbed her back. "Glad you're here."

"Thanks. Me too."

In a few minutes, the receptionist, Elizabeth, called them forward and let them know Dr. Boyle was ready for them. Zachary and Kenzie made their way to her office and made a little small talk to get settled into the session. Dr. Boyle opened their file in front of her to review the last session's notes.

"Any new developments that you would like to discuss? How have things gone the last couple of weeks?"

Zachary looked at Kenzie, his expression and body language indicating she should take this one. Dr. Boyle looked at Kenzie as well, eyebrows lifted in expectation.

Kenzie glanced at Zachary, wondering how much he wanted revealed and what he wanted to focus on.

"Well, Zachary's friend—our friend—Rhys, he had a breakdown, and we don't know all the reasons for that. He was hospitalized and has been through some therapy since then, which has been... worrying for both of us."

Dr. B nodded. "I'm sorry to hear that. What has been the biggest impact of this?"

Kenzie looked at Zachary again to see if he wanted to jump in, but he did not take the initiative.

"It's been stressful. As well as not knowing what precipitated this breakdown, he's also been put into an experimental therapy program that I had significant concerns about. And I know that it's probably affecting Zachary as well. Making it more difficult to sleep..."

"Zachary?" Dr. B. prompted.

"Yeah. It's been… challenging," Zachary agreed.

They both waited for him to elaborate. Zachary looked at Kenzie and then away.

"I don't know much about the cases that Kenzie has been working on. But I know a little bit. Things that have made it to the news and certain discussion forums. And… things that I have overheard."

Kenzie cut a glance toward him. She didn't think that she had said anything within his hearing that was confidential, but she would have to be more aware of that in the future.

"I know that there were abuses at Persons," Zachary said. "The facility where Rhys was being treated. I know that Kenzie was investigating a death—two deaths—there. And so, knowing that Rhys was there, has been very… has made me very anxious."

Dr. B nodded. "That makes sense. How has Rhys been?"

Zachary scratched the back of his neck. "The drug therapy that they did—he reacted to it. He's been agitated, hallucinating, talking and crying about when his grandpa was killed. I'm afraid he's never going to come out of it. That's how he'll be for the rest of his life."

"He should come back down off of it," Kenzie tried to reassure Zachary. "In the case studies that I was able to find, they came back down after a few days and recovered. It's just a matter of keeping him calm and treating him while he's still reacting. They don't know why some people react that way."

"I know that's what the doctors are *saying*," Zachary agreed. "But I'm still afraid we've lost him for good."

Kenzie nodded. She knew better than to try to argue with a feeling. Feelings, as they had often discussed in their sessions, could not be argued down with logic or controlled by the person feeling them. Their reactions and responses could be controlled, and some situations could be reframed to make the person better understand what they were feeling or relieve some of the negative feelings. Still, there was no such thing as "turning off" a feeling. Only of hiding or repressing it, actions which could cause negative emotions to grow over time.

"That's scary," Kenzie acknowledged. "That thought really scares me too. I try to focus on the likely positive outcomes. But that doesn't mean there aren't possible negative outcomes either."

Zachary nodded. He stared down at the carpet in front of his feet. "I don't know how to turn the negative thoughts off."

"Have you tried any mindfulness activities?" Dr. B asked. "Any anxiety-releasing exercises?"

Zachary tended to scoff at things like controlled breathing and visualization. He didn't say that they didn't work this time, but it was clear that he didn't think they would and that was why he hadn't tried anything.

"How about your antianxiety meds?" Dr. B asked. "That's why you have them. To help to get through rough spots like this."

Kenzie shook her head, but Zachary nodded, surprising her. He pressed his lips together and looked away. "Yeah. I have a couple of nights over the last week."

Kenzie was stunned. Zachary always resisted taking the antianxiety meds, complaining about how they made him groggy in the morning and that he could manage better without them. He always pushed back when she suggested he take them, though sometimes he would eventually agree that it was a good idea.

She was shocked that not only had he taken the meds on his own without any encouragement from her, but also that he had done it without her knowledge.

He was a grown man and, of course, he was perfectly capable of taking care of his own health and had done it for years before meeting her and been stable most of the time. He didn't need her to tell him to take his meds, and he didn't need to report back to her whether he had taken something.

But she had thought that she would know. She would recognize that his anxiety was ramping up, and then she would recognize that he had taken something for it, the dampening effect of the drug on his panic or intrusive thoughts.

"I didn't even know," she told him. "You didn't tell me you were feeling so bad."

Zachary shrugged.

"You can share that with me," Kenzie told him firmly. "I want to be there for you. To help you. You don't have to hide it from me."

"I wasn't… you just had so much on your plate already. You were trying to do what you needed to so that you could issue your report on the two deaths. And you were just as worried about Rhys as I was. You need to get your sleep so that you can get up in the morning for work. You don't need me pulling you down and causing you extra worries."

Kenzie couldn't think of what to say. She looked to Dr. Boyle for help.

"Zachary recognizes that you have had a lot of stress this week as you have been trying to work through these issues as well," Dr. B stated.

"Yes. I know I've been stressed too. But I don't want that to stop him from sharing with me when he's feeling bad. Especially…"

"Especially what?" Dr. B prodded after a few seconds of silence.

"Especially… at this time of year when we know he is vulnerable to worsening depression. Any changes in his mental health could have a significant effect on how he makes it through the season…"

Dr. B looked at Zachary. "Do you think you might need some more support, which you're pulling away from? Do you not want Kenzie to see how you're feeling in case your depression is worsening?"

"I don't know. I thought I was doing the right thing. That I was helping her and being supportive of her needs."

"And you were. But let's talk about your needs too. How would you rate your depression this past week, as compared to the same time last month?"

Kenzie still had to learn to use these kinds of qualifiers and scales when asking Zachary about his depression. Not just asking him if he was feeling okay or whether he thought he might be slipping into depression again.

Zachary was silent for a few minutes, considering the question. Then he finally let out a sigh. "I guess… on a scale from one to ten, I was a four or five this time last month. And maybe a… six this week."

Still low enough that Kenzie wasn't too concerned about it, but trending in the wrong direction. As they had all known that it would.

"Good," Dr. B pronounced. She didn't say that he needed to evaluate his depression meds or that she wanted to immediately increase them. She just let that sit for a bit.

Zachary eventually looked at her. "Good?"

"Good. Thank you for giving me a nice firm evaluation. How do you feel about that?"

"Well…" Zachary took a peek at Kenzie before looking back at Dr. B again. "It's not much of a change. And we're both worried about Rhys. It's normal for it to be worse this time of year, but I think it's not too bad yet."

Dr. B made a couple of notes on the file in front of her. "You're not concerned about it."

"No. I don't think we need to make any changes."

"Okay. Kenzie, how do you feel about it?"

"Worried…" Kenzie looked at him, but he kept his face toward Dr. B, not looking at Kenzie. "But I'm more worried about you feeling like you need to hide what you feel from me than I am about a slight change in your depression."

Zachary nodded. He didn't voice any defense for this behavior. They both understood that he had been conditioned by society and the many families and social workers he had dealt with over the years to hide his negative feelings and pretend to be a strong, stalwart provider who didn't have tender feelings of his own. It took a lot of trust and reconditioning to confess how he was feeling to Kenzie. He had done well the previous year, when he'd had to be admitted to the hospital, of revealing to her the depth of his depression and self-destructive feelings.

With some more work, she thought they could get to the point where he would tell her about his slightly-worse feelings directly instead of having to share them in couple's therapy with Dr. Boyle mediating between them. They were making progress. They hadn't needed to pry out of Zachary the feelings he was having now.

"Is there anything that would make it easier to share these feelings with Kenzie?" Dr. Boyle asked.

Zachary shrugged. "I don't think so. I just… don't want to stress her out more than she already is."

"If she told you that she took a sleeping pill because she was having trouble putting the investigation aside and going to sleep, would you be upset by that?"

"No." Zachary shook his head. "I'd be glad to know she was taking care of herself."

"Kenzie," Dr. B turned her attention to Kenzie. "Do you think you would be upset if Zachary told you that he took an anxiety pill in order to calm down his racing thoughts?"

"No."

"Do you think you could accept it without worrying that he needed further intervention?"

Kenzie rolled her eyes. She didn't like being made to feel like she let her worry get out of control. Because that wasn't true at all. She worried about Zachary but didn't harass him to take other medications, call Dr. B, or admit himself to psych. At least, she didn't think she did. Not usually.

"Yes, I think I could do that." She looked at Zachary. "I will try not to assume that it means anything more than that you needed to take one antianxiety pill to settle down and get a good sleep."

Zachary nodded. "I'll try to… make it more natural to tell you."

Dr. B looked satisfied. "I think the two of you will find it helpful if you can share feelings and strategies without it having to be a big, life-changing event. You've come a long way in developing trust and sharing your feelings, but you are still both pretty sensitive about upsetting the other person by disclosing your true feelings. We'll keep working on that."

Kenzie and Zachary both nodded.

"And I hope that next week, I'll hear positive news about your friend Rhys."

They bought ice cream on the way home, as was their tradition. Kenzie was trying not to watch Zachary, assessing whether he was feeling stressed and anxious. He would let her know. She didn't need to analyze everything he did and said to evaluate his mental state. He had been quiet about his feelings while she'd been working on the Persons cases. But she had still known that he had been worried and anxious about Rhys, even if they hadn't talked about it at length and he hadn't mentioned taking anxiety pills during the week.

"Peanuts and chocolate?" Zachary asked, looking over the ice cream flavors.

"Mmm," Kenzie shook her head. She didn't like peanuts or peanut butter in ice cream. "Butterscotch ripple?"

"Is there one with butterscotch and chocolate ripples? I think you deserve both."

Kenzie laughed. "No, I don't think so… we could get a butterscotch ripple and a chocolate ripple and have a scoop of each."

"Ah, good thought," Zachary agreed. "Or we could do the butterscotch ripple and…" he gestured dramatically to the toppings section nearby, "chocolate sauce on top."

"Ooh. Yes, I think you've nailed it. Is that what you want too, or do you want something else?"

"I'm good with that. And what we've already got in the freezer."

There were several pints of other various flavors in the freezer already. Kenzie added a few bananas to their basket. That at least made it look like they weren't just binging on ice cream. Though, of course, they would be part of their banana splits.

After checking out, it wasn't long before they were home. They had just put their bowls of ice cream on the table when the doorbell rang. Kenzie looked at Zachary.

"Are you expecting a delivery?"

"No." Zachary took out his phone to check the doorbell cam. He raised his brows. "It's your parents."

"What?" Kenzie stared at him in disbelief.

"Walter and Lisa."

Her father had shown up at her house once or twice unannounced, but Lisa never would. She would always check with Kenzie before she showed up. Generally, she just invited Kenzie to come see her if she wanted to talk to her about something. Walter and Lisa were divorced and hadn't lived together for years. It made no sense that they would show up together.

Zachary could be mistaken. It could be Walter and some other woman that he had been dating. Zachary had only met Lisa once or twice. He might mistake someone else for her, especially if Walter were dating someone of similar physical appearance to Lisa. He probably had a "type."

Even though he was a PI and part of his business was recognizing faces. The man was not infallible, and he was looking at a small screen.

Kenzie went to the door anyway. If it was Walter, she should be the one to answer it and either welcome him in or turn him away if she thought he was up to no good. With her concussion and seeing Rhys and it being a therapy day, which always wrung out her emotions, she was exhausted and didn't want to have to see anyone.

Especially Walter, who she always had to be wary of and try to figure out his motivations and whether he were being upfront with her. Or more accurately, to figure out how he was not being upfront with her. Walter always held something back. As a lobbyist, constantly negotiating and exercising power plays, he always needed something in his back pocket that he could bring out when negotiations broke down and more pressure was needed. It was second nature, whether it was because he was a lobbyist or whether he was a good lobbyist because that was the way he was made.

Kenzie took a deep breath and let it out slowly. She didn't have to let him in. She could tell him that it was a bad time, and they would have to set up another time to meet. He had shown up without calling or making an appointment first, so she was well within her rights to tell him that it simply wouldn't work. She opened the door.

It *was* Walter and Lisa. Kenzie gaped at them. "Mom? Dad? What is this? What are you doing here?"

Lisa smiled. "I'm sorry to descend upon you like this without any warning. But since you called this morning, we figured we should handle this sooner rather than later. And better off face to face."

Kenzie opened her mouth to object.

She didn't have problems telling Walter it wasn't a good time and sending him on his way. But Lisa was another matter altogether. She wasn't used to telling her mother no about anything.

"If we could come in, MacKenzie. We'll keep it as brief as possible."

Kenzie stepped back and motioned them in. Zachary stood at the end of the hallway. He stepped out of the way, ducking back into the kitchen. Kenzie followed her parents toward the living room. They could see into the kitchen, where she and Zachary had been preparing their splits. Lisa followed her eyes.

"Oh, we're interrupting your dinner. I'm so sorry."

"Well, no, we were just having some ice cream…" Kenzie didn't bother explaining the post-therapy-session ice cream tradition to Lisa. Wasn't she the one who used to take Kenzie out for ice cream after a trip to the doctor or dentist? "Would you like to join us?" Kenzie offered, rather than telling Zachary to put the ice cream away and they would have it later.

"I wouldn't say no to ice cream," Walter said jovially, immediately stepping into the kitchen.

Lisa looked less certain. She smoothed her blouse and skirt down, as if checking to make sure that her stomach was still flat. She was remarkably svelte for someone who spent so much time at fancy fundraising dinners. She didn't eat very much of the steak and lobster.

"Come on in, Mom," Kenzie encouraged. "It won't hurt to have a spoonful of ice cream."

Lisa entered the little kitchen, looking around as if she weren't sure she belonged there. "Well, maybe half a banana," she suggested, looking at the small bunch that sat on the table awaiting the banana splits.

"It's not really a banana split if all you eat is half of a banana," she told Lisa.

But Lisa had already made up her mind, and her banana split *would* consist of half a banana. Kenzie might be able to talk her into a drizzle of chocolate syrup, but she wasn't counting on it.

For a few minutes, they were occupied with getting their splits ready. Walter had to look through all the flavors of ice cream, weighing the merits of each one. Always one to make a careful, discerning choice. Kenzie and Zachary had already decided what they wanted, and Lisa was going with half a banana. Eventually, they were all finished dishing up and sat down at the table with their bowls, looking at each other.

Kenzie wanted to know what they were doing there.

You called and left messages for both of us this morning," Lisa said briskly. "So I assume you have at least some idea of what this is about."

Kenzie looked down at her ice cream and had a few spoonfuls, making sure to get lots of chocolate sauce in each one, before answering.

"I was calling you about Rhys."

Lisa nodded.

Zachary looked back and forth at them. "Why would you be calling her—them—about Rhys?" he asked. "They don't even know Rhys."

"No," Kenzie agreed. "But I mentioned the first day when Rhys was admitted to the hospital, talked about what had happened and how worried I was about him."

"We both were," Zachary agreed seriously, looking at Walter and Lisa. "And we still are."

Kenzie nodded. "But I think… well, I guess maybe I should have figured it out sooner. Where the grant for Rhys to get into Persons and into the trauma therapy study there came from."

"I did try to talk to you about it," Lisa said, "but you were so busy with everything else. You won't just stop and read an email. You get caught up in everything else and think that any of the family stuff is a lower priority. I don't know how to change that."

Kenzie rubbed her eyes and wished her head weren't pounding so much. Zachary looked at her, but wasn't following the conversation. Kenzie knew what was coming, but she had already been thinking about it for a few days, and Zachary was coming into it late in the game.

"Mom… it isn't that I don't think it is important. It's just that… other people can handle it. Before I started getting more involved in the foundation, you had other people to handle it. So I know you can do it without me."

"But we don't want to do it without you. It is *your* legacy. You need to step up and help run it and decide what you want to finance and what you do not. And you're a doctor. You have a much better understanding of the different causes than any of the non-professionals on the board."

"It isn't for me to run. Not yet, anyway."

"We don't want you to just take it over when we are gone," Lisa said. "What kind of parents would we be if we just dumped it on you at the end of the day? You need to learn the business and how to run it gradually so that you're ready for it when it is your turn to take over. You need to be trained and taught what to do and how to direct it."

"Okay. Yes," Kenzie agreed. "I agree with all of that. But I can't run it at the same time as I'm running the medical examiner's office. It's too much for me to take everything on."

"But you need to take more. You need to have a say in what is being financed and how. Otherwise…" Lisa sighed and shook her head.

Walter took up the conversational torch. "Otherwise, you end up in a mess like we find ourselves in now."

Zachary shook his head. "Should I even be here? It sounds like you're talking about family foundation stuff, and I am not part of that. I can work on other things while the three of you talk." He picked up his bowl as if to leave.

"No," Lisa and Kenzie said together.

They exchanged a look.

"This is about you too, Zachary," Lisa said firmly. "Not as a director of the foundation, but as someone who has an interest in how the foundation runs and the parties that it benefits."

Zachary shook his head. "That's for you and Kenzie to decide."

"If we are focusing our efforts on a mental health project, then shouldn't you have some say in it?" Walter asked. "You are the one who is most interested in and invested in deciding what mental health projects are the most viable and helpful programs. For the rest of us... it's just academic. We can look at numbers and talk about what has been funded in the past, but *you* are the one who knows the bones of the business. Which programs really need funding and are doing the most good."

Zachary had been happy to sit by while Kenzie and her parents discussed mental health issues in a general way. And while Tyrrell, his brother, helped to pick out the companies and programs that he thought would make the most difference, based on his experience with abuse, addiction, and family issues. Zachary had been happy to let them all do their thing and cheer them from the sidelines.

But Lisa was right; he was the one who had the most experience and the most insight into what programs would be the most impactful.

He looked uncomfortable. "I'm not part of the foundation..."

"What did you think of the program we put Rhys into?" Walter asked.

Zachary opened his mouth and then sudden understanding entered his expression. Until then, he had not guessed what Kenzie had—that the Kirsch family foundation was the anonymous donor who had reached out to Vera to sponsor Rhys's admission to the trauma program.

"That *you* put Rhys into?" he repeated.

"Well," Walter shrugged. "It was his grandmother who put him into the program, of course, but we are the ones who approached her with the idea and funded his admission to Persons. She would not have been able to afford to put him into the program herself. And he needed a trauma treatment program, didn't he?"

"Well, yes," Zachary agreed cautiously.

"But you wouldn't have put him into that one."

Zachary shook his head slowly. He shot a look at Kenzie, worrying about whether he was doing something wrong by admitting this. He didn't want to alienate her parents and cause some kind of rift between them and Kenzie. Kenzie nodded, trying to convey that it was okay to express his opinion on the matter. And of course, he already knew how she felt about the program. They had discussed it repeatedly. He had been right behind her in trying to dissuade Vera from putting Rhys into it.

"No," he admitted. "I wouldn't have put him into it. These drug trials are... controversial. Untested. And there have been some very negative experiences around them. Even if they show good results overall, they have to be properly regulated and supervised and some patients will react very badly to the medications. Like Rhys did."

"You anticipated that he might have a reaction to it?"

"The risks are too high. Especially with a teenager. They often have paradoxical reactions to psychiatric meds."

"Why?" Lisa asked.

"I don't know." Zachary looked at Kenzie. "Your daughter can tell you the whys better than I can. I just know that it's true. Kids don't react the same way as adults. They are the ones who start hearing voices or having suicidal thoughts even though it works just fine for most adults."

"Changing hormones," Kenzie shrugged. "The brain is rewiring itself. They metabolize drugs differently. They are more likely to be heavy drinkers or into recreational drugs and not tell their parents or doctor. We don't know all the factors."

"When Kenzie said that Rhys was in crisis and needed some kind of treatment soon, we acted," Lisa explained. "Maybe before checking things out carefully enough. Persons was strongly promoting this new trauma therapy program they were working on. It was being touted as the most revolutionary and successful trauma program, and they were the only ones in the state authorized to offer it to teens. It just seemed like the natural choice. It was close to his family. It was trauma therapy. It was something he hadn't tried before. It was the only one open to teens. All his family needed was the money to get into the program."

Zachary nodded. He kept his eyes down, not letting Lisa look at them. Kenzie put her hand briefly over his, not wanting him to feel badly for admitting that he wasn't impressed with the drug program and would have recommended against it. There was nothing wrong with revealing that he would not have recommended a program that they now knew had been all wrong for Rhys. Run by people who were, at the very least, looking the other way and ignoring the problems within the program.

"There are things that I can't tell you, Mom," Kenzie told them. "You'll hear some of them in the news over the next week or two. But I can't tell you myself. If you had approached me about this program and about funding it for Rhys, I would have told you no."

"But we couldn't approach you on a program at a facility you were already dealing with on another matter," Lisa pointed out. "You would have had to recuse yourself and not say anything about it, just like you can't say anything now. We knew you were investigating a death at the facility, and we couldn't talk to you about this."

Kenzie turned her palms upward in a pleading gesture. "If you knew I was investigating a death at Persons, then why would you think that Rhys going there for a program was a good idea?"

"People die in hospitals," Walter said baldly. "And from what we saw in the news, it was the result of an altercation with the staff, not anything to do with the therapy program. And there wasn't anything to suggest that the patient was part of that trial. The trial was not even mentioned, so we assumed it had nothing to do with his death."

"I don't get this," Kenzie said. "You just decided unilaterally that you would take Rhys and put him into this trauma program because you figured it was the best thing for him. You knew there might be a problem at that institution and that I was investigating it. Still, you didn't let that affect your decision. You didn't even bother to *tell* me that you had made this decision."

"It was… meant to be a nice surprise for you," Walter said lamely. "Later on down the line, when you found out about it and you were no longer involved in any investigation at Persons. You would find out that we were the ones who had put Rhys through this program, and would be impressed with how well Rhys did in the program, and you would be grateful that we had taken the initiative and put him into it."

"But it didn't work out that way," Lisa said, her eyes sad. "Clearly."

And if Rhys hadn't reacted so badly to the MDMA, maybe things would have worked out how her parents had planned. But there was always the concern that he would be abused in the program as Isah had been. Or that he would be given non-approved drugs, as Janice had been. Kenzie's parents hadn't stopped to thoroughly investigate the program and whether it was being run properly. Maybe they wouldn't have found out anything even if they had looked, but they had not taken any time to investigate it. Not when Rhys had gotten into the program the day after Kenzie had told Lisa about him.

"I think it's best," Kenzie said slowly, "if you don't pick out individuals you think will benefit from specific treatments. If you are going to fund mental health initiatives, then pick the study or the company doing it, or a special media campaign or whatever. Don't pick a person and interfere with their treatment."

"Interfere?" Lisa challenged. "You wanted to get him out of the hospital and into a program. That family would not have had the money to do that. They didn't have any options available to them."

It was true. Kenzie had been desperate to get Rhys out of the hospital, where he had not been getting any effective treatment as far as she could tell, and into a program where he could try something new, something that would lead to success. Lisa had responded to that urgency, but things had not worked out the way she had hoped.

56

We should go out to dinner," Walter suggested jovially, now that the serious business was complete.

Kenzie looked down at the remnants of the ice cream melted in the bottom of her bowl. "After ice cream?"

"Well, why not? You could eat again in a couple of hours, couldn't you? I never knew you to have a poor appetite. And your mother…" Walter shrugged. "She only ate half a banana. She can eat dinner."

Walter looked expectantly at Zachary, waiting for him to chime in that he could eat in a couple of hours.

"No," Kenzie said firmly. "I do not want to go out anywhere else today. And I don't want to make something at home or entertain you for the next few hours until everyone is hungry again, either. This has all been… it's been a really tough day, and I can't deal with any more stress. We'll have to take a rain check on dinner."

"Tomorrow?" Walter suggested. "My calendar is miraculously clear for dinner tomorrow. I was going to call around to set up a business dinner, but if I could eat with my daughter and her family, that would be much better."

Kenzie turned tired eyes toward her mother, waiting for her to announce that she had a fundraiser that she needed to be at. Lisa always had some kind of event that she needed to attend. If Kenzie wanted to get onto her social calendar, she needed to schedule it weeks in advance.

"I need to speak at a girls' empowerment evening in Montpelier," Lisa said. "But I am free after that. I don't have to stay to eat at that one. They're just having pizza or some kind of fast food afterward."

Lisa wouldn't stay for that. She would never have planned to in the first place, so she wouldn't have to talk her way out of it now. She had probably planned to go home for a home-cooked—or at least, home-warmed—dinner of chicken and rice or salad and a quiet evening.

"Well?" Walter looked at Kenzie expectantly. "What are the odds of both of us being available for supper at a moment's notice? If you tried, you probably couldn't find another night that we were both free between now and Christmas."

That was probably true. And even if they did find an evening that they could both make work, there was no guarantee that Zachary would be in any shape to go to it. Who knew how he would feel as they got closer to Christmas Eve. She looked at him, trying to read his expression and anticipate what he would want to do. He shrugged at her, indicating that she could agree to it if she wanted to. If not, she could use him as an excuse. He would follow her lead.

"Well, I suppose," Kenzie agreed, trying not to sound too reluctant. "If it works for both of you, that has to be some kind of a sign. When and where do you want to meet?"

Kenzie was eager to hit the sack, even though it was earlier than their usual bedtime. "I hope you don't mind," she told Zachary. "I'm exhausted. It's been such a busy day, and my brain is just wrung out. Even watching TV would be pointless."

"Then let's get to bed," Zachary agreed. No argument. Kenzie knew that getting to sleep early would be a problem for him. He might not even be able to get to sleep for a few more hours. It might screw up his sleep schedule for the rest of the night. And screwing up his sleep schedule was something that she didn't really want to do.

"Are you sure?" Kenzie checked. "You probably don't want to."

"If I don't fall asleep with you, I'll just get back up. Watch TV or work on some photographs until my body decides that it is ready for sleep. Then I'll come back in."

She was glad he didn't say he would just sleep on the couch. She was comforted by the fact that he would be at her side for the few hours that he slept. She could reach out in her sleep and touch him, warm and solid, in the bed beside her.

"Okay. Then I'm going to sleep."

Whether it was the concussion or just her general exhaustion, Kenzie fell asleep quickly and slept through the night, not even aware of whether Zachary had gotten up during the night. The next morning, she found him in the living room working on his computer, the smell of fresh coffee rich in the air. They had a pleasant breakfast, both quiet and thinking their own thoughts about Rhys and work and the planned dinner with Kenzie's parents that evening. Kenzie's head was not hurting as much as it had the previous day, so she hoped to put in a full day of work and fulfill all her usual responsibilities.

She parked her car in its usual spot in the parking garage attached to the building. As she walked from her car toward the elevator, she heard the hollow echo of heels hitting the concrete, which was matched in time to hers, off just a fraction of a second so that it was jarring to Kenzie's ears. She turned her head to see who was there, as the police station wouldn't open to the public for another hour. There wasn't anyone else who usually parked on the same level as Kenzie at the same time. She could hear the woman's shoes behind her, but couldn't turn her head far enough to see who it was without being obvious. She didn't want to look anxious or snoopy, so she didn't.

Not at first.

But the sound kept following her, and Kenzie's chest tightened. It set off all her jangly nerves. The ones that had become much more sensitive since her kidnapping. Something was wrong, and she didn't want this woman, whoever she was, anywhere near her. She stopped and turned around to confront her. She didn't care how paranoid she looked.

The woman following her, closing the gap between them with each step, was Dr. Richards.

W hat are you doing here?" Kenzie demanded.

There was absolutely no good reason for her to be in the building. Richards didn't have anything to do there. Even if she were a member of the public wanting to file a police report, that didn't give her access to a parking space in the garage. It didn't give her a security pass. And the police department complaints desk would not open for another hour.

"You come to my place of work uninvited," Dr. Richards challenged. "Why shouldn't I come to yours?"

"Actually, I was invited to your workplace," Kenzie pointed out. "I was invited there to review a death scene and retrieve a dead body."

"And then you were told that there was no reason for you to be there. That you didn't need to investigate it. And you still did. And you kept coming back, even after you were warned."

Kenzie narrowed her eyes at Dr. Richards. "You were the one who called in that threat that was left on my voicemail?"

"I don't know what threat you're talking about," Dr. Richards said unconvincingly. "Why couldn't you just stay out of it and mind your own business? Why did you have to come in and screw everything up for everyone? Do you know how many people rely on us? How many people we are providing an essential service for? And what do you think will happen to all those people if we have to close down?"

"I'm not closing you down," Kenzie told her. She looked around for a security guard. There was always a guard close by, someone who saw her to and from her car. Where was he today? Out to pick up a coffee or donut for breakfast? Taking a bathroom break? Why wasn't he there when Kenzie actually needed him? "I don't have the authority to shut you down, so I don't know what you're talking about. If you're dealing with problems with the police or other regulators, you need to talk to them, not me. I don't have anything to do with it."

"It's because of you and your inquiries. You snooping where you are not wanted or needed."

"I'm required by law to investigate every death that occurs at a mental institution," Kenzie pointed out. "I didn't write the law. I'm just following it. Did you think that all the abuses would never come to light? That you could just continue operating in the dark like you were doing forever, and no one would ever be the wiser?" She couldn't understand how anyone could think they could allow illegal human experimentation and physical and sexual abuse to run rampant in the institution and believe it would never get out to the authorities. Sooner or later, they were bound to be investigated for something. Then the dominoes would start to tumble, one after another, all in a row.

"I didn't know anything about any abuse," Dr. Richards snapped. "Do you think I would allow that to continue if I had known about it? Once I found out, I would have shut it down. And we would have been able to continue our efforts to help those who have been so terribly abused in the past, to help them to confront their demons and enjoy life again. To give them back their childhoods, their teens, the years they suffered in silence."

Kenzie thought about Rhys's silence and swallowed.

Your friends will benefit by you staying out of the way.

Of course Dr. Richards had been talking about Rhys. She knew he was a friend of Kenzie's because of the Kirsch family foundation. She knew that the foundation had sponsored his registration in the program. The donor might have been anonymous to Vera, but had to be properly accounted for on Persons's books.

"I did what I was required to do by law," Kenzie said. "It's not my fault you and the other doctors broke the law. You had to know there were problems with how the program was being run."

Dr. Richards's lovely face twisted into an angry scowl. "I'm supposed to know everything the other doctors are doing? Everything was set up the way it was supposed to be. We got all the approvals and ran it the way we were supposed to. What they did on their own is not my fault."

Kenzie watched Dr. Richards's hands warily. She didn't want to end up on the business end of a scalpel. She'd seen that movie before.

"Look. I'm sorry things turned out badly for you. I hope it all works out and you can continue running your facility. But people died." She met the woman's clear blue eyes. "Not just Leander and Janice. Others too. And who knows how many of the patients were abused by Dr. Miller? All of them? Just some of them? You're supposed to be healing people; instead, they're being put through additional traumas. Incapacitated by drugs and abused. How do you think they felt?"

Dr. Richards's lips pressed together. Despite her salon-fresh appearance, she wasn't looking so beautiful anymore. "I know how they felt!" she growled. "And I would have put a stop to it. I never had the chance. You just swept in and destroyed everything I built."

"Everything okay over here?"

Kenzie breathed a sigh of relief at the husky male voice that interrupted their conversation. A security guard in uniform moved toward them. "Bert."

He nodded. He recognized her, of course, and turned his gaze on Dr. Richards. Kenzie held her breath, worried that the guard would melt at the sight of her. Would assume, as they all did, that a beautiful, vulnerable-looking woman could not be a threat. That she was a friend of Kenzie's or someone who had wandered in by mistake or who needed help.

"What's going on here?" Bert demanded, taking a couple more steps toward Richards, his hand on his taser. "Are you causing trouble for Dr. Kirsch?"

He must have heard them arguing, heard the tone of Dr. Richards's accusations and complaints, even if he hadn't been able to discern the words.

"We're just having a conversation," Dr. Richards told him, giving him a warm smile. She was very good at what she did. Using her body to get what she wanted. Kenzie wondered fleetingly how often she herself used her feminine wiles without even realizing it. Harmless flirting to get out of a traffic ticket, to get into a show after the ticket booth had closed, or to explain her presence somewhere she hadn't been invited. It wasn't something she even thought of, just something inside her that turned on when the circumstances demanded it. How much of that had been ingrained by society? And how much by her mother, telling her how to always be gracious and still get what she wanted under every circumstance?

"You are not authorized to be in here," Bert said flatly, ignoring the smile and the charm. "Dr. Kirsch? You want me to call the police?"

"No." Kenzie gave Dr. Richards a look. "If she'll just leave on her own and not come back…"

Dr. Richards took a step back. No scalpel appeared. No attack seemed imminent. She was just a frustrated woman who had come to express her grievances. Not someone Kenzie needed to fear.

Still, she was relieved when Bert stepped forward to escort Dr. Richards off the property, not trusting her to leave voluntarily. He said a few words into his shoulder mike, alerting the other guards that he was dealing with a trespasser and calling for Pratt to check in with Dr. Kirsch.

Kenzie let her breath out slowly as she watched Bert escort Dr. Richards away. Pratt was there by the time Bert was out of sight.

"Everything okay, Dr. Kirsch? Another wacko?"

Kenzie chuckled. "Yeah," she agreed. "Escaped from a mental institution."

He shook his head. "Let me walk you to the door."

He escorted her in the other direction, watched her swipe her card to enter the corridor to the medical examiner's office, and waved a hand in farewell. "Don't you worry about anything, Dr. Kirsch. We'll keep our eyes open."

58

Kenzie would not have suggested Old Joe's as the restaurant to meet with her parents. She would have looked for something more sophisticated, more likely to satisfy Lisa's particular tastes. Probably something in the city, since Roxboro didn't have anything that fancy. But Zachary had gone ahead and set it up and, despite the image that Kenzie had built up in her head of socialites who would never lower themselves to eat at a mere steakhouse, they both seemed comfortable and happy to be there. Neither dithered over the menu and complained that they didn't have the right cuts or a world-class chef. Kenzie started to relax and feel more comfortable having Zachary and her parents at the same table.

She had built up the differences between them so much in her mind, creating a schism between them and the feeling that it would be impossible for them to break bread together and enjoy it. Which was silly because no matter how much money her parents had or how embroiled they were in their charities and politics, they had raised Kenzie. And they had raised Amanda, and she hadn't been a snob either. They had both always been down-to-earth people at home, expecting her to do her homework and chores, to have friends over, and to make messes and break things. Because that's what kids did. Kenzie had been allowed to play at the playground and to ride her bike around, to explore her independence and to fall and skin her knees. Parents like that were not the type who would refuse to go to a steakhouse or put on a show of not enjoying it.

"So, how are things going with your investigations?" Walter asked. "Are you still working on those deaths at Persons?"

It had only been a day since they last spoke, so Kenzie could be forgiven if she snapped and told him nothing had changed in the last twenty-four hours. But of course, it had. She had reviewed all the details with Dr. Cook and Dr. Wiltshire and published her findings on both Leander Isah's death and Janice Martin's.

"I finished with them today. Filed my reports. So they are now public, or will be whenever they get posted."

"Was Janice Martin a suicide?" Zachary asked, his head cocked slightly.

Kenzie studied him. His question suggested that he'd had doubts about it, but Kenzie had never told him about the inconsistent bruising she had found. She had kept it all to herself to ensure that nothing could leak to the press, even though she knew that Zachary was not the source of the leak.

"No," she said slowly. "Janice Martin did not commit suicide. She was strangled."

"Homicide." Zachary nodded, seeming unsurprised by this.

"How did *you* know?" Kenzie demanded.

He shrugged and sipped his water. "It was… a little too convenient. And in a place like that… we should not have been the ones who found her. They should have had her on a watch. And she said they were not allowed to be in their rooms alone during the day. Her door should have been wide open so that they could see if anyone was inside. And they should have had someone walking by there every fifteen minutes. She shouldn't have had the opportunity and, if she had, they should have discovered her immediately."

"So you figured that someone had staged it."

Zachary nodded. "Not easy, but if patients are not supposed to be in their rooms, they shouldn't be in the corridor where they could see something going down. They should be in the common areas, visiting like they were supposed to."

Kenzie let out a breath. "Yeah. Things just didn't add up. People *do* find ways to commit suicide in places like that. But... it didn't really fit."

"You could prove it?" he asked.

Kenzie nodded. "The bruises on her neck went the wrong direction."

"I don't know if this is really dinnertime conversation," Lisa protested.

Kenzie rolled her eyes. "Dad asked. Get after him."

"And the other one?" Walter asked, ignoring his ex-wife's objection. "Was it also homicide?"

"Not that I could prove definitively. It could have been, and certainly the things that they did to him contributed to his death, but I believe it was actually the MDMA. Accidental death. A reaction to the drug, whether they gave him too much or if together with the SSRI it triggered Serotonin Syndrome. His body was overheating, he was very agitated, and, in the end, his heart just gave out. Sudden cardiac death due to MDMA ingestion."

"How sad," Lisa observed. "They were trying to help him."

"Well... some of them were," Kenzie agreed. "But there were a lot of abuses going on there too. A lot of things that should never have happened. There was supposed to be oversight. Controls in place. But it didn't work out that way."

"You're talking about that doctor they arrested?" Walter asked. "Disgusting that a predator like him should be able to operate in a facility with such vulnerable patients."

Kenzie nodded. "And other things that they are still building cases for. He isn't the only one responsible for what happened to Isah."

"And you think he is the one who killed this woman too?"

"That would be my guess. But it's not up to me to build a case against him. Just to give the police whatever I can. I suspect... Janice Martin was talking too much. She told me Isah wanted out of the program before he died. And she had been talking about missing time and other issues she had with the program. I suspect he wanted to shut her up before she said too much to the wrong person."

Zachary and Kenzie's parents all nodded, looking appropriately shocked at what had happened. Zachary was looking at Kenzie, a frown of concentration on his face. Kenzie wasn't sure what he was thinking. Maybe it was about her cases or about something completely separate that he was working on. Or perhaps just trying to think of another conversational segue to keep her parents engaged.

"Do you know for sure that it was the drug that killed Isah?" Zachary asked.

He had worked enough cases where it had turned out that the ME's findings were wrong. He knew that they could make mistakes as easily as anyone else. Or not have been provided with the information they needed to make the right ruling.

"Sudden cardiac death can be caused by other things," Kenzie said slowly. "He could have been experiencing heart or respiratory problems when they walked him out of the room after the altercation in the cafeteria, or when he was faced with the police, who he feared. He could have had a sudden, devastating allergic reaction. To what, I don't know, but it is possible. They might have placed him in restraints when they took him back to his room or to an isolation room. Someone might have waited until everyone was asleep and then smothered him."

"If it was an allergic reaction, he would have had hives and a swollen throat," Walter said, "And if he was smothered, he would have had those red dots. Those petechiae."

"If this was a TV show, yes," Kenzie agreed. "Because they always have enough clues on TV to nail everything down beyond a reasonable doubt. But in real life… someone with an allergic reaction severe enough to stop their heart may have no other physical signs, even microscopic ones. It happens so quickly that there is no sign on the body. They are dead in seconds. And not all asphyxiation cases show petechial hemorrhaging. Seventy to eighty percent do, but not all of them. A medical examiner gathers all the information he or she can from all different sources: the body, the scene, the trace evidence, the witnesses. But sometimes, it is still not enough to make a final determination. We just give it the best shot we can, and then…" Kenzie shrugged. "Move on to the next case."

"It could have been a toxin," Zachary suggested. "Something rare that paralyzes all the muscles of the body so that he can't breathe. Or that stops his heart."

"And some of the tox screens may still come back with more information. But the preliminary testing doesn't show anything, and we can't test for everything in the world. We can test for things that seem likely based on the signs in the body. But there is no way to test for every substance in the world."

He stared off into space, clearly thinking of all the different things it could be.

"He was on MDMA," Kenzie said. "MDMA kills. Occam's Razor."

"When you see hoof prints, think horses, not zebras."

"Exactly," Kenzie agreed. "And speaking of nature, I need to answer a certain call… back in a minute."

59

Kenzie stepped into the back hallway of Old Joe's and paused to let her eyes adjust to the dim light before proceeding past the kitchen and toward the ladies' room.

When she returned from the bathroom, she stepped to the side for a tall, distinguished-looking patron headed toward the men's room. He barreled directly into her, smashing her into the wall.

"Hey!" Kenzie protested, outraged, "Look where you're—"

"Shut up." His hand closed over her mouth and pinned her head back against the wall tightly to prevent her from moving or speaking. Kenzie struggled to escape him and then realized who it was. She had only seen him once, on the occasion of Isah's death. One of the other doctors from Persons. Dr. Alvarez. But what was he doing there? And what did he think he was doing?

She tried to tell him to let her go but, with his hold on her, she couldn't. His eyes darted around, and he changed his grip to pull her away from the wall. He swept her toward the back emergency exit before she could even formulate the idea to fight back. She was out into the chilly night. The emergency door slammed back into place, and he pressed her against the outside wall, the rough red bricks biting into her head and back. His hand was still over her mouth, preventing her from saying anything.

"You should have listened!" he growled. "You should have minded your own business and just walked away! But you wouldn't listen. And you didn't die!" He shook his head and pressed her even more tightly against the wall, nearly smothering her.

Kenzie tried to fight back, but he was much bigger than she was, much stronger. Her mind went a mile a minute, adding up the things she hadn't accounted for.

Alvarez had been there when Kenzie went to pick up Isah's body. But why had he been there at night? It wasn't like with an emergency room, where they needed doctors there all the time. Everyone was asleep at night. There might have been a doctor on call if a patient was sick or needed something, but he would just give the nursing staff instructions over the phone.

Instead, he had told Nurse Craig to stay away from Isah in breach of their own protocols. And when they had discovered that he was dead, he had instructed the nurse to call a funeral home rather than the medical examiner's office. Alvarez, not Miller.

Had Isah already been dead when Alvarez told Nurse Craig that he was sedated and was not to be disturbed? He must have planned to obscure the time of death, giving his body longer to cool down to a normal temperature. Did he know about the problems Isah's hyperthermic state would cause in identifying his actual time of death?

Kenzie again tried to escape Alvarez's grip. What did he think he was going to do? Kidnap her? Kill her? She hadn't seen any weapon. He didn't take her to a car or van, which was good because she already felt nauseated and her head was throbbing. If she had to add a kidnapping to the horror of what was happening to her, she didn't know how she could handle it.

He had already tried pushing her out into traffic. That had failed and now here he was ready to try again, and who knew what he would do this time. A more direct approach?

Alvarez started to look around. Maybe it had just occurred to him that he hadn't really planned things out. What was he going to do now? Leave once he'd aired his grievances? Kill her? With what? His bare hands? A makeshift weapon? Kenzie tried again to squirm free of his grip. She tried to use her voice, even though he was not letting her speak. She could still get a noise out. A pleading sound. Something to remind him that she was human; he was holding a human life in his hands.

He looked at her, his eyes meeting hers for the first time. Kenzie stared into his dark eyes pleadingly. She tried to reach out to that hurt part of him that was causing him to lash out. He was frustrated. Disappointed. Like Dr. Richards, he'd had his dream pulled out from under him. The fact that it had happened because of his own choices made no difference. Not to him. He still felt the loss of his job and the nice set-up he'd had there. He blamed Kenzie for it but, if she could make him see her as a person, an individual, maybe he would let her go. Maybe it would make a difference.

She made another noise under his hand. Soft. Questioning. Like she was asking him if he was okay. If she could help him.

"It's *your* fault," Alvarez growled, clearly not getting the message she was trying to send him. "If you hadn't shown up, sticking your nose into something that was none of your business, it would all have been different. We could have kept Persons going. You've ruined everything."

Kenzie tried to make a sorrowful, apologetic noise. Her mind slid to Rhys. How he'd been silenced for so many years. How hard he had to try to make himself heard when he couldn't speak. She'd never appreciated how difficult that was. How lucky they were to communicate using words when Rhys was left with pointing, gesturing, sending them pictures and the occasional text to convey his feelings, questions, and needs. She wanted to help Rhys if she could. She didn't think they were done yet. They could still help Rhys. Just because the MDMA trial had not worked out well for him, that didn't mean it was the end of the road.

Alvarez gave Kenzie a little shake, bringing her thoughts back to him. It was as if he had sensed her drifting away from him. Maybe he was restricting the flow of air into her lungs and she was experiencing symptoms of oxygen deprivation.

"You're going to pay for this," Alvarez shouted, furious not to have her full attention. He wanted her to be afraid, terrified. He fed off of fear. That must have been one of the perks he got from working at Persons. Lots of traumatized people. Lots of anxiety and fear to go around. Especially if he were part of the abuse, either as a partner or an observer.

"Julio Alvarez!" a loud woman's voice called out. "Put your hands in the air and back toward me."

Dr. Alvarez stared into Kenzie's eyes. He didn't turn around to look at the cop who had called his name. He wasn't willing to give up his position of power, to have to relax, let Kenzie go, and hand himself over to someone else's authority. He was in a position of strength, threatening her, frightening her, and he was not going to let go.

Physically, Kenzie had no way of breaking free from him. He was too strong and none of her attempts to break free had been successful. None of them had even made him budge.

Kenzie could only think of one way to escape his power.

She closed her eyes.

60

"Look at me!" Alvarez's grip on Kenzie tightened, and she could feel his face get closer to hers. She could feel the proximity of his body, its warmth, his damp breath on her face.

She didn't open her eyes. She tried to relax her body as much as she could. Like when she was at the dentist and realized that she was holding her whole body rigid during a procedure and would force herself to relax all her muscles. To pretend that she was at a spa for some pleasant treatment, the buzzing of the drill or cleaning tool just white noise, drifting toward sleep.

Alvarez could feel her relax and started to panic. "No! No, come back here!" He shook her, grinding the back of her head into the rough brick wall. "No! That wasn't long enough!"

Kenzie refused to open her eyes again. She decided it would be good if he thought she had completely blacked out and loosened her knees, letting her body fall away from his, slipping down and to the side, so that he was trying to hold her up instead of just pinning her in place.

She heard a shout. Knew that Zachary was there with Garcia, too. He believed she was hurt, unconscious or dead. But she couldn't respond to the anxiety in his voice. She needed to do her part to get away from Alvarez and let the police do their jobs. The concrete below her feet was hard and studded with gravel and possibly broken glass. Not the best place to land in an unconscious state. She did the best she could to cushion her fall, but couldn't be obvious about it.

Alvarez turned away from her. The police were yelling at him, giving him instructions. Eventually, they managed to put him under arrest, search him, and cuff him without incident. He carried no gun. Or scalpel. But that didn't mean he couldn't have killed her. Kenzie watched the latter part of this process through her lids, cracked just slightly open, not moving. Not until they had him in cuffs.

Garcia hurried over to check on Kenzie as she sat up and started to brush the gravel from her arms and legs.

"Dr. Kirsch! Are you all right?" she asked earnestly, her accent stronger than usual, reaching out to take Kenzie's hand and to check her pulse.

Zachary was telling the other cops to let him through to go see Kenzie, and Garcia turned around and told them to let him. Zachary hurried over, crouching over to hug Kenzie and reassure himself that she was alive.

"Don't get up," he told her as she tried to get to her feet. "You passed out. Let the paramedics check you out—"

"I didn't faint," Kenzie told him. "I was shamming."

"What?"

"It was an act. He was getting off on my fear, on connecting with me and terrorizing me. So I shut him off."

Zachary blinked, considering this. "But I saw your eyes close. I saw you collapse."

"Just acting." Kenzie brushed gravel from her palms and looked down at her pants, which looked pretty bad after landing on the grimy sidewalk. There were specks of blood on her hands from the sharp gravel and glass. A tear in the knee of her pants and another graze. The opposite one from the one she'd hurt when he had pushed her into traffic. A matched set now.

Zachary put his hands out to steady her, but didn't touch her, watching to make sure that she was stable and then pulling back to let her have some space.

"Go tell Walter and Lisa I'm okay," Kenzie instructed him. "How did you know where I was and what was going on?"

"You're never long in the bathroom," he said with a shrug. "Not like some women. I could see you on my friends app. See that you weren't in the restaurant anymore. You didn't have any good reason to be in the back lane. GPS can be off, but… I couldn't see you in the back hall. And I knew it wasn't just one man."

"You knew…?"

"At Persons. One man couldn't have gotten Janice hung up in that position. The set-up would need at least two."

"Well… you might have mentioned that."

He smiled. "I was going to." He touched her cheek briefly, comforting her and confirming to himself that she was okay. "I'll go tell them you're all right. I'll get our bill, unless you want to stay for dessert."

Kenzie laughed. "No. I had ice cream yesterday. I think that will have to count for today, too. I don't think I could sit down at a table again tonight."

He left to go talk to her parents. Garcia shook her head slowly. "Are you sure you're okay? What did he say to you? Anything incriminating?"

"I don't know… it all happened so fast. It was more about blaming me for ending all the good stuff than admitting anything he had done."

"Oh, well. We've got plenty we can charge him with now, while we look at the situation and see what else we can prove."

"I guess he and Miller must have been working together."

Garcia nodded. "We'll play them off each other. See if we can get them to implicate each other."

"Dr. Richards showed up at work today. I was going to call you and tell you about it… and then I got distracted by other things."

"Oh? Is she part of this too? I was beginning to think she was just a dupe."

"I don't think she did anything. Just looked the other way. Played ignorant. I can't see her not knowing any of what was going on. Especially when those therapy sessions were being taped. She must have watched a few of them back in the beginning. Maybe before things got so advanced. But she must have known that the trial wasn't running the way it was supposed to."

"Why did *she* come to see you?"

"I don't know if she intended to do anything more than just complain about me screwing everything up for her. I was a little anxious she might be carrying a scalpel with my name on it. But security came along and got rid of her."

"I'll have a chat with her. Make sure it doesn't happen again."

"Thanks. I really don't want to have to keep worrying about people showing up and threatening me!"

"No, that's probably enough for one week." Garcia smiled. "I'm glad you're all right."

"And glad that Zachary called you instead of playing cowboy?"

"Good for him," Garcia agreed. "If Alvarez had been armed, holding you at gunpoint or knife point, he could really have put you in danger. But I suspect if we hadn't gotten here pretty quickly, Zachary would have been around back in that alley within a few minutes."

"Probably." Zachary didn't have the best impulse control. The fact that he had called Garcia and not run directly toward trouble surprised Kenzie. Maybe he was learning. Or maybe he had trusted her to take care of herself for a few minutes.

"What do you need from me?" Kenzie asked. "Can I give a statement tomorrow? I've got my parents here, and there is only so much drama I can deal with at once."

"Sure. Come by the office, and you can make a report tomorrow. We have enough to start proceedings based on what we saw."

61

W e were just hoping for an update on Rhys," Zachary said to Vera, his phone lying on the table with speakerphone enabled. "Has there been… any change?"

"He's doing better," Vera said cautiously. "The doctors say that the effects of the MDMA are wearing off. That his brain is… healing. Returning to the way that it was before the break. They hope… that there won't be any permanent damage."

"That's good news," Zachary told her.

Kenzie was glad to hear it. She felt terrible that her family had been part of the cause of what had happened to Rhys. If he'd been permanently damaged by that initial therapy session, she didn't know how she could handle it. Even though she had begged Vera to take Rhys out of the program. It was still partially her fault that he had been in it. Her family money. Her worry about Rhys expressed to her mother. She hadn't wanted it, but she still felt like it was her fault.

"Could we visit him again?" Zachary asked Vera, "Are they letting him see people?"

"I don't know…" Vera hesitated, and Kenzie didn't think it had anything to do with the hospital and whether they would allow Kenzie and Zachary in. "I suppose it would be good for him to see someone other than me. He always enjoys his visits with you."

Except for maybe the last one.

"Are we still on his approved visitor list?"

"Yes, of course. You can go see him anytime, if the hospital approves it. And I'm sure they will unless he is in therapy when you want to visit."

"We'll pick a time when he isn't in therapy. Maybe call ahead to be sure. Has he... said anything about what happened? Before, I mean. When Stanley found him."

Vera didn't answer right away. "I've been afraid to ask," she admitted eventually. "He's been through so much; I don't want to traumatize him more by bringing it up. I'm hoping that... maybe it was just one of those things. A virus. Sleepwalking. And that he'll just go on like normal."

As before, her first reaction was to ignore that there was a problem. To cover it up, forget that it ever happened.

"Do you mind if we ask him?" Kenzie asked. She didn't want to do something that was strictly against Vera's wishes. But she also didn't want Rhys to be left to deal with it himself, swimming in whatever sorrow or trauma might have triggered him again.

"Well... maybe that would be a good idea," Vera conceded. "And if you think it is something that I need to know about... or that his doctor does..."

"We'll let you know," Zachary agreed.

They were able to get in to see Rhys at the hospital. He was not in his room this time, but was well enough to be in the common areas without getting too agitated or disturbing the other patients. An orderly hovered nearby, keeping an eye on things, ready to step in if the situation became too much for Rhys. Kenzie tried to ignore him and to focus on the boy and how he was doing.

Rhys shook hands with Zachary, slapping him on the shoulder with his free hand. He didn't have the big smile he usually did when greeting Zachary, but at least he knew who they were and wasn't opposed to seeing them. He looked at Kenzie and hesitated, unsure how to greet her. Kenzie offered her hand, and when he took it tentatively, she leaned in and gave him a brief hug around the shoulders too. She often greeted him with a kiss on the cheek, but she didn't this time, worried it might be too much for him. She released his hand and motioned to the table where they could sit. Rhys looked at Zachary, and when he sat, Rhys did as well.

"How are you feeling?" Zachary asked. "You've been through a pretty tough time."

Rhys shrugged and nodded. He raised one hand and wobbled it back and forth. *So-so.*

"That drug therapy really affected you," Kenzie suggested. "Do you remember everything that happened?"

He shook his head.

"Boy, were you ever talkative," Zachary told him. "You just went on and on and on."

Rhys thought about that for a minute. He pointed tentatively at his head, then made a "blowing up" gesture, spreading his fingers apart to signify an explosion.

"Some people have a feeling of being opened up," Kenzie said. "Or of being able to see and experience things they couldn't before."

He pointed at her and nodded slightly. Maybe not a fully accurate description of his experience, but close enough.

"You talked a lot about when Grandpa Clarence was killed," Zachary told him.

Rhys looked at Zachary, but made no response.

"Do you remember that?" Kenzie asked him. "Vera didn't think you remembered anything about when your grandpa died. Or at least, not clearly."

Rhys pointed at himself and gave an emphatic nod.

"You remember what happened that day?"

He nodded again.

"Do you want to talk about it? To us, or your grandma, or a therapist? It might help to be able to talk about it instead of keeping it hidden all the time."

Rhys made a horizontal slicing motion with his hand. A definite *no*, and yet, there was something else behind it. As if Rhys were saying, *No, not about that.*

"You want to talk?" Kenzie tried.

He nodded. He looked at Zachary.

"Do you just want to talk to Zachary? I can give you guys some space. Go check out the gift shop and pick up some snacks."

The corner of his mouth twitched in a slight smile, but he shook his head.

"You want to talk to both of us?" Zachary asked. "Or just to Kenzie?"

He pointed to them each in turn.

"Okay." Zachary nodded. "We're both staying, then. Did you just want to visit, or was there something particular?"

A nod. Zachary rolled his eyes, recognizing that he'd trapped himself again, asking two questions and then not sure which Rhys was responding to.

"You don't want to talk to us about when Clarence was killed," Kenzie said.

He shook his head, agreeing with the statement.

"About the therapy?" Zachary asked.

He shook his head again.

"Did anyone hurt you when you were at Persons?" Kenzie asked. "Or… get inappropriate with you? Some of the doctors there were… doing a lot of things they shouldn't."

Rhys grimaced and shook his head again, adding a negating hand gesture as well. But there *was* something he wanted to talk to them about.

"Before that?" Kenzie suggested.

He nodded. Kenzie looked over at Zachary. Maybe Rhys wanted to talk to them about whatever had been on his mind lately. What might have triggered his fugue state, his inability to communicate with them at all.

"Something happened that upset you," Kenzie suggested. "Was it something going on at school? Were you being bullied?"

He pointed at her, then hesitated and shook his head. Kenzie was doing what she had just observed in Zachary. Peppering Rhys with too many questions, not giving him a chance to answer one at a time, which confused the process. She tried to slow down.

"Something happened that upset you," she repeated, making it a statement of fact. Something had sent him way off the rails. It was possible that it was just a virus or a hormone surge, or some developing psychosis, but she didn't think so.

Rhys nodded his agreement.

Something had upset him. It had sent him out on the streets looking for Stanley Green, a strong male role model. Someone who could help him.

Only whatever bothered him was too much for him to handle, even with Stanley's help. By the time he got there, things were spinning out of control.

"Something going on at school?" Zachary asked, trying to pick up where the disconnect had been. Rhys had started out with yes, and then drawn back.

Rhys shrugged and wobbled his hand back and forth. *Sort of.*

"Did someone at school threaten you?"

Rhys shook his head.

"Are they bullying you? Causing you problems?"

He shook his head.

Kenzie and Zachary looked at each other. Kenzie tried to fathom what would have upset Rhys enough that it had sent him into a fugue state. If not someone targeting Rhys, then maybe he had witnessed someone else being hurt? That could also be very traumatic. Especially given his history with his grandfather being killed, and then his aunt, and then Bridget being kidnapped. Rhys had shown himself to be a protector. Someone who had stepped forward when Madison had needed help, and Luke and Aster. And who had insisted that Zachary take care of himself and admit himself to the hospital when things had gotten too bad for him. Rhys was someone who cared deeply about other people. That had to be it.

"Is someone else being hurt or bullied?" Kenzie asked.

He didn't respond immediately, then nodded slowly.

"We want to help too," Zachary said. "I don't want to see any kids being hurt."

Rhys shook his head.

Another misstep. Kenzie wasn't sure how they had lost the thread. "Can you tell us who is being hurt or bullied?"

He looked around him, seeming unsure what to do. He pointed at himself and then made a phone gesture.

"Oh. Of course," Zachary dug his phone out of his pocket and slid it across the table toward Rhys. Rhys frequently communicated by messaging on his phone. His communications were severely curtailed if he wasn't allowed to have his phone during his stay in the psych ward.

Rhys shook his head and pushed the phone back, pointing insistently at himself. Then he turned his head to look at the orderly, nodding to indicate him.

"You want *your* phone."

Rhys nodded.

Zachary waved the orderly over. "Can you get Rhys his phone?"

The man looked stern. "Patients are not allowed to have their phones without supervision. We've had a number of incidents with… misuse. And then there is the issue of trying to work with someone on their mental health when all they will do is stare at the screen."

"Rhys's phone is an assistive communication device," Kenzie said firmly. "He needs it now to communicate with us. Please go get it."

The orderly opened his mouth to argue.

"I'm sure you wouldn't want to be accused of abusing the rights of a disabled person," Kenzie suggested. "Denying accommodations for communications under the *Americans with Disabilities Act—*"

"Okay, okay," the orderly held up his hand. "As long as you will be responsible for its use. If there are any issues…"

"There aren't going to be any issues," Zachary said. "He wants to be able to talk to us."

The orderly looked at Rhys for a moment, then nodded. "I'll bring it to you in a minute. I just need to sign it out."

Rhys nodded.

The orderly walked away. Rhys rolled his eyes. He pointed to Kenzie and with his brows raised, made a fingernail-polishing gesture against his chest.

"I can be pretty tough," Kenzie said with a laugh. "Just try bullying someone around me."

Zachary looked at Rhys and nodded his agreement. "She's not kidding."

Rhys grinned, the first genuine smile they'd seen from him since arriving. After a week of not seeing him smile, it was a relief. Kenzie felt a flood of warmth and, for the first time, she felt like Rhys would be okay. They hadn't done irreparable harm. He was on his way back, and he would be okay.

It was a few minutes before the orderly returned with Rhys's phone. He handed it to the boy with a nod, then retreated to his previous position.

Rhys held the phone close to him, then turned it on. The screen didn't light up. Kenzie closed her eyes in frustration. Had they let the battery drain in the time since Rhys had been admitted?

Frowning, Rhys held down the power button and, in a moment, the screen lit up as it rebooted. It still had juice. It had just been powered down.

They waited while the phone restarted, and all the texts and messages sent while the phone was off were delivered. A lot of messages. Kenzie was glad at the evidence that people had been concerned about Rhys. His absence had not gone unnoticed. Rhys waited, but didn't read through all the new messages. Eventually, the phone stopped flashing and buzzing and settled down again. Rhys tapped and swiped his way through his phone and then stopped. He held the phone against his chest for a minute and looked at Kenzie as if reconsidering whatever he had planned to show her.

"It's okay," Kenzie said. "We want to help you. It doesn't matter what it is."

Zachary nodded his agreement. "We're here for you, bud."

Rhys held it away from them for a moment longer, and then put the phone down on the table and slid it across to them.

Kenzie looked down at a photograph. The picture of a man's face. The pallid blue-gray skin was a tip-off even before Kenzie focused on the round, dark red hole in the man's forehead. Kenzie looked more closely. A lot could be accomplished with a little stage makeup. There were some experts in the business who were very good at what they did. Thrillers and zombie movies were a big thing. Realistic blood and gore. But she knew, looking at the man, that he was dead.

She looked back at Rhys. He knew it, too.

"Where did you get this?" Kenzie asked.

He shrugged.

"A friend? Someone at school?"

He nodded.

"And where did they get it?"

He shrugged and made a round, circulating gesture. He mimed sending messages out several times.

"It's going around school," Zachary interpreted. "Everybody's sending it around."

Rhys nodded.

"Do you know who it is?" Kenzie asked. "Where they got it?"

He shook his head. He pointed firmly at Kenzie, and then at the picture.

"You want me to find out."

Rhys nodded his agreement.

Kenzie looked at Zachary, and then stared down at the man in the picture. "Well then… I guess I'll look into it."

CAPTURED IN DEATH

For friends who speak up
Even when speaking up is impossible

1

I t wasn't the way Kenzie's cases normally came to her.

As an assistant to the medical examiner, she was used to bodies being brought in by van, laid out on the table and cleaned, ready for her to begin her postmortem. She would have some scene notes to peruse or, if she had gone out to the scene herself, she would have dictated the notes. Maybe she would be by herself, or maybe with Dr. Cook, who was substituting for Dr. Wiltshire while his broken hand was healing.

A very different scenario from the one she currently found herself in, sitting in the visiting area of the psych ward with Rhys sitting across from and Zachary next to her. Kenzie pulled her eyes away from the photograph on the phone she held in her hand to the serious Black teen who had handed it to her and was waiting for her to say something.

"Rhys, this needs to go to the police. They need to investigate. Do you even know who this is?"

Rhys, non-speaking as usual, spread his hands apart, palms up, in a gesture of helplessness. *Don't know.*

Zachary leaned in to look at the picture again, his face close to Kenzie's so she could smell his shaving cream. He usually sported a three or four-day growth of beard, which made him look like a homeless person or, at least, someone down on their luck. Someone people didn't want to make eye contact with and would forget as soon as they walked away. As a private investigator, he didn't want people to remember him. But today, he happened to be clean-shaven. His dark eyes were intense as he stared at the photograph. He ran a hand over his close-cropped dark hair.

"We don't even know if it is real," he pointed out. "It could be… stage makeup."

Kenzie didn't have to look again at the grayish skin or the bullet hole in the man's forehead to know that this was no makeup job. She had seen enough corpses in the course of her work to recognize one when she saw it, even in a picture.

"He's dead," she told Zachary with certainty. "It's real."

Rhys nodded his agreement. His dark skin kept him from looking pale, but his expression was pinched and worried. His frown deeper than usual. He had been through an ordeal, a mental collapse apparently triggered by this very picture, followed by a reaction to the drug used in the experimental treatment program he had been placed in, and then finally sedated to let him catch up on the sleep he needed and get back on track again.

It had been over a week since Stanley Green had found him wandering in the street in a fugue state. And if that fugue state had been triggered by viewing this picture, then the man in the picture had been dead for over a week and still hadn't shown up in the morgue.

Maybe he never would. Maybe his body had been dumped somewhere no one would find it.

Rhys held out his hand for his phone. Kenzie shook her head, not giving it back to him. "This is evidence. The police will want to look at the photograph's metadata and any other evidence on your phone. Where you got it from." Kenzie raised her eyebrows, asking again for Rhys to tell her where he had gotten the picture. How did a teenager end up with the picture of a murdered man on his phone? Who had sent it to him and why?

Rhys looked frustrated. Maybe he wanted to text her something on his messaging app. He relied on his phone for communication. He couldn't tell his story to her in gestures and facial expressions. Some things could be communicated that way, but he needed something more.

Kenzie slid her own phone across the table to him. "Send messages to Zachary's phone," she prompted.

Rhys picked up her phone with long, slender fingers and operated it quickly. He found the messaging app he wanted, swiped and tapped rapidly with his thumbs, and the first message popped up on Zachary's phone in a few seconds. Zachary held it so that he and Kenzie could see it at the same time, their heads close together.

Rhys had sent a picture of a dog, a recurring theme in his messages. This one was a cartoon picture of a basset hound dressed in a Sherlock Holmes deerstalker hat and peering into a magnifying glass.

Kenzie nodded. "I know you want me to look into it. To find out what I can. And I will… but this is a police matter. They will have to figure out where the picture came from and who it is. Until I actually see the body, there's not much that I can tell just by looking at a picture."

Rhys pointed at the picture of the dead man, rolling his eyes. What other information did Kenzie need than the fact that the man had been shot in the head? Wasn't that enough to determine cause and manner of death? It was glaringly obvious.

Then what was he expecting her to find out in her investigation? Was she supposed to be able to tell from the photograph who did it? Why?

"Okay, yes," she said as patiently as she could. "I can see that he was shot. Cause of death. I can't issue a medical examiner's report based on a photo. I don't know who it is or the circumstances surrounding his death. I mean, I do issue reports on John Does, but it still needs to go through the official channels for me to do that. I need human remains. Who did you get this from?"

He shrugged and made the ASL sign for "friend," both index fingers hooked together. A well-known sign, even though he did not generally use ASL to communicate, but relied on his own gestures and the phone pictures and short texts to get his message across.

"A friend from school?" Zachary asked.

Rhys nodded.

"And do you know where *he* got it from?"

Rhys shrugged. He had already communicated to them that it was something that had been circulating the school. His friend had gotten it from another friend, who had gotten it from another friend.

"What are they saying about it?" Kenzie asked. "They're not just sending it around by itself with no explanation."

He pointed at the phone and made a gun shape with his hand, complete with a jerk showing the gun had been fired.

"What?" Zachary asked. " 'Here is a picture of a man who was shot.' That's it?"

Rhys nodded. Kenzie wanted to search through his phone to see who it had come from and exactly what the attached text had said. But she didn't want to touch anything that the police would want to look at. It had probably been sent through an app where the message self-destructed, and all of that information was gone. But maybe the police techs could pull off information that had been deleted but not overwritten.

There was just one thing that she needed to do. If Rhys wanted her to investigate the man's death, she needed a copy of the picture. She didn't know what she could do for Rhys, but he needed to see that she was doing everything she could. He had trusted them with this information that he hadn't shown anyone else, and he was counting on her being able to make everything right.

She didn't know if she could do that, but she would do everything she could for him.

2

I'm going to send this to your phone," she told Zachary.

It might make more sense to forward it to her own phone. She would need it there eventually. But Rhys didn't need it popping up in his face again while he was holding her phone in his hands. It had been traumatic enough the first time.

And she would probably get Zachary to look at the photo's metadata to see if he could tell her anything about its origin.

Zachary nodded his agreement. Kenzie sent it to him, then slid Rhys's phone into her pocket. It would need to go to the police as evidence. Kenzie would get Rhys another phone. His grandmother, Vera, could probably not afford it. Kenzie didn't think she had much disposable income. But Kenzie didn't want Rhys to be left without a means to communicate beyond gestures.

"This whole thing," Kenzie motioned to the phone in her pocket. "I'm so sorry you had to deal with it. It must be really difficult after what happened to your grandpa."

Rhys nodded. His eyes dropped to the phone in his hand, but he didn't type anything immediately.

Until the drug therapy that Rhys had reacted to, they had all assumed that what had happened to Grandpa Clarence when Rhys was just five was long forgotten, or at least very murky in Rhys's memory. But the

MDMA had made Rhys voluble, overcoming his usual mutism, and he had related the images to them over and over again.

His grandfather murdered before his eyes. Shot in the head, like the man in the picture.

It wasn't that Rhys was afraid that the same murderer might have come back, that she had killed a second time and he might be in danger.

Because Rhys knew who the murderer was. He had always known, and he had lived with her for years after Grandpa Clarence's death. Because it had been his aunt Robin. She had since passed. so they all knew that it wasn't the same killer. Just the same cause of death.

Kenzie saw Rhys's lips moving. The same mantra repeated over and over again. Even though he didn't voice the words, she still recognized them.

Stop it. Just stop it.

Robin's words, the night she had killed her father.

"I know," Kenzie said softly. She leaned forward and put her hand over Rhys's briefly, unsure how he would respond to the physical contact. "This is terrible for you. Are you having a lot of flashbacks?"

After remaining unfocused for a few long seconds, Rhys's gaze finally returned to Kenzie's face. He cocked his head slightly as if he knew that Kenzie had said something but wasn't sure what it was or what she meant.

"I asked if you're having flashbacks," Kenzie said slowly, "If you keep remembering what you saw and felt the night that your grandpa was killed, there are things that you can do to try to reduce the impact of the flashbacks, to… get back to the present."

He held out one hand, palm out, inviting her to go on, eyebrows raised curiously.

"One method that helps Zachary is called anchoring." Kenzie looked at Zachary.

He nodded but didn't explain. His flashbacks were better than they had been, but he wasn't over them. The fire that had destroyed his childhood home and precipitated the rift in his family was still ever-present in his mind. Even if he wasn't having flashbacks, he was still aware of it. And although he could stand to be around a lit candle or small campfire now without being thrown back to that experience, other things still triggered flashbacks for him.

"You concentrate on your senses," she told Rhys, since Zachary didn't seem inclined to explain. "You name five things that you see, five things that you hear, five things that you smell or feel. Focusing on those things, on your senses and surroundings, helps minimize the flashback and anchor you to the present."

Rhys nodded slowly. He couldn't name the things he saw out loud and probably couldn't type them on his phone when he was in the throes of a flashback, but he could still focus on them and hopefully get himself out of a flashback faster.

"Maybe you could tell Vera about anchoring, too," Zachary suggested. "She can help talk Rhys through it."

Kenzie nodded. "*You* should probably talk to her rather than me."

Kenzie wasn't exactly in Vera's good books these days. Kenzie had been vocal about Rhys not going to Persons, the private psychiatric facility that had done the experimental drug protocol, for treatment. Kenzie had tried to tell Vera that it was too dangerous, that what they were doing there was not ethical, and that MDMA therapy was too risky for Rhys.

But Vera had been desperate. After years of not hearing Rhys's voice more than just a word or two here and there, and then his falling into the fugue state where he was completely uncommunicative, not even acknowledging that they were speaking to him, let alone trying to respond, she had been willing to risk anything for the miracle cure Persons had dangled in front of her.

Kenzie had been right. The fact did not endear her to Vera. Kenzie was sure Vera would feel awkward and embarrassed that she had gone ahead and done what Kenzie had warned her about and that the result had been negative, just as Kenzie had feared it would be. Kenzie being right about the therapy would be harder for Vera to forgive than being wrong would have been.

Zachary looked at Kenzie for a few seconds, reading this in her face, and eventually nodded. "I'll talk to her about anchoring," he agreed. "Walk her through how to do it." He looked at Rhys. "It does help. It doesn't make them go away completely, but it helps you to... not drown in the flashbacks."

Rhys gave a thumbs-up. He was all for anything that might help.

Kenzie wondered how he felt about the treatment that Vera had put him through. Did he understand that she had just been trying to help him? Did he resent being treated like an animal or a child with no understanding, with no choice in how she decided he should be treated? He hadn't been able to talk to her at the time, hadn't been able to understand or to express his wishes one way or the other, but that understanding wouldn't necessarily change his feelings about what had happened.

Feelings were not always logical. Kenzie sometimes found herself feeling completely opposite from what she wanted to sometimes. No matter how much she tried to talk herself into feeling a certain way, she couldn't control her primitive brain.

"So…" Kenzie took a deep breath and let it go.

They had asked him whether he wanted to talk about Grandpa Clarence and what he remembered. He had shown them the picture of the stranger and asked Kenzie to look into it. Kenzie didn't know how much success she would have in her assignment.

Rhys was looking tired and strained around the eyes. It was bound to be taking a lot of effort for him to act as normal as possible and socialize with them. He had been through a lot in the last couple of weeks, and it would take time for him to recover.

"So, I guess we should probably be going," Kenzie said, standing up and looking at Zachary to encourage him to do the same. "You're looking pretty tired," she told Rhys. "I don't want to wear you out. I'll talk to the police and get started on this… and one of us will bring you a new phone by the end of the day so you can use it to communicate. I don't know how long it will be before you get this one back. I assume they'll need it for a day or two to get all the information they need."

Rhys shrugged, looking unconcerned about whether he got the phone back or not. Kenzie supposed that if he got a new phone in the deal, he wouldn't be too upset about it, as long as he could still log back in to all of his accounts and not lose any information.

3

Kenzie and Zachary were quiet while they took the elevator back to the main floor and walked out to Zachary's car. Kenzie rubbed her temples. As much as she would like to pretend that she was back to full health, she couldn't deny that she was still having headaches, which she assumed were the result of her mild concussion.

Or maybe it was just this new headache that Rhys had handed her. How was she going to get anywhere on it?

"Who are you going to talk to?" Zachary asked, putting a slightly different spin on it.

Kenzie knew her share of homicide detectives. She could pick who she wanted to take it to and who would give it the most time and attention. Someone who was more likely to believe Rhys, a mentally ill teenager, and not to just brush the case off or say that since no one had found a body, it was obviously a faked photograph, and she could forget about it and just go about her normal business. And so could Rhys.

But how would Rhys go on as usual when the memories of his Grandpa Clarence's murder and the picture of the murdered man that had arrived on his phone stacked up to cause him even more mental distress than he had felt over the previous decade? How was he going to put his grandpa's murder behind him, relegating it to the past when this new face brought it all back again?

She had worked with Detective Elena Garcia on a couple of cases, but Garcia was more likely to be impatient and to roll her eyes at the paucity of the information. She would need a lot more concrete evidence before she would take something like that on. Tuttle and Baker had worked with Kenzie on the Wade homicides, and she considered them seriously before shaking her head. She was sure they had already taken enough flak for having to arrest the congressman's wife. They probably didn't need to take on anything controversial in the wake of that case.

Kenzie shook her head, thinking about it.

"What about Campbell?" Zachary suggested.

Kenzie considered him. He had come to her aid when her father had been missing, helping her sort that mess out and deal with the threats and unexpected developments involving the Russians. He wasn't strictly a homicide detective, but he was a good man to go to with a case that needed to be handled somewhat differently from the straightforward homicide cases Kenzie was used to dealing with.

"Yeah. He might be a good person," she agreed.

"He doesn't jump to conclusions," Zachary offered. "He listens."

"Do you think he'll believe it? That this is real?"

Zachary chewed on his lip. "I think he would consider it. He wouldn't automatically brush it off."

"Yeah."

They reached the car and Zachary disarmed the alarm and unlocked the doors.

"What do you think of the picture?" he asked.

"What do I think? I think someone needs to take it seriously. I don't know who this guy is or when or where he was killed, but someone needs to make sure that we find out."

"You think it's legitimate. That it is someone who was shot and killed."

"Yes." Kenzie looked at him. "You don't think so?"

"I reserve judgment. I don't know."

"You think it's a prank?" Kenzie's voice rose slightly, though she tried to keep it under control.

"I think you know a dead body when you see one."

"And I say it is a dead body."

Zachary nodded. He started the engine and pulled out of the parking space. "Then it is."

"Do you really believe that?"

"Yes." He said it firmly. No waffling. Not that he believed it if she believed it. If Kenzie were looking for an argument, she wouldn't get one from him.

The rest of the discussion on the way to the police station was whether Zachary should also go in with Kenzie. Would they be taken more seriously if both of them showed up, believing this was a real case that Campbell needed to look into? Or would Campbell wonder why Zachary needed to be there to prop up Kenzie's story?

Zachary didn't have any evidence independent of what Rhys had given Kenzie. She had the phone and the picture, and Rhys's brief explanation of where it had come from.

Ultimately, they decided it would be best if Zachary dropped Kenzie off. She worked in the basement of the police department so, when she was finished talking to Campbell, she could just go downstairs and work the rest of the day. Meanwhile, Zachary could go home and analyze the copy of the photo Kenzie had forwarded to him and see if he could find out anything about its origins.

Sergeant Joshua Campbell was at his desk and able to see Kenzie right away. She had been worried that he wouldn't be around, and then she would have to decide whether to leave a message, put it off, or pick someone else to talk to about it.

"Dr. Kirsch," Campbell greeted, standing up when she walked in and extending a hand. "It's great to see you. What can we do for you today?"

"Well… I'm in kind of a quandary," Kenzie admitted, sitting down in the guest chair in front of his desk and thinking about it. She had been trying to script out how the meeting would go ever since they had left the hospital, but she had been unable to come up with anything that made her happy. Of course, it would be great if he just agreed that it was a case that needed to be looked into and that it was an actual, legitimate murder and not some hoax. But she couldn't see a clear path toward getting him to agree with her on that point.

"I'm happy to help you out any way I can," Campbell offered with a smile. "Can I get you some coffee?"

"No, no. I'll get one when I get down to work."

"How's Zachary?" Campbell's eyes wandered to his computer, maybe checking the date to see how close they were to Christmas. "Is everything okay with him?"

"Yes, so far."

Campbell was aware of Zachary's seasonal depression and the suicidal thoughts that had landed him in the psych ward the previous year.

"He's on a different cocktail this year and I'm hoping it will work better," Kenzie told him.

"Good. Glad to hear it. So you aren't here about anything to do with him."

"No. This is… a new case. Maybe a case. Something I'm hoping you can investigate."

Campbell raised an eyebrow, waiting for Kenzie to get on with it.

Kenzie pulled Rhys's phone out of her pocket. She brought the picture up on the screen again and handed it to him.

Campbell looked at the picture for a few long seconds before focusing on Kenzie.

"Is this a threat? Did someone send it to you?"

"No. It was sent to a friend of ours. Rhys Salter. From what we can understand, it's circulating throughout his school. One of those… horror pictures that people gawk at. Like a bad car crash. Shock value. Curiosity. Have a look and pass it on to your friends."

Campbell blinked at her. Kenzie wasn't sure why he looked so confused. She shook her head, waiting for his response.

"Rhys Salter?" Campbell repeated.

"Yes. It was received by him. This is his phone."

"Is he related to Robin Salter, the woman who was murdered?"

"Oh." Kenzie nodded. She had forgotten that he had been involved in the case while Zachary had been investigating it. "Yes, this is Gloria's son. Robin's nephew."

"The mute boy."

"Selectively mute," Kenzie amended. "Yes. But he does have other ways to communicate, and he gave us this. Wanted us to pursue it."

Campbell pondered this. The picture on the phone disappeared as the screen shut off, and he pressed the button to bring it up again.

"This man appears to have been killed in the same way as Rhys's grandfather."

"Yes."

"And you don't find that odd?"

Kenzie shook her head, frowning. "No. What do you mean? What's odd about it? It is disturbing, for sure, but I don't know that I would call it odd."

"I'm thinking that perhaps… this boy has unresolved issues where his grandfather's murder is concerned. Maybe he sought out a picture of a man who was killed in the same way because he is trying to understand his feelings about what happened. Or trying to play it out in his mind again in order to try to control the outcome this time. You hear all the time about adult criminals who are trying to reenact something that happened to them as children in order to be in control of it. Because they had so little control as children."

4

You're not saying that you think Rhys killed someone because of what he witnessed." Kenzie's anger flared at the suggestion. "This boy has been through enough trauma without someone accusing him of being a killer."

"No, no," Campbell made a dampening movement with his hands, patting downward. "I'm not saying that he killed someone. I'm saying he might be trying to accept his feelings about the original murder. This could be his attempt to gain control or to examine those feelings from another perspective."

"No," Kenzie shook her head. "All it will take is one of us going to the school and finding out whether this picture has really been circulating the students like Rhys says it has been. But I can tell you, I believe him one hundred percent. I believe this picture was sent to him by someone else, out of the blue, and that it greatly disturbed him. He went into a fugue state. He's been hospitalized since he got this picture; it bothered him so much and brought back all those old feelings. This is *not* something that Rhys did himself."

"Okay, okay. It was a question that had to be asked. And even if it is circulating the school, that doesn't prove he didn't start it. He might have been the first one to send it around. He could control multiple fake accounts to keep it circulating. You don't know."

"I don't believe that. This is something that was sent to him and caused a great emotional shock. And he wants to know who it is and what happened. *That* is what he wants to resolve. He already knows who killed his grandfather. He doesn't need to resolve that."

"He may still be having a lot of emotional disturbance due to his grandfather's murder. He *is* still mute, isn't he?"

"He's… well, mostly, yes."

"So it hasn't been resolved."

"Not in that way. But there is no way to tell if he will ever be able to talk normally, even if he has fully accepted and integrated what happened to his grandfather. Sometimes those scars are just too deep."

Campbell nodded, looking at the picture. "So you are coming to me to… investigate this crime…?" He tapped the side of the phone.

"Well, yes. I can't really open an investigation from the medical examiner's office because I don't have a body. But maybe this is enough evidence for *you* to open a file and conduct some preliminary investigation…"

Campbell swiveled slightly to face his computer and typed a query. He scrolled through the screen, shaking his head.

"This doesn't appear to be a local death. Nothing on our system indicates that we have opened an investigation into a man who was shot in the head in the last few days."

"It would be longer ago than that."

"How long?"

"Closer to two weeks. Maybe longer, if the picture didn't start to circulate immediately."

"At two weeks, it should be on your table by now. If there was such a crime."

"Unless the body was dumped somewhere and just hasn't been discovered yet."

"I'm not sure how we're supposed to do anything if that is the case. But there's also nothing to indicate that this is a local murder. It could be hundreds of miles away. It could have been five years ago. It could be staged."

"It's not staged."

But Kenzie couldn't deny that he could be right about it not happening two weeks before. Or being local. She had assumed that the murder happened just before the picture started circulating at the school. Still, she had seen a number of stories make their rounds on social media every few years, showing up with a few details changed so that it was suddenly brand new again. Everyone was agog, not realizing it had happened five, ten, or even twenty years before.

"What about facial recognition?" she suggested. "If we could identify who the man is, we could narrow down the time and place. Find out whether it really is something that happened recently."

Campbell sighed. "I can get the techies to run it, see if they get any hits. I don't know whether the resolution is high enough or whether we have enough of his face to get a hit. The portrayals you see on TV of facial recognition are highly exaggerated. You need a full-frontal view, no profiles, with all of the landmarks visible. And only a fraction of felons are actually in the database yet. There are a lot of databases that are not accessible to us."

"It's *almost* straight on."

"Almost. That's why I said I'd see if they can get any hits off of it. But don't hold your breath. It isn't as easy as you see on TV. It's a very sophisticated technology, and it doesn't do as well in the wild as it does in controlled tests and fiction."

"So you'll open a file on it?"

"I'll need to open a file to log the evidence and have it examined," Campbell said, touching the phone again. "But I'm not opening it as a homicide. Only as 'disturbing peace by use of telephone.' Someone sending this disturbing picture to a minor, especially one who has previously witnessed a similar murder in his own family, could well be seen as an attempt to 'terrify, threaten, harass, or annoy.' "

Kenzie nodded her agreement. "Especially when you consider the outcome."

"Right. In the meantime…"

Kenzie waited for his question. "Yes…?"

"I assume you kept a copy of this."

Kenzie shrugged, her cheeks getting warm. "Well… yes."

"You might see if Zachary can trace the origin of the picture. If it has been circulating the internet for a few years, or if it is from a movie set, he may be able to identify it and confirm that it is not actually a current, local murder that needs to be solved."

"I already have him looking at it," Kenzie said. "I hadn't thought about finding out if it is already on the net somewhere, but I did ask him to check the metadata to see if it leads us anywhere."

"I'm sure he'll go the whole way. Photography is his thing. If he could do that, I would appreciate it. My techs' time is precious. I don't like to waste it on a wild goose chase. If he can narrow down whether it is really something that we need to look into… I would appreciate that."

"Sure. I'm sure he would be happy to loop you in."

"Good. I haven't talked to him for a while. We could do coffee and catch up."

5

After the talk with Campbell, Kenzie headed downstairs to the morgue. It was a late start, but she had warned Dr. Cook ahead of time. She and Zachary had needed to go see Rhys, and Kenzie had put in a lot of hours at the morgue lately. It wouldn't hurt them for her to take a couple of hours off. Better for her mental health than overworking herself for two weeks straight. Had it been that long since she'd had a break?

Kenzie sat down at her desk and dialed Zachary to tell him about her meeting with Campbell. As she checked her email and digitally filed a number of reports that had come in overnight, she filled him in on the details. Zachary agreed to do as Campbell had said and to do some image searches to see if he could find out where the picture had originated.

"He says you guys should get together for coffee," Kenzie said. "So if you can find anything, you should follow up. Maybe he has some other stuff they want to contract out. Or maybe he just wants to catch up with you."

"It has been a while," Zachary admitted, sounding far away. "I'll follow up."

"Good. And can you email me the photo? I want to have Dr. Cook take a look at it, too."

"Yeah? Okay. I can do that." She heard him typing rapidly. "There you go, on its way to you. Thanks for talking to Campbell. I'm glad he decided to look into it."

"Well, as a phone harassment case, not as a homicide. But I don't really care, as long as he can start pulling together some information to find out who the guy is and what happened to him."

"Well, we know what happened to him."

"Well… before that. And after that. Who did it, and why, and what happened to the body? Because Campbell says that nothing has shown up on their radar. No body."

"Maybe he's right and it's something that happened in Russia. Or ten years ago. We just assumed that it was something that had just happened, but…"

"Anything in the metadata?"

"Not much. From the looks of it, it was a screen capture somewhere along the way. The original metadata isn't still attached. Someone received it, grabbed a screenshot, and then forwarded that screenshot to someone else. And so on. Probably more than once. But if I can find other copies of it on the internet, I might be able to find something with the original metadata still attached. Or other information that could help us."

Kenzie sighed. "I suppose it was too much to expect someone to leave all the information attached to the photo. Geotags, dates, what kind of camera it was taken with. That would have been nice, wouldn't it?"

"No such luck," Zachary said, sounding a little too cheerful about it. "But I'll see if I can find other copies online. Maybe I'll have better luck that way."

Kenzie had the photo on her screen when Dr. Cook walked up to her desk to touch base on how they were going to be spending the day.

"Morning, Dr. Kirsch," he greeted, and his eyes slid over to her screen. He frowned. "I didn't get a call out today. What case is that?"

"Oh… actually, it isn't a case yet. The police are looking into it, but…"

"If there is a dead man and the police are looking into it, then why hasn't the medical examiner's office been called?"

"Because actually… we don't know where the photo came from. It could be nothing. It could be something that happened years ago or in another part of the world altogether. But it could also... be something that happened here a couple of weeks ago."

"I would think we would have the body on the table by now if it happened a couple of weeks ago."

"Maybe. I mean... if it was left out on the street where someone could find it. But if it was disposed of somewhere else... out in the Vermont woods... I mean, there are a lot of wild areas it could be hidden and not found for years."

"That has been known to happen," he admitted. "So... you're free-lancing now? Off finding your own bodies?"

"Well... it sort of fell into my lap." Kenzie's cheeks were warm. "That is... I have a friend who received this on his phone and wanted me to look into it. See whether it was legitimate or not. I don't know anything yet. I haven't had enough time to investigate it. And... we have other cases to work on, legitimate ones. Where the bodies are on our tables."

"Yeah." He didn't move on to their legitimate cases. "But nothing so urgent that we can't take a few minutes to examine an intriguing photograph. See what we can discern from it." He leaned on the high counter of her reception desk, looking at the photograph thoughtfully.

Kenzie turned her attention back to her screen. "Everyone's first reaction is that it can't be real. That it is just stage makeup or something. But..." Kenzie grimaced. "I've seen my share of dead bodies. More than most people. And that looks like a real dead body to me. The dead bodies on TV, with all of the makeup and special effects they have at their disposal, never look the same. They look like live people who are pretending to be dead. Or else like gruesome zombies too bloody and gory to be real."

Dr. Cook nodded his agreement.

Kenzie was suddenly uncomfortable with how close he was leaning to her. Cook was good-looking, with dark, longish hair and brilliant blue eyes, looking like a movie star who had wandered off some set and, while Kenzie had gotten used to being around him most of the time, he was a bit too close for comfort and she was a little bit too aware of his good looks. She leaned away from him, pushing her chair to the side slightly.

"Do you want me to send it to you?"

"No, this is fine." He seemed oblivious to her discomfort. "So we're looking at a small caliber bullet fired close to the head. Execution style."

Kenzie nodded. "A 22 round, maybe. Small entrance wound, not a lot of bleeding, no exit wound that we can see on the photograph, but obviously we can't see the back of his head."

"But there isn't a pool of blood under his head. And only a little bleeding from the forehead. So, I think it is probably still inside. Bounced around inside his skull until it lost velocity."

"Right," Kenzie agreed. In the enclosed space of the skull, a 22 could do a lot of damage as it ricocheted inside the skull.

"I don't see any other signs of violence on the body, but we can't see the whole thing. No way to tell if he was armed or had been in an altercation."

"It's not likely he shot himself."

"No," Cook agreed. "Few suicides go for the forehead. That's more likely to be in the mouth or under the chin, like you see in the movies."

Kenzie's skin crawled. She paused, waiting for the goosebumps and the knot in her gut to fade. She didn't like talking about suicide. She had investigated plenty of suicides, but few of them were by gunshot. It was a particularly violent and messy way to go. She couldn't help thinking about Zachary whenever she was talking about suicide. He had not attempted suicide in the time that they had known each other, but she knew he had when he was younger. Sometimes cutting and sometimes pills. Maybe other methods she didn't know about.

The previous year had been a difficult one, and Zachary had struggled with suicidal thoughts enough that he had admitted himself to the psych ward in order to keep himself safe and get back on track. It had been a scary time. In the days before he had admitted himself, he had taken the sharp knives from the butcher block in the kitchen and put them away out of sight so that he wouldn't be tempted by them. She had been afraid whenever she left him alone, worrying about how he would be while she was gone.

She shook off the dark thoughts and tried to focus her attention back on the photography.

"You okay?" Dr. Cook asked.

"Yeah, just… a bad feeling. It's nothing." She didn't want to get into any detail with him, but she also didn't want to deny her emotions. She didn't want to fall into morbid thoughts. She could stay removed from the situation and view it from a clinical perspective.

The victim was not anyone she knew. She cataloged what she could tell or guess from the picture. A long-haired blond man. Probably in his late twenties or early thirties. While his face didn't show a lot of extra weight, his stomach did strain against his waistband and shirt, as if he'd bought clothes a size too small or recently put on weight. He was not well-dressed. Not someone she could immediately identify as homeless, but he didn't look like he was comfortably situated. On the skids.

He looked like an aging street punk. Gone to seed. Someone who had spent too much time drinking or doping, or both. Not a crackhead, but not clean.

"How about the background?" Cook suggested. "When they examine pictures of hostages or child pornography, they always look at the background to see if they can find something that will help them to pinpoint the location."

Kenzie didn't find the background very helpful. The guy was lying on the pavement. There was no city skyline behind him, no store or business name they could pick up. Just a man lying on the street. She looked at Cook to see if he had discerned anything else from it.

"Well…" Cook looked for something to say. "It looks much easier on TV. There is always a historic building they can trace or some kind of mountain range or train station that they can use to triangulate the location."

Kenzie nodded. "It looks like half-light. Early morning or evening. Do you think it is a street, sidewalk, or back alley?"

They both studied it, trying to guess from the aggregate and any other indicators exactly what the surface was.

"Not a sidewalk," Cook said. "And no lines or curbs. It doesn't make much sense that he would be executed in the middle of the street where everyone could see. So… a back alley. That would be my guess."

That narrowed the possible locations down by about half, but still wasn't anywhere near the amount of information they would need to positively identify the location.

"I guess this wasn't terribly helpful," Cook admitted. "An interesting exercise, but I guess we'll have to rely on the cops to figure out who it is and where and when."

Kenzie nodded. "Yeah. I guess I'm not very good at a virtual autopsy."

"It's a little easier when you actually get to see the scene and get the body on your table. Not much we can test or investigate in this case."

Kenzie agreed. She closed the photo window. Dr. Cook stepped back. "Well, then, back to our regular programming," he announced with a smile.

6

It was late in the day when Kenzie stopped by the hospital to give Rhys the new phone she had picked up for him.

She had tried to balance the wishes of Rhys and his grandmother. Rhys would, of course, want the latest and greatest thing in cell phones. Whatever was the most popular or the newest release—something with all the bells, whistles, and latest features.

Vera, on the other hand, might be embarrassed if Kenzie got something too expensive, showing her up, making her feel like she couldn't provide for her grandson. So, Kenzie had bought a middle-of-the-road model. All of the features she thought that Rhys would really need, access to the streaming data he would need to be able to communicate most efficiently, with enough storage for him to be able to keep pictures and maybe install an actual AAC app to communicate with.

Rhys seemed unwilling or unable to use any alternative communication system. Kenzie wasn't sure whether it was because he was afraid he would look different or fail, or because his brain just would not fit into the confines of how the rest of the world felt he should be able to communicate. But he could not seem to be able to implement a language system that would let him tell them in detail what had happened the night Grandpa Clarence had been murdered. Robin's order to "Just be quiet" seemed to have taken such a hold on Rhys that he couldn't do anything but obey, no matter what communication methods might be available.

Vera was still at the hospital, which Kenzie hadn't anticipated. She had thought it would be late enough for Vera to be at home getting ready for bed. She smiled and warmly shook Kenzie's hand, but Kenzie sensed a lingering reserve.

"How nice of you to come."

"Thanks." Kenzie also shook hands with Rhys, and he looked at her with bright, expectant eyes. He knew why she had come back. Kenzie chuckled. She pulled out the phone she had set up for Rhys and handed it to him. Rhys beamed. He pressed the home button and started tapping and swiping to explore the new device and what he could do with it.

Vera was frowning at Kenzie. "Is your phone not working? He's very good at fixing them."

Kenzie looked at Rhys, who was too enthralled by the phone to pay any attention to the conversation. He had apparently not told Vera about the picture or why Kenzie had taken his phone away. She probably thought it was still locked away, as the psych ward did not normally permit the patients to use their phones, having run into some behavioral issues with other patients. When Rhys had let them know that he needed to show her something on his phone, Kenzie had insisted that Rhys be allowed to use it, as it was one of his only means of communication.

"Uh, no. This is Rhys's new phone." Kenzie tried to think of how to tell Vera what Rhys had shown them.

Vera was looking at her, shaking her head, trying to understand what was happening.

"It was… well, you know that something triggered Rhys's breakdown a couple of weeks ago," she said quietly.

Vera nodded. Of course she knew that. It had been the focus of her life from the moment Stanley Green called her to tell her he had found Rhys wandering the streets, unable to communicate with him.

"Well, Zachary and I were talking to Rhys about what had happened, and it turns out that there was a picture on his phone, one that was sent by a friend."

Vera's jaw dropped, shocked and horrified. "Was it… pornographic? I've warned him. I've told him that's what kids these days do, and he just can't get involved in that. He could be prosecuted if he ever participated in forwarding pictures like that." She glared at Rhys as he played with his phone.

"No," Kenzie said. "A picture was being forwarded around the school, but it wasn't pornography. It was… a picture of a murdered man." She said it baldly, getting the pertinent information out as quickly as possible. She didn't want there to be any question of what kind of picture she was talking about. It wasn't the time to be vague or use kind euphemisms. Vera needed to know what she was dealing with.

"A… murdered man!" Vera grasped Rhys's arm tightly and pulled him toward her.

Rhys was forced to look up from his phone to see what was going on. He looked at Vera's face, put his other hand over hers, and then looked at Kenzie for an explanation.

"Yes," Kenzie said, keeping her focus on Vera. "It was a picture of a man who had been shot, and it was very upsetting to Rhys. It brought back… a lot of old stuff." She couldn't bring herself to say Clarence's name or to allude more directly to his murder. "It was overwhelming to him. But now that he's feeling better," she put on a lighter, happier tone, "He would like us to find out who it is and what exactly happened to him. To make sure that it is handled properly."

That was probably a tactless thing to say. Kenzie hadn't planned her explanation out very well. Would Vera assume Kenzie meant they hadn't handled Clarence's death properly? Of course, they had not. They had covered up what had happened and Robin had never been brought to justice. Rhys had lived with the unpunished murderer for years. Now, Rhys wanted another killer brought to justice. Kenzie didn't know if she could find the killer or help see him convicted. But she would try. She would do everything within her power to identify the victim and his killer.

Vera looked at Rhys, licking her lips, swallowing hard. "Rhys…" Her tone was a mixture of horror and accusation.

"He hasn't done anything wrong," Kenzie told Vera. "He was just one recipient of the photograph, and he has asked for help."

"Well, we can't… we can't get involved in this. That kind of thing, it would just be too hard on Rhys. We don't want to get involved."

"I've already taken his phone to the police. I'm sorry if you think that was… that I was taking liberties and should have left it to you. It seemed like the right thing to do. So… they have his phone, and I brought this new one for him to use."

Rhys nodded. He let go of Vera's hand and picked it up to show her, pointing to the bright, crystal-clear screen and the icons and widgets he was already playing with.

Vera tried to smile, but she was clearly upset. "You just went ahead and did this without even talking to me?"

"I… yes. Rhys asked for my help, and I just went ahead and did it. I didn't think about anything else… I guess I thought he would tell you about it and that you would want me to do the same thing."

"He can't be involved in this." Vera shook her head and rubbed her eyes. "The police are going to want to talk to him and he's going to get dragged into something ugly. Something that has nothing to do with him. He should have just deleted the picture and forgotten about it."

Rhys looked at his grandmother reproachfully with that peculiar, sad-eyed frown that always reminded Kenzie of a basset hound. Kenzie didn't want to take sides or interfere with their relationship. Still, she had already done so, and they had the evidence from history that hiding things, burying them and trying to forget them, had done Rhys no good in the past. He had only been harmed by this strategy before.

"Vera… I don't think that would work or do any good for Rhys. He needs to… he wants to help. To feel like he has done something for this man."

"We don't even know him. You have no idea who he is!" Vera glared at Rhys. "You don't even know him from Adam, do you?"

Rhys shrugged and spread his hands out, agreeing with her. He had no clue who the dead man was. But why should that stop him?

"This is all a big mistake," Vera said. "Some joke email. A kids' prank. The police will write it off, warn us not to bother them with silly stuff like this in the future, and we can go on as before."

"They're going to look into it," Kenzie told her. "They are not labeling it a homicide. They don't know yet what it is. Nobody is in trouble for anything."

Vera shook her head grimly. "Well, you can expect that trouble is going to come looking for you."

Kenzie wasn't feeling great after the meeting with Vera. It was Friday night, date night. She and Zachary were supposed to be out exploring Vermont and their relationship with each other, enjoying themselves and relaxing.

But she didn't feel very relaxed. They had decided to go to a classic car show in Burlington. Kenzie didn't know a whole lot about cars, but she loved her "baby," a cherry red convertible—though the cooling weather meant that they were taking Zachary's more practical, nondescript surveillance car more often. Zachary didn't know much about cars either, so they were on equal footing, both interested in what looked shiny and retro without getting bogged down with engine configurations, exhaust pipes, or all-original-parts.

She tried to be cheerful and get into it. But despite the rows of beautiful cars, the food vendors, and the people offering various car services, she was still down in the dumps.

They sat down at a table with soft drinks and small servings of fries and mini donuts, fragrant with grease, yeast, and vanilla, and ate slowly, savoring the treat and the special time together. But Kenzie found her mind constantly distracted by Vera's reaction to Kenzie stepping in and taking over Rhys's phone and deciding what was best for him without any thought that his guardian might have a different opinion.

Kenzie's life experience had been very different from Rhys's or even Vera's. A white girl, growing up in a wealthy, privileged home, her biggest challenges had been related to her sister Amanda's illness. Rhys and Vera had to deal with prejudices against Blacks, especially in law enforcement and the legal system. They grew up fearing random police attention and unfair prison terms. Vera also dealt with the terror of Rhys not being able to speak to the police, being taken as a problem: having an attitude and being unable to explain himself verbally. The family's reaction to Clarence's murder had not been to seek justice, but to keep it quiet. To cover it up and turn away police suspicions.

Considering Campbell's reaction to finding out that Rhys was the boy who had been in possession of the picture of the man with a bullet in his head, Vera was right to believe that the police would think the worst of Rhys. That they would automatically see him as a troublemaker, either a criminal or an attention-seeker, rather than as a troubled boy who had been traumatized by what he had witnessed and then received on his phone. They did not see him as vulnerable and broken, but as a potential threat to public peace. Campbell was one of the good ones. Kenzie could only imagine what those who were *really* prejudiced would think.

She initially flinched when Zachary put his hand over hers. But she relaxed and looked at his face and forced a smile in response to his concerned expression.

"Are you okay?" Zachary asked. "You must be tired. It's been a long day, and with the concussion…"

"The concussion isn't a problem," Kenzie said. "I don't think I'm having any more symptoms. It was just very mild. But… I am tired."

"We'll head for home once we finish eating."

"Yeah, that would be good. I'll need some time to unwind before we go to bed."

He nodded. His eyes still searched her face, maybe sensing that there was more to it than just tiredness. But that was up to Kenzie to explain. He had already asked her if she was okay. He wouldn't push too hard for more than she had offered. He wouldn't dig down deeper unless it was really obvious that something was bothering her and, hopefully, she'd not given that much away.

"It's just Vera," Kenzie told him. "She was really not happy with me going ahead and taking Rhys's phone and the picture to the police."

Zachary nodded slowly. "I don't see how we could have done anything else. But… I guess I can see where she's coming from. He's her grandson, she's the boss and the one making decisions for him. And it is kind of… the second strike."

Kenzie winced. "Because I was against the MDMA therapy."

"Yeah. So that's twice when you've 'known better' than her what was best for Rhys."

"I suppose so. She was pretty upset."

"How was Rhys?"

Kenzie thought about it. If it was Rhys that she was trying to help, then she should probably focus on his reaction rather than Vera's. Vera was his caregiver for now but, in a few years, Rhys would be making his own decisions, and he was old enough now to defy Vera, riding across town when he was supposed to be at school, showing up at Stanley Green's late at night when he was supposed to be in bed. Vera might think that she knew what was best for Rhys, but how had Rhys felt about it?

Rhys had seemed happy. He had certainly liked getting the new phone, but that wasn't all there was to it. He had not bowed under Vera's opinion that taking the case to the police had been the wrong thing to do. He had still maintained that was what he wanted done. And she thought he seemed lighter for having passed that burden on to Kenzie. He no longer had to shoulder it alone and to figure out what to do and how to get justice for the murdered man. Instead, he could leave it to Kenzie and the police to sort out, and he could go back to being a kid.

Or at least, not as much. She suspected he would still think a lot about the dead man. And still have flashbacks to Grandpa Clarence's murder. Nightmares too. But at least he had taken one step, a constructive step to resolving the situation he found himself in once more. He wouldn't stand by and be a silent witness this time. His voice might have been silenced, but his brain and his body weren't, and he could still shout his story out to anyone who would listen.

Kenzie nodded her head slowly. "Rhys was okay with it. Happy, I think. Happier than before."

"I felt when we left there this morning that it was a relief for him to talk to us about it and to get you looking into it."

"I guess so. It's hard to hold things in." Kenzie closed her eyes and passed her hand over her lids, tired. "Even though it was really hard to talk to you and Dr. B about the... about the Russians..." She still had a hard time saying the word *kidnapping*. "I really did feel better about getting it out in the open and not having to keep it a secret anymore."

Zachary nodded. He ate a fry and stared away from Kenzie, ostensibly looking at a row of shiny Fords. But Kenzie knew he wasn't looking at them.

How many secrets was Zachary still hiding, trying to stuff down things that had happened in his life that he'd been forced to be quiet about? And how many times had something happened, like the assault by Archuro, and Zachary had done his best to forget it because it was so traumatic? She hoped that, somehow, he would be able to talk about more of those things.

8

Zachary confirmed the fact that he couldn't find any copies of the photograph of the dead man that had been in circulation prior to two weeks before, when Rhys had received it on his phone.

Once the picture had started circulating the school, there were a few instances where it had popped up on the internet in places that should have been secure, but were not to someone who knew the secrets of getting into such places. And it appeared more frequently on the deep web, where it couldn't be easily deleted or blocked by the content scrubbers searching for offensive material.

But none of the copies were more than two weeks old. And the picture seemed to have originated locally, though it had been distributed to some far-flung parts of the world very quickly.

"So, I think I should talk to some of the teachers and kids at the school and see if I can find out some more about it," Kenzie told Zachary over breakfast. "It may be that a few well-placed questions will crack this open, and we will be able to find out who that man was and where the message came from pretty quickly."

Zachary grimaced. "I don't think it will be as quick as you think. Kids aren't necessarily going to want to talk to you. They like their secrets. You're an adult, and not a trusted one."

"But I have to try, right? The only way I'm going to find out who forwarded it to whom is by asking. They still have the choice of whether to answer me or not. But I only need one or two people who will answer my questions."

"One or two people who know something," he clarified.

"Well, yes." Kenzie was slightly deflated. It wouldn't do to have a hundred students telling her they had no idea who the man was or why they had been sent the picture. She needed one or two people who knew what was going on.

"I know the principal over there," Zachary offered.

"At Rhys's school?"

"Yeah."

Kenzie sat up. "That would be great. How do you know him?"

"Her. I talked to her when I was looking for Madison. Principal Lakes. I'm sure she'll cooperate if you mention my name."

"Because you helped Madison?"

"Well, as far as they are concerned, Madison was fatally injured in a shootout on the highway, so I didn't do much to help her. But I also… broke a case regarding Principal Lakes's predecessor."

"*A case regarding* her predecessor?"

"Yeah. It turned out that she was… seeing some of her students socially."

It took a minute for his meaning to sink in. Kenzie's brows rose. "She was a pedophile?"

Zachary nodded.

"And you were the one who figured it out?"

"I can't take all of the credit. It was her husband who figured she was seeing someone behind his back. And the police who made the arrest."

"But you're the one who caught her with a student."

Zachary nodded.

Kenzie vaguely remembered something in the news a couple of years before about a principal dating a student. But she didn't think she had known at the time that Zachary had been the one to break it. It had been early in their relationship. Maybe just around the time she had met him.

"Well, I guess you're in the new principal's good books, then," she agreed. "Unless, of course, she has a similar leaning."

"No," Zachary shook his head quickly, getting red-faced, "She told me why she was having to rebuild everyone's trust after Principal Montgomery was arrested. She would have known better than to do anything like that, even if she did have… leanings." His face got redder still.

"Do you want to come with me, then?" Kenzie offered. "If I talk to the school on Monday, do you want to ride along and break the ice for me?"

He looked proud of himself. And well he should. Principal Lakes had good reason to be impressed with him after he both exposed a pedophile working in the school system and rescued a girl who was being trafficked. She had no way of knowing that Madison's story hadn't ended on the tragic note she thought it had. And she didn't know that Zachary had rescued Luke at the same time. And again, once more since then, had proven that Luke was not guilty of the murder he had been accused of.

Zachary had done a lot of good over the last few years. And maybe he could help Kenzie solve this case, too.

"Sure," Zachary agreed. "I'll make some time for it. Besides, you shouldn't be driving yet, anyway. You'll need someone to take you over there."

"My head is fine." At some point, he would have to let her start driving again. She was going to have to insist. But she needed him at the school, so she would let him drive her one more time before insisting on his letting her return to normal

---

Saturday and Sunday were more relaxing. Now that the deaths at the private psychiatric facility were off of her plate and Rhys was back in the public hospital where he was safe, she could take some time to rest and regenerate. She put in a couple of hours of work on Saturday and nothing on Sunday. She knew she had a slight backlog of bodies to catch up on when she returned to the office. But it would only take her and Dr. Cook a few days. There was nothing too controversial or unexpected. Unless something turned up in the postmortem examinations that gave her cause for concern, she should be able to deal with them quickly enough.

So, Monday morning, she and Zachary headed over to Rhys's school to see what they could find out about the picture's origin. Zachary had messaged the principal over the weekend so that she knew they were coming, though she didn't know any details about what was going on yet.

As expected, Zachary was an angel in her eyes, and she went out of her way to clear her schedule to see them.

Principal Lakes was a young woman. She was the type of young professional that always made Kenzie feel like she had wasted the first part of her life when others, like the principal, were building their careers early, hitting it hard and getting ahead before Kenzie had even figured out what she wanted to do with her life. It wasn't the money. She knew that principals did not make a lot. It was just the feeling that she had been left behind in the dust while the movers and the shakers had taken up their positions.

"Dr. Kirsch, it's very nice to meet you," Principal Lakes greeted, shaking her hand firmly, but not too hard. Just the right professional touch. "Why don't we all have a seat, and you can tell me what you're here about today?"

She gestured to the couch and chairs grouped at the end of her office opposite her desk, where a coffee carafe, mugs, and milk and sugar were waiting.

Principal Lakes gave Zachary a quick hug before letting him sit, making him blush. Kenzie enjoyed his discomfort.

They all sat down and helped themselves to the coffee. Principal Lakes asked Zachary how he was doing, and he answered her questions politely and professionally.

"So." Principal Lakes wrapped her hands around her mug. "What can I help you with today? I guess this has something to do with Rhys?"

Zachary looked at Kenzie, indicating it was time for her to take over.

Kenzie took a deep breath and let it out slowly to calm herself.

9

We found out from Rhys that there is a photograph circulating amongst the students, which is disturbing and impacted him quite significantly."

Principal Lakes shook her head. "Selfies? Nudes? We have talked to students about that before. I thought they were doing very well. But of course, that is from an administrator's perspective, and I don't see everything that happens on their phones. I do try to be aware of it, and we have frequent discussions about what is appropriate or not appropriate to have on their phones."

"No," Kenzie said. "Not selfies." She brought the picture up on her phone and handed it to Principal Lakes. She stared at it, frowning.

"What is this?"

"It appears to be a dead man. A man who was shot."

"This can't be real. It's probably off of some television show or movie."

"I will be very relieved if it turns out to be," Kenzie said. "But it is very realistic. As someone who deals regularly with dead bodies, I can tell you that. I don't believe it is from a movie. I think it is real."

"But where would students get such a thing? I suppose it's off of the internet—some crime scene photo. People have ways of repurposing material and using it to achieve their own goals. Maybe a student thought this looked disgusting and wanted to cause drama and upset people. Or maybe it was originally sent by a student interested in forensics or pathology, like you," Principal Lakes nodded to Kenzie. "It could be quite innocent, initially."

"We would like to figure out where it came from. To trace it back to its origin."

"Do you think that the students have done something criminal here? I don't see how they could be charged for this."

Kenzie thought about Campbell opening it as a phone harassment case. There were certainly things that students could be charged with for forwarding explicit or terroristic material to their friends. Even if they didn't intend any harm. But she wasn't about to tell Principal Lakes that her students could be arrested and charged for what they had unwittingly done.

"We just want to find out where the picture originated, to help us identify who he is and what happened to him."

"And you will not charge any students in this matter."

"I'm not a cop. I'm not charging anyone with anything."

"And you're a private investigator," Lakes looked at Zachary for confirmation. "So you're not laying any charges either."

"No, ma'am."

"Well, this is something that bears looking into." She meditated for a moment, considering the matter. "My first guess would be that it was a picture that someone found online, like I said. If it wasn't that, my next suspects would be the drama club."

Kenzie raised her brows. She had difficulty believing that a group of students could pull off something that looked so realistic with amateur makeup skills. But then, sometimes an amateur job could look more realistic than a professional one. Amateurs had certainly fooled experts with pictures in the past. And a group of dedicated hobbyists might have the ingenuity to pull off something like that. She remembered back when she was in school; students had been using oatmeal and food coloring to make fairly convincing zombies. Who had come up with the idea of oatmeal? Not likely a professional.

"If it was created by a group of kids," Zachary said slowly, "then wouldn't the apparent victim be a kid?"

Principal Lakes looked at him, lips pursed. "They could have talked an adult into being their test subject. We have the auto mechanics students working on people's cars and the hairdressing students cutting hair for other students or adults. It's not unusual to recruit an adult for help with practical application."

Zachary looked unconvinced. "We can talk to the drama club, but I suspect they would have used another student. This guy doesn't look old enough to be someone's parent. If it were a teacher, you would recognize him. They didn't just recruit some random guy off the street."

The principal looked at the photo again, for a bit longer this time, deep frown lines between her brows, clearly trying to figure out if she could identify the "victim."

"If you could let us talk to the drama club kids," Kenzie said, "that would be helpful. And if you could identify who some of Rhys's friends are, so we can talk to them about what they might know about the picture and its origins, that would also be great."

She should have asked Rhys for the names of his friends. That would have sped things up a little. She could just say who she wanted rather than rely on the principal to know who Rhys hung out with the most. But Rhys had been tiring and not as communicative at the end of their discussion. And Kenzie hadn't wanted to ask him anything about the picture in front of Vera. She knew when to keep her mouth shut.

"I can call a few people down to the office to talk to you," Principal Lakes offered slowly. "But this is not an official interview. This is just you, as a friend to Rhys, trying to help him with a personal problem. I don't want there to be any suggestion that the police are involved or that these interviews are being done on their behalf."

Kenzie and Zachary nodded. The police would probably have the very same request. They wouldn't want Kenzie and Zachary holding themselves out as police agents either.

"That's exactly what we want," Kenzie agreed. "We're just doing whatever we can to help Rhys. He's... had a pretty rough time."

"That boy," Lakes sighed. "I only know a little of what he's been through, but I know he's really had a tough life. I wish there was more that we could do to help him."

10

Apparently, drama kids slept in. Principal Lakes only managed to find a couple who had shown up for their morning classes on time. She rolled her eyes and shook her head at Kenzie.

"Free spirits. If I had skipped classes, my parents would have killed me. Or at least grounded me and pulled me out of drama club until I started behaving myself. These kids tend to be very bright. They keep their marks up okay despite missing classes and hanging out to smoke weed or work on their next production. Yes, I know they are smoking. There's not much we can do about it if they are off school property. It isn't like their parents don't know."

Kenzie couldn't imagine how her parents would have reacted if she had thought she could get away with skipping classes and smoking weed. Step one would have been grounding and visits to a therapist to work through her issues. They would probably have blamed it all on the difficulty of dealing with Amanda's condition. Step two, if that failed, would have been to ship her off to some foreign girls' school with strict security. Somewhere they could ensure that she wasn't involved in anything illicit and would not have the chance to escape until she was finished earning her high school diploma.

Walter and Lisa would not have put up with any nonsense. She was sure of that.

The first boy was named Graham. He was a sleepy-eyed youth wearing a knit hat even when he had come in from the cold and had a pair of sunglasses hooked over the collar of his t-shirt. Apparently, he was rebelling against the idea of rebelling by not wearing appropriately warm clothing in the nippy Vermont air. Instead, he was so cool that he could pull off wearing it indoors. Kenzie saw Principal Lakes's eyes take in the hat, consider making a fuss over it, and decide this wasn't a hill she was willing to die on. She just shook her head slightly and introduced Graham to Kenzie, explaining that she had some questions that might help out another student.

Graham gave her a sleepy smile as he sat with her at the table in the small meeting room. It was a nice room, not just a cheap round table and tubular chairs, but a sturdy wooden table, solid rather than laminated particle board, and padded swivel chairs that poofed and squished when Kenzie sat down. Pretty comfortable. Maybe where the principal, her vice principals, and upper-level staff sat down to sort things out with a weekly meeting.

Graham looked Kenzie over, smiling, and ignored Zachary. "So..." he leaned forward, giving her a better look at his acne scars, "how can I help you, beautiful?"

Kenzie laughed. She was a bit old for him. But he was a charmer. "Well, thank you. I'm glad to find you in such a helpful mood. I gather your friends all slept in this morning."

He chuckled. "We had a busy weekend. It's hard to get up Monday morning."

Kenzie didn't want to spend too much time on the preliminaries. She held her phone up for him to look at the picture. "I'm wondering if you know anything about this?"

Graham's eyes took in the body, looking unsurprised. Not shocked that she would have such a thing on her phone. "Yeah. I've seen that. It's not bad, huh? A little putty and corn syrup blood..."

"I'm with the medical examiner's office." Kenzie put the phone down on the table where they could both still see it. "This is not fake."

He shrugged. "You can't tell by looking at a picture."

"Look at the color of his skin. There's no red blood circulating through it."

"A little makeup." He leaned over to look at it more closely. "Probably a green base layer, with natural flesh tone and a little blue mixed together applied on top."

"So, is this your work?"

"Mine?" He sat back again. "No. I didn't do it. I'm just guessing. Telling you how I would have done it. I don't know whose work this is. It's good, but I could do better."

"You said that you had seen it before. Do you know where it came from? Principal Lakes said it was probably something pulled off of the internet. Maybe something from a movie."

He shook his head and chewed on his lip, thinking about it. "I haven't seen it online anywhere. Only being sent around the school. Don't know who did it. But that's not Hollywood."

"Oh?" Kenzie was amused at the assertion. As if he had seen everything that Hollywood had produced. "How do you know that?"

"Look at the asphalt." Graham leaned forward again and zoomed in on a patch of pavement beside the body. "Look at all of those cracks. That's from winter weather. Water getting down into little fissures and freezing and expanding. Pushing it apart. You don't see that in Hollywood. No ice."

"You know your concrete, do you?" Kenzie looked closely at the cracks, wondering if Graham could be right. He certainly made it sound like he knew what he was talking about.

"Asphalt," Graham corrected. "Not concrete."

"What's the difference?"

"Bitumen." He looked into her eyes, serious and engaged. "The sticky black stuff that holds it together. Concrete is different. Like sidewalks." At Kenzie's unspoken question, he sat back again, folding his arms across his chest. "My dad is in road construction. What do you think I do every summer?"

Kenzie laughed. "I see. So you do know your, uh, paving materials."

"Aggregates. Yeah, I do. Someday, if I put my mind to it, I could be the king of concrete," he said in a snobbish tone. He motioned to the phone. "This could all be mine."

She liked the cheeky kid. "How wonderful."

Graham snorted.

"So, where do you think this came from?" Kenzie asked.

He shrugged with one shoulder. "Like I said, Vermont, or somewhere with winter weather. And I don't think it came from TV. The lighting is bad."

"TV can't have bad lighting?"

"No director worth his salt would accept that. You need a second light source. Something to even it out. A fill light and diffusion panel." He cocked his head, considering. "I mean, they could be going for the unfinished look, like in Blair Witch Project, something that is supposed to look amateur. This doesn't look like it was done by a cinematographer."

"Do you think it could be real?"

He cocked his head in the other direction and considered, fiddling with the edge of his hat. "Well, I suppose it could be," he said eventually, grudgingly. "But I don't know. Does that bullet hole look authentic? I would go for something a little bigger. Build up the edges a bit to make it look deeper. This just looks… like it was slapped on."

"Well, I have seen a few real bullet holes in my time."

"And you don't think that's too small?" He peered at it again.

"I think it is a small caliber bullet."

"But it doesn't look like it would do any damage. This guy might still be walking around after being drilled by something like that."

"As long as they have enough penetrating force to get through the front of the skull, it doesn't matter if they come out through the back or not. They do a lot more damage by bouncing around inside."

"Oh." He nodded. "Cool."

Kenzie shook her head. "Not cool. So can you remember when you saw it the first time?"

"Uh…" he stared off into space for a bit. "Say… a couple of weeks, probably. I don't think I could tell you the exact day. But it hasn't been that long."

"And you don't have any idea where it came from? Who sent it to you?"

"I don't remember." He smiled and patted the pocket his phone was in. "And they self-destruct, so don't ask me to look it up for you."

"That's convenient."

"How else are we supposed to defend ourselves against parents and teachers who search our phones? If there's nothing for them to find, there's nothing to get upset about."

"And they won't get upset about a program that deletes a message after it is sent?"

"Teachers don't get upset about it. Parents might, but what are they going to do? Tell you that you can't message with your friends anymore?" He scoffed at this. "They can't stop you. They try, and you pick up a burner. Keep one phone for the 'rents and one for…" He motioned to Kenzie's phone on the table. "Stuff they wouldn't want to see."

"And that keeps everyone happy."

"You got it."

"Who else is in your drama club?"

He raised his brows. "Most of them aren't here right now. Principal can give you the information if she wants to. But I don't know you from Adam." He glanced over at Zachary, who he had been ignoring, but had not forgotten. "Or Eve," he amended.

"Do you know Rhys Salter?"

"Rhys?" He seemed to think about it for a moment. "Oh, the Black kid? Silent Salt? Yeah, I know who he is."

"But you don't know him personally?"

"No. He doesn't hang around with the drama kids." He gave a little laugh. "He could be a mime, I suppose. I'll bet he'd be good at that."

"He can communicate, even if he can't speak."

"Sure." He shrugged. "I know he can. That's why I said he'd be a good mime. But he doesn't run with my crew. Sorry."

"Do you know who would have sent him that picture?"

"One of *his* friends, I guess. Wouldn't make any sense for me or any of the drama geeks to send it. What do *we* know about him? I know we've been in the same school for years, but Rhys doesn't mix much. I don't really know much about him except that…" Graham trailed off. His eyes dropped to the photo on the phone.

Kenzie waited, not offering anything. She glanced at Zachary, who listened with interest but let her take charge of things. She had thought that he would be more involved, but suspected he was holding himself back from participating because Rhys had asked Kenzie to look into it, not him. So far, she thought she was doing a pretty good job of it. And she knew Zachary would help when she asked for it.

Graham scratched the back of his head under the hat, frowning slightly. "Didn't his grandfather get killed?" he asked. "Shot in the head or something!"

Kenzie nodded.

Graham shook his head. "That's messed up. Who would send that to him? That's like… making cripple jokes to an amputee. That's just wrong, man."

"It was pretty upsetting to him," Kenzie agreed. "But we don't know that he was being targeted. The photo was making its rounds through the school, so it isn't like he is the only one who got it."

"Yeah. It was making its way around," Graham agreed. "I got it a few times."

"But it didn't make its way to any social networks or discussion groups?"

"I dunno. Most of us, we don't hang out on the old-people social platforms. We might have accounts there that we post to now and then to keep them happy, but we've got our own places. Private servers. That kind of thing."

"Did any of the other drama kids make it in this morning?"

"A couple. But why are you looking at us? I mean, like I told you, we don't really know Old Salt. Talking to us isn't going to get you very far."

"Principal Lakes thought it was a good starting point. She thought that maybe the drama club had staged the picture. That it was some kind of prank you guys had pulled off. Or a picture you grabbed from the internet to get attention."

"Nah. None of us did that. I would have done a better job of it. Even if that *is* real… I could make something that looked *more* real. And more scary. This guy… he kind of looks soft. He doesn't look like someone who would get shot in the head. You want someone who is a real tough guy. Big and beefy, tattoos, bald. Mouth bleeding. Black eye, or at least a bruise under one of them. More blood. Bigger hole. Better lighting. I could really make it *pop*."

"Okay, I'm convinced," Kenzie said, holding her hands up. "The Concrete King wins."

Graham grinned at her. He stretched and settled his knit cap on his head. "I should probably be getting to class. It isn't like the teachers will hold the lessons for me. And the reason I'm here so early ain't because my parents are happy with my recent performance."

"Well, I appreciate you taking the time to talk to me. It was very… enlightening."

11

Principal Lakes escorted in a boy who seemed too small to be in high school. He had blond hair that was just a little too long to be called short and too short to really be called long. It curved around his face, making it appear more round. He looked about ten years old.

"This is Hugh. He is a friend of Rhys's."

Kenzie nodded to him. She was afraid she might appear too intimidating to the small boy if she stood up to shake his hand or greet him, so she stayed where she was. "Hi, Hugh. Thanks for coming to talk to us."

He looked at Principal Lakes, who gave him a small push of encouragement and then withdrew, pulling the door shut behind her. Hugh looked at the chairs and climbed up into one of them. The big, formal chair made him look even smaller, like a munchkin.

"Hi."

"Hi. I'm Kenzie Kirsch, and I guess Principal Lakes already told you I'm here to help Rhys."

"Don't know how you can help him when he's not here."

"Well, he can't be here right now, but we can. How long have you known Rhys?"

"I don't know. It's been, like, forever," The small boy made a motion to indicate something that had happened far in the past. Amusing, since he seemed like he couldn't have known Rhys for more than a minute. He was *so* young.

"And you guys are pretty good friends?"

"Well… we have some classes together. And sometimes… we eat lunch together. Stuff like that. I mean… it doesn't seem like much. We're just school friends. We don't hang out together outside of that." He rubbed his chin. "My parents don't like me to go anywhere else."

"You never went to Rhys's house?"

"Especially not to Rhys's house. Not when someone had been killed there." He shrugged dramatically. "I know it's silly, because it isn't like there was still a murderer lurking around there, but my folks are a little…"

"Overprotective?"

Kenzie didn't actually think they were being unreasonable. Despite what Hugh said, the murderer had still lived with Rhys for many years. She wasn't there anymore, but it hadn't been a random break-in like the Salters had told everyone. Kenzie didn't think that Hugh would ever have been in any danger there, but Rhys had been exposed to his grandfather's murderer daily, and no one knew what had gone on between them. Had she continued to threaten and terrorize Rhys for all those years? Or had she ignored him and pretended that the murder had never happened?

"Yeah, they're overprotective," Hugh agreed. "I've been sick a lot, and they worry about everything. Thinking that it might put me in danger."

Kenzie was disappointed that Principal Lakes hadn't managed to come up with someone a little bit closer than Hugh, who was "just a school friend."

"So… I guess you're wondering why we want to talk to you. It's about… this." Kenzie displayed the picture on her phone for an instant. She didn't want to leave it on too long and risk traumatizing the boy with something so graphic. His overprotective parents would not be thrilled with her for that.

Hugh's quick eyes caught the picture, cataloged it, and recalled it. His eyes widened.

"What's that?" he asked, pretending not to know.

"You already know what it is. I'm sure everyone around the school has a pretty good idea what it is."

Hugh looked down at the table and then out the window, but not back toward Kenzie's face.

"Some stuff gets forwarded between people, back and forth," he said eventually. "That doesn't mean I saw it or had anything to do with it."

"No. It doesn't. But we're trying to figure out where it came from originally. It's important to figure out what happened and whether this is a legitimate picture."

He rolled his eyes. "It's not real."

"How do you know?"

His eyes flicked back toward Kenzie's phone, which was turned off.

"Never trust anything without a source. It's fake news. It's just some picture someone photoshopped. Not *real*. I told Rhys it wasn't real."

"Did you?"

Hugh nodded. "He was freaking out over it. I told him it was nothing. That he should just delete it and forget about it if it bothered him."

"What did he say to that?"

Hugh crossed his hands in a big X sign, and pushed it away from him. A gesture that Kenzie had seen Rhys make. *No. Definitely not.*

Kenzie nodded, chuckling a little that she could actually see and hear Rhys in her head, telling her no.

"So he didn't think ignoring it was the right thing to do."

"No." Hugh looked at Kenzie as though she were a child that he had tried to explain something elementary to. "Rhys isn't the kind of guy who would look the other way."

"Did that ever get him into trouble?" Zachary inserted.

Kenzie looked at him, surprised, but stayed silent, letting Hugh answer the question.

"Sometimes it did," Hugh admitted. "He'd get smacked around by the bigger guys. Or get in trouble with a teacher for talking back." He shook his head. "Kind of funny, when he hardly ever says a word."

"But he can make himself understood," Zachary said.

"Yeah." Hugh smiled. "He can."

"Who smacked him around?" Kenzie asked.

Hugh looked wary. "Just guys. Rhys took care of himself. Don't mess things up for him."

"How bad was it?"

"They all knew he was kind of a teacher's pet. The staff all felt sorry for 'that poor Salter boy.' So anyone who wanted to rough him up had to be pretty careful. And not go overboard. He fared better than some of us."

He apparently read Kenzie's face and quirked a smile at her. "And yeah, they feel protective of me because I'm so tiny, too, so I don't do so bad."

"Do you think one of those people who beat up on him might have sent him the picture to intentionally upset him?"

Hugh shook his head slowly as he considered it. "No… I don't think any of them are that inventive. Or that bright."

Zachary snickered. Hugh looked at him, spreading his hands wide as he asked the question. "I mean, you know how it is, right? These bullies are either meatheads, or they're these all-stars who are killing it in academics as well as sports, but still never had an original thought. They might be able to answer textbook questions but, as far as coming up with something inventive like torturing Rhys by sending him pictures of dead bodies…?" Hugh shook his head. "No way."

"I thought you didn't believe this was a real dead body," Kenzie said.

"Well… I don't know. I doubt it. Who would be sending out pictures of real dead bodies?"

"Just one, as far as I know. Were there more?"

"No, no. Just that one. But I saw it a few times. It was one of those posts that no matter how many times you slap it down and delete it, people keep forwarding it to you again."

"And Rhys too?" Zachary asked.

"Yeah. I guess. We all did."

"That would be pretty hard to deal with," Zachary reflected. "He couldn't just delete it and forget about it even if he wanted to. Because every time he tried, it just landed in his inbox again."

"And if each time, it causes flashbacks and distress…" Kenzie said. She didn't need Zachary or any psychology textbook to tell her it wasn't going to do much good for his mental health.

"He was getting worse, wasn't he?" Zachary asked Hugh. "Even his grandma knew that he was having more trouble at school. Getting into fights, getting upset with the resource room teacher. They were worried about him before he broke down."

"He probably should have just deleted the app. Or set up a new account," Hugh admitted. "I thought it would stop, or he'd get over it. If I knew he was gonna go off the rails like that..."

"What would you have done?" Kenzie asked.

"I dunno. I'm just a kid," Hugh pointed out. "He should have, like... gone to his therapist. Told his grandma. Gone to someone who could help him. What was *I* supposed to do?"

"I'm not blaming you," Kenzie told him gently. "And he did go to a family friend to try to get help. But maybe he got the picture again before getting there, and it pushed him over the edge."

"Is he okay now?" Hugh asked, his eyes wide. "No one will tell us what's been going on with him, when he'll be home again, or anything."

"He's doing better, but still not ready to go home. It's been pretty difficult for him." She didn't tell him about the residential care facility, about how he had reacted to the drug therapy. It would be up to Rhys how much he wanted to reveal to his friends about what had happened.

"Can we go see him?" Hugh asked. "He came to see me in the hospital before. If I can go and talk to him..."

"I don't know. I'll ask him and his grandmother about putting you on the visitor list, and then I'll let you know. I'm not sure he's ready for more visitors yet. He might need some more time."

Hugh looked down. "It was pretty bad, wasn't it?"

"Yes."

"I should have done something. I should have talked him into seeing someone or called his grandma. She would have helped, if she had known."

"You did what you could by being his friend," Zachary reassured him. "It wasn't your responsibility to push him into treatment. He had to decide that for himself. Or... for this to happen so that they could admit him." Zachary met Kenzie's eyes. "It can be really hard when you're doing everything you can for someone you love, but they're not ready to do what you think they should."

Hugh gave a heartfelt sigh. "You're right about that."

Kenzie nodded her agreement.

12

As Hugh stood up to leave, he paused, looking at Kenzie one more time. "You should talk to Ayla."

Kenzie nodded. "Okay. Who is she? A girlfriend?"

Hugh looked at her, frowning, and shook his head. "Just a friend," he said firmly. "Rhys doesn't have any girlfriends."

Kenzie was not surprised by this. She knew that Rhys was interested in Luke, or at least had been in the past. She didn't know if he was also interested in girls. He had been interested in Madison when she had gone missing, but maybe that had just been friendship. Zachary would have a better idea. It had been his case, nothing to do with her. Other than when she'd had to help him clean things up.

She glanced over at Zachary and decided that it was best not to ask whether Rhys had a boyfriend, or whether he was interested in both genders. She didn't want to disclose anything if he wasn't "out" to Hugh.

"Ayla," Hugh repeated. "You should talk to her."

Principal Lakes confirmed that Ayla was one of the kids she planned to have Kenzie and Zachary talk to and that she was present. She checked the girl's schedule and had her called to the office. In a few minutes, Ayla showed up, a shy Black girl with her hair pulled into a large bun. She looked at Kenzie and Zachary suspiciously, not too keen to talk to them.

"It's about Rhys," Lakes explained to her. "They're trying to help him out. You know that he's… sick in the hospital, right?"

Ayla chewed on her thumbnail. "He's not sick."

"Well, what would you call it, then?" Principal Lakes challenged. "Whether it is physical or emotional, he is not well. He is in the hospital, and Dr. Kirsch and Zachary are trying to help him."

Ayla folded her arms across her chest. Looking thoroughly uncomfortable and blocked off. "I don't know anything. He just didn't come to school one day. And someone said he was in the hospital. That's all I know."

"Could we talk to you for just a few minutes anyway?" Kenzie coaxed. "We won't take too much of your time, and you might know something that can help us."

Kenzie didn't want to discuss the photo in the main office where people could overhear. Once behind closed doors, she could explain it to Ayla and see if she knew anything more than the other kids did about where the photo came from or who had sent it to Rhys.

They all waited. Finally, Ayla rolled her eyes and consented to go into the meeting room to talk to Kenzie and Zachary. Kenzie reintroduced herself and tried to connect with the girl, assuring her that they didn't believe she had done anything wrong. They simply wanted to see if she had any information that could help with Rhys's case.

"I don't know what's going on with Rhys," Ayla said stubbornly. "We're friends, but he didn't tell me personal stuff. Like about his illness or anything. We just hung out together sometimes." She shrugged. "When you're, like, two of the only Black kids in the school, you stick out like a sore thumb. People think that you belong together. I don't think we're that much alike in anything but our skin color. Maybe our grandmas. But I can't tell you what was going on with him before he had his… breakdown."

"Did you notice that something was going on with him? That he was getting in trouble, having fights, distressed about something?"

"Yeah, I know he was fighting. So what?"

"Did you know why? What was going on with him?"

"He was a Black teenager. They get in fights. Especially in a school like this, surrounded by…" She made a surrendering gesture as if she didn't know what to call the other students. "These people."

"White? Privileged? Jerks?" Kenzie offered.

"All of the above. Yeah. So it was unusual, but it wasn't, you know? Everybody is going to blow sooner or later. You can't just… keep dealing with it all the time."

"We think that the reason for Rhys's behavior and the breakdown, was this." Kenzie showed her the picture briefly, as she had with Hugh, turning it off again right away.

"That picture? That was disgusting. I don't know why everyone shared it and acted like it was such a big deal. Why do I want that on my phone?"

"Do you know who was circulating it?"

"Everyone. I got it more than once."

"Who do you think started it? And was it targeted at Rhys?"

"Why would it be…" Ayla trailed off. "Because of his grandpa, you mean? Well, I guess… but it wasn't like they looked anything like each other."

"What do you mean?" Zachary asked.

"I mean, his grandpa was an old Black man. Nothing like this weirdo white guy all gone to seed. They don't look anything alike. Why would it bother Rhys?"

"Because both men were shot in the forehead. We know that it bothered Rhys, gave him flashbacks to his grandfather's murder."

"Yeah?" Ayla looked thoughtful. "I don't know why it would. They don't look anything like each other."

"They don't have to. Flashbacks can be triggered by just one thing. A smell. A color. A bullet in the forehead. It doesn't matter if the rest of the circumstances are the same or not."

"Oh. Okay, then…"

"Do you know who started sending the picture around? Was it the boys who were bullying him? The jocks? One of the kids that he got in a fight with before the breakdown?"

"No, I don't think so. Why would any of them have that? Something like that, it probably came from the losers."

Kenzie raised her brows and blinked.

She shouldn't be surprised. She'd heard enough kids called losers at school. It just surprised her that a minority, someone on the outside, would use the term so casually.

"What losers would that be?"

"Kids who are on their way to dropping out. They're only at school half the time, if that, they're doing drugs or drunk all the time, they're failing, don't have anyone to keep them on the straight and narrow." Ayla shrugged. "The losers."

"Do you have anyone in particular in mind?"

"I don't know them personally," Ayla said. "Why would I hang with that crowd? I don't do drugs. I'm not a loser."

"You must know some of the kids who do. You must have certain kids in mind."

"I don't know them," Ayla insisted. "They hang out back behind the bleachers. Or at the convenience store across the street. Smoking and doing their sh—doing whatever they want. You ask me, those are the kids who started this going around."

"Why them? What makes you think it could be them?" Zachary asked.

"It's just the kind of thing that they would do. Starting rumors, excitement, looking for negative attention. How do I know why? I just know that they are the kind of people who want to disrupt things. To make people feel bad."

Zachary accepted this. Kenzie nodded. At least it was somewhere to start. Maybe Ayla just had an instinct and didn't really know where it came from. Or maybe there was more to it and she had seen the photo being forwarded by members of that group.

"Anyone in particular in that group?" Kenzie prodded.

Ayla opened her mouth to answer, then closed it and shook her head. "I think... no, I don't know. I have no idea. I don't run with that group at all."

"Does Rhys know any of them? Would one of them have sent it to him because they were friends? Or because they thought it would bother him?"

"I don't know." Ayla chewed on her thumbnail again. "He didn't hang out in any of those places. But sometimes... Rhys knew things. He kind of... fades into the background and he hears things. People know he won't repeat anything they say, so they don't worry about him being around."

"So he might have heard something. One of them might have said something around him."

"Maybe. He cared about things, you know? Cares. Like… people who fly under the radar. Who aren't very popular, just living on the edge… That could get him in trouble."

It already had, Kenzie knew. He was the one who had put Zachary on to Madison's case when she had gone missing. Others had brushed it off, but Rhys had not been willing to. And he had pictures on his phone that had been instrumental in figuring out what was going on with her and, eventually, in finding her.

Sometimes, knowing things got people into trouble.

13

Should we see if we can make contact?" Zachary asked Kenzie, making it sound like he was talking about getting in touch with extraterrestrials rather than a group of kids.

"I suppose they won't necessarily cooperate with Principal Lakes in coming to talk to us," Kenzie said, thinking about the dynamics.

"If they're even in the school. It is Monday morning, and that crowd tends not to be early."

"You think we should wander over to the bleachers or the convenience store? See if they're around?"

Kenzie wasn't sure if they would be found at either of those places. If they were hung over after a weekend of partying, they might still be home in bed. She looked at her watch. She had told Dr. Cook that she would be late getting in, but she should try to get to the medical examiner's office before long.

"Chances are, their parents at least got them out of bed and kicked them out of the house this morning," Zachary said, seeming to read her mind. "And they won't be inclined to run this early in the morning."

Kenzie chuckled. "You think they would try to run away from us? I doubt it. We can't exactly make them talk to us. They would know that."

"If someone has a guilty conscience, they're not going to stay around to find out who we are and if we are with the cops."

She conceded the point. But would they think they had anything to be guilty about if all they had done was to forward a creepy picture to a friend? She supposed there were other things that they might be guilty of that she had no idea about.

"Sure. Which do you think is the most likely place to get them?" Zachary had a better insight into their minds than Kenzie. She hadn't exactly been part of the popular cheerleader crowd in high school, but she hadn't been one to hang out with the goth kids smoking out behind the school, either. Zachary had been more on the fringes. Maybe not one of the kids Ayla would classify as a "loser," but not part of any of the clubs or cliques, either.

"Convenience store," Zachary said with certainty. "If they've got coffee…"

Kenzie wouldn't mind getting another coffee herself. It seemed like it had been a long time since her cup at breakfast. "Convenience store it is," she agreed.

They stopped to thank Principal Lakes for her cooperation in their investigation. They didn't tell her that they were going to look for the loser kids to interview them. It was outside of school. They didn't need her permission and she didn't need to know about it.

"I hope it was helpful," Lakes said, looking doubtful about the possibility. "I'll keep my ears open and see if I can find out anything about that photo or who might have started forwarding it around. I wish there was more I could do for Rhys. Will you tell him that I said hello?"

"We'll pass it on," Kenzie agreed. "I'm sure he'd be comforted to know that you were thinking about him."

"I've always been concerned about Rhys and trying to make his school experience positive. You know, as a principal, you tend to attach to certain kids, those who have particular needs. I wish there was more I could do for Rhys."

They said their goodbyes and, rather than walking to Zachary's car, headed across the street toward the convenience store for a cup of coffee.

"My perception of principals as an adult is really different than it was as a kid," Zachary confessed as they walked, pondering what they had heard that morning.

"Yeah? I guess mine is too. They were an authority figure when I was a kid. If you had to go to the principal's office or got singled out for some kind of attention, that was a really bad thing. If a principal had a special interest in you, like Principal Lakes has in Rhys, that would not be seen as a positive thing."

Zachary nodded. "I remember some of the principals I banged heads with… they were really hard cases. Or that's how I saw them. Looking back, I suppose they were just trying to keep order in their school and keep everyone safe. Trying to keep an eye on the troublemaker."

"I'm sure they didn't see you as a troublemaker," Kenzie protested. The Zachary that she knew was a quiet, thoughtful, caring man. He got attached too easily and had problems letting go of the people who had been a part of his life—certainly not a fighter or rabble-rouser.

"Don't kid yourself," Zachary laughed. "A foster kid who had burned the house down and destroyed his family? Big red flag right there. Spent half my time in institutions rather than families. No friends. Impulsive. Couldn't sit still or read or focus on the work. I was every teacher's nightmare. I practically lived in the principal's office at some schools."

"But those things are all misperceptions. You weren't a bad kid. You'd been through some terrible experiences. You had disabilities. If they had focused on helping you instead of seeing you as a bad kid…"

"I'm sure some of them were trying to help me. Probably most of them were. But I didn't see that. I saw them as a threat. Dangerous. Adults who would punish and hurt me." He shook his head. "I don't remember any principals hitting me. Looking back, I can see the compassion. But I couldn't then. Adults were not to be trusted."

They entered the convenience store, filled "to go" cups, and stood in line waiting to pay, not talking, just thinking over what had been said. Kenzie wondered about the "loser" kids. How many of them were struggling like Zachary had, with learning disabilities and early trauma that had put them at odds with the rest of the world? Kids who had not learned to trust and *couldn't* behave the way they were expected to even if they tried.

And why try, when they knew they were bound to fail anyway?

They left the convenience store and stood sipping their coffees, looking around at the various other people coming from and going to the store. Zachary nodded toward a group of kids who were ostensibly waiting for the bus but, since school was in, they obviously should have been heading into the school rather than going anywhere else. They had undoubtedly been told before that they weren't allowed to loiter around the door and the parking lot of the convenience store, so they instead stood around an area where people were expected to stand around. They just weren't actually interested in getting on the bus.

Kenzie nodded in agreement. Zachary led the way, wandering closer to the bus stop, ignoring the kids initially.

The kids quieted and watched them; then, as they decided Kenzie and Zachary were no threat and were just waiting for the bus, their conversations picked up again. Kenzie eavesdropped on their discussions, which were mainly school gossip and celebrity news.

One of the oldest boys kept eyeing them and eventually turned to them, confronting them directly. "Who the hell are you? I haven't seen you around here before. What are you doing, hanging around here and listening in on our conversations?"

Kenzie wasn't sure how to respond. Deny that she was listening? Suggest she had just as much right to be there as anyone else?

Zachary's response was to pull his coat closer, as if he were cold, and to look around him suspiciously. That immediately had the kids checking for other watchers as well. They drew closer together and the boy's voice dropped lower and quieter.

"Never seen you here before," he repeated.

Zachary nodded. He looked around again, very obviously. He nodded at the school across the street. "You guys attend there?"

"Depends what you mean by attend," one of the girls said. She had dyed black hair and several nose rings and other piercings.

The other kids laughed appreciatively at her response.

"Young guy I know goes there," Zachary said. "Sometimes," he added, tilting his head toward the girl to refer to her joke.

They chuckled at this. "Who?" the boy who had confronted them asked. "And why would you be talking to us about it? You some kind of pedo?"

"Rhys."

Kenzie expected him to use Rhys's full name and explain why they were there, but Zachary didn't. He was spare with his words, which seemed to keep the kids on the hook rather than immediately running him off because they didn't like extra observers around.

"Rhys," the boy repeated, looking at Zachary. "Skinny Black kid?"

Zachary nodded. "Doesn't talk a lot," he contributed.

This brought an explosive laugh from the boy and snickers from the other kids. "Doesn't talk a lot!" the boy repeated loudly. "Kid never says a word!"

Zachary nodded his agreement.

The laughter died down, and they waited for him to say why he was there, listening to them, talking to them, but he didn't offer any further explanation. The kids stood around looking at each other, asking questions with their eyes until the leader again pursued it with Zachary.

"Rhys ain't been around lately. I heard he was sick."

Zachary nodded his agreement. He shifted, sliding his hand out of his pocket with his phone. They watched him warily, but phones were normal. Phones were not guns or something sinister. They all had phones practically grafted into their hands. Zachary had the picture ready. He turned the phone screen on, flashed the picture of the dead man, and turned it off again.

The students shifted and looked at each other uncomfortably. Zachary slid the phone back into his pocket.

"Anyone else seen that? I'm guessing you have. I'm guessing it's been on all of your phones sometime in the last couple of weeks."

There were nods and shrugs, no one admitting it directly or offering any more information, but no one denying it.

"Who's she?" one of the girls asked, indicating Kenzie.

"She's a friend of Rhys's, too," Zachary informed them. "He asked her for help."

"What kinda help? We don't know the guy. Sure, we seen him around the school, but that isn't the same as knowing him. None of us can help you. Or her. Or Rhys."

14

That picture's been going around for a couple of weeks," Zachary said. "The same as Rhys has been away for a couple of weeks."

"You saying that one has something to do with the other?" another of the boys demanded. He was shorter than the others, but still taller than Zachary. He was heavyset and powerful-looking. Someone who lifted weights or did other heavy work. He could mash either one of them without a second thought.

Zachary nodded. He sipped his coffee. His brief answers and silences seemed to get to the group, who wanted to know what he was all about and why he was talking to them. There were more comments being tossed back and forth between them as they tried to figure out what was going on with this strange man and woman who came to ask them questions and then didn't ask questions or give any information.

Zachary looked around again. "This probably isn't the best place to talk."

"This is fine. Ain't no one here but us and you."

"They might have…" Zachary bent over as if to look under the bus bench and then around him again. Acting paranoid. Kenzie had seen him paranoid before, really paranoid, and recognized that this was just an act.

"What? Bugged our bus stop? Come on, man. I heard that Salter was in the psych ward. Is that where you came from? You some loony tune that he talked into helping him with some crazy mission? This is safe. This is our place, and no one has bugged it."

"That's some kind of crazy, man," another boy contributed.

"This guy," Zachary tapped the phone in his pocket. "You ever seen him before? You know who he is?"

There were head shakes around the group. They were elbowing each other now. Making quiet and not-so-quiet jokes about Zachary's sanity. About him coming there on some mission for some crazy kid about some unknown guy no one had ever seen before, who got himself shot in the head.

"It's a picture," the young man who had initially confronted them said with exasperation. "Just a picture of some dead dude."

"Some *really* dead dude."

He shook his head, "You're either dead or not dead. You don't get any deader."

"No, I mean… not fake dead. Not a costume or a prank. Not makeup or Photoshop. Actually dead dead."

Until now, everybody immediately protested that the photo was fake, but the young man was the exception.

"Yeah, probably. Looks dead enough for me. So what? Why do you care?"

"Rhys."

"Why does Rhys care? I mean, really. Unless he's the one who killed him, why give it a second thought? It's some stranger, right? No one knows. It's a shocking picture. That's why you send it around. No way to tell who the guy is or what happened to him, so you make up a story. How you knew the guy or saw him after he was whacked. Or he's your cousin or something. You tell everyone you saw the guy. The dead dude. You touched him or you took his picture."

"But the picture has already been circulating around the school, so people know it wasn't you," Zachary countered.

"They don't know. Not if they don't know where it came from first."

"So that's it? You just send it around so that you can brag that you know the guy or saw it happen? No one will believe you."

"Doesn't matter if they believe it or not. It's just something to do."

"So you don't know him. You don't really know anything. All you got is a picture."

The boy nodded his agreement. "Yeah. You got it. All I got is a picture. I don't know this dude. I don't care what happened to him. It's just like... a meme. Something to share."

"Do you know who shared it first? Who started it going around the school?"

"Could be Rhys himself. How do I know?"

"You didn't start it. Do you know who sent it to you?"

The kids looked back and forth at each other. There had been a temperature shift. Kenzie found it hard to define, but something had happened. They had gone from laughing at Zachary and his paranoia and being unconcerned about the two strangers who had shown up in their territory, to suddenly guarded, wanting to get them out of there. And Kenzie had no idea what had changed.

"Look," a girl said. She was medium height, a little heavy, with straight brown hair and a wide, flat nose. She wore a t-shirt with a jacket, and jeans with a red bandana tied around the thigh. "You should stay out of stuff that isn't any of your business. This guy, whoever killed him, he wouldn't want you poking your nose into it and asking a lot of questions. You should just stay out of it; forget you ever saw anything. Tell Rhys to forget he ever saw anything." Her dark eyes were serious. "You don't want to get involved."

Kenzie breathed in slowly and let her breath out again. Did they know? It was the first sign that someone knew something about what was actually going on. Where the photo had come from, who it was. There wouldn't be any danger from an anonymous person. From someone killed on the other side of the world months or years ago. There would only be danger if it were current and local.

"It actually is my business," she said, venturing to speak for herself to these teens at last. "I am with the medical examiner's office, and poking my nose into suspicious deaths is exactly what I do."

The girl stared at her, mouth hanging open in shock for a minute before she realized and closed it.

"If you know something about who this is and what happened to him, I want to know about it," Kenzie said. "If you know where that picture was taken... who it was that started circulating it... those are things I need to know about."

"You're like those CSI folks?" the boy asked, speaking over the dark-haired girl before she could respond. "You collect and run all that evidence from the crime scene!"

"No, most of that has usually been done by the time I get the body. Sometimes, I'm at the scene before the crime scene techs, examine the body, and release the crime scene to them. But usually, I'm at the medical examiner's office and do post-mortem examinations when they are brought in."

"Cool." He seemed impressed by this. "Anyone who works with dead bodies is chill in my books."

"She *has* to keep chill," Zachary told him. "Have you ever been in the morgue? It's like working in a meat locker."

The boy snorted, then covered his mouth, hiding an unexpected smile. "Dude."

Kenzie rolled her eyes. She was used to Zachary's terrible jokes about the morgue and the bodies she worked on.

"Look," she addressed the group of youth in a confidential tone, leaning forward. The others drew in closer, whether intentionally or unconsciously drawn in by her tone. "I don't know who might actually know something about this body—who he is, where he came from, what happened to him—but if you do know something, you can reach me through the medical examiner's office. I'd really like to know what you know." She kept her hands out of her pockets and didn't pull out any business cards for them. They wouldn't take them, and if they did, they would just throw them away the minute she walked away. But they were internet savvy; they could certainly find the number for the medical examiner's office with a quick search.

The teens looked at each other, and no one offered anything. They were circling the wagons, drawing closer to each other to protect anyone who might be vulnerable. They knew something; Kenzie was sure of that now. But she wasn't going to get it out of them, and certainly, they wouldn't give it up to the police if they ever became involved.

Zachary touched Kenzie on the shoulder and made a small shuffling motion to indicate they were done and it was time to leave. Kenzie nodded. She looked at the kids again, meeting as many of their eyes as she could, and then followed Zachary's lead to walk away from them.

15

They know something," Kenzie told Zachary as they got into the car and prepared to head over to the medical examiner's office.

"Yeah," he agreed. He looked solemn and thoughtful.

"Do you think they know who the guy is? Or just where the photo came from?"

"I don't know." Zachary shook his head slowly as he considered. "It was hard to get a good read on everyone at the same time. Very cautious… but I don't know who they are protecting, or why."

"What changed?"

"What changed?" Zachary repeated, frowning.

"Something changed there near the end. Before they decided to shut us out."

"Mmm." He nodded his agreement. "I think that maybe, up until then, they didn't realize that someone in the group was involved. I don't think it was until then that they all realized it was anything but a meme being forwarded around because they thought it was something cool. But then… they suddenly realized that someone knew something or was involved somehow. And then they wanted us out."

Kenzie nodded. It made sense to her. She just wished she had been quick enough to catch the shift and see who had known something. She hoped that whichever one it was would call or email her at the medical examiner's office, but she expected that was probably a lost cause. Zachary had already spoken his thoughts earlier. He hadn't trusted any adults. Those teens sharing with each other out by the bus stop would never trust an adult—certainly not a stranger who had never done anything for them.

Kenzie was at her desk working through her email filing and responses when Dr. Wiltshire called. She looked at the Caller ID and picked it up, glad for the chance to talk to him. She had Dr. Cook there as a substitute to help provide Kenzie with any extra manpower she needed when Dr. Wiltshire was on disability leave, waiting for his broken hand to heal. But there were some things that the young, handsome substitute just could not help Kenzie with.

"Doctor," she greeted cheerfully. "How are you doing?"

"Healing slowly. You should see all the lovely colors it has been turning to."

Kenzie could well imagine. The external fixator device holding Dr. Wiltshire's bones in place while they knit together left his hand much more visible than a regular cast would have, so she had been able to see, each time he came in, the black and blue bruises, gradually turning to green and yellow. A little more gruesome than the leaves changing color on the trees, marking the passing of the year, but just as colorful.

"And how is the pain? And your head?"

"Getting gradually better," he said,. "As I need to take fewer painkillers, the brain fog is clearing, leaving me with more workable time. I know it will be a while before my hand is healed enough to work, but I am glad to at least be getting my brain back."

"Yeah." Kenzie was sympathetic to Dr. Wiltshire's plight. At least when she wasn't inconvenienced by his absence. Those times when she needed him to be there for her, she could get quite irritable about the lengthy waiting process for herself rather than him. "Before we get into anything else, I'm wondering if you remember a case from some years back…"

"With this head, I can't promise you anything. But… tell me what you can, and I'll try to remember."

"It was a man who was shot in the head during a supposed burglary. He died instantly and the case was closed."

Dr. Wiltshire didn't volunteer anything, so Kenzie kept going, trying to give him enough information that he would remember it, without tainting his memories.

"An older man, Black, right in the forehead. Sitting at his dinner table."

"Ahh," Dr. Wiltshire's voice held promise. "Yes, yes. I do remember that one. Felt bad for the family. No one was expecting such a thing. It was a good neighborhood. Quiet town. Home invasions simply aren't our speed here."

"But it wasn't a home invasion."

"Not as we have come to define them, no. The police thought that the homeowner and burglars had startled each other. He didn't know there was anyone in the house, so he was just sitting at his table eating. And they didn't think he was home so, when they saw him, they were taken off guard and reacted reflexively. They probably wouldn't have done it if they had been thinking things through. They could have just left again without being caught."

"It turned out it wasn't a robbery," Kenzie said. "It was just staged to look that way. As it turned out, it was actually his daughter who did it. You reopened *her* death when Zachary got involved in it."

"Salter," Dr. Wiltshire recalled.

"That's right."

"The daughter did it? Was that proven?"

"The family admitted to covering it up but, by that time, the daughter was dead, so there wasn't really any point in gathering the evidence to prove it."

"So… why are you asking me about this case now? What bearing does that have on anything? If he was murdered, and the murderer is dead, why are you bringing it up now?"

"There was a grandson, a witness to the murder."

"The son of the woman who killed him?"

"No. Grandson through another daughter."

"Okay. I seem to remember something about that when the Salter woman's case was reopened. He was missing, wasn't he?"

"They both were, for a while. So… he's having some trouble now."

"Is it any wonder?"

Kenzie gave a little laugh. "No. This is just my roundabout way of saying… there has been another death. Apparently unrelated. But he was a… witness of sorts. Saw a picture of it, and it triggered a breakdown. Because… on the surface, it was the same as his grandfather's death."

"Shot."

"Yes. Same type of thing. Execution style. Shot to the head."

"And you are asking, in your roundabout way, about the previous murder because…"

"I'm wondering… what you remember about it. Trying to figure out if there are any other connections that I have missed, aside from it being a shot to the head."

"Do you expect there to be?"

"No. I don't think that one had anything to do with the other. It's just that… I think I should know all of the similarities between the two if I am going to help Rhys to work through it."

"I see. Well, I'm afraid I don't remember much more than we have already discussed."

"Was there anything unusual about the death? Anything notable about the face? I'm grasping at straws here… there probably isn't anything else that ties the two together."

"Any similarities between the victims? An older Black man?"

"Uh, no. Young white man. In the street, not in his house. I haven't looked at the pictures of Clarence, but I don't imagine there are a lot of similarities between them physically."

"Pictures should still be on the system. You should be able to access the old autopsy file still. It was ten years ago, but we're still on the same system."

Kenzie hadn't even thought to look. She had just thought about the physical box being shoved away in a warehouse somewhere, along with rows and rows of similar packages. It hadn't even occurred to her that it would still be on the computer.

"Oh, that's great. I'll look it up." Kenzie was already tapping the keys to bring it up on a search for Clarence Salter. There was an immediate hit. Kenzie clicked on it and immediately saw the main picture on the file, a headshot of Clarence in death. Lying on the autopsy table. Small caliber bullet through the forehead. While the victims looked nothing alike, the similarities between the mode of death were striking. It was not surprising that Rhys had been so upset by receiving the photo of the unknown dead man.

And had received it over and over again, several times. It must have seemed like a nightmare, having that image show up on his phone repeatedly, triggering flashback after flashback.

"Poor Rhys," she murmured.

"You found it?" Dr. Wiltshire asked.

"Yeah. Thanks. I'll read through the file and see if there were any other similarities between them."

"Who is the second victim?"

"We don't actually know who he is yet."

"A John Doe?"

"I can't even open a case yet. We don't have the body. Just a picture."

"Well, you can't autopsy that."

"No," Kenzie agreed. "Dr. Cook and I went over as much as we could… but you really can't tell very much from the photo."

16

Kenzie looked up at the sound of footsteps approaching down the long, tiled hallway from the elevator. From the man's bearing, he was a cop, maybe with military training, so she was not concerned by his approach. She nodded when he reached her.

"How can I help you?"

He was not in uniform. A plain-faced young man. They seemed to be putting them through the academy younger and younger, the older she got. There had been a time when all policemen were older than she was. But that time was long past.

"I'm Detective Saul, ma'am," he introduced himself, holding out a large hand to shake.

Kenzie stood up so that he wasn't towering over her and shook his hand briefly. "Detective." He was young to have achieved that title already. "Good for you. What can I do for you?"

"Well, actually, I'm here to report to you. Sergeant Campbell brought me in on the phone harassment case. And I thought I would fill you in on what we have discovered so far."

It took just a split second for Kenzie to remember that the phone harassment case was actually Rhys Salter's dead guy photo. She nodded her head eagerly.

"I'm glad that he's got someone looking into it. I don't suppose... that you've been able to find much out." No one at the school had mentioned anything about being contacted by the cops, so she had wondered whether they even had anyone looking into it and making inquiries, or if the new file was only populated with the details she had provided him. The picture, Rhys's phone, and Rhys's name and details.

"Not much we can do," Detective Saul acknowledged. "Not insofar as actually finding a body, which I gather from Campbell is what you are hoping for."

Kenzie shrugged. "No geo coordinates, unfortunately."

"No," he agreed with a slight frown. "Nothing like that."

"And no real clues in the picture. Other than the asphalt he is laying on, which I am told is consistent with Vermont asphalt, not Hollywood asphalt."

His brows climbed his forehead. "You have an asphalt expert on staff?"

"Just a consultant," Kenzie said with a laugh.

"We have been trying to track the progress of the photograph through the various platforms or programs it was transferred through since it first appeared in the school."

"Have you had much luck with that?"

"Unfortunately, the most popular messaging apps that teens use are the ones that delete the message and any attachments after they are read."

Kenzie nodded. "Which makes it kind of hard to track what hands— or phones—it has gone through."

"Exactly. I am told there aren't any signs of it before it started circulating through the school. Which means that it likely originated with someone at the school."

"You mean that one of them *took* the picture?"

Up until that point, Kenzie had been assuming that someone at the school had received it from someone outside of the school and then circulated it to his friends. She hadn't considered the possibility that it had actually been taken by one of the students.

"We don't know for sure. In fact, we can't even be sure that it was a real picture and not something created in a graphics program. But... it is a possibility that it is, in fact, a local death, and was taken by a student."

"Do you... know who that might be? Who started circulating it?"

She thought about the kids at the bus stop. Protecting each other. Protecting the person who had taken the picture. Had the person who took the picture been the killer? It seemed unlikely that anyone else would just happen to stumble over a body and take a picture of it. And start circulating it to their friends or other students. On the other hand, why would they kill someone and then start circulating the picture to their friends? That didn't make much more sense.

Kenzie supposed that such things did happen. People were arrested all the time for a crime that they had committed and posted about in an online public forum.

Saul looked at her, his eyes discerning. "Do *you* know who it might be?"

"No... we talked to some of the kids this morning, but I don't know... if any of them took it, or why they would."

"If I could get their names from you, I can talk to them and push a little more. See what I can find out."

"I don't actually know any names. They were just standing at the bus stop."

"You didn't get any names when you knew that they might know something?"

"Well, no. I didn't find anything concrete. I'm hoping one of them will come forward about what they know, but... I don't know how likely that is."

"Not very likely without any names."

"They didn't tell me anything. I just got a feeling they knew something about where the picture had come from."

Saul looked at her, his lips pressed tightly together in a thin, straight line. Clearly, not impressed with her investigative efforts. "Well... that's too bad. I hope we'll be able to track down the photo's origin. If it is legitimate. Sometimes, these things are just pranks, you know. Kids trying to get people upset or to get attention."

"I don't get that feeling in this case. I mean... if they wanted attention for it, wouldn't they be talking about it instead of covering it up?"

"Maybe. But they might only be looking for attention from a certain person or small group. They might not have intended it to get out to the public."

Kenzie supposed that was true.

"If you find anything out, be sure to give me a call," Saul told her. He took out a business card and snapped it down onto her desk. "That's my direct line. If there is *anything* on this case, give me a call to talk it over. We want to be kept in the loop. In fact, you should not be investigating it yourself. Leave that to us. You stick to bodies."

"If I had his body, I would."

Saul chuckled. "Leave it to us. If these pictures are of someone who was really killed, we'll figure it out soon enough. I'm sure you have enough other cases on your plate already. Or rather, on your table." He laughed at his joke.

Kenzie nodded. As soon as she finished her computer work, she had a couple of bodies to roll out and start working on.

"All right." Saul smiled. "Be sure to call me if you hear anything from your contacts." He patted her desk before walking away.

17

Kenzie worked late, since she had missed so much of the morning following up with the interviews at the school. When she got home, it was long past dinner time. Zachary had already warmed up a microwave dinner and Kenzie had settled for a sandwich from the vending machine down the hall. Kenzie showered off the sweat and stresses of the day and settled down on the couch to at least have some relaxed time with Zachary. Kenzie wasn't in any mood for discussion. She was ready to skip straight to mindless TV drivel.

When Kenzie's phone vibrated, she wanted to ignore it but knew she could not. She needed to at least make sure it was not a call-out to a scene of death that she had to attend. She pulled it out of her pocket to look at the screen and sighed.

Not a call out. But not a call that she could ignore, either. Lisa Cole Kirsch. Kenzie rolled her eyes at Zachary and swiped to answer the call.

"Hi, Mom."

"MacKenzie. It's nice to hear your voice, dear. It's been a little while since we last spoke."

"Yeah, sorry about that," Kenzie lied. "I've been busy."

"You have to be careful not to get too wrapped up in your work. That is a challenge your father has always had. He gets so embroiled in his work that he forgets to spend time with loved ones."

"I know. We've talked about that before. He and I. That's one of the dangers of doing the work you love. You get so into the work that you forget to balance it out with other things."

"Exactly," Lisa agreed. "And I don't want to see that happen to you and for you and Zachary to grow apart."

"Well, right now, I'm sitting in front of the TV with him, getting ready to watch a movie."

"Watching a movie is not exactly a relationship-building activity," Lisa's voice was disapproving. "You need to do something other than sit in front of the TV together. You need to talk with each other. Go out places. Don't fall into the trap of thinking that TV is all you need to be entertained and have a happy relationship."

"I know that, Mom. We do other things. But today has been a long day. We were out together this morning. Tonight, I just need to unwind and have some time *not* to think of anything."

"Of course. I'm sorry, I shouldn't be interfering."

Kenzie hated it when her parents interfered or asked personal questions, and then said they shouldn't, still expecting her to answer their questions despite the apologies.

"How *are* you and Dad?" Kenzie asked, turning the conversation to her mother instead.

"Oh, well, the same as usual, I suppose. We are both busy with our own things. He will be coming to dinner next Sunday, if you would like to join us…"

Kenzie cleared her throat and thought about her schedule. "Usually, Zachary and I like to see the Petersons on a Sunday if we have the time. Not every week, but we haven't been there for a few because of the cases I have been working. It's a lot harder right now with Dr. Wiltshire being away."

"I thought that you had someone subbing in now."

"I do… but with Dr. Wiltshire, he did stuff independently and had me fill in where he needed to. With Dr. Cook, it's sort of the other way around. I do everything I can, and he fills in on the stuff I can't get to. And I don't really give him the run of the office. I know that technically, if he's subbing for Dr. Wiltshire, he is my superior. But really, it is my office, my responsibility, and I want to make sure that he doesn't… mess anything up."

"Good thing you are not a control freak," Lisa teased.

"I know, I know. I need to let him do more and trust him to get stuff done the right way, even if it means giving up control. But…" She trailed off.

"So, dinner on Sunday…?"

"I'll have to see."

"I think we should at least get equal time with Zachary's parents. It's the first time that I've asked you to dinner. We want to get to know Zachary better and to spend some quality time with our daughter."

Secretly, Kenzie was still mad at her parents for interfering with Rhys's treatment plan and not informing her. She didn't want to meet with them or to spend some nice social time together. She didn't even want to talk on the phone with them. It was an effort to act as if nothing had happened and be civil.

"I hear what you're saying," she said neutrally. "But it will depend on what other commitments we have made. I'll get back to you."

"MacKenzie…"

It wasn't a whine, but the tentative beginning of something else. And Kenzie didn't want to talk to her about something else. She wanted to hang up now and watch the movie with Zachary. He was watching her with a concerned expression, wondering what was happening.

"What, Mother?"

"I'm sorry… for that business with your young friend. You know that my intentions were good. We just happened to pick a program that did not work for him. We had no way of knowing that he would react to the drug. You do see that, don't you?"

"You should have talked to me about it."

"I couldn't when you might have a conflict of interest. We wanted to help you and your friend with something he needed, to surprise you later when you were no longer working on any cases at that facility. We thought it lined up perfectly and would be a real help for Rhys."

"Well, it wasn't, and I would have told you that if you had bothered to ask. But you didn't. You just went in there anonymously, interfered with the treatment of someone we love, and ended up causing harm that I could have warned you about if you had asked me instead of going off on your own and thinking you knew what was best for him! You're not a doctor."

Lisa was silent.

"I'm sorry, Mom," Kenzie realized as she said it that she was doing just what she had just observed that her parents did, apologizing for something she was not sorry about. "I know that I'm probably being unfair to you. But what you did caused real damage. And could have killed him. Saying that your intentions were good is… just not good enough."

"No," Lisa agreed quietly. "We should have done our due diligence. And maybe we should have waited until you had cleared your cases there and could go over a treatment plan with you. But it sounded so good, and you said that his condition was serious and that he needed treatment as soon as possible."

Kenzie held her tongue. They would just keep going around in circles over the same material again and again. There was no point in rehashing it when both had a valid argument. Kenzie was convinced she was right and Lisa should not have interfered.

"I'll let you know about Sunday," she told Lisa firmly.

"Thank you. I would appreciate knowing as soon as you are able to decide."

"Have a good night. We'll talk later."

Kenzie didn't wait to see if Lisa would terminate the call and pressed the red button to end it herself.

Zachary's finger hovered over the remote, not starting the movie. "What was that about? Your mother wants us to come for dinner?"

"Yes. She thinks she ought to get equal time with Lorne and Pat. That we should split between them instead of always going to the Petersons'."

"Well, she might have a point there," Zachary conceded. "I don't want to neglect your mom and dad and your relationship with them. I've said before that we should spend time with them if we can. But I didn't think she was really interested in things like family dinner."

"She's not. She's never suggested it until now. So why should I be concerned with giving her equal time? Your family has spent much more time and effort getting to know us. My parents are always occupied with their own social events."

"If they're opening up to other possibilities now, then maybe we should take it onboard and try to give them some time too."

"We had to leave right in the middle of Pat's breakfast last time. We need to make that up to him. That's more important than dropping everything and running because my mom decided to play hostess and invite us over for once."

"Maybe you could offer a different date instead? The next weekend? Or give us a weekend at home and then see if she's available the following weekend?"

"Yeah. Maybe something like that. I'm just not inclined to jump through hoops for her. She said that Dad is coming this Sunday. That's why she wanted all of us."

"Maybe he could come in a couple of weeks."

"Yeah. I agree. If it's that important to them, they should be making some effort to work with our schedule, not force us to theirs. To hers."

"I don't know if anyone is trying to *force* anything."

Kenzie sighed. "You have your parental issues, and I have mine."

He smiled at that. Kenzie knew that her parental issues were minor compared to his. The abuse, neglect, and abandonment he had been through made her arguments with her parents occasionally stepping on her toes seem small and petty. She should be happy that she still had parents in her life. That they were good people at their core. That she could rely on them.

"Maybe you should bring it up with Dr. Boyle at couple's therapy," Zachary suggested.

"I think I need a whole different therapist to deal with all of that," she joked.

"Well, you could, you know," Zachary pointed out seriously.

"Yeah. I know. But I really don't think it's anything I need therapy for. It's just normal parent-child dynamics and me trying to assert my independence while they're trying to keep me a dependent child."

Zachary shrugged, backing off of it. He knew what it was like to have someone pushing therapy at him when he wasn't ready for it or didn't think it was necessary. She had been on the other side of the table enough times to recognize that he was trying to be helpful in his suggestion, not to irritate or tease her. But it wasn't something that she needed. She could handle her parents without a third party mediating.

18

Kenzie noted the police department transfer number on the caller ID of her desk phone and pressed the button to take the call. The dispatcher greeted her warmly.

"Looks like we've got a body dump for you, Dr. Kirsch."

"Well, things have been pretty quiet around here. I guess we needed a little excitement. What are the details?"

"Body found in a dumpster." The dispatcher gave her the location details. "From the sounds of it, this one is pretty ripe. You'll want a mask."

"Ripe because of what else is in the dumpster or ripe because of decomp?"

"Decomp. The reporting LEO said that it was not a fresh kill. And there were… certain familiar noises in the background of the call indicating that it was not a particularly pleasant scene."

Kenzie chuckled. Few death scenes were pleasant. And even fewer dump sites. It sounded like at least one of the law enforcement officers at the scene had lost his lunch over it. As the dispatcher had suggested, Kenzie had better make sure she had all of her gear with her, including a mask. It wouldn't completely block the smell, but it would help a little. Once the body was in the morgue, she could turn on the big exhaust fans that would clear most of the decomp smell while she was working. The rest she would get used to, as she always did.

She put in a call to Carlos to let him know she would need help with transportation. He promised to have the van ready to go in fifteen minutes. She texted George to tell him that she would need him to help in autopsy and also gave him a heads-up about the state of the body. She looked over the remaining emails and paperwork she had to deal with, and decided none of it took precedence over the new body. She locked her computer, tidied her desk, and went to Dr. Cook's office to talk to him.

She knocked on his open door and entered the room, not speaking until she was sure he was not on his phone. It was difficult to tell, sometimes, with his Bluetooth earpiece.

"I've got a call-out," she told him. "Something ripe that will need to be handled fairly quickly. Are you free this afternoon?"

"Oh, yes, please."

Kenzie laughed. "Just what you were hoping for, right? I'll let you know more when I see the scene. Dispatcher said it was a dump, so I'm not sure how much we will know about the cause of death or the actual scene of death."

"If we're lucky, maybe it was a bum who smelled particularly rancid even before he died."

Kenzie grinned. She waved at him and left to deal with the new victim.

Zachary had finally relented and let Kenzie drive herself in her own car, deciding that she was well enough and not dealing with any more concussion symptoms. So, rather than waiting for Carlos, she headed to the dump site ahead of him. Roxboro was not the big city and it did not take long to get there. It was obvious she had arrived at the right place from the police vehicles with flashing lights left on and the yellow tape strung around the scene.

She parked her car well away from the other vehicles, not wanting it to get scratched or clipped with their coming and going. Carlos would need room to drive the ME's van up. She got out of the car and locked it securely behind her. One of the uniformed officers on crowd control stopped her as she walked up to the tape.

"Crime scene, ma'am. You'll have to wait—"

"ME's office," Kenzie told him, pulling out her ID and showing it to him.

"Oh." He looked at her for a minute as if he couldn't quite believe it.

Probably because of the little red convertible. Most MEs didn't ride around town in something so flashy. But Kenzie would get as much use as she could out of it before winter hit full force, making it impractical for longer trips. She could still use it for the short drives to and from the office, but for anything that was too far, it wasn't easy to keep the car warm enough for comfort during the winter months.

"So…?" Kenzie motioned to the dump site.

The officer nodded. "Oh, yeah. Go ahead."

He lifted the tape for her to duck under. Kenzie stopped at the edge of the perimeter to pull on coveralls, put booties on over top of her shoes, a hair net and cap over her curls, and gloves. Ready to go, she picked up her bag and headed for the knot of people surrounding the dumpster and chatting with each other.

"Dr. Kirsch," one of the figures turned to her and she could make out the shape of Detective Cameron under the protective gear.

"I would shake," Kenzie offered, then shrugged. She obviously couldn't touch him and not contaminate anything. "What have you got for me?"

"I'm not sure how much they've told you, but this one is pretty nasty. Been here a while. I guess this bin doesn't get checked very often. I don't know how often it is supposed to be collected, but it looks like it's been a few weeks, at least."

"Pleasant."

Kenzie walked over to the dumpster. A step stool had been set up so she could get up to the right level to look down at the pile of rotting trash and a putrefying corpse that, as the others had already said, had been there for an extended time.

She looked at the longish blond hair, the size and shape of him, and the damage to the middle of his forehead. She felt suddenly dizzy and unstable on the top step of the stool and held on to the edge of the dumpster, contaminating her gloves. Detective Cameron was at her elbow and guided her back down the steps.

"You okay, Dr. Kirsch?"

Kenzie stood there, frozen, for a few seconds, reviewing everything in her mind. She had not been expecting to find him there. And yet, she had. She had been waiting for him to show up.

She stripped off her gloves, unzipped her coveralls, and reached deep into her pocket to pull out her phone.

"You get a call?"

Kenzie shook her head. She woke and unlocked her phone, then tapped through her photos until she found the one she wanted. She turned the phone around and showed it to Cameron. He stared.

"You think that's the same guy?"

Kenzie nodded. "Looks like it to me."

Cameron took the phone from her and walked up the step stool without touching anything to steady himself. He held the phone out in front of him and looked down at the corpse, viewing the images side by side. He nodded and stepped back down to hand Kenzie her phone.

"There you are. Yup. I'd say we've got your man. But how exactly did you have his picture before getting here? And who is he?"

"I don't have a name for him yet. Maybe now that we have fingerprints, we can get an ID."

"And you already have his picture because…"

"Because it's been circulating the local high school for the past few weeks."

"Ah. And someone contacted you to determine whether it was a real body or a hoax."

"More or less," Kenzie agreed. "I'm glad he finally showed up. While he was still identifiable as being the same person."

"Well, I'd never be able to tell by the face, but the hair and clothing are the same and the bullet hole is in the right place."

Kenzie nodded. She took a deep breath and headed back toward the dumpster, doing up her coveralls and pulling out a fresh pair of gloves.

"You okay to go up there again?" Cameron asked solicitously.

"Sure, I'm fine. It just gave me a turn when I saw him and realized who it was. That's all."

He nodded understandingly. "I can see why that would be a little startling!"

The second time looking down at the John Doe who had finally surfaced, Kenzie was able to look around appraisingly, looking for anything that had been dumped along with the body.

"There is a tarp. He was probably carried on top of or inside it. Make sure the tech guys get that."

"Right."

"You're going to have to sift through the contents for the gun. It might have been disposed of here at the same time."

She didn't see anything else that was relevant to the murder. She knew it was a dump site and was unlikely to provide many clues about where the man had come from or what had happened to him before and after he was shot. She didn't expect to get much from the body itself. However, she might get lucky and be able to get some trace evidence from his clothing that would be a clue as to where he had lain in the street, the vehicle he had been transported in, or something about the person who had transported him from one location to the other.

If she were really *really* lucky, maybe the dead man would have skin cells under his fingernails.

<h1 style="text-align:center">19</h1>

Kenzie had a little time when she returned to the office to check for any emails or messages left while she had been gone and to fill Dr. Cook in on the basics of the body dump. She had helped Carlos load the liquifying remains into the van. He and George would offload, and George would do the initial work to take pictures of the remains, remove and catalog the clothes, and prepare what was left for autopsy.

"This is the body you were looking for?" Dr. Cook asked.

"Uh… yes. The one who we had a picture of."

"So I guess it was not a prank."

"I guess not," Kenzie agreed. She decided she'd better call Sergeant Campbell and tell him the same thing. His phone harassment case could now be transitioned to a homicide, and the preliminary work that Detective Saul had done in tracking the origin of the photo could be used for the basis of when the man had been killed and who was there to take a picture of the body at the time. They had a head start on that, despite the age of the corpse.

She and Dr. Cook went to the autopsy and dressed and scrubbed, getting ready to begin as George finished separating the clothes from the decomposing flesh. Kenzie was glad for the good ventilation and the modern equipment that allowed her to quickly raise and lower the autopsy tables, make a recording by tapping the floor button with her foot, or give the computer instructions using voice commands and keywords. All of that made it so much simpler than it would have been ten or twenty years before when everything had to be done by hand, having to stop the autopsy in order to do anything else.

Once everything was ready, she tapped the floor button and began recording the John Doe's file number, the date and time, and her and Dr. Cook's names. She began with the gross examination—an appropriate appellation given the state the body was in—carefully describing everything she saw. While she knew that the man had been dead for over two weeks, she could not rely solely on her knowledge about the timing of the picture being circulated around the school to date the man's death. He obviously hadn't been killed after that date, but he could have been killed before. The decomposition and insect activity would give them a timeline. From her initial observations, two weeks was a pretty good estimate.

The body was bloated and red. As Cameron had observed, the face was unrecognizable. Without the photo on her phone, she would have had to order a forensic reconstruction done in order to visualize the face. There had been plenty of insect activity, with very little flesh left where the bugs had been active. The clothing had protected the body to some degree, and it was more intact than Kenzie would have hoped. Even so, there was very little to autopsy.

She had paused for long enough in her narration for Dr. Cook to speak up. "Would you like me to collect the fingernails and test them for a secondary DNA source?"

"Uh, yeah, that would be good." Kenzie waited for him to do so, looking at the body and trying to figure out what else would be constructive. She wasn't sure any organs would be intact if she opened him up. She worried that she wouldn't even be able to shift the body to look at the back and front without damaging it significantly. George and Carlo had done very well to get it onto the table intact. She hadn't thought they would be able to get him out of the dumpster in one piece.

"You're not going to be able to do much to manipulate it," Cook advised. "I don't think it's going to hold together. Maybe check each limb individually, but not the torso. We'll see what's left on the table in the end."

Kenzie nodded. For the recording, she described the appearance of the head wound, describing it as it was rather than as she had seen it in the photo. Since John Doe's death, it had become enlarged, harder to identify as a small-caliber bullet wound. But she had a better view of the hole in the skull and might be able to identify the size of the bullet and other factors from that.

She carefully picked up each of the limbs, describing any markings or tattoos still visible. The hands were in pretty bad shape, in an advanced state of decomposition, but Kenzie thought she might be able to get fingerprints from a couple of them. Maybe only partial prints, but it was possible they could still be helpful in identifying him. She examined each finger in turn and, with Dr. Cook's help, rolled each one that had any intact skin left that they might be able to pull a print from. In the end, only a couple looked like anything more than blotches on the screen. But with those two partials, it was possible that they would be able to get an ID.

She logged the weight of the remains, even though she knew it was far lower than the man would have weighed in life. Height was still reasonably accurate.

"Okay." She looked at Dr. Cook and then back down at the man again. "Do we do anything else? I'm not sure what a full autopsy would reveal at this point. The organs are liquifying."

"Some samples for tox screens. X-rays. While you know that he died from a bullet to the head—as far as we can tell—we want to build a picture of anything else we could before that point. Was he drunk? Was he in a fight? Those things could inform the ruling."

"Sure."

She proceeded on that basis. It was fascinating, and somewhat poignant to see how a body started to return to nature within a couple of weeks. Before long, if they did nothing to halt the process of decomposition, nothing recognizable would remain of their John Doe but the bones.

The X-rays didn't show any recent breaks. There were a few old, healed fractures, the recalcified areas brighter white on the X-ray. Nothing significant that Kenzie could see. He had not lived a sedentary life. But she couldn't classify which breaks were accidents, which were from fights, and which might have resulted from abuse. He might just have been unlucky.

Unlucky enough to get a hole in his head.

They worked efficiently to collect tissues and fluids needed for tests.

"We should retrieve the bullet, I guess," Kenzie suggested.

Dr. Cook agreed. They took an X-ray to determine the position of the bullet so that they wouldn't have to dig around looking for it. Kenzie took films from several different angles so that the police would have as much information as possible about the murder weapon and how the man had been killed.

"A .22," Kenzie observed as she put the bullet into a shallow dish and gently washed and dried it off before bagging it as evidence. "Like we thought from the photo. It isn't too badly deformed. Maybe they'll be able to match the ballistics to a known weapon."

"With any luck. If we get both—DNA and ballistics—there might not be anything left for the police to figure out."

Kenzie smiled. It would be rare to luck out with that much physical evidence. But one never knew.

20

Zachary had been at his therapist's while Kenzie was doing her autopsy, so he was tired when he got home and ready for ice cream and a relaxing evening. Kenzie told him about finding the John Doe, hesitant to suggest they go see Rhys and give him the news. But she didn't have to ask.

"We should go to the hospital," Zachary said immediately. "I know it doesn't *really* make any difference that the body has turned up... it doesn't prove anything except that he was really dead, and it wasn't just a Photoshop job. But I think he should know. It's important to him."

"Are you sure you're up to it? I can go alone if you aren't. He'll understand you're tired today and will come the next time."

"I'm seeing him at his worst. It doesn't really matter if I'm a little tired."

"If you're sure. I don't think he would mind."

"I'm going," he said firmly.

"Okay. We'll have a bite to eat, and then we can go."

She saw Zachary looking longingly toward the freezer. "You can have ice cream after dinner. Not for dinner."

"Sometimes we have ice cream for dinner."

"Not today."

Zachary grunted. He opened the freezer anyway but reached for a frozen dinner instead of ice cream. He took it out, then put it back away. Then he went to the cupboard and grabbed a can of Chicken and Stars soup.

It might not be what she would have picked out for supper, but it was better than the ice cream. If he needed the familiar comfort food after his session, that was his choice. How many times did Kenzie pick salad over something carb-filled, creamy, and satisfying? Not as often as she should.

They worked around each other in the kitchen, making separate meals. Zachary might go for the childhood favorite, but it wasn't high on Kenzie's list.

"So he was shot?" Zachary asked, introducing the subject of the autopsy.

Kenzie smiled and nodded. That much Zachary knew already. "Yes, .22 caliber. We got the bullet for ballistics. That's about all of the hard evidence that we have at this point. We'll see if anything shows up in any other tests. We're checking for DNA, in case the victim and the shooter had close contact. But there was no sign that he had been in a fight, so I'm not confident he got close enough to touch or scratch the gunman."

"But it was fired from close by?"

"No skin charring that I could see, so not a contact wound. But I would still guess that it was pretty close."

"Anything else at the scene?"

"Well, we don't have the murder scene. Only a dump site. The police are checking the dumpster for anything that might be related."

"Lucky them."

Kenzie nodded. "At least I get a morgue with good exhaust fans for the autopsy. I'm afraid they don't get the same for the garbage dive."

"At least it isn't one hundred degrees out."

"There's that. I still don't imagine they'll be too happy about it. Dirty, smelly business. Especially when you have a corpse marinating on top of everything. But if the gun or anything else is in the bin, they need to find it."

"You don't have any other trace evidence or avenues of investigation?"

"I'll go through the clothes with a fine-toothed comb tomorrow. You never know, we might find hairs, fingerprints, who knows what."

"Yeah. You never know. It might be right there under your nose."

They ate their dinner without ceremony. Kenzie didn't want to take any longer than she had to, knowing they both wanted to get home as soon as possible after the hospital visit. When they signed in at the hospital to visit Rhys, they found Vera there. Kenzie shouldn't have been surprised. She knew that Vera spent a lot of time at the hospital with Rhys. He didn't likely have anyone else visiting him. But she had imagined that they would have Rhys to themselves again and be able to update him on the John Doe.

Rhys was in the visitor area at a table with Vera. He jumped to his feet when he saw Zachary and Kenzie coming. He immediately shook hands with Zachary, clasping tightly and slapping him on the shoulder. He looked at Kenzie and leaned in for a hug. Kenzie put her arms around his shoulders and squeezed him tightly before releasing him.

"Hey, Rhys, how are you doing?"

He was recovering from his ordeal, his eyes looking less hollow than they had. His mood seemed lighter. Maybe they had him on a new medication. Or maybe it was not having to look at that oppressive image on his phone any longer. It must have bothered him to have to keep looking at the picture as it was forwarded to him repeatedly. She assumed he had logged in to all his social networks on the new phone. Hopefully, everyone had seen the picture and grown bored with it, and it was no longer making its rounds.

"Vera," Zachary greeted, and put his hand out to shake. Vera gave him a smile that still seemed a little forced, but she took his hand and then clasped it with her other hand so that his was sandwiched between both of hers.

"Hello, Zachary, Kenzie. It's nice of you to come see Rhys."

"I hope we're not interrupting," Kenzie ventured, giving Vera the opportunity to tell them that it was not a good time and they should leave.

"No, no. We run out of things to say after a while."

Rhys laughed silently at this, drawing a chuckle out of Zachary. Vera patted her hair, looking embarrassed.

"Well, of course, that's never stopped us before," she said good-humoredly.

They all sat back down around the table. Kenzie saw that Rhys had his phone in his pocket and was glad they were letting him hold on to it, at least while he had a visitor there, so that he could communicate more easily.

"You're looking better," Zachary commented, looking Rhys over. "You're feeling a bit better?"

Rhys nodded his agreement. He looked at Kenzie and raised his brows. Kenzie understood that he wanted to know how she had fared on investigating the picture of the John Doe, but wasn't sure she wanted to jump directly into the subject, especially with Vera there. She glanced over at Vera, wondering if she had any thoughts of going home now that Rhys had other visitors. She would probably be going home anyway so that she could go to bed.

"Rhys will be coming home soon," Vera contributed. "It will be nice to have him back again. It has been hard having him away for so long." She patted Rhys's arm affectionately. He put his hand over hers briefly.

"That's great news. I'm glad you're doing so much better," Kenzie told Rhys.

He gave a small smile and nodded. He pulled his phone out of his pocket and navigated to his messaging app. Her own phone buzzed and displayed a picture of Snoopy lying on top of his red doghouse, looking happy and comfortable. *Home.*

"Will it be hard to get caught up with school?"

Rhys rolled his eyes at this. He slumped in his seat and let his head fall back in mock exhaustion.

"He'll probably need some help," Vera said, "but we'll get him back on track."

"That's good."

"We met a couple of your friends," Zachary told Rhys.

Rhys turned his face to Zachary, raising his brows in inquiry.

"Hugh and Ayla," Zachary told him. "We were asking them when that picture had started circulating around the school."

"They seem nice," Kenzie contributed.

Rhys nodded his agreement. He didn't seem overwhelmingly positive about Zachary and Kenzie having met his friends. Maybe he hadn't thought that they would need to go to his friends when making inquiries about the dead man. Maybe he had thought that Kenzie would just be able to go to the morgue and look through unclaimed bodies to find the man and give

Rhys a rundown on who he was and what had happened to him. Or that she would be able to tell him that the body had been claimed and he was back with his people, at rest. Maybe the killer had already been caught and was behind bars. All of that would be good and would let him know that everything was okay without ever having to talk to anyone at the school.

He raised his brows at Kenzie, wanting to know what she had found out.

Kenzie looked at Vera, but she wasn't leaving.

"So, we looked into the picture you got on your phone," Kenzie started awkwardly. "That's why we were talking to your friends and some of the other kids at the school. When I looked into recent deaths, I couldn't find anything that matched the picture. No one was even sure whether it was local or recent. A lot of people thought that it might have been a prank."

Rhys's jaw set, and he shook his head adamantly.

"No, I know it was real," Kenzie agreed. "I just ran into some opposition with people not believing it."

He nodded, and, after a moment, pointed at his own chest. Kenzie studied him, trying to interpret the gesture. "Did you run into that too? Where people didn't believe it was a legitimate picture? That it was just some kind of joke or hoax?"

He nodded. Kenzie wondered who he had shown it to. Had it just been in discussions with friends, or had he gone to someone at the school and tried to convince them to look into it? Maybe to the school resource officer? If he had, word had not gotten back to the principal. Lakes had never seen the picture before Kenzie had shown it to her. Or at least, not that she was admitting. But would she admit it if she realized that it was the picture that caused Rhys's breakdown? She wouldn't want to admit that she hadn't taken Rhys seriously or that she had ignored something that she knew was circulating among the student body.

Kenzie nodded her understanding. "So I ran into the same thing, even though I'm an adult and work with the medical examiner. Someone who knows a thing or two about dead bodies."

Hopefully, it would make Rhys feel better to know that it hadn't just been him. It hadn't been just because he was a kid, or a minority, or had communication difficulties. Even Kenzie, the expert, had run into the same challenges.

She shifted in her chair, trying to get comfortable in the hard seat that was clearly not designed with comfort in mind.

"I did get the police to open an investigation into the picture," Kenzie told Rhys. "Not a homicide investigation, but an investigation into phone harassment, the picture being circulated around the school to upset people. It was the only thing he could do without a body or even a missing person report on the victim."

"I'm sure it was just a kid's prank," Vera said. "Why would anyone be passing around pictures of a real dead body? That's just… inappropriate."

Rhys shook his head, frown lines between his brows.

Kenzie put her hand on Rhys's arm to try to keep his attention on her. "Then today, they found the body."

"What?" Vera's voice was weak. This was not what she had wanted to hear.

"No one could even confirm until today that this was even a real person or a real death," Kenzie said. "Even though it looked real, it's true that it could have been some kind of makeup job or Photoshop manipulation. They can do a lot of things to make it look realistic. But as Rhys thought, it wasn't just a hoax. It wasn't just a meme being passed around school to disgust or upset people."

Rhys nodded his agreement. His eyes were riveted on Kenzie.

"But it was real," Kenzie said. "All of it. The man, the bullet wound in his head. A picture being taken of him after his death. I had him on my table this afternoon."

She could see Rhys breathing heavily.

"Are you okay, Rhys? Is this too much?"

He made a calming gesture with his hands.

"You're okay?"

A nod.

"You're sure? If it's making you feel extra anxious or panicky, you could get a sedative or spend some time talking to your therapist."

He moved his hands in a horizontal line. *No.*

Kenzie held his gaze for a moment to make sure that he wasn't getting too upset. He nodded encouragingly.

"The police have opened a homicide file now. I did the autopsy this afternoon. As much as I could do with the shape the body was in."

She probably shouldn't go into too much detail about the state of the man's remains.

"They will be trying to identify him. Now that we have some data, his DNA and fingerprints, hopefully, they will be able to figure out who he is, and we will be one step closer to finding out what happened to him."

Rhys nodded.

"I'm sorry that it took so long for the body to be found," Kenzie said. "It might have been easier on you if they had been able to confirm right away that he was deceased and opened an investigation into it. Knowing that it was circulating the school would have informed their investigation, helped them to sort out the origin of the photo sooner."

He cocked his head, questioning.

"They don't know who took the picture or started it circulating yet," Kenzie told him. "But they're working on it. It will be a higher priority now that it is a homicide rather than just phone harassment."

Rhys tapped something into his phone, and Kenzie looked down at hers when it buzzed. It was a gif of a spinning globe. Kenzie let Zachary see it and tried to think of what Rhys was trying to say. Zachary pursed his lips.

"Where did you find it?" he suggested.

They both looked at Rhys, who nodded and pointed to Zachary to confirm the question.

"It had been left in a dumpster," Kenzie told him. "One that wasn't emptied regularly. So it was longer than it should have been before someone found it."

Rhys pinched his nose.

"Oh, yes," Kenzie agreed with a laugh. "It was not a pleasant experience for the police, I'll tell you that."

He pointed to Kenzie, eyebrows up.

"Or to me. Well, no, but I've got good ventilation in the morgue, so it wasn't too bad. And I'm used to it to a certain degree. My job stinks."

They all chuckled over this.

"Well," Vera's huff clearly indicated she was attempting to change the subject. "I'm glad that Rhys can finally put his mind at ease about this whole situation. I don't know what happened or how that picture ended up on his phone, but now that he knows it is being taken care of, he can put it out of his mind and look to the future. What we need to focus on now is Rhys getting out of here soon and the outpatient treatment he will be following. The hospital has recommended a couple of therapists."

"Good," Zachary approved. He looked at Rhys. "I really didn't want to be in therapy, but it has helped me a lot. And it has helped Kenzie and me; we've done couple's therapy to help with that. You might want to do some family therapy with Vera as well as individual therapy. It could help you to communicate better."

Rhys rolled his eyes.

"I know it's not fun," Zachary emphasized. "I know you don't feel like doing it. But it does make a difference."

Rhys made a motion to his back, which Kenzie assumed was a reference to the past and the therapy he had done previously.

"Even if you had a bunch of therapy in the past," Zachary said. "It can still be useful."

Rhys shrugged.

"You're lucky they're going to fund the therapy," Vera told Rhys. "So we can afford it. We can afford to get someone good, not just whoever we can get with my benefits."

Kenzie looked at Vera, her throat tightening. "Who is funding it?" she asked, even though, of course, it was none of her business.

"The anonymous donor," Vera said. "The one who was paying for the experimental therapy at Persons. They said that since it didn't work out, since he reacted to the drug, they would fund something else. Whatever therapy we chose."

Kenzie happened to know who the anonymous donor was. The Kirsch family foundation. She was irritated to learn that they were still funding Rhys without even telling her about it. After the last debacle, she thought they were going to tell her whenever they did something that impacted her family and close friends. They had kept the experimental treatment a secret from her because of a potential conflict of interest, but there was no reason to keep the ongoing funding from her. Unless they thought she would be upset about it for some reason.

If they were letting Vera and Rhys choose what kind of therapy they thought would be best instead of funneling Rhys into a particular program, which Kenzie had told Vera was too risky, then the only reason she had to be angry about it was because they were doing it behind her back. Again.

She shook her head. Vera stared at her, frowning, trying to figure out what Kenzie was expressing her disapproval of.

"You just said he needed therapy. Why would you be opposed to an anonymous donor funding it?"

"Sorry," Kenzie said, trying to lighten her voice. "I was just thinking of something else. I didn't mean to scowl at you." She pasted a smile on her face. "That's great. I'm glad that money will not be a deterrent and you can get Rhys whatever treatment the two of you decide is best."

"It won't be that drug therapy," Vera told her in a tentative voice.

"No, I know that. I think it would be too risky after what happened the first time. Even if they lowered the dose, he might still react to it, and we don't want to do what could be irreparable damage."

Vera nodded her agreement, looking relieved.

Vera had been pretty insistent about Persons and their therapy before. She had stood up to Kenzie and ended up being wrong. She was probably worried that Kenzie would think she was making a bad choice again and didn't want to draw her disappointment.

"Will you be glad to be out of here and back at school?" Kenzie asked, turning her attention back to Rhys.

He made a face and shook his head.

"You don't want to go back to school?"

He nodded.

"You'll be glad to see your friends again, won't you? That will be nice."

He nodded, but didn't seem too excited about it. Kenzie remembered Hugh saying they were just school friends and didn't see each other outside of school. And Ayla didn't seem that close to him, even though Hugh suggested they talk to her. If those were Rhys's two best friends, and he didn't even see them outside of school hours, she could see why he wasn't too excited about going back to see them. He might be lonely at the hospital, but he would be lonely at home with just Vera to keep him company and lonely at school with just one or two friends to hang out with.

"Did you ever think of getting into one of the clubs?" Zachary asked.

Rhys looked at him and widened his eyes. *What clubs?*

Zachary shrugged. "I don't know. I always thought being in the photography or yearbook club would be fun. I couldn't ever be in any clubs or extracurricular activities, but I thought those might be cool. You wouldn't have to talk a lot for them."

Rhys nodded, but didn't look that interested. Maybe he wasn't interested in photography or they didn't have a photography club. Kenzie didn't know what Rhys was interested in.

"If there are any clubs you are interested in, we could help out with them," Kenzie said. "If there is some equipment you need to buy."

Vera looked at Rhys, but he just shook his head and didn't indicate any interest. "I think our Rhys is just a homebody," she said. "That's where he wants to be the most."

22

———

Sorry I couldn't get down yesterday to watch the autopsy," Campbell told Kenzie when he arrived at her desk. "I meant to get down for it, but too much was happening. A bunch of noise upstairs about other issues, and then finding a DB in the dumpster that somehow the medical examiner knew about before the police did kind of set some people's nerves on edge. As much as I explain that I can't be walking around to all the dumpsters in town looking for new bodies, they don't seem to understand that it is all just up to chance."

Kenzie smiled and shook her head. "I guess you're going to have to up your game. Make a list of high-priority dumpsters. Have them checked every day. Any time there is a body part, no matter how small, you make sure it is reported to you immediately…"

He grinned, "That's how new policies come to be," he agreed. "So, the autopsy?"

"You didn't really miss anything. Nothing that you would probably want to see, anyway." She grimaced. "The body was so old it was half liquid. It's a wonder it didn't burst when we took it out of the dumpster or during transport. There wasn't a lot that I could do with him. I got some fingernails, a couple of fingerprints, sent some DNA off to the lab for analysis and searched CODIS, but other than that… there was nothing remarkable. We couldn't tell much more from the body than we could from the picture. In some ways, the picture is more helpful. Oh, and I did get the slug that was in his head. That's been sent to ballistics in case they can identify the gun it came from, but I'm not that hopeful."

"Identifying features? Tattoos?"

"I took pictures of what I could. But anywhere his skin was still intact, the colors were not great. Someone who knew him well might be able to identify them."

"And nothing to indicate there might be another cause of death?"

"Shot to the head seems most likely. I am also getting a tox screen, just in case there are any complicating factors. If he was drunk or drugged, if he was poisoned. It isn't comprehensive, but we do what we can. If you tell me to look for another substance, I can do that."

"Nothing at this point. We need to identify the guy before we can find out much more about what happened to him."

Kenzie nodded. "We've got a few avenues for identification. Hopefully, one of them works out."

"Until then, what happens to the remains?"

"We've taken a few slides and samples to be held for future tests. If he is not claimed in the next few days, we'd best send them for cremation. His cremains can be held for any relatives who pop up much more easily than the soupy mess we've got in there now. Getting gradually soupier."

Campbell wrinkled his nose. "Thank you for that image."

"Like I say, you should be glad you didn't watch the autopsy. I don't think you would have enjoyed it quite as much as our less... aromatic patients."

Campbell laughed. "Dr. Kirsch, you are a ghoul."

"If you hadn't figured it out by now, you're not the investigator I thought you were."

***

Kenzie had thought that Campbell might stick around to be there while she examined John Doe's clothing in detail. But after hearing her summary of the autopsy, he apparently decided that he'd heard enough and retreated to his office.

Kenzie took each item of clothing one at a time, laying them all out on the autopsy table. She didn't usually spend so much time on the clothes but, given the state the body was in, she hoped to glean a few more details from the clothing, which was in better shape. A bloodstain on the shirt could indicate an injury that she hadn't been able to see on the body due to its advanced state of decomposition and predation. Or it could indicate an injury to his attacker and another DNA profile to be analyzed.

Other trace evidence might give her a better idea of where he had been when he was killed. It was unlikely that they could narrow it down to one site or a handful of places as they always could on TV, but it would give them a better idea of where to look—and who knew? Maybe they would be able to find the death scene and additional evidence. Unlike in *Bones,* she didn't have a botanist or entomologist on staff but, if she identified something of interest, she could track down an expert to tell her about it and whether it was significant.

She stretched the t-shirt out and smoothed the wrinkles the best she could. She took a couple of pictures of it, front and back, looking for any stains or tears or trace evidence that might be important. There were a few long, blond hairs on his collar that she assumed were the victim's own, but she carefully preserved them and marked the exhibits so that they could be analyzed and compared with the his hair, just in case they were from his girlfriend or assailant. She turned the shirt over and photographed and examined the back as well. Neither side presented much of interest. Kenzie bagged it separately and moved on to the jeans.

Nothing identified what stores the victim shopped at. He hadn't been buying designer clothes or jewelry. If Kenzie were to guess, she would say that he'd either had the clothes for a long time or he had gotten them at a thrift store or mission. Cheap, old, and worn.

The knees of the jeans were worn, but not torn. He had probably not been kneeling on the pavement—or asphalt—before he was shot. There was no motor oil, no particularly special soil that she could analyze to find out where he had been lately. Using tweezers, she pulled everything she could find out of the pockets. A couple of nearly unreadable receipts. Some loose change.

The jean jacket was similar to the pants. Nothing remarkable. Nothing that looked out of place.

That left her with a belt, socks, shoes, and bandana. No identifying phone or wallet. No weapons. Kenzie photographed and examined each piece. She looked closely at the belt, hoping it would have a unique buckle or something else that the victim had purchased as a special treat or been given as a gift by a family member or close friend. But it looked like a belt she could have purchased off the shelf in any department store. Not a collector's piece. No inscribed belt buckle. Just a generic, off-the-shelf belt.

23

I'm just not sure what you're doing here."

Kenzie paused as she stepped out of the morgue and heard raised voices. She cocked her head. Dr. Cook and…?

"This is my office. I have every right to be here," Dr. Wiltshire shot back.

"Of course, it's your office," Dr. Cook replied, his voice still louder than necessary. "But why are you here now? Today? I have everything under control. You are supposed to be off. Healing. Until your hand has healed, there isn't anything for you to do here."

"I want to keep on top of the new cases. See what's going on. See if Kenzie needs anything."

"That's why I'm here."

"I know her better than you do."

Kenzie rolled her eyes. They were fighting over her? Over the morgue? Acting territorial over dead bodies? She put the bagged and tagged clothing where it belonged and followed the voices to the boardroom, where both men stood while engaging in what sounded like a heated discussion, but was really quite ridiculous. Neither one had a leg to stand on. It was Dr. Wiltshire's office. Dr. Cook was legitimately there as his substitute. Either one could be there, doing whatever duties they were able to perform.

"What's going on?" Kenzie asked, to get their attention. It was already evident what was going on.

"Kenzie," Dr. Wiltshire turned toward her. His red face got a little redder. He smiled at her, forced and frozen looking. "I just thought I would check in. See how everything is going."

Kenzie nodded. "We're doing pretty well. Keeping up, for the most part."

Dr. Wiltshire nodded. "Good…"

"Dr. Cook has been very competent," Kenzie said, looking at him and giving a nod of acknowledgment. "It's been very good to have someone else here to lean on while you're healing."

Dr. Cook looked like he wanted to say something aggrieved, like "I'm the good guy here," but he restrained himself, nodding back to Kenzie. "Dr. Kirsch and I have been able to stay on top of things so far. She is also very competent."

Kenzie chuckled to herself. Wasn't it great that they could all get along?

The two men still had the puffed-up appearance of tomcats confronting each other over their territory. She hoped that her words would soothe the savage beasts and put a stop to the caterwauling.

"Did you want to go over this new John Doe with me?" she invited Dr. Wiltshire. "We've done the autopsy—what little we could do with the advanced state of decomposition—and I've just finished going over the clothing. I could use your guidance on anything else we should do before incinerating what is left."

Dr. Wiltshire nodded and looked authoritative. "Certainly. Of course. You want to do it here?" He motioned to the boardroom table. He knew, of course, that Dr. Cook was already established in his office. He couldn't really kick him out just to assert his dominance when Dr. Cook was legitimately there to substitute and keep things running smoothly during Dr. Wiltshire's recovery.

Kenzie nodded. She went to the computer attached to the AV equipment in order to navigate to the files so they could blow up the pictures and imaging on the big screen.

"I'll leave you to it, then," Dr. Cook said stiffly. "Anything I should know about on the examination of the clothing, Dr.—uh—Kenzie?"

While he had refused to call her by her first name before, he had apparently changed his mind now that he'd heard Dr. Wiltshire calling her Kenzie.

"No, nothing significant. I wish I could say that we have more than we do."

"It's understandable. We can't force the issue. It is whatever it is."

Kenzie nodded her agreement. Dr. Cook retreated to the office and Dr. Wiltshire sat down at the table. Kenzie shook her head and did not ask, "What was that all about?"

She already knew Dr. Cook had been listening to rumors about Dr. Wiltshire losing his money gambling and possibly having his hand broken by some enforcer trying to persuade him to pay up. If he was going to listen to nonsense like that, it wasn't particularly surprising that he would end up in a showdown with Dr. Wiltshire when they met in person.

Kenzie was sure Dr. Wiltshire was not a gambler and his hand had just been hurt in an accident. He had suggested at one point that he might have broken it while golfing. But he'd been too embarrassed about the circumstances to explain it in any detail to Kenzie. Maybe it had been golfing, and maybe it had been something else. But some kind of mob enforcer? Kenzie couldn't see it.

"First, the picture that started to circulate before the body was found," Kenzie announced, pulling up the photo of their John Doe. The picture she had seen many times on her phone and was now looking at on the big screen. Amazing that such a substantial person, looking like he had been dead only for minutes, could be changed so quickly to the fragile, dissolving body that had been discovered in the dumpster, and then fell to pieces under Kenzie's knife. But it only took days for the decomposition process to really kick in, moving from the just-dead corpse to something almost unrecognizable.

Dr. Wiltshire gazed at the picture for a moment, his eyes flickering to each detail, trying to catalog it and gather all of the information he could from this postmortem picture.

"Right," he agreed. "And have the police had any success in determining the origin of this picture?"

"Not yet. I should have asked Campbell if they had found anything else when he was here earlier, but I didn't. I just figured if there was anything new, he would have told me. The timeframe is about two weeks. That's all. It was being circulated at a local school, but they don't know who the first person was to start sending it to their friends there."

"How does a high school student get a picture of a dead body like that? Not one that has been on movies or in the news, but just fresh, when there has been no police involvement?"

Kenzie didn't like to think about it. When she pictured Rhys or one of the students she had talked to about the picture being in a position to either see the murdered man and snap a photo, or to be sent the picture by the actual killer or someone else on the inside, she felt sick. They were supposed to be at school, sheltered, getting an education that would serve them well in the real world. They should not be around murdered men or people who happened to have photos of recently murdered men.

"I wish I could tell you. I think I know the group that started distributing it, but not the one person that sent it to that group to start with. They're… well, disadvantaged, I guess. Not drop-outs, but close to it. On the edge."

Dr. Wiltshire nodded. He didn't pursue it and ask for more details about the "loser" kids that Hugh had pointed her toward. He wasn't one for conducting personal interviews. He preferred to let the evidence speak for itself, and, where the evidence could not speak, to remain silent.

Kenzie brought up a couple of photos showing the body first in the dumpster where it had been found, and then on the autopsy table, prepped and ready to be processed. Dr. Wiltshire didn't flinch. He had seen plenty of bodies in advanced decomposition in his day.

"About two weeks into decomp," Kenzie advised. "Quite advanced."

"Well, you got him here in one piece. That was pretty good work."

Kenzie nodded. She ran through the high points of the autopsy and what tests they had done or requested. Then she brought up the pictures of the clothing she had just taken.

"See anything significant?" she asked. "I hate to just toss the clothes in a bag and say that there wasn't anything noteworthy. But other than a few hair follicles, there wasn't really much to find."

"Some cases, you just don't have enough evidence," Dr. Wiltshire agreed. "Unfortunate, but in real life, unlike a TV drama, cases go unsolved. John Does may never be identified. As many tools as we have at our disposal, it is still not possible to solve every crime."

They both stared at the screen, searching for any small clue that would give them a "Eureka" moment and push the case forward.

"Maybe the police will find something. Or the fingerprints or DNA will give us an identity."

Kenzie shook her head. "I'd really like to know what he was doing here to get himself shot in the head."

24

At home that evening, Kenzie repeated her frustration at being unable to find out anything else about the man who had been killed, even his identity. She had hoped they would get results back from the fingerprints, but they might not have been clear enough, half decomposed as they were, for any kind of match. A DNA result could take weeks or months. Campbell had said that they did not want to show his face on TV or the media until they had exhausted all other means of identification. Doing so would result in a flood of calls, most of which would be nonsense and a waste of resources. It was clear that no one was looking for the man. There was no matching missing person report in Vermont or the surrounding states. They had even checked for matches across the border in Canada and come up dry.

"And everything he was wearing was generic?" Zachary asked. "Nothing that identified where he might have come from or if he was even local?"

"No. Brands you could get at any department store. Nothing new. Nothing traceable."

She brought up the pictures of the clothes on her phone and let Zachary flip through them to see if they jogged anything for him.

Zachary stopped, and Kenzie reached to take the phone back from him. He didn't hand it over, but turned it around and showed her the picture of the bandana.

Kenzie nodded. She had seen bikers use them as do-rags, teens using them as masks, and a number of other decorative uses. "Yeah, so? You see a lot of those around. They're trendy with the kids."

"You don't remember seeing anyone else with one of these recently?"

Kenzie shook her head slowly. But Zachary's words triggered half a recollection. Something tickled at the back of her brain, and she struggled to bring it forward into conscious thought. *Had* she seen one recently? She must have, if Zachary said that she had. And he had been with her at the time, so that narrowed down where she might have seen it. She closed her eyes and ran her fingers through her hair, trying to dredge it up.

"No?" Zachary asked.

Kenzie shook her head and opened her eyes. "No. Where?"

"At the school."

It flashed into her mind. "The losers."

"One of them."

Kenzie had seen one tied around her thigh. She'd thought it an eighties fashion throwback. "One of the girls. I remember." She shrugged. "So they must be getting popular again."

"Were they the same color?"

Kenzie rolled her eyes. "Yes… I would say both were that same shade of red."

Zachary nodded slowly, handing her phone back to her. "Gang colors."

"What?" Kenzie shook her head. "No. Gangs don't even wear colors anymore. They dress just like anyone else to make it harder for the police to identify them."

"The bigger gangs, sure. But some of the little ones that float around and aren't into big money laundering or drug trafficking operations. Some of them do."

Kenzie stared down at the picture of the bandana. "And you think this identifies John Doe as a gang member. And that girl at the school."

"That's what they're for. To make it easier for members to identify each other. Or to identify rivals who infringe on their territory."

They were at the school the next morning to talk to Principal Lakes.

Kenzie knew that they needed to pass what they knew on to Detective Saul so that he would be able to trace the victim's identity, any rival gangs, and all of the details needed to solve the case. But she wanted to talk to the girl with the bandana first, to see if she had been the one to start circulating the photograph. That was the part of the investigation that Kenzie felt she needed to follow up on personally. That was what had affected Rhys, and what she had agreed to follow up on for him. Where that photo had come from.

Obviously, she couldn't do anything for John Doe now. It wasn't a matter of protecting him. They would try to bring his killer to justice, but she wanted to understand why the girl had started passing around the photo. Was it some kind of brag or trophy? Had she wanted to upset Rhys or other students in general? Did she realize the kind of damage that she had done just by sending out the photo, even if she'd had nothing to do with the execution? Even if she hadn't even seen what happened or taken the picture herself.

People experienced disconnect with the internet and other methods of social communication. They were separated from the consequences of their actions. They did cruel things to others because they could hide behind a screen name, avatar, or anonymous phone number, and no one would know who they were. And they would never know what harm they had done.

Kenzie did her best to describe the girl to Principal Lakes, with Zachary providing a few additional details that she had missed. Lakes nodded slowly.

"That sounds like Emily Cross." She sighed. "She's had a few problems this year. I wish I could say that she couldn't be involved in anything like this, but unfortunately… some kids go astray and there isn't much you can do to reach them…"

Kenzie tapped the name into her phone. "If we could get her contact information… We'll check out the bus stop where they were hanging out before, but she might not be there this time. I might need to reach her at home or on her phone."

"We can't really give out students' personal information."

"This is for the medical examiner's office. And it is related to a police investigation into a homicide."

"I know that." Lakes was hesitant. "But the police would come to me with a warrant, not just a verbal request. I can comply with a warrant and not get in any trouble for it. But giving the information out to just anyone…"

Zachary gave her a charming smile. "This isn't just anyone. You know me. I've protected your students before. We're trying to protect Rhys and others like him. We just want to talk to Emily about what happened and the consequences of sharing a photo like that."

Kenzie could see that Lakes wanted to give in. But she was still hesitant. "If it was the police…"

"I'm sure they'll be around later. You're not giving away anything you shouldn't. You're just… releasing it a bit early. So that we can talk to Emily before the police talk to her and she clams up. You know she's not going to talk once the police get involved. I think we can do some good here."

"Well… I think what I'll do is write down the information that the police will need. And I'll give it to them when they come for it. I can't give it to you. But I'll just step out and see whether she has shown up for her first-period class. If she has, I'll have her called to the office so you can talk to her."

Kenzie watched Lakes tap a search into her computer and then write down Emily's name and her personal contact information very neatly on a memo page from the block near her pen holder. "I'll just be a moment," she told Kenzie and stepped out of her office, shutting the door behind her.

Before Kenzie could move, Zachary was out of his seat and positioned his phone in front of the note. He snapped a picture and sat back down. He assumed a casual stance, looking as if he were just scrolling through the social networks on his phone, waiting for the principal's return. It couldn't have taken more than three seconds.

Kenzie opened her mouth to say something to him when her phone buzzed. She looked down at it in time to see the message come from him, with an image attached. Now, she was part of the conspiracy. She had Emily's covertly obtained contact information as well. She stared at Zachary.

"I can't believe you could move that fast."

Zachary grinned. "It's all about taking the opportunities when they pop up."

Lakes gave them plenty of time before she returned with a cup of coffee. She set it down on her desk and smiled at them as she sat in her chair.

"Emily is not in her first-period class, unfortunately. I'm sorry about that. But I can't say I'm surprised. She has been truant quite a lot lately. She's barely hanging on by a thread. She'll be expelled before long."

"Do you know what's going on with her?" Kenzie asked. "Is she involved in something that's keeping her away from school?"

Of course, she already knew this, but she was curious how much the school knew of what was happening and how deep Emily's involvement with the gang was. Was she just flirting with danger, or was she deeply involved with the gang and the violence they perpetrated?

"Unfortunately, it's pretty hard to know what is happening with all the kids. We've tried to talk to her. I've talked to her, her teachers have, her guidance counselor has." Lakes sighed. "But she just doesn't want the help. She doesn't want to talk to anyone about what is going on with her. I assumed there are issues at home. Maybe drugs. A lot of the kids in the group that she is hanging out with are involved in drugs. Not heavily, but... enough to get them into trouble."

"Gangs?"

"Gangs? No, not that I know of. There are some groups and cliques, but I think I would know if there was any gang involvement. It's a pretty safe neighborhood. We haven't had to worry about that."

Maybe Emily was an exception. Or maybe Zachary was wrong and she had just been making a fashion statement. Emily might have just purchased the bandana at a department store and had no idea that it was the same color as the symbol being used by a gang in the area. Or she could be imitating the gang, knowing they used the red bandana. Just wanting to look tough or like she belonged to something.

"Well..." Kenzie looked at Zachary. "Shall we see if we can find her?"

Zachary nodded his agreement. "Thanks for your help," he told Lakes. "I understand why you couldn't give us the information we were looking for. Just pass it on to the police when they get around to making their inquiries..."

Lakes smiled and nodded. "I will. Nice to see you again, Zachary."

25

They left the school and headed toward the convenience store.

"Coffee?" Zachary suggested.

"Haven't you already had enough?" Kenzie asked with a laugh. He'd had at least two cups before leaving the house that morning and another supplied by the school while they had been waiting for Lakes to get out of her early morning staff meeting.

"I could always have another."

"I would be so wired if I had that much."

He shrugged. "It just makes me more focused. Mild stimulant."

"Well, you'll be super focused if you have another one."

He shrugged, and they headed directly to the bus stop instead of going to the convenience store first. There were a few kids at the bus stop. Fewer than there had been earlier in the week. They looked at Zachary and Kenzie, faces tightening, not as open to talking to them as they had been the last time.

"What are you guys doing here again?" the older boy they had talked to before demanded.

"Following up," Kenzie said in what she hoped was a casual, soothing voice. Like they just needed to confirm something that they already knew. She looked over the faces of the kids there, disappointed to find that Emily was not there. She wasn't at the school. She wasn't out with her friends. Maybe she was still home, in bed asleep. If she were hanging out with a gang, she might have been out with them late at night or in the early morning hours. Lakes said she had been truant a lot.

"We ain't interested in following up with you," the boy said in a tough voice. Kenzie shrugged it off. Of course he was going to pretend to be a tough guy. That didn't mean he was or she should respond to him as if he were.

"Where's Emily?"

The kids exchanged concerned looks with each other. They didn't like Kenzie looking for her, asking for her by name.

"Is she okay?" Zachary asked.

They kept close together as a group, huddled together, watching and listening to each other, communicating more by expression and body language than the whispers that passed between them.

The boy gave Zachary a measuring look. "Why? What do you mean?"

"I just want to make sure… that nothing happened to her. With all of this stuff going on… I wanted to make sure that she is safe."

"What stuff? Why wouldn't she be?"

Zachary didn't say anything. Kenzie waited to see if he were going to contribute something else, but he didn't. He just looked at her, then looked back at the boy again.

The boy looked at his friends, frowning.

"How long has it been since you saw her?" Kenzie asked.

"She's been around," he said with a shrug.

"Devon," one of the girls murmured, a bit of a whine in her voice.

"Shush," he told her. "Keep it to yourself."

But the others were starting to get antsy about the situation as well.

"She hasn't been at school," one of them pointed out.

"In how long?" Kenzie asked. "We saw her here on Tuesday. Have you seen her since then?"

"Why are you guys here stirring everything up?" Devon demanded. "It ain't any of your business what Emily or any of us are doing. Who cares? You live in a different world."

Kenzie had to admit that was true. But there was a certain point where their lives intersected. Two points now.

"It actually is my business," she said. "Especially now that we have the body."

"You have the body?" one of the girls screeched. "What body? Emily?"

"Would she be here asking after Emily if she had Emily's body on ice?" Devon asked. "Think about it, stupid."

"Well, what is she asking about, then? Em is in trouble? Are you telling me that picture was actually real? I mean, we were just laughing at it, saying how unreal it looked. That it could be really real. It was just another one of her stories."

He shook his head and made a "zip it" gesture. "Shut up, Clarissa."

But Clarissa looked at Kenzie appealingly. "What happened to her? Where is she? You know something about what is going on?"

"If you'll tell me what you know, we can sort this out a lot faster. I don't want Emily to come to harm, so if you guys could help out so that we can make sure nothing happens to her…"

"Why would something happen to her?"

"She's a witness," one of the others pointed out, her voice low, trying to keep Kenzie and Zachary from being able to make out what she was saying. "Right? How do you take a picture of a body like that without someone seeing you? And if they catch you taking a picture, or they know that you've been spreading it around, what do you think they're going to do? Just laugh it off? Someone has already killed at least once. You think Emily planned to be the next one?"

"Do you know the name of the man in the picture?" Kenzie asked. "If Emily was the one who showed it to you or sent it to you, did she tell you his name? Even just his first name or an alias? It would be really helpful to be able to identify him."

"I don't know what you're talking about."

"She never told you the name of the man in the picture?"

There were a few headshakes, but no one answered aloud. Devon, the apparent leader of the group, was trying to keep everyone quiet and keep them from saying too much. But they were not listening to him. They would not have made a very good gang. Kenzie assumed that they were just a group of friends and there was no hierarchal structure that would put Devon over anyone else's head.

"What is the name of the gang she is in?"

"Emily isn't in a gang," Devon scoffed.

"We know she's in a gang," Zachary said dismissively. "The same one as the dead man was in. He was killed and that puts her in danger too.

What was he involved in? Why was he taken out? If the two of them were close…"

It was interesting to watch the dynamics between the members of the group. Zachary clearly knew how to talk to them and communicate with them better than Kenzie did. He had been closer to the street, closer to gangs and teen dropouts and the grittier aspects of the street than Kenzie ever had been. She had been raised in a privileged home, had everything she needed, had never had to worry about being suspended or expelled, drugs, or gang involvement. She had no idea how to talk to these kids other than just being direct in her questions and answers. Zachary led them in different directions, pretended to know things that he didn't, and held back instead of giving them everything he knew.

"Whatever Emily was involved with, that's her own business," Devon declared. "Doesn't have anything to do with me. With us." He motioned to the rest of the kids in the group. "We're not in any gangs. We're just hanging out. Having a smoke and talking. Nothing illegal about that."

Forget the part about it being illegal for minors to buy cigarettes or be truant from school.

They weren't concerned with those kinds of things. Murder was on a whole different plane from any minor complaints about how they were spending their time.

The other kids, particularly the girls, objected to his declaration that Emily's concerns were not theirs. They took care of each other. Watched each other's backs.

"And how is she watching our backs?" Devon demanded. "If she's involved with someone getting killed, or some other stupid gang stuff, and she brings that back to us, you think anyone is going to care that we weren't involved in it? We're going to get painted with the same brush. I don't know about you, but I don't want to end up with a bullet in *my* forehead."

They quieted, thinking about this. Still looking at each other, exchanging glances back and forth while they weighed what Devon had said. Deciding whether to follow his lead or go out on a limb on their own, risking his wrath and unsure how the rest of the group would take it.

The girl, Clarissa, finally spoke up again, addressing Kenzie. "I don't know where Emily is. Haven't seen her for a couple of days. I don't know how long, for sure. I lose track of the days unless it's the weekend."

"Have you talked to her?" Kenzie asked. "Messaged her? Or has she been completely silent since then?"

They looked at each other. Clarissa played with a stud in her lip, looking uncertain.

"I don't know."

"Can you call her? See if she answers?"

She rolled her eyes at this suggestion. "We don't call each other. Who wants to talk on the phone? We message. Or whatever."

Kenzie choked back her own reaction at this. Today's kids behaved differently from the way she had, growing up in the world of landlines and no internet, talking forever on a cordless phone with her friends. Lisa eventually got Kenzie her own line, so the main house line would be available when Lisa wanted it.

But kids who had grown up with devices in their pockets and instant messaging preferred that over actually speaking to each other voice to voice. If they did talk, it was probably in a video or gaming group.

"Could you message her right now?"

Out of the corner of her eye, Kenzie saw Zachary give her a quick shake of the head. He was right, of course. Kenzie should try to get to Emily before anyone could tell her that some stranger was looking for her. If Emily knew people were looking for her, she would stay out of sight.

"She didn't want to talk to you guys then," Clarissa said. "Why would she want to talk to you now?"

"Maybe she wants to get her story out there before everyone knows about the dead man. Maybe she needs some protection. Or maybe she just wants to get it off of her chest. Maybe she has been posting about what she saw because she was traumatized by it."

"Traumatized?" Devon snorted. "She was proud of herself. Acting all big and important for having taken that picture."

So she *had* been the one to take the picture, not just an early recipient. Kenzie thought about that, wondering what all of the implications were. How had she been there? Who knew she had been there? Why had she taken the picture? Why had she shared it? Kenzie couldn't understand why Emily had acted the way that she had. There didn't seem to be any logic to it.

But then, people often behaved in illogical ways. Even when Kenzie knew that something she was doing was illogical, that didn't stop her from doing it. She considered herself a logical, reasoning person, but she still did things she knew didn't make sense. She made an emotional decision. A split-second reflex. A compulsion. Magical thinking. There were a lot of reasons for behaving illogically.

26

Do you think anyone will be home at Emily's house?" Kenzie asked Zachary as they walked back away from the kids to get into the car.

"Who knows what her schedule is like? Some people work during the day, some don't. Since you're out right now, we may as well check and find out. Or maybe Emily herself will answer the door. Then we would at least know that she is home and safe." He shook his head. "I hate to think of her out with the gang somewhere after someone in the gang turns up dead and she takes a picture of him. That's not… that doesn't show a good sense of self-preservation."

Kenzie chuckled. "That's different from how I would have put it, but you're absolutely right. I have no idea how she is mixed up with this gang or what she is doing, but it doesn't strike me as particularly wise to be disseminating pictures of a dead gang member so indiscriminately."

"No. I don't think so. There's a code in these groups. You start sharing gang business around in other places, and you break the code. I wouldn't want to be in her place."

"She's so young. You really think she's a member of a gang?"

"She's not that young. Teens are prime recruits for gangs. And when you're dealing with family memberships, kids of established gang members, they can easily be brought up while they're still in single digits.

Eight or nine years old. Start running courier for the gang, standing as lookout, anything like that. They're born into it."

Kenzie couldn't even picture it. Gang members as young as that? But surely they wouldn't be considered full members. Wouldn't be expected to keep all of the gang's rules.

They were driving Zachary's car. He put the address he had photographed into the GPS and started driving without waiting for directions. He obviously knew what area of town it was in even if he didn't know the exact street or house.

"How much do you know about gangs like this?" Kenzie asked.

"Not a lot. I don't know what kind of gang it is, whether they are a local chapter of a bigger gang or it is a small juvenile gang that is just a bunch of friends who got together and play at being tough guys. I don't know if they have something to prove. Whether Emily is a full gang member or has to perform some challenge to be initiated into the gang. I don't know why your John Doe was killed."

There were a lot of questions to be answered. There wasn't any one gang template that would fit over the situation and give them all of the answers they were looking for.

The GPS started giving instructions, which Zachary followed until they got to the address. It wasn't far away. Roxboro wasn't a big town, and Emily had to be close enough to the school to attend there.

It was an older neighborhood. Houses that had been there for a long while and had not withstood the test of time very gracefully. Many had long grass and unkempt yards, paint peeling off of the house, maybe an abandoned, rusty car sitting in the middle of the driveway or yard, sometimes up on blocks, sometimes with a missing tire, propped up by a jack.

"Nice," Kenzie said, shaking her head.

She immediately regretted it. Who was she to judge these people by how much time or money they had to maintain their homes? They clearly didn't have much of anything and did the best they could with the little they had. Was she better than they were just because she made more money, having come from a family that made more money and allowed her to get the education she had in order to pursue an interest in medicine?

"Sorry," she said to Zachary, shaking her head at the inappropriateness of her judgment.

He shrugged. She was sure he had probably heard much worse judgments his whole life, at least all of his growing-up years, which had been very lean. He had been on the other side.

They stepped carefully up the slightly wobbly steps to the house and rang the doorbell. Kenzie couldn't hear the bell ringing inside the house, so she followed up with a firm knock on the door, which should rouse anyone within.

They waited for a few minutes, looking around, watching the rest of the neighborhood, while the neighborhood watched them. Even though it was the middle of the workday for many people and the middle of the school day for the kids, there were a good number of people out and about, sitting on front porches, working on cars, and taking the dogs for a walk.

Eventually, they could hear footsteps inside, and the door handle turned. A woman opened the door and looked at them. Her skin was whiter than Emily's, her face narrower and more finely-boned. Emily didn't look enough like her for Kenzie to be sure that they were biologically related.

"Hi. We're looking for Emily Cross?" Kenzie asked.

"She's not here. It's a school day. She's at school."

"We just came from there. I was hoping she would be here."

"Who are you?" The woman leaned forward and looked Kenzie up and down. She glanced at Zachary, but discounted him as unimportant and continued to speak to Kenzie. "You her probation officer or something? You're not from the school."

"Is she on probation?"

The woman looked at her suspiciously. "Who are you?"

"I'm… with law enforcement, but I'm not her probation officer. I didn't realize she was on probation."

Mrs. Cross shrugged as if it didn't make any difference. And Kenzie didn't suppose it did. She hadn't said anything to the mother that would give her any cause for concern or explain why Kenzie was there or should know that Emily was on probation.

"She's not at the school. If she's not here, then where do you think she is?"

"I don't know. She'll show up sooner or later."

"When was the last time you saw her?"

The woman rubbed her forehead. She shook her head. "I don't know. It s been a crazy week. We have been on opposite shifts, so I don't really see her."

Kenzie couldn't imagine not even knowing where her teenager was for a week. Not even knowing when the last time she had seen her was.

"That must be difficult," she said sympathetically. "And tough for Emily. So… is there a friend she might be with? A boyfriend?"

"Em doesn't have a boyfriend," Mrs. Cross said immediately, shaking her head. She was awfully sure about it for someone who didn't even know when the last time she saw her daughter was.

"Oh, Okay. You don't know where else she might be hanging out?"

The woman scratched the back of her neck. "I don't know. Who did you say you were?"

"I'm with the medical examiner's office," Kenzie finally admitted. "Someone that Emily knows was killed recently, and I wanted to make sure that she is okay."

27

M rs. Cross blinked, frowning, trying to make sense of what Kenzie was telling her. She shook her head and stepped back from the door, motioning for them to enter.

"You'd better come in."

Kenzie entered and Zachary followed her in, his head turning back and forth as he looked around the house. Kenzie realized she should probably be more aware of her surroundings, her "head on a swivel," as the cops liked to say. But she was too focused on the woman in front of her, leading her into the untidy front room that smelled of stale smoke, where a TV was playing too quietly to make out the words.

Mrs. Cross motioned for them to seat themselves, and the two of them tried to shift things around to make a place where they could sit comfortably.

"Who died?" Mrs. Cross demanded, "What are you talking about? A friend from school?"

Kenzie shifted uncomfortably, not sure what to say. She didn't want to show Emily's mother the picture of the man to see if she could identify him. Emily had probably never introduced him to her family, if they were in a gang together. There was no point in showing the dead body to Mrs. Cross, something that would just upset her. But she also wanted the woman to understand how concerned they were for Emily's welfare and to find out what she knew and why she had done what she had.

"A man that Emily knew… from the neighborhood," she said after a period of consideration. "He was killed… violently. I don't know if Emily was around when it happened, but it seems likely. She definitely knew about it." Kenzie stopped short of revealing that they knew Emily had seen John Doe's dead body. That might be revealing too much.

"A man?"

"A… young man. But… older than Emily."

"Who?"

"I don't know his name. I was hoping that Emily could help me with that."

"You don't know his name? How do you know that she knows him?"

"From her phone. You know kids… and their apps."

She thought that the reference had been too oblique, but Mrs. Cross rolled her eyes as if this were something she complained about often. Maybe it was. Kenzie didn't have to deal with teens and their phones in her line of work. She only knew what she did from absorbing it from the culture around her.

"Yeah, I know," Mrs. Cross agreed. "Why don't you ask her friends where she is? Have them look on *their* magical apps and tell us where she is right now."

"We didn't find her friends terribly helpful," Zachary inserted dryly.

Mrs. Cross snorted. "I would guess not."

"You're not impressed with her friends?" Kenzie asked with a laugh.

"You know… once upon a time, she was a very nice, sweet girl. I remember when she was a toddler, she just charmed the pants off of everyone. Even when she started school, the teachers all loved her, and she was so helpful. I think she thought she was one of the teachers, not one of the students, because she was always trying to do things with the grown-ups and talked about the kids her age like they were little kids she was taking care of instead of friends her own age."

Mrs. Cross stared off into the distance, then rubbed her eyes as if she were looking through a fog.

"She was such a nice little girl. But she didn't stay that way. When she was ten, eleven, she wanted to be off on her own. Leave her alone. Don't talk to her. Don't ask her about her friends or school or anything. And then the rest started creeping in… the hair stuff. Piercings that I certainly had not approved. Tattoos. Clothes that were… not little girl clothes. I would have been happy if she had just worn jeans and a t-shirt. But she had to be… too grown up. For a while, I thought things were better. She was in one of the early-morning clubs at school, and it was like she was happy again." She sighed. "I wonder whatever happened to that little girl sometimes. Whatever happened to my little girl?"

"That must be difficult. I know mothers and daughters can have complicated relationships."

"I just wish… that I *had* a relationship with her. I really don't. We're like… two people who live in the same house. That's all. We don't talk. We don't eat together. I don't know when the last time was that we went out shopping together. I used to take her shopping for school clothes at the beginning of each school year. Kids don't really do that anymore. Start school with new outfits. I guess it's… gauche. Not cool."

"She's had a lot of truants this year?" Kenzie suggested.

"Yeah, sure. It isn't like I can force her to go to school. Even before I was working shift, I couldn't. It isn't like I could physically force her into the car. If I told her she had to go, she would just tell me no. What am I going to do? Take something away from her? Ground her? There wasn't anything to take away from her. She barely had anything. The way we live… paycheck to paycheck… there aren't any extras. And grounding her? How can I keep her here when I'm not here?"

"That would be pretty difficult," Kenzie admitted.

"They won't let you chain them up," Zachary added.

This made Mrs. Cross chuckle. "It would be so much easier if you could."

"Well…" Kenzie sighed. "I guess there isn't really anything else I have to ask you. If you don't know where Emily is, you don't know where she is. Do you think she would answer the phone if you called her?"

"She never does."

"If you texted her?"

"Maybe." Mrs. Cross pulled her phone out and tapped the screen several times.

"I wouldn't ask her where she is," Zachary advised. "That will just put her off and warn her that someone is looking for her. Is there something you would normally text her out of the blue? That you're just checking in to see how she is? You want to take her out to dinner? Can't find your tablet?

"My hair dryer." Mrs. Cross shook her head in disbelief. "She is always taking it and leaving it somewhere else. And the girl never actually looks like she's done her hair. She looks like she just rolled out of bed. So what does she need a hair dryer for?"

"To dry her fingernails?" Kenzie suggested.

"Maybe so." Mrs. Cross pondered this. She tapped her phone and sent a text off to her daughter. "I don't know if she'll answer. Sometimes she just ignores me."

She scrolled up through her conversations.

"She texted me Wednesday."

"And she sounded okay?"

The woman shrugged. "Seemed like it. I guess so. It was just… routine stuff. You know. Sort of roommate stuff, since we're hardly mother and daughter anymore."

Kenzie nodded, not sure what to say to this. They all sat there waiting for the beep that would indicate Emily had texted her mother back. Mrs. Cross sat looking at the phone. Nothing happened. Eventually, she looked around the room.

"I really need to clean this place up. I don't think she's going to answer me. Maybe she went to the school after you were looking for her. She's not allowed to use her phone during classes."

"That's probably it," Zachary agreed.

Kenzie nodded. She didn't think that any of them actually believed it, but she didn't want to do anything to make Mrs. Cross feel worse. It was bad enough that she didn't know where her daughter was, hadn't seen her in days, and had no idea where she could be or who she might be with. She wasn't going to be in a very happy mood when they left her to her own thoughts.

"Thank you for your help," Kenzie told her. "I'm sorry we couldn't answer more of your questions. Do you think that you could ask Emily to call me when you see her next?" Kenzie got out one of her business cards and handed it to Mrs. Cross. "I'd really appreciate it."

"Sure, of course," Mrs. Cross agreed.

But Kenzie left wondering if Mrs. Cross would ever see her daughter again.

28

There wasn't much more that Kenzie and Zachary could do. Kenzie needed to get to the office to continue with her regular work. The medical examiner's office did make inquiries to assist in their postmortem examinations and reports, but actual detective work was sort of outside of her purview. There was only so much she could do without raising eyebrows.

"Sorry we weren't able to get anywhere," Zachary told her.

"No, it's fine. I didn't know if we would be able to find anything. I should just leave it to the police and their investigation, but I thought that since Emily was one of the kids at the school, and we were trying to help out Rhys, I might be able to get somewhere with it. I'll just let Campbell and Detective Saul know what we found out and let them look into it."

"Do you want me to do any more investigating? Checking into Emily's background? Investigating gangs in the area?"

"No, it's fine. You've got your own cases to work on. The police are already on it, so we shouldn't be duplicating their efforts and getting in their way."

Zachary held Kenzie's gaze for a moment, trying to read her. She hated it when he tried to interpret what she was saying instead of just listening to what she said. Yes, there were times when she said she was fine with something when she was not, but he should still listen to what she said, until she was ready to tell him otherwise.

"Really," Kenzie assured him. "The police will take care of it. I don't want you to waste resources on it. You have enough to do."

In truth, she had no idea how many cases he had and how much of his time was spoken for. But he seemed to have plenty to keep him busy and she didn't know whether he would be able to get any further on the case anyway. And she didn't want to be accused of hiring a private investigator or involving a related party without authorization.

"Okay," Zachary agreed finally. "I'll drop you at the office and pick you up later. Are we going out tonight?"

Kenzie tried to remember what they had lined up for date night. The previous week had been the car show. She thought that tonight was just a walk in the park. It would be chilly and the sun would go down early, so she would need to get out of work in good time. Or failing that, choose another activity.

"Yes. For sure. If I don't get out in time to go to the park..."

"You're already going into the office late, so it probably wouldn't be a good idea to leave early. Why don't we plan something else tonight? A movie. Something we can start late that won't take any special planning or a lot of effort."

"Yeah, that sounds good. If you're looking for something to do today when you break for lunch, see what's showing. Otherwise, we'll look at the listings when I get home."

"Or just go over there and look at the posters and pick something on the fly."

"Oooh, that's living dangerously." Kenzie grinned. "That sounds great, actually. I think a movie is a good idea."

Zachary smiled and gave her a quick kiss before she exited the car.

Campbell said he would come down to talk to Kenzie when he was free, so she could get started on her regular work and not lose time waiting for him upstairs. It was nearly lunchtime before he came down to find her.

"We have some progress on your John Doe," Campbell told her as he stood by her desk. "First thing we got any results back on was ballistics."

Kenzie had not been confident that they could match the bullet to anything, so this was good news.

"The gun has a history?"

"Been used before in an armed robbery. A shot fired into the ceiling, not into a person," Campbell reassured her.

"Was it a gang?"

He raised his brows and looked at her. "Was it a gang," he repeated slowly. "Do you know something about gang involvement in this case?"

"It was Zachary who made the connection," Kenzie said. "I was frustrated not to be able to get anywhere on the identification, and I showed him the clothing. We were trying to figure out if there was anything identifiable, anything that we could trace back to a particular source that would tell us something about the victim or his identity."

Campbell nodded. "And Zachary's got a good eye," he acknowledged. "What did he see?"

"There was a bandana. I didn't think anything of it, but he thought it might be a gang identifier. Gang colors."

"Not too much of a stretch," Campbell admitted. "Although most of the gangs don't use identifiable colors anymore. They prefer to stay under the radar. Wear them to funerals or other public events where they want to show their solidarity but, most of the time, they keep them under wraps to make it harder for the police or the casual observer to identify them as gang members. Keep the heat off."

"Zachary said that some of the smaller local gangs still use them."

"Yep. He's right. Especially ad hoc neighborhood gangs. They want to be visible. Want people to know that it is their territory, and that there are gang members around. Be able to quickly identify rival gang members and allegiances when they are fighting over city blocks."

"Even here in Roxboro?"

"No town is too small for one or two gangs. That might be all they can support, but one or two—you really need two; a single gang can't survive in a vacuum—yeah. Even if it is just a few members. They like to swagger around, bully citizens. Pretend they're tough and independent. James Dean syndrome."

Kenzie chuckled at the reference to the cultural icon from *Rebel Without a Cause*. The kids today probably had no idea who James Dean was, but they still needed something to rebel against. Still needed to fight for dominance. In a poor neighborhood like the one Emily lived in, it was vital to have something to fight against and fight for.

"So do you know which gang uses red bandanas around here?"

"Yeah, there are a couple of small gangs, and I know one of them wears red. I'll get details from someone who knows the situation a bit better. And in answer to your question, the robbery wasn't necessarily a gang action, but I wouldn't be surprised to find that it was perpetrated by gang members or was used to fund gang activities."

"But they weren't wearing colors when they did it?"

"That would make things a bit too easy for the detectives investigating it. They're not completely stupid, these kids."

"We think that the girl who started circulating the picture of the murdered man was a member of the same gang."

"Oh?"

"She was wearing the bandana when we saw her the first time. We thought—or I thought—it was just a fashion statement. Zachary was the one who put the two bandanas together to come up with the theory that they are both members of the same gang. We went back to the school to talk to her today to see if we could get the name of the John Doe from her. But she was gone. The group of friends she hangs out with, who are not all gang members, said that she hadn't been around much since we talked to them."

"What day was that?"

"It was Tuesday that we talked to them before. And then this morning. They weren't sure if they had seen her since then."

"Do you have a name? We'll look into it. Drop by her house and talk to her folks. See what's been going on with her."

"We actually…. dropped by there this morning already. Her mom was home; doesn't know when she saw her daughter last."

"Is she a missing person?"

"I wouldn't say so. Not that her mom has reported missing, anyway. She said that they don't see much of each other. Mom works shift. The girl—Emily Cross is her name—has missed a lot of school. Sounds like she doesn't get there very often. I have the address and phone number. I'll text them to you,"

"You got them from her friends?" Campbell raised an eyebrow in disbelief.

"Well… let's just say that we managed to get them when we went by the school to talk to her friends."

Campbell coughed into his fist, laughing. "Okay, let's go with that," he agreed. "Zachary was with you?"

"How did you guess?"

"Well, the first clue is saying 'we' but, even without that, I would still have guessed. He has a remarkable talent for getting information out of people."

"He knows some people over there. Apparently, he got the previous principal busted."

"Ah, yes. That was a nasty case that did not endear the school administrators to the parents and community."

Kenzie thought of how Zachary had not only gotten the information from Principal Lakes, but had also managed to draw out the "loser" kids that Emily hung out with, holding back information and making them ask him about it, instead of the other way around. He knew people.

"He's a talented private investigator," she agreed.

"So, with all of that, I suppose I don't need to tell you the dead man's identity."

"Do you know who he is?" Kenzie asked eagerly. "We didn't manage to get a name. He's older than the school kids and, if they knew who he was, they weren't telling. Emily's mom said that Emily didn't have any boyfriends and she doesn't know who her friends are."

"Always nice to have such involved parents," Campbell said dryly.

"I don't think it's entirely her fault. I think she would like to do more. But it is tough when she's not home at the same time. Single parenting. Shift work. Teenagers. It's a pretty difficult scenario."

Campbell nodded. "Thank goodness for my own parents and their stability," he said simply.

"Were you ever a rebellious teen?"

"When we played cops and robbers, I was always the cop."

"Ah." Kenzie nodded. "So you didn't struggle to figure out what direction you wanted to go. This was always your end game."

"Pretty much, yeah. So I was careful not to do anything as a teenager that might disqualify me from being able to serve as a law enforcement officer. That helped to keep me on the straight and narrow. No drugs. No arrests."

"And you have a name for our John Doe?" Kenzie brought the conversation back to the critical revelation. She hated having unidentified bodies in the morgue. Every body had a name. Every body should be identified. She didn't like anyone going to potter's field without a name. Even if they went unclaimed, they shouldn't go unidentified.

29

Your victim's name is Trevor Mercer."

Kenzie immediately wrote it down on the pad next to her and pulled up the file on the computer to substitute Trevor Mercer for John Doe.

"Great! How was he identified?"

"Fingerprints. Not a great match. Not enough index points to be sure of the ID, but enough to get a pop on the system to check it out. Comparing the initial picture to his driver's license. Showing his next of kin a sanitized photo. They're going to give us DNA and dental records to verify."

"Perfect," Kenzie nodded. With all of those things, they could be sure they had the right man, even with the advanced state of decomposition. She had retrieved enough DNA for the lab to profile, and his dental work was entirely intact. No baseball bat or bullet to the teeth. She had already done the X-rays needed for the comparison, once they tracked down the last dentist that Mercer had gone to.

"So who was he?" she asked. "He must have a record if you got a hit on fingerprints."

"Just low-level stuff, no felonies. And he was only ever arrested or convicted in Ohio."

"Ohio! Well, he was a little way from home. Is that where his family is?"

"Yes. He got in some trouble as a teen. Got himself out of there, ran away to New York. Ended up in Vermont." Campbell shrugged, spreading his hands apart. "Don't ask me how or why. So we're trying to track his movements now in Vermont, but there isn't a lot. He stayed below the radar."

"Maybe he had a cousin or friend in Vermont."

"Probably. There is not a big draw for criminals to come from New York to Vermont. Retired couples, maybe. People who want to run B&Bs or take over a family maple operation. But criminals?"

Kenzie nodded her agreement. She saw enough crime, working for the medical examiner's office, but it was mostly local. Some cartels from other countries. But it wasn't somewhere that usually drew much interest from petty criminals in nearby states. Unless they were trying to escape something. Start over again.

"And do you know if he was in the gang? The one you were talking about that wears red?"

"I will be looking into it. The bandana is a good lead. It's hard to know who is in what gangs when the criminals don't advertise it."

"He wasn't the owner of the gun?"

"Not originally. But it has gone through several hands since it was registered, and it is pretty hard to say whether he ever owned it or not. These guys tend not to register the transfers."

"Well, someone should talk to them about that," Kenzie teased.

"Yes. I'm sure if they realized it was their civic duty, they wouldn't be so negligent."

Kenzie laughed. "Well, I hope this helps you figure out what happened to him. I'm very relieved to have a name. I don't like them to be unidentified."

"I'm sure his family will be grateful to know what happened to him, too. Maybe not happy about what happened to him or about the state of the remains when we found him, but at least they won't have to spend decades wondering whatever happened to them."

Kenzie reported Campbell's findings to Zachary when she took a break for lunch. He listened to the details and was happy to hear that Campbell had agreed that Emily and Mercer were members of the same gang and would follow up about it.

"We're getting closer," he said, pleased. "Or rather, you're getting closer. The police are getting closer. They'll be able to figure out where he was and what happened to him if they keep digging. The main work—identifying him and the connection between him and Rhys's school—has been done."

"I hope that they can work it all out. I still don't understand why Emily would circulate his picture to her friends and acquaintances at school."

"Maybe it was… some kind of memorial. Making sure that he wouldn't be forgotten. The more people she got it to, the more of a 'legend' he would become. He would leave a footprint. A legacy. Instead of being a nameless, faceless guy the local gang had just offed, he became… a face they would remember, anyway."

"Still nameless."

"As far as we know. Maybe when she started to circulate it, it included his name. But later in the process, the name wasn't forwarded to Rhys, or the message that contained his name was erased, but Rhys managed to save the photograph. But even nameless, he would still be remembered."

Kenzie nodded in agreement. "And for someone like Rhys… that picture is imprinted on his memory forever. He will never forget it."

"Oh, *Rhys.*"

Kenzie could tell from the tone of his voice that he had just remembered something.

"Yes? Rhys what?"

"He was discharged today. He's back home."

"Oh!" Kenzie felt some of the tension go out of her. She hadn't been aware that she had been holding herself so stiff. "That's good to hear. I'm very glad about that."

"Yeah. It's always better to be at home than the psych ward. When you're feeling well enough to be home, I mean."

"Of course. I knew what you meant. Sometimes the hospital is a necessity. I'm glad that he's recovered enough that he and Vera and the doctors all feel like he can be home now."

"Me too. I might go over to see him this afternoon. Take him a burger or something and just chill at home where he is comfortable."

"That sounds good. You should."

"I think I will," Zachary agreed. "I'm not being very productive today. I keep starting on other things, but I don't get anywhere. Keep thinking about Emily and Rhys."

Kenzie could understand that. She was feeling somewhat distracted herself. At least the Mercer case was actually something she was supposed to be working on, so she could obsess over it and still be considered to be doing her work.

"I'll see you tonight. We'll do the movie thing, maybe go out for supper, and you can tell me how Rhys is."

30

They had a good evening. Kenzie was glad to get away from work and to try to put all of her files to the side for a while. She worked hard at the office and, when she left, it was time to hang up her scalpel and spend time with Zachary or do other things she needed to. She wanted to be fully present in those other things, not with half of her brain working on her medical examiner work, while the other half tried to keep up with her social or personal life.

She remembered how much Walter had focused on his work when she was a child. There was no escaping it. When the Senate was in session, he was away all the time, dealing with bills that should pass and those that shouldn't, wining and dining politicians, developing his strategies and constantly obsessed with achieving his ends. On those rare occasions he was home and spent time with his family, he always brought up his work, what he was doing, what frustrations he was dealing with. Everything there was to know about whatever cause he was working on. Sometimes, it was exciting, and Kenzie was interested in seeing how he worked things out, fascinated with the complex processes he worked through, with how much knowledge he had to have to perform his job. He made everything seem exciting and important.

But over the years, she had learned that everything was not exciting and important. Bills that were defeated kept popping up again and again in later sessions, under other names and sponsors. Bills that passed did not change the world as Walter had promised they would. The world moved slowly. The frenetic pace at which Walter had tried to get everything done didn't mean anything. The pace did not continue once a bill was passed. It was in someone else's bailiwick then, and changes happened slowly and gradually. What passed in one session might become too bloated and bogged down to go anywhere. Or it might be reversed again in the next session.

She didn't want to be like her father. She wanted to give the people in her life enough of her time and intention to know they were important and brought her joy.

So she deliberately put all work concerns aside for the night and just enjoyed her time with Zachary.

They had a good visit, watched an action movie that both of them liked, and spent a little quiet time before bed to unwind and make sure that they were ready for sleep.

Kenzie woke up with a start. Someone was shaking her arm and, as she awoke she realized her phone was ringing. Not the loud ring tone of a call-out, but the muted buzzing of her phone vibrating against the side table.

Kenzie grunted and tried to say something coherent to Zachary, the person who had obviously been shaking her. She fumbled with her phone, pulled it off of the charge cord, and held it up to her ear while trying to swipe the slider on.

"Hello?"

"Is this… the medical examiner? It's Clarissa."

Kenzie blinked hard, trying to wake herself up and make the connections.

"Clarissa?" she repeated.

"You said call you about Emily and anything we knew about her."

Kenzie sat up in bed, trying to make sense of the girl's voice on the other end of the call.

"Clarissa… about Emily."

"Yes," the girl said impatiently. "You said to call you."

"Yeah. I'm glad you did. You just caught me off guard. I'm sorry. I'm just getting my thoughts in order now."

"Emily knew him. The guy who died. Who was shot."

"Yes, I know she did. And she was the one who took his picture and started circulating it around, too, wasn't she?"

"Maybe. I guess so."

"They were both in the same gang together?"

"I don't know if it is a gang," Clarissa temporized.

"Well, it isn't a social club."

Clarissa laughed weakly at that. "Well… I don't know. A lot of these guys call themselves clubs now, instead of gangs."

"I don't care what they call themselves. As long as we can figure out how Emily and Trevor Mercer were involved with each other and sort out what went wrong."

"You know his name?"

"Yes. Maybe you were hoping that you would be the one to tell me that. If you were, then thank you for at least calling to tell me that part. But there are a lot of other details that are still missing from the picture."

"Trevor… she didn't even call him that. She called him by his last name. Mercer."

"Did she talk about him a lot?"

"I don't know. Sometimes she talked about him. Sometimes, she didn't want to talk about anything to do with the gang. She just pretended that they didn't even exist."

"Was she involved in… the criminal aspects of the gang? Or was it just another family to hang out with?"

"I guess they were like a family," Clarissa agreed. Kenzie rubbed her eyes, trying to remember what she knew about Clarissa and what the girl looked like. She had been one of the crowd. White face, blond, kind of tangled hair, if Kenzie were remembering the right girl. Young looking. But they all looked young. She couldn't believe how young the teenagers looked now that she was older.

When she was that age, she had figured she was no different from an adult. She'd been mature, but that didn't mean she made all the right choices. Clarissa was racking up her mistakes. Skipping school. Doing whatever the "losers" who hung out together did. She knew her friend was involved in a gang, even if she wasn't herself. She had known about the dead man and yet had lied to Kenzie and Zachary when they had asked if she knew who he was and who had started circulating the picture. Everything she had done had shown that she wasn't ready for adult responsibility yet.

Then again, not all adults were ready for it, either.

Kenzie drew in a long breath and let it out. "So you called me, Clarissa. What did you want to tell me? Other than Mercer's name and the fact that they were in a gang together. Because I already knew all of that."

"You didn't know it earlier," Clarissa sounded pouty.

"No. But things can move fast in an investigation. That's why you should tell us everything you know when we first ask, so we can get out ahead of the ball instead of playing catch-up the whole time."

"Yeah... well, Emily wouldn't want me to be telling you all of this stuff. But I figured... I don't want her to get hurt. I'm worried. She's not answering any messages. I thought... she would be back. We could talk. She could tell me what I should or shouldn't say. I could tell her to talk to you about it, because you could help her. But... I don't know what's happened."

"When was the last time you heard from her?"

"I'm not sure. Wednesday or Thursday."

"Did she tell you what was going on? Anything about why Mercer was killed? Why she was sharing his picture with everyone?"

"No. She said..." Clarissa paused, trying to gather her thoughts. "She said that she had to stay clear of the cops, that it wasn't safe. So I knew she didn't want to talk to you guys."

"What did she think the police were going to do? Did she see Mercer killed?"

"I don't know. Yes. She was really freaked out. She said that everything had gone wrong. She wanted to get out. She wanted to find some way to be safe."

"She wanted to get out of the gang? Out of town? What?"

"I don't know."

"Were she and Mercer friends? Or just both in the same gang?"

"They're family, those guys."

"And I know that. She needed some structure and support. She didn't feel like she was getting it at home. Her mom was always out and didn't have the time for her. And I guess she wasn't getting all of the support she needed from you guys at school, either, if she felt the need to join the gang."

"We couldn't all get together outside of school time," Clarissa said defensively. "Some of us got parents at home. Curfews. Bed checks at night. We can't all get out at night or whenever we want to."

"So…" Kenzie persisted. "How close was Emily to Mercer?"

"They were… you know… getting together. They liked each other."

"They were intimate?" Kenzie clarified.

Clarissa snorted. "Whatever you want to call it. Yeah. Some stuff was going on. But they weren't… like… exclusive. Boyfriend and girlfriend or anything."

"If she liked him, why didn't she report to the police when he was killed? Why did she send those photos to other kids instead of letting the police know that something had happened to him? Doesn't she want whoever killed him to be punished for it? And then she doesn't have to be afraid. The person who killed him will be behind bars, and she will be safe."

"No, no. She said that she couldn't. I don't know all the details, but she said she couldn't talk to any police about it."

Kenzie knew that the police spent all kinds of money on programs to introduce kids and cops to each other so that they could develop good, trusting relationships and so, when something happened to a kid, he didn't feel like he had to be afraid of the cops. He would know he could go to them with his problem and they would help him. There were resource officers in the school and the community. The police went to community events, let kids sit in the police cars or police helicopter. All so the kids didn't think they had something to fear from the police.

And did it do any good? Kids got to be Emily's age, and they didn't trust any adults, especially those who wore uniforms.

"Well…" Kenzie rubbed her eyes. "I appreciate you calling to let me know some of these details. It is really helpful. I want to help Emily, and that's pretty hard if she won't have anything to do with me. If she'll come to me, I can introduce her to the policeman who is in charge of the case. He's really nice. I've been involved in other cases with him. He's always been very helpful and calm and good to work with. I think that once she knew him… she would feel differently."

"Yeah. I don't think she's going to take that advice."

"If you see or hear from her, please tell her that. I'm a woman and not a cop, and I think she could approach me without worrying that I would turn her into a suspect. I'm a nice person. You know Rhys Salter? You ask him. He can tell you that I'm a good person and I've helped him out before. My boyfriend and I have both helped him."

"Oh yeah, Salter. Well, he won't talk to me, will he?" Clarissa laughed.

"He can still communicate. He can tell you that we are trustworthy."

"Even if you are, I know the police *aren't*. So that's not going to happen."

Kenzie shook her head. "Okay, Clarissa. You do whatever you think is best. Let Emily get into trouble because she won't listen to good advice and turn in a killer."

She waited momentarily to see if Clarissa had anything to say to that, and then ended the call.

31

That sounded interesting," Zachary commented.

Kenzie lay back down and felt for the side table to lay her phone down again. Her head was throbbing, and she hated how she felt after being dragged out of a sound sleep and having to talk on the phone and sound coherent. Would she be able to get back to sleep now that she'd woken up?

"I don't know why she bothered to call me," Kenzie groaned. "She didn't have any new information. Certainly nothing that she needed to wake me up for."

"But she didn't know what you already knew."

"Not really. But there's no reason she couldn't have waited until morning. It's just rude to wake people up in the middle of the night."

Zachary put one arm around Kenzie, snuggling her close against him. "She probably did it on purpose."

"To make me mad? To show her power over me?"

"Maybe. Or maybe because she wanted to catch you off balance. To make sure you didn't have a way to call the police or figure out where she was."

"I don't need to know where she is right now. She's probably at home. She was talking about curfews and bed checks. And I know where she'll be tomorrow. Or rather, on Monday. So I don't need to know where she is tonight."

"Unless she was with Emily."

Kenzie opened her eyes and stared into the soft, velvety darkness. "What?"

"If she was with Emily tonight, and that was why she called you, then she wouldn't want you to be able to trace her there. So she calls you at night, out of a deep sleep, so you won't be able to put the police on to her until it's too late."

"Do you think that's what she was doing?"

"I don't know. Just one possibility. She could also have called you because she couldn't sleep. Maybe she was worried about Emily and couldn't settle in until she'd called you to talk about it."

"Yeah."

"Either way… there's not much you can do about it. If Emily doesn't want to be found, Clarissa isn't going to tell you how to find her."

"How did you know that?"

"It was obvious from your side of the conversation that she wasn't giving it up. Emily is in hiding. She doesn't want to be found."

"She said the last time she talked to Emily was Wednesday or Thursday."

"Maybe. Or maybe they are together. She may not tell you the truth."

"Of course not," Kenzie agreed. Even though she knew this was true, she still always expected people to tell her the truth, or some version of it, to start with. She had to remind herself that even she herself didn't tell the truth, or the whole truth, all the time. "Do you think they are together? That Emily is okay?"

"I think Clarissa would be more worried if she thought that Emily was in real danger. It didn't sound from your conversation like she feared Emily being discovered or killed at any moment."

"No. She wasn't acting like that."

"Then whether they are together or not, Clarissa doesn't necessarily believe she is in any real danger."

"She's just repeating what Emily said. And she thinks Emily is being paranoid."

She felt Zachary nod. He readjusted his grip on her. "Yeah. probably."

"Emily doesn't think it is safe to talk to the police either."

"Most kids don't."

"Yeah. That's what I was just thinking. And I don't even know why that is, because most kids do not have experiences where the police have been violent toward them or have treated them unfairly. Most kids haven't even had any contact with the police, and they still have this... rift."

"Yep," Zachary agreed. He breathed into her hair. "We should probably be quiet; let you settle down to sleep again."

"What about you?"

"Don't worry about me."

He wouldn't go back to sleep, she knew. But Kenzie staying awake wouldn't make any difference to his sleep. There wasn't anything she could do to make him relax and go back to sleep.

There was a message on Kenzie's work voicemail from Detective Saul, asking her to call him back about developments on the case. He didn't know that Clarissa had called Kenzie, of course, but maybe he suspected she had more information than she had given Sergeant Campbell. Campbell had only wanted the general structure of what Kenzie knew. Maybe Saul wanted to dig down deeper. Kenzie felt like they should be getting somewhere with the investigation but that they were not moving fast enough.

She often felt that way, though. The timelines seen on TV versus what happened in real life were very different. A case was not solved in a day or two. There was a lot of investigation and case building to do before they had enough information to lay charges. As Zachary had indicated, they couldn't just take Clarissa or anyone else at their word. The police needed evidence to verify Clarissa's story. Where her phone GPS said she had been. Whether she'd been exchanging calls with Emily or a burner phone. Whether what she said about Emily's and Mercer's relationship was true.

She called Saul back and, getting his voicemail, left him a message to follow up with her when he was ready. They could put their heads together and review what each knew.

Saul showed up while Kenzie was working on another autopsy. He stood in the observation room until she noticed him.

"Oh, hi." Kenzie looked back down at the body she was finishing up with. "I didn't know you were there. How long have you been standing there?"

"Just a few minutes. I didn't want to startle you."

Kenzie appreciated it, but thought it was more than a little creepy to have him standing there watching her silently when she didn't even know he was there. It was common courtesy for a cop to announce himself when he entered the room if she were already in the middle of a procedure.

"Uh, next time, just say hi. I'd rather know you were there waiting for me."

He shrugged.

"I'm just about finished with this post. Do you mind waiting another five minutes? Then we can grab the conference room and run through everything."

"Sure. No problem. Who are you working on now?"

Kenzie filled him in on the details. "Natural death. Just unattended. Guy had a massive coronary. Everyone knew he was a ticking time bomb. He'd probably been told that half a dozen times himself. Looks like he had regular medical appointments when it would have been brought up."

"No rare poisons? Family members waiting to inherit? Business rivals?"

"Nope. From all indications, just died in his sleep. Well, he probably woke up for a few seconds or minutes before he died, but there isn't anything to suggest foul play."

"I guess they can't all be so interesting."

"No, a lot of the postmortems we do are just boring old natural deaths or accidents. There isn't usually a big mystery or conspiracy around them."

32

Kenzie finished all that she was going to do and stripped off her gloves. George would clean up and close the incisions. Kenzie was out of Saul's line of sight for a couple of minutes while she pulled off the rest of her protective clothing. Then she motioned for him to follow her and took him to one of the smaller meeting rooms. They both sat down.

"So, what can you tell me so far about Mercer?" Saul inquired. "I guess I already know cause and manner of death. But you have also been making other inquiries."

"Yes. As you know from Sergeant Campbell, Mercer was in a gang before he died. And one of the kids that we talked to the other day was in the same gang. They both had a red bandana, which I guess they used to show that they were members of the gang when they wanted it to be known."

"So you have a witness."

"I'm not sure yet what she witnessed, and what she might have just happened across lately. I don't have her story yet. The girl's name is Emily Cross. She's only sixteen, and I guess she and Mercer were involved despite the difference in their ages."

"Emily Cross."

"Yeah. I tried to follow up with her home address, but she wasn't there. Her mom isn't sure when she was last home. She could be staying with a friend somewhere."

"Or the gang."

"Right." Kenzie nodded. "I guess you could watch the gang to see if she is with any of them."

"Do you have the names of her friends at school?"

"Not really. The principal might be able to help you. I know a couple of first names, but that's all. She could give you full names and contact information. I couldn't exactly get a warrant for that information, but you could."

She didn't tell Saul how she had gotten Emily's home address, and he didn't ask her.

"Right," Saul agreed. "We'll be sure to follow up with them. And her friend that you know, the one who started all of this."

"Rhys."

"Yes. I should talk to him directly. Do you suppose they would let me into the psych ward to do an interview?" Saul made a face. "I suppose I'm going to have to explain in court why I think a psych patient's testimony is reliable."

"He is out of the hospital. He was released yesterday."

"Oh. So I could see him at home or at the school."

"I don't know if he'll be at school on Monday," Kenzie said. "He might still need some more time before he is ready to go back. But he'll be at home today and tomorrow."

"Good. And he lives with his parents?"

"With his grandmother. She has raised him, either by herself or with her husband or daughter—the boy's mother—since he was born. It's just the two of them right now."

"What happened to the mother?"

Kenzie shrugged as if she didn't know or it was unimportant. Saul really didn't need to know those details. If Kenzie just glossed over them, he probably wouldn't pursue it. Kids were left alone or with grandparents for a lot of reasons.

"But…" she approached the topic delicately, "as far as talking to him goes, did Sergeant Campbell tell you about him?"

"What about him?"

"Uh, that he is selectively mute?"

"He's a mute?"

"He speaks occasionally, but usually only a word or two at a time."

"Does he use sign language, then? I need an interpreter?"

"No. He uses some gestures, but not sign language. And he uses his phone messaging app."

"Oh, of course. It's all texting with kids these days."

"Well…" Kenzie tried to give him a sense of what he would be dealing with, worried that he was getting the wrong impression. "He doesn't text full sentences."

"I know." He waved a hand at her. "No punctuation. I've seen the ways kids text. No periods and half the time no vowels. But I can figure it out."

"No, what I mean is, he will just use a word or two, and pictures or gifs. It's kind of like… trying to solve a word puzzle."

"Charades?"

"Well, there are some similarities for sure," Kenzie admitted. "It's a mixed bag. His grandma will be able to help you to figure out what he means. But she is *not* happy about him being involved with all of this. You might run into some problems with her. She wasn't happy with Rhys coming to me about it and taking his phone, making a police report without her. And I guess I kind of overstepped my bounds there. I just acted because Rhys asked me to. I didn't stop to get permission from Vera."

"Has Campbell talked to her?"

"Not as far as I know. But he's not telling me about every step of the investigation. He… he knows Rhys and Vera from a previous case. So he might have decided not to bother because of the difficulty in communicating with Rhys. He has the phone, and Rhys didn't know where the pictures originated. They were circulating around the school; Rhys didn't know Emily directly."

"Do you know that for sure?"

"Uh… well, I guess not for sure. I haven't talked to him since we identified Emily as the source. Maybe he does know her, but they were not close friends. The kids that Emily hangs out with knew who Rhys was, but it didn't sound like any of them knew him personally."

Saul nodded. He pulled out his notepad and made a few notations so that he would remember this information later. Emily Cross. Rhys Salter.

Probably something about their family situations and Rhys being selectively mute.

"Okay. That is helpful. I can definitely follow up on that. And you don't know any of Emily's close friends?"

"No." Kenzie wondered about Clarissa and whether she ought to tell Campbell and Saul about her. Clarissa hadn't provided any additional information, and whether Emily was staying with her was up for speculation. Kenzie hadn't heard anything on the call the previous night that would indicate that Emily had been with Clarissa. Kenzie didn't know Clarissa's last name or where she lived. Saul would need to get that information from the school anyway. "The principal is your best bet. There was a boy named Devon and a girl named Clarissa. And other kids. They are… not always at the school. They tend to be truant a good deal. So you may be able to find them there, and maybe not."

Saul jotted down the names. "Good."

"Was there anything else on Rhys's phone?" Kenzie asked.

He glanced at her, startled by the question. Maybe she wasn't supposed to be asking him any questions about the case. He was in charge of the investigation into the phone, now the homicide. It wasn't Kenzie's place to be asking about what he had found.

"Anything else?" he asked. "Like what?"

"I just didn't know whether you would be able to get anything else. Maybe there were other pictures he had saved. Or conversations in his messaging app. I don't know. I don't think he knows Emily directly but, if he does, then he might have other relevant information."

"Yeah, we're looking into all of that. The electronic forensics guys." He made a gesture to indicate that they were all working on it upstairs.

Kenzie supposed that, like everything else, this took longer in real life than it did in a one-hour cop show on TV. And there was likely a backlog. Would there be any kind of rush on it now that it had turned out to be an actual murder case? Or would they assume that since the murder had already occurred that there was no reason to hurry the results along?

In the meantime, Rhys had his new phone, so Kenzie didn't have to worry about his being unable to communicate. But she might ask him again whether he knew anything else that he hadn't told her. And whether Rhys knew Emily. When he had gone to Zachary about the trouble that Madison had been in when she had been involved with human traffickers, he had known a lot more about her and the people around her than anyone else. People tended to discount Rhys. The fact that he was mute meant that he was not likely to repeat anything that he had heard, so they just ignored him.

But Rhys had ways of communicating what he knew. And maybe it was time to find out if he knew more than he had initially revealed about the picture of the body and where it had come from. He might have known all along that it had originated with Emily and was just trying to keep her out of harm's way. Emily was concerned about the police giving her trouble, and maybe Rhys was too. Maybe she had talked him out of helping out in any other way, so that the only thing he could think of to do was to show the medical examiner the dead body.

When Kenzie returned to her desk, she found an envelope from the archives storage company. She sat down and grabbed the scissors to slit it open. Out of the plastic packet she pulled an old file, dusty, the color of the folder having degraded over time, two-toned where the info tab had been exposed to light, but the rest of the folder had been squashed up against its neighbors.

Salter, Clarence

Rhys's grandfather. The murder that he had been witness to very early in his life. Five years old. He had been the only one in the house with Grandpa Clarence and the killer. And the killer had been his own aunt.

But the people who had compiled this file had not known those details. They just knew the physical description of the victim, a bare bones description of the scene, and how he had died. When Kenzie started to skim through the description, she only found a couple of lines about Rhys. According to what the medical examiner had been told, he had been in the house, asleep. The police investigation had suggested that Grandpa Clarence had been killed in a burglary gone bad. The burglars had not known that there was anyone in the house. Maybe they had rung the doorbell or knocked on the door before breaking in, but Clarence, hard of hearing, hadn't heard them.

He had been sitting in his kitchen at the table, eating a bowl of spaghetti. The burglars had stepped in and pulled the trigger, driving a bullet straight into his forehead, killing him instantly.

In Clarence's case, it had not been a .22 caliber round, but a steel-cased .45, and it had not stopped inside his skull, but had continued on a downward trajectory, through his brain stem and out the back of his skull—as close to being killed instantly as anyone could hope for. If he had looked up in time to see the woman standing in front of him, he might have had a second or two to recognize that she was holding a gun on him and, when she had pulled the trigger, his consciousness had ended.

Not a bad death for Clarence.

Not so great for the five-year-old who had been in the house. The Salters had insisted that Rhys had slept through it and that the trauma he had experienced had just been because he had suddenly lost the grandpa he idolized without understanding what had happened to him.

But as Zachary and Kenzie had discovered, that had been a lie.

When Vera and Gloria had gotten home that day, they had known immediately what had happened. Robin's violence had been escalating before the murder. Her rage over minor irritants had led to a number of incidents already. However, at that point, her family had been more concerned about hiding what was happening than about getting her proper treatment. Or maybe that was unfair, and it had not progressed to the point where they could have her admitted involuntarily for assessment. Or maybe she had been assessed and released, and the doctors did not consider her a danger to anyone.

But they had definitely covered up the murder. They said it was a burglary, that no one but Clarence and sleeping Rhys had been home. They had moved home electronics into a pile so that it looked like a break-in had been in progress. They said they had found Rhys still asleep in his bed. Vera and Gloria had never changed their story or told anyone what had really happened.

But when Zachary had been helping Madison and Luke to escape from the human trafficking cartel, and Luke had been skimmed across the head by a bullet, it had been painfully obvious that Rhys had seen his grandfather after he had been shot, if not actually witnessed the shooting. He had immediately devolved into repeating the words he had said over and over again after Clarence's death—Robin's familiar warning, "Stop it! Just stop that!"

Kenzie had thought that was probably the only evidence they would ever have that Rhys had seen Clarence's face after he was killed. None of the Salters were willing to talk about it.

But after his MDMA therapy, Rhys's mouth had again been opened. He had been unable to stop talking and obsessing over the memories. And Kenzie had learned a lot more about that day as the words spilled out like they never had before, and maybe never would again. It had been disjointed, never the whole picture

or sequence at once. Maybe he had only been able to take it in in fractured bits. Or maybe his brain had broken it apart to store the memories separately because it was too overwhelming and terrible to have to see and hear the whole thing as a coherent whole. Or maybe the therapies over the years had helped him access some parts but not others.

Maybe it was the MDMA itself and that was how hallucinogenics always worked. Kenzie had never studied hallucinogenic therapy in detail.

As Kenzie read through the clinical autopsy report, Rhys's words echoed in her brain, and she pictured the horrific event.

At the scene survey, subject was found to be still seated at the kitchen table where he had been shot.

Grampa eating 'getti. Grampa eating red 'getti.

Attacker entered the kitchen from the living room area after apparently breaking in and gathering electronics to be stolen from the home. On discovering that the homeowner was, in fact, present, the intruder shot the victim in the forehead as he sat.

Grampa, no! Put away! Be a good girl.

The bullet traveled on a downward trajectory, through the brain stem, causing immediate death.

The noise! Loud! Grampa sit. Red 'getti. Red 'getti.

Victim had been eating spaghetti and meatballs with red sauce. Forward blood spatter on table and dishes noted, photographed, and measured, as well as exit wound spatter. No voids, no discrepancies.

Grampa eating 'getti.

Rhys had cried. It was not often that a teenage male would dare show tears to the world, and Kenzie didn't know if he had cried as a five-year-old when Vera and Gloria had arrived home. But under the influence of the MDMA, he had cried in horrified gasps, the tears pouring down his face.

Grampa! Grampa!

And then a switch from his frantic sobs to Robin's repeated,

Stop it! Just stop it!

Several times, as he told the story, Rhys collapsed onto the bed and lay in a fetal position after recounting the gunshot, curled up, hands over his head, shaking in terror. When it became too much, he would switch off and talk about the spiders he saw crawling on the walls or repeating other nonsensical phrases, convinced that they meant something, or that Kenzie and Zachary would understand if he just kept repeating them.

It was heartbreaking. Kenzie could picture the little boy he had been, just five years old, terrified by the gunshot. His Grandpa Clarence, previously a central figure in his life, sitting motionless in the chair where he had just been eating, a spaghetti-red hole in his head, red spatter across the table, unresponsive to Rhys's screams as Robin picked him up and put him back to bed, where he had supposedly been when his mother and grandmother returned home.

The police had taken Vera and the others at their word and written it up as a murder during a burglary. The burglars were never caught. They hadn't taken anything from the scene, but had fled after firing on the old man. They had left no fingerprints, no hair or other trace evidence that could be used to find them. Clarence was the only one who had seen them, and he couldn't tell anyone.

3 4

Kenzie paged through the pictures, and then finally closed the file. Would it do anyone any good to bring the real story to light now? Would anyone other than Vera and Rhys care what had really happened? They already knew. It would be part of their family history forever, no matter how hard they worked to hide it. The killer could never be prosecuted because she was dead. The file could be closed, which might help the police stats a little. But being such a cold case, who would even look at the statistics?

It was a tragic case. She hadn't really learned anything from the file that she hadn't known from Rhys's own mouth. Maybe the technical stuff, like the bullet going through the brain stem. But anything that was important, she had already known.

But she felt like she had needed to see it, needed to read through the dry narrative to pull together all of the pieces of the puzzle into a coherent whole.

She tidied up her desk and put things away. It was a Saturday, so she had no particular schedule she needed to follow. She didn't officially have to be at the morgue at all. She just liked to spend a little extra time getting caught up on the bits she couldn't get done during the week.

"Dr. Kirsch," Nathan, one of the regular security guards in the parking garage, raised a hand to wave at her. "Have a great weekend!"

"Thank you, Nathan. You too. You got some time off after this?"

"I'm working tomorrow. I'll take my weekend Monday and Tuesday."

"Well, enjoy your weekend then."

He nodded, smiling at her. "I sure will."

He watched her walk to her car and get in, then nodded as she drove off.

Kenzie drove to the Salter home. She had a few things she wanted to talk to Rhys about. She didn't think that Saul would be able to get anything out of him. If Rhys didn't want to talk to him, if he didn't think that Emily would want him to talk to Saul, he would just shut down. He wouldn't respond to any questions, and there wouldn't be anything that Saul could do about it. Even if Rhys had been subpoenaed to give testimony in a case, they couldn't force him to. He had a well-documented psychological condition that prevented him from being able to communicate through any conventional means.

Kenzie wasn't sure that Rhys's usual means of communication would even be taken as sworn testimony if he were willing to try. He could give a yes or no head shake to a question, with an unbiased third party interpreting his answers for the court clerk, but how would they interpret dog gifs, photos, and gestures without codified meanings? Would a word or two typed into a messaging app be enough for a judge to agree that his meaning had been clear?

But he would do his best to communicate with Kenzie. He had a bit of a crush on her and never refused to see or talk to her. Kenzie rang the doorbell and was a little surprised when it was answered by Zachary. He laughed at her expression.

"I did say that I might stop by to see Rhys," he reminded her. "Did you forget that?"

"It seems like days ago," Kenzie confessed. "Yeah. It completely slipped my mind."

"So you don't want to see me."

"Well..." Kenzie walked in the door. "I always want to see you, but I came to see Rhys."

"Hello, Kenzie," Vera greeted, getting up from the couch. "I want to thank you for helping Rhys out with this. I know I wasn't too positive about it before, but even if it isn't what I want, I am still grateful to you for helping Rhys."

Kenzie gave her a brief hug. "Of course. I'll always help Rhys whenever I can."

"He's in his room," Zachary said. "I just came out to open the door for you because Vera saw you pull up."

It did help to have a recognizable vehicle! Kenzie glanced out the window at her little red convertible and smiled. She walked with Zachary to Rhys's bedroom. He stood up from his bed to give her a hug.

"Hey, it's good to see you. I'll bet you're glad to be home," Kenzie told him.

He released her from the hug and nodded vigorously. When she thought about all he had been through the last few weeks... no kid should have to go through what he had recently. And as a child. He had been lucky to be raised by loving grandparents, which was probably the only reason that he had managed to get through the traumatic experiences he had. And even with that, he had not escaped unscathed. Kenzie wished she could take back the choices that his family had made both before and after Clarence's death. They had been too afraid of the system to stop the abuses within the family.

They all looked for places to sit down. Zachary had claimed the swivel chair at Rhys's study desk. Rhys sat on the bed. There was no other chair and not a clear place to sit on the floor. Though she was sure that Rhys and Vera would not have let her sit on the floor anyway.

"Why don't we go out to the living room?" she suggested. "It would be more comfortable."

Zachary looked at Rhys, who shook his head. He motioned for Kenzie to sit on the end of the bed, patting it like he was trying to call a cat or dog to jump up. Kenzie sat down. Rhys probably wanted his room's privacy so Vera didn't have to overhear what they discussed. As much as Vera loved Rhys and was grateful that Kenzie had agreed to help him, she still did not like the police interfering with their lives.

She would probably not even let Detective Saul come over to interview Rhys. She would tell him no, that she didn't want Rhys talking to law enforcement about anything.

"So, what have you guys been talking about?" Kenzie asked Zachary, hoping to ease into the conversation gradually.

"Mostly… how he's feeling about going back to school. If there is anyone he's interested in. What he likes best about school…"

Kenzie rolled her eyes. "Well, I guess I have school questions too. I hope you haven't talked him out."

Rhys made an expansive gesture to Kenzie, inviting her questions.

Kenzie sighed, trying to decide where to start. "I want to ask you questions, but I don't want to upset you, and some of these things might be upsetting."

He nodded seriously.

"I don't want you to think I'm accusing you or anyone else of doing something wrong. Okay? I don't know much about what happened, and I need you to tell me more about it."

Rhys nodded again. He pointed at Kenzie. *Take it away.*

"Was it Emily who sent you the picture? Or someone else?"

He rocked his hand back and forth uncertainly.

"You don't know who sent it? Why not? Was it sent anonymously?"

He shook his head. He ticked off his fingers as if enumerating a list of points.

"It was sent to you several times," Zachary said. "I remember you said that. You kept deleting it, and it kept coming back again."

Rhys pointed at him in agreement.

"Okay, you got it several times. Did you get it from Emily?"

Rhys pursed his lips, then nodded.

"The first time you got it, was it from her?"

Rhys shook his head slowly and shrugged. *Not sure.*

"Right. You got it several times, and it gets muddled after a while. But you know that one of the times you got it, it was from Emily."

He nodded.

"Did she send any message with it? Or was she just sending out the picture without any text?"

Rhys shrugged. Kenzie thought he was being intentionally evasive. "Were you and Emily friends?"

He shook his head.

"You didn't hang out with those kids at all."

He shook his head again.

"But you knew who she was?"

Rhys nodded. He made a circular motion with his finger pointing up. Kenzie hazarded a guess. "Everybody knew who she was."

He grinned and pointed at her. *You got it.*

Kenzie had a feeling that Emily was a person who liked attention. She did what she could to get it. Had that been the only reason for sending around the picture of Mercer? She couldn't get past the fact that they had been close. It didn't make sense that she would circulate his death picture just because she hoped it would go viral. Kenzie didn't think that was her motivation.

"And did everybody know that she was the one who started circulating the picture?"

Rhys shook his head. He pointed to himself and made a slashing movement with his hand.

"You didn't?"

He nodded his agreement.

"You got it from her, but you didn't know that she was the one who had started it. You thought she was just one of the people forwarding it around."

Rhys agreed.

"Did you find out that she was the one who took the picture?"

Rhys stared back at her.

"Was Emily the one who took the picture?"

He shrugged. He frowned and shook his head. *Don't know, don't think so.*

"Did you talk to her about the picture at all?"

A shrug.

"Did you talk to her, message her, ask her if she was okay?"

Rhys pointed and nodded at the last suggestion.

"You asked her if she was okay?"

He nodded again.

"What did she say?"

Rhys frowned and shook his head.

"You don't remember?" Kenzie asked.

He shook his head. He pointed to the space beside him and shook his head, still frowning.

"Emily said she was not okay?"

A nod.

"Did she ask for your help? Is that why you wanted me to get involved once you were feeling better?"

He shook his head.

"She didn't want help?"

Another shake.

Kenzie had only seen Emily briefly, but she tried to call up a picture of the girl in her mind. To imagine that they were talking to each other. She tried to call on all of the information her mother had given about her, to get a sense of the girl's background and personality. Emily was independent. She hung out with a gang. She was separate from her mother at home, more like roommates operating on different shifts than mother and daughter. She was not going to school often and, when she did, she was hanging around with the wrong crowd. She had a boyfriend, even if she wasn't calling him that. She thought she was grown up. That she could do everything on her own without her mother's help or anyone else's.

"Did you know the man in the picture was her boyfriend?"

Rhys shook his head.

"Did you know that the both of them were in a gang?"

His eyebrows shot up.

Kenzie nodded. "Yes. In a gang. I suspect that's where she hung out when she wasn't at school. She wasn't at home very often."

Rhys nodded.

"Had you ever walked her home? Did you know where she lived?"

Negative. Kenzie wasn't sure she believed they didn't really know each other or ever talk, but she didn't think Rhys had anything to do with her disappearance or the gang.

35

D o you think that Emily could have been the one to shoot him?" Kenzie asked finally. She had to ask. It had been niggling away at the back of her mind ever since she had found out that Emily and Mercer were in the gang together and had been getting to know each other even more intimately.

Intimate partner violence was a frequent cause of the violent deaths that Kenzie saw come through her autopsy. Knives, guns, fists, stairs, everything she could think of. Emily wasn't exempted by her age. And Mercer had been older than she was. Bigger and stronger. If he had come after her and she'd had to defend herself...

But if she had killed him in self-defense, she could have gone to the police. She could have told them about it. And why circulate his picture if she had killed him in self-defense?

What if it had been an initiation? Her ticket into a full-blooded member of the gang? Kenzie had heard that gangs didn't actually require murders to get in. That sort of initiation was a thing of the past. But she didn't believe it. Maybe the number of gangs that had demanded it had been exaggerated, so people thought that was the only way to get into any gang. But there were still those that required some kind of evidence that an inductee was willing to do whatever it took to get into the gang of their choice.

Rhys's eyes were wide. He shook his head. He made a large X with both hands and pushed them away from him in an adamant "No!"

"Do you know for sure she didn't do it?"

He repeated the gesture.

"Do you know who did? Or you just don't think that she could do something like that?"

There was a stubborn set to Rhys's jaw. He didn't answer.

Kenzie studied him for a minute, then nodded. "Did you have any other pictures or messages on your phone from Emily?"

He shook his head.

"Did you delete everything?"

He hesitated, then shrugged.

Everything except for that one picture, Kenzie thought. He had kept that to show to her. He had deleted it several times, but it kept coming back until he couldn't handle it anymore.

Zachary had sat back and remained quiet throughout most of the conversation, but spoke up now. "Did you upload anything to the cloud before deleting it from the phone?"

Rhys raised his brows. He shrugged.

"What did you keep?" Kenzie asked.

Rhys rolled his eyes up toward the ceiling and didn't answer.

"More pictures?"

Still no answer.

"Pictures of Mercer, the dead man?"

He shook his head.

"Pictures of Emily?"

He shrugged, looking away from her.

"Download them," Zachary ordered. "Let's have a look."

Rhys spread his hands out wide. *Why?*

"You don't know. There might be other clues in those photos that you didn't recognize."

Rhys didn't pick up his phone or make any move to do so.

"Rhys… do you know where Emily is?" Kenzie asked.

He shook his head.

"I would really like to talk to her, but she hasn't been back to her house or school the last few days. And of course now it is the weekend, so she won't be back to school before Monday. If you know where she's hanging out, it would be helpful…"

Rhys made a show of pointing to his closet, then shaking his head. He bent over as if to look under his bed and then shook his head. He shrugged.

"I'm not saying that you've got her hidden somewhere, or even that she's hiding. Maybe you could message her and let her know that we would like to talk with her."

Rhys shook his head.

"You wanted me to help, Rhys. How am I supposed to help you if you don't let me? I need to talk to Emily. You know I'm not going to do anything to hurt her. I promise I'm not asking just so I can turn her over to the police. I want to make sure she's okay and find out what she knows about Mercer's death." Kenzie shook her head. "You can't just start circulating pictures of a dead man and expect not to have to answer questions."

Zachary chuckled. "I think that's pretty sound advice," he agreed.

36

Rhys was being pretty stubborn. He didn't want to download the pictures of Emily, and he didn't want to send her a message, yet he still expected Kenzie's help.

"You wanted me to look into Mercer's death," Kenzie coaxed. "His death reminded you of your grandpa's death and you didn't want another murder to go unsolved. You wanted to make sure that this man got justice."

Rhys looked down at his hands, fiddling with his phone. He nodded slightly.

"You saw what happened to your grandpa. That was really hard on you. You still see it all the time."

He looked up at her, surprised. He probably didn't remember much of what he had said when he'd had the MDMA therapy, but Kenzie had been struck by how many times he had gone back to Clarence's death. He repeated phrases and bits of what he had seen over and over again, and she didn't think that was just because of the drugs. She believed that was how Rhys's brain always worked, stuck in a loop, constantly obsessing over how Clarence had died, seeing his face again and again. Or maybe constantly. Maybe it never went away, even for a second.

"You didn't want to be stuck with Mercer's face in your head all the time too. Or it kept bringing back the pictures of Clarence. It was just too much. And you needed someone to help you with that."

Rhys pointed to Kenzie, agreeing.

"Yeah. You know I'm always playing with dead bodies," Kenzie joked, trying to lighten the mood. "So I can handle it. I can figure out who he is and what happened to him and make sure that his killer is brought to justice. So that Mercer can be at rest. So that you can let him go."

Rhys squeezed his eyes shut. Maybe Kenzie was making things worse by talking about it.

"I'm sorry. I just want to help. Let's find a way to help Emily and to help the police find out who it was that killed Mercer. I believe you that it wasn't Emily. You know her, right?"

Rhys looked at Kenzie again. He nodded his head vigorously.

"You understand other people a lot better than most of us do." Kenzie shrugged. "Maybe it's the nonverbal communication thing. You can read their body language and facial expressions better. You can see things that are going on under the surface. Beyond what everyone else sees."

The same was true of Zachary, but for different reasons. He had grown up in such a hostile environment, never knowing who he could trust, moving from one home to another after the fire when he was ten. He had to learn to read the people around him for survival. He wasn't a kid who could ever behave the way he was expected to. As hard as he tried, he could never be the perfectly behaved kid who wouldn't make waves and could please his foster parents or caregivers. Therefore, he had to know when to duck.

Rhys eyed Zachary and Kenzie, and finally reached for his laptop computer rather than his phone. The sticker declaring it the property of his school was big and bold, but starting to wear off. He opened it and touched the fingerprint recognition pad to unlock it. No need to type in a password. With the laptop screen facing Rhys rather than Kenzie, she could only see his fingers skating over the trackpad. She couldn't tell what he was doing with it. It was a few minutes before he turned the computer around so they could look at the pictures on the screen. Zachary left the office chair and sat on the bed with Kenzie. His weight depressed the mattress, making Kenzie fall against him. She snuggled into position and he put an arm around her while they both looked at the first picture Rhys had pulled up on the laptop.

Kenzie saw the girl they had been looking for. Emily, whom she had only seen briefly, mixed in with the crowd of "lost" kids, trying to blend in and fly under the radar. Straight dark hair, flat nose, piercings. She wore blue jeans and an autumn jacket left unzipped. Fake leather with a warm lining and collar. Recent. She wouldn't have worn that in the summer.

She was glancing toward the camera, unsmiling. Nervous? Was she aware that her picture was being taken, or had Rhys been covert, not giving away what he had been doing?

"She's pretty," Kenzie said, not sure what else to say. But Emily really wasn't. She was plain and looked like she'd been sleeping rough for a few days. Kenzie searched for anything in the picture that she could use. Something that would tell her where Emily was or what had happened that day. Or why Emily would circulate the picture of her dead boyfriend.

Rhys nodded. After a few seconds, he turned the computer around and swiped the trackpad to view the next picture. He turned it back to them.

Emily with her group of school friends. Not a "me and the gang" picture where she was laughing with them and enjoying the halcyon days of her youth. Not one that she would look back at in twenty or thirty years as she fondly remembered the kids she used to hang out with in those years before taking on the responsibilities of adulthood. They smoked or hung out together, few of them actually looking at each other. Emily's dark eyes stared off into the distance. She looked lost, alone in the crowd, and hurting. Kenzie's heart squeezed. What had this girl been through in her life that others had no idea of? All the secret hurts and troubles were there on the surface, visible but unreadable.

"She looks so alone," Zachary murmured, echoing what Kenzie was thinking. Alone in the crowd.

Rhys nodded his agreement. Maybe that was what had stood out to him. How alone she was, just like Rhys.

Zachary pointed at the bandana, tied around Emily's leg like it had been the day they had seen her. "She wears the gang colors at school. That means there are either other members of her gang or the rival gang in the school. Probably both. But she's not hanging out with them. She's probably a new member."

"You don't think that shooting Mercer was her initiation, do you?"

Zachary shook his head. "Killing a member of your own gang wouldn't be an initiation. Unless he was known to be dirty. And even then, that would most likely be left to a more senior gang member so that a recruit couldn't mess it up."

That made sense. The gang wouldn't want to eliminate its own members. It had been a ridiculous thought.

"But you think she was new to the gang."

He nodded. "Yeah. Which would explain why she's hanging out with other kids at school instead of the gang. She hadn't made the transition from one 'family' to the other."

"And the guy in the gang that she liked the best didn't go to the school. Mercer was quite a bit older than her. In his twenties. If she joined the gang to be with him, or he had suggested that she do it, she might not actually like anyone else in the gang."

Zachary nodded. "You don't join a gang because you like all of its members. You join it for protection. You might like one person, or one person might have taken you under his wing or recruited you. But there are probably people associated with the gang that you really don't like and have to put up with anyway."

Rhys pointed at Zachary, eyebrows raised questioningly. Zachary shook his head.

"I was never in one. There were times when I considered it… but I was never in one place for long. Becoming a gang member would mean running away, and I always hoped… that I would find a family I belonged with. I saw what happened to the kids who ran away and ended up on the street. I might have envied them for a while, but things never turned out well. They had more freedom, but freedom to do what?"

Rhys and Kenzie both nodded. Zachary was lucky that he hadn't made that choice. It would have been even harder for him to climb out of poverty and homelessness, addiction, and violence, than it had been to pull himself up by his bootstraps and set himself up as a private investigator as he had.

They looked at a couple of other pictures of Emily. She wasn't smiling in any of them. They could usually spot the red bandana tied around her neck or hair, around an arm or leg. They were all school pictures taken by

Rhys, so nothing showed her with Mercer, the rest of the gang, or her mother. Just candid shots of Emily by herself or hanging out with her group of friends, smoking or staring off into the distance.

37

See if you can set up a meeting with her," Kenzie urged. "Either with you or with me, whichever one you think she'll agree to more easily. She needs to tell her story. Just like you needed to talk about what happened to your Grandpa Clarence, she needs to be able to tell someone what happened. Why else do you think she was forwarding pictures of him to everyone?"

Rhys looked at Kenzie for a minute, thinking about it.

Kenzie might have overstepped her bounds. Did she really know what Rhys needed? What Emily needed? Was she just being manipulative, saying what she thought had the best chance of convincing Rhys to do what she wanted him to?

Eventually, Rhys picked up his phone. He tapped it a few times and frowned, trying to decide what to write to Emily. Or what picture to send her. He finally moved again, tapping out a couple of words and sending the message to her with an electronic *whoosh*.

He looked at Kenzie and Zachary, taking a deep breath and letting it out in a sigh. None of them knew if Emily would respond to Rhys. She might not trust him. She might be busy with other things or have switched phones. People did unpredictable things and, with a stressor like her boyfriend being shot and killed, probably in front of her, who knew what she might have done?

Was she in hiding or simply not going to school? It could certainly be "too much" for her while dealing with other things. Would her friends at school know where to find her? Would the police be able to pick up her trail?

Rhys's phone vibrated and he looked down at it. He glanced at Kenzie and then down at the phone again. Kenzie watched him think things through, find a gif to send back, and enter another word. Then they were waiting again.

It always fascinated Kenzie how Rhys used language. It wasn't just that he couldn't speak aloud whenever he wanted to. He could only use any form of communication in a limited way. A few words or a picture or gesture to express what he wanted to. She wondered if he thought in sentences or only in pictures or some other way, and had to translate each thought into something he could communicate with the people around him.

She leaned against Zachary, comfortable with his closeness, patiently waiting for Rhys to have his conversation with Emily and, hopefully, convince her to come out of hiding to meet with him.

Rhys looked at her several times, but seemed satisfied each time that she was not hovering, not angry that the process was taking time. How could Kenzie think that it wouldn't take time? Emily would need to ask a lot of questions before she was ready to meet with a stranger, or even with Rhys. She had been traumatized by the loss of her boyfriend. She probably didn't know who she could trust.

Kenzie's phone vibrated, and she slid it out of her pocket to have a look at it. It wasn't Rhys, texting her on the side to let her know how things were going, but Lisa.

Dinner tomorrow?

Kenzie almost groaned aloud. She had forgotten that Lisa and Walter wanted her and Zachary to come over for family dinner in Burlington, instead of going down to see Lorne and Pat. She held the phone so that Zachary could see it over her shoulder.

"Do you want to?" he murmured.

"No."

"Do you want me to talk you out of it? Or you want to use me as an excuse?"

"We had already planned to go see the Petersons, hadn't we?"

"You said your parents don't usually manage to get the same time off."

"I know," Kenzie grumbled. "But they're not going to get equal time. They might think they're going to, but there is no way they'll be free every couple of weeks. It will be twice a year, maybe."

"That sounds manageable."

Kenzie grunted an acknowledgment, thinking about it. She didn't like to give in to Lisa, just out of general principles. Hadn't she just been thinking about how she hadn't been a rebellious teen but had always tried to be responsible and to do what her parents wanted her to? Maybe she hadn't been rebellious as a teen, but she was certainly feeling her oats now, wishing her parents would recognize that she was an adult and lived an independent life, no longer tied to them.

What was the difference? Was it just because she was older and her brain had matured? Or because she was with Zachary now? Maybe there was something about starting her own little family unit that had set off her rebelliousness.

Or maybe she had been rebellious for years and just not recognized it in herself. Pretended that it wasn't really there.

Rhys grunted and nudged Kenzie with his toe. She looked at him.

He tapped his wrist, the universal sign for *what time?*

"What time can I meet with Emily? Any time. I'll make time."

His eyes dropped to his phone again.

Kenzie looked at her own phone. "I'm just going to tell Lisa I can't do it this weekend. Maybe they'll leave me alone then. If they don't, then we can find a time that works better."

"You wanted to spend more quality time with your parents. To do more with them."

"I thought you were supposed to be talking me out of it."

"I offered. You didn't answer, which I think means that I'm *not* supposed to talk you out of it."

"Hmm."

He was right, of course. Both in assuming that she didn't actually want him to talk her out of it and that she had promised to start spending more quality time with her parents. And a weekend dinner was perfect. Not too long. No pressure. Not a holiday or an assignment. Just dinner.

Another message popped up on her phone while she was looking at it.

Burlington tomorrow

She thought it was just her mother pressing her again, then realized that the message had actually come from Rhys, sitting across from her, looking at her to see whether that was good.

"In Burlington?" Kenzie frowned at Rhys. "Is that where she is?"

Rhys pointed at his phone screen and raised his brows questioningly.

"Yes, of course I'll meet her in Burlington tomorrow." Kenzie laughed. "It looks like I'm going to be there anyway. What time?"

He splayed his fingers. *Five.*

"Okay. Tell her yes and find out where I'm supposed to meet her. Or give her my number and she can text me the details." She looked at Zachary. "I guess she decided to get out of town for a while."

He nodded. "Probably a good idea. Roxboro is a small town, especially if you're in a gang. There is only a limited number of places you can go. It's too easy to find people."

"Even on the street?"

"Especially on the street. People see your movements. Report on you. You don't know who might have seen you. It's everybody's business where you have been and where you are going. When I went back to Clintock trying to find Robbie Elder, you wouldn't believe how fast word was out about who I was looking for, who I had met with, all of that. People were watching me before I managed to figure anything out."

"But you were well-known there."

"I hadn't been back for years. And Emily is well-known here. Especially if she was involved with someone in the gang. Someone who got killed. You can bet there are plenty of stories floating around about how he got killed and what her involvement was."

"Do you think she was involved?"

"No… not in the way you are thinking. I don't think she did it. But she was involved with him, and she was involved in his death, which you know, because she had a picture of it."

"Right. We just don't know what that involvement was."

Kenzie's phone buzzed again, this time with a pin on a map. She looked at it and nodded. "Okay. I'll meet her there," she relayed back to Rhys. "Let her know I'll be there. And maybe Zachary too, since we'll be going to Burlington together for dinner with my family. You can vouch for Zachary. Tell her that he isn't going to bother her or get in anyone's way."

Rhys looked at Zachary for a minute before nodding his agreement. Was he worried that Zachary would scare Emily off? That it would turn into another high-risk case like Madison's? Or was he remembering how Zachary had helped him in the past? Found him and Bridget when she had been kidnapped. He knew that Zachary was reliable and would help out a teenager in need without question.

He lowered his head and started another message to Emily. Kenzie worried about whether she would understand everything Rhys said—or didn't say. She worried that Emily would get something wrong, and she and Kenzie wouldn't meet, or something about Kenzie would set Emily off and she would be angry or afraid.

She just wanted everything to go smoothly.

38

Kenzie checked the time on her phone again. She caught Zachary looking at her.

"What time do you think we should leave?" she asked. "Should we be in Burlington before the meeting in case she calls back to say she wants to move it up?"

"I don't think she'll do that. She knows that you're coming from Roxboro. She knows that switching the time would mean you couldn't meet with her. It's possible that she will, but if she does, she's doing it to sabotage the meeting. Not because you weren't there in good time."

"What time do you think we should leave?"

He just smiled. "I don't think I've ever seen you so anxious about a meeting before."

"Well, is it any wonder? I'm not usually meeting with witnesses. Or volatile teenagers. Or gang members."

He laughed. "You'll do fine. You've talked to her before. You know she's not scary."

"She's not scary? Who are you kidding? Teenagers are terrifying."

"She didn't do anything to hurt or aggravate you before when you met her. She actually stayed pretty quiet. She didn't mock or bully you or pretend that she was so tough. Her mom seemed to think that she was a pretty good kid. I know she's been rebellious and hanging out with a gang, but her mom didn't talk about how violent she has been lately, or volatile, or using drugs. She sounds like she's lonely. Looking for help."

"But even kids looking for help can be pretty... angry."

Zachary nodded, conceding the point. Kenzie wondered what he had been like as a teenager. She knew he had been depressed, alone, and abused, but how had he shown that to the outside world? Had he been withdrawn? Angry? Swinging from one extreme to the other? From what he and Lorne had said, he had been a pretty good kid, just hyperactive and unable to control his impulses. He hadn't been the kid that you had to worry might bully or beat up other kids in the family. He hadn't been the one who would stand up to an authority figure, challenging or even attacking them. But were their recollections accurate or rose-colored after years of denial?

"She's going to be okay," Zachary assured her. "Emily is just looking for someone who will help her."

"Okay." She would have to rely on his assurances. He read people. He knew kids. He knew what it was like to be in the position Emily was in now, not knowing who to trust or how to get help. "I'm sure you're right. It's going to be fine."

He looked at the time on his phone. "We can leave in an hour or so if you like. We'll stop for ice cream when we get there and ruin our appetites."

Kenzie laughed. At least they would have a few hours to burn off the ice cream before dinner. Like many of those in their social set, Walter and Lisa ate dinner later than Zachary and Kenzie normally did. So an afternoon snack was probably not a bad idea. Maybe the ice cream would help her to de-stress.

"Sounds good," she agreed.

It was a good thing she didn't have to wait too much longer, because she was unable to get any work done in that time. She couldn't concentrate on anything. Whenever she tried to settle into something, her head was somewhere else. She kept thinking about Rhys and his grandfather's death. About Emily and her boyfriend's death. Parallel paths. Things that others in their social groups probably couldn't relate to. Had Emily known anything about Rhys's history? Enough to recognize a kindred spirit? Was it just coincidental? Or had Rhys sought her out to tell her about it? Kenzie still wasn't convinced that Rhys hadn't known who

Mercer was or that Emily was the person who started circulating the pictures before Kenzie had made those discoveries. But she didn't have any evidence to back the feeling up.

They took Zachary's car to Burlington. It was easier on gas, warmer in the crisp fall weather, and less noticeable on the street. They didn't want to attract attention when meeting with Emily. Kenzie let Zachary drive, but regretted it. He loved driving, so she didn't like to take that away from him, especially when it was his car. But she found herself at loose ends and wished she had something to keep her hands and mind occupied instead of just staring out the window, wishing they were there, and she didn't have to wait any longer.

They stopped for ice cream, as promised, but were only halfway through eating it when Kenzie's phone buzzed, and she saw it was Emily.

Where are you?

They weren't expected at the meeting location for another hour, so Kenzie wasn't sure why Emily was already texting her and demanding to know her location.

Having ice cream, she texted back. *Meeting you in an hour.*

Meet sooner?

Kenzie showed the phone to Zachary and raised her brows. He had been sure that Emily wouldn't do this. She wouldn't be playing games with them, trying to disrupt the scheduled meeting. But…

Maybe. When and where?

Emily proposed meeting in fifteen minutes at a different mall. Kenzie calculated the driving time in her head, along with how long it would take them to get to her car, and to walk from the car to the location inside the mall.

Can't make it in under twenty.

20 min then

"Okay, I guess we're on the move," Kenzie said.

"We can walk and eat."

They were finished eating their ice creams by the time they reached the car.

"You know where it is?" Kenzie asked. She had grown up in Burlington and he had not.

"Yeah, I'm good."

He drove faster than she would have and arrived within ten minutes.

They looked around for any sign of Emily as they got out of the car, but didn't see her. They walked briskly into the mall and found the location she had designated for the meeting. They were there ahead of schedule.

"Not bad," Kenzie told Zachary. At least they were not late. Emily probably would be. Kenzie had an idea she knew how it would go down. Emily would not arrive right away. She would be watching them from a distance, maybe looking down from the second story. Making sure that they didn't have any police or other watchers with them, and that they weren't talking to other people on comms. All of the stuff that she had seen on TV.

But Kenzie and Zachary were not TV show cops or spies. They were just a couple of people there to see if they could help Emily sort things out in her life and maybe help bring her boyfriend's killer to justice. There weren't going to be any fireworks, no police descending into the mall from helicopters. There were no undercover cops pushing baby carriages or cleaning up trash. Just Kenzie and Zachary.

Kenzie's phone vibrated. She looked at it.

Meet me by the fountain

Kenzie looked around. The fountain was new since she had hung out there as a teenager. They checked the nearest directory and walked to the fountain. They moved slowly, like window shoppers or tourists rather than law enforcement officers trying to meet with a material witness.

They circled the large fountain. Kenzie checked her pockets and tossed a couple of pennies in, launching them toward a frog's wide open mouth and missing by a mile. Zachary laughed, but he didn't show off his own prowess.

"I was never any good at sports," he told her.

Kenzie wasn't sure that throwing money into a fountain counted as a sport.

"Hey."

39

Kenzie turned and saw Emily sitting on a bench, hunched over inside her coat, a cap pulled down low over her face. Pretty hard to recognize if they didn't know who they were looking for.

"Hi," Kenzie greeted, giving Emily a warm smile that she hoped would help to calm her. "I'm glad you agreed to meet with me. How are you?"

Emily shrugged. She indicated the space on the bench next to her. Large enough for only one person. Kenzie sat down. Zachary withdrew a short distance away. He could still see them and hear them if voices were raised, but probably wouldn't hear anything that was said in a normal speaking voice or lower. Especially with the white noise of the fountain covering it.

"Your mom was worried about you," Kenzie tried. "She didn't know where you were. Are you staying here in Burlington, or is it just a place to meet?"

"It's where we're meeting." Emily looked around restlessly. Her hands were in her pockets. Kenzie hoped that she didn't have a weapon on her. Even if she had only brought something for self-defense, Kenzie still didn't want to sit within arm's reach.

"Is this where you've been since Tuesday when we came by the school?"

"It doesn't matter where I've been," Emily snapped.

Kenzie took the hint and stopped asking questions. She waited for Emily to take control of the conversation.

"Rhys said that you're the medical examiner," Emily stated. "You, like, cut all the dead people."

Kenzie thought about that for a minute. She didn't need to correct the inaccuracies, but tried to analyze what Emily needed to hear.

That she was an expert.

That she was trustworthy.

That she wasn't there to arrest Emily or drag her in for questioning on the death of her boyfriend.

"Yes, I work at the medical examiner's office, doing autopsies and making other inquiries to find out what happened to the people who end up on my table."

"And… you got Trevor now?"

"Yes. I'm sorry I didn't have him any earlier, but his body was not discovered for quite some time."

"They dumped him somewhere. I didn't know where."

Kenzie nodded. She didn't fill Emily in on the details. She didn't need to know he'd been left in a dumpster or the state of the remains when he was finally discovered.

"So you know it wasn't just made up, now," Emily said. "It wasn't just… a prop or a prank. It was *real*." Tears sprang to her eyes.

Kenzie reached over to pat Emily's leg to comfort her, but Emily jerked away.

"I know," Kenzie agreed soothingly. "I know that you weren't just trying to get attention. I don't know why you were circulating his picture to everyone, but I don't think it was because you were trying to… sensationalize what happened."

"No," Emily agreed in a small voice.

"Do you want to talk to me about what happened?"

"I don't want to… but I want you to know about Trev. So I guess I have to."

Kenzie nodded and waited.

"He didn't deserve to die." Emily swore. "I can't believe that I saw it, right in front of my own eyes. It was like a play or something, not like it really happened in real life. You know how many times I've seen people killed like that on TV or in GTA or something? You don't think about what it would be like to see it happen in real life."

"No. They say that violent shows and games desensitize us to death and violence. But I'm not sure that's the case."

"We always joke around about number of kills and being a criminal in first person shooter games and stuff, how it makes us tough or macho or something. But seeing it happen in real life… it wasn't anything like one of those games."

Kenzie had to school herself not to reach out and touch Emily. The girl wasn't looking for physical comfort. She had another agenda. Or she had agreed to follow Kenzie's agenda, since she was the one who had set up the meeting.

"So… how did it happen? Was there a fight?"

Kenzie was pretty sure it hadn't been a fight. It had been deliberate. Execution style. But she wanted to get Emily talking about it. Let her tell her story.

"No. It just… it was like it came out of nowhere, and my brain still doesn't understand what happened. I was with the gang. Or, we had been." Emily rubbed her forehead, wincing and frowning. "Then… it was Trev and me, and he was talking about that stupid cop. I just… I thought it would all blow over again, and him and me would spend some time…" She shrugged. "I just wanted to be with him. Didn't want all of the politics."

"What stupid cop?" Kenzie tried to get up to speed on what Emily was talking about.

"That stupid cop who was always making trouble. Like, if he caught you with a boosted car, then he wouldn't bust you if you… traded up for it. Like… if you were peddling coke, he wanted his cut of it if he was going to let it go. He was always here and there, stickin' his nose into everything. And since he got guys to trade information, he always knew something that was going on, and would use that to get more leverage…"

"A dirty cop? He was taking bribes for not making arrests?"

"Not bribes," Emily protested, though that was certainly how the police department would have seen it. "He was *taking* it. He wasn't saying, like, if you pay me, I'll look the other way. He would walk in, take what he wanted, and say you couldn't report him for it because he had something on you. You couldn't complain. All you could do was take it."

"So more like blackmail than a bribe."

"Yeah… maybe. I don't know what the hell to call it. Who cares? He was in it to squeeze everything he could from the gang members. Or other people in the neighborhood. Guns, drugs, girls, stolen stuff. It didn't matter. He didn't want to do the work to get it legitimately. Just to take it from somebody else."

"How long had this been going on?"

"Months. I don't know. As long as I was hanging around with them. You just had to watch out for this guy. Make sure he didn't see you doing anything. Didn't look at you and decide he wanted something you had."

Kenzie nodded, making a noise for Emily to go on.

"Trev was going on about him again, how he was screwing everything up and someone needed to kill him. Just shoot him in the head and get it over with." Emily swallowed hard and kept going.

"I was trying to get him to settle down. Like, no one was doing anything to him and he could just enjoy himself… enjoy being with me, and not worry about anything else. He'd wrecked enough other good times by obsessing over this cop and everything he was doing. Just… have a little time together," Emily said it in a coaxing voice, as Kenzie was sure that she had that night.

"But he wouldn't pay any attention to me. I tried to take him away from there so we could go somewhere private. Another flop or someplace private. He was acting drunk, all jelly legs and stumbling around in the street, but he hadn't had that much to drink."

"Maybe his drink had been spiked?"

"I don't know. I was with him, so I don't see how it could have been. But he was all… agitated. Yelling about the stupid bent cop and how he was ruining everything. He grabbed me and shook me, and it scared me. I didn't even know if he could see me anymore, or if he was seeing someone else. He wasn't talking to me. I'm not sure what was going on. He hadn't used. Hadn't for days."

"If he hadn't used, maybe he was in withdrawal. People can halluci-nate in withdrawal. Get very agitated. Lots of mood swings and paranoia and not understanding that people are trying to help them."

"I don't know, maybe." Emily pulled her elbows in, hands still in her jacket pockets, holding her arms against herself like she was cold. Hunching down inside the jacket to hide from the world. "He was all sweaty and his eyes were funny. You would have thought he was on drugs, but it wasn't that."

Kenzie frowned, nodding. "And the whole time, he was complaining about the dirty cop."

"Yeah. I mean, I hated the guy too, but I didn't want to spend all of my time thinking about him, looking over my shoulder to make sure I wasn't being watched."

"Who was this cop?"

"I don't know his name. Trev called him…" Emily looked away from Kenzie for a moment, rubbing her forehead and laughing weakly. "He called him Deputy Donut. I don't know his real name. I always stayed away from him as much as I could. He didn't wear a uniform, so I never saw his name badge or anything. It was always just Deputy Donut. Not to his face; he woulda killed anyone who called him that to his face. But they liked dissing him when he wasn't around."

"And he was with the gang unit? Not a patrol officer, if he didn't wear a uniform."

"I don't know. I never asked anything about who he was or what department he worked with. Why would I? I didn't want anything to do with the guy."

"Why was Trevor so upset about him that night? What had he done?"

"I dunno if he had done anything new, or if it was just… overflowing from the rest of the times he'd caused Trev trouble. He was really angry, but I kind of thought he was just amped up about something else. It was all the usual stuff. Deputy Donut thinking that he could get away with whatever he liked. Ripping us off."

"Had he taken something that day?"

"I don't know. How would I know?" Emily protested, frustrated with Kenzie's questions. "I was at school during the day. I went over, thinking Trevor and I could have some time together. You know, hang out, enjoy each other's company. Instead, we'd had to do stuff with the gang, and then when everyone broke up to go their different directions, and I thought we could finally have some alone time, then Trev was going off the rails about Deputy Donut and how he'd ripped him off, and he was going to do something to get even."

"What?"

"I don't know. I don't think he, like, had a plan. He was just spouting off. Just because he said he was going to do something, that doesn't mean he was. He said a lot of things."

"Okay. And then what happened?"

4 0

Emily bent over, burying her face in both hands, elbows braced against her knees. This was clearly the crisis point. She had avoided going any further in her narrative because she didn't like where it ended up.

Kenzie was quiet, giving Emily a chance to regain her composure.

Emily swore. "I could really use a drink. Do you have anything? I need something to take the edge off."

"No. Sorry."

Emily lifted her head. "Pills? You're a doctor. You must be able to get some benzos or something, right?"

"I don't have anything. Try taking some deep breaths. Count them out, nice and long."

"I don't want to breathe," Emily muttered.

Kenzie caught Zachary's amused glance toward them. He could obviously hear some of what was being said and sympathized with Emily's irritation at being told just to breathe. Zachary probably had meds on him Emily would appreciate getting her hands on. Some nice strong anti-anxiety pills, for one thing. Zachary didn't like to take them most of the time, but they were helpful in heading off a panic attack if he took them in time.

"You're going to be okay," Kenzie reassured Emily. "Why don't you tell me what happened? Just take your time. Then we'll figure out what to do."

She sniffled and cleared her throat. "Then Deputy Donut shows up. The worst timing ever. He starts taunting Trevor and hitting on me. Saying he can take whatever he wants. You know, like he could have me too. He'd… some of the girls… you gave him what he wanted. What else were you gonna do? Get thrown in jail over some stupid, trumped-up charge? End up at the mercy of the COs and other inmates anyway? At least with Donut, it's over fast and you can go on with your life and forget about it." Emily shook her head, closing her eyes.

"So Trevor thought the cop was going to assault you?"

"I don't know. I guess so. I don't know if he would have. It seemed like what he really cared about was getting Trevor's goat. I don't know if he heard all of what Trevor was saying about him and wanted to get back at him. I just don't know what he was after."

"And then…?" Kenzie didn't want to lead Emily, but she wanted to hear the rest. This was what she had come for. And Emily wanted to get it off of her chest. Kenzie was sure Emily would not have come if she didn't want to tell her story.

"It was just… like… a standoff between them. An argument."

"Did it get physical?"

Emily shook her head. "Stupid Deputy Donut pulled a gun and pointed it at Trevor's head. Told him that if he didn't do what he was told and quit bellyaching about it, he was going to get his head blown off. Trevor laughed. He could barely stand. Looked like he was going to pass out any minute. He said Donut couldn't push him around, couldn't make him do anything he didn't want to. What was he gonna do, arrest him? For talking?"

"And what did he say about that?"

"He pulled the trigger. Just like that, no more arguing. Trevor said that he wouldn't, that he couldn't do anything, and he pulled the trigger. And…" Emily choked up. "Trev just went down."

Kenzie didn't have any trouble picturing it. She had seen the photo. Mercer lying there on the pavement with a bullet hole in his forehead. She shook her head in horror.

"How did you react? What did you do? That must have been terrifying."

"I just… I don't even know. Maybe I screamed, maybe not. I think I said something to him. Swore, tried to hit him or take the gun away. I wasn't… I didn't know what I was doing. Didn't know what to do. He kept telling me to settle down. Slapped me." Emily shook her head. "Like, maybe that works on TV, but I can tell you in real life, someone slapping me across the face just makes me want to take them on. You don't slap me."

Kenzie nodded.

"He said… he said he would take care of everything. I just had to stay quiet. If I didn't want to get popped too, I'd better keep my mouth shut. He could make both of us disappear, and people would think we had just run off together. No one would even look for us."

"So you listened to him."

"What was I supposed to do?" Emily demanded.

"You did what you had to to survive."

"He went to get… I don't know, a tarp or something. I didn't understand what he was doing. That's when I took the pictures." Emily swallowed. She looked around her as if she'd never seen the mall before, hadn't even known where she was. Eyes wide and startled to find herself there.

Kenzie supposed she had been so deep in the recollection that it was disorienting to return to the present.

"If he did something to me too… I didn't want anyone to think we had just run off together. I wanted everyone to know we were dead, not running off to New York to start over or something like that."

"So you sent the picture out to all your friends."

Emily nodded. "I wanted… I don't know what I wanted. I was just going on instinct. I got outta there. Went home to bed." She turned wondering eyes to Kenzie. "I don't know how I could just go to sleep! I shouldn't have even been able to sleep. Not after seeing that."

"People shut down after something like that," Kenzie reassured her. "It doesn't mean that you weren't upset by what happened. Devastated. It's just your brain's way of dealing with something overwhelming. It wasn't because you didn't feel anything; it was because you felt too much. Too much emotion, danger, stress, not knowing what to do next. That's why you slept."

"I slept all weekend. Not just like… sleeping in in the morning and getting up late. But I just slept right through. I'd wake up to go to the bathroom, maybe check my messages for a minute, and then crawl back into bed and… go back to sleep again."

Kenzie nodded understandingly. "And he didn't come to your house? Did he know your name or where you lived?"

"No, I don't think so. I don't know if he even knew my name. Trev just called me Em or Babe most of the time. And I would tag with the letter M. So he wouldn't have known it was short for Emily."

"And the rest of the gang, they didn't know that either?"

"No. It was just me and Trevor. He's the reason that I…" She shrugged uncomfortably. "I got into the gang stuff with him because that was what he was into. But I wasn't in it before that."

41

Kenzie thought through the story. It would need to be verified, of course. She needed to call Sergeant Campbell and Detective Saul to tell them of the developments. They would not be happy to find out they had a dirty cop in their ranks. And not someone who had stopped at harassing the young gang members. He hadn't broken the law just by stealing drugs and guns from them. Or by coercing the girls to do what he told them to. He had murdered one of them, apparently in cold blood.

Who was he? Was he working for someone else? Was he even part of the Roxboro police department, or some other city, state, federal, or private organization? People sometimes mistakenly classified everyone who looked remotely like law enforcement as being cops when they were not. If "Deputy Donut" was not in uniform, Emily probably only knew he was a cop from what others in the gang said.

"What did this guy look like?" Kenzie asked. "Could you identify him? Do other people in the gang know his real name?"

Emily wiped her eyes. "I don't know. He was a cop. White guy, middle-aged, not some young rookie. Dark hair and eyes. I guess I'd recognize his picture." She sniffled. "I don't know his name, but some of the others might. But I don't know if I'm going back there."

"Does your mom know where you are? Are you staying with a friend?"

"I haven't told her. I'll let her know… sometime. When things have blown over."

"Where are you staying? A friend? A shelter?"

Emily shook her head. "I don't want anyone to be able to find me."

"But I'll need to be able to get ahold of you after I talk to the cops and make sure that everything is safe. If I bring you some pictures to look at, how will I find you?"

"Send them to my phone."

Kenzie supposed that having Emily's phone number gave her a way to communicate with the girl and for the police to trace her location, so she didn't push it further. She didn't want to scare Emily away. It was a big deal for her to be talking to Kenzie and knowing that Kenzie was going to go to the police when her boyfriend had been killed by a crooked cop.

"If he was working with gangs, then he was probably anti-gang unit or narco squad or something like that," she suggested to Emily.

"Yeah, I guess so. I don't know. I never asked. They knew who he was, but he wasn't any beat cop." She wiped at her nose with her sleeve. "What else would he be?"

"If he's federal, he could be DEA. Or something else."

"Long as I never have to see him again, I don't care what kind of cop he is."

Kenzie nodded. She tried putting a hand on Emily's shoulder and, this time, the girl didn't jerk away. Maybe she had become comfortable enough with Kenzie that she didn't fear her anymore. Or maybe telling the story had just left her so exhausted that she didn't have the energy to protect herself. Kenzie rubbed her back gently.

"You must be so tired. You were really brave to come here to talk to me today."

"Rhys said you're okay."

"Rhys is a pretty special guy himself. You would think that with all of his problems, he would be focused on himself, but he always seems to be watching and worrying about other people."

Emily gave a little laugh. "Yeah. Pretty amazing."

"How well do you know him?"

Emily sniffled and rolled her neck, probably stiff after sitting hunched over. "I've gone to school with him since we were little kids. But I don't really know him. Just… you know, always going to the same school, you know who people are. Especially if they're like him. You know, special needs."

"He has a lot of challenges," Kenzie acknowledged.

"I've been paired with him for group work because they mostly mainstream him. He does some resource room work but, mostly, he's in the regular classes."

"How do group projects go?"

She shook her head. "He's good at little cartoon pictures and lettering on posters. Finding pictures of stuff and research on the internet. But he doesn't write stuff out and he can't help with an oral presentation. Except, like, advance slides or use the pointer."

At least she'd been able to find things for Rhys to do. Kenzie had often wondered what things were like for Rhys at school.

She didn't imagine that everyone accommodated him quite so well. There would be those who just ignored him and didn't involve him in a project at all or who complained to their parents about being paired with him.

"So that's why you had Rhys's number? Because you'd worked with him on group collaborations before?"

Emily hesitated, then nodded. "Yeah. Because of that."

"Yeah? So you texted about what you needed to do for the project…"

She shrugged.

"Why would you send him the picture of Trevor? Didn't you know anything about his history?"

Emily blinked at Kenzie. "What do you mean?"

"You don't know what happened to him when he was little?"

Emily shook her head. "I told you I've known him since we were little. What are you talking about?"

"About his grandfather being murdered."

She continued to shake her head. "No, I don't know anything about that."

"He was shot in the head."

Emily's mouth dropped open. She stared at Kenzie. "What? Are you kidding me?"

"No joke," Kenzie said, shaking her head. "His grandfather was killed the same way as Trevor Mercer. When you sent him the picture… and he kept getting it from others as well… he was very upset about it. He ended up in the hospital for a while."

"Because of those pictures?" Emily swore and shook her head. "I never meant to do anything that would hurt him. He's a nice guy, I wouldn't do that."

"I don't imagine he was the only one upset by you broadcasting a picture of a murdered man to their phones. A lot of people would find that upsetting."

Emily was immediately defensive, her voice rising. "Well it was upsetting to me to see it and to think that Donut might make me disappear too, so excuse me for trying to make sure that someone would know the truth!"

"Why didn't you call for help? If you were afraid to call the police because of the dirty cop, why not call your mom? Or another trusted adult? A news reporter? There are better ways to get help."

Emily just looked at Kenzie and shook her head. She had no trust in adults. It shouldn't have surprised Kenzie that the only way she could think of to help herself, in the panic of the moment, had been to reach out to her friends, and that the medium had been a texted picture, their usual means of communication.

Kenzie just wished Rhys hadn't been one of the recipients.

She put up her hands to indicate that she was backing off. "I'm sorry. I guess I'm just feeling protective of Rhys. You did what you could to protect yourself. And you're still doing what you can to keep yourself safe. When you are in mortal peril, that's the only thing you can think about."

Emily pushed some of her long hair back over her ear, frowning at Kenzie. "Are you making fun of me?"

"No. I'm serious. When your life is in danger, you don't think about anyone else or about the long-term consequences of your actions. You just try to survive."

Emily didn't say anything, obviously wondering where Kenzie got this bit of wisdom. Kenzie shrugged. She didn't tell Emily anything from her personal experience. It really wasn't the time, and she didn't share those things easily.

42

Kenzie wished she didn't have somewhere to go after the meeting with Emily. She wanted to get back to Roxboro. She wanted to talk to Campbell or Saul about what she had found out; make sure they would follow up on it all and be able to identify Emily's "Deputy Donut."

But she had agreed with Lisa and Walter to come over for family dinner after the meeting with Emily. That meant it really didn't matter how tired or unsociable she felt; she still had to be at the house as she had promised.

"I don't know why they didn't pick a restaurant," Kenzie told Zachary as they wound their way down the long drive that approached the house. "It would have been easier. No cooking or catering involved. It would be a lot easier to cancel at the last minute if I didn't know she'd gone to all of the effort to do it herself."

"Maybe that's why."

"What?"

"Maybe she knew it would be harder for you to cancel at the last minute if she did the work herself."

Kenzie shook her head. "That's really devious."

"Not like your mother?"

"Totally like her," Kenzie contradicted.

Zachary laughed. Kenzie stared out the window. She should have realized herself that it was part of the plan to get her to the house and to make sure she stayed for a while to visit. If it had just been a restaurant reservation, it would have been a lot easier for Kenzie to just say that she was too tired from the day's events and go home.

The house was beautiful as they approached. Even though Kenzie hadn't been there much over the past few years, it still felt like coming home to see the bright, warm lights of the house at the end of the long drive.

"It looks like a fairy-tale castle," Zachary said.

Maybe not quite that grand, but it *was* pretty. Clean lines, lots of small lights that twinkled in the dark and lit it evenly across all of the above-ground levels. It was more of a chalet than a castle, but she could see Zachary's point. It wasn't like any place he had ever lived.

"It is pretty," she agreed. "Just park over there."

He pulled in against the curb where Kenzie pointed.

"Stay there," he told Kenzie, putting his hand on her leg for an instant. He was out of the car and quickly circled to her door before she could figure out why he had told her to stay put. He pulled the door open and offered his hand.

Kenzie took Zachary's hand, her face flushing, and stood up. He held on to her hand and they walked together to the front door. Kenzie knew her mother was probably watching out the window and would have seen Zachary's chivalrous gesture from inside. Which was why he had done it. To show them that he was a gentleman and knew how to take care of their daughter.

It was doubly impressive because he had not been raised that way. Kenzie didn't imagine any foster family training the boys to open the doors for the girls. No one would take the time for that. The girls would be expected to open the doors for themselves just like anyone else. Chivalry was not something taught in public schools, either.

The front door opened as they approached. Walter stood there, beaming at them, and ushered them inside. Lisa crossed the entrance hall to greet them, Lola walking politely at her side, not running and barking as she had the previous year. Lisa had obviously been working on her training.

"MacKenzie, my dear. It is lovely to see you," Lisa greeted, giving her a perfunctory hug and bussing both cheeks. She did the same with Zachary, who managed not to look too awkward at the greeting.

"The house looks great, Mom," Kenzie told her.

"Thank you. I hope you will enjoy your time here."

"Of course we will."

"Shall we begin with drinks?" Walter suggested, leading the way to the study, where a fire was already burning in the grate. "Have a seat. Make yourself comfortable. Wine for you, MacKenzie? As I remember, Zachary, you're not much of a drinker. Would you like to start with a cognac, or do you prefer Coke? Soda and lime?"

Zachary looked at Kenzie, his eyes questioning. Kenzie nodded. "Whatever you prefer. It doesn't matter."

"No pressure," Walter assured him. "We have a full range of beverages. If you would prefer a fruit juice, coffee, tea?"

"Well, Coke sounds good."

"I'll have a glass of wine with dinner," Kenzie said. "Just a sparkling water right now."

Walter acted as the bartender, getting everyone what they wanted. Lisa sat down on the couch with Lola at her feet, and motioned for her daughter and Zachary to sit down wherever they liked.

"Well, this is nice. We should have done this a lot earlier. How long have the two of you been seeing each other now?" Lisa asked.

Kenzie cleared her throat. "Well, it's been a couple of years, at least."

"Yes, we certainly should have done this before now. I am going to try to have something more often in the future. There's no reason we can't make time to do something as a family. We make time for everything else!"

Kenzie had to admit that, as much as she would like to say she was too busy with work and other engagements to have dinner with her family, she still had to eat, and it wasn't that much of a sacrifice to have a meal with them every few months. She shouldn't be so resistant to the idea.

"So, how is everything going?" Walter asked. "With your work? Any interesting cases for either one of you?"

"Well, neither of us can really talk about our cases," Kenzie said. "We can't give away anything confidential."

"Of course not," Walter agreed. "But there are probably still a few interesting tidbits that you could share, without any… identifying features."

"Some insurance work," Zachary said with a shrug. "Surveillance, reconstruction, checking backgrounds, that kind of thing. Skip traces. It's all pretty routine right now, nothing really big."

"But we don't really want those big cases too often," Kenzie said with a laugh. "They can be kind of stressful and take a lot of hours. Every now and then is fine!"

Zachary sipped his Coke and nodded. "Yeah, you're probably right."

"And yours, MacKenzie?" Walter prompted.

Kenzie looked at Lisa. "Uh… most people prefer that we don't discuss autopsies around dinner time. If they want to know anything about my job at all."

Lisa nodded. "I really don't think we need that kind of thing around the dinner table, Walter."

"We aren't around the dinner table yet."

"But I'd prefer we keep our appetites. Really. It's one thing for MacKenzie to choose such an… unusual line of work. I really don't think we need to discuss any of the details." She cleared her throat. "Ever."

Zachary chuckled. "It's actually one of the things that attracted me to Kenzie, Mrs. Cole Kirsch. The fact that we could discuss forensic and medical stuff over dinner or wherever. Most people don't consider it… polite."

"Oh, call me Lisa, Zachary," she corrected. "Mrs. Cole Kirsch is too much of a mouthful. Much too formal."

Zachary nodded, but didn't immediately say, "Lisa," to show that he would. It would probably take a while before he was comfortable with it, but he called Kenzie's father Walter, and he generally didn't like people calling him Mr. Goldman, so he would adjust to calling Lisa by her first name soon enough.

43

"Why don't you tell us what you're working on?" Zachary suggested, including both parents in his invitation. "You must have some good causes you are working on right now."

Kenzie's parents were always eager to discuss their work, so she was sure that wouldn't be a problem. She smiled her approval at Zachary.

"Well, yes, of course," Lisa agreed. "I'm sure Kenzie probably keeps you updated on what the foundation is doing…"

Zachary glanced over at Kenzie. "Well… I follow a little about what she and Tyrrell discuss…" Tyrrell was Zachary's younger brother, whom they had hired to help Hillary with any administrative work for the Kirsch family foundation. "But I'm afraid I'm not up-to-speed on it other than that."

Lisa arched an eyebrow and looked at Kenzie in reproof. Kenzie wondered just what information Lisa expected her to share with Zachary. She had always worked on the assumption that most of what she had to do with the foundation was confidential.

"She's probably told you we are working more with mental health causes now," Lisa suggested.

"Yes," Zachary agreed rather explosively. "Oh, yeah, I knew that. I'm really glad to hear it. Not enough people put money into mental health, and it is so important. Despite all we have learned about mental health and resilience, we are still very slow to recognize and treat it, and there is a lot of stigma."

"You don't think we're doing better with the stigma?"

"Better, yes. But it's still there. If you had two good candidates for a job, but you knew one of them had mental health challenges, which would you go with?"

"Well, I suppose it's only natural that I would go with the one who didn't have known mental health challenges," Lisa admitted.

"Hmm."

Lisa pursed her lips. "I'm being honest. That's what you wanted, isn't it?"

"You didn't ask what challenges the other candidate might have."

"Well… no." Lisa's cheeks turned slightly pink. "But I would assume in an example like that, you would give me the challenges on both sides to compare. And then I would decide based on the known factors for both."

"Do your candidates tell you what all of their challenges are? Physical disabilities or disease? Single parenthood? Caring for aging parents? On the verge of divorce? In debt? Mobility or accessibility concerns?"

"No," Lisa admitted. "I guess everybody has some challenges that they are coping with. We don't always know what they are when we hire someone."

"But without knowing what the challenges of both candidates were, you were willing to drop one candidate just because they had a mental illness."

Lisa nodded. "I guess so. I will say we have been very happy with Tyrrell's performance. I knew when we hired him that he had a number of challenges. We were willing to put the time into training him, knowing that he might have certain… attendance or quality issues."

"He really likes the job," Kenzie said. "And I think from what Hillary has said that he's been a good asset. She's been giving him more and more responsibility."

"He has been very helpful," Lisa agreed. "And I think he's more than proven his worth. Even if we do, at some point, have to put money into rehabilitation or a temp to cover him while he gets back on his feet again… hiring him was still the right choice and worth it to the foundation. Not just as a social experiment, but really a beneficial employer-employee relationship."

Kenzie hoped that resolve would hold if Tyrrell did fall off the wagon and had to go back into rehab. It was one thing to say it as a hypothetical. It might be a different story when they faced it in real life. When they had to deal with declining work quality and it cost real money to put him through rehab and get someone to fill in for him. Then, they would see how Lisa really felt about the cost of addiction and mental health issues and the ability of employers to handle them in a constructive, supportive way.

"How is your young friend?" Walter asked, leaning forward. "The boy."

"You know his name," Kenzie said in irritation. "Why can't you call him by his name like a real person instead of calling him our young friend?"

"Oh, of course," Walter said quickly. "How is Rhys? He continues to show improvement?"

"I assume you know as well as I do, since you are still involved in funding his care."

Walter didn't look like he appreciated Kenzie's tone.

"Well, dear." He cleared his throat. "You sound upset that we are providing him financial support. I thought you would appreciate it."

"I thought you were getting out of his case and leaving him alone. Letting Vera and Rhys make the decisions about what he needed."

"We are," Lisa protested. "He isn't in Persons or in that drug therapy anymore. We told his grandmother she could put him into whatever program she thought would work best for him. It's totally her decision, not ours. We're just writing the checks."

"That's good. I just…" Kenzie shook her head. "I don't know. I don't like the foundation being involved after what happened."

"You think it would be better for us to drop our support when he needs it the most? Say that we made a mistake and he didn't respond the way we had hoped to the therapy we chose, so now we're going to dump him and they're on their own again."

"No," Kenzie admitted. "I don't want that. I know I'm being ridiculous. I don't know what it is that I expect. Of course I still want him to be funded and get treatment. Just not from the family foundation. Not after what they—we—did."

Lisa and Walter exchanged glances. "Well…" Lisa considered this.

"We could look at some of our partners and the causes that we have funded and see if any of them would take on Rhys's case. There wouldn't be any change from Vera's perspective, but you would not have to worry about us being involved or you having any conflict."

"Or you knowing what was going on with him. I think it's… I don't think it's appropriate for me or my family to know anything about Rhys's mental health or treatment. Other than what he decides to tell us directly."

Zachary had another drink of his Coke. "I hadn't really thought about it like that. It makes sense, though. I see where you're coming from."

"I guess… we'll look at transitioning his funding to someone else," Lisa agreed. "If that's really what you want."

"That's how it should have been done in the first place."

44

Zachary was quiet on the way home, as was Kenzie. It had been a long day and they had worked through a lot of emotional stuff with Emily and then had the aggravation of dealing with Kenzie's parents. Not that Walter or Lisa had done anything wrong; Kenzie just found them challenging to deal with. They made her feel awkward and immature. The rest of the time—or most of the rest of the time—she felt like a competent adult. But with her parents, she always felt like she had to fight to prove herself.

She wasn't even sure what made her feel that way. Looking at her parents' behavior objectively, she couldn't identify anything they did wrong, any tone or nuance or hint that they didn't think of her as a grown-up. But she still felt small and unsure around them.

"Are *you* okay?" she asked Zachary, when they were almost home.

He startled in his seat, surprised by her sudden query.

"Yeah, yeah, I'm fine," Zachary assured her.

"Good."

Kenzie returned to her own thoughts. But after a few more miles, an alarm started to ring in her head.

"Fine?" she repeated. "Did you just tell me you're *fine?*"

It was one of their rules from therapy. No social brush-off. No saying that they were fine. Or good. The answer to "How are you feeling?" or

"Are you okay?" or any similar question needed to be thought out, heartfelt, and honest.

"Uh… yeah, I guess I did."

She waited for him to amend his answer and come up with something more real. He said nothing.

"So how are you really?" Kenzie pressed. "I'm pretty tired. Feeling… kind of mentally wrung out." She hoped that her honest assessment would help him on the way.

After a few minutes of silence, Zachary spoke up. "I'm… feeling down. Nothing serious. Just… post-party crash, I think. I need time and space to process. Get out of my own head. A movie or a job or something. I'm just…" He sighed. "I don't know. Feeling a bit low."

"Did we do too much today? It was probably too much, wasn't it? I should have had dinner with my parents another day. Told them that we couldn't make it this week. It was too much to do after the meeting with Emily, and we stayed there for hours."

Kenzie looked at the time on the dashboard clock and tried to calculate how many hours they had been at her mother's house. Unlike dinners at home, which were usually a quick affair, leaving time for other evening activities, the dinner with her parents had dragged out to fill the entire evening, with pre-dinner drinks and conversation, courses served separately for dinner, and postprandial coffee and more conversation. Kenzie had felt the lack of discussion topics halfway through the pre-dinner drinks. After that, it had all been Lisa and Walter feeding her conversational topics that ranged from personal to political.

"It was all too much for one day," Kenzie repeated.

"It's fine. When we visit Mr. Peterson, it takes half a day with the driving and visiting too. And I'm happy to stay there over a weekend. We can spend a few hours with your parents. It's only fair."

"But they're not comfortable like Lorne and Pat. It's more of… an ordeal."

She thought Zachary would chuckle at this, but he just sighed. "It's fine, Kenzie. I told you, it's just my post-party crash. I would feel the same way no matter who it was. It just takes a lot of energy to stay turned on for something like that, and I feel it afterward, even when it's been a really good visit. And it was nice to see your parents. It's good for you to do things with them."

Kenzie looked for a way to argue. She wanted to protect him and his mental health. To do whatever was the best for him. She didn't like his feeling bad after a dinner that she had set up.

But then, she knew that even after a meeting with Lorne or with Joss or Tyrrell, he tended to have that low-energy dip as well. It was hard for her to understand. She did feel emotionally spent after the emotional interview with Emily and spending all night trying to please her parents and stay engaged with them. But she didn't feel that way after every interaction. She was fine after a day with the Petersons, a work meeting, or a lunch with a friend. She felt energized and up, a pleasant afterglow. For Zachary, the more excited and energized he was by a social gathering, the worse he felt in the hours following it.

"Well," she tried to keep a logical, positive tone in her response. "It's good that we could spend the time with my parents. And you just need a little recovery time. That's not the end of the world."

"No," Zachary agreed. "I'm used to it. Just need a little time."

Kenzie was still anxious about his mental state the rest of the night, but she tried to keep it to herself and to give him the space he needed to recover. He didn't need her hanging over him, nagging him to tell her how he was feeling and if he needed to take anything or arrange an additional visit with Dr. Boyle.

And even though she wanted him to take something that would help, she was still concerned when she saw him taking a sleep aid before bed, which he usually resisted. She couldn't help but be concerned that things were really bad if he was taking extra meds to get through the night.

But she forced herself to paste a smile on her face and keep her mood light and pleasant as she got ready for bed. The sleep aid would ensure he had a good night's sleep, so important to maintaining his mental health, and he would feel better in the morning.

45

Kenzie called Sergeant Campbell as soon as she got into the office the next day, hoping to catch him before he got involved in meetings. But there was no answer. She considered whether to go upstairs to find him, but it would probably just be a waste of time. He wasn't likely sitting at his desk declining her call. If he didn't answer, he was already engaged with something else. She left him a brief message to get back to her ASAP.

She was eager to share the information she had gleaned from the meeting with Emily Cross. Maybe eager was not quite the right word, since she dreaded having to tell him that a dirty cop was involved in the killing and whatever other crimes he had committed in his interactions with the gang over the past few months. But he needed to know, and the case could not be solved until he had all the details.

There would still have to be an investigation. They wouldn't just take Emily at her word. She could be lying. Accusing a cop because they wanted him off the street. Because she wanted to cover for whoever had really killed Mercer. Because she had done it herself. She couldn't assume that everything Emily had said had been true. She had lied or hidden other things. She had her own agenda.

But Kenzie believed the story Emily had told. It rang true. The emotions were genuine, or else Emily was a *very* good actor.

After leaving a message for Campbell, she hung up the phone and got on with her other work. It wasn't like she didn't have anything else to do. She would leave the police case to the police and take care of her work at the medical examiner's office. The work she had been hired to do.

She had been working for a couple of hours, trying to sort out a slew of reports that had all come back from the lab at the same time. There had been a backlog of weeks on tox results, and everything had suddenly come through simultaneously. A piece of equipment that hadn't been working must have just been brought back online. Or a lab tech who had been on vacation had returned and had started to run the backlog of waiting tests.

The desk phone rang, and Kenzie picked it up without looking at it. "Medical Examiner's Office, Kenzie speaking."

"Ah, Kenzie," it was a familiar voice. "You sound like you're very busy today."

Kenzie looked away from her computer screen. "Dr. Wiltshire. How are you?"

"Well, I wish I could say I was one hundred percent and coming back in next week, but I'm afraid it will still take more time to get rehabilitated."

"It is never as quick as you want it to be, is it?" Kenzie sympathized. "I hope it will heal quickly, but you shouldn't push it too much. Make sure that you're really ready and that you're not going to set your healing back by trying to do too much too soon."

"I know. I will take care of myself and will listen to the doctors and physiotherapist."

"Good."

"I wonder if you would be free for lunch today. I know you work through lunch a lot of days, but could I convince you to take a break and eat at a table today?"

"Uh, yeah, of course. Did you want to come here?"

"I'll come to you, and then we can walk together from there."

Kenzie wondered if he suggested walking her because of what had happened the last time she had ventured out from the medical examiner's office for lunch and had been pushed into traffic. She had, luckily, not been badly injured. It could have been much worse. But that wouldn't happen again if someone were with her.

It seemed like no time had passed before Dr. Wiltshire approached her desk. She looked at the clock and saw that it was nearly noon. And she was still trying to get all the toxicology reports printed and filed.

"Oh, doctor! Good to see you." Kenzie looked for a way to take care of all the printouts quickly so she could go with him.

"You look snowed under! Are you not getting the assistance you need while I'm away?"

"No, it's just the lab. They were backed up. And now… I guess they aren't. They sent everything we've been waiting for through last night."

"Well, that's good news. Glad to hear it."

Kenzie nodded. "I'll get it cleared up today. It's just a lot of paper to deal with all at once."

He waited patiently while she cleared her desk and locked her drawers. It was a pain to do in the middle of the day, but she couldn't just leave work out on her desk.

"All right, that's it." Kenzie grabbed her jacket and they headed up to street level, discussing what restaurant to go to.

She had no idea why he wanted to have lunch with her. Was there a purpose behind it or was he just restless? When he had been working, they had rarely eaten together. Unless he brought donuts.

Maybe he was lonely and wanted to be brought in on any interesting cases she'd had recently. But she didn't think so. He must have other people that he saw socially.

He wanted a sit-down restaurant, not just a fast-food joint. They picked out an Indian restaurant with a buffet so they could serve themselves immediately, and both sat down with plates heaped with curry, fragrant rice, chutneys, and naan bread. They tasted and exclaimed over the various dishes.

"So, I'm sure you're wondering why I wanted to meet," Dr. Wiltshire said eventually.

Kenzie nodded. She hoped it was not to announce that his hand was not going to recover fully and he had to retire. If he left, would Dr. Cook take over? Or would he only stay for the interim, and there would be yet another doctor to get used to? Another boss who would have different procedures and expectations?

"No need to look so concerned," Dr. Wiltshire quickly reassured her.

Maybe he had decided to tell her the real story behind how he had hurt his hand. There had been a lot of rumors about it. She didn't want to believe that he had been involved in anything shady or fooling around on his wife. He'd hinted that it was a golfing accident, and she was willing to believe that, as unlikely as it seemed. People could break bones in all kinds of improbable ways. He might have slammed it in a car door, or tripped over a cat, or punched a wall when he was angry. Though she didn't think it was that. From what she had seen of his bruised hand and the bits that were pinned in place by the external fixator, he hadn't sustained boxer's fractures. It looked more like a crush injury.

Dr. Wiltshire caught her eyes on his hand and the space-age-looking fixator cage around it. He raised his brows and shook his head. "It's looking better, don't you think? Now that the bruising has faded?"

"Much better," Kenzie agreed. "Is there still a lot of pain?"

"Not much, as long as it doesn't get jarred. Sleeping is getting easier. The first little while there... unless I was heavily medicated, I wasn't getting any rest at all."

She remembered how scattered, foggy, and irritable he had been whenever he had come in to review and sign documents. Between the pain, the painkillers, and no sleep, it was no wonder he'd been in such bad shape.

"But this isn't about me," Wiltshire went on. He leaned back in his chair and dabbled a piece of naan bread in his curry. "I wanted to talk to you about your position in the office."

"Oh." Kenzie's stomach plummeted. She wished she hadn't eaten so much curry already, as it threatened to make a reappearance. She gripped the table, took a deep, calming breath, and did her best to keep her voice steady. "What about it?"

46

"I told you," Dr. Wiltshire touched her arm lightly. "There's no need to look so grim. Everything is fine, Kenzie."

"But you need to talk to me about my position."

He stared at her. His concerned expression changed to a twinkle. "You're not getting fired," he said with a laugh.

Kenzie took another deep breath and held it. "Suspended?" she suggested. "Flayed?"

"None of the above. Your work has been exemplary, Kenzie, especially how you have stepped up while I have been gone. I know it hasn't been easy. You've had to deal with a couple of very big, very public cases, as well as taking on new responsibilities and coping with a bigger workload. I know you have Dr. Cook now, and he is able to take up some of the slack, but that has still left you in charge of making sure that everything runs smoothly."

Kenzie nodded. She didn't demur and say that it had been nothing. It had been difficult. It was great to get the additional experience to put on her curriculum vitae, but she'd had a few sleepless nights herself and still had to be able to function during the day and to get the work done, despite any additional challenges. Dr. Cook was a professional and was willing to do whatever work Kenzie pointed him at, which was a big help once he had signed on. But there were things that she didn't want to turn over to him, and he approached his work differently from Dr. Wiltshire, causing a number of friction points.

"I have been talking to my superiors, and they are aware of… your handling of the Wade case and the exposure of what was going on at Persons, and agree that you are a professional and deserve to be recognized for your work. The work that you are doing, since it isn't going away anywhere."

"Okay. Well, that sounds good."

"It is. I told you. This isn't anything negative. You can relax."

He waited, while Kenzie demonstrated her level of relaxation by taking a deep breath and leaning back in her seat. He smiled.

"Up until now, you have been my administrative assistant, taking on an increasing role in the medical practice, learning more about performing postmortem procedures, getting as much practical experience as I could give you. You have been an assistant in the medical examiner's office, but you have not carried the title of Assistant Medical Examiner."

Kenzie held her breath. She had hoped that this would come sooner or later. Still, advancement opportunities were few and far between in a small town, and when they would come was unpredictable. They didn't follow the more regular models in the bigger cities, where one could expect a particular title or recognition after a certain length of time, provided they didn't screw things up too much.

"The Health Commissioner will announce your appointment as an Assistant Medical Examiner tomorrow." Dr. Wiltshire beamed at her.

Kenzie couldn't suppress the grin that nearly split her face in half. "That's great! Thank you. I had no idea that you were thinking of making any changes."

"Well, I know better than to promise anything the bureaucracy hasn't yet approved. It's a surefire way to get yourself in hot water when people don't get what they have been promised."

"I guess so," Kenzie agreed. She had learned more about bureaucracy and red tape in the years that she had been working at the medical examiner's office than in all the years listening to her father talking about politics and everything involved in getting a bill passed. When Walter talked about it, it was just her dad complaining about problems at the office. It was different when it was her own office that was affected.

Kenzie's phone buzzed. She glanced down at it briefly and saw that it was Sergeant Campbell. She wanted to talk to him, but their conversation would be more than a three-second exchange. She would need time and attention to cover everything with him. She sent the call to voicemail and slid the phone away again.

"Is that Zachary?" Dr. Wiltshire asked. "You'll want to tell him right away."

"I will. That was just something else. A call that is going to take quite a while, and I don't want to interrupt our conversation with it. If I'm on my lunch break, then I should enforce those boundaries, right?"

"See? You're already sounding more like an entitled professional."

They both laughed.

"Thank you for doing this, doctor. I really appreciate it. Thank you so much for your confidence and for pushing that through."

"Everybody but me will be glad that I broke my hand. Good things will come of this! I appreciate all the help you have given me since you took on this position. You have always been willing to jump in and do what needed to be done, even if it was something beneath you, like making coffee, straightening out someone else's mess, or staying late to ensure that a postmortem got done so the family could claim the body. You've been willing to take on more and more responsibility, and you have learned and progressed a lot in the time you have been with me."

Kenzie's face burned with Dr. Wiltshire's praise, but she lapped it up. She really needed to hear everything he had to say. She had been diligent, a hard worker, always pushing to be everything that Dr. Wiltshire expected her to be. And it was paying off.

"Does the change in title come with… improved compensation?" she asked tentatively.

Not that she needed the money. Even if her salary had not been enough to support her modest lifestyle, she still had a trust fund she could draw on as well. Usually, she only drew from the trust to divert money to worthy causes, not herself, but she didn't have to. She could have lived on it quite well.

"Yes," Dr. Wiltshire confirmed. "There will be an appropriate increase in compensation to go with the title. You are doing the work of two or three people, including that of the medical examiner. We can pay you the appropriate salary and still make out like bandits."

"Awesome." Kenzie was glad that not only did she get the salary she deserved for the job, but that the Department of Health did not resent the promotion and think that she should still be paid little more than a receptionist for the medical work she was doing. "That's great."

"Zachary will be proud."

"Yes, he will," she agreed. "And my parents. Though they still aren't sure what to think of me working at the medical examiner's office."

He chuckled. "Most people find it quite morbid. They don't see it like you and I do. All of our good work, the people we help, and the interesting mysteries we are involved in unraveling. What more could you want from a job?"

"Live patients, maybe. Not me; don't get me wrong, I'm not saying I want live patients. Especially not on the autopsy table. I'm saying other people think it's not really medical work if it isn't done on live patients. And that I would be happier with live patients than with dead ones."

He shook his head slowly. "Do you know how aggravating live patients are? You think it's difficult working with the next of kin around here. Just imagine what it would be like if you had to listen to the patients' complaints too. This is the quietest medical facility you will ever work at."

"I've always found our patients to be fairly easy to get along with," Kenzie agreed with a chuckle.

"We've got the best job in the world, I'm telling you."

Kenzie nodded. She decided she could afford to eat a few more bites of her curry. Her stomach was much happier now that she had heard Dr. Wiltshire's news. She was very pleased not to be fired and have to look for a new job. Especially since she would be lucky to find another medical examiner job in the state, let alone in Roxboro. The opportunities were few and far between.

47

Kenzie returned to the office feeling light and buoyant rather than weighed down by her heavy meal. She and Dr. Wiltshire said their goodbyes outside the building and then she headed back down to the morgue to pick up where she left off on her filing.

She saw Dr. Cook hanging around her desk as she returned, and quickly looked at her phone to see how late she was getting back. She hadn't really been thinking about the time while she was with Dr. Wiltshire, her actual boss, and he was controlling the schedule. She could afford to take a nice leisurely lunch with her boss, who had just given her a plum promotion.

"Sorry," she said. "You were looking for me?"

Dr. Cook smiled. With his movie star good looks, he looked like an ad for dental work. "Oh, that's all right," he told her. "Did you… get any good news?"

"Oh, you knew about this, did you?" Kenzie asked with a laugh. "I thought you were going to be upset I took so long to get back."

"No, no. Honestly, you can take a long lunch whenever you want. It's your office, and I know you put in the hours, whether you take a lunch break or not. You're here late, on weekends, answering call-outs in the middle of the night. You don't need to punch the clock."

That was the way that Kenzie felt about it. Still, she hadn't been sure whether Dr. Cook would see her as lazy or trying to take advantage of Dr. Wiltshire's good graces when she took a long lunch, an afternoon off for couple's therapy, or came in late in the morning after working a call out in the middle of the night.

"Okay. Well, I'm back if you need anything." She looked at him expectantly.

"Honestly, I was only here to see if you were back yet so I could congratulate you."

Kenzie grinned. "Thank you! That's very nice."

"Now, what do you need *me* to work on this afternoon? I saw there was a whole stack of stuff that came in from the lab."

"I've got that under control for now. Speaking of tox screens, though…"

She gave him a few instructions before sitting at her desk and pulling out the lab reports to finish collating.

Kenzie tried to reach Sergeant Campbell, with no answer again, so she left him a message and went back to work. She was searching through slides in the fridge for a misfiled sample when her cell phone rang. She pulled it out to see Campbell's name.

"Hey! I've been trying to reach you."

"And I've been trying to reach you. But I've been foiled all day by meetings. You're free now?"

"Yes," Kenzie confirmed, though she continued to look through the fridge for the sample she was looking for. "Do you want to come down here, or do you want me to come up there?"

"I guess it depends on whether you have anything to show me down there."

"No. I don't have any evidence. Just… information."

"Why don't you come upstairs, then. I'll get a fresh pot of coffee going."

He wouldn't be the one to put it on; someone on his team would. Kenzie suspected that whatever coffee brewing technology they now had in the break room had outstripped the sergeant's skills.

"I'll be right up."

She checked the fridge once more, then left it. She left a note for George that she was looking for the sample, left it stuck to the fridge door, and then went upstairs to talk to Sergeant Campbell.

"Hey, I hear congratulations are in order," he said as he shook her hand in greeting.

"Did everyone know except me?"

"Probably. A promotion like this has to go through a lot of channels, to make sure everyone is on the same page. But I don't think there were too many roadblocks along the way."

Kenzie hoped not. But she thought about her suspension and a couple of warnings about conflicts of interest or other issues and had to wonder. Did all those things get wiped out now that she was being promoted?

"You don't think my… family connections are a problem?" she asked Campbell.

"I don't think so. In fact, I think your family connections were a bonus, not a deterrent."

"They're not concerned about conflicts of interest or political pressure? That I'll cave because my mother or father want me to rule a certain way?"

"That certainly hasn't been our experience in the past." Campbell chuckled. "You've been pretty determined to keep your family and your family name out of all of the medical examiner's office business."

Kenzie had. But she thought that people still perceived that she could be swayed by family pressures.

Campbell led her to an interview room where coffee service had been set up. One of the more comfortable rooms.

"All right, let's get to it. You said that you had some information to pass on to me. About the Mercer case?"

"Yes."

"You haven't found any other physical evidence on the case? Nothing else showed up in the autopsy?"

"No. But there are some tests still pending. I'm not going to change my mind about the cause and manner of death, but I might have more information to add about the state of his health before his death."

Campbell nodded and took a long sip of his coffee. "Yes. Of course. That makes sense."

"The big thing is that I managed to get into contact with Emily."

<h1 style="text-align:center">48</h1>

Sergeant Campbell raised his brows. "Emily? And she is…?"

"She was Mercer's girlfriend inside the gang."

"Ah, right. The gang girl. Wearing colors like he was. You managed to talk to her? I'm surprised she would say anything at all to you."

"Rhys managed to talk her into it."

"For someone who can't speak, that boy is awfully persuasive."

Kenzie laughed. "Yeah, you're right about that. I didn't know if he'd be able to talk her into it, but it didn't take him that long. And probably a lot fewer words than it would have taken me."

"Probably. So tell me what you managed to find out from her."

"Well…" Kenzie shifted in her seat and took a sip of the coffee. She tried to think of the best place to start. "She had some interesting things to say. The thing that I'm most concerned about is that she said the guy that shot Mercer… was a dirty cop."

Campbell scowled and shook his head. "It's not that surprising that she would suggest such a thing. She's trying to get the pressure off of herself and the other members of the gang. We knew from our investigation and your confirmation of Emily and the suspect wearing colors that he was from a gang. Being killed execution-style with a bullet to the head is not an uncommon method for some of these gangs. We're looking at the gangs as suspects, trying to figure out whether he was shot by someone in his own gang by a rival or maybe for a double-cross, or whether it was someone from the other gang. So along comes…"

"Emily."

"Along comes Emily to say that, oh no, it wasn't one of the gangs. It was a cop."

Kenzie nodded slowly. "I can see why you might be suspicious of the source, but Emily was very emotional. I know she is afraid of the killer and that he could come after her. She was very close to Mercer. She took his death pretty hard. All of this felt very… raw and real. Not made up."

Campbell sighed. He wrote down a few notes in his notepad. "Of course we will follow up on every lead, this one as well as any others we have come across. Just don't set your heart on her being right. It might have just been a story to throw the police off the trail."

"She is afraid of the police because he was the one who did it. That was why she would only agree to talk to me, not to you."

"That may be. Or it might just be because gang kids don't like to talk to cops. Does this girl have the name of the cop who is supposed to have done it?"

"No. She said that they all just called him by a nickname. So she never knew what his real name was."

"And he didn't wear a uniform. How did she know he was a cop? Did she see his ID? Did he arrest her?"

"No, she was just told by other members of the gang that he was."

"That's not particularly convincing. No name. No reliable source. That's how these investigations go, unfortunately. Everyone has plenty of gossip and speculation about what happened, but no evidence. We hear a hundred different versions of what happened, each one a little different, but no one has the evidence to go with it, and a hundred people who didn't actually see what happened, who are not witnesses…"

"But Emily saw what happened. She took the picture and sent it to her friends. We know that she saw it happen."

"We know that she was in possession of a single picture. And that she circulated it to friends for no particular reason. That doesn't mean she saw the murder take place or that she knows who did it."

"Right," Kenzie agreed. "I'm sorry. That's true. I'm assuming that she is the one who took the pictures. And the reason she circulated them to her friends was that if the killer made her disappear too, her friends would know that she and Mercer hadn't just run away together. They would at least know what had happened to him."

Campbell considered this for a minute before nodding. "That's the first explanation with the ring of truth. I really couldn't find anything else that fit, other than that kids like to circulate pictures to each other and she didn't really understand the difference between a cute meme from Facebook and an actual murder in the impact that they would have on people. She was just looking for a lot of views."

"I don't think that was it at all."

"Neither do I. Every kid understands the difference between circulating something real and circulating something funny or clever. They probably understand it better than we do. Society is changing, but they are the ones who are on the cutting edge and understand what is now socially acceptable."

"So you believe that she saw Mercer killed and thought that her own life might be in danger."

"I believe she might have forwarded the picture because she was afraid of what might happen to her. That's not quite the same thing."

"I asked her whether she would look at some photos and help us to identify the killer. There can't be that many cops who are involved with the gang. It should be pretty quick to identify him, shouldn't it?"

"Do you know what kind of crap I would get from the patrolmen's association if I showed a gang kid a lineup of cops and asked her which one killed her boyfriend? I'd be lynched. I can't do that."

"Oh." Kenzie nodded slowly. She hadn't thought about an anti-cop bias and how it would look in court if it came out that the witness had only been shown photographs of cops when trying to identify the killer. The union wasn't the only organization that would have a problem with that. "But she is willing to help."

Campbell shrugged. "We'll see what kind of help she is when push comes to shove. You think she'll come in if I call her?"

"Well, not call in here… but maybe meet with you somewhere more public. And I don't know if she has a way to get from Burlington to Roxboro reliably."

"From Burlington?"

"That's where she is right now. Or where she was yesterday when I talked to her. I think she will stay there for a while, but I can't be sure. She wasn't giving me any details about her living arrangements."

"You'd better give me her details. You have her phone number?"

Kenzie opened her phone to find the information and gave it to him.

"How about Rhys's phone?" she asked Campbell. "Was there anything else useful on it? I asked Detective Saul, and he said that your forensic IT guys were still looking at it."

"Who?"

"Detective Saul."

"And who is he?"

"He's the homicide detective that you put on the case…" Kenzie's voice faltered as she realized she had never talked to the two of them together and Campbell had never referred to Saul's part in the investigation. She had relayed the same information to each of them separately.

Sergeant Campbell shook his head, frowning. "No. There is no Detective Saul on the case."

49

Kenzie realized she was sitting with her mouth open, and closed it. She shook her head.

"How could Detective Saul not be a part of your investigative team?" she asked. "He's a homicide detective."

"No, he's not. I know of one Detective Saul, but he doesn't have anything to do with this case. I've worked with him a couple of times on other cases." Campbell pressed his lips together, thinking about it. "He's in the narcotics unit."

"Narcotics. What would he be doing on the case?"

"I've talked briefly with narcotics, following up on the gang connection, but they weren't aware of anything unusual happening. They couldn't identify Mercer from his photo. Not an active enough player. Maybe he was new to the gang."

"So maybe that's how he knew about the case. I was sure he said that you had put him on it, and he was working on finding out who Mercer was and who had started circulating the picture to the kids at the school. You put him on it."

"I didn't. He might have heard about it at a briefing, just because we put the word out about the picture and the phone, trying to get some traction on it, to see if we could identify the players involved."

"Maybe that's what he meant. But I did get the impression that he was working with you…"

"Maybe you misunderstood. Maybe he just said I was the one who had opened the case. I wouldn't necessarily be talking to him directly unless he found something worth reporting."

That soothed Kenzie's anxieties. It explained the whole setup. She had gone to Sergeant Campbell with the picture of the dead man. He had opened the phone harassment case. But since he couldn't identify the players, it was only natural that he spread the news to various other departments to see if anyone knew them. Detective Saul had figured it might be gang- or drug-related. It looked like an execution, so gangs were the obvious suspects. Of course the narcotics division, the acting anti-gang unit, would be in on it. Saul had come to Kenzie for more details, had mentioned that it was Campbell's case, and she had assumed that Saul was on Campbell's team.

An easy misunderstanding.

"Yeah, that must be it," she agreed. "So, were the forensic IT guys able to find anything on the phone that might be helpful? Rhys had other pictures of Emily. Conversations that he'd had with her. I know he deleted them, but sometimes that stuff can be restored, right? I know that Rhys wasn't telling me everything he knew. Maybe he thought that it wasn't relevant, or that he could hold it back without it affecting the investigation. Personal stuff, maybe."

Campbell shook his head. "I want to hear more about Detective Saul and his involvement."

"I've just been keeping him apprised of the investigation. He wanted to know the players, when I talked to anyone, that kind of thing. I've tried to keep both of you as up-to-date as I can on developments."

"So does he know that Emily is in Burlington?"

"Uh, no. I know he was going to try to talk to her, but her mom had said that she hadn't been home, so I warned him that he might not be able to find her."

"But you didn't tell him that you had found her."

"No," Kenzie agreed. "Not yet."

Campbell pulled out his phone and made a call, asking for Saul's phone number. Kenzie waited while he tried to reach Saul. He disconnected the call without leaving a message when he got to voicemail. He looked at Kenzie.

"Do you have a description of the cop that Emily said was involved?"

"No, it's pretty generic. White guy. Middle-aged. Dark hair and eyes." Kenzie considered the description. "But it couldn't be Saul. He's pretty young."

"Yeah, but your 'middle-aged' is coming from a teenager. Our perspectives change. That just means he was older than twenty."

"Saul couldn't have been much more than that."

Campbell chuckled. "He was thirty if he was a day. He could pass for twenty, yes. That comes in handy in narco. To you and me, he seems young. But to a kid Emily's age? She can tell he's no teenager."

"You think he's the dirty cop?" Kenzie shook her head in confusion. "I thought you didn't believe there was a dirty cop."

"I said we would have to follow up on all leads. It was probably an internal gang dispute or a rival gang, but… it bothers me that Saul would talk to you and not at least mention to me and my team that he was pursuing leads. Why didn't he keep us looped in on it?"

"Because he couldn't find Emily? He hadn't talked to her yet, so he didn't have anything to report?"

"But it would have been common courtesy for his team and mine to talk to each other. Coordinate talking to witnesses, instead of both calling the same person independently."

"He's young. Maybe he was just being a…" Kenzie searched for an appropriate moniker. "An eager beaver. A hot dog. Thinking that he had what it took to solve the case himself and be the hero."

"I won't deny that we have our fair share of hot dogs in the department," Campbell admitted. "It's possible. I just want to make sure that he is on a leash." He looked down at his phone, picked it up, and made another call. This time, it sounded like he was talking to an equal. He shot the breeze with his colleague for a few minutes before turning to the question he wanted answered.

"Your young Detective Saul. Is he around?"

Campbell was silent while he waited for the answer.

"Yeah, I already tried his number. No answer. I was hoping you knew where he was."

Another silence. "Yeah. Tell me, was he interested in this homicide that we picked up? The dead guy on the phone. You know, the one I opened up." Campbell frowned at the reply. "No? He didn't mention anything about it to you? He's been talking to the medical examiner's office about it. Implied that he knew some of the players."

It was difficult to follow everything that was being said from only hearing Campbell's side of the conversation. But the gist was clear. Saul's sergeant hadn't known of his interest in the case.

"You guys know the players in the gangs. You didn't recognize the guy in the phone picture? We identified him as Trevor Mercer." He listened for a moment. "Yeah. Small time, just moved here recently. Foot soldier, if he had any responsibility. He had a girlfriend in the gang too…"

Kenzie shook her head. "He was the one who brought her in, so she had even less experience with them."

"Oh." Campbell relayed this information to the other cop. "Never mind, she was an even smaller fish than he was. Totally inexperienced."

Campbell hit the speaker button and laid his phone on the table.

"So, what's the deal?" the sergeant on the other end inquired. "Have you got a beef with Saul? If he's been trying to help with the case, I'm not sure what you're calling about. Leave him a message and coordinate with him."

"Our witness says that there was a cop involved in the death," Campbell explained reluctantly. "I don't have any evidence that is true. But Saul talking to the medical examiner and being involved in this without me knowing about it is a little unusual. And without telling you about it, either. I'd understand if he just wanted the limelight, wanted to be a big hero here. But he's not even talking to you about it?"

"What do you mean there was a cop involved in the death?" the gravelly voice of the other sergeant was cautious.

"Mercer was supposedly killed by a dirty cop."

"Where are you getting this?"

"It's the first I've heard of it, so I'm making inquiries. I'm not accusing Saul or anyone else. The witness could be covering up her own guilt here. But Saul has been making inquiries and getting information from the medical examiner and elsewhere. I would like to talk to him."

"Well, I would too," the narcotics sergeant answered. "I don't want my men going rogue or pursuing other cases without me knowing about it. I'll get ahold of him and get back to you."

"Okay. Appreciate that. Thanks."

Kenzie sat back in her chair, thinking this all through. It was a lot to take in at once. She had come up to talk to Campbell, believing that she had some additional information that would need to be investigated, not sure whether to believe Emily's story of there being a cop involved or not. She wanted to believe that, if it was a cop, it was someone from a state or federal agency, not one of the locals.

Zachary had been involved in a couple of cases in the past that included police corruption, and it was difficult to know how to proceed. It wouldn't help anyone for Kenzie to withhold all of the information she had from the local police department. That gave them no chance of solving Mercer's death. But if there was police corruption involved, then she needed to be careful not only of officers whose behavior was suspect— like Saul, who had professed to be investigating the case under Campbell's auspices— but also those who might be aware of what was going on and had looked the other direction. Or who had profited from the corruption. Or who had gotten involved themselves. Being able to identify one dirty cop was not the end of it. The corruption could run deep.

Or it might be just one rogue cop.

50

So, where do we go from here?" Kenzie asked Sergeant Campbell. "I mean… I don't have anything else to tell you, but now I'm really worried. Saul knows who I am. What if he comes back to me for more information? What if he follows me to see if I'm in contact with Emily? Or follows Rhys?"

"Don't jump to conclusions, first of all. There is no proof that he has done anything illegal or inappropriate. He might just have been interested in what he heard on the case and looked into it on his own time. And if he was the cop who killed Mercer… there is still no reason to believe he is a danger to you or anyone else. You don't know what might have transpired between him and Mercer. But he hasn't shown any inclination to harm you or Emily or anyone else in the case. You haven't felt threatened by him in any way before this?"

"No, not at all." He had come down to see her in the morgue, but had not given her any reason to fear him. He had acted like a cop. Like any other cop she had met. Just gathering evidence, finding out what the autopsy had shown, listening to what witnesses had to say. Nothing had seemed the slightest bit out of character.

"Take the usual precautions. Keep your car in the parking garage. Make sure you aren't followed home. Vary your routes, keep an eye on the rearview mirror and spot-check what cars are visible throughout your trip. Don't go anywhere you wouldn't want him to follow you."

"What about when I'm at home? We have a security system, but…"

"You're usually with Zachary. Two sets of eyes plus a robust electronic system hardwired to a professional security company are pretty good measures. Keep it armed and stay aware."

Kenzie nodded. She thought about getting out of her car and walking to the house and her heart started pounding hard and fast. That was a weak point. When she was in her car, she had a layer of protection between herself and any outside parties. She could keep the doors locked. She could drive away. She could ram her way through human obstacles. And once in the house, she had several layers of protection. She knew it took the security company only two or three minutes to get armed guards to the house. The system had been tested before.

But when she got out of the car, she was vulnerable. Anyone could drive up, jump out of a van, grab her, and carry her off.

"Kenzie, are you okay?" Campbell asked in concern. "Can I get you something…? A glass of water…?"

She breathed heavily, feeling again the hands closing around her, throwing her in the back of the van. She felt her head hitting the floor, pain blossoming from the impact point.

The terror of not knowing what was going to happen to her. They had her under their complete control. They could take her anywhere, do anything.

Sergeant Campbell got up from the table and returned a moment later with a cold glass of water, which he put on the table in front of Kenzie.

"Put your head between your knees," he suggested to Kenzie, placing a hand on her back. "Are you feeling faint?"

"No… no, just…" Kenzie puffed, unable to find the words to even begin to describe what she was feeling.

"You're hyperventilating. You'll make yourself pass out. Have a drink. Count out your breaths."

Kenzie grasped the cold glass, but couldn't drink. She was too nauseated. Breathing too fast. She wasn't in control of her own body anymore.

"Zachary."

Campbell reached out and pushed the button on Kenzie's phone and held it down. "Call Zachary," he instructed.

The computer voice answered and the ringing tone sounded. After a couple of rings, Zachary picked it up.

"Hey, Kenzie."

"This is Campbell," the sergeant announced. "I'm with Kenzie and she's having a little trouble. Can you talk her through this? Tell me what to do?"

"Kenzie?" Zachary's voice was worried. "What's going on?"

Kenzie breathed hard, unable to answer coherently. Campbell's other hand was still on her back, pressing firmly as if trying to hold her in place.

"She's hyperventilating," Campbell relayed. "Does she have panic attacks?"

"She was kidnapped," Zachary told him. "Kenz, how about anchoring? Can you tell me five things you see?"

Kenzie tried to slow her breathing down enough to speak. "Campbell… table… chairs…" She gulped and hiccuped. "Coffee. Water."

"Good. Five things you hear."

"You. Phone." Kenzie tilted her head and tried to interpret the outside noises she could make out through the closed conference room door. "Voices. Ringing phone. Photocopier."

"You said phone twice," Zachary said in a slightly teasing tone.

"I think she meant two different phones," Campbell said helpfully.

"What can you smell?" Zachary prompted.

Each prompt got progressively harder to answer, but they slowed things down and made Kenzie concentrate on something other than the thoughts that had originally triggered her, which she didn't want to return to.

"Deodorant," Kenzie said, her body's rising heat and sweat triggering the scent of her own protection. "Sweat. Laundry soap. Dust."

"How are you doing?"

She took a deeper breath. "Okay."

"Okay?" he repeated. "You don't sound okay. What happened?"

"Don't really want to think about it," Kenzie said, "and trigger another reaction."

"Okay. You and Campbell are together? How's it going, Joshua?"

"Kenzie and I have just been discussing this Mercer case," Campbell informed him. "You're aware of the broad strokes?"

"Yeah."

"You know that Kenzie's witness, Emily, says that there was a dirty cop involved?"

"Yeah. I was going to look into that some more. See if I could help identify who it was if there really was a cop. She could be covering for herself or someone else she knows."

"There's a slight possibility that it might be Detective Saul, a cop who has been talking with Kenzie about the case."

"Detective Saul. Really? I thought he was one of yours."

"He is *not* one of mine. I have talked to his commanding officer, and they will have him in to try to sort this whole thing out. Why he was investigating, what he knows, if he has an alibi for the night Mercer was killed."

"Okay. Good. Sounds like you're on top of it."

"But there are security concerns. Kenzie has concerns."

"Yeah. Of course," Zachary agreed. "How are you doing, Kenzie? Still breathing?"

Kenzie forced herself to keep her breathing slow and steady. "Yeah."

"Uh… why don't I invite Mario over for dinner and to watch the game tonight?" Zachary suggested. "He can tail you home. We'll all be watching. Three sets of eyes. We'll keep you safe."

Kenzie concentrated on the image of Zachary and tubby Mario Bowman walking her up the sidewalk from her car to the house.

Only she wouldn't be parked at the curb. That was silly. She would be parked in her own garage. Safe from the view of any outside parties. A big garage door to keep them out. A locked door between the garage and the house to keep everything secure. All doors monitored and alarmed. She wouldn't be in parked at the curb like before.

"Yeah," she agreed. "That sounds good."

"Okay. I'll give him a call. Are you going to stay with Campbell for now? When are you going to come home?"

Kenzie ran her hands over her face, massaging tension points that were suddenly pulsing with pain. She was exhausted. "I don't know. Give me a while to decide."

"Sure. If you're not up to driving, I can Uber over and drive you home in your car. Or I can pick you up in mine and just leave yours in the parking garage for the night."

"Don't know yet."

"Or you could leave yours in the garage and drive home with Mario."

"Maybe."

"Okay. Do you want to stay on the line, or do you want to call me later when you've had some time?"

"I'll call."

"I always want to sleep after a panic attack," Zachary told her. "It's okay if you want to go to sleep. Grab the couch there or come home early."

"Thanks. Okay. Yeah."

Zachary made a kissing noise. "Call me, Kenz, when you're ready."

"Okay." Kenzie tapped the red button to end the call. She sat there looking at the phone, breathing, counting her breaths, in and out, slowly.

Campbell removed his warm hand from her back and sat down close to her.

"You were kidnapped? No wonder you're panicking. I'm sorry, I didn't know that."

"No. Didn't tell anyone. Even Zachary." She blew out her breath. "For months."

"Good grief. How did he not know?"

"He was in the hospital. It was only for a few hours."

"Well, you've got every right to be concerned about your security. I'll talk to the patrols in your area about rolling by your house regularly."

"You don't need to… especially if Mario is going to come by."

"I'll see what I can do. You stay here while I make a few calls."

"I could go back downstairs. Do some work."

"You could," he admitted. "But you'd just end up having to redo it again later."

Kenzie gave a short laugh. He was probably right about that.

She felt guilty about not going straight back down to the morgue to continue her work. She had already taken time out for lunch.

"I'm getting a promotion," she told Campbell.

"Yeah. I know."

"Did we already talk about it?"

"Briefly."

"Oh, yeah."

51

Maybe it should have bothered Kenzie that Zachary and Mario Bowman seemed to be taking it in turns to walk around the interior of the house, looking out through all of the windows, checking the settings on the security system and making sure that the outdoor cameras were still functioning as they should. It should have made her anxious to have them acting so restless and wary.

But she wasn't anxious. She felt like an animal tucked safely in its den. Warm and cozy and well-protected. No predators could get in. She could rest easy. She looked back at her panic attack of earlier in the day, rolled her eyes, and laughed at herself for breaking down. Yes, she had been through something awful. One time. It had been over in a few hours, and she had not been mistreated while they had held her. The injury to her head had been accidental. They didn't hit her or even put her in handcuffs. They shut her in a room with a bed, didn't abuse or threaten her, and fed her delicious, nourishing soup.

She had refused therapy for the trauma, but she had discussed the incident in couple's therapy a few times as the experience had impacted her relationship with Zachary. She felt that she had put it behind her now. It had just been a fluke that thinking about her security when she got home had triggered panic. Normally, she was just fine with it.

As fine as she could be.

841

That didn't mean that she was totally over the nightmares. Or that she could talk about kidnapping as if it weren't something that struck her deeply. But she could function on a day-to-day basis and not spend all of her time thinking about it. She wasn't disabled by it. Zachary's experiences had been much worse and he had been able to get through being triggered by fire. Exposure was the key. Not avoidance.

But that didn't mean she needed to talk and think about it all the time. Kenzie pushed the thoughts away and tried to concentrate on the show that Zachary had put on. A silly heist movie, filled with spy gear and car chases, witty repartee, and double entendres. Just the kind of thing they all needed to put the kidnapping and Mercer's murder out of their minds for a while.

It wasn't Saul. Kenzie was sure it wasn't Saul.

He wouldn't have been so bold, coming to talk to her repeatedly, getting all the details he could about the investigation. Getting Emily Chase's name and information about what she had done. Kenzie telling him about Rhys and his disabilities. If he had been the one who had killed Mercer, he would have left town immediately. Or at least as soon as they started to gather more information about what had happened. When Mercer's body was discovered. If he had been the killer, he would have left town at that point.

He wouldn't have just kept visiting Kenzie and pretending to be on the case.

Kenzie wasn't sure when she fell asleep. It wasn't a typical night. She was tired from the panic attack. Zachary had been right about that. He had said that he just wanted to sleep after an attack, and Kenzie felt the same way, but she resisted it. She wanted to show someone—herself or Zachary, or maybe Mario, she wasn't sure which—that she was stronger than that. That she could just bounce back.

Even if she was weak enough to succumb to a panic attack, she was strong enough to carry on afterward. Like Superwoman.

Zachary had promised Mario that they would watch the game together. However, Zachary had probably had to look up what game was playing, since he wasn't at all into sports. So after the heist movie, they had put the game—football—on the TV, and had watched it together, between shifts pacing around the house and looking out the windows. Kenzie sat on the couch and pretended to read a book, turning the page every now and then. But she really had no idea of the words on the page. She was just glad to be there, safe and sound, protected by the security system on the outside and the units that would respond to it, and her partner and a cop on the inside.

She didn't think that she had fallen asleep on the couch. Zachary wouldn't have been able to carry her to her bed. Mario, though a bigger man, was considerably out of shape and probably wouldn't carry anything bigger than a pizza to bed. So she must have gotten there under her own power, but she couldn't remember doing so.

"Zachary?"

"I'm here."

She heard the rustle of sheets as he stirred beside her, the soft click of his putting his computer or phone on the bedside table. Then he was cuddling up against her, putting his arms around her.

"Are you okay?" he murmured in her ear. "You're safe here."

"I know. I just wondered where you were."

"I'm not going anywhere."

"What time is it? You should go to bed."

"I am in bed," he pointed out.

"You should go to sleep," Kenzie clarified. Though of course, he knew exactly what she meant. "You need to get your sleep, too."

"Too early for me to go to sleep."

She couldn't stir herself enough to check the time. She must have dropped off early. Nine o'clock, maybe. It was dark outside, but Zachary would never go to bed that early.

"Soon," she told him. "Don't stay up too late."

"Okay."

He stayed there like that, with his arms around her, just breathing in her ear, until she fell asleep again.

Kenzie didn't know how much later it was when she heard Zachary moving around and distant voices again. She rubbed her eyes and looked at the window to verify that it was still nighttime, and no light was creeping in around the blinds. Her body told her that it was late at night. Or very early in the morning. Maybe Zachary was seeing Mario off. She had thought that he would spend the night on the couch, just to reassure Kenzie that everything was okay, but maybe he had decided that it wasn't worth wrecking his back over.

They had a spare room. He could sleep in there. But then he wouldn't be near any of the ingress or egress points, which made it a silly place to station a guard.

"Zachary?" Kenzie called softly. "Is Mario leaving?"

She would tell him to tell Mario goodbye for her. And thank you for coming when she called him, regardless of how ridiculous it was to need an out-of-shape policeman eating chips in front of the TV while she slept.

A dark form paused in the bedroom doorway. Zachary.

"No, Mario is staying the night."

"Aren't you going to sleep? I thought you were coming to bed with me."

"I was just answering the phone. Go back to sleep."

"Is everything okay?" Kenzie rubbed her eyes. Who was calling in the middle of the night? Sergeant Campbell checking in on her? The security company providing a report that they had driven by and everything looked clear? Someone else that Zachary had touched base with in an effort to improve the security of the house?

"Go back to sleep. We can talk in the morning."

But something told Kenzie that everything was not well.

"What is it? What's wrong?"

Zachary didn't answer for a moment. Kenzie's body wanted to go back to sleep, but her brain kicked into high gear at Zachary's silence. She reached over and turned on the bedside lamp to illuminate him and keep herself from falling back asleep again before he could tell her.

"Zachary?"

She could see, squinting at him in the warm lamplight, that his expression was grave.

"It's Rhys."

52

"Rhys?" Kenzie's heart raced.

She had been so worried about protecting herself, making sure that Saul couldn't come back after her, that she hadn't thought about the others who might need protection.

Rhys.

He didn't have a state-of-the-art home security system protecting him, with armed guards just minutes away. He didn't have Zachary. Or Mario with his gun. All Rhys had was an aging grandmother who took sleeping pills at night and didn't even notice when he decided to take off on his own.

Kenzie slid her feet over the side of the bed. She was still wearing the yoga pants she had put on to relax before bed and hadn't changed into her jammies. Not that there was any difference other than the appropriateness of each in Kenzie's mind for their utility.

"What happened to Rhys? Is he okay?"

"We don't know." Zachary licked his lips and swallowed. "Nobody knows anything yet, except that he isn't home."

"Vera called?"

"Yes."

"He might just be out for a walk. Taking off to visit with someone, like he's done before."

"Exactly. We know he doesn't always stay home in bed like he is supposed to."

The last time, he had been in a fugue state, wandering near Stanley Green's house. Not a good place for a young, vulnerable teen.

"Has she called Stanley?"

"Yeah. He's gone out to drive around, see if he can see Rhys anywhere. I turned the lights on outside," Zachary nodded to the front of the house. "And I called Tyrrell to give him a heads-up."

Tyrrell lived in Zachary's old apartment, which Rhys had been to before and could conceivably show up at if he were in a confused state.

"What else? Has she called the police?"

"Yes. They know that he is a vulnerable individual and have opened a file. They're starting with the basics. Searching the neighborhood in case he's just wandered off. Asking about acquaintances, if they'd had a fight, all that kind of thing."

"Asking whether he's a witness in a murder case?" Kenzie asked.

"They've been filled in on what we know. Campbell's already been contacted."

"What about the other cop he called? Saul's commanding officer? Have they found Saul?"

"No. He's still not answering. He's not at home. Hasn't reported in for his shift at work."

"He was supposed to be there?"

Zachary nodded. "But he just didn't show up."

Kenzie's heart was pounding. "What if he has Rhys?"

Zachary swallowed strenuously and nodded. "That is being considered."

"Why didn't you wake me up? You should have!"

"There wasn't anything you could do that we weren't already doing. You might as well get your sleep. Be well-rested in the morning. See if you can notice anything with fresh eyes that we might have missed."

"What about tracing Rhys's cell phone?"

"It's turned off."

"Then he didn't just wander away."

"I don't think so. It's possible that he took it with him and he just ran out of juice. Forgot to plug it in at the end of the day, or it wasn't properly connected. I've had a time or two when I plugged my phone in before going to bed and then woke up in the morning and it was dead. Because it wasn't plugged in the right way or the cord was faulty."

"Well, yes. It could happen. But most of us are pretty careful to make sure that it doesn't. And Rhys relies on his phone for communication. He's going to make sure that it doesn't run out of juice."

"Mistakes happen. Technology fails."

But it was a brand-new phone.

Kenzie stood up. "Is there anyone else here? Is it just you and Mario?"

"Yes. Just us. Campbell stopped by for a few minutes to check in on things, but he's gone over to Vera's."

"I should go over there. Sit with her."

"Are you sure you want to go out? I thought… you would want to stick around here."

"Because I'm afraid? It's obvious that Saul decided Rhys was the most vulnerable and went after him. He's in the wind now. He's not coming after me. He got everything he could from me before I realized what was happening. He's not coming over here."

Zachary looked at her for a minute, then nodded.

"Let me grab my purse and splash some water on my face, and then we can go," Kenzie told him.

53

Rhys kept his head down, chin to chest, pretending he had fallen asleep. People thought that he was stupid. That he couldn't understand what was going on. He learned a lot by just keeping his head down and pretending not to hear anything.

The bad cop drove into the darkness, his headlights dim on the country road. Just his running lights on. Hardly enough to make out the shape of the road ahead. Because he didn't want to attract the attention of anyone who might live nearby, Rhys assumed. Though it was hard to believe that anyone lived out there in the trees. Maybe some farmers or hunters.

Rhys shifted, flexing his wrists, pushing outward on the bonds that held him. He looked up at the sky and wondered if, had he known his constellations better, he would be able to tell where he was by the stars in the sky. As it was, he only knew the big and little dipper and the north star, though he was never actually sure which one was the north star. Venus was brighter, and he always thought he should be able to follow the morning star instead of the north star to get where he wanted to go.

But being a city kid, he wasn't navigating anything by the stars.

They pulled off of the gravel that wasn't really a road anymore, into the trees. Rhys thought they were going to run directly into one of the trees. Maybe the bad cop had fallen asleep and gone off the road by accident. But he stopped before he hit the trees. He punched Rhys in the arm.

"Wake up, kid."

Rhys raised his head. The bad cop shoved him into the door. "Get out."

He felt for the door handle, but it wasn't in the same place as in Grandma's car, and he couldn't find it in the dark. The cop reached across him and found it, clicked it open, and pushed the door, giving Rhys another shove to encourage him to get out of the car.

He considered running into the trees. It was the one time he was out of the cop's reach. He could probably outrun the cop in a few minutes. He was a fast runner and the cop looked soft and slow. Em said he took drugs, which meant his body was in bad shape. Maybe he even had heart damage.

It would serve him right if he had a heart attack chasing Rhys.

But Rhys was still in handcuffs, and he didn't know where he was or where to find people or to run to. He could run into a river or off a cliff. Or just into a nest of poisonous snakes. There could be other people out there that were working with the bad cop. And the cop was armed. Rhys couldn't outrun a bullet. If the cop got a good shot at him… Rhys knew how it turned out on TV. Down he would go, and no one would ever find him out here in the wilderness. Grandma would never even know what had happened to him. Maybe she would think that he had run away. That he didn't love her and want to stay with her anymore.

He didn't want her to die thinking he had run away from her.

As much as he wanted to be grown up and have a place of his own and be independent of all of the people who told him what to do or thought they knew what was best for him better than he did himself, he didn't want that.

By the time he had finished thinking through whether or not to run, it was too late. The moment had passed. The bad cop was around the car and grabbed him by the arm. Rhys resisted initially, but the cop was strong despite his drug use, and Rhys knew that he wouldn't win anything in a fight. Especially not against an armed man. He just wanted the cop to know that he wasn't going easily. He wasn't beaten.

Rhys couldn't see ahead of him as the cop led him into the trees. Was this it? The cop had brought him out here just to kill him and leave his body there to rot? Was the only reason he had left Rhys alive because it was easier to get Rhys somewhere walking under his own power than it was to transport a dead body?

"Keep walking," the cop growled, holding on to him, but forcing Rhys to walk a little ahead of himself. Rhys stumbled, unable to see where to put his feet. The ground was uneven with rocks, roots, and branches under his feet that threatened to trip him and make him fall on his face.

But the cop didn't push him faster than he could go. As Rhys's eyes adjusted to the dark, he saw a building through the trees. Not a big house, but bigger than the fishing shack Rhys and his mother had gone to when she had been on the run. Rhys assumed that was where the bad cop wanted him to go, and aimed his steps toward the front door of the cabin. This seemed to suit bad cop, since he didn't growl at him again, and was patient as Rhys's feet found their way through the invisible obstacles.

"Nice to have a hostage who doesn't talk back, for once," the bad cop said, and laughed. The noise was harsh in the silence of the woods. Rhys wondered. How many other people had he brought out here? And what had happened to them? Had they left under their own power, or were their bodies still out here, buried in shallow graves somewhere beyond the house?

He wished he had the power to say something smart to bad cop, like an action movie hero. They always had something quick and clever on their lips. They didn't struggle to put together language like Rhys did, and then to push the words out of his mouth and throat.

A mute action hero. Now that would be something.

It would never work. How would anyone know how smart he was? How he felt about things? How would they know the difference between when he was being quiet because he didn't want to give away his thoughts and when he was being quiet because he couldn't get out the thoughts he wanted to share? How would they know whether his smile was genuine or hiding pain? He wouldn't be able to get the girl. He wouldn't even be able to finish training with whatever law enforcement agency initially hired him. He couldn't go rogue if he were never hired in the first place.

The cabin loomed up ahead of him. It was actually bigger than he had thought. It was hard to tell at night from a distance. He stopped walking, and the cop pushed him forward again, one hand still firmly on his arm.

Right up to the door, where Rhys stopped again. Was someone going to let them in? How many people did bad cop have helping him?

But the cop didn't knock or ring the doorbell. He jingled keys as he juggled them out of his pocket and found the one he needed, then pushed Rhys to the side slightly in order to unlock two locks. He opened the door and pushed Rhys ahead of him into the pitch-black room. Rhys's toe caught on the lip of the doorframe and he yelped a little as he tripped and then recovered his balance.

The cop reached around the doorframe and found a switch. He flipped it on, and the room was suddenly flooded with light. Rhys squinted and his eyes teared up before they adjusted to the new environment.

There were not a lot of lights, but it still seemed painfully bright. And it would be visible to neighbors or anyone traveling down the road they had driven in on. Did the cop want to give away their location? Did he not care? Maybe there were no neighbors close enough to care about it. Maybe no one else used the road.

How was anyone going to find Rhys? He was still trying to figure out how he would get in touch with Zachary or Kenzie to tell them where he was. His phone had GPS on it. He could send them coordinates. But to do that, he had to be able to get his phone out and find a way to send them a message without the cop knowing about it. It wasn't going to be as easy as it had been when he was with his mother.

And it had almost been too late by the time he had managed to communicate his location then.

54

The trip to Vera's house had never taken so long. Kenzie refused to look at the speedometer as Zachary drove. She knew that he would speed. And he wouldn't get caught; he never did. He would have made a good race car driver, and at night there was little traffic on the roads.

So how could it take so long to get there?

Kenzie resisted the urge to look at the time on the radio or on her phone. It didn't take long to get to Vera's house. Roxboro was not the big city.

Finally, they pulled up to the Salter house. Or a few houses down from it, as there were police vehicles and other dark, nondescript vehicles parked in front of it. It wasn't like the scene when Bridget's twins had been kidnapped. That had happened out in the open and the police knew from the start that it had been an abduction rather than just a kid sneaking out at night. In Rhys's case, they were probably still trying to keep it from attracting too much attention. No point in attracting the attention of all of the neighbors if Rhys had just left on his own, without any coercion, and not as the result of a psychological break. The lights on the police vehicles had been turned off, and there was not a crowd of cops and technicians outside, setting up bright lights and stringing crime scene tape.

Zachary and Kenzie both got out of the car quickly. There was no waiting for Zachary to open the car door for her today. They didn't exactly sprint up the sidewalk, but it was definitely a fast walk.

There was a cop just inside the front door trying to keep control of the scene. He put a hand out to stop Zachary and Kenzie.

"Hold on. Names and roles, please."

"Zachary Goldman and Kenzie Kirsch," Zachary informed him. "Friends of the family. We're here to help."

"Sorry, you're going to have to talk to the family later. It's vital that we get the police investigation off the ground as quickly as possible."

"Ask Sergeant Campbell."

The cop looked surprised at Zachary knowing the name of one of the ranking officials there. "Wait here, please."

He motioned to another cop across the living room to keep an eye on them, and retreated to the hallway that led to the bedrooms, where Vera and Campbell apparently were.

Zachary jiggled impatiently and Kenzie found it difficult not to do the same. She wanted to talk to Campbell. To give Vera a hug and reassure her that everything would work out okay. She wanted to reassure herself that everything would be okay. When Rhys had disappeared the last time, he had been in very bad shape mentally. Had something else happened to trigger him? Had he been released from the hospital too early? Or was it actually an abduction? She hated not knowing.

After what seemed like a long time, the cop returned and motioned for Zachary and Kenzie to enter.

"Sorry. We don't want the place to be overrun," he explained.

"Of course not," Zachary agreed. "Do you want us to wait out here or can we go back and see the bedroom?" His eyes were bright as he looked around the room, taking everything in.

Kenzie imagined that if she were looking over a body or deeply involved in an autopsy, Zachary would see the same kind of calculation in her eyes as she saw in his. While she could see everything he could see around the room, she wasn't thinking everything through the same way he was. His brain was working through all of the scenarios, he was looking for every little thing that was out of place or might give him some clue as to what had happened that night. A voluntary disappearance? Rhys going out to meet another teen? That was the best-case scenario. If he were somewhere nearby, at a friend's house or some meeting place.

"Come on back," Campbell told Zachary, appearing in the hallway behind the officer.

Zachary and Kenzie headed for the bedroom. Kenzie hung back. There were already too many people in the room. It was crowded with Vera, Campbell, Zachary, and a couple of crime scene investigators looking for any evidence that would help them figure out what had happened.

"Zachary! Thank you for coming," Vera told him, moving forward for a hug.

Zachary nodded, giving her a squeeze and letting her go. Kenzie remembered how it had been when Gloria had disappeared with Rhys. Vera had been on the wrong medications and had been confused and muddled, not sure what was happening. It might have been kinder when she didn't know what was going on. The fear and anxiety in her eyes now was painful to see.

"I'm so sorry," Kenzie told her. Vera left the bedroom to hug Kenzie in the hallway. Her grip was tight.

"We will find him," Vera said fiercely. "I know we will find him! After all that boy has been through in his life, this will not be the end."

Kenzie tried to swallow a lump in her throat. Vera's strength made her feel weak and vulnerable. "What do you think happened?"

"I don't know." Vera's eyes were dry. Her gaze was direct and unwavering. "We are going to find out."

"What do you know so far?" Zachary asked, seemingly of the room in general.

"Not much yet," Campbell said. "Vera got up to check on Rhys and make sure that he was settled for the night. He wasn't there. When she checked the rest of the house, she found that his shoes, coat, and phone are gone. The front door was left unlocked. He did not take keys or a wallet with him."

Kenzie frowned, trying to puzzle that through. "Well, that doesn't sound like a kid who's taken off to meet friends or go to a party somewhere. If he was going out to something he didn't want Vera to know about, he would have taken keys with him to lock up and let himself back in again."

Vera was still holding on to Kenzie's arm tightly. "Yes, I agree," she confirmed.

"Why did you get up to check on him?" Zachary asked.

"He hasn't been sleeping soundly since his breakdown. I like to look in and make sure that he's okay. If he's restless or having nightmares, I'll sit up with him for a while. And of course… he just left that night without me knowing it, and I didn't want that to happen again. I wanted to know if he left the house, even if it was just because he didn't want me to know he was sneaking out."

She released Kenzie's arm and massaged the knuckles on each hand. Kenzie didn't know if that was because they were hurting her or if it was a nervous gesture.

"Sometimes kids sneak out," Vera went on. "If that's what he needed to do… then fine. He could sneak out, as long as I knew about it."

Kenzie smiled and shook her head at this. "Then it's not exactly sneaking, is it?"

"If he doesn't tell me, it's still sneaking. If I don't tell him that I know about it, then he thinks he's gotten away with something and he feels stronger and more independent. And…" Vera gave Kenzie a sly look out of the corner of her eye, "I can use his guilt over sneaking out to make him do other things for me."

Kenzie couldn't help laughing, despite the seriousness of the situation. "You are very devious," she told Vera.

"I've raised two girls. Now, girls and boys may not be the same, but they all need a chance to spread their wings. And to have rules and structure the rest of the time."

Kenzie nodded at her wisdom. "I wonder if my parents knew about things I was doing and just never told me."

"You can be sure they did. Not everything, maybe, but parents know. It's best to just keep quiet about it until you need to use it. And even then… you don't mention it directly. Just say that you're so glad that they are willing to help you and don't sneak around like your friend's child or grandchild."

"That sounds very well-thought-out."

"If he didn't take his keys and wallet with him, then he didn't leave of his own free will," Zachary said, bringing them back to the important point.

"But that doesn't mean he was forced," Kenzie said. "If he was sleep-walking or in a fugue, then he could easily have left things that he would need at home."

"What about video?" Zachary asked. "You don't have a doorbell camera. Do any of your neighbors?"

Vera motioned to Campbell. "I think he is already looking into that."

Sergeant Campbell nodded. "Yes. We are canvassing. Just eyeballing each house right now, we'll start ringing doorbells on houses that have cameras at a more decent hour."

"You're putting neighbors' sleep above Rhys's safety?" Zachary challenged.

"It doesn't help us if people are angry at being woken up and tell us that the video is not recorded anywhere, and it is. Then we've just shot ourselves in the foot and lost a potentially rich source of information because we didn't respect the neighbors' sleep."

Zachary frowned. He didn't like this answer, but didn't seem to have an argument against it. If people told the police that they didn't have a recording, they couldn't exactly demand it. They couldn't say anyone was impeding an investigation. There would be no way to prove whether or not they were telling the truth. The cops would just be out the footage that they could have offered. Having to wait a few hours was a risk, but Campbell was trying to weigh each risk carefully.

"Of course, if people are looking out their windows to see what is going on, we can politely ask them if they have any footage," Campbell said. "We just can't go around indiscriminately ringing doorbells at this time of night. I can tell you from experience that it will backfire."

"What else?" Kenzie asked. "Zachary said that Rhys's phone is off?"

"Yes," Campbell admitted. "We're watching for it to come back online, but at the moment, all we know is that it was here when it went offline. No chance of following it for a few blocks so that we at least know what direction he left in."

"And it could just be a faulty battery," Kenzie suggested.

Campbell shrugged. "At this point, I am assuming that is not true. I think the chances that his phone would accidentally run out of juice in the middle of the night, at the same time as he goes sleepwalking or wanders off in a fugue are pretty slim. I don't think that's what happened."

Kenzie had to admit that it didn't sound too likely. "What about an Amber alert? Have you put one out?"

"It will be going out shortly. First, we had to satisfy ourselves that it was a likely abduction. And that the situation would be helped by an Amber alert. Because of course… if it was Saul or a dirty cop who took him, then he gets the Amber alerts, and it will tip him off to the fact that we know Rhys is missing. When otherwise, he wouldn't know that until much later. Keeping him in the dark might give us an advantage."

"But you decided to go ahead. so you don't think it gives you any advantage."

"Having weighed both sides, we decided to go ahead with the alert. If he is somewhere people might see him… it will help us more than hinder us."

55

Kenzie's phone buzzed. At first, she just ignored it. What she was doing was far more important than what anyone could be messaging her about. But gradually, as the follow-up reminders to check her message buzzed, she realized that it was still the middle of the night. Who would be texting her at this hour?

She pulled the phone out of her pocket and looked at it. Zachary glanced at her with an irritated look that quickly switched to the same realization.

"Who is it?" he asked.

"Just a second…" Kenzie had to unlock her screen in order to see her messages. For the sake of privacy, her own and others', she did not allow text messages to display on her lock screen. It was a number she did not recognize and, for a moment, Kenzie's heart fell. Just some spammer from some country on the other side of the world where it was daytime. But she glanced at the message, and it was not spam. "It's Emily."

Campbell and Zachary both waited for more information. Vera raised an eyebrow and shook her head slightly. "Who?"

"The girl who sent Rhys the picture of the dead man. She's the one who witnessed his death. The one who… started all of this."

"She didn't start it," Zachary pointed out sensibly. "She was caught in the middle of it. She was recruited into a gang. She witnessed a murder. Neither thing was something she had planned to do."

Kenzie looked at Vera and saw her lips tighten. They were both thinking the same thing. That Emily could still have made different decisions. Decisions that wouldn't have negatively affected Rhys, and possibly other students and people in Emily's community.

But Emily was a kid. And the choices that she had made could not be changed now. It was best to just forget about the past and any part of the blame that might be hers and move on.

Kenzie looked at the message. "She said that Rhys started messaging her." She looked at Campbell. "I thought you said you were watching for his phone to come back online."

"We are." Campbell pulled out his own phone to see if he'd missed any messages from the team. "Hang on."

They waited while he called to check with his IT guys, and shook his head.

"Rhys's phone has not come back online."

Kenzie looked down at her phone. "And this is not the same number that she was sending me messages from before. It might not be Emily. And she might not be getting anything from Rhys. So what is this?"

"What does she say?" Zachary asked.

"She said that Rhys started messaging her. She initially ignored it because she didn't know who it was, but it was Rhys, and he was asking her to meet with him."

"Where is he?"

Kenzie tried to think of the best reply to send to Emily. Was it Emily? And if so, how had she gotten a message from Rhys when his phone wasn't online? Maybe it was a message from the kidnapper. From Deputy Donut, as Emily had referred to him.

How do I know who this is? she finally texted, hoping the direct approach would work best. Emily must know that she would need proof. That she couldn't just assume that anyone who messaged her was telling the truth and was who they claimed to be.

There was no immediate response from Emily. Kenzie waited impatiently. How long could it take to type a message that somehow verified who Emily was?

DD only knew me as M, was the not-so-lengthy reply that Kenzie finally received.

And then another piece of the puzzle.

til you told DD my name

Kenzie read both replies aloud to Campbell and Zachary, even though they made her wince.

"Who is DD?" Vera asked plaintively, upset about being out of the loop and not knowing what they were talking about.

"Deputy Donut," Kenzie said. "A nickname for the dirty cop."

She didn't say Detective Saul. Not until that was proven.

"Okay. So it is Emily," Zachary said, ignoring the sender's accusation. "She got a new phone or is using a burner she already had stashed. But is it really Rhys she is messaging with?"

Kenzie nodded. She texted back to Emily. *How u know it is Rhys?*

They again had to wait for Emily to figure out what to say or to compose it on her keyboard.

Eventually, the answer came through. Not words this time. Instead, it was a picture of a pug with a Sherlock Holmes deerstalker hat on its head and a pipe in its mouth. Kenzie sighed. She showed it to Vera, who was still standing beside her, and then stepped into the bedroom to show it to each of Zachary and Campbell.

"I guess she recognizes Rhys's communication style," Zachary confirmed.

"Give me the number she's texting from," Campbell ordered. Kenzie tapped it on her screen so that she could see the full number and then read it out to him.

"We'll get a trace on it and see where she is," Campbell advised. "And then we can see who she is exchanging texts with too."

"I can just ask her what number he is texting from."

"Don't trust witnesses to tell you the truth," Campbell advised. "Then you won't be disappointed when they lie."

"Trust but verify," Kenzie said, repeating something she had heard on TV.

Campbell shook his head. "Don't trust." He cleared his throat and shrugged. "We're going to take a two-pronged approach. You need to keep messaging with Emily. Get everything you can out of her. She already trusts you, so you just have to make sure not to do anything that will make her back off. Don't ask too many questions. I will get the tech guys on to it, but it will take time to track the number Rhys is texting from and to trace his phone."

"He might not be using text messaging. It might be an app."

Campbell grimaced. If Rhys and Emily were using another app instead of straight text messaging, then it would be that much harder to find the phone they needed to trace.

"Right. Maybe ask her that, but not right away. Like I said, not too many questions."

Kenzie nodded. "Okay." She worked on breathing slowly and regularly.

They were making progress. They would find Rhys. They would bring him back safe.

Kenzie went back out to the living room and sat down where she would be able to text more comfortably with Emily. She didn't want to be looking at Rhys's room, reminded of his absence there. And standing in the hallway was awkward and made her anxious for Emily's answers to come faster than they did.

She sat down with the phone on her knee.

Where is Rhys? Did he say?

Emily's reply was quicker to this question. *wont say DD there probly wont let him*

Kenzie was sure that Emily had probably asked. Had probably wanted to know all of the details. But Rhys's communications were being monitored by Saul, if he was the kidnapper. He couldn't say anything the man didn't first approve.

Is DD Detective Saul? Kenzie typed.

dont know

Kenzie looked around her. People were coming and going, but none of them were of any help to her. "Zachary?"

He was at her side in a minute, looking at the phone expectantly.

"Not anything from Emily," Kenzie said, waving her hand at it. "Can you get a picture of Detective Saul that I can send to Emily? To find out if that's her Deputy Donut?"

"Sure," Zachary agreed. He returned to the hallway, to ask Campbell for a picture, Kenzie assumed.

Why did Rhys send you a message? Kenzie asked Emily.

DD wants to talk to me.

Kenzie wasn't surprised. Of course the dirty cop wanted to talk to her. He wanted to see how much of a threat she was. Or he wanted to take her out so that she was no longer a threat. Since Emily was the person who could identify him as the killer, he probably wanted her to disappear permanently. So that she could never cause any trouble for him again.

Don't agree to it, Kenzie warned.

u think im stupid?

Sorry. Just worried about you. Are you still in Burlington?

There was a long pause during which Kenzie watched the flashing dots and tried not to be too impatient. She tried to think of other things instead of how they were going to get Rhys out of the situation he was in. What work she had to do at the office. What her priorities were. When would her promotion be announced to the public? She hadn't seen any paperwork on it yet. Didn't have anything but Dr. Wiltshire's assurance that she was being promoted.

Her phone vibrated. She looked back down at it.

worried bout Rhys. DD is crazy

I know. We're worried too. Do you have any idea where they are?

trying 2 figure out. something with stars?

Kenzie had no idea what that meant. *What?*

*he keeps *starring* words*

Like for emphasis? Bolding?

R never does that

"Okay," Kenzie murmured to herself. What was Rhys trying to communicate by starring words? If he didn't usually do it, he was trying to communicate something. Highlighting words that would combine to form a separate, hidden message?

Tell me the words he starred.

no must today do it

All words that someone might normally emphasize in a conversation. Kenzie shook her head. That wasn't it.

What else has he said to you about where he is or what he wants?

What DD says. Meet or Ill hurt people. Rhys mom kids from school all of them

They must still be in Roxboro, then. All of those are people who live here.

More dots. They kept starting and then stopping and Kenzie didn't know if she was writing and deleting her responses or just couldn't think of what to write.

Are you in Burlington or Roxboro? Kenzie tried again to get an idea of where the girl was. Was she in the same city as the killer? Several hours away? Did Saul know that she had gone to Burlington? Did Rhys? The kids kept things from the adults, Kenzie was sure, and she didn't know how much Emily had told Rhys about what had happened with Mercer and the gang and the dirty cop, and how much she had kept a secret.

How much she still might be keeping a secret from all of them even now. The way she told the story, she was innocent of any responsibility in Mercer's death and had only been afraid for her life.

u dont need 2 know

56

Kenzie had to admire the girl. She knew how to protect her privacy. Emily had reached out to Kenzie for help but, apparently, her trust did not extend to telling Kenzie where to find her. But Campbell would soon know.

Kenzie got another message, but when she looked down at her screen, it was not there. There wasn't anything since Emily's last comment. She tapped out of the screen and saw that the OS said she did have another message but, when she tapped that, she saw the new message wasn't in her conversation with Emily, but under Zachary's name. She pulled up the message and saw Detective Saul's picture. It looked like maybe it was his police academy graduation photo. Kenzie texted Zachary back a thank you, then she copied and pasted the picture into her conversation with Emily.

Is that DD?

The response from Emily was a string of expletives.

Does that mean yes?

Another long string of expletives combined with Emily's reply, which boiled down to a "yes."

Kenzie sent a text back to Zachary, confirming that Emily had identified Saul as the cop who killed Mercer. She felt numb. She had been hoping that Emily would say no. That they'd been all suspicious of the cop for no reason. It was just an innocent mistake. Kenzie wanted the dirty cop to belong to another law enforcement organization. Or to not actually be a cop at all, just someone who had pretended to be one to scam everybody.

How could a cop she had known and not suspected of anything be guilty of murder? Not an accidental shooting or a shooting in the line of duty. He had, from Emily's description, killed Mercer in cold blood.

If Emily were telling the truth. But right now, that was all that they had to go on.

Kenzie could hear Campbell's raised voice in the back hallway. He was not happy about something. Obviously, he wasn't fighting with Vera. He wouldn't do that. One of his own crime scene investigators? Kenzie knew them, and they were well-trained. She would have deferred to them on any procedure to be followed or evidence to be collected.

That left Zachary.

Kenzie was right. Within a minute, Campbell and Zachary were both back in the living room. Zachary positioned himself between Campbell and Kenzie, his face intent and body language tense.

"What's the matter?"

"You sent Emily Chase a photo of Detective Saul and asked her if he was the killer?" Campbell demanded.

"Uh…" Kenzie couldn't very well deny it. She looked at Zachary and back at Campbell. "Yeah. I figured that was the best way to find out who we were dealing with. She said she didn't know his real name. We were at a disadvantage, not knowing whether it was Detective Saul or if she was talking about someone else."

"I told you I wouldn't let her look through pictures of cops."

Kenzie cleared her throat. Yes, he had been very clear about that point. Kenzie couldn't say that she had somehow misunderstood. Campbell had not wanted to throw a bunch of cops under the bus. Hadn't wanted her to pick out someone who was completely innocent and identify him as a killer.

But they'd already had reason to suspect Saul. It wasn't just blindly choosing a bunch of police officers and letting her pick anyone she pleased to say that it was the dirty cop.

"I thought since we already figured it was Saul, it wouldn't hurt to get a confirmation." Kenzie looked at Zachary. "You told him that was why I needed the picture, didn't you?"

Zachary didn't answer.

Campbell looked at Zachary. "Oh, this is on you too, is it? You're the one who found the picture for her."

"Yes."

Kenzie was just getting caught up on what had happened. She had thought that Sergeant Campbell had given the picture of Saul to Zachary, but he had not. Zachary had done what he did best—searched out the needed information—and had given it to Kenzie without checking with Campbell first. And Campbell would not have approved Kenzie using it for that purpose.

"Oh… I'm sorry. I thought that you had given it to Zachary when I asked for a picture to send to Emily. I… should have known you wouldn't want me to send it to her."

"You've tainted this witness. You've shown her a picture of one person, and named that person as a suspect, and it will now be firmly entrenched in her mind as the person she saw kill Mercer. If that was actually what happened and not just something she made up."

Kenzie rubbed her forehead. "I didn't realize."

"You know we have rules about showing pictures to witnesses. Photo lineups. Not tipping off a witness that you are looking at a certain person."

"Yes." Kenzie looked down at her phone. She couldn't very well take it back now. Emily had seen what she had seen. If she testified against Saul in court, if they could arrest him for the murder and get her up on the stand, she would be forced to say that she had been shown a single picture. And the identification would get thrown out. "She was pretty vehement."

She turned the phone and showed it to Zachary, but not to Campbell. Campbell wouldn't care. It wouldn't convince him that Kenzie had done the right thing. And she hadn't. Not if she had screwed up that identification so badly. And she was supposed to be a professional, the person getting promoted to assistant medical examiner.

Or maybe she wouldn't. Maybe she would just be fired.

Zachary looked at Emily's message and chuckled. He swiped down the rest of the conversation, his eyes going quickly over their words.

"Stars?" he asked.

"I don't know what it means. I thought maybe the starred words in their conversation would make a message, but it doesn't make sense."

"What's that?" Campbell asked.

"Emily says that Rhys keeps putting stars in his messages. But she doesn't know why. It isn't something he usually does."

"Maybe it means that he is not the one sending the messages. Or that he is not the one with the phone in his hands."

Kenzie shook her head slowly. "Emily was sure that it was Rhys she was messaging with. He was sending her the kind of messages that Rhys does. He has a… unique messaging style."

"So I recall," Campbell agreed. He thought about it. "But Rhys could be telling Saul what to write in the messages, but the punctuation, the starred words, are Saul's own additions."

"How would Rhys tell him what to put?"

"He could…" Campbell's forehead wrinkled as he thought it through. "He could be writing it down. Or he could have another phone and is typing his own messages, and then Saul is retyping them on the phone he controls. Making sure that Rhys can't send a secret message."

"Why would he do that? And if he did, then why would he add something that might tip Emily off to the fact that it isn't Rhys typing?"

"That doesn't seem very likely, does it? Unless he copied the stars from what Rhys typed on his own phone."

"And then we're back to why are the stars there?"

"And we know that Rhys isn't typing on his own phone," Zachary said, "since it is turned off. So Saul would have had to get two new phones, one for Rhys to type to him on and one for him to contact Emily with. More money, more complications, and the possibility that Rhys could be doing something with one phone while Saul is doing something with the other. He'd have to have eyes on Rhys's phone all the time to make sure he wasn't sending any secret messages. He'd have to be looking at his own phone and Rhys's all the time."

Kenzie nodded at this. It made sense. She didn't think that there were two phones. And even if there were, Rhys was the one who had put the stars into the messages. They had to mean something.

"You remember when Gloria took him?" Zachary asked Kenzie. "He sent me messages to give us information about his location. Even when he could have just said, 'the fishing cabin Grandpa took us to,' he didn't. His problem isn't just with being unable to say things out loud. I don't believe that he even thinks in words. He thinks in images. Or in concepts. And the more stressed he is, the harder it will be to convert those concepts into words."

"And this time, it is even harder, because he's got someone looking over his shoulder and reading all of those messages to make sure that he doesn't say anything that would tip us off."

Zachary nodded his agreement.

"So this is a picture," Kenzie said, closing her eyes. "He's sending two messages at once. What Saul tells him to, and a picture."

57

Rhys watched bad cop out of the corner of his eye as the man paced back and forth across the cold, spare room like a tiger in a cage at the zoo. Back and forth, back and forth, getting more and more agitated. Rhys had thought that he would settle down once he was in contact with Emily but, rather than being reassured that she was no longer in Roxboro and hadn't talked to anyone, he was acting like everything was falling apart.

He watched Rhys like a hawk. There was no opportunity for him to send an extra message to Emily, turn on location sharing, or install another app. All he could do was to send the messages bad cop told him to write and to try to keep everything from blowing up. He didn't want bad cop going after Emily. He wanted to keep them apart and to try to calm things down. If Emily was still in Burlington, that was good.

He thought that she would message Kenzie. They had been in contact, and Rhys figured that once Emily knew he was in trouble, she would reach out to Kenzie and maybe to Zachary.

"Tell her she has to meet me," bad cop growled at Rhys.

He shrugged and spread his hands out a little, as much as the handcuffs would allow him to. He had already sent that message to Emily more than once. Sending it again would not help anything.

"Do it!" the cop snapped, smacking Rhys across the back of the neck and head.

Rhys jumped. It didn't hurt that much, but his heart raced even faster, and it was all he could do not to jump up from the table and find some-place to hide.

There was nowhere to hide. But that's what his body and brain wanted him to do. His instincts were so strong that it was hard to keep himself pasted to the chair. He tried to look calm, like he wasn't bothered at all by the cop or anything he did, but he was sure that every thought was probably written on his face. He wasn't good at hiding his emotions. Not when that was often the only tool he had to communicate.

He popped up the gifs and jumped from one category to another, looking through the app's frequently used gifs to try to home in on related ones that would express what he wanted. He wished he had his own phone and photo stream. But they weren't available. The only thing the cop would let him install was his messaging app, so that he would be able to send Emily the messages the cop insisted he send.

"Come on," bad cop growled, watching over Rhys's shoulder. "Tell her she has to meet. She doesn't have any choice. The only way I will let you go is if she meets with me. Shows me her phone. Shows me that she's gotten rid of all of the pictures. Then she can run away wherever she wants to."

Rhys doubted that the cop would let Emily go anywhere. He already knew he had made a mistake letting her go the first time. Not realizing that she had taken a picture and would send it out to others. She had been in shock. All she could do was go home and go to bed. That was what Emily had told him. She had been too panicked to do anything but snap a couple of pictures of the man she had seen killed and get out of there. It wasn't until she awoke from her first hibernation that she'd sent them out to friends. And then she'd gone back to sleep again, staying in bed for days like she had the flu.

Rhys understood. He knew that mind-numbing feeling that had pressed against his consciousness. That desire to withdraw. The letting go. It was easier to be gone than to face the pain and the panic. Even now, as he searched for a gif to send to Emily, he was fighting hard to stay present. He worked through the exercise Kenzie had suggested. *Five things you see. Five things you hear. Five things you smell.*

He finally found a gif that he thought worked, a meme from one of the TV shows he used to watch as a kid, with text across it. "Meet me halfway."

"Not 'halfway,'" bad cop growled, slapping Rhys's hand back before he could press Send. He grabbed the phone to delete the image and went back to the gifs Rhys had been looking at.

"This one," he pointed.

Rhys wrinkled his nose. A dancing black girl from some talent show franchise Rhys had never watched, with "Meet me" across the bottom. The band name? The song name?

Emily would know that Rhys hadn't picked it out.

He went ahead and sent it anyway. It wasn't like she didn't know the cop was there, reading every message, telling him what to send.

No meeting, Emily texted back.

"She meets with you or I'm going to start cutting off fingers," bad cop threatened, his voice going high and strained, like someone had run over his foot. "Or better yet, I'm going to shoot your kneecaps off!" He raised his gun and pointed it first at one of Rhys's knees and then the other. "Tell her!"

Rhys pointed at the pile of guns and boxes of ammunition that bad cop had stacked on one of the kitchen counters.

"What?" the cop demanded.

Rhys raised the phone with both hands, pointing it at the guns and miming taking a picture.

"You want to send her a picture of my artillery? Go ahead. Send it to her. Tell her I'll use whatever I have to. She *is* going to come to me, one way or the other."

Rhys frowned. Palms up, he moved his hands back and forth. *Here?*

Bad cop scowled and didn't come up with an answer. Rhys didn't know how he thought Emily would get out there to meet with him. She would need a map. And a car. She couldn't just take the bus out into the middle of nowhere. She couldn't get a ride share that would take her all the way out there, where she might have an accomplice lying in wait to rob the guy. She would need a car she had control of and the GPS coordinates.

While the cop thought about that, Rhys composed a message, snapping a photo first of the pile of weapons, and then of his own knees, showing through frayed holes in his blue jeans. Grandma hated that he wore jeans with holes in them. Rhys hated that his knees were so thin and knobby. He wanted to be big and strong like Stanley Green. Like the wrestlers he saw on TV. Massive bodies. No one would push him around then. No one would grab him by the arm and drag him off like he was a little kid.

He tried not to think about how Emily would feel when she saw the threat. How she already felt knowing that the guy she had liked in the gang had been killed. Sick with guilt. Horrified that such a thing had happened while she looked on.

He knew that feeling. That sick, gut-wrenching, mind-numbing feeling. A sinking, heavy, crushing feeling. He felt it all the time when he thought about Grandpa Clarence and what had happened that day, something that he had been unable to stop. Something that could happen again to someone else he loved.

Predators lurked everywhere. Not just outside the house in the shadows, like on TV. But inside. Inside the house. Inside the family. People he knew and loved could do terrible things to each other and to him. People could die while he stood by and watched and did nothing to stop it.

He hoped that Emily would not break down and agree to meet. Unless he and Emily could work out a way between them to set bad cop up. To keep him from being able to hurt Emily. Or anyone else. If they could do that, it was worth whatever pain Rhys had to suffer to get there. If he could just prevent anyone else from getting hurt.

He scrolled through the gifs, trying to think of how they could do it.

5 8

Kenzie's phone started buzzing and buzzing, several messages coming in right on top of each other. She pulled herself away from the argument with Campbell and Zachary to look at her phone. Her heart beat fast, worried about what was going on. Why had Emily suddenly ramped up the messages? Kenzie half expected her phone to ring with a call from the girl before she had a chance to read the messages. She could see as she checked her notifications screen and switched to the texting app that a couple of the messages were graphics.

Campbell and Zachary went quiet, waiting to find out what Kenzie had received.

The last message from Emily was a shrieking line of OMGs, big and bold and repeated all the way across the screen. Kenzie swallowed hard and scrolled up to see the earlier messages.

The first message was calm. *DD keeps saying he wants to meet and I say no.*

Then, a scream emoji, followed by the pictures. They were photographs rather than popular gifs.

A counter stacked with guns and ammunition boxes.

Two skinny brown knees protruding through frayed holes in blue jeans. A selfie. Someone seated at a kitchen table. Apparently, the same semi-rustic room as the guns were in. Both showed matching furnishings.

873

DD gonna kneecap R if I dont meet!

Kenzie felt ill. She was glad she was already sitting down, because she didn't think she could have remained on her feet. She felt the blood drain from her face, leaving her dizzy, white sparkles obscuring her vision here and there.

"Kenzie?" Zachary rushed to her side. He sat beside her and put his arm around her, leaning over to look at her phone. Kenzie held it toward him, not looking him in the face.

Zachary swore. "He's got guns. Plenty of guns, and he's threatening to harm Rhys if Emily won't meet."

Campbell leaned over for a look. He raised his voice to speak to one of the other cops. "How close are we to getting the location of that phone?"

A detective across the room, with his phone to his ear, covered the front mic and shook his head at Campbell.

"That's not her phone number. It's part of a block of numbers reserved by an app for people who want to send messages anonymously. We're trying to find out from the company who has purchased it, and to get their information, but they won't comply without a subpoena. Same song from Ms. Kirsch's phone provider. We're working on it from both directions."

"They know that there is a minor in danger?"

"They don't care."

Campbell growled. "Forward me those pictures," he told Kenzie. "We'll see if we can get any information from them."

"Most messaging apps strip the EXIF data," Zachary told him.

Campbell shook his head. "Not all of them. Some of the most popular ones are still unprotected. If they have location data embedded, we can find out in two minutes."

Much faster than they could get the information from the phone or app companies. Kenzie forwarded the two pictures to Campbell, hoping that it would help. She enlarged them on her screen.

"Does that look like somewhere in town to you? Or in Burlington?" she asked Zachary.

He studied it, frowning. "Outdated finishings and fixtures. If it's in town, it's in a very old area." He zoomed in on the corner of the window, caught in the picture of the guns. It blurred before Kenzie could see anything significant, but she wasn't sure what he was looking at. Zachary panned over the ugly tile backsplash with orange bunches of flowers on it, along the wall to the edge of the fridge.

"What do you see?" Kenzie asked impatiently.

He zoomed out more and pointed to the plugin. "There's a two-pronged plugin. No ground."

"That's old. How long has it been since you could wire a house like that?"

"In the city?" Zachary shook his head. "I'd have to look it up. It's been decades."

"In the city?" Kenzie repeated. "Then they're *not* in the city."

"Maybe not," Zachary agreed.

"The stars. The stars he keeps throwing into his messages."

"You can't see stars like that in the city!" Zachary instantly saw where Kenzie was going. "It's incredible when you get out of the city, away from all the streetlights, and can see the stars. Rhys is a city boy. Other than those fishing trips with his grandpa, when was the last time he was out of the city like that?"

Kenzie laughed, shaking her head. "He couldn't very well put pictures of trees or a cabin in his messages. Saul would have known he was trying to give hints about his location."

"Campbell," Zachary interrupted Campbell, who was talking to one of the tech guys. About whether there was any location metadata attached to the pictures, Kenzie assumed. "He's in a rural area. Away from the city. Do you know if he owns any land outside the city? A grandparent's place? Something way out in the sticks?"

Campbell glared at him, still angry about their sending the picture of Saul to Emily.

"How do you know that?"

"Look at the pictures. Old finishings and fixtures. The wall around the windows looks like plaster, not drywall. The plugin is a two-prong. The fridge has rounded corners, and it's not because it's retro. It's original. Maybe even gas-powered."

Campbell blinked, looking at it. "I was only looking at the guns. I can see the finishings are old, but... to be that old and still in use... you're right. It's probably rural. I've already got them looking for any city properties in Saul's name. I'll have it expanded… to the whole state, and any parent's or grandparent's name that we can find."

"Look for obituaries for grandparent names. Any grandparents on Facebook are probably too dialed in to modern technology not to have replaced the wiring by now."

Campbell nodded. "Yeah. Probably right. If we can get this guy before he hurts anyone…"

Kenzie's heart felt like ice. Saul was a dangerous person. Someone who had already killed and was trying to cover up his first mistake. And the second mistake—letting Emily go. He had misjudged her, thought that she wasn't a threat to him, when the truth was that she wasn't prepared to stay quiet and just let him murder. She knew that her safety hinged on her exposing him rather than pretending that she hadn't seen what she had.

He had killed one man already and was threatening to kill another—one Kenzie knew.

Kenzie's phone buzzed, and she looked down at it. She had taken far too long to follow up on Emily's last message. Emily would think that Kenzie had abandoned her.

But the buzz wasn't a notification of a message from Emily. It was an email from Dr. Cook, following up on a toxicology test she had asked him to order from the lab the previous day. Kenzie looked at the living room window. It was starting to get light out. She hadn't realized that so much time had passed. Cook was at the medical examiner's office even earlier than Kenzie would have guessed. It was no wonder she could never get there before he did.

She messaged Emily, trying to think of words that might comfort her. To let her know that they weren't just ignoring what she had sent and her concerns about Rhys being tortured to convince her to meet with him.

Following up on leads, she promised Emily. *Hang on. Stay where you are.*

Wherever she was. Kenzie wished she knew. But Emily wasn't about to tell anyone, and had already shown herself to be more resourceful than they had expected. Kenzie was afraid that when they managed to trace Emily's phone to a location, they would find out that was spoofed too. Fake phone number. Fake location. She was worried about a corrupt cop. So she wasn't about to give the police any information that might lead them to her.

After sending the message to Emily, she switched over to the email received from Dr. Cook. She opened the attached report to see what they had found.

Zachary was looking at her a few minutes later, craning his neck and getting closer to her to try to see what she was reading. But the type was too small for him to be able to see it clearly, and she knew that, even if it was large enough, he would have had a difficult time reading it. The paragraphs were densely written and full of measurements and figures. Not dyslexia-friendly.

"What is it?" Zachary asked when he realized Kenzie was looking at him.

"It's a tox screen on Mercer."

Zachary laughed and shook his head. "Why would you do a tox screen on Mercer? You already know how he was killed. Bullet to the brain."

"That's what killed him," Kenzie agreed. "But he would be dead now even if he hadn't been shot in the head."

"What?"

Campbell turned around and looked at Kenzie as well, obviously having overheard this little tidbit and echoed Zachary's inquiry. "What?"

Kenzie nodded, looking from one to the other. "He was too impatient. Couldn't wait. If he had, he could have saved himself a bullet."

"From the looks of things, he doesn't need to have any concerns about running out of ammunition," Campbell said dryly. "I wouldn't want to jump to any conclusions, but it looks like the reports of Saul taking weapons and other contraband from the gang members and keeping it for himself were true."

That made sense. And he had stashed them in the cabin to prevent anyone from stumbling across them too easily. If there were accusations from the gang members that led to his apartment being searched, no one would find anything.

Except for at least one of the guns, which he had used to shoot Mercer. So that the weapon could only be traced back to the gang and street violence rather than back to him.

"What would have killed him if he hadn't been shot?" Zachary pressed.

"Methanol."

He frowned. "Isn't that just alcohol?"

"It's alcohol, but not the right kind. It's very toxic."

"So… who poisoned him?"

"Probably the same person who killed him, since most people don't have several murderers out to get them."

"From the sounds of it, this guy could have."

Kenzie shrugged. "Maybe. That will have to be investigated. The police will have to look into it."

"Was he poisoned, or could it have been accidental?" Campbell asked.

"Accidental is possible, but rare. Then again, murder by methanol is pretty rare too. But it is possible, and you do hear about it every now and then. Or at least, medical examiners do." Kenzie smiled. "Not everyone spends as much time reading interesting postmortems as we do."

"So what did he do? Spike Mercer's drink?" Zachary asked.

"Probably. Emily said that he was acting drunker than he should be. So he was drinking booze. Which actually helps the body to metabolize methanol. Ethanol is an antidote to methanol poisoning."

"So maybe Saul didn't give him enough methanol. Or didn't realize that the stuff would be counteracted by regular alcohol. What made you check?" Zachary cocked his head to the side slightly.

"Emily. It just sounded… like more than a simple drink. Staggering, blind drunk… sweating, dilated pupils. Or rather, she said his eyes were funny."

"Good catch," Campbell told her. "I would never have guessed that there was another contributing factor. The photo itself looked pretty conclusive."

Kenzie nodded.

"And I wouldn't have thought there was… enough of him left to test for toxins."

"Well, luckily, there was enough in his system that we were still able to test for methanol and formate, one of its metabolites. It wasn't cause of death, but if we want a full picture… we want to find those things. One thing we notice with poisoners is that they often don't kill the first time they try. They might go through several different poisons or increasing doses over a period of time. Humans can be remarkably resilient, and many poisoners don't give enough of the poison, or the body… er, expels it before it can take full effect."

"I've heard of that a few times before," Campbell admitted. "Spouses especially. They have access to their partner's food, so they mix a little in, thinking it will just take a little, and then they'll be gone, all neat and quiet. But they get sick and end up in the hospital or are over it after a couple of days. And then the spouse has to move to another poison or more direct action."

"Like shooting the guy in the head."

"Not as many people survive that," Campbell said dryly.

"No. Not nearly as many."

59

Kenzie exited the email report without replying to Dr. Cook. He wouldn't expect her to be at the office for several hours yet, so she didn't need to give away that she was already awake and explain to him that... what? That she wouldn't be in because she was dealing with Rhys's abduction? It wasn't exactly her job, but she couldn't see herself being able to go to the office and do anything else while they were trying to find Rhys and negotiate with Saul.

She reopened the message thread with Emily. She wasn't going to think about anything else yet. She was just going to deal with Emily and figure out how they would make sure Rhys got home safe and sound.

It wasn't like a TV series, where you knew that everyone would get home safely in the end. In real life, there were no such assurances. He was in the hands of a killer. A murderous cop intent on clearing the board so that there wasn't anyone left to testify against him.

Without Emily, they didn't have any proof that Saul was the one who had killed Mercer. They couldn't connect the gun with him. It was doubtful that they would get anyone in the gang to talk about Saul and how he had been harassing and taking advantage of the members of the gang. It didn't look good for them. They wouldn't want to sully their reputations.

We think Rhys is in a remote location, Kenzie texted Emily. *Did DD ever talk about owning a place in the woods? Going there for a vacation or a party?*

It was a while before Kenzie saw the dancing dots pop up. Was Emily busy texting with Rhys? She wondered if Rhys would be able to think of more reasons to take pictures that might help them pin down the location of the cabin.

Never talked to him, Emily texted back. *Not friends.*

What about when he talked to Mercer? Or someone else in the gang?

dont know

There were more dots, so Kenzie waited to see what else Emily had to share.

Hes gonna hurt Rhys

Kenzie swallowed. There was a lump in her throat. All of those guns. Rhys, a gangly teenager, there all by himself with no one to protect him.

dont know what to do, Emily confessed.

You need to talk to the police, Kenzie typed back. *Call me and you can talk to cop in charge.*

no

Leaning with her elbow on her knee, Kenzie ground her fist into her forehead. As if massaging her aching muscles would get her brain working better.

You want me to help, but you won't give me anything to work with.

Kenzie received several files all at once. She tapped the first, which was another photo. This one, she thought, Rhys had taken covertly. Not a message from his captor. He caught a back view of Saul, and part of a facial profile as he bent down close to the kitchen counter. Not to inspect the guns and ammunition but, Kenzie thought, to snort coke.

She hadn't thought she could feel any worse about the situation. She swore and looked at Zachary, who was studying his phone, working whatever magic he could to figure out where Rhys was being held.

"He's doing coke."

After a moment, Zachary looked up from his phone, pulling himself away from whatever he had been focused on. His expression was bleak. "Tell me you're kidding."

"You know I wouldn't joke about something like that, even if it wasn't a dire situation like this."

Zachary nodded. "He might be tired. Looking for an energy boost."

"Well, he won't be going to sleep now."

She had been hoping, in the back of her mind, that sooner or later, Saul would have to sleep. And that would give them some time to chase him down and give Rhys a break. Rhys must be terrified. Kenzie remembered how afraid she herself had been when…

Kenzie pushed the thought out of her mind, scrolling down from the picture to look at the other file Emily had sent. This one was a video. Kenzie couldn't make sense of the screen to begin with. The camera was pointed at the table or floor rather than being held up where Rhys would be able to film his captor or something else in the room that would give them clues as to where the cabin was.

Then she realized that it was the audio Rhys had been trying to capture. She pressed the up-volume control to get it as loud as possible. She could hear Saul in the background, muttering and growling, talking to himself. She couldn't make out the whole thing as he moved around the room.

"Thinks she's smarter than anyone else… can't get away with it… not going to this time, I know better this time, and there's no way she's not going down. She thinks she can control this?" He swore, cussing out whoever he was talking about. A partner? Emily? Kenzie herself? Who was he going after next? Was he giving up on Emily and going to a new part of his plan, or was he trying a new approach to get her?

Had Rhys broken down and given Saul what he needed in order to find Emily? Maybe he had switched to the friends app on Rhys's phone and found Emily's phone location through that? Kenzie believed she herself was safe. But who would Saul go after next? Emily had said that he had threatened her mother and the other kids at school. Maybe one of them was next. Maybe he would just keep grabbing and torturing people close to Emily until he found the key needed to get her to meet with him?

"You'll see," Saul snarled on the recording, "no stupid female is going to get the better of me."

Campbell had been out of the room talking to one of the numerous law enforcement officers who had overrun the house. He returned, looking even more tired and frustrated than he had, if that were possible. He looked at Zachary and then at Kenzie.

"No luck on the photos. No geolocation tags."

Kenzie nodded her understanding. "And property ownership?"

"Going to take a while to find everything we need, especially if it is in a family member's name." Campbell looked around the living room. "Someone needs to do a coffee run."

A younger officer near the door put up his hand. A rookie who had probably been relegated to the fringes of the investigation, appointed to watch the door and the property outside to make sure that no one unauthorized walked in, and he was now eager to get out and do something. Anything. "I'll do that. What do you want?" He pulled out a notebook to start a list.

"Don't get individual orders. You can get it by the box at the place up the street. It's twenty cups or something. Get that."

The young man nodded, put his notebook back away, and walked out of the house. Campbell looked at Kenzie. "You look about as bad as I feel."

Kenzie held her phone up. "Umm… Emily sent a couple more files."

"Forward them to me."

Kenzie did so. Campbell's phone dinged, and he looked at the picture and then opened the video file. He looked confused, then did the same thing as Kenzie had, turning the volume up so that he could hear what had been recorded. He shook his head slowly. "This guy is a walking time bomb. We're doing our best to find him…"

He glanced around the room, probably looking for Vera, but she was not in the room. Maybe she had gone to her own room to lie down or cry in privacy.

Campbell just continued to shake his head. "We're doing our best," he repeated, but Kenzie heard the resignation in his voice. He was worried they wouldn't be able to do anything before Saul had a meltdown or took the next step in his plan.

Kenzie wasn't ready to give up yet. She tapped a message to Emily.

Where are you? We will come to you.

Staying at Vera's house wasn't getting them anywhere. That wasn't where the action was. Kenzie could receive messages nearly anywhere. But Saul had gotten himself far away from the Salter house before he had started messaging Emily; they weren't going to find anything useful at the house. If Emily were still in Burlington, or Rhys thought she was still in Burlington, that might be where Saul was headed next. If Kenzie could do anything to get closer to them and possibly prevent Saul from being able to reach her….

She waited for a reply from Emily, rubbing the muscles around her eyes. She had not gotten enough sleep and, now that the adrenaline was starting to fade, she was really feeling the strain. It was a good thing that Campbell had ordered some caffeine. They were all going to need it.

She continued to wait, but there were no further messages from Emily. She looked at Zachary.

"She's gone silent."

"Check your bars."

Kenzie looked at the top of the screen. "They look fine."

Kenzie sent another text to Emily, but received no response.

"I don't know if it is going through."

"Try sending me something."

She sent a brief test message to Zachary, and his phone immediately lit up.

"That worked," Kenzie mused. "What's going on with Emily all of a sudden?"

Zachary took a deep breath and let it out. "Emily has turned off her phone."

60

Kenzie knew immediately that Zachary was right. Emily didn't like being pushed to talk to the police. Texting with Kenzie wasn't getting her any closer to helping Rhys out. The messages Rhys kept sending her just confirmed that Saul was escalating, that he was working his way up to torturing Rhys to convince Emily to meet with him. And he had other people on his hit list if Emily didn't respond to the torture and death of Rhys. Her mother. Her friends. Saul would just keep going until she listened to what he said.

And did they really think that a fifteen-year-old girl was going to stand up to such intense pressure? Saul was a cop. He had guns. He had Rhys. He had all the power. The only way for Emily to stop it was to give in.

"We have to find them," she said urgently. "We need to know where Saul and Rhys are."

Zachary shook his head. "No. We're too late now. By the time we figure it out, he'll be gone. He needed somewhere to take Rhys where people wouldn't see him, and to access his weapons and coke. But he's not going to meet Emily there. Even if she has a car, he's not going to want to give her directions to drive to his hideout. She could call the police and send them to him. He won't want her to come to his safe ground."

"Okay." All of that made sense. "But Emily has shut off her phone, so she is going somewhere and doesn't want the police to be able to track her or for me to be able to reach her. She's given up on us."

Kenzie couldn't accept that she had failed. Emily had reached out to her. They'd had a connection. Why hadn't she been more careful not to push Emily too far? Why hadn't Kenzie said something to give her hope that they would be able to save Rhys before anything happened to him?

"So where would they meet?" Kenzie asked. "Where is Saul going to set up a meeting?"

It was an impossible question to answer, and they both knew it.

"I think we need to go," Zachary said, looking around.

Kenzie knew that look. If she didn't get on board, he would end up leaving without her, off chasing a possible lead.

"Okay," she agreed. She looked at Campbell. "There's no point in us sticking around here. I don't think there's anything to find."

"No," he agreed. "I don't know how much longer I'll be here. Probably just long enough to get a couple of cups of coffee onboard. Maybe then I'll know what to do next." He rubbed his forehead, undoubtedly feeling the same fatigue that Kenzie herself felt after being woken up in the middle of the night and thrown into an emergency situation. "Might call in the feds. They have more resources. Might be able to do some things with technology that we can't."

"On TV, they can turn someone's phone back on remotely," Kenzie contributed.

"Yea. Maybe they'll be able to do that," Campbell said tiredly. But he didn't sound very hopeful. Maybe, like so many of the other things that law enforcement was seen doing on TV, that was just another wave of the magic wand, like always being able to identify the origin of the trace soil left in the tread of someone's shoes. "Thanks for coming by. And for what you were able to squeeze out of Emily." Campbell nodded to Kenzie. "Hopefully, it will turn out to be useful in the long run."

He had, apparently, given up on the short run. When Kenzie thought about Rhys, she wanted to cry. He had been so brave, finding ways to bury clues in his messages to Emily and sneak additional ones to her, despite his challenges and a murderer hanging over him, rapidly going off the rails.

They said goodbye to Campbell and left before the coffee arrived. Kenzie regretted that part. She really could use a boost. But she knew that if she didn't leave with Zachary, he would go rogue. And she didn't want to be left behind trying to catch up with him while he ran off trying to save the world by himself.

Again.

They walked out to the car in silence. Zachary took the wheel, looking aside at Kenzie.

"Are you okay?"

"No, not really. You?"

He shrugged and grunted. No words were really needed. Kenzie understood. He pulled away from the curb. Kenzie had no idea where they were going. Maybe just to drive around aimlessly while they spit-balled ideas.

"Do you think she's still in Burlington?" Zachary asked.

Kenzie thought about it. She had asked more than once, but Emily had never answered, other than to tell her that she didn't need to know. Kenzie closed her eyes, but that didn't help. She reviewed the string of texts on her phone.

"No."

"No, you don't think she's in Burlington?"

"No. If she was in Burlington, she probably would have been okay with telling me that. She was far enough away that even if I wanted to get to her, it would take a couple of hours to get there. Even if we could get a location on her phone and knew where she was, she had a cushion of a couple of hours."

"But here, she doesn't," Zachary pointed out the obvious.

"Exactly. If she's in Roxboro and we go looking for her… we could get there in a few minutes."

"Especially if we have her phone location."

"But we don't, and she knows that," Kenzie tried to follow all of the clues to their conclusion. "So she must be somewhere we could find her just by what we know about her."

Zachary nodded. He had apparently followed this chain of logic as well, and that was why he'd wanted to get away from the Salter house. Emily wasn't there. But she was somewhere close by. And she was getting ready to act. That was why she had shut off her phone. She was no longer looking for help.

"She is somewhere we know about." Kenzie considered it. "Home or the school. Or wherever the gang hangs out. But I never got where that is from Campbell or Emily. Is it like in the old books and movies? Do they have a specific territory? A clubhouse or home base?"

"I don't think it would be with the gang. Emily already knows that the other gang members will listen to Saul and let him get away with whatever he wants. They've let him get away with ripping them off; why would she trust them to protect her interests when they haven't protected their own?"

"Maybe now that people know what he's been doing, they'll stand up to him. Or Emily thinks they will."

Zachary shook his head again. And Kenzie trusted him. He had good instincts. If Zachary didn't think that Emily would go to the gang, if he was that sure of himself, he was probably right. He knew human behavior. He could read people.

"So, home or the school. Or somewhere else?" Kenzie asked.

"I think home is too dangerous. I don't think she would agree to meet him there. Not where he could get close to her mother. Home is *her* safe space. Her den. Her cocoon. When she witnessed Mercer's murder and was in shock, she went home to sleep. Not the place you would take someone who was a threat to you and your family."

"So the school." Kenzie looked at the time. "Her friends won't be there yet. But if he is an hour or two away at his cabin then, by the time he gets here, some of the early birds will be starting to show up at the school. Not her friends, maybe, but some of the staff. Early morning clubs. Orchestra practice."

"He'll want to meet somewhere away from people. She'll want to meet somewhere close to people."

Kenzie nodded, thinking about it. The only place they had met with Emily had been at the bus stop across from the school, next to the convenience store. But Emily couldn't meet with Saul there. It was out in the open, where everyone would see. He couldn't bring Rhys there at gunpoint. He would never agree.

Would he have Rhys with him? Or would he leave Rhys stashed somewhere?

"Behind the school?" Kenzie suggested. "In the parking lot?"

"Not bad," Zachary admitted. "But still out in the open. Even in an isolated corner, he won't be able to ensure that no one sees them. As a cop, he'll want to make sure there is a way in and a way out, and that they can't be observed while he is there."

"Somewhere inside the school."

"Yeah."

"It won't be unlocked yet," Kenzie objected.

"It will be soon. At least a couple of the doors. And Saul has ways of opening locked doors, so that isn't a limitation. He knows how vulnerable a door is, even if it is locked. Pick it or kick it."

"Right. Okay. Inside, then. Where does Emily feel safe inside the school?"

They drove in silence for a while, both of them considering the matter.

61

By the time they got to the highway, the stars had faded and the sky was brightening. Rhys was rarely up in time to see the sunrise. Would it be the last one he ever saw?

The bad cop concerned him even more now. He had been worried during the drive to the cabin, wondering how he would survive the ordeal. The cop had grabbed him and handled him like he was just a doll and not a real person. He was rough and wanted to show Rhys he was in charge. The least little thing that Rhys did that didn't comply with his instructions or expectations resulted in a smack or a threat. But it wasn't like he'd gotten beaten up. He'd still been okay when he got to the cabin. Scared, but in one piece.

He wasn't sure how far they were going to make it in the car. The coke affected bad cop's driving. He was fast and reckless, and honking horns followed them everywhere they went. A couple of times, he even tapped someone's bumper when they didn't get out of the way fast enough, and they took one guy's side mirror off when bad cop skimmed past with only inches between the two cars. Rhys hung on to the door and the emergency brake and tried not to cry out every time it looked like they would end up in an accident.

The whole time, the cop kept up a running monologue, like he had been doing while pacing at the cabin. Rhys didn't know whether he was talking to Rhys, to himself, or to someone else he saw or heard in his head. He railed at the drivers, about Em, about Mercer, the gangbanger he had killed. He yelled about his boss and the other cops he worked with. And Kenzie, too. How she was wrong about everything and didn't have any idea what was going on and he'd heard that she had made mistakes on other autopsies.

They were headed back into Roxboro. Rhys still had the phone. The cop hadn't thought to take it away from him when they had started back toward the city. Rhys had casually slid it into his pants pocket, and bad cop had been so amped up, angry, and distracted that his eyes had slid right over Rhys without any indication that he had seen Rhys pocket it.

The cop had been mad when Emily had shut off her phone. He wanted to be in control, and the fact that he could no longer communicate with Emily at all had him frantic. He threw things across the cabin, making Rhys duck and flinch. As much as he tried to show no reaction to anything that bad cop did, he couldn't control his body. The cop kept insisting that Rhys message Emily again to make her turn the phone on, and Rhys kept showing him the *User Offline* message on the screen. He thought the cop was going to throw the phone across the room. Then he would have no way to communicate if Emily decided to turn her phone back on or if he were somewhere the cop couldn't see him for a minute. He could message someone else for help.

Then they had to go outside to see if they could get a better signal and get a message to send from there.

Rhys knew what had happened. He knew that Emily had shut off her phone after her last message. But the cop didn't want to listen to anything Rhys had to say or to take the time to figure it out. Rhys knew that more messages and going outside or even to the highway would not make any difference.

Em was so strong. Tiring of the cop's threats, she had just told him where she would be, and then turned off her phone. There were no more negotiations. Emily was done. The cop could curse and complain as much as he liked, throw as many things as he wanted, but none of that would change anything. He could crash the car, flip it over, and wreck half a dozen cars on the highway, and it wouldn't change anything. Emily was out of touch and the only way to talk to her was to go where she was. That was what bad cop had wanted all along anyway, wasn't it?

They nearly sideswiped a semi, making Rhys let out an inadvertent yelp. The cop swore and swerved and gave the other driver the finger and kept driving with his pedal to the metal like he was some Indy racer. Rhys knew they were never going to make it. The stupid, stoned cop would kill them both before they could even make it back to Roxboro.

But somehow, they did it. They got back into the city, and the cop even slowed down once he hit the city streets and did not swear and gesture as much. Maybe the initial kick of the cocaine was wearing off, or he had exhausted enough of his fury, or was now thinking about meeting Emily and what he would say and do to her when that happened.

Rhys touched the phone in his pocket. He wanted to look at their messages again, to see whether Emily had understood everything he had told her. But he already had the whole conversation in his head. He was sure they had understood each other, despite bad cop's determination to control everything.

There were a few cars in the parking lot at the school. Not a lot, but people were starting to arrive to prep for classes, have a coffee, or attend one of the early-morning clubs. Emily had enjoyed her early-morning activities before she and Mercer had become friends. She'd been part of a different crowd then, and Rhys had seen her more often. He didn't like the kids she hung out with now, staying on the outskirts of school society when she wasn't hanging out with Mercer and the gang.

She used to get up early in the morning. Now, she was rarely up by the time school started. Sometimes, she got there in the morning and sometimes not before noon. He missed the way things used to be. It was Mercer's fault that she had changed so much. And now Mercer was gone, but things wouldn't go back to how they used to be.

Bad cop pulled his car into one of the slots that was supposed to be reserved for staff members. Rhys didn't suppose it mattered. Was someone going to give him a ticket? Have it towed? What difference would that make now?

62

Zachary and Kenzie didn't find Emily so much as a result of careful deduction and logic, narrowing down where she would be based on everything they knew about her and what the chances were that she would make certain choices. Instead, they walked through the school, avoiding anyone else and trying doors to see what was unlocked. They stuck to the quieter areas of the school, especially the basement, assuming that for a clandestine meeting, they would prefer a location away from the busy hallways. The early-morning enrichment clubs had started up, and they tried to avoid the kids who were there early and to look like they belonged there and knew where they were going.

Kenzie found a door unlocked and swung it open, only to find a small group of students gathered in a circle, talking.

"Oh, sorry," Kenzie said, ready to close it again. Then she stopped.

A couple of faces looked familiar. She gave herself another second or two to remember them before withdrawing. She jerked her head to invite Zachary to follow her, and when they were both in the room, they shut the door again.

"Um, this is the drama club," a high-pitched, nasally voice told them. "I don't know who *you* are, but this is our room. Talk to Mr. Jefferson."

Kenzie looked carefully at each one of them. Then she returned her gaze to Graham. The one who had told her that he could produce a much more realistic picture of a corpse than the one Emily had taken. Even though the one that Emily had taken had, in fact, been an actual corpse

"Hey," she said. "You remember me?"

Graham's eyes slid toward a closed door on the other side of the room before looking back at Kenzie.

"You can't be here," he said. "Like Chantelle said, we have the room booked."

The girl who had told them that already nodded, a superior, challenging look on her face.

"Is she here?" Kenzie asked.

"I'm right here," Chantelle said in a huff.

"Not you." Kenzie looked back at Graham. "Emily."

"You know where it is," bad cop growled at Rhys, giving him a shove forward with the barrel of the gun.

Rhys didn't think it was a good idea for him to still have the gun out when he was in the middle of the school. There weren't a lot of kids there yet, but it wouldn't be long before the hallways were full and they were in danger of being accidentally shot by the jumped-up cop.

"Hurry it up," the cop told him. "Don't make this difficult. The more trouble you cause me, the worse things are going to be for your friend."

Rhys looked back at the cop, nodding, letting him see that Rhys was complying with his instructions. But rather than speeding up, he slowed very slightly. The cop might think he could force Emily and Rhys to do whatever he wanted to, but Rhys still had some control over the situation. The cop couldn't force him to go any faster, even if he did have a gun. How would shooting Rhys help him at this point? He would lose his guide and have to find his way to Emily's meeting place. While dealing with a school on lockdown.

"The theater," bad cop repeated. "You know where it is. And if you try to lead me in another direction, I can look it up on the floor plan or ask someone else. I don't need you."

If he didn't need Rhys, then why didn't he let him go?

He continued to walk slowly along, looking in the other open classroom doors. Wondering if he would run into any teachers along the way or anyone else he knew. He didn't like walking through the school when it was so quiet. It was creepy.

They reached the stairs and Rhys indicated that they had to go down. The cop didn't seem to like the idea, but he looked at the signs and saw a placard for the theater, so he nodded and Rhys started down the stairs ahead of him.

They could hear other activity. The orchestra was practicing. There were shouted instructions and grunts from the direction of the gymnasium. The early-morning programming was in full swing.

The phone in Rhys's pocket started chirping. He pulled it out to check to see what was happening, then remembered that the cop was watching. He might not want the man to see the message or messages on the phone and tried to shove it back down before the cop could realize what was going on.

"What is it?" bad cop said sharply.

Rhys shrugged and kept going. Bad cop closed in on him when he reached the bottom of the stairs, grabbing him by the shoulder and shoving the barrel of the gun into his ribs with a smack that was bound to leave a bruise. Rhys gasped and held his side.

"Let me see. Give it to me."

The phone had been silent since Emily had shut off her phone. The incoming messages could only mean one thing... she was back online again. And if she was online, she could see his location. She had requested to track his live location through the messaging app in one of the last messages they had exchanged. Bad cop, pacing and arguing with himself, breaking down and going off the rails, had not seen the message request, and Rhys had quickly deleted it from the message thread as soon as he had granted permission.

So Emily knew that he was in the school now.

Rhys wrapped his hand around the phone and didn't give it to the cop.

Bad cop didn't spend any time arguing about it. He grabbed Rhys's arm and then pried Rhys's fingers away. He was strong. As tightly as Rhys tried to hold on to it, he couldn't prevent the cop from stealing it. Bad cop looked at the screen and gave a bark of laughter. He handed it back to Rhys.

"Tell her good riddance!"

Rhys looked down at the message on the screen.

Im so sorry Rhys its the only way I can end it

Rhys didn't send a response, and the cop didn't force it. Rhys walked a little more quickly toward the theater. They wanted to get the timing just right.

They were almost there when the report echoed from the theater.

Bad cop swore under his breath and shoved Rhys again, hurrying him toward the theater and what they would find there.

Rhys pushed his way through the side door that led into one of the wings of the theater. It was silent as a tomb. Rhys hurried across the empty wing toward the stage.

A couple of spotlights were turned on so that the scene on the stage was brightly lit. Rhys let out a howl.

"Emily!"

Bad cop had been reaching for him again, whether to slow him down or to push him forward, Rhys didn't know, but he fumbled and fell back slightly in surprise at Rhys using his voice. Rhys ignored his reaction and rushed up to Emily.

63

Emily sat slumped in one of the stage chairs. An upholstered chair with wings and arms. Maybe even the one used in *Arsenic and Old Lace*, the classic murder mystery performed by the school almost every year. The gun that Emily had held in her hand had dropped to the floor.

In the side of her forehead was a bullet hole every bit as vivid as the one Emily had caught in her pictures of Mercer. Every bit as gruesome as the one Rhys had first seen in his grandfather's forehead, repeated in his head thousands upon thousands of times since.

The pink flush was gone from her cheeks as her blood ceased to circulate, already taking on the gray pallor of death. There was a trail of blood down her cheek and a fine spatter on the chair. They wouldn't be able to use it as a stage prop again. Not unless they re-covered it. Rhys grasped Emily's hands, still warm, but limp. Rhys felt her wrist and then her throat for a pulse. He turned to the cop and tried to get out the words he had practiced in his head.

She's dead!

His lips formed the words, but no voice came to his aid.

The cop's eyes were wide with surprise. He stared at Rhys and could clearly understand the words without needing to hear them. Besides, he could see for himself. He had seen enough bodies to know the difference between living and dead at a glance.

"Saves me a bullet," he snapped.

He considered Rhys for a moment, and Rhys thought that he was going to grab him by the arm again and drag him off, as he had before. Then the cop just turned and walked out, sliding his gun into a concealed holster as he went.

Rhys watched him walk back through the curtain and listened carefully for the noise of the door as he left the same way they had come in. He squeezed Emily's hands and waited.

64

Saul moved quickly through the hallway, mapping out his escape plan. With Emily out of the way, there was no longer anyone who could tie him directly to Mercer's killing, but he still didn't plan to stick around town. His cover had been blown and, whether or not they could officially accuse him of anything, he knew he wouldn't ever have a responsible position with the police department again. Even if they couldn't fire him with cause, because they couldn't prove what he had done, they could sit him in front of a computer all day. Or at the public-facing desk at the precinct, dealing with civilian complaints all day. That would drive him away faster than any criminal investigation.

He had plenty of guns, money, and drugs. He had criminal contacts who would help him to disappear. He could get away cleanly and they could never put anything on him. He could start life somewhere else.

A school bell rang, and Saul could hear doors closing. It seemed odd to be closing doors instead of opening them as the students arrived for classes.

He was moving much more quickly toward his car than he and Rhys had walked when they entered the school to find the theater. Of course the boy had not wanted to move very fast. He knew that things would not turn out well when Saul and Em had their face-to-face discussion.

As it had turned out, things had gone much better than Saul had expected. He laughed to himself. Nice of her to do the dirty work for him. She had known what was coming and had taken the coward's way out rather than to have to face him.

He hit the crash bar on the exit door and got three steps out in the parking lot toward his car before realizing anything was wrong.

"Freeze! Hands in the air, Saul!"

Saul looked around, taking in the guns pointed at him from several directions. Cops sheltering behind cars, over roofs, around corners. It must have been all the active officers on duty, and maybe a few who should have been home, too.

He searched for a way out, his mind racing. The coke made him think faster, but even this juiced-up version of his brain was not coming up with any great solutions. He could pull his gun and shoot it out but, with so many weapons aimed at him, he didn't stand a chance, and suicide by cop was not an honorable way to go out.

They didn't have enough to arrest him for Mercer's death. He was sure about it. The boy's kidnapping? Maybe. But he couldn't testify. And Saul hadn't been the one to pull the trigger on Emily. He could find a way to plead extreme emotional distress or confusion from the drugs. He could get bail and then run for it. He knew how to foil an ankle monitor.

He turned around, looking in all directions. He already knew there was no physical escape. He raised his hands to shoulder level.

"Take a picture."

Kenzie looked down at Emily, who was still slumped in the chair, eyes closed, her mouth barely moving when she spoke.

"What?"

"Before I move or take any of this off. You need to take a picture for me."

Rhys finally moved from his position, holding Emily's hand and looking stricken. He rose to his feet and looked for the best angles to take some pictures from. He still looked upset, and Kenzie wanted to get him to his grandma and maybe to the hospital as quickly as possible. The two kids seemed to be too occupied with the staged scene and makeup to worry about real life just yet.

Rhys got the pictures he wanted and tapped Emily on the shoulder. She opened her eyes and looked at him.

"Got them?"

Rhys nodded.

Emily stretched and yawned widely, displaying her tonsils for all to see. She looked at Kenzie, not at all embarrassed. "I don't think I got a wink of sleep last night. I'm gonna go home and sleep for a week."

"You're going to need to talk to the police first. And maybe get checked out by a doctor."

"A doctor? What for?"

Kenzie looked at the bullet wound in the side of Emily's head, which she knew wasn't real, and tried to come up with an answer. "I know you haven't been physically hurt, but you've been through a lot of traumatic stuff the last couple of weeks. You should talk to someone."

"I don't need to. Not right now. What I need is sleep. And knowing my boy is back!" Emily grabbed Rhys and gave him a hug, making him laugh. Kenzie was sure that if his skin were lighter, they would have been able to see him blushing. Emily rubbed Rhys's tight black curls roughly. "Rhys is the one who needs to see a doctor." She pulled back from him a little to look him in the face. "I was so scared he was going to hurt you. When he said he was going to shoot you in the knees, and you sent the video with him sounding so whacked out…"

Rhys nodded. He wiped his forehead dramatically with the back of his hand.

Kenzie studied Rhys, looking for any signs of injury. "Did he hurt you? Did he touch you at all?"

Rhys waved her question away as inconsequential. Kenzie shook her head. "Rhys. He was acting crazy. He was threatening you. He killed that other young man. I didn't know if… I didn't know how we were going to get you back safely." Her voice cracked a little, and she let it. It wouldn't hurt him to know how emotional she was about it. How much she and Zachary cared.

He nodded and looked down for a minute, and she thought he was probably thinking about how close he had come and how he himself had wondered if he would make it. He must have been terrified, no matter how casual he was trying to act about it now.

"We did it. Everybody is safe," Emily said, pulling Rhys to her again, to hug him sideways and then keep her arm wrapped around his shoulders. "But I don't know how you got here," she told Kenzie, "Did Rhys share his location?"

Emily knew that she hadn't shared hers. Kenzie shook her head. "No. And it would have been nice if one of you had thought to do that. You could share with each other, but not with us?"

Emily rolled her eyes and looked away. "Didn't want you tracking me. Didn't need more cops showing up to wreck everything. All you wanted to do was sic the cops on me."

"That's not true. We were trying to help you and Rhys."

"By bringing the cops in," Emily reasserted. Kenzie wasn't going to be able to talk her out of her opinion that the cops would have just ruined everything and gotten Emily or Rhys killed.

But then, it had been a cop who had killed Mercer. Did Kenzie really think that she could talk Emily out of how she felt about that? That, okay, there was one corrupt cop, but there were no more and they would all behave just exactly how they had been trained? It was a hard sell.

As they spoke, cops were starting to drift into the theater. There hadn't been time to get them in place before Saul arrived with Rhys. They'd barely had enough time to get the stage set before Saul had gotten there. Emily had been watching their location on her phone, so they had known how close they were and there had not been time to get the police there before his arrival.

Campbell climbed the stairs to the stage and walked up casually. Though he was obviously tired, he looked much better than the last time Kenzie had seen him, when he had been worried that they had lost Rhys. That the boy was about to be tortured and killed by a coked-up dirty cop. Now that both teens were safe and Saul was in custody, Campbell's limbs were loose and his face unlined. Back to the cool, friendly cop that Kenzie knew. He looked Emily over, studying the makeup.

"Well, that's convincing. I guess it helps to have a coroner doing your makeup."

"It wasn't me," Kenzie said. She looked around for the drama club kids, who were still hanging back. "Graham told me he could do a better job of making up a dead person than the photo I had." She grinned at Campbell, sharing the joke that her picture *had* been of a dead person.

"And I gotta say, he came through. I just helped with a few small adjustments."

Graham stood back from them, blushing.

"You did it," Kenzie told him again. "Saul never had a doubt that Emily was really dead."

"It was the blood spatter," Graham said. "That was you."

"No. That zombie skin tone..." Kenzie disagreed.

Emily fingered the fake bullet wound. She caught Rhys staring at it. For an instant, Kenzie saw concern flash across her face. Then she was swaggering and making faces at Rhys. "You gonna have nightmares about zombie girl now? This is the stuff of your worst nightmares, isn't it?" And it probably *was*, but Emily was trying to make it comic now, to erase anything serious or scary from the experience. She moved her lips in weird, exaggerated shapes, threatening to kiss Rhys, making him laugh and pull back from her, holding his hands up to stop her. He opened his mouth to say something, but no words came out, and he just shook his head and mouthed "no, no, no," as Emily fooled around, trying to make him laugh harder.

Emily had good instincts. Kenzie thought that maybe a bullet wound in the head would be less traumatic for Rhys to remember, with the addition of Emily and her silly faces and teasing. Maybe now, when the images of Grandpa Clarence came up, he would be able to push them away instead of obsessing over them.

65

Things moved slowly, as they always did when there was a crime scene to be processed and witnesses to be interviewed. And Kenzie herself was one of the witnesses this time, trying to describe the thought processes that had brought them to the school and how they had helped to stage the scene before Saul had arrived. *And* had called the police. Kenzie emphasized that they had promptly contacted the authorities as soon as they became aware of the situation.

Principal Lakes came to talk to the police and to Zachary and Kenzie. And she gave Emily and Rhys both quick, tight hugs to let them know that she had been concerned about them and was glad that things had worked out so they were safe. Rhys ducked his head and looked embarrassed, and Emily returned the hug with a big one of her own. Kenzie couldn't believe how different Emily looked with a smile on her face. The sullen, withdrawn girl that she had met earlier was gone. She was back to that chipper, happy girl her mother had missed.

"Things are going to change around here," Principal Lakes warned, putting a hand on either side of Emily's face and looking her in the eyes. "I want to see you back in the drama club and stirring things up around here. I don't like the way that girl disappeared."

Emily nodded, swallowing a couple of times. "I miss it too. It's been…" She trailed off, not sure what to say.

904

"Don't let yourself get swallowed up by someone else's personality. You're special just the way you are."

"Special," Emily repeated mockingly.

"You are," Principal Lakes told her. "I don't care what anybody has to say about it."

"Okay." Emily gave a little laugh. She was stuck being "special" but seemed to be okay with that.

"And you…" Lakes looked at Rhys. "You're always getting mixed up in things."

He shrugged and looked away.

"He hears things," Kenzie said. "He's quiet and people forget that he's there, but he sees and hears things no one else does."

Rhys nodded his agreement.

"I don't know why you won't hang with the drama club," Emily told Rhys. "You're a really good actor."

He shrugged.

"I mean it," Emily said. "Do you think just anyone could have sold that performance? What would have happened if he hadn't believed I was dead?"

Kenzie had a hard time believing how smoothly it had gone. Saul had not even hesitated. He had believed that Emily was dead one hundred percent and, with that task taken care of, had been prepared to just disappear. If only the police hadn't been stationed outside to nab him as soon as he left the school.

"Let's get these kids to their parents," Campbell said. Principal Lakes had decided to keep the school open for the day, even though the students who were there were too distracted to focus on their studies. The school was the only form of childcare and supervision that a lot of those families had. But Rhys and Emily were going home. To catch up on their sleep, if nothing else.

Kenzie joined hands with Zachary, and they walked out of the school to the designated area in the parking lot where the parents and several medical professionals were waiting. Vera held out her arms for Rhys, crying as she approached. He swallowed and smoothed the expression on his face to keep from giving away how emotional he was and walked into her arms. Vera held him close, eyes closed, squeezing him hard.

Emily's mother was there too. Standing beside Vera, She looked uncertain, watching Emily approaching, not sure how to act. Their hug was more awkward. They appeared to be less emotional than Vera, but Kenzie saw each of them wipe a tear away.

"Hey," Emily's mom said. She sniffled. "You know where my hair dryer is? I haven't been able to find it."

Emily laughed. She hooked a thumb back toward the school. "Art room. I was using it to dry papier mache."

"Don't take my stuff without asking," Mrs. Cross told her sternly. She tightened her grip. "Especially don't take *you* away. I hate that."

"Okay," Emily laughed and sobbed, holding on to her. "I'll ask first next time."

EPILOGUE

Kenzie was glad to be at the Petersons'. Somewhere she always felt welcomed and cared for and could just relax and be herself. There were no expectations like when dining with her parents. No need to be perfect or "switched on" the whole time.

"So, it sounds like you've had a pretty eventful few weeks," Lorne commented, as everyone dished up Pat's homemade gnocchi. "A promotion, a gangland murder, and a kidnapping?"

Kenzie sipped her drink, then took a few long breaths, waiting for her heart to slow down. She wanted to be able to talk about what had happened calmly, without having to relive her own abduction. She paid attention to the coldness of the glass, the sweetness of the peach spritzer, and the hearty, spicy smell of the marinara sauce, trying to dwell on the moment and not to let herself slide back.

"Yes, it's been kind of crazy," she admitted. "I'm really glad that everything turned out okay. I wasn't sure that it would." She swallowed. "Things were looking pretty grim there for a while when Saul was holding Rhys and threatening to hurt him and anyone else Emily knew." She looked at Zachary, passing the question off to him.

"It was pretty intense," Zachary agreed. "Trying to figure out where he had Rhys, where he was going to meet Emily, and trying to figure out how to stop him and get Emily and Rhys somewhere safe." He shook his head. "Emily and Rhys had already concocted this whole thing. I'm not sure how, which they had to hide their messages in plain sight."

"They must be on the same wavelength," Pat commented.

Zachary and Kenzie nodded. "It can be challenging to communicate with Rhys at the best of times," Kenzie agreed. "They practically had to be telepathic to set Saul up like that. But they did it. A picture here, a word there. Emily, at least, was able to write whatever she wanted to. Rhys was more limited."

"But he still did things like typing the stars around words in his messages," Zachary agreed. "I think the two of them know each other a lot better than either of them is willing to tell."

"And the gang member who was killed? Was her romance with him just a sham?" Lorne asked.

"No. Definitely not," Kenzie shook her head. "Probably nothing good would ever have come from it even if she and Mercer had run away together somewhere they could be safe, but Emily really did have feelings for him. It's hard as a teenager… those relationships don't last, but that doesn't make them less real. I think that Emily and Rhys are just good friends."

"Hopefully, Emily will turn her life back around now that Mercer is gone," Zachary offered. He rubbed the bridge of his nose. "Principal Lakes is going to make an effort to keep her in school and away from the gang."

"And Rhys too," Kenzie contributed. At Zachary's confused look, she clarified. "I think that Emily is going to be his special project too."

"And maybe he'll be Emily's. She wanted him to get into the drama club."

"Is there a funeral for the young man who was killed?" Lorne asked. "A chance to say goodbye and get some closure around his death? It must have been difficult for her to deal with his death the way things happened."

"No, his cremains are being shipped back to Ohio. Where he originally came from. I guess that's where his parents are. I hope Emily gets some therapy to help her to work through it."

"And Rhys? I hope someone is working with him," Lorne said. "That's a lot of trauma to work through."

Kenzie swallowed and just nodded.

"We'll make sure he gets some help," Zachary supplied. "He's already in therapy. But so far... the last few days, he's seemed stable. Better than he was before."

"As long as he's not just masking." Lorne raised one brow speculatively. "It could all come tumbling down later."

"I think that the thing that bothered him the most was the picture," Kenzie said. "It made the memories of Clarence's death that much more real. Now that justice has been served, and he had a part in it, maybe he feels like he got his power back. That he isn't trapped anymore, forever a five-year-old with the adults making all of the decisions."

And maybe Kenzie had gotten a bit of her power back too, helping to get Rhys away from his kidnapper after she had been powerless to escape her own.

Maybe now they could both feel a measure of peace.

Did you enjoy this book? Reviews and recommendations are vital to making a book successful.

Please leave a review at your favorite book store or review site and share it with your friends.

Don't miss the following bonus material:
Sign up for mailing list to get a free ebook
Read a sneak preview chapter
Other books by P.D. Workman
Learn more about the author

DON'T MISS A THING! GET THE LATEST NEWS AND A FREE EBOOK

Kenzie was bent over her computer finishing up her notes and reports on the death of an elderly man, Casey Earl, when Dr. Cook approached her desk. He walked with a sense of purpose but did not have a stack of paperwork in his hands, so Kenzie straightened up expectantly. She brushed a few dark curls away from her face.

"What's up?"

"Feel like attending a death scene?"

"Sure," Kenzie agreed. She saved and closed her documents and started to tidy her desk. "What have we got?"

"Man found dead in his apartment. Paramedics were called to the scene. Nothing they could do; he'd been lying there dead for some time."

Kenzie nodded. Probably not anything too unusual about it. Someone who had died in his sleep, maybe a heart attack or stroke.

"How long is 'for some time'?" she asked cautiously. It could be anywhere from a few hours to a few weeks, and she wanted to be prepared for what she would find.

"Sometime today," Dr. Cook told her with an understanding grin. It always threw her for a loop when he smiled like that. He had the face of a movie star, not an experienced pathologist. Most of the time, she didn't really see his good looks anymore. They had worked together for a few months while Dr. Wiltshire was on medical leave, and once she'd worked over a few dead bodies with him, her consciousness of his appearance had faded. She didn't notice it unless he did something like smile at her in that relaxed, understanding way.

Whew. Zachary was lucky she didn't believe in office romances.

"Nice and fresh," Kenzie approved. "That's good. Looks like natural causes?"

Cook pursed his lips. "I will leave that up to you to determine; I would not want to bias you in any way."

Of course not. Kenzie nodded her agreement. "I'll let Carlos know we've got a transport. He and George can stand by for when I am done."

"I already paged him. He should be there by the time you're ready for him."

"Great." Kenzie opened her mouth to ask for the address when a text arrived on her phone. When she swiped the screen to reveal it, she saw it was the information she needed. He must have sent it as he had approached her desk, but had taken a minute to arrive. She read the address and nodded. "Okay, thanks. I'll get on this."

If it was pretty clear that it was a natural death, Kenzie should have the death scene cleared and the body back at the medical examiner's office within a couple of hours.

+++

Kenzie parked her "baby," a cherry red convertible, in front of the apartment building, ignoring the tow-away zone. The parking permit hanging from her rearview mirror identifying her as being from the medical examiner's office would prevent her car from being impounded. At least, it should. She popped the trunk to retrieve her small scene-of-death kit. She would be quickly in and out. The body would not need to be autopsied immediately. It might not require an autopsy at all if the man was elderly and his doctor informed her that he had a history of heart disease or was being treated for some other potentially fatal condition.

There was an elevator to the third floor. A good size for transport. Everything looked like it would fall into place, and they would not have any difficulties. She walked down the hall to apartment 302 and found the door standing open. Peering in, she could see the paramedics standing in the living room chatting while waiting for her arrival. She nodded and stepped in. She was not familiar with the paramedics, so she introduced herself. They would not expect a stranger to walk in off the street, but sometimes, people got overly curious and stepped into death scenes without authorization.

"Dr. Kenzie Kirsch," she advised them, holding out her hand. "Assistant Medical Examiner."

"Oh, doctor." The female paramedic shook her hand. "Thank you for getting here so quickly. Sometimes we have to hang out for hours."

Roxboro was a small town, so they really shouldn't have to wait a significant amount of time at any death scene. Except that being a small town meant that there were a limited number of people who could do the job, and if there were several deaths to attend to in a day, there might be a delay in getting to one of them. But that rarely happened. Since Kenzie didn't know the paramedic, she might have moved there from the city, where it was more likely that she would have to wait for a death scene investigator to arrive.

"Great, well, if you would like me to—" Kenzie stopped herself and studied the two other people in the room. A young man and woman in their late twenties or early thirties. The man's children? Grandchildren? Maybe one of them was a nursing care provider or aide? "Hi. I'm sorry. I'm Dr. Kenzie Kirsch. Medical examiner's office. Are you the ones who discovered the body?"

They both nodded.

"I'm Rachel Evans," the young woman introduced herself. She hugged herself tightly. "This is kind of weird. I'm a nurse practitioner."

"Mr. Robertson's care worker?" Kenzie asked expectantly.

"No." She shook her head vigorously, her eyes widening. "No, I was his girlfriend."

"Oh, I'm sorry." Kenzie's cheeks heated. How much younger than Robertson was his girlfriend? She didn't like putting her foot in her mouth like that. She should know better than to make assumptions. "I just assumed when you said you were a nurse…"

"No." The pretty blonde was flushing as well. "I should have told you. I don't know why I said I was a nurse before I told you about our relationship. I just mean, that's what is so weird. I deal with sick people, deal with death all the time, but I feel like… I don't know. It was just so surprising to find him like that."

Kenzie nodded understandingly. "It's not the same when it is someone you know. If he wasn't in your care, you didn't think of him that way. Had he been ill for a long time? Actually—" Kenzie held up her hand to prevent Rachel from answering the question. "Let me examine the body and the scene before you say anything. I don't want to be influenced by anything else." She turned to face the other person in the room, the young man. "And are you…?"

She didn't want to put her foot in it again by asking him if he was Mr. Robertson's son, so she left the sentence hanging, waiting for him to complete it.

"I'm his roommate."

"Oh, okay." Kenzie felt uneasy as she looked toward the bedroom. If the girlfriend and the roommate were both in their early thirties, then she had might have been wrong in her assumption that the man who had died had been elderly like Casey Earl, whose file she had just closed, or even middled-aged. He was probably around their age. "What did you say your name was?"

"Alex Collins."

"Okay. If you would just stay out here…" Neither of them appeared to be inclined to follow her into the bedroom. "Which room is it?"

"Last one at the end of the hall."

PREVIEW CHAPTER 2

Kenzie nodded and stepped away to examine the body. She didn't want to be influenced by anything else they might have to say. One of the paramedics, the woman, trailed along behind her. Always best if there were two witnesses to corroborate each other's testimony if there were ever any questions as to what had taken place at the death scene.

Kenzie went through the door standing open at the end of the hall. The room was warm, the blinds drawn, like he had still been sleeping, maybe feeling sick. Or maybe he was a shift worker. He could be a medical professional like his girlfriend, someone she had met on the job.

Robertson was still in the bed. The paramedics had not moved the body to the floor to examine him or to do CPR. They knew a dead man when they saw one. Robertson lay as if asleep, partially on his side. He was a young man, like his girlfriend and roommate.

It was a queen-size bed that took up most of the small room. There was already a faint odor of death. He had been there most of the day, if she had to guess just by the stuffiness of the room. She moved closer to him, pulling on gloves. In the artificial lighting, his skin seemed to have a yellowish cast. He was overweight, puffy and bloated, his belly hanging out from under the t-shirt he had worn to bed. Someone who had not, at first glance, taken good care of himself.

Kenzie touched his neck to confirm death. His flesh was waxy. Rigor had set in. Nothing about the body suggested that it had been moved after death. Kenzie looked slowly around the room. There were several pill bottles on the side table, which she examined one at a time. A statin for high cholesterol. An SSRI antidepressant. Xanax for anxiety. All prescribed by the same doctor.

Kenzie pulled evidence bags out of her scene of death kit and sealed each one individually. She looked through the drawer of the side table to see if there was anything more. She found over-the-counter remedies. Antacids, allergy pills, painkillers, cold and sinus. The same as she would find in practically any bedroom or bathroom cabinet. She bagged each one.

Pulling out her phone, Kenzie looked up the prescribing physician online and called his office.

"Dr. Brandon is with a patient at the moment," the receptionist advised. "Did you want to set up an appointment?"

"This is Dr. Kirsch from the medical examiner's office. I need to talk to him about the death of one of his patients."

"Oh, dear!" the receptionist sounded concerned. "I'm sorry to hear that. I will have him call you back. Can I get your number? And the name of the patient so he can review the file before calling you?"

"Patient's name is Scott Robertson." Kenzie gave her phone number. "If I could get him to call me back as soon as possible. I am at the death scene right now, and I don't want to release it until after I have talked to Dr. Brandon."

"I'll try to have him call you before his next patient. We do have a busy practice…"

"I understand that. And hopefully, he does not have the ME's office calling him about too many of them. It is quite important that he take the time to call me back."

"I will let him know."

Kenzie sighed. "Thank you."

There wasn't much else for her to do. She would do a full examination of Robertson in the morgue, but it appeared that he had not been in good health and there were no preliminary indications that it was anything other than a natural death.

The room was not exactly neat, but there was no sign of any violence there, either. No sign of a struggle. Robertson was in bed, where he had likely been since the night before. There were no visible injuries. His laptop sat on his desk, along with his phone and a few other items that any self-respecting burglar would have taken.

As she looked around the room, there was a noise in the closet. Kenzie froze, her heart racing.

Was there someone in there? Even though she had been thinking of a burglar, there was no sign of any burglary. If it had been burgled, why would the thief have stayed in the room for hours to risk discovery by the girlfriend or roommate? Obviously, he couldn't show himself once they had shown up, and then the paramedics had come, and then Kenzie, so there hadn't been any time in which someone could sneak out from the time the body was discovered.

Kenzie had heard of cases where a burglar had fallen asleep in the middle of his burglary and been discovered at the scene. She looked at the bed, but there was no sign that anyone had been sleeping there other than Robertson. She didn't think that a burglar would have lain down next to a corpse. But then, she wouldn't have thought they would lay down at all, much less fall asleep in the midst of a burglary.

"Is somebody there?" she asked in a loud voice.

The paramedic, who had followed her to the bedroom but was stationed outside the door due to the lack of space inside the room, stuck her head in the door.

"Did you call me?"

"No, there's… I think there's someone in the closet."

The paramedic looked at the door, closed most of the way but still slightly ajar. She turned and shouted back to the others in the living room. "Is there anyone else in the apartment?"

Kenzie could hear Rachel and Alex coming down the hall toward them, arguing about something. It sounded like an old argument, something they had hashed over many times before and barely had the energy to get mad about now.

"You know she isn't allowed in there! You're supposed to keep track of her," Rachel insisted.

"I do. Who left the door open? It wasn't me."

"You're not supposed to let her roam everywhere."

Alex marched into the bedroom, forcing Kenzie to step back so that she was squeezed against the bed. He paid no attention to her and walked over to the closet door, pulling it open with a whoosh.

"Cuddles!" He snapped. "Get out of there! You know you're not supposed to be in there!"

Kenzie couldn't help grinning as he bent over to push things around the bottom of the closet, coming out with an armful of fluff.

"This is Cuddles," Alex said unnecessarily. The fluffy tricolor cat glared at Kenzie, ears folded back. "Sorry. She's not supposed to be in here; she must have snuck in while we were calling the paramedics. We were both kind of in a panic. We weren't expecting… something like this."

Now that he had retrieved the cat, he stopped and stared at Robertson's body on the bed. His cheeks turned pink and he swore.

"I didn't mean to just barge in here like that. I kind of forgot myself… I'm sorry." He shook his head.

"If you could just step out with Cuddles, that would be great. We don't want her contaminating the scene or getting in the way."

"I told you!" Rachel was saying in the hall. "If you're going to have a cat, you need to keep it shut in your room. It can't just be wandering all over the apartment. I told you before that she aggravates Scott's allergies!"

She suddenly went quiet.

"Well, she isn't going to aggravate them anymore, is she?" Alex sighed. "I *am* sorry. I said that. Neither of us was watching her when we went to call the ambulance and answered the door. She just snuck in. It was unintentional. Normally, she couldn't get into Scott's room; that was why she was so curious about it."

"She shouldn't have the run of the apartment. You shouldn't have even gotten the cat while he was living here. It's common courtesy. You talk to the people in the household before you bring an animal in. Scott would never have agreed to a cat. His allergies were so bad."

So Cuddles was the reason for the antihistamines in the side table. Kenzie felt sorry for Robertson, who had not been in good health, to have had this additional trial to deal with. Not just the allergy, but the ongoing fight with his roommate about it and the contention between his girlfriend and his roommate. It wouldn't have been easy for him to deal with on top of his illness.

"Why don't we go back out to the living room," she suggested. "It is going to be a while before I can transport the body. I may as well ask a few questions while I am waiting."

ABOUT THE AUTHOR

P.D. Workman is a USA Today Bestselling author and multi-award winner, renowned for her prolific output of over 100 published works that span various genres. With a knack for crafting page-turners, Workman captivates readers with everything from cozy mysteries like the Auntie Clem's Bakery series to gripping young adult and suspense novels.

Her stories resonate deeply as she masterfully weaves sensitive themes— such as childhood trauma, mental illness, and addiction—into compelling narratives that evoke a powerful emotional response. Readers are drawn to her unique voice and empathetic portrayal of complex issues.

With each new release, fans eagerly anticipate another thrilling blend of thought-provoking storytelling and relatable characters that define P.D. Workman's brand as an author of unforgettable page-turners—gripping tales that leave a lasting impact long after the last page is turned.

> P. D. Workman, does not shy from probing the deep psychological scars of childhood trauma, mental illness, and addiction. Also characteristic of this author, these extremely sensitive issues are explored with extensive empathy, described with incredible clarity, and portrayed with profound insight.
>
> — —KIM, GOODREADS REVIEWER

Some of Workman's titles have been translated into Spanish, French, Portuguese, German, and Italian.

Workman began writing at an early age and is a prolific reader as well as writer. She is also passionate about teaching and learning, expresses her creativity through art and cooking, and loves exploring the Calgary parks and green spaces where the Parks Pat Mysteries are set. She was a legal assistant for many years and has done extensive charitable work.

Workman was born and raised in Alberta, Canada, and is married with one adult son.

Please visit P.D. Workman at pdworkman.com to see what else she is working on, to join her mailing list, and to link to her social networks.

If you enjoyed this book, please take the time to recommend it to other purchasers with a review or star rating and share it with your friends!

tiktok.com/@pdworkmanauthor

facebook.com/pdworkmanauthor

x.com/pdworkmanauthor

instagram.com/pdworkmanauthor

amazon.com/author/pdworkman

bookbub.com/authors/p-d-workman

goodreads.com/pdworkman

linkedin.com/in/pdworkman

pinterest.com/pdworkmanauthor

youtube.com/pdworkman

Find P.D. Workman's books at

PDWORKMAN.COM

Scan the QR code below